MISSION OF
HONOR

Baen Books by David Weber

Honor Harrington:

On Basilisk Station	Honor Among Enemies
The Honor of the Queen	In Enemy Hands
The Short Victorious War	Echoes of Honor
Field of Dishonor	Ashes of Victory
Flag in Exile	War of Honor
At All Costs	Mission of Honor

Honorverse:

Crown of Slaves (with Eric Flint)
Torch of Freedom (with Eric Flint)
The Shadow of Saganami
Storm from the Shadows

edited by David Weber:

More than Honor	Changer of Worlds
Worlds of Honor	The Service of the Sword

Mutineers' Moon	The Excalibur Alternative
The Armageddon Inheritance	
Heirs of Empire	Bolos!
Empire from the Ashes	Old Soldiers

In Fury Born	Oath of Swords
	The War God's Own
The Apocalypse Troll	Wind Rider's Oath

with Steve White:

Crusade	The Shiva Option
In Death Ground	Insurrection
The Stars At War	The Stars At War II

with Eric Flint:

1633
1634: The Baltic War
Torch of Freedom

with John Ringo:

March Upcountry	March to the Sea
March to the Stars	We Few

with Linda Evans:

Hell's Gate
Hell Hath No Fury

MISSION OF HONOR

DAVID WEBER

MISSION OF HONOR

This is a work of fiction. All the characters and events portrayed in this book are fictional, and any resemblance to real people or incidents is purely coincidental.

Copyright © 2010 by David Weber

A Baen Books Original

Baen Publishing Enterprises
P.O. Box 1403
Riverdale, NY 10471
www.baen.com

ISBN 13: 978-1-4391-3361-3

Cover art by David Mattingly

First printing, July 2010

Distributed by Simon & Schuster
1230 Avenue of the Americas
New York, NY 10020

Library of Congress Cataloging-in-Publication Data

Weber, David, 1952–
  Mission of honor / David Weber.
       p. cm.
  "A Baen Books Original."
  ISBN 978-1-4391-3361-3 (hardcover)
  1. Harrington, Honor (Fictitious character)—Fiction. 2. Space warfare—Fiction.
  3. Women soldiers—Fiction. I. Title.
  PS3573.E217M57 2010
  813'.54—dc22

                                                    2010009369

10 9 8 7 6 5 4 3 2 1

Pages by Joy Freeman (www.pagesbyjoy.com)
Printed in the United States of America

For Megan, Morgan, and Michael Paul,
the centers of the universe Sharon and I live in.
When you guys get around to reading this,
remember it was for you.

Just like all the rest of my life.

Your Mom and I love you.

DECEMBER 1921 POST DIASPORA

"To understand Solly foreign policy, we'd have to *be* Sollies...and nothing would be worth *that*!"

—Queen Elizabeth III of Manticore

Chapter One

ANY DICTIONARY EDITOR stymied for an illustration of the word "paralyzed" would have pounced on him in an instant.

In fact, a disinterested observer might have wondered if Innokentiy Arsenovich Kolokoltsov, the Solarian League's Permanent Senior Undersecretary for Foreign Affairs, was even breathing as he stared at the images on his display. Shock was part of that paralysis, but only part. And so was disbelief, except that *disbelief* was far too pale a word for what he was feeling at that moment.

He sat that way for over twenty seconds by Astrid Wang's personal chrono. Then he inhaled explosively, shook himself, and looked up at her.

"This is *confirmed*?"

"It's the original message from the Manticorans, Sir," Wang replied. "The Foreign Minister had the chip couriered straight over, along with the formal note, as soon as he'd viewed it."

"No, I mean is there any independent confirmation of what they're *saying*?"

Despite two decades' experience in the ways of the Solarian league's bureaucracy, which included as the Eleventh Commandment "Thou shalt *never* embarrass thy boss by word, deed, or expression," Wang actually blinked in surprise.

"Sir," she began a bit cautiously, "according to the Manties, this all happened at New Tuscany, and we still don't have independent confirmation of the *first* incident they say took place there. So—"

Kolokoltsov grimaced and cut her off with a wave of his hand. Of course it hadn't. In fact, independent confirmation of the first New Tuscany Incident—he could already hear the newsies capitalizing *this* one—would take almost another entire T-month, if Josef Byng had followed procedure. The damned Manties sat squarely inside the League's communications loop with the Talbott Sector. They could get word of events there to the Sol System in little more than three T-weeks, thanks to their never-to-be-sufficiently-damned wormhole junction, whereas any direct report from New Tuscany to Old Terra would take almost two months to make the journey by dispatch boat. And if it went through the Meyers System headquarters of the Office of Frontier Security, as regulations required, it would take over eleven T-weeks.

And assuming the Manties aren't lying and manufacturing all this evidence for some godforsaken reason, any report from Byng has to've been routed by way of Meyers, he thought. *If he'd shortcut the regulations and sent it directly by way of Mesa and Visigoth—like any admiral with a* functional *brain would have!—it would've been here eight days ago.*

He felt an uncharacteristic urge to rip the display unit from his desk and hurl it across the room. To watch it shatter and bounce back in broken bits and pieces. To curse at the top of his lungs in pure, unprocessed rage. But despite the fact that someone from pre-Diaspora Old Terra would have estimated his age at no more than forty, he was actually eighty-five T-years old. He'd spent almost seventy of those years working his way up to his present position, and now those decades of discipline, of learning how the game was played, came to his rescue. He remembered the *Twelfth* Commandment—"Thou shalt never admit the loss of thy composure before thine underlings"—and actually managed to smile at his chief of staff.

"That *was* a silly question, wasn't it, Astrid? I guess I'm not as immune to the effects of surprise as I'd always thought I was."

"No, Sir." Wang smiled back, but her own surprise—at the strength of his reaction, as much as at the news itself—still showed in her blue eyes. "I don't think anyone would be, under these circumstances."

"Maybe not, but there's going to be hell to pay over this one," he told her, completely unnecessarily. He wondered if he'd said it because he still hadn't recovered his mental balance.

"Get hold of Wodoslawski, Abruzzi, MacArtney, Quartermain, and Rajampet," he went on. "I want them here in Conference One in one hour."

"Sir, Admiral Rajampet is meeting with that delegation from the AG's office and—"

"I don't care who he's meeting with," Kolokoltsov said flatly. "Just tell him to be here."

"Yes, sir. Ah, may I tell him why the meeting is so urgent?"

"No." Kolokoltsov smiled thinly. "If the Manties are telling the truth, I don't want him turning up with any prepared comments. This one's too important for that kind of nonsense."

"So what's this all about, anyway?" Fleet Admiral Rajampet Kaushal Rajani demanded as he strode into the conference room. He was the last to arrive—a circumstance Kolokoltsov had taken some care to arrange.

Rajampet was a small, wiry man, with a dyspeptic personality, well suited to his almost painfully white hair and deeply wrinkled face. Although he remained physically spry and mentally alert, he was a hundred and twenty-three years old, which made him one of the oldest human beings alive. Indeed, when the original first-generation prolong therapy was initially developed, he'd missed being too old for it by less than five months.

He'd also been an officer in the Solarian League Navy since he was nineteen, although he hadn't held a space-going command in over half a T-century, and he was rather proud of the fact that he did not suffer fools gladly. (Of course, most of the rest of the human race was composed almost exclusively of fools, in his considered opinion, but Kolokoltsov could hardly quibble with him on that particular point.) Rajampet was also a formidable force within the Solarian League's all-powerful bureaucratic hierarchy, although he fell just short of the very uppermost niche. He knew all of the Navy's ins and outs, all of its senior admirals, the complex web of its family alliances and patronage, where all the bodies were buried . . . and precisely whose pockets were filled at the trough of the Navy's graft and corruption. After all, his own were prominent among them, and he personally controlled the spigots through which all the rest of it flowed.

Now if only the idiot knew what the hell his precious Navy was up to, Kolokoltsov thought coldly.

"It seems we have a small problem, Rajani," he said out loud, beckoning the gorgeously bemedaled admiral towards a chair at the table.

"It bloody well *better* not be a 'small' problem," Rajampet muttered, only half under his breath, as he stalked across to the indicated chair.

"I beg your pardon?" Kolokoltsov said with the air of a man who hadn't quite heard what someone had said.

"I was in the middle of a meeting with the Attorney General's people," Rajampet replied, without apologizing for his earlier comment. "They still aren't done with all the indictments for those damned trials, which means we're only just now getting that whole business with Technodyne sorted out. I promised Omosupe and Agatá"—he twitched his head at Omosupe Quartermain, Permanent Senior Undersecretary of Commerce, and Permanent Senior Undersecretary of the Treasury Agatá Wodoslawski—"a recommendation on the restructuring by the end of the week. It's taken forever just to get everyone assembled so we could sit down and talk about it, and I don't appreciate being yanked away from something that important."

"I can understand why you'd resent being interrupted, Rajani," Kolokoltsov said coolly. "Unfortunately, this small matter's come up and it needs to be dealt with ... immediately. And"—his dark eyes bored suddenly into Rajampet's across the table—"unless I'm seriously mistaken, it's rather closely related to what got Technodyne into trouble in the first place."

"What?" Rajampet settled the last couple of centimeters into his chair, and his expression was as perplexed as his voice. "What are you talking about?"

Despite his own irritation, Kolokoltsov could almost understand the admiral's confusion. The repercussions of the Battle of Monica were still wending their way through the Navy's labyrinthine bowels—and the gladiatorial circus of the courts was only just beginning, really—but the battle itself had been fought over ten T-months ago. Although the SLN hadn't been directly involved in the Royal Manticoran Navy's destruction of the Monican Navy, the consequences for Technodyne Industries had been profound. And Technodyne had been one of the Navy's major contractors for four hundred years. It was perfectly reasonable for Rajampet, as the chief of naval operations, to be deeply involved in trying to salvage something from the shipwreck of investigations, indictments, and show trials, and Kolokoltsov never doubted that the admiral's attention had been tightly focused on that task for the past several T-weeks.

Even if it would have been helpful if he'd been able to give a modicum of his attention to dealing with this other *little problem,* the diplomat thought grimly.

"I'm talking about the Talbott Cluster, Rajani," he said out loud, letting just a trace of over-tried patience into his voice. "I'm talking about that incident between your Admiral Byng and the Manties."

"What about it?" Rajampet's tone was suddenly a bit cautious, his eyes wary, as instincts honed by a T-century of bureaucratic infighting reared their heads.

"It would appear the Manties were just as pissed off as their original note indicated they were," Kolokoltsov told him.

"And?" Rajampet's eyes turned warier than ever and he seemed to settle back into his chair.

"And they weren't joking about sending their Admiral Gold Peak to inquire into matters on the ground in New Tuscany."

"They weren't?" The question came from Wodoslawski, not Rajampet, and Kolokoltsov glanced at her.

She was twenty-five T-years younger than he was—a third-gerneration prolong recipient with dark red hair, gray eyes, and quite an attractive figure. She was also fairly new to her position as the real head of the Treasury Department, and she'd received it, following her predecesor's demise, only as a compromise between the other permanent senior undersecretaries. She knew perfectly well that she'd been everyone else's second choice—that all her current colleagues had allies they would really have preferred to see in that slot. But she'd been there for over a decade, now, and she'd solidified her powerbase quite nicely.

She was no longer the junior probationary member of the quintet of permanent undersecretaries who truly ran the League from their personal fiefdoms in the Foreign Ministry, Commerce Department, Interior Department, Department of Education and Information, and Treasury Department. She was, however, the only one of them who'd been out-system and unavailable when the first Manticoran diplomatic note arrived. As such, she could make an excellent claim to bearing no responsibility for how that note had been handled, and from her expression, Kolokoltsov thought sourly, she was thoroughly aware of that minor fact.

"No, Agatá," he said, moving his gaze to her. "No, they weren't. And just over a T-month ago—on November the seventeenth, to be precise—Admiral Gold Peak arrived at New Tuscany...to find Admiral Byng still there."

"Oh, shit," Permanent Senior Undersecretary of the Interior Nathan MacArtney muttered. "Don't tell us Byng opened fire on *her*, too!"

"If he did, I'm sure it was only because she provoked it!" Rajampet said sharply.

"With all due respect, Rajani," Permanent Senior Undersecretary of Education and Information Malachai Abruzzi said tartly, "I wouldn't bet my life on that." Rajampet glared at him angrily, and Abruzzi shrugged. "As far as I can tell from the Manties' first note, none of their ships did a damned thing to provoke him the *first* time he killed several hundred of their spacers. That being so, is there any reason we ought to assume he wouldn't just as cheerfully kill a few thousand more for no particular reason?"

"I'll remind you," Rajampet said even more sharply, "that none of us were there, and the only 'evidence' we have of what truly happened was delivered to us, oh so generously, by the *Manties*. I see no reason to believe they'd be above tampering with the sensor data they provided to us. In fact, one of my people over at Operational Analysis commented at the time that the data seemed suspiciously good and detailed."

Abruzzi only snorted, although Kolokoltsov suspected he was tempted to do something considerably more forceful. The vast majority of the Solarian League's member star systems looked after their own educational systems, which meant, despite its name, that Education and Information was primarily concerned with the *information* half of its theoretical responsibilities. Abruzzi's position thus made him, in effect, the Solarian League's chief propagandist. In that role, it had been his job to find a positive spin to put on Josef Byng's actions, and he'd been working on it ever since the Manties' first diplomatic note reached Old Chicago.

So far, he hadn't had a lot of success. Which wasn't too surprising, Kolokoltsov thought sourly. When a Solarian admiral commanding seventeen *battlecruisers* opened fire without warning on three *destroyers* who didn't even have their wedges and sidewalls up, it was going to be just a trifle difficult to convince even the Solarian public he'd been justified. Nor was there much chance that any reports or sensor data the Navy finally got around to providing were going to make things any better—not without an awful lot of "tweaking" first, at least! Rajampet could say whatever he liked about the data the Manties had provided, but Kolokoltsov agreed with Abruzzi's original analysis. The Manties would never have sent them falsified data. Not when they knew that eventually the League would be receiving accurate tactical data from its own people.

"All I'll say, Rajani," Abruzzi said after a moment, "is that I'm just glad the Manties haven't leaked this to the newsies . . . yet, at least. Because as hard as we've been trying, we haven't been able to find a way to make *them* look like the aggressors. And that means that when this *does* hit the 'faxes, we're going to find ourselves in a very difficult position. One where we'll probably have to *apologize* and actually offer to pay reparations."

"No, damn it!" Rajampet snapped, betrayed by anger into forgetting, at least briefly, his former wariness. "We can't establish that kind of precedent! If any pissant little neobarb navy decides the SLN can't tell *it* what to do, we're going to have a *hell* of a problem out in the Verge! And if Byng's been forced into another exchange of fire with them, we have to be even more careful about what sort of precedents we set!"

"I'm afraid you're entirely correct about *that* one, Rajani," Kolokoltsov said, and his frigid tone snapped everyone's eyes back to him. "And, unfortunately, I'm equally afraid Nathan's mistaken about the Manties' degree of discretion where the newsies are concerned."

"What the hell do you mean?" Rajampet demanded. "Go ahead—spit it out!"

"All right, Rajani. Approximately ninety minutes ago, we received a second note from the Manticorans. Under the circumstances, the fact that we decided to opt for a 'reasoned and deliberate' response to their original complaint—and refused to let anyone think we were allowing ourselves to be rushed by any Manticoran demands—may have been less optimal than we'd thought. I don't imagine getting our response to their *first* note a couple of days after they banged off their *second* note to us is going to amuse Queen Elizabeth and her prime minister very much.

"And the reason they've sent us this second note is that when Admiral Gold Peak arrived in New Tuscany she issued exactly

the demands the Manties had warned us about in their first note.
She demanded that Byng stand down his ships and permit Manticoran boarding parties to sequester and examine their sensor
data relative to the destruction of three of her destroyers. She
also informed him that the Star Empire of Manticore intended
to insist upon an open examination of the facts and intended to
hold the guilty parties responsible under the appropriate provisions
of interstellar law for the unprovoked destruction of their ships
and the deaths of their personnel. And"—Kolokoltsov allowed his
eyes to flip sideways to Abruzzi for a moment—"it would appear
it wasn't all part of some sort of propaganda maneuver on their
part, after all."

"I don't—" Rajampet's wrinkled face was darken and his eyes
glittered with fury. "I can't believe anyone—even *Manties!*—would
be stupid enough to really issue *demands* to the Solarian Navy!
They'd have to be out of—I mean, surely this Gold Peak couldn't
possibly have thought she'd get *away* with that? If Byng blew her
damned ships into orbital debris, the only person she's got to
blame for it is—"

"Oh, he didn't blow up any of her ships, Rajani," Kolokoltsov
said coldly. "Despite the fact that she had only six battlecruisers
and he had seventeen, *she* blew *his* flagship into . . . what was it
you called it? Ah, yes! Into '*orbital debris.*'"

Rajampet froze in mid-tirade, staring at Kolokoltsov in disbelief.

"Oh, my God," Omosupe Quartermain said quietly.

Of everyone present, she and Rajampet probably personally disliked Manticorans the most. In Rajampet's case, that was because
the Royal Manticoran Navy declined to kowtow satisfactorily to
the Solarian League Navy's supremacy. In Quartermain's case, it
was because of how deeply she resented Manticore's wormhole
junction and its merchant marine's dominance of the League's
carrying trade. Which meant, among other things, that she had
a very clear idea of how much damage the Star Empire of Manticore could do the League's economy if it decided to retaliate
economically for Solarian aggression.

"How many ships did the Manties lose *this* time?" she continued in a resigned tone, clearly already beginning to reckon up
the restitution the Star Empire might find itself in a position to
extort out of the League.

"Oh, they didn't lose *any* ships," Kolokoltsov replied.

"*What?*" Rajampet exploded. "That's goddammed *nonsense!* No Solarian flag officer's going to roll over and take something like that without—!"

"In that case, Rajani, I recommend you read Admiral Sigbee's report yourself. She found herself in command after Admiral Byng's... demise, and the Manties were kind enough to forward her dispatches to us along with their note. According to our own security people, they didn't even open the file and read it, first. Apparently they saw no reason to."

This time, Rajampet was clearly bereft of speech. He just sat there, staring at Kolokoltsov, and the diplomat shrugged.

"According to the synopsis of Admiral Sigbee's report, the Manties destroyed Admiral Byng's flagship, the *Jean Bart*, with a single missile salvo launched from far beyond our own ships' effective range. His flagship was *completely* destroyed, Rajani. There were no survivors at all. Under the circumstances, and since Admiral Gold Peak—who, I suppose I might also mention, turns out to be none other than Queen Elizabeth's first cousin and fifth in line for the Manticoran throne—had made it crystal clear that she'd destroy all of Byng's ships if her demands were not met, Admiral Sigbee—under protest, I need hardly add—complied with them."

"She—?" Rajampet couldn't get the complete sentence out, but Kolokoltsov nodded anyway.

"She *surrendered*, Rajani," he said in a marginally gentler voice, and the admiral closed his mouth with a snap.

He wasn't the only one staring at Kolokoltsov in horrified disbelief now. All the others seemed struck equally dumb, and Kolokoltsov took a certain satisfaction from seeing the reflection of his own stunned reaction in their expressions. Which, he admitted, was the *only* satisfaction he was likely to be feeling today.

On the face of it, the loss of a single ship and the surrender of twenty or so others, counting Byng's screening destroyers, could hardly be considered a catastrophe for the Solarian League Navy. The SLN was the biggest fleet in the galaxy. Counting active duty and reserve squadrons, it boasted almost eleven thousand super-dreadnoughts, and that didn't even count the thousands upon thousands of battlecruisers, cruisers, and destroyers of Battle Fleet and Frontier Fleet... or the thousands of ships in the various system-defense forces maintained for local security by several of the League's wealthier member systems. Against that kind of firepower, against such a massive preponderance of tonnage, the destruction of a single battlecruiser and the two thousand or so people aboard it was less than a flea bite. It was certainly a far, far smaller relative loss, in terms of both tonnage and personnel, than the Manticorans had suffered when Byng blew three of their newest destroyers out of space with absolutely no warning.

But it was the *first* Solarian warship destroyed by hostile action in centuries, and no Solarian League admiral had *ever* surrendered his command. Until now.

And that was what truly had the others worried, Kolokoltsov thought coldly. Just as it had *him* worried. The omnipotence of the Solarian League Navy was the fundamental bedrock upon which the entire League stood. The whole purpose of the League was to maintain interstellar order, protect and nurture the interactions, prosperity, and sovereignty of its member systems. There'd been times—more times than Kolokoltsov could count, really—when Rajampet and his predecessors had found themselves fighting tooth and nail for funding, given the fact that it was so obvious that no one conceivable hostile star nation, or combination of them, could truly threaten the League's security. Yet while they might have had to fight for the funding they *wanted*, they'd never come close to not getting the funding they actually *needed*. In fact, their fellow bureaucrats had never seriously considered cutting off or even drastically curtailing expenditures on the Navy.

Partly, that was because no matter how big Frontier Fleet was, it would never have enough ships to be everywhere it needed to be to carry out its mandate as the League's neighborhood cop and enforcer. Battle Fleet would have been a much more reasonable area for cost reductions, except that it had more prestige and was even more deeply entrenched in the League's bureaucratic structure than Frontier Fleet, not to mention having so many more allies in the industrial sector, given how lucrative superdreadnought building contracts were. But even the most fanatical expenditure-cutting reformer (assuming that any such mythical being existed anywhere in the Solarian League) would have found very few allies if he'd set his sights on the *Navy's* budget. Supporting the fleet was too important to the economy as a whole, and all the patronage that went with the disbursement of such enormous amounts was far too valuable to be surrendered. And, after all, making certain *everyone else* was as well aware as they were of the Navy's invincibility was an essential element of the clout wielded by the League in general and by the Office of Frontier Security, in particular.

But now that invincibility had been challenged. Worse, although Kolokoltsov was no expert on naval matters, even the synopsis of Sigbee's dispatches had made her shock at the effective range—and deadliness—of the Manticoran missiles abundantly clear even to him.

"She *surrendered*," Permanent Senior Undersecretary of the Interior Nathan MacArtney repeated very carefully after a moment, clearly making certain he hadn't misunderstood.

Kolokoltsov was actually surprised anyone had recovered that quickly, especially MacArtney. The Office of Frontier Security came under the control of the Department of the Interior, and after Rajampet himself, it was MacArtney whose responsibilities and... arrangements were most likely to suffer if the rest of the galaxy began to question just how invincible the Solarian Navy truly was.

"She did," Kolokoltsov confirmed. "And the Manties did board her ships, and they did take possession of their computers—their fully *operable* computers, with intact databases. At the time she was 'permitted' to include her dispatches along with Admiral Gold Peak's so we could receive her report as promptly as possible, she had no idea what ultimate disposition the Manties intend to make where her ships are concerned."

"My God," Quartermain said again, shaking her head.

"Sigbee didn't even dump her *data* cores?" MacArtney demanded incredulously.

"Given that Gold Peak had just finished blowing one of her ships into tiny pieces, I think the admiral was justified in concluding the Manties might really go ahead and pull the trigger if they discovered she'd dumped her data cores," Kolokoltsov replied.

"But if they got all their data, including the secure sections..." MacArtney's voice trailed off, and Kolokoltsov smiled thinly.

"Then they've got an enormous amount of our secure technical data," he agreed. "Even worse, these were *Frontier Fleet* ships."

MacArtney looked physically ill. He was even better aware then Kolokoltsov of how the rest of the galaxy might react if some of the official, highly secret contingency plans stored in the computers of Frontier Fleet flagships were to be leaked.

There was another moment of sickly silence, then Wodoslawski cleared her throat.

"What did they say in their note, Innokentiy?" she asked.

"They say the data they've recovered from Byng's computers completely supports the data they already sent to us. They say they've recovered Sigbee's copy of Byng's order to open fire on the Manticoran destroyers. They've appended her copy of the message traffic between Gold Peak and Byng, as well, and pointed out that Gold Peak repeatedly warned Byng not only that she *would* fire if he failed to comply with her instructions but that she had the capability to destroy his ships from beyond his effective range. And, by the way, Sigbee's attested the accuracy of the copies from her communications section.

"In other words, they've told us their original interpretation of what happened to their destroyers has been confirmed, and that the admiral responsible for that incident has now been killed, along with the destruction of his flagship and its entire crew, because he rejected their demands. And they've pointed out, in case any of us might miss it, that Byng's original actions at New Tuscany constitute an act of war under interstellar law and that under that same interstellar law, Admiral Gold Peak was completely justified in the actions she took. Indeed," he showed his teeth in something no one would ever mistake for a smile, "they've pointed out how restrained Gold Peak was, under the circumstances, since Byng's entire task force was entirely at her mercy and she gave him at least three separate opportunities to comply with their demands without bloodshed."

"They've *declared war* on the Solarian League?" Abruzzi seemed unable to wrap his mind around the thought. Which was particularly ironic, Kolokoltsov thought, given his original breezy assurance that the Manticorans were only posturing, seeking an entirely cosmetic confrontation with the League in an effort to rally their battered domestic morale.

"No, they haven't declared war on the League," the diplomat replied out loud. "In fact, they've *refrained* from declaring war ... so far, at least. I wouldn't say there's any give in their note—in fact, it's the most belligerent diplomatic communication I've ever seen directed to the League, and they've made no bones about observing that a *de facto* state of war already exists between us because of *our* flag officer's actions—but they've made it clear they aren't prepared to foreclose all possibility of a diplomatic resolution."

"*Diplomatic resolution?*" Rajampet exploded. He slammed one fist down on the conference table. "*Fuck* them and their 'diplomatic resolutions'! They've destroyed a Solarian warship, killed Solarian naval personnel! I don't care whether they *want* a war or not—they've *got* one!"

"Don't you think it might be a good idea to at least look at Sigbee's messages and the data the Manties have sent along, Rajani?" MacArtney demanded tartly. The admiral glared at him, and MacArtney glared right back. "Didn't you hear what Innokentiy just said? Gold Peak took out *Jean Bart* from outside Byng's effective missile range! If they outrange us that badly, then—"

"Then it doesn't goddammed *matter!*" Rajampet shot back. "We're talking about frigging battlecruisers, Nathan. *Battlecruisers*—and Frontier Fleet battlecruisers, at that. They don't begin to have the antimissile defenses a ship-of-the-wall does, and no battlecruiser can take the kind of damage a waller can take! I don't care how many fancy missiles they've got, there's no way they can stop Battle Fleet if we throw four or five hundred superdreadnoughts straight at them, especially after the losses they've already taken in their damned Battle of Manticore."

"I might find that thought just a little more reassuring if not for the fact that all reports indicate they apparently just finished taking out something like three or four hundred *Havenite* SDs in the same battle," MacArtney pointed out even more acidly.

"So what," Rajampet more than half-sneered. "One damned batch of barbarians beating on another one. What's that got to do with *us?*"

MacArtney stared at him, as if he literally couldn't comprehend what Rajampet was saying, and Kolokoltsov didn't blame MacArtney at all. Even allowing for the fact that all of this had come at the CNO cold...

"Excuse me, Rajani," the diplomat said, "but don't our ships-of-the-wall and our battlecruisers have the same effective missile range?" Rajampet glowered at him, then nodded. "Then I think we have to assume *their* ships-of-the-wall have at least the same effective missile range as *their* battlecruisers, which means they outrange us, too. And given the fact that the Republic of Haven has been fighting them for something like, oh, twenty T-years, and is still in existence, I think we have to assume they can match Manticore's combat range, since they'd have been forced to surrender quite some time ago if they couldn't. So if the Manties managed to destroy or capture three or four hundred *Havenite* superdreadnoughts, despite the fact that they had equivalent weapon ranges, what makes you think they couldn't stop *five* hundred of our ships if they outrange us significantly? At least the Havenites could shoot back, you know!"

"So we send a *thousand*," Rajampet said. "Or, hell, we send twice that many! We've got over two thousand in full commission, another three hundred in the yards for regular overhaul and refit cycles, and over *eight* thousand in reserve. They may've beaten the crap out of the Havenites, but they got the shit shot out of them, too, from all reports. They can't have more than a hundred of the wall left! And however long-ranged their missiles may be, it takes hundreds of laser heads to take out a single superdreadnought. Against the kind of counter-missile fire and decoys five or six hundred of our wallers can throw out, they'd need a hell of a lot more missiles than anything they've got left could possibly throw!"

"And you think they wouldn't still be able to kill a lot of our ships and a lot of our spacers?" Wodoslawski demanded skeptically.

"Oh, they could *hurt* us," Rajampet conceded. "There's no way in the universe they could *stop* us, but I don't doubt we'd get hurt worse than the Navy's ever been hurt before. But that's beside the point, Agatá."

Her eyebrows arched skeptically, and he barked a short, sharp—and ugly—laugh.

"Of course it's beside the point!" he said. "The *point* of this is that a jumped up neobarb Navy's opened fire on the SLN, destroyed one of our warships, and captured an entire Solarian task group. We can't let that stand. No matter what it costs, we have to establish that no one—*no one*—fucks with the Solarian Navy. If we don't make that point right here, right now, who else is likely to suddenly decide *he* can issue ultimatums to the fleet?" He turned his glower on MacArtney. "You should understand that if anyone can, Nathan!"

"All right," MacArtney replied, manifestly unhappily. "I take your point." He looked around the conference table at his civilian colleagues. "The truth is," he told them, "that big as it is, Frontier

Fleet can't possibly be everywhere it needs to be—not in any sort of strength. It manages to maintain nodes of concentrated strength at the various sector HQs and support bases, but even they get stretched pretty thin from time to time. And most of the time, we send a single ship—at most a division or two—to deal with troublespots as they turn hot because we can't afford to weaken those concentrated nodes by diverting more units from them. And what Rajani's saying is that because we're spread so thinly, there are a lot of times when we don't actually have the firepower on the spot to enforce our policies. But what we *do* have on the spot is a representative of the entire Navy. Under the wrong circumstances, an unfriendly power may well have enough combat power to destroy whatever detachment we've sent out to show it the error of its ways. But they don't, because they know that if they do, the *rest* of the Navy—however much of it it takes—is going to turn up and destroy *them*."

"Exactly," Rajampet agreed, nodding vigorously. "That's *exactly* the point. I don't care how damned justified the Manties may have thought they were. For that matter, I don't care how 'justified' they may actually have *been*, and I don't give a damn whether or not they were operating within the letter of interstellar war. What I care about is the fact that we have to make an example out of them if we don't want to suddenly find ourselves eyeball-to-eyeball with other neobarbs, all over the galaxy, who suddenly think *they* can screw around with the Solarian League, too."

"Wait." Malachai Abruzzi shook himself, then looked at Kolokoltsov. "Before we go any further, what did you mean about their 'discretion' where the newsies were concerned, Innokentiy?"

"I mean they officially released the news of Byng's attack on their destroyers—*and* their response to it—the same day they sent us this note," Kolokoltsov said flatly. Abruzzi stared at him in obvious disbelief, and Kolokoltsov smiled thinly. "I imagine we should be hearing about it shortly," he continued, "since, according to their note, they intended to release the news to their own media six hours after their dispatch boat cleared the Junction headed for Old Terra."

"They've already *released* the news?" Abruzzi seemed stunned in a way even the news of *Jean Bart*'s destruction had failed to achieve.

"That's what they tell us." Kolokoltsov shrugged. "When you get right down to it, they may not have a lot of choice. It's been two months since the first incident, and the communications loop from New Tuscany to Manticore's only about three weeks. Word of something this big was bound to leak to their newsies pretty damned quickly after Byng managed to get himself blown away." Rajampet's eyes glittered at his choice of words, but Kolokoltsov didn't especially care. "Under the circumstances, they probably figured they couldn't keep it under wraps much longer even if they tried, so they'd damned well better get their version of it out first—especially to their own people."

"Then the bastards really have painted us all into a corner," Rajampet snarled. "If they've gone ahead and broadcast this thing to the entire galaxy, we've got even less choice about how hard we respond."

"Just hold on, Rajani!" Abruzzi said sharply. The admiral glared at him, and he glared right back. "We don't have any idea at this point how they've positioned themselves on this. Until we've at least had a chance to see the spin they put on it, we aren't in any position to decide how we want to spin our own response to it! And trust me on this one—we're going to have to handle it very, very carefully."

"Why?" Rajampet snapped.

"Because the truth is that your idiot admiral was in the *wrong*, at least the first time around," Abruzzi replied coldly, meeting the admiral's eyes glare-for-glare. "We can't debate this on their terms without conceding that point. And if public opinion decides he was wrong and they were right, and if we handle this even slightly wrong, the hullabaloo you're still dealing with over Technodyne and Monica's going to look like a pillow fight."

"If it does, it does," Rajampet said flatly.

"You do remember the Constitution gives every single member system veto power, don't you?" Abruzzi inquired. Rajampet glared at him, and he shrugged. "If you wind up needing a formal declaration of war, don't you think it would be a good thing if nobody out there—like, oh, *Beowulf*, for example—decided to exercise that power?"

"We don't need any frigging declarations of war! This is a clear-cut case of self-defense, of responding to an actual attack on our ships and personnel, and the judiciary's interpretation of Article Seven has always supported the Navy's authority to respond to that kind of attack in whatever strength is necessary."

Kolokoltsov started to respond to that statement, then made himself pause. Rajampet had a point about the judiciary's interpretation of Article Seven of the League Constitution . . . historically, at least. The third section of that particular article had been specifically drafted to permit the SLN to respond to emergency situations without waiting weeks or months for reports to trickle back to the capital and for the ponderous political mechanism to issue formal declarations of war. It had not, however, been intended by the Constitution's drafters as a blank check, and if Rajampet wanted to move the Navy to an actual war footing—to begin mobilizing additional superdreadnoughts from the Reserve, for example—*someone* was going to point out that he needed the authorization of that same formal declaration. At which point someone else was going to support Rajampet's position.

At which point we'll wind up with a constitutional *crisis, as well as a military one,* Kolokoltsov thought grimly. *Wonderful.*

He wondered how many of his colleagues grasped the true gravity of the threat they faced. If Rajampet was able to crush Manticore quickly after all, this would almost certainly blow over, as many another tempest had over the course of the League's long history. But if the Navy *couldn't* crush Manticore quickly, if this turned into a succession of bloody fiascoes, not even the most resounding ultimate victory would be enough to prevent seismic shockwaves throughout the entire tissue of bureaucratic fiefdoms which held the League together.

He suspected from Abruzzi's attitude that Malachai, if no one else, had at least an inkling of just how dangerous this could turn out to be. Wodoslawski probably did, too, although it was harder to tell in her case. Rajampet obviously wasn't thinking that far ahead, and Kolokoltsov honestly didn't have a clue whether or not MacArtney and Quartermain were able to see beyond the immediate potential consequences for their own departments.

"I agree with you about the historical interpretation of Article Seven, Rajani," he said out loud, finally. "I think you'd be well advised to consult with Brangwen about the precedents, though. And to make sure the rest of her people over at Justice are onboard with you for this one."

"Of course I'll check with her," Rajampet replied a bit more calmly. "In the meantime, though, I'm confident I've got the authority to respond by taking prudent military precautions." He smiled thinly. "And there's always the old saying about the best defense being a strong offense."

"Maybe there is," Abruzzi said. "And I'll even agree that apologizing later is usually easier than getting permission first. But I'd also like to point out that this one's quite a bit different from 'usually.' So if you intend to sell that to the Assembly in a way that's going to keep some of the busybodies over there from demanding all sorts of inquiries and holding all kinds of hearings, we're going to have to prepare the ground for it carefully, anyway. Some of those people over there think they really ought to be in charge, you know, and the ones who think that way are likely to try to use this. As long as there's no strong public support for them, they aren't going to accomplish much—all the inertia in the system's against them. But if we want to deny them that public support, we're going to have to show everyone that you not only have that authority but that we're in the *right* in this particular confrontation."

"Despite what you just said about my 'idiot admiral'?" Anger crackled in Rajampet's voice.

"If the adjective offends you, I'm sorry." Abruzzi didn't waste a lot of effort on the sincerity of his tone. "But the fact remains that he *was* in the wrong."

"Then how in hell do you think we're going to convince that 'public support' of yours we're in the *right* if we smash the Manties like they deserve?" Rajampet sneered.

"We *lie*." Abruzzi shrugged. "It's not like we haven't done it before. And, in the end, the truth is what the winner says it is. But in order to rebut the Manties' version effectively, I have to know what it is, first. And we can't make any military moves until after I've had a chance to do the preliminary spadework."

"Spadework." This time, Rajampet's sneer was marginally more restrained. Then he snorted harshly. "Fine. You do your 'spadework.' In the end, it's going to be my superdreadnoughts that make it stand up, though."

Abruzzi started to shoot something back, but Omosupe Quartermain interrupted him.

"Let's not get carried away," she said. The others looked at her, and she shrugged. "No matter what's happened, let's not just automatically assume we've got to move immediately to some sort of military response. You say they haven't ruled out the possibility of a diplomatic settlement, Innokentiy. Well, I'm sure the settlement they have in mind is us making apologies and offering *them* reparations. But what if we turned the tables? Even the

Manties have to be capable of doing the same math Rajani just did for us. They have to know that if push comes to shove, any qualitative advantage they might have can't possibly stand up to our *quantitative* advantage. So what if we were to tell them we're outraged by their high-handedness, their unilateral escalation of the confrontation before they even had our response to their first note? What if we tell them it's our position that, because of that escalation, all the additional bloodshed at New Tuscany was *their* responsibility, regardless of how Byng may have responded to their ultimatum? And what if we tell them *we* demand apologies and reparations from *them* on pain of an official declaration of war and the destruction of their entire 'Star Empire'?"

"You mean we hammer them hard enough over the negotiating table, demand a big enough kilo of flesh for leaving them intact, to make sure no one else is ever stupid enough to try this same kind of stunt?" Abruzzi said thoughtfully.

"I don't know." Wodoslawski shook her head. "From what you said about the tone of their note and what they've already done, don't we have to assume they'd be willing to go ahead and risk exactly that? Would they have gone this far if they weren't pre-pared to go farther?"

"It's easy to be brave *before* the other fellow actually aims his pulser at you," Rajampet pointed out.

Several of the others looked at him with combined skepticism and surprise, and he grunted.

"I don't really like it," he admitted. "And I stand by what I said earlier—we can't let this pass, can't let them get away with it. But that doesn't mean Omosupe's idea isn't worth trying, first. If they apologize abjectly enough, and if they're willing to throw this Gold Peak to the wolves, and *if* they're ready to cough up a big enough reparation, then we'll be in the position of graciously restraining ourselves instead of hammering their pathetic little 'Star Empire' flat. And if they're still too stupid to accept the inevitable," he shrugged, "we send in however much of Battle Fleet it takes and squash them like a bug."

It was obvious how he expected it to work out in the end, Kolokoltsov thought. And the hell of it was that even though Quartermain's idea was probably worth trying, Rajampet was even more probably right. Wodoslawski was obviously thinking the same thing.

"I think we ought to do some risk-benefit analysis before we go embracing any military options," she said. "Omosupe, you're probably in a better position over at Commerce to come up with what kind of impact it would have if Manticore closed down our shipping through the wormholes they control. For that matter, just pulling their merchantships off the League's cargo routes would probably hit our economy pretty damned hard. But whether that's true or not, I can tell you even without looking at the numbers that our financial markets will take a *significant* hit if the Manties disrupt interstellar financial transactions as badly as they could."

"So we take an economic downtick." Rajampet shrugged. "That's happened before, even without the Manties getting behind and pushing it, and it's never been more than a short-term problem. I'm willing to concede this one could be worse, but even if it were, we'd still survive it. And don't forget this, either, Agatá—if we go all the way, then when the smoke clears, the Manticoran Wormhole Junction will belong to the *Solarian League*, not the Manties. That ought to save your shippers a pretty penny in transit fees over at Commerce, Omosupe! And even if it doesn't," he smiled avariciously, "all those fees would be coming to the *League*, not Manticore. Relatively speaking, it probably wouldn't mean all that much compared to our overall gross interstellar product, but it sure as hell ought to be enough to pay for whatever the war costs! And it would be an ongoing revenue source that brings in a nice piece of pocket change every year."

"And it would get the Manties out of our hair in the Verge, too," MacArtney said slowly. "It's worst over around Talbott right now, but I don't like the way they've been sniffing around the Maya Sector, either."

"Slow down, everybody," Kolokoltsov said firmly. They all looked at him, and he shook his head. "Whatever we do or don't do, we're *not* going to make our mind up sitting around this conference table this afternoon. That's pretty much what we did with their first note, isn't it? Correct me if I'm wrong, but that doesn't seem to have worked out all that well, does it? And, for that matter, Malachai's right on the money about the way we have to handle this for public consumption. I want to see how the Manties are spinning this in the 'faxes, and before we start suggesting any policies, I want us to *think* about it this time. I want all the data we have analyzed. I want the best possible models of what they've really got militarily, and I want a realistic estimate on how long military operations against the Manties would take. I'm talking about one that uses the most *pessimistic* assumptions, Rajani. I want any errors to be on the side of caution, not overconfidence. *And* I want to see some kind of numbers from you and Agatá, Omosupe, about what a full-scale war with Manticore could really cost us in economic and financial terms."

There was silence around the table—a silence that was just a bit sullen on Rajampet's part, Kolokoltsov thought. But it was also thoughtful, and he saw a high degree of agreement as he surveyed his fellow civilians' faces.

"At this moment, I'm strongly inclined to agree with Rajampet's reasoning," Nathan MacArtney said after several seconds. "But I also agree with you and Agatá about looking before we leap, Innokentiy. And with Malachai about doing the spadework ahead of time, as well. For that matter, if the Manties have taken out Byng's task force, there can't be much left in-sector for us to be launching any offensives with. I know for damn sure that Lorcan Verrochio isn't going to be authorizing any additional action by the handful of Frontier Fleet battlecruisers and cruisers he's got left in the Madras Sector, at any rate! And I don't think the Manties are going to go looking for yet another incident while this one's hanging over their heads."

"I doubt they are either," Kolokoltsov agreed. "On the other hand, I think we need to put together a new note pretty quickly. One that makes the fact that we're distinctly unhappy with them abundantly clear but adopts a 'coolheaded reason' attitude. We'll tell them we'll get back to them as soon as we've had an opportunity to study the available information, but I think we need to get that done more quickly than we did last time around. Unless there are any objections, I'll 'recommend' to the Foreign Minister that we get a stern but reasonable note off no later than tomorrow morning."

"Suit yourself," Rajampet said, and there might have been just a flicker of something in his eyes that Kolokoltsov didn't really care for. "I think it's going to come down to shooting in the end, but I'm more than willing to go along with the attempt to avoid it first."

"And there won't be any unilateral decisions on your part to send reinforcements to Meyers?" Kolokoltsov pressed, trying hard not to sound overtly suspicious.

"I'm not planning on sending any reinforcements to Meyers," Rajampet replied. "Mind you, I'm not going to just sit here on my arse, either! I'm going to be looking very hard at everything we can scrape up to throw at Manticore if it comes to that, and I'm probably going to start activating and manning at least a little of the Reserve Fleet, as well. But until we all agree a different policy's in order, I'll leave the balance of forces in the Talbott area just where it is." He shrugged. "There's damn-all we can do about it right now, anyway, given the communications lag."

Kolokoltsov still wasn't fully satisfied, and he still didn't care for that eye-flicker of whatever it had been, but there was nothing concrete he could find fault with, and so he only nodded.

"All right," he said then, and glanced at his chrono. "I'll have full copies of the Manties' note, Sigbee's report, and the accompanying technical data distributed to all of you by fourteen-hundred."

Chapter Two

"I CAN'T BELIEVE THIS," Fleet Admiral Winston Kingsford, CO, Battle Fleet, half-muttered. "I mean, I always knew Josef hated the Manties, but, still..."

His voice trailed off as he realized what he'd just said. It wasn't the most diplomatic comment he could possibly have made, since it was Fleet Admiral Rajampet who had personally suggested Josef Byng as the CO of Task Group 3021. Kingsford had thought it was a peculiar decision at the time, since the task group was a Frontier Fleet formation and Byng, like Kingsford, was a Battle Fleet officer. He'd also expected Fleet Admiral Engracia Alonso y Yáñez, Frontier Fleet's commanding officer, to resist Byng's appointment. For that matter, he'd expected *Byng* to turn it down. From a Battle Fleet perspective, a Frontier Fleet command had to be viewed as a *de facto* demotion, and Josef Byng had certainly had the family connections to avoid it if he'd chosen to.

All of which suggested it might not be a good idea to even hint at "I told you so" now that things had gone so disastrously awry.

"Believe it," Rajampet said heavily.

The two of them sat in Rajampet's luxurious office at the very apex of the Navy Building's four hundred stories. The view through the genuine windows was spectacular, and in another thirty or forty years it would almost certainly belong to one Winston Kingsford.

Assuming he didn't screw up irretrievably between now and then.

"Have you looked at the technical material yet, Sir?" he asked.

"Not yet." Rajampet shook his head. "I doubt very much that you'll find any clues as to secret Manticoran super weapons in it. Even if they've got them, I'm sure they'll have vacuumed the sensor data before they sent it on to us. And since Sigbee surrendered *all* of her ships, I'd imagine they did a pretty fair job of vacuuming her computers, too. So I don't think we're going to get a lot of insight into their hardware out of this even if they do oh-so-graciously return our property to us."

"With your permission, Sir, I'll hand this over to Karl-Heinz and Hai-shwun, anyway."

Admiral Karl-Heinz Thimár commanded the Solarian League Navy's Office of Naval Intelligence, and Admiral Cheng Hai-shwun commanded the Office of Operational Analysis. OpAn was the biggest of ONI's divisions, which made Cheng Thimár's senior deputy... and also the person who should have seen this coming.

"Of course," Rajampet agreed, waving one hand brusquely. Then his mouth tightened. "Don't hand it over until I've had a chance to talk to Karl-Heinz first, though. Someone's got to tell him about Karlotte, and I guess it's up to me."

"Yes, Sir," Kingsford said quietly, and gave himself a mental kick for forgetting Rear Admiral Karlotte Thimár, Byng's chief of staff, was—*had* been—Karl-Heinz's first cousin.

"Actually, getting them started on this is probably a damned good idea, even if we're not going to get much in the way of hard data out of it. I want the best evaluation OpAn can give me on these new missiles of theirs. I don't expect miracles, but see what you can get out of them."

"Yes, Sir."

"And while they're working on that, you and I are going to sit down and look at our deployment posture. I know the entire Manty navy's a fart in a wind storm compared to Battle Fleet, but I don't want us suffering any avoidable casualties because of overconfidence. Kolokoltsov has a point, damn him, about the difference in missile ranges. We're going to need a hammer they won't be able to stop when we go after their home system."

"*When* we go after their home system?" Kingsford stressed the adverb, and Rajampet barked a grating laugh.

"Those civilian idiots can talk about 'if' all they want to, Winston, but let's not you and I fool ourselves, all right? It's not 'if,' it's 'when,' and you know it as well as I do. Those Manticoran pricks are too arrogant to recognize what their real options are. They're not going to go for this ultimatum of Quartermain's, and in the end, that means we'll be going in. Besides—"

He broke off rather abruptly, and Kingsford raised one eyebrow at him. But the CNO only shook his head, waving his hand in another brushing away gesture.

"The point is," he continued, "that it's going to come to shooting in the end, no matter what sort of 'negotiations' anyone may try to set up. And when it does, the strategy's actually going to be pretty damned simple, since they've only got one really important star system. They don't have any choice, strategically. If we go after Manticore itself, they *have* to stand and fight. No matter how long-ranged their missiles may be, they can't just cut and run, so I want to be sure we've got enough counter-missiles and point defense to stand up to their missile fire while we drive straight for their planets. It may not be pretty, but it'll work."

"Yes, Sir," Kingsford said yet again, and he knew his superior was right. After all, that concept lay at the bottom of virtually all of Battle Fleet's strategic doctrine. But however much he might agree with the CNO about that, his brain was still working on that aborted "Besides" of Rajampet's. Something about it bothered him, but what...?

Then he remembered.

I wonder... Did he even mention Sandra Crandall and her task force to the others? And while I'm wondering, just how much did he have to do with getting her deployed to the Madras Sector in the first place?

It took all of his self-control to keep his eyes from narrowing in sudden, intense speculation, but this was definitely not the time to ask either of those questions. And even if he'd asked, the answers—assuming Rajampet answered him honestly—would only have raised additional questions. Besides, however far into this particular pie Rajampet's finger might be, the CNO was covered. Byng's assignment, while not precisely routine, wasn't completely unprecedented. It was certainly justifiable in the wake of the Battle of Monica and all the charges and counter charges *that* had spawned, as well. And, equally certainly, Crandall had the seniority to choose, within reason, where to carry out her training exercises. So if it just *happened* she'd picked the McIntosh System for Exercise Winter Forage (or whatever she'd decided to call it in the end), and if that just *happened* to mean Task Force 496 was barely fifty light-years away from the Meyers System, that didn't *necessarily* indicate any collusion on Rajampet's part.

Sure it didn't, he thought. *And I'll bet that answers my first question, too. Hell no, he didn't tell them. And he's covered no matter what happens, because she's undoubtedly made up her own mind by now what she's going to do, and he can't possibly get orders to her in time to stop her. So, really, there was no point in telling them, was there?*

Winston Kingsford hadn't commanded a fleet in space in decades, but he had plenty of experience in the tortuous, byzantine maneuvers of the Solarian League's bureaucracy. And he was well aware of how much Rajampet resented his own exclusion from the cozy little civilian fivesome which actually ran the League. Minister of Defense Taketomo's real power was no greater than that of any of the other cabinet ministers who theoretically governed the League, but Defense was—or damned well *ought* to be, anyway—at least as important as Commerce or Education and Information. It had a big enough budget to be, at any rate, and it was critical enough to the League's prosperous stability. Yet Rajampet had been denied his place at the head table, and it irritated the hell out of him.

But if we should just happen to get into a real, genuine war for the first time in three or four hundred years, all of that could change, couldn't it? Kingsford thought. *I wonder how many people Rajani would be willing to kill to bring* that *about?*

Despite his own trepidation, Kingsford felt a certain grudging admiration. It was always possible he was wrong, of course. In fact, he wouldn't have thought Rajampet had that sort of maneuver in him. But it wasn't as if Winston Kingsford felt any inclination to complain. After all, if Rajampet pulled it off, it was Kingsford who would eventually inherit that increased prestige and real political clout. And if everything went south on them, it wouldn't be *Kingsford's* fault. All he would have done was exactly what his lawful superior had instructed him to do.

It never even crossed his mind that in most star nations what he suspected Rajampet of would have constituted treason, or a reasonable facsimile thereof. For that matter, under the letter of the Solarian League Constitution, it *did* constitute treason—or, at the very least, "high crimes and misdemeanors," which carried the same penalty. But the Constitution had been a dead letter virtually from the day the original ink dried, and what someone else in some other star nation, far, far away, would have called "treason" was simply the way things were done here in the Solarian League. And, after all, *somebody* had to get them done, one way or another.

"Well, Sir," he said, speaking for the recorders he knew were taking down every word, "I can't say I'm looking forward to the thought of having any more of our people killed, but I'm afraid you're probably right about your civilian colleagues' hopes. I hope not, of course, but whatever happens there, you're *definitely* right about our in-house priorities. If this thing does blow up the way it has the potential to, we'd better be ready to respond hard and quickly."

"Exactly." Rajampet nodded firmly.

"In that case, I'd better be getting the technical data over to ONI. I know you want to tell Karl-Heinz about Karlotte yourself, Sir, but I'm afraid we're going to need to move pretty quickly on this if we're going to have those models and analyses by tomorrow morning."

"Hint taken," Rajampet said with a tight smile. "Head on over to his office. I'll screen him while you're on the way over. Probably be a good idea to give him something else to think about as quickly as possible, anyway."

Elizabeth III sat in her favorite, old-fashioned armchair in King Michael's Tower. A three-meter Christmas tree—a Gryphon needle-leaf, this year—stood in the center of the room in the full splendor of its ornaments, mounting guard over the family gifts piled beneath its boughs. Its resinous scent filled the air with a comforting perfume, almost a subliminal opiate which perfected the quiet peacefulness which always seemed to surround King Michael's, and there was a reason it was here rather than somewhere else in Mount Royal Palace. The stumpy, ancient stonework of the tower, set among its sunny gardens and fountains, was a solid, comforting reminder of permanence in Elizabeth's frequently chaotic world, and she often wondered if that was the reason it had become her and her family's private retreat. She might well conduct official business there, since a monarch who was also a ruling head of state was never really "off duty," but even for business purposes, King Michael's Tower was open only to her family and her personal friends.

And to some people, she thought, looking at the tall, almond-eyed admiral sitting sideways in the window seat across from her, with her long legs drawn up and her back braced against one wall of the window's deep embrasure, who had become both.

"So," the Queen said, "what did your friend Stacey have to say over lunch yesterday?"

"My friend?" Admiral Lady Dame Honor Alexander-Harrington arched one eyebrow.

"I think it's a fair choice of noun." Elizabeth's smile was more than a little tart. "Mind you, I don't think anyone would have given very high odds on that particular friendship's ever happening, given the way you and her father first met."

"Klaus Hauptman isn't actually the worst person in the world." Honor shrugged. "Admittedly, he made an ass out of himself in Basilisk, and I wouldn't say we got off on the right foot in Silesia, either. And, to be honest, I don't think I'm ever going to really *like* him. But he does have his own sense of honor and obligations, and that's something I can respect, at least."

The cream-and-gray treecat stretched out on the window sill raised his head and looked at her with quizzically tilted ears. Then he sat up, and his true-hands began to flicker.

<He's smart enough to be scared of you,> his agile, flashing fingers signed. <And he knew what Crystal Mind would do to him if he didn't admit mistakes.>

"'Crystal Mind'?" Elizabeth repeated out loud. "Is that what the 'cats call Stacey?"

"Yes," Honor replied, but she was looking at the treecat. "I don't think that's entirely fair, Stinker," she told him.

<"Fair" is a two-leg idea,> he signed back. <The People think better to be accurate.>

"Which is one of the reasons I, personally, prefer treecats to most of the two-legs I know," Elizabeth agreed. "And, for that matter, Nimitz's estimate of Hauptman the Elder's personality is closer to mine than yours is."

"I didn't put him up for sainthood, you know," Honor observed mildly. "I only said he isn't the worst person in the world, and he isn't. Arrogant, opinionated, frequently thoughtless, and entirely too accustomed to getting his own way, yes. I'll grant you all of that. But the old pirate's also one of the most honest people I know—which is pretty amazing, when you get down to it, given how rich he is—and once he figures out he has an obligation in the first place, he's downright relentless about meeting it."

"That much," Elizabeth conceded, "is true. And"—the Queen's eyes narrowed shrewdly, and she cocked her head—"the fact that he's so strongly committed to stamping out the genetic slave trade probably helps just a tad where you're concerned, too, doesn't it?"

"I'll admit that." Honor nodded. "And, frankly, from what Stacey had to say, he's not taking the possibility of Manpower's involvement in what's going on in Talbott what someone might call calmly."

"No, I suppose not."

Elizabeth leaned back in her armchair, and the treecat stretched along its top purred buzzingly as the back of her head pressed against his silken pelt. He reached down, caressing her cheek with one long-fingered true-hand, and she reached up to stroke his spine in return.

"He's not exactly alone in that reaction, is he, though?" she continued.

"No."

Honor sighed and scooped Nimitz up. She gave him a hug, then deposited him in her lap, rolled him up on his back, and began to scratch the soft fur of his belly. He let his head fall back, eyes more than half-slitted, and her lips quirked as he purred in delight.

In point of fact, Elizabeth's last question was its own form of thundering understatement, and she wondered what the response on Old Terra was like. By now, their newsies had to have picked up the reports coming out of Manticore, and it wouldn't be very long before the first Solarian reporters started flooding through Manticore, trying to get to Spindle and New Tuscany to cover the story.

"I'm sure you have at least as good a feel for how people are reacting to all this as Stacey does," she pointed out after a moment.

"Yes, and no," Elizabeth replied. Honor looked a question at her, and the Queen shrugged. "I've got all the opinion polls, all the tracking data, all the mail pouring into Mount Royal, analyses of what's being posted on the public boards—all of that. But she's the one who's been building up her little media empire over the

last T-year and a half. Let's face it, the newsies are actually better than my so-called professional analysts at figuring out where
public opinion is headed. And I'm sure she's also hearing things
from her father's friends and business acquaintances, as well. For
that matter, you move in some fairly rarefied financial circles
yourself, Duchess Harrington!"

"Not so much since I went back on active duty," Honor disagreed. "Willard and Richard are looking after all of that for me
until further notice."

Elizabeth snorted, and it was Honor's turn to shrug. What she'd
said was accurate enough, but Elizabeth had a point, as well. It
was true that Willard Neufsteiler and Richard Maxwell were basically running her own sprawling, multi-system financial empire at
the moment, but she made it a point to stay as abreast of their
reports as she did those from Austen Clinkscales, her regent in
Harrington Steading, and those reports frequently included their
insights into the thinking of the Manticoran business community.
And, for that matter, of the *Grayson* business community.

"At any rate," she went on, "Stacey hasn't had her 'media empire'
all that long. She's still working on getting everything neatly organized, and I think there are aspects of the business which offend
her natural sense of order. But, I have to admit, the fact that she's
so new to it also means it's all still fresh and interesting to her."

"So she did bring it up at lunch!" Elizabeth said a bit trium-
phantly, and Honor chuckled. But then her chuckle faded.

"Yes, she did. And I'm pretty sure she said basically what your
analysts are already telling you. People are worried, Beth. In
fact, a lot of them are scared to death. I don't say they're scared
as badly as some of them were immediately after the Battle of
Manticore, but that still leaves a lot of room for terror, and this
is the *Solarian League* we're talking about."

"I know." Elizabeth's eyes had darkened. "I know, and I wish
there'd been some way to avoid dumping it on all of them. But—"

She broke off with an odd little shake of her head, and Honor
nodded again.

"I understand that, but you were right. We had to go public
with it—and not just because of our responsibility to tell people
the truth. Something like this was bound to break sooner or
later, and if people decided we'd been trying to hide it from them
when it did..."

She let her voice trail off, and Elizabeth grimaced in agreement.

"Did Stacey have a feel for how her subscribers reacted to the fact that we already sat on the news about what happened to Commodore Chatterjee for almost an entire T-month?" the Queen asked after a moment.

"Some of them are upset about the delay, but she says e-mails and com calls alike are both running something like eight-to-one in support of it, and the opinion poll numbers show about the same percentages." Honor shrugged again. "Manticorans have learned a bit about when and how information has to be . . . handled carefully, let's say, in the interest of operational security. You've got a pretty hefty positive balance with most of your subjects on that issue, actually. And I think just about everyone understands that, especially in this case, we have to be wary about inflaming public opinion. And not just here in the Star Kingdom, either."

"That's my read, too," Elizabeth agreed. "But I'm still not entirely happy about mentioning the possible Manpower connection." She sighed, her expression worried. "It's bad enough telling people we're effectively at war with the Solarian League without telling them we think a bunch of nasty genetic slavers may be behind it all. Talk about sounding paranoid!"

Honor smiled wryly. Yet again, Elizabeth had a point. The notion that any outlaw corporation, however big, powerful, and corrupt it might be, was actually in a position to manipulate the military and foreign policy of something the size of the Solarian League was preposterous on the face of it. Honor herself had been part of the discussion about whether or not to go public with that particular aspect of Michelle Henke's summary of her New Tuscan investigation's conclusions. It really did sound paranoid—or possibly just like the ravings of a lunatic, which wasn't all that much better—but she agreed with Pat Givens and the other analysts over at ONI. Lunatic or not, the evidence was there.

"I agree some people think it's a little far fetched," she said after a moment. "At the same time, a lot of other people seem to be looking very hard at the possibility Mike's onto something. And, to be perfectly frank, I'm just as happy to have that aspect of it out in the public 'faxes because of the possible out it gives those idiots on Old Terra. If Manpower really was behind it, maybe it will occur to them that cleaning their own house—and letting their public know they're doing it—is one response that might let both of us step back from the brink. If they can legitimately lay the blame on Manpower, then maybe they can admit they were manipulated into a false position. They've got to know that if they'll only do that, we'll meet them halfway at the negotiating table. And after what already happened to them in Monica, and with Technodyne, surely the groundwork for that kind of response is already in place!"

"Sure it is. And you can add in the fact that they're going to be pissed as hell at Manpower when they realize we're right. So they've got all sorts of reasons to climb on board and do exactly what you're suggesting. But they're not going to."

Elizabeth's expression was no longer worried; now it was grim, and Honor frowned a question at her.

"If they'd been going to be reasonable, they never would've taken better than three weeks just to respond to our first note. Especially when their entire response amounted to telling us they'd 'look into our allegations' and get back to us. Frankly, I'm astounded they managed to leave out the word 'ridiculous' in front of 'allegations.'" The Queen shook her head. "That's not a very promising start...and it *is* very typically Solly. They're never going to admit their man was in the wrong, no matter *how* he got there, if there's any way they can possibly avoid it. And do you really think they're going to want to admit that a multi-stellar that isn't even based in a League star system—and *is* involved up to its eyebrows in a trade the League's officially outlawed—is able to manipulate entire squadrons of their battlecruisers and ships-of-the-wall?" She shook her head again, more emphatically. "I'm afraid a lot of them would rather go out and pin back the uppity neobarbs' ears, no matter how many people get killed along the way, than open any windows into corners of the League's power structure that are that filled with dirty little secrets."

"I hope you're wrong about that," Honor said quietly, and Elizabeth's lips twitched.

"I notice you only 'hope' I am," she said.

"I'd prefer a stronger verb myself," Honor acknowledged. "But..."

"'But,' indeed," Elizabeth murmured. Then she pushed herself more briskly upright in her chair. "Unfortunately, I don't think either of us can afford to treat ourselves to any of those stronger verbs of yours. Which, along with thinking about the possibility of past errors, brings me to what I really wanted to ask you about."

"Four days," Honor said, and Elizabeth chuckled.

"That obvious, was I?"

"I have been thinking about it a bit myself, you know," Honor replied. "The ops plan's been finalized, even if everyone hopes we won't have to use it; Alice Truman's running the fleet through the rehearsal exercises; and I'm just about finished up with my briefings from Sir Anthony. So, about four days."

"You're sure you don't want a couple of more days with the fleet yourself?"

"No." Honor shook her head, then smiled. "Actually, I could probably be ready to leave even sooner than that, especially since I'm taking Kew, Selleck, and Tuominen with me. But if it's all the same to you, I'm not going anywhere until after I've celebrated Raoul's and Katherine's first Christmas with Hamish and Emily."

"Of course 'it's all the same' to me." Elizabeth's face softened with a smile of her own, and it was her turn to shake her head. "It's still a bit hard sometimes to remember you're a mother now. But I always figured on your at least having Christmas at home before we sent you off. Are your parents going to be there, too?"

"And Faith and James. Which, by the way, made Lindsey happy, when she found out about it. This would've been the first Christmas she hadn't spent with the twins since they were a year old."

"I'm glad for all of you," Elizabeth said. Then she inhaled deeply. "But getting back to business, and allowing for your schedule, you're sure about how you want to go about this?"

"I wouldn't go so far as to say I was sure about it, and I'm not going to pretend I'm anything anyone would be tempted to call an expert at something like this, either. I just think it's the best shot we've got...and that we can at least be pretty sure of getting their attention."

"I see." Elizabeth looked at her for several seconds, then snorted. "Well, just remember this little jaunt was your idea in the first place. Mind you, now that I've had time to really think about it, I think it's a *good* idea. Because whether you were right in the beginning or I was"—her expression sobered once more—"it would be a really, really good idea for us to get at least one forest fire put out. If this entire situation with the League turns out as badly as I am afraid it could, we're not going to need to be dealing with more than one problem at a time."

✧   ✧   ✧

Honor Alexander-Harrington stood as James MacGuiness ushered the tallish man in the uniform of the Republican Navy into her Landing mansion's office. Behind her, beyond the crystoplast wall and the office balcony, the dark blue waters of Jason Bay were a ruffled carpet under a sky of dramatic clouds and brilliant late-afternoon sunlight, patterned in endless lines of white-crested waves as a storm pushed in from the open sea, and Honor supposed that made a fitting allegory, in many ways, for her relationship with her visitor.

"Admiral Tourville," she said, rising and extending her hand across her desk while Nimitz sat upright on his perch and cocked his head thoughtfully at the Havenite.

"Admiral Alexander-Harrington." Lester Tourville reached out to shake the offered hand, and she tasted his own flicker of ironic amusement. His lips twitched in a brief almost-smile under his bushy mustache, and she released his hand to indicate the chair in front of her desk.

"Please, take a seat."

"Thank you," he said, and sat.

Honor settled back into her own chair, propped her elbows on the armrests, and steepled her fingers in front of her chest as she contemplated him. The two of them had, as the newsies might have put it, "a history." He was the only Havenite officer to whom Honor had ever been forced to surrender; the man she'd defeated at the Battle of Sidemore in the opening phases of Operation Thunderbolt; *and* the fleet commander who'd come perilously close to winning the war for the Republic of Haven five months earlier.

But as Andrew always says, "close" only counts with horseshoes, hand grenades, and tactical nukes, she reminded herself.

Which was true enough, but hadn't prevented the Battle of Manticore from killing better than two million human beings. Nor did it change the fact that Honor had demanded the surrender of his intact databases as the price for sparing his surviving super-dreadnoughts. She'd been within her rights to stipulate whatever terms she chose, under the rules of war, yet she'd known when she issued the demand that she was stepping beyond the customary *usages* of war. It was traditional—and generally expected—that any officer who surrendered his command would purge his computers first. And, she was forced to concede, she'd had Alistair McKeon

do just that with his own data when she'd ordered him to surrender his ship to Tourville.

*I suppose if I'd been going to be "honorable" about it, I should
have extended the same privilege to him. He certainly thought I
should have, at any rate.*

Her lips twitched ever so slightly as she remembered the seething
fury which had raged behind his outwardly composed demeanor
when they'd finally met face-to-face after the battle. Nothing
could have been more correct—or icier—during the "interview"
which had formalized his surrender, but he hadn't known about
Honor's ability to directly sense the emotions of those about her.
He might as well have been bellowing furiously at her, as far
as any real ability to conceal his feelings was concerned, and a
part of her hadn't cared. No, actually, a part of her had taken its
own savage satisfaction from his anger, from the way his sense
of failure burned so much more bitterly after how agonizingly
close to total success he'd come.

She wasn't proud of the way she'd felt. Not now. But then the
deaths of so many men and women she'd known for so long had
been too fresh, wounds too recent for time to have stopped the
bleeding. Alistair McKeon had been one of those dead men and
women, along with every member of his staff. So had Sebastian
D'Orville and literally hundreds of others with whom she had
served, and the grief and pain of all those deaths had fueled her
own rage, just as Tourville's dead had fanned his fury.

*So I guess it's a good thing military courtesy's as iron bound as
it is,* she thought. *It kept both of us from saying what we really
felt long enough for us to stop feeling it. Which is a good thing,
because even then, I knew he was a decent man. That he hadn't
taken any more pleasure in killing Alistair and all those others
than I'd taken in killing Javier Giscard or so many of Genevieve
Chin's people.*

"Thank you for coming, Admiral," she said out loud, and this
time there was nothing halfway about his smile.

"I was honored by the invitation, of course, Admiral," he replied
with exquisite courtesy, exactly as if there'd been any real question about a prisoner of war's accepting an "invitation" to dinner
from his captor. Nor was it the first such invitation he'd accepted
over the past four T-months. This would be the seventh time
he'd dined with Honor and her husband and wife. Unlike him,

however, Honor was aware it would be the last time they'd be dining together for at least the foreseeable future.

"I'm sure you were," she told him with a smile of her own. "And, of course, even if you weren't, you're far too polite to admit it."

"Oh, of course," hc agreed affably, and Nimitz bleeked the treecat equivalent of a laugh from his perch.

"That's enough of that, Nimitz," Tourville told him, wagging a raised forefinger. "Just because *you* can see inside someone's head is no excuse for undermining these polite little social fictions!"

Nimitz's true-hands rose, and Honor glanced over her shoulder at him as they signed nimbly. She gazed at him for a moment, then chuckled and turned back to Tourville.

"He says there's more to see inside some two-legs' heads than others."

"Oh?" Tourville glowered at the 'cat. "Should I assume he's casting aspersions on the content of any particular two-leg's cranium?"

Nimitz's fingers flickered again, and Honor smiled as she watched them, then glanced at Tourville once more.

"He says he meant it as a general observation," she said solemnly, "but he can't help it if *you* think it ought to apply to anyone in particular."

"Oh, he does, does he?"

Tourville glowered some more, but there was genuine humor in his mind-glow. Not that there had been the *first* time he'd realized the news reports about the treecats' recently confirmed telempathic abilities were accurate.

Honor hadn't blamed him—or any of the other POWs who'd reacted the same way—a bit. The thought of being interrogated by a professional, experienced analyst who knew how to put together even the smallest of clues you might unknowingly let slip was bad enough. When that professional was assisted by someone who could read your very thoughts, it went from bad to terrifying in record time. Of course, treecats couldn't really read any human's actual *thoughts*—the mental... frequencies, for want of a better word, were apparently too different. There'd been no way for any of the captured Havenites to know that, however, and every one of them had assumed the worst, initially, at least.

And, in fact, it was bad enough from their perspective as it was. Nimitz and his fellow treecats might not have been able to read the prisoners' *thoughts*, but they'd been able to tell from their emotions whenever they were lying or attempting to mislead. And they'd been able to tell when those emotions spiked as the interrogation approached something a POW most desperately wanted to conceal.

It hadn't taken very long for most of the captured personnel to figure out that even though a treecat could guide an interrogator's questioning, it couldn't magically pluck the desired information out of someone else's mind. That didn't keep the 'cats from providing a devastating advantage, but it did mean that as long as they simply refused to answer, as was their guaranteed right under the Deneb Accords, the furry little lie detectors couldn't dig specific, factual information out of them.

That wasn't enough to keep at least some of them from bitterly resenting the 'cats' presence, and a significant handful of those POWs had developed a positive hatred for them, as if their ability to sense someone's emotions was a form of personal violation. The vast majority, however, were more rational about it, and several—including Tourville, who'd had the opportunity to interact with Nimitz years before, when Honor had been *his* prisoner—were far too fascinated to resent them. Of course, in Tourville's case, the fact that he'd done his dead level best to see to it that Nimitz's person had been decently and honorably treated during her captivity had guaranteed that Nimitz liked *him*. And, as Honor had observed many times over the five decades they'd spent together, only the most well armored of curmudgeons could resist Nimitz when the 'cat set out to be charming and adorable.

He'd had Tourville wrapped around his furry little thumb in less than two weeks, despite the still thorny emotions crackling between the Havenite officer and Honor. Within a month, he'd been lying across Tourville's lap and purring blissfully while the admiral almost absently stroked his coat during meetings with Honor.

Of course, I have to wonder how Lester would react if he knew I can read his emotions just as well as Nimitz can, she reflected for far from the first time.

"I'm sure he didn't mean to imply anything disrespectful," Honor assured Tourville now, and the Havenite snorted.

"Of course he didn't." The Republican admiral leaned back in his chair and shook his head. Then he cocked that same head at Honor. "May I ask what I owe the pleasure of this particular invitation to?"

"Mostly it's a purely social occasion," Honor replied. He raised a skeptical eyebrow, and she smiled. "I did say mostly."

"Yes, you did, didn't you? In fact, I've discovered, if you'll forgive me for saying so, that you're most dangerous when you're being the most honest and frankly candid. Your hapless victim doesn't even notice the siphon going into his brain and sucking out the information you want."

His amusement, despite a bitterly tart undertone, was mostly genuine, Honor noted.

"Well, if I'm going to be frank and disarming," she said, "I might as well admit that the thing I'd most like to 'siphon out of your brain' if I only could would be the location of Bolthole."

Tourville didn't quite flinch this time. He *had*, the first time she'd mentioned that name to him, and she still couldn't decide if that stemmed from the fact that he knew exactly how vital a secret the location of the Republic's largest single shipyard—and R&D center—was, or if he'd simply been dismayed by the fact that she even knew its codename. In either case, she knew she wasn't going to pry its location out of him, assuming he actually knew what it was. He wasn't an astrogator himself, after all, although he undoubtedly knew enough about it for someone to have put the pieces together and figured out the actual location with his cooperation. Expecting Lester Tourville to cooperate over something like that would be rather like a Sphinxian woodbuck's expecting to negotiate a successful compromise with a hungry hexapuma, however, and that was one piece of data which hadn't been anywhere in any of the computers aboard his surrendered ships. It once had been, no doubt—they'd confirmed that at least half his surrendered ships had actually been built there—but it had been very carefully (and thoroughly) deleted since.

And exactly why anyone should be surprised by that eludes me, she thought. *It's not as if Haven hasn't had plenty of experience in maintaining operational security. Of course they were going to make sure there was as little critical data as possible stored in the computers of ships heading into a battle like that one! Quite aside from any demands by arrogant, unreasonable flag officers for anyone who wanted to surrender, there was no way to be sure we wouldn't capture one of their wrecks and find out the security failsafes hadn't scrubbed the computers after all. And only drooling idiots—which, manifestly, Thomas Theisman, Eloise Pritchart, and Kevin Usher are* not—*would fail to realize just how critical Bolthole's location is! It's not as if we haven't been trying to figure it out ever since the shooting started back up, after all. And I'm sure they know how hard we've been looking, even if we haven't had much luck cracking their security. Of course, we'd've had* better *luck if we'd still been up against the Legislaturalists or the Committee of Public Safety. We don't have anywhere near as many dissidents to work with, anymore.*

"Bolthole?" Tourville repeated, then shrugged. "I don't know what you're talking about."

He didn't bother trying to lie convincingly, since both of them knew he wouldn't get away with it anyway, and the two of them exchanged wry smiles. Then Honor sobered a bit.

"To be honest," she said, "I'm actually much more interested in any insight you can give me—or are willing to give me—into the Republic's political leadership."

"Excuse me?" Tourville frowned at her. They'd touched upon the political leaders of the Republic several times in their earlier conversations, but only glancingly. Enough for Honor to discover not only that Operation Beatrice had been planned and mounted only after Manticore had backed out of the summit talks Eloise Pritchart had proposed, but also that Tourville, like every other Havenite POW who'd been interrogated in the presence of a treecat, genuinely believed it was the Star Kingdom of Manticore which had tampered with their prewar diplomatic exchanges. The fact that all of them were firmly convinced that was the truth didn't necessarily mean it *was*, of course, but the fact that someone as senior and as close to Thomas Theisman as *Tourville* believed it was a sobering indication of how closely the truth was being held on the other side.

In fact, they all believe it so strongly that there are times I'm *inclined to wonder,* she admitted to herself.

It wasn't a topic she was prepared to discuss with most of her fellow Manticorans, even now, but she'd found herself reflecting on the fact that the correspondence in question had been generated by Elaine Descroix as Baron High Ridge's foreign secretary. There wasn't much Honor—or anyone else who'd ever met High Ridge—would have put past him, including forging the file copies of diplomatic correspondence to cover his backside, assuming there was any conceivable advantage for him in having been so inflammatory in the first place. Actually, if anyone had asked her as a hypothetical question whether someone with Eloise Pritchart's reputation (and Thomas Theisman as a member of her administration) or the corrupt politicos of the High Ridge Government were more likely to have falsified the diplomatic exchanges which had been handed to the newsfaxes, she would have picked the High Ridge team every time.

But there are too many permanent undersecretaries and assistant undersecretaries in the Foreign Office who actually saw the original messages. That's what it keeps coming back to. I've been able to talk to them, too, and every one of them is just as convinced as every one of Lester's people that it was the other *side who falsified things.*

"There are . . . things going on," she told Tourville now. "I'm not prepared to discuss all of them with you. But there's a pretty good chance that having the best feel I can get for the personalities of people like President Pritchart could be very important to both of our star nations."

Lester Tourville sat very still, his eyes narrowing, and Honor tasted the racing speed of the thoughts she couldn't read. She *could* taste the intensity of his speculation, and also a sudden spike of wary hope. She'd discovered the first time they'd met that the sharp, cool brain behind that bristling mustache was a poor match for the "cowboy" persona he'd cultivated for so long. Now she waited while he worked his way through the logic chains, and she felt the sudden cold icicle as he realized there were *several* reasons she might need a "feel" for the Republic's senior political leaders and that not all of them were ones he might much care for. Reasons that contained words like "surrender demand," for example.

"I'm not going to ask you to betray any confidences," she went on unhurriedly. "And I'll give you my word that anything you tell me will go no further than the two of us. I'm not interrogating you for anyone else at this point, Lester. This is purely for my own information, and I'll also give you my word that my reason for asking for it is to prevent as much bloodshed—on either side—as I possibly can."

He looked at her for several seconds, then inhaled deeply.

"Before I tell you anything, I have a question of my own."

"Go ahead and ask," she said calmly.

"When you demanded my surrender," he said, gazing intently into her eyes, "was it a bluff?"

"In what sense?" She tilted her head to one side.

"In two senses, I suppose."

"Whether or not I would have fired if you hadn't surrendered?"

"That's one of them," he admitted.

"All right. In that sense, I wasn't bluffing at all," she said levelly. "If you hadn't surrendered, and accepted my terms in full, I would have opened fire on Second Fleet from beyond any range at which you could have effectively replied, and I would have gone right on firing until whoever was left in command surrendered or every single one of your ships was destroyed."

Silence hovered between them for several moments that seemed oddly endless. It was a taut, singing silence—a mutual silence built of the understanding of two professional naval officers. And yet, despite its tension, there was no anger in it. Not anymore. The anger they'd both felt at the time had long since vanished into something else, and if she'd had to pick a single word to describe what the two of them felt now, it would have been "regret."

"Well, that certainly answers my first question," he said finally, smiling crookedly. "And I suppose I'm actually relieved to hear it." Her eyebrows arched, and he snorted. "I've always thought I was a pretty good poker player. I would've hated to think I'd misread you quite that badly at the time."

"I see." She shook her head with a slight smile of her own. "But you said there were two senses?"

"Yes." He leaned forward, propping his forearms on his thighs, and his eyes were very sharp. "The other 'bluff' I've been wondering about is whether or not you really could have done it from that range?"

Honor swung her chair from side to side in a small, thoughtful arc while she considered his question. Theoretically, what he was asking edged into territory covered by the Official Secrets Act. On the other hand, it wasn't as if he was going to be e-mailing the information to the Octagon. Besides...

"No," she said after no more than two or three heartbeats. "I couldn't have. Not from that range."

"Ah." He sat back once more, his crooked smile going even more crooked. Then he inhaled deeply. "Part of me really hated to hear that," he told her. "Nobody likes finding out he was tricked into surrendering."

She opened her mouth to say something, then closed it again, and he chuckled. It was a surprisingly genuine chuckle, and the amusement behind it was just as genuine, she realized. And it was also oddly gentle.

"You wanted my databases intact," he said. "We both know that. But I know what else you were going to say, as well."

"You do?" she asked when he paused.

"Yep. You were going to say you did it to save lives, but you were afraid I might not believe you, weren't you?"

"I wouldn't say I thought you wouldn't *believe* me," she replied thoughtfully. "I guess the real reason was that I was afraid it would sound . . . self-serving. Or like some sort of self-justification, at least."

"Maybe it would have, but that doesn't change the fact that Second Fleet was completely and utterly screwed." He grimaced. "There was no way we were going to get out of the resonance zone and make it into hyper before you *were* in range to finish us off. All that was going to happen in the meantime was that more people were going to get killed on both sides without changing the final outcome at all."

Honor didn't say anything. There was no need to, and he crossed his legs slowly, his expression thoughtful.

"All right," he said. "With the stipulation that any classified information is off the table, I'll answer your questions."

Chapter Three

"SO YOU'RE SATISFIED with our own security position at the moment, Wesley?"

Benjamin IX, Protector of Grayson, leaned back in his chair, watching the uniformed commander in chief of the Grayson Space Navy across his desk. Wesley Matthews looked back at him, his expression a bit surprised, then nodded.

"Yes, Your Grace, I am," he said. "May I ask if there's some reason you think I shouldn't be?"

"No, not that *I* think you shouldn't be. On the other hand, I have it on excellent authority that certain questions are likely to be raised in the Conclave of Steadholders' New Year's session."

Matthews' expression went from slightly surprised to definitely sour and he shook his head in disgusted understanding.

The two men sat in Benjamin Mayhew's private working office in Protector's Palace. At the moment, the planet Grayson's seasons were reasonably coordinated with those of mankind's birth world, although they were drifting slowly back out of adjustment, and heavy snow fell outside the palace's protective environmental dome. The larger dome which Skydomes of Grayson was currently erecting to protect the entire city of Austen was still only in its embryonic stages, with its preliminary girder work looming against the darkly clouded sky like white, furry tree trunks or—for those of a less cheerful disposition—the strands of some vast, frosted spiderweb. Outside the palace dome, clearly visible through its

45

transparency from the bookcase-lined office's window, crowds of children cheerfully threw snowballs at one another, erected snowmen, or skittered over the steep, cobbled streets of the Old Town on sleds. Others shrieked in delight as they rode an assortment of carnival rides on the palace grounds themselves, and vendors of hot popcorn, hot chocolate and tea, and enough cotton candy and other items of questionable dietary value to provide sugar rushes for the next several days could be seen nefariously plying their trade on every corner.

What *couldn't* be clearly seen from Matthews' present seat were the breath masks those children wore, or the fact that their gloves and mittens would have served the safety requirements of hazardous materials workers quite handily. Grayson's high concentrations of heavy metals made even the planet's snow potentially toxic, but that was something Graysons were used to. Grayson kids took the need to protect themselves against their environment as much for granted as children on other, less unfriendly planets took the need to watch out for traffic crossing busy streets.

And, at the moment, all of those hordes of children were taking special pleasure in their play because it was a school holiday. In fact, it was a planetary holiday—the Protector's Birthday. The next best thing to a thousand T-years worth of Grayson children had celebrated that same holiday, although for the last thirty T-years or so, they'd been a bit shortchanged compared to most of their predecessors, since Benjamin IX had been born on December the twenty-first. The schools traditionally shut down for Christmas vacation on December the eighteenth, so the kids didn't get an extra day away from classwork the way they might have if Benjamin had been thoughtful enough to be born in, say, March or October. That little scheduling *faux pas* on his part (or, more fairly perhaps, on his mother's) was part of the reason Benjamin had always insisted on throwing a special party for all the children of the planetary capital and any of their friends who could get there to join them. At the moment, by Matthews' estimate, the school-aged population of the city of Austen had probably risen by at least forty or fifty percent.

It was also traditional that the Protector did no official business on his birthday, since even he was entitled to at least one vacation day a year. Benjamin, however, was prone to honor that particular tradition in the breach, although he'd been known to use the fact that he was officially "off" for the day as a cover from time to time. And it would appear this was one of those times. Events were building towards the formal birthday celebration later this evening, but Matthews was among the inner circle who'd been invited to arrive early. He would have found himself in that group anyway, given how long and closely he and Benjamin had worked together, but there'd obviously been other reasons this year.

The high admiral regarded his Protector thoughtfully. This was Benjamin's fiftieth birthday, and his hair was streaked progressively more thickly with silver. Not that Matthews was any spring chicken himself. In fact, he was ten T-years older than Benjamin, and his own hair had turned completely white, although (he thought with a certain comfortable vanity) it had remained thankfully thick and luxuriant.

But thick or not, we're neither one of us getting any younger, he reflected.

It was a thought which had occured to him more frequently of late, especially when he ran into Manticoran officers half again his age who still looked younger than he did. Who *were* younger, physically speaking, at least. And more than a few *Grayson* officers fell into that same absurdly youthful-looking category, now that the first few generations to enter the service since Grayson's alliance with Manticore had made the prolong therapies generally available were into their late thirties or—like Benjamin's younger brother, Michael—already into their early forties.

It's only going to get worse, Wesley, he told himself with an inescapable edge of bittersweet envy. *It's not their fault, of course. In fact, it's nobody's fault, but there are still a lot of things I'd like to be here to see.*

He gave himself a mental shake and snorted silently. It wasn't exactly as if he were going to drop dead of old age tomorrow! With modern medicine, he ought to be good for at least another thirty T-years, and Benjamin could probably look forward to another half T-century.

Which had very little to do with the question the Protector had just asked him.

"May I ask exactly which of our esteemed steadholders are likely to be raising the questions in question, Your Grace?"

"Well, I think you can safely assume Travis Mueller's name is going to be found among them." Benjamin's smile was tart.

"And I expect Jasper Taylor's going to be right beside him. But I understand they've found a new front man—Thomas Guilford."

Matthews grimaced. Travis Mueller, Lord Mueller, was the son of the late and (by most Graysons) very unlamented *Samuel* Mueller, who'd been executed for treason following his involvement in a Masadan plot to assassinate Benjamin and Queen Elizabeth. Jasper Taylor was Steadholder Canseco, whose father had been a close associate of Samuel Mueller and who'd chosen to continue the traditional alliance between Canseco and Mueller. But Thomas Guilford, Lord Forchein, was a newcomer to that particular mix. He was also quite a few years older than either Mueller or Canseco, and while he'd never been one of the greater admirers of the social and legal changes of the Mayhew Restoration, he'd never associated himself with the Protector's more strident critics. There hadn't been much question about his sentiments, but he'd avoided open confrontations with Benjamin and the solid block of steadholders who supported the Sword and he'd always struck Matthews as less inclined than Mueller to cheerfully sacrifice principle in the name of "political pragmatism."

"When did Forchein decide to sign on with Mueller and Friends, Your Grace?"

"That's hard to say, really." Benjamin tipped his swiveled armchair back and swung it gently from side to side. "To be fair to him—not that I particularly want to be, you understand—I doubt he was really much inclined in that direction until High Ridge tried to screw over every other member of the Alliance."

Matthews snorted again, this time out loud. Like Benjamin himself, the high admiral strongly supported Grayson's membership in the Manticoran Alliance. Not only was he painfully aware of just how much Grayson had profited, both technologically and economically, from its ties with the Star Kingdom of Manticore, but he was even better aware of the fact that without the intervention of the Royal Manticoran Navy, the planet of Grayson would either have been conquered outright by the religious lunatics who'd run Masada or at best have suffered nuclear or kinetic bombardment from space. At the same time, he had to admit the High Ridge Government had proved clearly that the Star Kingdom was far from perfect. In his considered opinion, "screw over" was an extraordinarily pale description of what Baron High Ridge had done to his alliance so-called partners. And like many

other Graysons, Matthews was firmly of the opinion that High
Ridge's idiotic foreign policy had done a great deal to provoke
the resumption of hostilities between the Republic of Haven and
the Star Kingdom and its allies.

As far as the high admiral was personally concerned, that simply demonstrated once again that idiocy, corruption, and greed
were inescapable elements of mankind's fallen nature. Tester knew
there'd been more than enough traitors, criminals, corrupt and
arrogant steadholders, and outright lunatics in *Grayson* history!
Indeed, the name "Mueller" came rather forcibly to mind in that
connection. And for every Manticoran High Ridge, Matthews
had met two or three Hamish Alexanders or Alistair McKeons
or Alice Trumans, not to mention having personally met Queen
Elizabeth III.

And then, of course, there was Honor Alexander-Harrington.

Given that balance, and how much Manticoran and Grayson
blood had been shed side by side in the Alliance's battles, Matthews was prepared to forgive the Star Kingdom for High Ridge's
existence. Not all Graysons were, however. Even many of those
who remained fierce supporters of Lady Harrington separated
her in their own minds from the Star Kingdom. She was one
of *theirs*—a Grayson in her own right, by adoption and shed
blood—which insulated her from their anger at the High Ridge
Government's stupidity, avarice, and arrogance. And the fact that
she and High Ridge had been bitter political enemies only made
that insulation easier for them.

"I'm serious, Wesley." Benjamin waved one hand, as if for
emphasis. "Oh, Forchein's always been a social and religious
conservative—not as reactionary as some, thank God, but bad
enough—but I'm pretty sure it was the combination of High
Ridge's foreign policy and Haven's resumption of open hostilities
that tipped his support. And, unfortunately, he's not the only one
that's true of."

"May I ask how bad it actually is, Your Grace?" Matthews
inquired, his eyes narrower.

It wasn't the sort of question he usually would have asked,
given the Grayson tradition of separation between the military
and politics. Senior officers weren't supposed to factor politics
into their military thinking. Which, of course, was another of
those fine theories which consistently came to grief amid the

shoals of reality. There was a difference, however, between being aware of the political realities which affected the ability of his Navy to formulate sound strategy or discharge its responsibilities to defend the Protectorate of Grayson and of becoming involved in the formulation of political policy.

"To be honest, I'm not really certain," Benjamin admitted. "Floyd is taking some cautious political soundings, and I expect we'll have a pretty good idea within the next week or so of who else might be inclined in Forchein's direction."

Matthews nodded. Floyd Kellerman, Steadholder Magruder, had become Benjamin's chancellor following Henry Prestwick's death in the attempt to assassinate Benjamin and Elizabeth III. He'd also been Prestwick's understudy for the last two years of the old chancellor's tenure, and the Magruders had been Mayhew allies literally for centuries. Lord Magruder hadn't yet developed the intricate web of personal alliances Prestwick had possessed, but he'd already demonstrated formidable abilities as both an administrator and a shrewd politician.

"Having said that, however," the Protector continued, "I'm already pretty confident about *where* the problem is going to come from... and what our problem children—however many of them there turn out to be—are going to want." He shook his head. "Some of them wouldn't have supported us sticking with Manticore against Haven this time around if the Protector's Own hadn't already been involved at Sidemore. Their position is that High Ridge had already violated Manticore's treaty obligations to us by conducting independent negotiations with Haven, which amounted to a unilateral abrogation of the Alliance. And while we do have a mutual defense treaty outside the formal framework of the overall Alliance, one whose terms obligate us to come to one another's support in the event of any attack by an outside party, the Star Kingdom's critics have pointed out that the Republic of Haven did not, in fact, attack Grayson in Operation Thunderbolt despite our involvement in defending *Manticoran* territory. The implication being that since High Ridge chose to violate Manticore's solemn treaty obligations to us—along with every other party to the Alliance—there's no reason we should feel legally or morally bound to honor our treaty obligations to them if doing so isn't in the Protectorate's best interests.

"And—surprise, surprise!—the way the Manticorans' expansion into the Talbott Sector's brought them into direct collision with the Solarian League has only made the people who are pissed off with Manticore even less happy. And to be honest, I can't really blame anyone for being nervous about finding themselves on the wrong end of a confrontation with the League, especially after the way High Ridge squandered so much of the Star Kingdom's investment in loyalty.

"Of course, none of our vessels have actually been involved in operations anywhere near Talbott, but we do have personnel serving on *Manticoran* warships which have been. For that matter, over thirty of our people were killed when that idiot Byng blew up the destroyers they were serving in. Which gives the people who worry about what may happen between the League and the Manticorans—and, by extension, with *us*—two legitimate pieces of ammunition. The Sollies may view the participation of our personnel, even aboard someone else's ships, in military operations against the League as meaning we've already decided to back Manticore, and I don't think it would be totally unfair to argue that the people we've already lost were lost in someone else's fight. Mind you, *I* think it should be obvious to anyone with any sort of realistic appreciation for how Frontier Security and the League operate that standing up to the Sollies should be *every* independent 'neobarb' star system's fight. Not everyone's going to agree with me about that, unfortunately, and those who don't will be airing their concerns shortly. Which brings me back to my original question for you. How satisfied *are* you with the system's security?"

"In the short term, completely, Your Grace." Matthews' response was as firm as it was instant. "Whatever High Ridge and Janacek might have done, ever since Willie Alexander took over as Prime Minister, especially with Hamish as his First Lord of Admiralty, our channels of communication have been completely opened again. Our R&D people are working directly with theirs, and they've provided us with everything we needed to put Apollo into production here at Yeltsin's Star. For that matter, they've delivered over eight thousand of the system-defense variant Apollo pods. And they've also handed our intelligence people complete copies of the computer files Countess Gold Peak captured from Byng at New Tuscany, along with specimens of Solly missiles, energy weapons, software systems—the works. For that matter, if we want it, they're more than willing to let us have one of the actual battlecruisers the countess brought back from New Tuscany so we can examine it personally. So far, we haven't taken them up on that. Our people in Admiral Hemphill's shop are already seeing everything, and, frankly, the Manties are probably better at that sort of thing than we are here at home, anyway.

"Based on what we've seen out of the Havenites, I'm confident we could successfully defend this star system against everything the Republic has left. And based on our evaluation of the captured Solarian material, my best estimate is that while the Sollies probably could take us in the end, they'd need upwards of a thousand ships-of-the-wall to do it. And that's a worst-case estimate, Your Grace. I suspect a more realistic estimate would push their force requirements upward significantly." He shook his head. "Given all their other commitments, the amount of their wall of battle that's tucked away in mothballs, and the fact that they'd pretty much have to go through Manticore before they got to us at all, I'm not worried about any known short-term threat."

He paused for a moment, as if to let the Protector fully absorb his own confidence, then drew a deep breath.

"In the *long* term, of course, the Solarian League could pose a very serious threat to the Protectorate. I agree with the Manties' estimate that it would take years for the SLN to get comparable technology into production and deployed. I think some of the individual system-defense forces could probably shave some time off of how long it's going to take the SLN in particular, and the League in general, to overcome the sheer inertia of their entrenched bureaucracies, but as far as I'm aware, none of those SDFs are in anything like the Star Kingdom's—I mean the Star *Empire's*—league. For that matter, I don't think any of them could come close to matching our combat power for quite a lengthy period. But in the end, assuming the League has the stomach to pay the price in both human and economic terms, there's not much doubt that, barring direct divine intervention, the Sollies could absorb anything we and the Manticorans combined could hand out and still steamroller us in the end."

Benjamin puffed his lips, his eyes worried, and rotated his chair some more. It was very quiet in the office—quiet enough for Matthews to hear the creaking of the old-fashioned swivel chair—and the high admiral found himself looking out the window again, at the throngs of children.

I'd really like for someone to grow up on this planet without having to worry about wars and lunatics, he thought sadly, almost wistfully. *I've done my best to keep them* safe, *but that's not the same thing.*

"I wish I could say I was surprised by anything you've just said," Benjamin said at last, pulling Matthews' eyes back to him. "Unfortunately, it's about what I expected to hear, and I don't doubt Mueller and Friends, as you call them, have reached about the same conclusions. They already think of us as 'Manticoran lackeys' who put Manticore's interests ahead of Grayson's. That's going to dispose them to take the least optimistic possible view, shall we say, of our long-term strategic position. Nor do I doubt that they're going to be perfectly ready to share their thoughts on the subject with their fellow steadholders."

"Your Grace, I could—"

"No, you *couldn't*, Wesley," Benjamin interrupted. The high admiral looked at him, and the Protector smiled tartly. "I'm sure, High Admiral Matthews, that you would never suggest to the Lord Protector that it might be possible for you to prevaricate or even mislead the Conclave of Steadholders if you were called to testify before them."

Matthews closed his mouth and sat back in his chair, and Benjamin chuckled harshly.

"Don't think I wouldn't appreciate the offer, if you'd ever been so lost to all sense of your legal and moral responsibilities as to make it. But even if I were tempted to encourage you to do any such thing, and even if it wouldn't be both morally and legally wrong—which, granted, aren't always exactly the same things—it would only blow up in our faces in the long run. After all, it's not exactly like it would take a hyper physicist to realize just how damned big the League is. If we tried to pretend the Sollies couldn't kick our posterior in the long run, we'd only look and sound ridiculous. Or, worse, like we were trying to carry water for the Manties. So I doubt you'd be able to do much good... in that respect, at least."

Matthews nodded slowly, but something about the Protector's tone puzzled him. He knew it showed in his expression, and Benjamin chuckled again, more naturally, when he saw it.

"I said I don't want you to mislead anyone about the long-term threat the League could pose, Wesley. I never said I didn't want you to underline your confidence in our *short*-term security, if you're actually confident about it."

"Of course, Your Grace." Matthews nodded with no reservations. In fact, even though he'd scrupulously used the phrase "any known short-term threat" in his response to the Protector's question, in his own mind a better one would have been "any *conceivable* short-term threat."

"Good." Benjamin nodded back. "One thing we scheming autocrats realized early on, High Admiral, is that *short-term* threats have a far greater tendency to crystallize political factions, for or against, than long-term ones do. It's the nature of the way human minds work. And if we can get through the next few months, the situation could certainly change. For example, there's Lady Harrington's mission to Haven."

Matthews nodded, although he suspected he hadn't succeeded in keeping at least a trace of skepticism out of his expression. As the Grayson Space Navy's uniformed commander, he was one of the handful of people who knew about Honor Alexander-Harrington's planned mission to the Republic of Haven. He agreed that it was certainly worth trying, even if he didn't exactly have unbridled optimism about the chances for its success. On the other hand, Lady Harrington had a knack for accomplishing the improbable, so he wasn't prepared to totally rule out the possibility.

"If we can manage to bury the hatchet with Haven, it should be a major positive factor where the public's morale is concerned, and it would certainly strengthen our hand in the Conclave," Benjamin pointed out. "Not only that, but if anyone in the Solarian League realizes just how steep our present technological advantage is, and couples that with the fact that we're not being distracted by the Republic anymore, he may just figure out that picking a fight with Manticore is a game that wouldn't be worth the candle."

"Your Grace, I can't disagree with anything you've just said," Matthews said. "On the other hand, you and I both know how Sollies think. Do you really believe there's going to be a sudden unprecedented outburst of rationality in *Old Chicago*, of all places?"

"I think it's *possible*," Benjamin replied. "I'm not saying I think it's *likely*, but it is possible. And in some ways, this makes me think about a story my father told me—an old joke about a Persian horse thief."

"Excuse me, Your Grace?"

"A Persian horse thief." Matthews still looked blank, and Benjamin grinned. "Do you know what 'Persia' was?"

"I've heard the word," Matthews admitted cautiously. "Something from Old Earth history, wasn't it?"

"Persia," Benjamin said, "built one of the greatest pre-technic empires back on Old Earth. Their king was called the 'shah,' and the term 'checkmate' in chess comes originally from 'shah mat,' or 'the king is dead.' That's how long ago they were around.

"Anyway, the story goes that once upon a time a thief stole the shah's favorite horse. Unfortunately for him, he was caught trying to get off the palace grounds with it, and dragged before the shah in person. The penalty for stealing any horse was pretty severe, but stealing one of the shah's was punishable by death, of course. Still, the shah wanted to see the man who'd had the audacity to try to steal a horse out of the royal stables themselves.

"So the shah's guardsmen brought the thief in, and the shah said, 'Didn't you know stealing one of my horses is punishable by death, fellow?' And the thief looked at him and said 'Of course I knew that, Your Majesty. But everyone knows you have the finest horses in all the world, and what horse thief worthy of the name would choose to steal any but the finest?'

"The shah was amused, but the law was the law, so he said 'Give me one reason why I shouldn't have your head chopped off right this minute.' The horse thief thought about it for a few moments, then said, 'Well, Your Majesty, I don't suppose there's any legal reason why you shouldn't. But if you'll spare my life, I'll teach your horse to sing.'

" 'What?' the shah demanded. 'You claim you can actually teach my horse to *sing*?' 'Well, of course I can!' the thief replied confidently. 'I'm not just a *common* horse thief, after all, Your Majesty. I don't say it will be easy, but if I can't teach your horse to sing within one year, then you can chop off my head with my blessings.'

"So the shah thought about it, then nodded. 'All right, you've got your year. If, at the end of that year, you haven't taught the horse to sing, though, I warn you—a simple beheading will be the *least* of your problems! Is that understood?' 'Of course, Your Majesty!' the horse thief replied, and the guards hauled him away.

" 'Are you crazy?' one of them asked him. 'No one can teach a horse to *sing*, and the shah's going to be even more pissed off when he figures out you lied to him. All you've done is to trade having your head chopped off for being handed over to the torturers! What were you *thinking*?' So the thief looks at him and says 'I have a year in which to do it, and in a year, the shah may die, and his successor may choose to spare my life. Or the *horse* may die, and I can scarcely be expected to teach a *dead* horse to sing, and so my life may be spared. Or, *I* may die, in which case it won't matter whether or not the horse learns to sing.' 'And if none of those things happen?' the guard demanded. 'Well, in that case,' the thief replied, 'who knows? Maybe the horse *will* learn to sing!'"

Matthews chuckled, and the Protector's grin broadened. Then it slowly faded, and he let his chair come back upright, laying his forearms on his desk and leaning forward over them.

"And in some ways, that's where we are, isn't it?" he asked. "We've been too closely allied with Manticore for too long, and we've already had personnel involved in active combat with the SLN. If the League decides to hammer the Star Kingdom over something that was clearly the League's fault in the first place, what makes anyone think they'll hesitate to hammer any of the uppity neobarbs' uppity neobarb friends, at the same time? What's one more star system when you're already planning on destroying a multisystem empire, with the largest independent merchant marine in the entire galaxy, just because you can't admit one of your own admirals screwed up by the numbers?"

Matthews looked back at his Protector, wishing he could think of an answer to Benjamin's questions.

"So that's where we are," the Protector repeated quietly. "In the long term, unless we're prepared to become another nice, obedient Frontier Security proxy and go around bashing other 'neobarbs' for the League, I'm sure they'll decide one of their flag officers should have another unfortunate little accident that gets our Navy trashed along with Manticore's before *we* turn into a threat to them. So all I can see for us to do is the best we can and hope that somewhere, even in the Solarian League, someone's going to be bright enough to see the shipwreck coming and try to avoid it. After all," Benjamin grinned again, this time without amusement, "the horse really may learn to sing."

✧   ✧   ✧

"All right, boys and girls," Commander Michael Carus said. "It's official. We can go home now."

"Hallelujah!" Lieutenant Commander Bridget Landry said from

her quadrant of his com display. "Not that it hasn't been fun," she continued. "Why, I haven't enjoyed myself this much since they fixed that impacted wisdom tooth for me."

Carus chuckled. The four destroyers of the Royal Manticoran Navy's Destroyer Division 265.2, known as "the Silver Cepheids," had been sitting a light-month from Manticore-A for two weeks, doing absolutely nothing. Well, that wasn't exactly fair. They'd been sitting here maintaining a scrupulous sensor watch *looking for* absolutely nothing, and he was hardly surprised by Landry's reaction.

No, I'm not, he admitted. *But somebody had to do it. And when it comes to perimeter security for the entire star system, better safe than sorry any day, even if it does mean somebody has to be bored as hell.*

DesDiv 265.2 had been sent to check out what was almost certainly a sensor ghost but which could, just possibly, have been an actual hyper footprint. It was extraordinarily unlikely that anyone would have bothered to make his alpha translation this far out, be his purposes ever so nefarious, since his impeller signature would certainly have been detected long before he could get close enough to the Manticore Binary System to accomplish anything. But Perimeter Security didn't take chances on words like "unlikely." When a sensor ghost like this one turned up, it was checked out—quickly and thoroughly. And if the checker-outers didn't find anything immediately upon arrival, they stayed put for the entire two T-weeks SOP required.

Which was precisely what the Silver Cepheids had just finished doing.

"Should I assume, Bridget," Carus said, "that you have some pressing reason for wanting to head home at this particular moment?"

"Oh, how could you possibly suspect anything of the sort?" Lieutenant Commander John Pershing asked from the bridge of HMS *Raven*, and Lieutenant Commander Julie Chase, CO of HMS *Lodestone* chuckled.

"I take it your senile old skipper is missing something?" Carus said mildly.

"She's got one of those creative archaism thingies," Chase said.

"That's creative *anachronisms*, you ignorant lout," Landry corrected with a frown.

"Are you going off to play dress-up *again*, Bridget?" Carus demanded.

"Hey, don't you start on me!" she told him with a grin. "Everyone's got her own hobby—even you. Or was that someone else I saw tying trout flies the other day?"

"At least he eats what he catches," Chase pointed out. "Or is it that what catches him eats him?" She frowned, then shrugged. "Anyway, it's not as silly as all those costumes of yours."

"Before you go around calling it silly, Julie," Pershing suggested, "you might want to reflect on the fact that 'the Salamander' is an honorary member of Bridget's chapter."

"What?" Chase stared at him from her display. "You're kidding! *Duchess Harrington's* part of this silly SCA thing?"

"Well, not really," Landry said. "Like John says, it's an honorary membership. One of her uncles is a real big wheel in the Society on Beowulf, and he sponsored her back, oh, I don't know... must've been thirty T-years ago. I've actually met her at a couple of meetings though, you know. She took the pistol competition at both of them, as a matter of fact."

"There you have it," Carus said simply. "If it's good enough for the Salamander, it's good enough for anyone. So let's not have anyone abusing Bridget over her hobby anymore, understand? Even if it is a remarkably silly way for an adult human being to spend her time, at least she's being silly in good company. So there."

Landry stuck out her tongue at him, and he laughed. Then he looked sideways at Lieutenant Linda Petersen, his astrogator aboard HMS *Javelin*.

"Got that course figured for us, Linda?"

"Yes, Skipper," Petersen nodded.

"Well, in that case pass it to these other characters," Carus told her. "Obviously, we have to get Commander Landry back to Manticore before she turns back into a watermelon, or a pumpkin, or whatever it was."

Commodore Karol Østby leaned back in the comfortable chair, eyes closed, letting the music flow over him. Old Terran opera had been his favorite form of relaxation for as long as he could remember. He'd even learned French, German, *and* Italian so he could listen to them in their original languages. Of course, he'd always had a pronounced knack for languages; it was part of the Østby genome, after all.

At this moment, however, he found himself in rather greater

need of that relaxation than usual. The seven small ships of his command had been creeping tracelessly about the perimeter of the Manticore Binary System for over a T-month, and that wasn't something calculated to make a man feel comfortable. Whatever those idiots in the SLN might think, Østby and the Mesan Alignment Navy had the liveliest possible respect for the capabilities of Manty technology. In this case, though, it was the Manties' turn to be outclassed—or, at least, taken by surprise. If Østby hadn't been one hundred percent confident of that when Oyster Bay was originally planned, he was now. His cautious prowling about the system had confirmed that even the Alignment's assessment of its sensor coverage had fallen badly short of the reality. Any conventional starship would have been detected long ago by the dense, closely integrated, multiply redundant sensor systems he and his personnel had painstakingly plotted. In fact, he was just a little concerned over the possibility that those surveillance systems might still pick up something soon enough to at least blunt Oyster Bay's effectiveness.

Stop that, Karol, he told himself, never opening his eyes. *Yes, it* could *happen, but you know it's not very damned likely. You just need something to worry about, don't you?*

His lips twitched in sour amusement as he acknowledged his own perversity, but at the same time, he was aware that his worrier side was one of the things that made him an effective officer. His subordinates probably got tired of all the contingency planning he insisted upon, yet even they had to admit that it made it unlikely they would truly be taken by surprise when Murphy decided to put in his inevitable appearance.

So far, though, that appearance hadn't happened, and Østby's flagship *Chameleon* and her consorts were past the riskiest part of their entire mission. Their own reconnaissance platforms were the stealthiest the Alignment could provide after decades of R&D and more capital investment than he liked to think about, and those platforms hadn't transmitted a single byte of information. They'd made their sweeps on ballistic flight profiles, using purely passive sensors, then physically rendezvoused with their motherships to deliver their take.

And, overall, that take had been satisfying, indeed. Passive sensors were less capable than active ones, but the multiple systems each platform mounted compensated for a lot of that. From the numbers of energy sources they'd picked up, it appeared the ships the Manties currently had under construction weren't as far along in the building process as intelligence had estimated. If they had been, there'd have been more onboard energy sources already up and running. But at least Østby now knew exactly where the orbital yards were, and the *external* energy sources his platforms had picked up indicated that most of them had projects under-way. From the numbers of signatures, and the way they clustered, it looked as though more than a few of the yards were at early stages of their construction projects, and he hoped that didn't mean intelligence's estimate of the Manties' construction times was off. It was hard to be certain, given how cautiously he had to operate, but if all those new projects meant the yards in question had finished their *older* projects ahead of estimate...

And the fact that the Manties seem to be sending all their new construction off to Trevor's Star for working up exercises doesn't help, either, he admitted sourly.

Which was true enough—it didn't help one bit. Still, there was a lot of work going on in those dispersed yards of theirs, and while his estimates on what their space stations were up to were more problematical, he had no doubt there were quite a few ships under construction in those highly capable building slips, as well.

And we know exactly where they *are,* he reminded himself.

Now it was just a matter of keeping tabs on what their recon platforms had located for them. He'd really have preferred to send the platforms through on another short-range sweep closer to their actual execution date, but his orders were clear on that. It was more important to preserve the element of surprise than it was to monitor every single detail. And it wasn't as if there'd been any effort to conceal the things Østby and his people were there looking for. People didn't normally try to hide things like orbital shipyards (even if they'd wanted to, Østby couldn't imag-ine how someone would go about doing it), nor did they move them around once they were in position. And if anyone did move them, *Chameleon* and her sisters would be bound to know, given the distant optical watch they were keeping and the fact that the impeller wedge of any tug that started moving shipyards would certainly be powerful enough to be detected by at least one of the watching scout ships.

So all we have to do now is wait, he told himself, listening to the music, listening to the voices. *One more T-month until we put the guidance platforms in place.*

That was going to be a little risky, he admitted in the privacy of his own thoughts, but only a little. The guidance platforms were even stealthier than his ships. Someone would have to almost literally collide with one of them to spot them, and they'd be positioned well above the system ecliptic, where there was no traffic to do the colliding. He would have been happier if the platforms had been a little smaller—he admitted that to himself, as well—but delivering targeting information to that many individual missiles in a time window as short as the Oyster Bay ops plan demanded required a prodigious amount of bandwidth. And, despite everything, it was highly likely the Manties were going to hear *something* when they started transmitting all that data.

Not that it was going to make any difference at that late date, he reflected with grim pleasure. Everything he and his squadron had done for the last three and a half T-months all came down to that transmission's handful of seconds . . . and once it was made, nothing could save the Star Empire of Manticore.

Chapter Four

"HAVE YOU GOT A COPY of that memo from Admiral Cheng?" Captain Daud ibn Mamoun al-Fanudahi asked, poking his head into Captain Irene Teague's office.

"*Which* memo?" Teague rolled her eyes in an expression she wouldn't have let any other Battle Fleet officer see. In fact, she wouldn't have let al-Fanudahi see it as recently as a month or so ago. Displaying contempt—or, at the very least, disrespect—for a flag officer was always risky, but even more so when the officer doing the displaying was from Frontier Fleet and the object of the display was from Battle Fleet. And especially when the flag officer in question was the Frontier Fleet officer in question's CO.

Unfortunately, Irene Teague had concluded that al-Fanudahi had been right all along in his belief the "preposterous reports" of the Royal Manticoran Navy's "super weapons" weren't quite so preposterous after all. A point which, in her opinion, had been abundantly proved by what had happened to Josef Byng at New Tuscany. And a point which apparently continued to elude Cheng Hai-shwun, the commanding officer of the Office of Operational Analysis, to which she and al-Fanudahi happened to be assigned.

"The one about that briefing next week," al-Fanudahi said. "The one for Kingsford and Thimár."

"Oh."

Teague frowned, trying to remember which of her voluminous correspondence folders she'd stuffed that particular memo into.

Half the crap she filed hadn't even been opened, much less read. No one could possibly keep track of all of the memos, letters, conference reports, requests, and just plain garbage floating around the Navy Building and its annexes. Not that the originators of all that verbiage felt any compulsion to acknowledge that point. The real reason for most of it was simply to cover their own posteriors, after all, and the excuse that there simply weren't enough hours in the day to read all of it cut no ice when they produced their file copy and waved it under one's nose.

She tapped a command, checking an index. Then shrugged, tapped another, and snorted.

"Yeah. Here it is." She looked up. "You need a copy?"

"Bang one over to my terminal," al-Fanudahi replied with a slightly sheepish grin. "I don't have a clue where I filed my copy. But what I really needed was to see if Polydorou or one of his reps is supposed to be there."

"Just a sec." Teague skimmed the memo, then shrugged. "No mention of it, if they are."

"I didn't remember one." Al-Fanudahi grimaced. "Not exactly a good sign, wouldn't you say?"

"Probably not," Teague agreed, after a moment. "On the other hand, maybe it *is* a good thing. At least this way if they listen to you at all, he'll have less warning to start covering his arse before someone starts asking him some pointed questions."

"And just how likely do you really think that is?"

"Not very," she admitted.

If Cheng had so far failed to grasp the nature of the sausage machine into which the SLN was about to poke its fingers, Admiral Martinos Polydorou, the commanding officer of Systems Development was in active denial. The SysDev CO had been one of the masterminds behind the "Fleet 2000" initiative, and he was even more convinced of the inevitability of Solarian technological superiority than the majority of his fellow officers.

In theory, it was SysDev's responsibility to continually push the parameters, to search constantly for improved technologies and applications. Of course, in theory, it was also OpAn's responsibility to analyze and interpret operational data which might identify potential threats. Given that al-Fanudahi's career had been stalled for decades mostly because he'd tried to do exactly that, it probably wasn't surprising Polydorou's subordinates were unlikely to disagree with him. After all, Teague was one of the very few OpAn analysts who'd come to share al-Fanudahi's concerns... and he'd specifically instructed her to keep her mouth shut about that minor fact.

"There might be a better chance of getting some of those questions asked if you'd let me sign off on your report, Daud," she pointed out now.

"Not enough better to risk burning your credibility right alongside mine." He shook his head. "No. It's not time for you to come out into the open yet, Irene."

"But, Daud—"

"No." He interrupted her with another headshake. "There's not really anything new in Sigbee's dispatches. Aside from the confirmation their missiles have a range from rest of at least twenty-nine million kilometers, at any rate, and that'd already been confirmed at Monica, if anyone'd been interested in looking at the reports." He shrugged. "Someone's got to keep telling them about it, but they're not going to believe it, no matter what we say, until one of our units gets hammered in a way that's impossible even for someone like Cheng or Polydorou to deny. Everybody's got too much of the 'not invented here' syndrome. And they don't want to hear from anyone who disagrees with them."

"But it's only a matter of time before they find out you've been right all along," she argued.

"Maybe. And when that happens, do you think they're going to *like* having been proved wrong? What usually happens to someone like me—someone who's insisted on telling them the sky is falling—is that if it turns out he was right, his superiors are even more strongly motivated to punish him. The last thing they want is to ask the advice of someone who's told them they were idiots after the universe demonstrates they really were idiots. That's why it's important you stay clear of this. When the crap finally hits the fan, you'll be the one who had access to all of my notes and my reports, who's in the best position to be their 'expert witness' on that basis, but who hasn't been pissing them off for as long as they can remember."

"It's not right," she protested quietly.

"So?" Teague had seen lemons less tart than al-Fanudahi's smile. "You were under the impression someone ever guaranteed life was fair?"

"No, but..."

Her voice trailed off, and she gave her head an unwilling little toss of understanding. Not *agreement*, really, but of acceptance.

"Well, now that that's settled," al-Fanudahi said more briskly, "I was wondering if you'd had any more thoughts on that question of mine about the difference between their missile pods and tube-launched missiles?"

"About the additional drive system, you mean?"

"Yeah. Or even about the additional drive *systems*, plural."

"Daud, I'm on your side here, remember, and I'm willing to grant you that they might be able to squeeze one more drive into a missile body they could shoehorn into a pod, but even I don't see how they could've put in *three* of the damned things!"

"Don't forget our esteemed colleagues are still arguing they couldn't fit in even two of them," al-Fanudahi retorted, eye a-gleam with combined mischief, provocation, and genuine concern. "If they're wrong about that, then why couldn't *you* be wrong about drive system number three?"

"Because," she replied with awful patience, "there are physical limits not even Manties can get around. Besides—"

Daud ibn Mamoun al-Fanudahi leaned his shoulders against the wall of her cubicle and smiled as he prepared to stretch the parameters of her mind once again.

Aldona Anisimovna walked briskly down the sumptuously decorated hallway. It wasn't the first time she'd made this walk, but this time she was unaccompanied by the agitated butterflies which had polkaed around her midsection before. And not just because Kyrillos Taliadoros, her personal enhanced bodyguard, walked quietly behind her. His presence was one sign of how monumentally her universe had changed in the last six T-months, yet it was hardly the only one.

Then again, everyone else's universe is about to change, too, isn't it? she thought as they neared their destination. *And they don't even know it.*

On the other hand, neither had she on that day six T-months ago when she and Isabel Bardasano walked into Albrecht Detweiler's office and Anisimovna, for the first time in her life, learned the *real* truth.

They reached the door at the end of the hall, and it slid open at their approach. Another man, who looked like a cousin of Taliadoros' (because, after all, he was one), considered them gravely for a moment, then stepped aside with a gracious little half-bow.

Anisimovna nodded back, but the true focus of her attention was the man sitting behind the large office's desk. He was tall, with strong features, and the two younger men sitting at the opposite ends of his desk looked a great deal like him. Not surprisingly.

"Aldona!" Albrecht Detweiler smiled at her, standing behind the desk and holding out his hand. "I trust you had a pleasant voyage home?"

"Yes, thank you, Albrecht." She shook his hand. "Captain Maddox took excellent care of us, and *Bolide* is a perfectly wonderful yacht. And"—she rolled her eyes drolly at him—"so *speedy*."

Detweiler chuckled appreciatively, released her hand, and nodded at the chair in front of his desk. Taliadoros and Detweiler's own bodyguard busied themselves pouring out cups of coffee with the same deftness they brought to certain more physical aspects of their duties. Then they withdrew, leaving her with Albrecht and his two sons.

"I'm glad you appreciate *Bolide*'s speed, Aldona." Benjamin Detweiler set his cup back on its saucer and smiled slightly at her. "And we appreciate your using it to get home this quickly."

Anisimovna nodded in acknowledgment. The "streak drive" was yet another thing she hadn't known anything about six months ago. Nor, to be frank, was it something she would have expected out of Mesan researchers. Like most of the rest of the galaxy, although for rather different reasons, she'd been inclined to think of her home world's R&D community primarily in terms of biological research. Intellectually, she'd known better than most of humanity that the planet of Mesa's scientific and academic communities had never restricted themselves solely to genetics and the biosciences. But even for her, those aspects of Mesa had been far more visible, the things that defined Mesa, just as they defined Beowulf. *Well, if it surprised me, I imagine that's a pretty good indication of just how big a surprise it's going to be for everyone else, too,* she thought dryly. *Which is going to be a very good thing over the next few years.*

The streak drive represented a fundamental advance in interstellar travel, and there was no indication anyone else was even close to duplicating it. For centuries, the theta bands had represented an inviolable ceiling for hyper-capable ships. Everyone had known it was theoretically possible to go even higher, attain a still higher apparent normal-space velocity, yet no one had ever managed to design a ship which could crack the iota wall and survive. Incredible amounts of research had been invested in efforts to do just that, especially in the earlier days of hyper travel, but with a uniform lack of success. In the last few centuries, efforts to beat the iota barrier had waned, until the goal had been pretty much abandoned as one of those theoretically possible but practically unobtainable concepts.

But the Mesan Alignment hadn't abandoned it, and finally, after the better part of a hundred T-years of dogged research, they'd found the answer. It was, in many ways, a brute force approach, and it wouldn't have been possible even now without relatively recent advances (whose potential no one else seemed to have noticed) in related fields. And even with those other advances, it had almost doubled the size of conventional hyper generators. But it worked. Indeed, they'd broken not simply the iota wall, but the kappa wall, as well. Which meant the voyage from New Tuscany to Mesa, which would have taken anyone else the next best thing to forty-five T-days, had taken Anisimovna less than thirty-one.

"Now," Albrecht said, drawing her attention back to him, "Benjamin, Collin, and I have skimmed your report. We'd like to hear it directly from you, though."

"Of course," she replied, "but—" She paused, then gave her head a tiny shake. "Excuse me, Albrecht, but I actually expected to be making this report to Isabel."

"I'm afraid that won't be possible." It wasn't Albrecht who answered her; it was Collin, and his voice was far harder and harsher than Albrecht's or Benjamin's had been. She looked at him, and he gave a sharp, angry shrug. "Isabel's dead, Aldona. She was killed about three months ago . . . along with everyone else in the Gamma Center at the time."

Anisimovna's eyes widened in shock. Despite her recent admission to the Mesan Alignment's innermost circles, she still had only the vaguest notion of what sort of research had been carried on in the Alignment's various satellite centers. The only thing she'd known about the Gamma Center was that, unlike most of the others, it was right here in the Mesa System . . . which implied it was also more important than most.

"May I ask what happened?"

She more than half expected him to tell her no, since she presumably had no operational need to know. But Isabel had become more than just another of her professional colleagues, and Collin surprised her.

"We still don't have all the pieces, actually," he admitted. "In fact, we never will. We do know someone activated the self-destruct security protocols, and who it was. We're still guessing at some of the events leading up to that, but given that Isabel was on her way to take him into custody, we're pretty sure *why* he activated them."

He paused, expression grim, and Anisimovna nodded. If she'd had a choice between pressing a self-destruct button and facing what would be euphemistically described as "rigorous questioning," she would have chosen vaporization, too.

"What we still can't prove is exactly what he was up to before Isabel became suspicious of him. We're sure we've figured out his basic intentions, but we've had to do most of the figuring from secondary sources. There aren't any *primary* sources or witnesses left on our side, aside from the one low-level agent who seems to be the only person to've done everything right. But there's reason to believe the Ballroom was involved, at least peripherally."

"The *Ballroom* knew about the Gamma Center?" Astonishment and a sudden pulse of panic startled the question out of her. If the ex-genetic slave terrorists of the Ballroom had discovered that much, who knew how much *else* they might have learned about the Alignment?

"We don't think so." Collin shook his head quickly. "We do have a few . . . witnesses from the other side, and based on their testimony and our own investigations, we've confirmed that Zilwicki and Cachat were here on Mesa and—almost certainly—that the Center's head of security made contact with them."

Anisimovna knew her eyes were huge, but not even an alpha line could have helped that under these circumstances. Anton Zilwicki and Victor Cachat had been here on Mesa *itself*? This was getting better and better by the second, wasn't it?

"None of the evidence suggests they'd come expressly looking for the Center," Collin went on reassuringly. "We know how the traitor discovered they were here in the first place, so we're confident they didn't come looking to make contact with *him*, at any rate. It looks like he decided, for reasons of his own, that he wanted to defect and jumped at the chance when he realized they were here. In fact, we have imagery of him actually meeting Zilwicki—that's what made Isabel suspicious in the first place. Zilwicki hadn't been IDed from the imagery before she went looking for . . . the defector, but she did know that low-level agent I mentioned had already fingered him as a Ballroom peripheral. Unfortunately, the first person he reported that little fact to was the Center's chief of security."

He smiled thinly at Anisimovna's grimace.

"Yes, that was convenient for him, wasn't it?" he agreed. "We think that's what triggered the decision to defect, and it also put him in a position to keep anyone higher up the chain from realizing Zilwicki was on-planet. The only thing that screwed him up was the original agent's suspicions when one of his bugs caught them meeting in a seccy restaurant. We were just lucky as hell our man had the gumption and the balls to go directly to Isabel. Unfortunately, 'lucky' is a relative term in this case. Our man didn't know his 'Ballroom peripheral' was Anton Zilwicki, so Isabel didn't realize it either. If she had, she would have approached the whole thing differently, but she clearly had no idea how serious the security breach really was, and she decided to handle it personally, quickly, and, above all, quietly. Which, however reasonable it may've seemed, was a mistake in this case. When he realized Isabel was coming for him, the defector was able to trigger the charge under the Center. He took the whole damned place—and all of its on-site records and personnel—with him. Not to mention one of Green Pines' larger commercial towers—and everyone inside *it*—when the charge went off in its sub-basement."

Anisimovna inhaled suddenly, sharply. She might have known the Gamma Center was in the Mesa System, but she'd never guessed it might be located in one of the system capital's bedroom suburbs!

"The only good points were that it was a Saturday and early, so most of the Center's R&D personnel were safely at home, and the defector had apparently set up a fallback position to take out Zilwicki and Cachat in case they stiffed him. He used it, and we're ninety-nine-point-nine-nine percent sure he managed to kill both of them . . . even if it did take *another* nuke to do the job. So they're both dead, at least. But not"—his jaw muscles tightened, and he eyes went terrifyingly cold—"without another Ballroom bastard using a nuke on Pine Valley Park. On a Saturday morning."

Anisimovna's stomach muscles clenched. She knew Collin's family lived just outside Green Pines' central park. His children played there almost every weekend, and—

"No," he said more gently as he saw the shock in her eyes. "No, Alexis and the kids weren't there, thank God. But most of their friends were. And on a more pragmatic level, we picked up two of the local seccies Zilwicki and Cachat used." This time his smile was a terrible thing to see. "They've been dealt with, but not before they told us everything they ever knew in their lives, and, to give the devil his due, they both insisted Zilwicki and Cachat never intended to nuke the park. In fact, it wasn't *their* idea, either. One of their fellow lunatics apparently went berserk and made the decision on his own."

Anisimovna knew she looked shell-shocked, but that was all right. She *was* shell-shocked.

"On the other hand," Collin continued, "having three separate nukes go off in *Green Pines* on a single day isn't the sort of thing you can cover up. We took the position that we intended to conduct a *very* thorough investigation before we leveled any charges—which was true enough—but we knew we'd eventually have to go public with *some* explanation. No one wanted to admit the Ballroom could get through to pull something like this, but we decided that was the least of the evils available to us. In fact, once the seccies confessed, we decided we could charge that Zilwicki was the mastermind behind the whole thing. Which, in a way, he was after all."

"We considered adding Cachat to the mix," Albrecht said, "but he wasn't the kind of public figure Zilwicki was after that expose of Yael Underwood's 'outed' him a couple of years ago, and he managed to keep his involvement with Verdant Vista under the radar horizon. Nobody knows who the hell he was, and we couldn't come up with a plausible way to explain how *we* knew, either. Under the circumstances, we decided that trying to link Haven to it as well would be too much for even the Solly public to take without asking questions—like what two agents from star nations at war with each other were doing on Mesa together—we'd rather not answer. Fortunately, no one in the League expects a bunch of Ballroom terrorists to act rationally, and we've been chiseling away at 'Torch's' claim that it's not *really* a Ballroom safe harbor ever since we lost the planet. That made Zilwicki's involvement even jucier."

His eyes glittered, and Anisimovna nodded. Once-in-a-lifetime propaganda opportunities like this one were gifts from heaven, and she understood the temptation to ride it as far as possible. At the same time, she was glad Albrecht had recognized that claiming it as a joint Manticoran-Havenite operation would have strained even the League public's credulity to the breaking point.

Probably about the only thing that could *do that,* she thought, *but under the circumstances...*

"At any rate," Collin said, resuming the narrator's role, "we officially completed our investigation about a week ago, and since neither Zilwicki nor Cachat is around to dispute our version of events, we've announced Zilwicki was responsible for all three explosions. And that the nukes represented a deliberate terror attack launched by the Ballroom and the 'Kingdom of Torch.' The fact that Torch's declared war on us made that easier, and our PR types—both here and in the League—are pounding away at how it proves any Torch claims to have disavowed terror are bullshit. Once a terrorist, always a terrorist, and *this* attack killed thousands of seccies and slaves, as well."

He showed another flash of teeth.

"Actually, it only got a few hundred of them, but no one off Mesa knows that. And enough seccies disappeared when the regular security agencies came down on them after Zilwicki and Cachat's little friends confessed that no one in the seccy or slave communities who does know better is going to say a word. That's not going to help the Ballroom's cause any even with other slaves. And as far as anyone else is concerned, the whole operation was a deliberate attack on a civilian target with weapons of mass destruction—*multiple* weapons of mass destruction. We're going to *hammer* them in the Sollie faxes, and having a known agent of Manticore involved in it gives us another club to use on the *Manties,* as well."

There was silence in the office for several seconds. Then Albrecht cleared his throat.

"I'm afraid that's the reason you won't be making your report to Isabel after all, Aldona," he said.

"I see."

Anisimovna considered asking about the nature of the research which had been carried out in the Gamma Center, yet she considered it neither very hard nor for very long. That was information she clearly had no need to know, but she was glad Isabel had caught the traitor before he'd managed to pass whatever it had been on to anyone else. For that matter, taking out Zilwicki and Cachat was going to hurt the other side badly down the road. And she could appreciate the way the disaster could be used as a public relations weapon against Torch and the Ballroom. But the price...

"I'm sorry, Aldona." She looked up, surprised by the gentleness in Albrecht's voice. She was almost as surprised by that as she was to feel the tears hovering behind her eyes. "I know you and Isabel had grown quite close," he said. "She was close to me, too. She had her sharp edges, but she was also a very clear thinking, intellectually honest person. I'm going to miss her, and not just on a professional level."

She met his eyes for a second or two, then nodded and inhaled deeply.

"I imagine she's not the only person we're going to lose, now that everything is coming more or less into the open," she said.

"I imagine not," Albrecht agreed quietly. Then he gave himself a shake and smiled at her. "But in the meantime, we have a lot to do. Especially since, as you put it, 'everything is coming more or less into the open.' So, could you please go on with your report?"

"Of course." She settled back in her chair, forcing her focus back on to the report she'd come here to give in the first place, and cleared her throat.

"Things went essentially as planned," she began. "Byng reacted almost exactly as his profile had indicated he would, and the Manties cooperated by sending three of their destroyers, not just a single ship. When *Giselle* blew up, Byng instantly assumed the Manties had attacked the station and blew all three of them out of space. Personally, I suspect there may actually have been a fourth Manty out there, given how quickly Gold Peak responded. *Someone* must have told Khumalo and Medusa what happened, at any rate. The turnaround time suggests it had to be either a warship or a dispatch boat, and I'm inclined to wonder if a dispatch boat would've had the capability to monitor and control current-generation Manty recon platforms. No one in Byng's task force or on New Tuscany ever saw any additional Manties, but Gold Peak arrived with detailed sensor information on the entire first incident, and someone must have provided it to her. Just as someone must have been there in order to get their response force back so fast.

"That's actually the part of the operation I'm least satisfied with," she said candidly. "*I* didn't think there was anyone else out there at the time, either, and I'd hoped I'd have a little more time to work on tying New Tuscany more securely into our plans. I didn't, so when the Manties did turn up, New Tuscany pretty much left Byng to sink or swim on his own."

She shrugged.

"He managed to sink quite handily, actually, although I could wish Gold Peak had pushed him under a little more enthusiastically. She settled for blowing up just his flagship, and from everything I could see before Captain Maddox hypered out, it looked as if Sigbee was going to comply with all of Gold Peak's demands without further resistance."

"That's exactly what happened," Benjamin told her. Her eyebrows rose, and he chuckled grimly. "The Manties released their version of what happened at New Tuscany—both incidents—nine days ago. I'm sure it's all over Old Terra by now. According to the Manties, they got everything from Sigbee's secure databases."

"Oh, my," Anisimovna murmured, and it was Albrecht's turn to chuckle.

"Exactly," he said cheerfully. "Hopefully, this whole thing is going to spin out of the Manties' and the Sollies' control without any more direct interference on our part—aside from whatever we can milk out of Green Pines, that is. But, if it looks like it's not, we can always start leaking some of that secure information ourselves, as well. So far, the Manties seem to be trying to respect the confidentiality of anything from the databases that doesn't pertain directly to their own problems with the Sollies. I don't know if those arrogant idiots in Old Chicago have even noticed that, but I'm sure they'll notice if the 'Manties' suddenly start leaking all of those embarrassing contingency plans of theirs to the media."

"That *would* be . . . discomfiting for everyone concerned, wouldn't it?" Anisimovna observed with an almost blissful smile.

"It most certainly would. Of course, so far, it doesn't look like we're going to need to do very much more to fan that particular flame. At the moment, Kolokoltsov and his colleagues don't seem to have missed very many things they could have done wrong." Albrecht's smile was evil. "And our good friend Rajampet is performing exactly as expected."

"And Crandall?" Anisimovna asked.

"We can't be positive yet," Benjamin replied. "We couldn't give Ottweiler a streak drive, so it's going to be a while before we hear anything from him. I don't think there's much need to worry about her response, though. Even without our prompting, her own natural inclination would be to attack as soon and hard as possible. And"—his smile was remarkably like his father's—"we happen to know her appreciation of the Manties' technology is every bit as good as Byng's was."

"Good." Anisimovna made no effort to hide her own satisfaction. Then she frowned. "The only other thing that still worries me is the fact that there was no way for me to hide my fingerprints. If New Tuscany's looking for some way to appease Manticore, they're damned well going to've told Gold Peak about *our* involvement. Or as much about it as they know, at any rate."

"Unfortunately, you're exactly right," Albrecht agreed. "They did roll over on us, and the Manties have broadcast that fact to the galaxy at large. On the other hand"—he shrugged—"it was a given from the outset that they were going to find out in the end. No one could have done a better job of burying his tracks than you did, so don't worry about it. Besides," he grinned nastily, "our people on Old Terra were primed and waiting to heap scorn on the 'fantastic allegations' and 'wild accusations' coming out of Manticore. Obviously the Manties are trying to come up with some story—any story!—to justify their unprovoked attack on Admiral Byng."

"And people are really going to buy that?" Anisimovna couldn't help sounding a bit dubious, and Detweiller gave a crack of laughter.

"You'd be astonished how many Sollies will buy into that, at least long enough to meet our needs. They're accustomed to accepting nonsense about what goes on in the Verge—OFS has been feeding it to them forever, and their newsies are used to swinging the spoon! Their media's been so thoroughly coopted that at least half their reporters automatically follow the party line. It's almost like some kind of involuntary reflex. And even if John Q. Solly *doesn't* swallow it this time for some reason, it probably won't matter as long as we just generate enough back-ground noise to give the people making the important decisions the cover and official justification they need." He shook his head again. "Like I say, don't worry about it. I'm completely satisfied with your performance out there."

Anisimovna smiled back at him and nodded in mingled relief and genuine pleasure. The assignment she'd been handed was one of the most complicated ones she'd ever confronted. It hadn't come off perfectly, but it hadn't had to come off *perfectly*, and from everything they'd said, it sounded as if the operation had accomplished its goals.

"And because I *am* satisfied," Albrecht told her, "I'm probably going to be handing you some additional hot potatoes." She looked at him, and he snorted. "That's your reward for pulling this one off. Now that we know you can handle the hard ones, we're not going to waste you on easy ones. And, frankly, the fact that we've lost Isabel is going to have us looking harder than ever for capable high level troubleshooters."

"I see." She put as much confidence and enthusiasm into her voice as she could, but Albrecht's eyes twinkled at her.

"Actually," he told her, "now that you've reached the center of the 'onion,' you'll find that, in a lot of ways, my bark is worse than my bite." He shook his head, the twinkle in his eyes fading. "Don't misunderstand. There are still penalties for people who just plain fuck up. But, at the same time, we know the sorts of things we're assigning people to do. And we also know that sometimes Murphy turns up, no matter how carefully you plan, or how well you execute. So we're not going to automatically punish anyone for failure unless it's abundantly obvious they're the *reason* for the failure. And, judging from the way you've handled this assignment, I don't think that's likely to be happening in your case."

"I hope not," she replied. "And I'll try to make sure it doesn't."

"I'm sure you will." He smiled at her again, then leaned forward in his chair, crossing his forearms on the edge of the desk in front of him.

"Now, then," he continued more briskly. "It's going to be another couple of T-weeks before anyone can 'officially' get here from New Tuscany. That means the Manties are going to have that much more time to get their version of events out in front of the Sollies. Worse than that, from the Sollies' perspective, it's going to be leaking into the League's media through the wormhole network faster than the government's version of events can spread out from Old Terra. From our perspective, that's a good thing...probably. It would take an old-fashioned miracle for those numbskulls in Old Chicago to do the smart thing and offer to negotiate with the Manties, so I think we can probably count on them to take the ball and run with it where . . . creative reinterpretation, shall we say? . . . of events in New Tuscany is concerned. Despite that, it's entirely possible that there's at least one—possibly even two—honest newsies on Old Terra. That could have unfortunate repercussions for the way *we* want to see this handled. Fortunately, we have people strategically placed throughout the League's media, and especially on Old Terra.

"What I want you to do now, Aldona, is to sit down with Collin and Franklin. They'll bring along some of our own newspeople, and the three of you will work with them to come up with the most effective way to spin what happened in New Tuscany to suit *our* needs. Given our allegations about Green Pines, a goodsized chunk of the Solly media is going to be salivating for anything that puts Manticore in a bad light, which should help a lot, and now that you've brought us all that raw sensor data from both incidents—not to mention those nice authentication codes—we can get started on a little creative reinterpretation of our own for the Sollies. I've got a few ideas on how best to go about that myself, but you've demonstrated a genuine talent for this sort of thing, so sit down and see what you can come up with on your own, first. Thanks to the streak drive, we've got two weeks to massage the story here on Mesa any way we have to before it could possibly get to us by any normal dispatch boat. I want to use that time as effectively as possible."

"I understand."

"Good. And, in the meantime, although you really don't have the need to know this, there's going to be another little news story in about two more T-months."

"There is?" Anisimovna glanced around, puzzled by the sudden, predatory smiles of all three Detweilers.

"Oh, there certainly is!" Albrecht told her, then waved at Benjamin. "Tell her," he said.

"Well, Aldona," Benjamin said, "in about another two months, a little operation we've been working on for some time, one called Oyster Bay, is going to come to fruition. And when it does—"

JANUARY 1922 POST DIASPORA

"I've got a bad feeling about this...."

—Admiral Patricia Givens, RMN
CO, Office of Naval Intelligence

Chapter Five

CAPTAIN (JG) GINGER LEWIS was not filled with confidence as she headed down the passageway aboard HMSS *Weyland* towards Rear Admiral Tina Yeager's office. It wasn't because she felt any worry over her ability to discharge her new duties. It wasn't even because she'd started her career as enlisted, without so much as dreaming she might attain her present rank. For that matter, it wasn't even because she'd just been assigned to the Royal Manticoran Navy's primary R&D facility when all her actual experience had been acquired in various engineering departments aboard deployed starships.

No, it was because she hadn't seen a single happy face since she'd arrived aboard *Weyland* half an hour before. Most people, she suspected, would have felt at least a qualm or two at being the new kid, just reporting in, when something had so obviously hit the rotary air impeller.

I wonder if it's just over here in R&D or if Aubrey and Paulo are about to get the same treatment? she wondered. Then she snorted. *Well, even if they are, Paulo has Aubrey to take care of him.*

The thought made her smile as she remembered Aubrey Wanderman's first deployment. Which, by the strangest turn of events, had also been *her* first deployment. She'd been quite a few years older than him, but they'd completed their naval training school assignments together, and she'd sort of taken him under her wing. He'd needed it, too. It was hard to remember now how *young* he'd been or that it had all happened almost fourteen T-years years ago. Sometimes it seemed like only yesterday, and sometimes it seemed like something that had happened a thousand years ago, to someone else entirely. But she remembered how shiny and new he'd been, how disappointed he'd been at being assigned to "only" a "merchant cruiser"... until, at least, he'd discovered that the captain of the merchant cruiser in question was then-Captain Honor Harrington.

Her smile faded just a bit as she remembered the clique of bullies and would-be deserters who'd made Aubrey's life a living hell, at least until Captain Harrington had found out about it. And the way she'd found out about it had been when their attempt to murder a certain acting petty officer by the name of Ginger Lewis had failed and Aubrey, who'd fallen under the influence of Chief Petty Officer Horace Harkness and HMS *Wayfarer*'s Marine detachment, had beaten their ringleader half to death with his bare hands. She was still a bit surprised she'd survived the sabotaged software of her EVA propulsion pack, and she knew she hadn't emerged from the experience unscarred. Even now, all these years later, she *hated* going EVA—which, unfortunately, came the way of the engineering department even more than anyone else.

Still, there was a world—a *universe*—of difference between that once-bullied young man and Senior Chief Petty Officer Aubrey Wanderman.

And, she thought a bit enviously, *neither he nor Paulo is going to have to report in to someone with the towering seniority of a flag officer. Lucky bastards.*

Her woolgathering had carried her successfully down the passage to Rear Admiral Yaeger's door. Now, however, she bade a regretful farewell to its distraction and stepped through the open door.

The yeoman seated behind the desk in the outer office looked up at her, then rose respectfully.

"Yes, Ma'am?"

"Captain Lewis," Ginger replied. "I'm reporting aboard, Chief."

"Yes, Ma'am. That would be Delta Department, wouldn't it, Ma'am?"

"Yes, it would." Ginger eyed him speculatively. Any flag officer's yeoman worth her salt was going to keep up with the details of her admiral's appointments and concerns. Keeping track of the comings and goings of officers who hadn't even known themselves the day before that they were about to be assigned to *Weyland* was a bit more impressive than usual, however.

"I thought so, Ma'am." The yeoman's expression didn't actually change by a single millimeter, yet somehow he managed to radiate a sense of over-tried patience—or perhaps a better word would have been exasperation. Fortunately, none of it seemed to be directed towards Ginger.

"I'm afraid the admiral's unavailable at the moment, Ma'am," the yeoman continued. "And so is Lieutenant Weaver, her flag lieutenant. It's, ah, an unscheduled meeting with the station commander."

Ginger managed to keep her eyes from widening. An "unscheduled meeting" with *Weyland*'s CO, was it? No wonder she'd sensed a certain tension in the air.

"I see...Chief Timmons," she said after a moment, reading the yeoman's nameplate. "Would it happen we have any idea when Admiral Yeager might be free?"

"Frankly, Ma'am, I'm afraid it might be quite some time." Timmons' expression remained admirably grave. "That's why I wanted to confirm that you were the officer Delta's been expecting."

"And since I am?"

"Well, Ma'am, I thought in that case you might go down to Delta and report in to Captain Jefferson. He's Delta Division's CO. I thought perhaps he might be able to start getting you squared away, and then you could report to the admiral when she's free again."

"Do you know, Chief, I think that sounds like a perfectly wonderful idea," Ginger agreed.

✧   ✧   ✧

"Well, *that* was an interesting cluster fuck, wasn't it?"

Vice Admiral Claudio Faraday, the commanding officer of HMSS *Weyland*, was known for a certain pithiness. He also had a well-developed sense of humor, although, Tina Yeager noted, there was no trace of it in his voice at the moment.

"Would it happen," Faraday continued, "that tucked away somewhere in your subordinate officers' files, between their voluminous correspondence, their instruction manuals, their schedules, their research notes, their ham sandwiches, and their entertainment chips, they actually possess a copy of this station's emergency evacuation plan?"

He looked back and forth between Yaeger and Rear Admiral Warren Trammell, her counterpart on the fabrication and industrial end of *Weyland*'s operations. Trammell didn't look much happier than Yaeger felt, but neither was foolish enough to answer his question, and Faraday smiled thinly.

"I only ask, you understand," he continued almost affably, "because our recent exercise would seem to indicate that either they don't have a copy of the plan, or else none of them can read. And I hate to think Her Majesty's Navy is entrusting its most important and secure research programs to a bunch of illiterates."

Yaeger stirred in her chair, and Faraday's eyes swooped to her.

"Sir," she said, "first, let me say I have no excuse for my department's performance. Second, I'm fully aware my people performed much more poorly than Admiral Trammell's."

"Oh, don't take all the credit, Admiral," Faraday said with another smile. "Your people may have performed more poorly than Admiral Trammell's, but given the underwhelming level of Admiral Trammell's people's performance, I very much doubt that anyone could have performed '*much* more poorly' than they did."

"Sir," Captain Marcus Howell said diffidently, and all three of the flag officers looked in his direction. Aside from Yaeger's and Trammell's flag lieutenants—whose massively junior status insulated them from the direct brunt of Admiral Faraday's monumental unhappiness—he was the junior officer in the compartment. He was also, however, Faraday's chief of staff.

"Yes, Marcus? You have something you'd care to add?"

"Well, Sir, I only wanted to observe that this was the first emergency evacuation simulation *Weyland*'s conducted in the last two T-years. Under the circumstances, it's probably not really all that surprising people were a little . . . rusty."

"'Rusty,'" Faraday rolled the word across his tongue, then snorted harshly. "If we use the term in the sense that a hatch sealed shut by atmospheric oxidation is 'rusty,' I suppose it's appropriate." The smile he bestowed upon Howell should have lowered the temperature in his office by at least three degrees, but then he grimaced. "Still, I take your point."

He gave himself a shake, then turned his attention back to Yaeger and Trammell.

"Don't think for a moment that I'm any happier about this than I was ten seconds ago. Still, Marcus does have a point. I'm not a great believer in the theory that extenuating circumstances excuse an officer's failures where his duty is concerned, but I suppose it's a bit early to start keelhauling people, too. So perhaps we should simply begin all over again from a mutual point of agreement that everyone's performance in the simulation was ... suboptimal."

In fact, Yaeger knew, it had been far, far worse than "suboptimal." If she were going to be honest about it—which she really would have preferred avoiding if at all possible—his initial, delightfully apt choice of noun had much to recommend it as a factual summation.

As Howell had just pointed out, emergency evacuation exercises had not been a priority of Rear Admiral Colombo, Faraday's immediate predecessor. For that matter, they hadn't been a *high* priority for the station commander before that, either. On the other hand, that CO had been a Janacek appointee, and *nothing* had been very high on his priority list. By contrast, Colombo possessed enormous energy and drive, which helped explain why Admiral Hemphill had just recalled him to the capital planet as her second-in-command at BuWeaps. But, Yaeger admitted, Colombo had been a tech weenie, like her. She didn't think he'd ever held starship command, and he'd been involved in the R&D side for over thirty T-years. He'd been conscientious about the administrative details of his assignment, but his real interest had been down in the labs or over in the fabrication units where prototype pieces of hardware were produced.

"Sir," she said now, "I'm serious about apologizing for my people's performance. Yes, Captain Howell has a point—it's not something we've exercised at. But the truth is, Sir, that an awful lot of my people suffer from what I can only call tunnel vision. They're really intensely focused on their projects. Sometimes, to be honest, I'm not sure they're even aware the rest of the universe is out there at all." She shook her head. "I know at least one of my division heads—I'd prefer not to say which—heard the evacuation alarm and just turned it off so it wouldn't disturb his train of thought while he and two of his lead researchers were discussing the current problem. I've already, ah, *counseled* him on that decision, but I'm afraid it was fairly typical. Which is my fault, not theirs."

"It's your fault, Admiral, in the sense that you're ultimately responsible for the actions of all personnel under your command.

That doesn't excuse their actions—or inaction. However, judging by the overall level of performance, I'd have to relieve three-quarters of the officers aboard this station if I were going to hammer everyone who'd screwed up. So we're not going to do that."

Faraday paused, letting the silence stretch out, until Trammell took pity on his colleague and broke it.

"We're not, Sir?" he asked.

"No, Admiral," Faraday said. "Instead, we're going to fix the problem. I'm afraid it's probably symptomatic of other problems we're going to find, and—to be fair, Admiral Yeager—I can actually understand why a lot of the R&D people think the rest of us are playing silly games that only get in the way of the people— them—doing serious work. From a lot of perspectives, they've got a point, really, when you come right down to it."

Yaeger was actually a bit surprised to hear Faraday admit that. Claudio Faraday was about as far removed from Rear Admiral Thomas Colombo as it was possible for a human being to be. He had effectively zero background on the research side. In fact, he was what Admiral Hemphill had taken to calling a "shooter," not a researcher, and Yaeger felt positive he would rather have been commanding a battle squadron than babysitting the Navy's "brain trust."

But that, she was beginning to suspect, might actually be the very reason he'd been chosen for his new assignment. It was more than possible Colombo had been recalled to BuWeaps not simply because his talents were needed there, but because certain recent events had convinced someone at the Admiralty House that HMSS *Weyland* needed the talents of someone like Claudio Faraday equally badly.

"I fully realize I've been aboard for less than one T-week," Faraday continued. "And I realize my credentials on the R&D side are substantially weaker even than Admiral Colombo's. But there's a reason we have an emergency evacuation plan. In fact, there's an even better reason for us to have one than for *Hephaestus* or *Vulcan* to have one. The same reason, in a lot of ways, that we back all of our data up down on the planetary surface every twelve hours. There is one tiny difference between our data backups and the evac plan, however." He smiled again, a bit less thinly than before. "It would be just a bit more difficult to reconstitute the *researchers* than their research if both of them got blown to bits."

The silence was much more intense this time. Four months ago, Yaeger might have been inclined to dismiss Faraday's concerns. But that had been before the Battle of Manticore.

"We all know the new system-defense pods have been deployed to protect *Weyland*," the vice admiral went on after a moment. "For that matter, we all know the Peeps got hammered so hard it's not really likely they're going to be poking their noses back into Manticoran space anytime soon. But nobody thought it was very likely they'd do it in the first place, either. So, however much it may inconvenience our personnel, I'm afraid I'm going to have to insist we get this little procedural bump smoothed out. I'd appreciate it if you'd make your people aware that I'm not exactly satisfied with their performance in this little simulation. I assure you, I'll be making that point to them myself, as well."

He smiled again. Neither Yaeger nor Trammell would ever have mistaken the expression for a sign of pleasure.

"What you are *not* going to tell them, however, is that I have something just a little more drastic in mind for them. Simulations are all well and good, and I'm perfectly prepared to use them as training tools. After all, that's what they're intended for. But as I'm sure you're both aware, it's always been the Navy's policy to conduct live-fire exercises, as well as simulations. Which is what we're going to do, too."

Yaeger managed to keep her dismay from showing, although she was fairly certain Faraday knew exactly what she was feeling. Still, she couldn't help a sinking sensation in the pit of her stomach as she thought about the gaping holes the chaos of an actual physical evacuation of the station was going to tear in her R&D schedules.

"I fully realize," Faraday continued as if he'd been a Sphinxian treecat reading her mind, "that an actual evacuation will have significant repercussions on the station's operations. Because I am, this isn't something I'm approaching lightly. It's not something I want to do—it's only something we *have* to do. And because we not only need to test our actual performance but convince some of your 'focused' people this is something to take seriously, not just something designed to interrupt their work schedules, we're not going to tell them it's coming. We'll go ahead and run the additional simulations. I'm sure they'll expect nothing less out of their new, pissed-off, pain-in-the-ass CO, and they'll bitch and

moan about it with all the creativity of really smart people. I
don't care about that, as long as they keep it to themselves and
don't force me to take note of it. But, hopefully, when we hit
them with the actual emergency order—when it's *not* a simple
simulation—they'll at least have improved enough for us to get
everyone off the station without someone getting killed because
he forgot to secure his damned helmet."

✧   ✧   ✧

Captain Ansten FitzGerald tipped back in his chair as Commander Amal Nagchaudhuri stepped into the briefing room with
an electronic tablet tucked under his arm.

"Have a seat," the captain invited, pointing at a chair across
the table from his own, and Nagchaudhuri settled into it with a
grateful sigh. FitzGerald smiled and shook his own head.

"Are you anywhere near a point where you can actually sit down
for a couple of hours with a beer?" he asked, and Nagchaudhuri
chuckled sourly.

It had never occurred to the tall, almost albino-pale commander
that he might find himself the executive officer of one of the
Royal Manticoran Navy's most powerful heavy cruisers. He was
a communications specialist, and posts like that usually went to
officers who'd come up through the tactical track, although that
tradition had been rather eroded over the past couple of decades
by the Navy's insatiable appetite for experienced personnel. On
the other hand, very few XOs had inherited their positions under
circumstances quite like his, which had quite a bit to do with
his current weariness.

"By my calculations, it won't be more than another T-year before
I can take a break long enough for that, Sir," he replied. "Ginger
was one hell of an engineer, but we're *still* finding things that
managed to get broken somehow." He shrugged. "Most of what
we're finding now is little crap, of course. None of it's remotely
vital. I imagine that's one reason Ginger hadn't already found it
and dealt with it before they transferred her out. But I'm still
annotating her survey for the yard dogs. And the fact that BuPers
is pilfering so enthusiastically isn't helping one damned bit."

FitzGerald nodded in understanding and sympathy. He'd held
Nagchaudhuri's position until *Hexapuma*'s return from the Talbott
Quadrant. He was intimately familiar with the problems the com-
mander was experiencing and discovering, and the XO's frustration

came as no surprise—not least because they'd all anticipated getting the ship into the yard dogs' hands so quickly.

FitzGerald's eyes darkened at that thought. Of course they'd expected that! After all, none of them were psychic, so none of them had realized the Battle of Manticore was going to come roaring out of nowhere only five days after their return. *Hexapuma*'s damages had kept her on the sidelines, a helpless observer, and as incredibly frustrating as that had been at the time, it was probably also the only reason FitzGerald, Nagchaudhuri, and the cruiser's entire complement were still alive. That cataclysmic encounter had wreaked havoc on a scale no one had ever truly envisioned. It had also twisted the Navy's neat, methodical schedules into pretzels...and the horrendous personnel losses had quite a bit to do with how Nagchaudhuri had ended up confirmed as *Hexapuma*'s executive officer, too.

"Well," he said, shaking off the somberness memories of the battle always produced, "I've got some good news for once. Rear Admiral Truman says she's finally got a space for us in R&R."

"She does?" Nagchaudhuri straightened, expression brightening. Rear Admiral Margaret Truman, a first cousin of the rather more famous Admiral *Alice* Truman, was the commanding officer of Her Majesty's Space Station *Hephaestus*, and HMSS *Hephaestus* happened to be home to the Repair and Refit command to which *Hexapuma*'s repair had been assigned.

"She does indeed. Captain Fonzarelli will have docking instructions for us by tomorrow morning, and the tugs will be ready for us at oh-nine-hundred."

"That's going to piss Aikawa off," Nagchaudhuri observed with a grin, and FitzGerald laughed.

"I imagine he'll get over it eventually. Besides, he was due for a little leave."

Ensign Aikawa Kagiyama had been one of *Hexapuma*'s midshipmen on her previous deployment. In fact, he was the only one still aboard her. Or, rather, assigned to her, since he *wasn't* onboard at the moment.

"I guess we can always ask *Hephaestus* to delay our repairs a little longer. Long enough for him to get back from *Weyland* for the big moment, I mean," Nagchaudhuri suggested.

"The hell we can!" FitzGerald snorted. "Not that I don't appreciate the way he looked after me after Monica, or anything. I'm sure he'll be disappointed, but if we delay this any longer just so he can be here for it, his loyal crewmates would probably stuff him out an open airlock!"

"Yeah, but he's fairly popular. They *might* let him have a helmet, first," Nagchaudhuri replied with an even broader grin.

"And they might not, too." FitzGerald shook his head. "No, we'll just let this be his little surprise when he gets back."

"I hope he's enjoying himself," Nagchaudhuri said more seriously. "He's a good kid. He works hard, and he really came through at Monica."

"They were *all* good kids," FitzGerald agreed. "And I'll admit, I worry about him a little. It's not natural for the XO to have to *order* an ensign to take leave. Especially not someone with his record from the Island!"

"He has been well behaved since we got back from Monica," Nagchaudhuri acknowledged. "You don't think he's sick, do you?"

"No, I think it's just losing all his accomplices." FitzGerald shrugged. "With Helen off as the skipper's new flag lieutenant, and with Paulo assigned to *Weyland* with Ginger, he's sort of at loose ends when it comes to getting into trouble. For which we can all be grateful."

"That depends. Are we going to get a fresh complement of snotties for him to provide with a suitably horrible example?"

"I doubt it." FitzGerald shrugged again. "Given the fact that we're going to be sitting in a repair dock for the next several months, I imagine they'll be looking for something a bit more active for snotty cruises. Besides, even if we get a fresh batch, he's an ensign now. I think he'd actually feel constrained to set them a good example."

"Somehow I find it difficult to wrap my mind around the concept of Aikawa being a *good* example for anyone—intentionally, I mean. At least without having Helen around to threaten him if he doesn't!"

"Oh, come now!" FitzGerald waved a chiding finger at the XO. "You know perfectly well that Helen never threatened him. Well, not *too* often, anyway."

"Only because she didn't have to make it explicit," Nagchaudhuri countered. "One raised eyebrow, and he knew what was coming."

Chapter Six

PRESIDENT ELOISE PRITCHART raked stray strands of platinum-colored hair impatiently from her forehead as she strode into the subbasement command center. In contrast to her usual understated elegance, she wore a belted robe over her nightgown, and her face was bare of any cosmetics.

The head of her personal security team, Sheila Thiessen, followed close behind her. Unlike the President, Thiessen had been on duty when the alert was sounded. Well, not precisely *on* duty, since her official shift had ended five hours earlier, but she'd still been on-site, wading through her unending paperwork, and she was her well-groomed, fully clothed, always poised normal self.

Despite which, she thought, the hastily-dressed President still managed to make her look drab. In fact, the President always made everyone around her seem somehow smaller than life, especially at moments of crisis. It wasn't anything Pritchart *tried* to do; it was simply what genetics, experience, and her own inherent presence did for her. Even here, even now, awakened from what had passed for a sound sleep in the months since the twin hammer blows of Javier Giscard's death, then the disastrous Battle of Manticore, despite the ghosts and sorrow which haunted those striking topaz eyes, that sense of unbreakable resolve and determination was like a cloak laid across her shoulders.

Or maybe that's just my imagination, Thiessen told herself. *Maybe I just need for her to be unbreakable. Especially now.*

Pritchart crossed quickly to the comfortable chair before her personal command and communication console. She nodded to the only two members of her Cabinet who'd so far been able to join her—Tony Nesbitt, the Secretary of Commerce, and Attorney General Denis LePic—then settled into her own seat as it adjusted to her body's contours.

Nesbitt and LePic both looked tense, worried. They'd been working late—the only reason they'd been able to make it to the command center this quickly—and both had that aura of end-of-a-really-long-day fatigue, but that didn't explain their tight shoulders and facial muscles, the worry in their eyes. Nor were they alone in their tension. The command center's uniformed personnel and the scattering of civilian intelligence analysts and aides threaded through their ranks were visibly anxious as they concentrated on their duties. There was something in the air— something just short of outright fear—and Thiessen's bodyguard hackles tried to rise in response.

Not that the anxiety level about her came as any sort of surprise. The entire Republic of Haven had been waiting with gnawing apprehension for almost half a T-year for exactly this moment.

Pritchart didn't greet her cabinet colleagues by name, only gave them that quick nod and smiled at them, yet her mere presence seemed to evoke some subtle easing of their tension. Thiessen could actually see them relaxing, see that same relaxation reaching out to the people around them, as the President took her place without haste then settled back, shoulders squared, and turned those topaz eyes to the uniformed man looking down from the huge smart wall display at one end of the large, cool room.

"So, Thomas," she said, sounding impossibly composed. "What's this all about?"

Admiral Thomas Theisman, Secretary of War and Chief of Naval Operations for the Republic of Haven, looked back at her from his own command center under the rebuilt Octagon, a few kilometers away. Given the late hour, Thiessen suspected that Theisman had been in bed until a very short time ago himself. If that was the case, however, no one would have guessed it from his faultless appearance and impeccable uniform.

"Sorry to disturb you, Madam President," he said. "And, to be honest, I don't have any idea what it's all about."

Pritchart raised one eyebrow.

"I was under the impression we'd just issued a system-wide Red Alert," she said, her tone noticeably more astringent than the one in which she normally addressed Theisman. "I'm assuming, Admiral, that you had a *reason* for that?"

"Yes, Madam President, I did." Theisman's expression was peculiar, Thiessen thought. "Approximately"—the Secretary of War glanced to one side—"thirty-one minutes ago, a force of unidentified starships made their alpha translations ten light-minutes outside the system hyper limit. That puts them roughly twenty-two light-minutes from the planet. The gravitic arrays detected them when they reentered normal-space, and our original estimate, based on their hyper footprints, was that we were looking at forty-eight ships-of-the-wall and/or CLACs, escorted by a dozen or so battlecruisers, a half dozen CLACs, and fifteen or twenty destroyers. They appear to have brought along at least a dozen large freighters, as well—most likely ammunition ships."

Thiessen felt the blood congeal in her veins. Those had to be Manty ships, and if they were, they had to be armed with the new missile systems which had broken the back of the Republic's attack on the Manticore Binary System. The missiles which gave the Royal Manticoran Navy such an advantage in long-range accuracy that they could engage even the Haven System's massive defenses with effective impunity. And which were undoubtedly loaded aboard those ammunition ships in enormous numbers.

Well, we've wondered where they were ever since the Battle of Manticore, she thought grimly. *Now we know.*

From the com display, Theisman looked levelly into Pritchart's eyes.

"Under the circumstances, there didn't seem much doubt about who they belonged to or why they were here," he said, "but it's taken us a while to confirm our tentative IDs at this range. And it turns out our initial assessments weren't quite correct."

"I beg your pardon?" Pritchart said when he paused.

"Oh, we were right in at least one respect, Madam President—it is the Manties' Eighth Fleet, and Admiral Harrington *is* in command. But there's an additional ship, one we hadn't counted on. It's not a warship at all. In fact, it appears to be a private yacht, and it's squawking the transponder code of the GS *Paul Tankersley.*"

"A *yacht*?" Pritchart repeated in the careful tone someone used when she wasn't entirely certain she wasn't talking to a lunatic.

"Yes, Ma'am. A yacht. A Grayson-registry yacht owned by Stead-holder Harrington. According to the message she's transmitted to us from one Captain George Hardy, the *Tankersley*'s skipper, Admiral Harrington is personally aboard her, not her fleet flagship. And, Madam President, Captain Hardy has requested permission for his ship to transport the Admiral to Nouveau Paris with a personal message to you from Queen Elizabeth."

Eloise Pritchart's eyes widened, and Thiessen sucked in a deep breath of astonishment. She wasn't alone in that reaction, either.

"Admiral Harrington is coming *here*, to Nouveau Paris. Is that what you're saying, Tom?" Pritchart asked after a moment.

"Admiral Harrington is coming to Nouveau Paris *aboard an unarmed private yacht* without first demanding any assurances of safety from us, Ma'am," Theisman replied. Then his lips twitched in what might have been a smile under other circumstances. "Although," he continued, "I have to say having the rest of Eighth Fleet parked out there is probably intended as a pretty pointed suggestion that it would be a good idea if we didn't let anything ... untoward happen to her."

"No. No, I can see that," Pritchart said slowly, and now her eyes were narrow as she frowned in intense speculation. She sat that way for several moments, then looked at LePic and Nesbitt.

"Well," she said with a mirthless smile, "*this* is unexpected."

" 'Unexpected?' " Nesbitt barked a laugh. "It's a hell of a lot more than that as far as *I'm* concerned, Madam President! If you'll pardon my language."

"I have to agree with Tony," LePic said when Pritchart quirked an eyebrow in *his* direction. "After the Battle of Manticore, after everything else that's happened ..."

His voice trailed off, and he shook his head, his expression bemused.

"Have we replied to Admiral Harrington's request yet, Tom?" Pritchart asked, returning her attention to Theisman.

"Not yet. We only received her message about five minutes ago."

"I see."

Pritchart sat for perhaps another ten seconds, her lips pursed, then inhaled deeply.

"Under the circumstances," she said then with a faint smile, "I'd really prefer not to be recording messages sitting here in my bathrobe. So, Tom, I think we'll just let you handle this stage of

things, since you look so bright-eyed and spiffy. No doubt we'll
need to get Leslie involved later, but for right now, let's leave it
a matter between uniformed military personnel."

"Yes Ma'am. And what would you like me to tell her?"

"Inform her that the Republic of Haven is not only willing
to allow her vessel to enter planetary orbit, but that I personally guarantee the safety of her ship, herself, and anyone aboard
the—*Tankersley*, was it?—for the duration of her visit with us."

"Yes, Ma'am. And should I discuss those superdreadnoughts
of hers?"

"Let's not be tacky, Admiral." The President's smile grew briefly
broader. Then it vanished. "After all, from Admiral Chin's report
there's not much we could do about them even if we wanted to,
is there? Under the circumstances, if she's prepared to refrain
from flourishing them under our noses, I think we ought to be
courteous enough to let her do just that."

"Yes, Ma'am. Understood."

"Good. And while you're doing that, it's time I went and got
into shape to present a properly presidential appearance. And I
suppose"—she smiled at Nesbitt and LePic—"it might not hurt
to drag the rest of the Cabinet out of bed, either. If *we* have to
be up, they might as well have to be, too!"

Admiral Lady Dame Honor Alexander-Harrington kept her face
calm and her eyes tranquil as she sat gazing out the viewport of
the *Havenite* shuttle. Only those who knew her very well would
have recognized her own anxiety in the slow, metronome-steady
twitching of the very end of the tail of the cream and gray treecat
draped across her lap.

Captain Spencer Hawke, of the Harrington Steadholder's Guard,
Colonel Andrew LaFollet's handpicked successor to command her
personal security team, was one of those few people. He knew exactly
what that twitching tail indicated, and he found himself in profound
agreement with Nimitz. If Hawke had been allowed to do this *his*
way, the Steadholder wouldn't have come within three or four light-
minutes of this planet. Failing that, her entire fleet would have been
in orbit around it, and she would have been headed to its surface
in an armored skinsuit aboard a Royal Manticoran Navy assault
shuttle, accompanied not just by her three personal armsmen, but by
a full company of battle-armored Royal Manticoran Navy Marines.

Preferably as the Manticoran Alliance's military representative for the signing ceremony as she accepted the unconditional surrender of an abjectly defeated Havenite government amid the smoking ruins of the city of Nouveau Paris.

Unfortunately—or perhaps fortunately—he also knew the Steadholder better than to suggest any such modest modification of her own plans. The Steadholder wasn't one of those people who vented volcanic rage when she was displeased, but it would have taken a hardier soul than Hawke's to willingly confront the ice which could core those almond-shaped brown eyes and the calm, reasonable scalpel of that soprano voice as she dissected whatever minor *faux pas* had drawn one to her attention.

Nonsense! he told himself. *I'd risk it in a minute if I thought it was really critical.* He snorted. *Yeah,* sure *I would!* He shook his head. *No wonder Colonel LaFollet was going gray.*

He glanced at Corporal Joshua Atkins and Sergeant Clifford McGraw, the other members of the Steadholder's personal detachment. Oddly enough, neither of *them* looked particularly calm, either.

There are times, he reflected, *when I actually find myself envying one of those armsmen with a cowardly, stay-at-home steadholder to look after. It's got to be easier on the adrenaline levels.*

✧   ✧   ✧

Honor needed no physical clues to recognize the tension of her armsmen. Their emotions flooded into her through her empathic sense, and even if they hadn't, she knew all three of them well enough to know what they had to be thinking at this moment. For that matter, she couldn't find it in her to be as irritated with them this time as she'd been upon occasion, either. The fact that what was happening was her own idea didn't make her feel any less nervous about it, herself.

Oh, stop that, she told herself, caressing Nimitz's ears with her flesh and blood right hand. *Of course you're nervous! But unless you wanted to come in shooting after all, what choice did you have? And at least Pritchart seems to be saying all the right things—or Thomas Theisman's saying them for her, anyway—so far.*

That was a good sign. It had to be a good sign. And so she sat still in the comfortable seat, pretending she was unaware of the mesmerized gaze the Havenite flight engineer had turned upon her as he came face to face with the woman even the Havenite newsies called "the Salamander," and hoped she'd been right about Pritchart and her administration.

Eloise Pritchart stood on the shuttle landing pad on the roof of what had once again become Péricard Tower following Thomas Theisman's restoration of the Republic.

The massive, hundred and fifty year-old tower had borne several other names during People's Republic of Haven's lifetime, including The People's Tower. Or, for that matter, the bitterly ironic one of "The Tower of Justice" ... when it had housed the savagely repressive State Security which had supported the rule of Rob Pierre and Oscar Saint-Just. No one truly knew how many people had vanished forever into StateSec's basement interrogation rooms and holding cells. There'd been more than enough, however, and the grisly charges of torture and secret executions which the prosecutors had actually been able to prove had been sufficient to win a hundred and thirty-seven death sentences.

A hundred and thirty-seven death sentences Eloise Pritchart had personally signed, one by one, without a single regret.

Pierre himself had preferred other quarters and moved his personal living space to an entirely different location shortly after the Leveller Uprising. And, given the tower's past associations, a large part of Eloise Pritchart had found herself in rare agreement with the "Citizen Chairman." Yet in the end, and despite some fairly acute personal reservations—not to mention anxiety over possible public misperceptions—she'd decided to return the presidential residence to its traditional pre-Legislaturalist home on the upper floors of *Péricard* Tower.

Some of her advisers had urged against it, but she'd trusted her instincts more than their timidity. And, by and large, the citizens of the restored Republic had read her message correctly and remembered that Péricard Tower had been named for Michèle Péricard, the first President of the Republic of Haven. The woman whose personal vision and drive had led directly to the founding of the Republic. The woman whose guiding hand had *written* the constitution Eloise Pritchart, Thomas Theisman, and their allies had dedicated their lives to restoring.

The well worn thoughts ran through her brain, flowing beneath the surface with a soothing familiarity, as she watched the Navy shuttle slide in to a touchdown. It was escorted by three more

shuttles—assault shuttles, heavily laden with external ordnance—
which went into a watchful counter-grav hover overhead, and even
more atmospheric sting ships orbited alertly, closing all air space
within fifteen kilometers of the tower to *any* civilian traffic as the
passenger shuttle settled towards the pad with the crisp, professional
assurance only to be expected from Thomas Theisman's personal
pilot. Lieutenant (JG) Andre Beaupré hadn't been selected as the
chief of naval operations' full-time chauffeur at random, so he'd been
the logical choice when Theisman decided he needed the very best
pilot he could lay hands on to look after their unexpected visitor.

*And so Thomas damned well should have, given the fact that
almost everybody thinks we already tried to assassinate her aboard
her own flagship!* Pritchart told herself tartly. *And even though we
know we didn't do it, no one else does. Worse, there have to be
enough lunatics in a city the size of Nouveau Paris for someone
to make an unofficial effort to kill the woman who's systematically kicked our Navy's ass for as long as anyone can remember.
No wonder Thomas opted for such overt security! God knows the
last* thing *we could afford would be for something to happen to
Harrington—Alexander-Harrington, I mean. No one in the entire
galaxy would ever believe it was really an accident.*

Her mouth twitched sourly with the memory of another accident
no one in the galaxy would ever believe had been genuine. The
complications left by that particular mishap had a lot to do with
why it was so vital to handle this visit with such exquisite care.

*And maybe—just maybe—actually bring an end to all this
butchery, after all,* she thought almost prayerfully.

The shuttle touched down in a smooth whine of power, and
Pritchart suppressed an urge to scurry forward as the boarding
ladder extended itself to the airlock hatch. Instead, she made
herself stand very still, hands clasped behind her.

"You're not the only one feeling nervous, you know," a voice
said very quietly in her right ear, and she glanced sideways at
Thomas Theisman. The admiral's brown eyes gleamed with the
reflected glitter of the shuttle's running lights, and his lips quirked
in a brief smile.

"And what makes you think I'm feeling nervous?" she asked tartly,
her voice equally quiet, almost lost in the cool, gusty darkness.

"The fact that *I* am, for one thing. And the fact that you've got
your hands folded together behind you, for another." He snorted

softly. "You only do that when you can't figure out what else to do with them, and that only happens when you're nervous as hell about something."

"Oh, *thank* you, Tom," she said witheringly. "Now you've found a fresh way to make me feel awkward and bumptious! Just what I needed at a moment like this!"

"Well, if being pissed off at me helps divert you from worrying, then I've fulfilled one of your uniformed minions' proper functions, haven't I?"

His teeth gleamed in another brief smile, and Pritchart suppressed a burning desire to kick him in the right kneecap. Instead, she contented herself with a mental note to take care of that later, then gave him a topaz glare that promised retribution had merely been deferred and turned back to the shuttle.

Theisman's diversion, she discovered, had come at precisely the right moment. Which, a corner of her mind reflected, had most certainly not been a simple coincidence. Maybe she'd rescind that broken kneecap after all. Their little side conversation had kept her distracted while the hatch opened and a very tall, broad shouldered woman in the uniform of a Manticoran admiral stepped through it. At a hundred and seventy-five centimeters, Pritchart was accustomed to being taller than the majority of the women she met, but Alexander-Harrington had to be a good seven or eight centimeters taller even then Sheila Thiessen, and Thiessen was five centimeters taller than the President she guarded.

The admiral paused for a moment, head raised as if she were scenting the breezy coolness of the early autumn night, and her right hand reached up to stroke the treecat riding her shoulder. Pritchart was no expert on treecats—as far as she knew, there *were* no Havenite experts on the telempathic arboreals—but she'd read everything she could get her hands on about them. Even if she hadn't, she thought, she would have recognized the protectiveness in the way the 'cat's tail wrapped around the front of his person's throat.

And if she'd happened to miss Nimitz's attitude, no one could ever have missed the wary watchfulness of the trio of green-uniformed men following at Alexander-Harrington's heels. Pritchart had read about *them*, too, and she could feel Sheila Thiessen's disapproving tension at her back as her own bodyguard glared at their holstered pulsers.

Thiessen had pitched three kinds of fits when she found out President Pritchart proposed to allow armed retainers of an admiral in the service of a star nation with which the Republic of Haven happened to be at war into her presence. In fact, she'd flatly *refused* to allow it—refused so adamantly Pritchart had more than half-feared she and the rest of her detachment would place their own head of state under protective arrest to prevent it. In the end, it had taken a direct order from the Attorney General and Kevin Usher, the Director of the Federal Investigation Agency, to overcome her resistance.

Pritchart understood Thiessen's reluctance. On the other hand, Alexander-Harrington had to be just as aware of how disastrous it would be for something to happen to Pritchart as Pritchart was of how disastrous it would be to allow something to happen to her.

What was it Thomas told me they used to call that back on Old Earth? "Mutually assured destruction," wasn't it? Well, however stupid it may've sounded—hell, however stupid it may actually have been!—at least it worked well enough for us to last until we managed to get off the planet. Besides, Harrington's got a pulser built into her left hand, for God's sake! Is Sheila planning to make her check her prosthesis at the door? Leave it in the umbrella stand?

She snorted softly, amused by her own thoughts, and Alexander-Harrington's head turned in her direction, almost as if the Manticoran had sensed that amusement from clear across the landing pad. For the first time, their eyes met directly in the floodlit night, and Pritchart inhaled deeply. She wondered if she would have had the courage to come all alone to the capital planet of a star nation whose fleet she'd shattered in combat barely six T-months in the past. Especially when she had very good reason to feel confident the star nation in question had done its level best to assassinate her a T-year *before* she'd added that particular log to the fire of its reasons to . . . dislike her. Pritchart liked to think she would have found the nerve, under the right circumstances, yet she knew she could never really know the answer to that question.

But whether *she* would have had the courage or not, Alexander-Harrington obviously did, and at a time when the Star Kingdom's military advantage over the Republic was so devastating there was absolutely no need for her to do anything of the sort. Pritchart's amusement faded into something very different, and she stepped forward, extending her hand, as Alexander-Harrington led her trio of bodyguards down the boarding stairs.

"This is an unexpected meeting, Admiral Alexander-Harrington."

"I'm sure it is, Madam President." Alexander-Harrington's accent was crisp, her soprano surprisingly sweet for a woman of her size and formidable reputation, and Pritchart had the distinct impression that the hand gripping hers was being very careful about the way it did so.

Of course it is, she thought. *It wouldn't do for her to absent-mindedly crush a few bones at a moment like this!*

"I understand you have a message for me," the President continued out loud. "Given the dramatic fashion in which you've come to deliver it, I'm prepared to assume it's an important one."

"Dramatic, Madam President?"

Despite herself, Pritchart's eyebrows rose as she heard Alexander-Harrington's unmistakable amusement. It wasn't the most diplomatic possible reaction to the admiral's innocent tone, but under the circumstances, Pritchart couldn't reprimand herself for it too seriously. After all, the Manticorans were just as capable of calculating the local time of day here in Nouveau Paris as her own staffers would have been of calculating the local time in the City of Landing.

"Let's just say, then, Admiral, that your timing's gotten my attention," she said dryly after a moment. "As, I feel certain, it was supposed to."

"To be honest, I suppose it was, Madam President." There might actually have been a hint of apology in Alexander-Harrington's voice, although Pritchart wasn't prepared to bet anything particularly valuable on that possibility. "And you're right, of course. It is important."

"Well, in that case, Admiral, why don't you—and your armsmen, of course—accompany me to my office so you can tell me just what it is."

Chapter Seven

"SO, WOULD YOU PREFER we address you as 'Admiral Alexander-Harrington,' 'Admiral Harrington,' 'Duchess Harrington,' or '*Stead-holder* Harrington'?" Pritchart asked with a slight smile as she, Honor, Nimitz, and a passel of bodyguards—most of whom seemed to be watching each other with unbounded distrust—rode the lift car from the landing pad down towards the president's official office. There'd been too little room, even in a car that size, for any of the other Havenite officials to accompany them, since neither Honor's armsmen nor Sheila Thiessen's Presidential Security agents had been remotely willing to give up their places to mere cabinet secretaries.

"It does get a bit complicated at times to be so many different people at once," Honor acknowledged Pritchart's question with an answering smile which was a bit more crooked than the President's. And not just because of the artificial nerves at the corner of her mouth. "Which would *you* be most comfortable with, Madam President?"

"Well, I have to admit we in the Republic have developed a certain aversion to aristocracies, whether they're acknowledged, like the one in your own Star Kingdom, or simply *de facto*, like the Legislaturalists here at home. So there'd be at least some... mixed emotions, let's say, in using one of your titles of nobility. At the same time, however, we're well aware of your record, for a lot of reasons."

For a moment, Pritchart's topaz-colored eyes—which, Honor had discovered, were much more spectacular and expressive in person than they'd appeared in any of the imagery she'd seen—darkened and her mouth tightened. Honor tasted the bleak stab of grief and regret behind that darkness, and her own mouth tightened ever so slightly. When she'd discussed the Republic's leadership with Lester Tourville, he'd confirmed that Eighth Fleet had killed Javier Giscard, Pritchart's longtime lover, at the Battle of Lovat.

That, in effect, Honor Alexander-Harrington had killed him.

Her eyes met the President's, and she didn't need her empathic sense to realize both of them saw the knowledge in the other's gaze. Yet there were other things wrapped up in that knowledge, as well. Yes, she'd killed Javier Giscard, and she regretted that, but he'd been only one of thousands of Havenites who'd died in combat against Honor or ships under her command over the past two decades, and there'd been nothing personal in his death. That was a distinction both she and Pritchart understood, because both of them—unlike the vast majority of Honor's fellow naval officers—had taken lives with their own hands. Had killed enemies at close range, when they'd been able to see those enemies' eyes and when it most definitely *was* personal. Both of them understood that difference, and the silence hovering between them carried that mutual awareness with it, as well as the undertow of pain and loss no understanding could ever dispel.

Then Pritchart cleared her throat.

"As I say, we're aware of your record. Given the fact that you come from good yeoman stock and earned all of those decadent titles the hard way, we're prepared to use them as a gesture of respect."

"I see."

Honor gazed at the platinum-haired woman. Pritchart was an even more impressive presence face-to-face than she'd anticipated, even after Michelle Henke's reports of her own conversations with the President. The woman carried herself with the assurance of someone who knew exactly who she was, and her emotions—what the treecats called her "mind-glow"—were those of someone who'd learned that lesson the hard way, paid an enormous price for what her beliefs demanded. Yet despite the humor in her voice, it was clear she truly did cherish some apprehension about her question, and Honor wondered why.

She used Mike's title as Countess Gold Peak... but only after she'd decided to send Mike home as her envoy. Did she do that as a courtesy, or to specifically emphasize Mike's proximity to the throne? An emphasis she wanted enough to use a title she personally despised?

Or is the problem someone else in her Cabinet whose reaction she's concerned about? Or could it be she's already looking forward to the press releases? To how they're going to address me for public consumption?

"Under the circumstances," Honor said after a moment, "if you'd be more comfortable with plain old 'Admiral Alexander-Harrington,' I'm sure I could put up with that."

"Thank you." Pritchart gave her another smile, this one somewhat broader. "To be perfectly honest, I suspect some of my more aggressively egalitarian Cabinet members might be genuinely uncomfortable using one of your other titles."

She's fishing with that one, Honor decided. Most people wouldn't have suspected anything of the sort, given Pritchart's obvious assurance, but Honor had certain unfair advantages. *She wants an indication of whether I want to speak to her in private or whether whatever Beth sent me to say is intended for her entire Cabinet.*

"If it would make them feel uncomfortable, then of course we can dispense with it," she assured the President, and suppressed an urge to chuckle as she tasted Pritchart's carefully concealed spike of frustration when her probe was effortlessly—and apparently unknowingly—deflected.

"That's very gracious—and understanding—of you," the Havenite head of state said out loud as the lift slid to a halt and the doors opened. She waved one hand in graceful invitation, and she and Honor started down a tastefully furnished hallway, trailed by two satellitelike clumps of bodyguards. Honor could feel the President turning something over in her mind as they walked. Pritchart didn't seem the sort to dither over decisions, and before they'd gone more than a few meters, she glanced at the tall, black-haired woman who was obviously the senior member of her own security team.

"Sheila, please inform the Secretary of State and the other members of the Cabinet that I believe it will be best if Admiral Alexander-Harrington and I take the opportunity for a little private conversation before we invite anyone else in." Her nostrils flared, and Honor tasted the amusement threaded through her undeniable anxiety and the fragile undertone of hope. "Given the admiral's dramatic midnight arrival, I'm sure whatever she has to say will be important enough for all of us to discuss eventually, but tell them I want to get my own toes wet first."

"Of course, Madam President," the bodyguard said, and began speaking very quietly into her personal com.

"I trust that arrangement will be satisfactory to you, Admiral?" Pritchart continued, glancing up at Honor.

"Certainly," Honor replied with imperturbable courtesy, but the twinkle of amusement in her own eyes obviously gave her away, and the President snorted again—more loudly—and shook her head.

Whatever she'd been about to say (assuming she'd intended to say anything) stayed unspoken, however, as they reached the end of the hall and a powered door slid open. Pritchart gave another of those graceful waves, and Honor stepped obediently through the door first.

The office was smaller than she'd anticipated. Despite its obviously expensive and luxurious furnishings, despite the old-fashioned paintings on the walls and the freestanding sculpture in one corner, it had an undeniably intimate air. And it was obviously a working office, not just someplace to receive and impress foreign envoys, as the well-used workstation at the antique wooden desk made evident.

Given its limited size, it would have been uncomfortably crowded if Pritchart had invited her entire Cabinet in. In fact, Honor doubted she could have squeezed that many people into the available space, although the President's decision against inviting even her Secretary of State had come as something of a surprise.

"Please, have a seat, Admiral," Pritchart invited, indicating the comfortable armchairs arranged around a largish coffee-table before a huge crystoplast window—one entire wall of the office, actually—that gave a magnificent view of downtown Nouveau Paris.

Honor accepted the invitation, choosing a chair which let her look out at that dramatic vista. She settled into it, lifting Nimitz down from her shoulder to her lap, and despite the tension of the moment and the millions of deaths which had brought her here, she felt an ungrudging admiration for what the people of this planet had accomplished. She knew all about the crumbling infrastructure and ramshackle lack of maintenance this city had suffered under the Legislaturalists. And she knew about the riots which had erupted in its canyonlike streets following the Pierre coup. She knew about the airstrikes Esther McQueen—"Admiral Cluster Bomb"—had called in to suppress the Levelers, and about the hidden nuclear warhead Oscar Saint-Just had detonated under the old Octagon to defeat McQueen's own coup attempt. This city had seen literally millions of its citizens die over the last two T-decades—suffered more *civilian* fatalities than the number of military personnel who'd died aboard all of the Havenite ships destroyed in the Battle of Manticore combined—yet it had survived. Not simply survived, but risen with restored, phoenixlike beauty from the debris of neglect and the wreckage of combat.

Now, as she gazed out at the gleaming fireflies of air cars zipping busily past even at this hour—at those stupendous towers, at the lit windows, the fairy-dusting of air traffic warning lights—she saw the resurgence of the entire Republic of Haven. Recognized the stupendous changes that resurgence had made in virtually every aspect of the lives of the men, women, and children of the Republic. And much of that resurgence, that rebirth of hope and pride and purpose, was the work of the platinum-haired woman settling into a facing armchair while their bodyguards, in turn, settled into wary watchfulness around them.

Yes, a lot of it was her work, Honor reminded herself, one hand stroking Nimitz's fluffy pelt while the reassuring buzz of his almost subsonic purr vibrated into her. *But she's also the one who declared war this time around. The one who launched Thunderbolt as a "sneak attack." And the one who sent Tourville and Chin off to attack the home system. Admire her all you want, Honor, but never forget this is a dangerous, dangerous woman. And don't let your own hopes lead you into any overly optimistic assumptions about her or what she truly wants, either.*

"May I offer you refreshment, Admiral?"

"No, thank you, Madam President. I'm fine."

"If you're certain," Pritchart said with a slight twinkle. Honor arched one eyebrow, and the President chuckled. "We've amassed rather a complete dossier on you, Admiral. The Meyerdahl first wave, I believe?"

"Fair enough," Honor acknowledged the reference to her genetically enhanced musculature and the demands of the metabolism which supported it. "And I genuinely appreciate the offer, but my steward fed me before he let me off the ship."

"Ah! That would be the formidable Mr. MacGuiness?"

"I see Officer Cachat and Director Usher—oh, I'm sorry, that would be Director *Trajan*, wouldn't it?—really have compiled a thorough file on me, Madam President," Honor observed politely.

"*Touché*," Pritchart said, leaning back in her chair. But then her brief moment of amusement faded, and her face grew serious.

"If you won't allow me to offer you refreshments, however, Admiral, would you care to tell me precisely what it is the Queen of Manticore sent you to accomplish?"

"Of course, Madam President."

Honor settled back in her own chair, her flesh and blood hand still moving, ever so gently, on Nimitz's silken coat, and her own expression mirrored Pritchart's seriousness.

"My Queen has sent me as her personal envoy," she said. "I have a formal, recorded message for you from her, as well, but essentially it's simply to inform you that I'm authorized to speak for her as her messenger and her plenipotentiary."

Pritchart never twitched a muscle, but Honor tasted the sudden flare of combined hope and consternation which exploded through the President as she reacted to that last word. Obviously, even now, Pritchart hadn't anticipated that Honor was not simply Elizabeth III's envoy and messenger but her direct, personal representative, empowered to actually *negotiate* with the Republic of Haven.

The possibility of negotiations explained the President's hope, Honor realized. Just as the disastrous military situation her star nation faced and the possibility that Elizabeth's idea of "negotiating" might consist of a demand for unconditional surrender explained the consternation.

"Her Majesty—and I—fully realize there are enormous areas of disagreement and distrust between the Star Empire and the Republic," Honor continued in that same, measured tone. "I don't propose to get into them tonight. Frankly, I don't see any way we'd be remotely likely to settle those disputes without long, difficult conversations. Despite that, I believe most of our prewar differences could probably be disposed of by compromises between reasonable people, assuming the issue of our disputed diplomatic correspondence can be resolved.

"As I say, I have no intention or desire to stray into that

territory this evening, however. Instead, I want to address some-thing that will very probably pose much more severe difficulties for any serious talks between our two star nations. And that, Madam President, is the number of people who have died *since* the Republic of Haven resumed hostilities without warning or notification."

She paused, watching Pritchart's expression and tasting the President's emotions. The Havenite hadn't much cared for her last sentence, but that was all right with Honor. Honor Alexander-Harrington had never seen herself as a diplomat, never imagined *she* might end up chosen for such a mission, yet there was no point trying to dance around this particular issue. And she'd offered Pritchart at least an olive *leaf,* if not a branch, with the phrase "*resumed* hostilities."

As Pritchart had pointed out to her Congress when she requested a formal declaration of war, no formal peace had ever been concluded between the then-Star *Kingdom* of Manticore and the Republic of Haven. And while Honor wasn't prepared to say so, she knew as well as Pritchart that the lack of a peace treaty had been far more the fault of the High Ridge Government than of the Pritchart Administration. She wasn't prepared to agree that High Ridge's cynical political maneuvering and sheer stupidity *justified* Pritchart's decision, but it had certainly contributed to it. And despite the surprise nature of Thomas Theisman's Operation Thunderbolt, it had been launched against a target with which the Republic was still legally at war.

Just as long as she doesn't decide we're willing to let her off the hook for actually pulling the trigger, Honor reflected coldly. *We'll meet her part way, acknowledge there were serious mistakes— blunders—from our side, as well, and that we were still technically at war. But she's going to have to acknowledge the Republic's "war guilt," and not just for* this *war, if this is going to go anywhere, and she'd better understand that from the beginning.*

"Her Majesty fully realizes the Republic's total casualties have been much higher than the Star Empire's since fighting resumed," she continued after a handful of seconds. "At the same time, the Republic's total population is also much larger than the Star Empire's, which means our fatalities, as a percentage of our population, have been many times as great as yours. And even laying aside the purely human cost, the economic and property damages have been staggering for both sides, while the tonnage of warships which have been destroyed may well equal that of every other declared war in human history.

"This struggle between our star nations began eighteen T-years ago—twenty-two T-years, if you count from the People's Republic's attack on the Basilisk Terminus of the Wormhole Junction. And despite the position in which we find ourselves today, even the most rabid Havenite patriot must be aware by now that, despite all of 'Public Information's' propaganda to the contrary, the original conflict between us began as a direct consequence of the People's Republic's aggression, not the Star Empire's.

"But because we saw that aggression coming, our military buildup to *resist* it began forty T-years before even the attack on Basilisk, so for all intents and purposes, our nations have been at war—or preparing for war—for over sixty T-years. Which means we've been actively fighting one another—or preparing to fight one another—since I was roughly four T-years old. In a very real sense, my Star Empire's been at war, hot or cold, against Havenite aggression, in one form or another, for my entire life, Madame President, and I'm scarcely alone in having that 'life experience' or the attitudes that come with it. After that long, after that much mutual hostility and active bloodletting, either side can easily find any number of justifications for distrusting or hating the other.

"But there are two significant differences between this point in the struggle between Manticore and Haven and almost any other point, Madam President. The first of those differences is that we're no longer dealing with the *People's* Republic. Your new government has claimed your primary purpose is the complete restoration of the old Republic of Haven, and I accept that claim's validity. But you've also chosen, unfortunately—for whatever combination of reasons—to resume the war between Haven and Manticore, which leads many—indeed, most—Manticorans to doubt there's any true difference between you and the Legislaturalists or the Committee of Public Safety.

"I hope and believe they're wrong. That *this* Havenite regime does care how many of its citizens are killed fighting its wars. That it does want to safeguard the enormous progress it's made recovering from generations of misrule and domestic political brutality. And that it does feel some sense of responsibility to see as few as possible of its people, military or civilian, killed rather than simply feeding them into the furnace of political ambition and spinal-reflex aggression.

"Which brings us to the second significant difference. To be blunt, and as I have no doubt you and Admiral Theisman realize just as well as Queen Elizabeth does, the Star Empire's present military advantage is even more overwhelming than it was at the time of the admiral's coup against Saint-Just. We can, if we choose to do so, drive this war through to a decisive, unambiguous military victory. We can destroy your fleets from beyond any range at which they can effectively counterattack. We can destroy the infrastructure of your star systems, one by one, and for all of the undoubted courage and determination of your naval personnel, they can't stop us. They can only die trying—which I, for one, have no doubt they would do with the utmost gallantry."

She looked directly into Eloise Pritchart's tawny eyes, watching their expressionless depths even as she tasted the combination of fear, frustration, and desperation concealed behind them.

"There are those in the Star Empire who would prefer, in no small part because of that history I just mentioned, to do exactly that," she said flatly. "And I'd be lying to you if I didn't admit Her Majesty is strongly inclined in that direction herself. If, as I assume you have, you've had access to Internal Security's and State Security's secret files, I'm sure you understand why Queen Elizabeth personally hates Haven and distrusts all Havenites with every fiber of her being. I suspect just about anyone would feel that way about a star nation which murdered her father, murdered her uncle, her cousin, and her prime minister, and *attempted* to murder her."

Pritchart said nothing, only nodded slightly in acknowledgment of Honor's point, but Honor tasted a confusing whirlpool of emotion within the President. Obviously, Pritchart had learned about the assassinations—including King Roger's—before Honor told her, and, equally obviously, she wasn't surprised someone with Elizabeth's fiery disposition would find it impossible to forget such offenses. Yet there was a strand of personal regret, as well. An understanding that someone as wounded as Elizabeth had every right to her fury, and a sense of sorrow that so much pain had been inflicted.

"Immediately following the Battle of Manticore," Honor resumed, "our own losses were severe enough to preclude our launching any fresh offensives. I'm sure your own analysts reached that conclusion, as well. Now, however, our new construction and our repair of damaged units have reached a point at which we can detach sufficient vessels to launch decisive attacks on your star systems without exposing our own system to attack. And, to be brutally frank, the situation in the Talbott Quadrant is nowhere near as close to resolved as we'd believed it was."

She paused again, tasting Pritchart's reaction to *that* revelation. The Havenite President would have been more than human if she hadn't experienced a surge of hope that Manticore's possible preoccupation elsewhere would work in Haven's favor. Yet there was also an even sharper strand of wariness, and Honor suppressed a desire to smile sardonically. She and her political advisers had discussed whether or not she should raise that particular point with Pritchart. Now, tasting the other woman's mind-glow, she knew she'd been right; Pritchart was too smart not to see the possible downside for Haven, as well.

Still, I might as well make certain we're both on the same page.

"We continue to hope for a diplomatic resolution in and around Talbott," she said, "but I won't pretend we're confident of achieving one. Failure to do so will obviously have potentially serious repercussions for the Star Empire, of course. I'm sure you and your advisers are as well aware of that as anyone in Manticore. But you need to be aware of this, as well."

She held Pritchart's gaze with her own.

"The threat of a direct conflict with the Solarian League is one we simply cannot ignore. Obviously, it's also one of the reasons we're seeking to compose our disagreements with the Republic. Any star nation would be insane to want to fight the Solarian League under any circumstances, but only one which was stupid, as well as insane, would want to fight the League and anyone else *simultaneously*. At the same time, I'm sure your own analysts have come to some of the same conclusions we have where the Solarians' war-fighting technology is concerned. In case they haven't, I can tell you that what's happened so far has confirmed to us that the SLN is considerably inferior technologically at this time to either the Star Empire or the Republic. Obviously, something the size of the Solarian League has plenty of potential to overcome tech disadvantages, but our best estimate is that even if they were ready to begin putting new weapons systems into production tomorrow, we'd still be looking at a period of at least three to five years of crushing superiority over anything they could throw at us.

"The reason I'm telling you this is that you need to understand that while we don't want to fight the League, we're a long way from regarding a war against the Sollies as tantamount to a sentence of death. But we're not prepared to fight the Solarians at the same time someone whose technology is as close to equal to ours as yours is comes at us from behind. So as we see it, we have two options where the Republic is concerned.

"One, and in many ways the less risky of them from our perspective, would be to use that technological superiority I spoke about a few minutes ago to destroy your infrastructure in order to compel your unconditional surrender. In fact, one month ago, I was instructed to do just that, beginning with this very star system."

It was very, very quiet in Eloise Pritchart's office. The emotions of the President's bodyguards were a background of taut anxiety and anger restrained by discipline, yet Honor scarcely noticed that. Her attention—and Nimitz's—were focused unwaveringly upon Pritchart.

"But those instructions were modified, Madam President," she said softly. "Not *rescinded*, but ... modified. Her Majesty's been convinced to at least consider the possibility that the Republic of Haven truly isn't the *People's* Republic any longer. That it was not, in fact, responsible for the assassination of Admiral Webster on Old Earth, or for the attempted assassination of Queen Berry on Torch. To be honest, she remains far from convinced of either of those possibilities, but at least she recognizes them *as* possibilities. And even if it turns out the Republic *was* responsible, she's prepared to acknowledge that killing still more millions of your citizens and military personnel, destroying still more trillions of dollars worth of orbital infrastructure, may be a disproportionate response to the Republic's guilt.

"In short, Madam President, the Queen is tired of killing people. So she's authorized me to deliver this message to you: the Star Empire of Manticore is prepared to negotiate a mutually acceptable end to the state of war between it and the Republic of Haven."

The President didn't even twitch a muscle. Her self control was enormous, Honor thought. Which it had no doubt had to be for her and Javier Giscard to survive under the eternally suspicious, paranoid eye of a megolamaniac like Oscar Saint-Just for so many years. She might have been carved from stone, yet her sudden burst of incredulous joy, leashed by discipline and wariness, was like a silent explosion to Honor's empathic sense. However eager she might be for an end to the fighting, this woman was no fool. She knew how difficult "negotiations" might prove, and she was as aware as Honor herself of how many bloody years of hostility, anger, and hatred lay between the Star Empire and her own star nation.

"No one in Manticore expects that to be an easy task, even assuming that, in fact, the Republic wasn't responsible for the assassinations which led Her Majesty to reject the summit *you* had proposed. Nonetheless, Her Majesty is prepared to make a best-effort, good faith attempt to do just that, and I've been authorized to begin that negotiating process for her and for the Star Empire.

"At the same time, however, Her Majesty has instructed me to tell you she is not prepared to stretch these negotiations out indefinitely. Given what I just told you about the situation in Talbott, I'm sure you understand why, and I fully realize that you here in Nouveau Paris feel—with what I recognize as good reason—that it wasn't the Republic of Haven which failed to negotiate in good faith following the overthrow of the Saint-Just regime. Her Majesty was opposed to the stance of the High Ridge Government at the time, but the peculiarities of our constitutional system prevented her from simply removing him and replacing him with someone more responsive to the duties and responsibilities of his office. And, frankly, no one in Manticore had any reason to believe his intransigence, arrogance, and ambition would contribute to an active resumption of the war between Haven and the Star Empire. She, like virtually all Manticorans, regarded the situation primarily as a domestic political struggle—one which might have diplomatic implications, but certainly not as one likely to spin out of control into an active resumption of the war. Under those circumstances, she was unprepared to provoke a constitutional crisis to remove him rather than waiting until that same ambition and arrogance led to his inevitable eventual fall from office. I have no doubt that, as President, you've experienced similar difficulties of your own."

Despite all her own self-discipline and focus, Honor nearly

blinked at the sudden white-hot explosion of mingled fury, frustration, and something which tasted remarkably like...guilt?... that roared up inside Eloise Pritchart with her final sentence. It was, in some ways, an even stronger emotional spike than the President had shown when she realized Elizabeth was willing to negotiate after all, and it puzzled Honor almost as much as it surprised her. Most of all, because it didn't seem to be directed at Manticore or High Ridge. It seemed to be aimed somewhere else entirely, and a corner of Honor's mind whirred with speculation as it considered the hours of political briefings which had preceded her departure for the Haven System...and occupied much of the voyage, for that matter.

But she couldn't allow herself to be distracted, and so she continued, her voice as level as before.

"Her Majesty deeply regrets her inability to call High Ridge to heel, and she's prepared to acknowledge the Star Empire's fault in that respect. Nonetheless, she and the current Grantville Government are firmly resolved to move forward with a *prompt* resolution of this conflict. If it can be resolved over the negotiating table, the Star Empire of Manticore is prepared to be as reasonable as circumstances permit in order to achieve that end. As an indication of that, I've been instructed to tell you that the only two points which the Star Empire will insist *must* be publicly and acceptably addressed in any peace settlement are the question of precisely who falsified the diplomatic correspondence between our two star nations and why, and a public acknowledgment of who actually resumed hostilities. The question of reparations must also be placed on the table, although the final *resolution* of that question may be open to a later round of negotiations. It is not, however, the Star Empire's intention to insist upon cripplingly punitive terms, and Her Majesty hopes it will prove possible to completely regularize relations—commercial, scientific, and educational, as well as diplomatic—between our star nations as part of the same negotiating process. Manticore desires not simply an end to the killing, Madam President, but a beginning to a peaceful, mutually advantageous relationship with Haven based upon mutual respect, mutual interests, and—ultimately, at least—mutual friendship.

"If, however, it proves impossible to negotiate an end to hostilities in what Her Majesty considers a reasonable period of time, the offer to negotiate will be withdrawn."

Honor met Pritchart's gaze squarely, and her voice was unflinching.

"No one in the galaxy would regret that outcome more than I would, Madam President. It's my duty, however, to inform you that if it happens, the Star Empire will resume active operations. And if *that* happens, the Royal Manticoran Navy will destroy your star nation's Navy and its orbital industry, one star system at a time, until your administration, or its successor, unconditionally surrenders.

"Speaking for myself, as an individual, and not for my Star Empire or my Queen, I implore you to accept Her Majesty's proposal. I've killed too many of your people over the last twenty T-years, and your people have killed too many of mine."

She felt Javier Giscard's death between them, just as she felt Alistair McKeon's and Raoul Courvoissier's and Jamie Candless' and so many others, and she finished very, very softly.

"Don't make me kill any more, Madam President. Please."

Chapter Eight

"WELL?"

Eloise Pritchart looked around the table at her assembled Cabinet. They sat in their normal meeting room, surrounded by a seamless, panoramic three hundred and sixty-degree view—from a combination of true windows and smart wall projections—of the city of Nouveau Paris. The sun was barely above the horizon, with a lingering tinge of early dawn redness, and none of her secretaries or their aides looked especially well rested.

"I think it's certainly dramatic," Henrietta Barloi replied after a moment.

The Secretary of Technology, like Tony Nesbitt at Commerce, had been one of the late, distinctly unlamented Arnold Giancola's supporters. Like Giancola's other allies within the Cabinet, her horror appeared to have been completely genuine when Pritchart revealed the near certainty that Giancola, as the previous Secretary of State, was the one who'd actually manipulated the diplomatic correspondence which had led the Republic to resume military operations. The President had no doubt their reactions *had* been genuine, but that didn't change the fact that Barloi and Nesbitt remained the two cabinet secretaries who continued to nourish the greatest suspicion—not to mention resentment and hatred—where the Star Empire of Manticore was concerned.

Despite which, as far as Pritchart could tell, Barloi's response was more a throwaway remark, sparring for time, than anything resembling the notion that Haven should reject the opportunity.

"'Dramatic' is one way to put it, all right," Stan Gregory, the Secretary of Urban Affairs agreed wryly.

He was one of the secretaries who'd been out of the city last night. In fact, he'd been on the opposite side of the planet, and he'd been up and traveling for the better part of three hours to make this early morning meeting. Which didn't keep him from looking brighter-eyed and much more chipper than Pritchart herself felt at the moment.

"Dropping in on you literally in the middle of the night was a pretty flamboyant statement in its own right, Madam President," he continued. "The only question in my mind is whether it was all lights and mirrors, or whether Admiral Alexander-Harrington simply wanted to make sure she had your attention."

"Personally, I think it was a case of . . . gratuitous flamboyance, let's say." Rachel Hanriot's tone could have dehumidified an ocean, despite the fact that the Treasury Secretary was one of Pritchart's staunchest allies. "I'm not saying she's not here in a legitimate effort to negotiate, understand. But the entire way she's made her appearance—unannounced, no preliminary diplomacy at all, backed up by her entire fleet, arriving on the literal stroke of midnight in an unarmed civilian yacht and requesting planetary clearance . . ."

Her voice trailed off, and she shook her head, and Denis LePic snorted in amusement.

"'Gratuitous flamboyance' or not, Rachel," the Attorney General said, "it certainly did get our attention, didn't it? And, frankly, given the way things've gone ever since Arnold got himself killed, I'm in favor of anything that moves us closer to ending the shooting before everything we've managed to accomplish gets blasted back to the stone age. So if Alexander-Harrington wanted to come in here naked, riding on the back of an Old Earth elephant, and twirling flaming batons in each hand, I'd still be delighted to see her!"

"I have to go along with Denis—assuming the offer's sincere and not just window dressing designed to put Manticore into a favorable diplomatic light before they yank the rug out from under us anyway," Sandra Staunton said. The Secretary of Biosciences looked troubled, her eyes worried. She'd been another Giancola supporter, and, like Nesbitt and Barloi, she continued to cherish more than a little suspicion where the Star Empire was concerned.

"Given how Elizabeth reacted to the Webster assassination and the attempt on Torch, and with the Battle of Manticore added to her list of 'Reasons I Hate Haven' on top of that, this entire out-of-the-blue offer of some sort of last-minute reprieve just rings a little false to me. Or maybe what I'm trying to say is that it seems *way* too good to be true."

"I know what you mean, Sandy." Tony Nesbitt's expression was almost equally troubled, and his tone was subdued. But he also shook his head. "I know what you mean, but I just can't see any reason they'd bother. Not after what *they* did to *us* at Manticore."

He looked rather pointedly at Thomas Theisman, and the Secretary of War returned his gaze levelly.

"I fully realize Operation Beatrice failed to achieve what we'd hoped to achieve, Tony," Pritchart said. "And I also fully realize the decision to authorize it was mine." Nesbitt looked at her, instead of Theisman, and her topaz gaze met his without flinching. "Under the circumstances, and given the intelligence appreciations available to both the Navy and the FIS at the time, I'd make the same call today, too. *We* weren't the ones who'd canceled a summit meeting and resumed military operations, and I fully agreed with Thomas that the only real option they'd left us—since they'd broken off negotiations and wouldn't even *talk* to us about any other possible solution—was to try to achieve outright military victory before they got their new weapon system fully deployed. As nearly as we can tell, we were almost right, too. None of which changes the fact that we were wrong, and that I authorized what turned out to be the worst military defeat our star nation has ever suffered."

There was silence in the Cabinet Room. Describing the Battle of Manticore as the "worst military defeat" the Republic of Haven or the People's Republic of Haven had ever suffered—in a single engagement, at least—while accurate, was definitely a case of understatement. Nor had Pritchart tried to conceal the scope of the disaster. Some details remained classified, but she'd refused to change her policy of telling the Republic's citizens the truth or abandon the transparency she'd adopted in place of the old Office of Public Information's propaganda, deception, and outright lies. Some of her political allies had argued with her about that—hard—because they'd anticipated a furious reaction born of frustration, fear, and a betrayed sense of desperation. And, to some extent, they'd been right. Indeed, there'd been calls, some of them infuriated, for Pritchart's resignation once the public realized the magnitude of the Navy's losses.

She'd rejected them, for several reasons. All of her cabinet secretaries knew at least one of those reasons was a fear that Giancola's unprovable treason would come out in the aftermath of any resignation on her part, with potentially disastrous consequences not just for the war effort but for the very future of the Constitution all of them had fought so hard to restore.

Yet they also knew that particular reason had been distinctly secondary in her thinking. The most important factor had been that the President of the Republic was not simply its first minister. Under the Constitution, Pritchart was no mere prime minister, able to resign her office and allow some other party or political leader to form a new government whenever a policy or decision proved unfortunate. For better or worse, for the remainder of her term, she was the Republic's head of state. Despite all the criticism she'd taken, all the vicious attacks opposition political leaders (many of them longtime Giancola allies) had launched, she'd refused to abandon that constitutional principle, and all the muttered threats of impeachment over one trumped-up charge or another had foundered upon the fact that a clear majority of the Republic's voters and their representatives still trusted *her* more than they trusted anyone else.

Which, unfortunately, wasn't remotely the same thing as saying they still trusted her judgment as much as they once had. And that, of course, was another factor she had to bear in mind where any sort of negotiations with Manticore might be concerned.

And where any admission of what Giancola had done might be concerned, as well. Which was going to make things distinctly sticky, given that it was one of the two points upon which the Manticorans were going to demand concessions.

"I doubt very much," she continued in that same level voice, "that anyone in this room—or anywhere on the face of this *planet*—could possibly regret the outcome of the Battle of Manticore more than I do. But you do have a point, Tony. After what happened there, and given the fact that there's no reason they can't do the same thing to us again whenever they choose to—which, I assure you, Admiral Alexander-Harrington didn't hesitate to point out to me, in the most pleasant possible way, of course—I see little point in their attempting some sort of negotiating table treachery. And unlike the rest of you—except for Tom, of course—I've actually met the woman now. She's... impressive, in a lot of ways. I don't think she's got the typical politician's mindset, either."

"Meaning what, Madam President?" Leslie Montreau asked, her eyes narrowing slightly.

"Meaning I think this is the last woman in the universe I'd pick to sell someone a lie," Pritchart said flatly. "I don't think she'd accept the job in the first place, and even if she did, she wouldn't be very *good* at it."

"I'd have to say that's always been *my* impression of her, Madam President," Theisman said quietly.

"And everything the Foreign Intelligence Service's been able to pick up about her suggests exactly the same thing," LePic put in.

"Which doesn't mean she couldn't be used to 'sell us a lie' anyway," Nesbitt pointed out. "If whoever sent her lied to *her*, or at least kept her in the dark about what they really had in mind, she might very well think she was telling us the truth the entire time."

"Ha!" Pritchart's sudden laugh caused Nesbitt to sit back in his chair, eyebrows rising. The President went on laughing for a moment or two, then shook her head apologetically.

"I'm sorry, Tony," she told the commerce secretary, her expression contrite. "I'm not laughing at you, really. It's just that... Well, trust me on this one. Even if all the wild rumors about treecats' ability to tell when someone's lying are nonsense, this isn't a woman I'd try to lie to, and Javier and I lied with the galaxy's best under StateSec! I have to tell you that I had the distinct impression that she could see right inside my skull and watch the little wheels going round and round." She shook her head again. "I don't think *anyone* could sell her a bill of goods that would get her out here to play Judas goat without her knowledge."

"Pardon me for saying this, Madam President," Walter Sanderson, the Secretary of the Interior, said slowly, "but I have the distinct impression you actually *like* her."

Sanderson sounded as if he felt betrayed by his own suspicion, and Pritchart cocked her head, lips pursed as she considered what he'd said. Then she shrugged.

"I wouldn't go quite that far, Walter. Not yet, anyway. But I'll admit that under other circumstances, I think I *would* like her. Mind you, I'm not going to let her sell me any air cars without having my own mechanic check them out first, but when you come down to it, one of the first rules of diplomacy is picking effective diplomats. Diplomats who can convince other people to trust them, even like them. It's what they call producing 'good chemistry' at the conference table. I know she's not a diplomat by training, but Manticore has a long tradition of using senior naval officers as ambassadors and negotiators. It's paid off for them surprisingly well over the years, and I'm sure that was part of their thinking in choosing her, but I also think it goes deeper than that."

"Deeper, Ma'am?" Montreau asked.

"I think they chose her because she *wanted* to be chosen," Pritchart said simply. She looked across at Theisman. "Now that I've had a chance to actually meet her, Tom, I'm more convinced than ever that your notion of inviting her to the summit *we* proposed was a very good one. Wilhelm's analysts got it right, too, I think. Of everyone in Elizabeth's inner circle, she probably is the closest thing we've got to a friend."

"*Friend!*" Nesbitt snorted harshly.

"I said the *closest thing we've got* to a friend, Tony. I don't think anyone could accuse her of being a 'Peep sympathizer,' and God knows this woman's not going to hesitate to go right on blowing our starships out of space if these negotiations don't succeed! But she genuinely doesn't *want* to. And I don't think she feels any need to insist on unduly punitive terms, either."

Nesbitt glanced around at his fellow cabinet secretaries, then turned back to Pritchart.

"With all due respect, Madam President," he said, "I have a sneaking suspicion you've already made up your mind what 'we're' going to do."

"I wouldn't put it quite that way myself," she replied. "What I've made my mind up about is that we're going to have to negotiate with them, and that unless their terms are totally outrageous, this is probably the best opportunity we're going to get to survive. And I'm not talking about the personal survival of the people in this room, either. I'm talking about the survival of the Republic of Haven . . . and of the Constitution. If we ride this one down in flames, we won't 'just' be taking thousands, possibly millions, of more lives with us." Her eyes were cold, her voice grim. "We'll be taking everything we've fought for with us. All of it—everything we've done, everything we've tried to do, everything we've wanted to accomplish for the Republic since the day Tom shot Saint-Just—will go down with us. I'm not prepared to see that happen without doing everything I can to avoid it first."

Silence fell once more. A silence that agreed with her analysis yet remained intensely wary, even frightened, of what she proposed to do to avoid the outcome she'd predicted.

But there was more than wariness or fear in the wordless, intense glances being exchanged around that table, Pritchart realized. Even for those like Nesbitt and Barloi who most disliked and distrusted Manticore, there was a blazing core of hope, as well. The hope that an eleventh-hour reprieve was possible, after all.

"How does Admiral Alexander-Harrington propose to conduct the negotiations, Madam President?" Montreau asked after several moments.

"I think she's willing to leave that largely up to us." Pritchart's voice was back to normal, and she shrugged. "I'd say she has firm instructions, but my impression is that when she describes herself as Elizabeth's plenipotentiary, she's serious. However 'firm' her instructions may be, I think Elizabeth chose her because she trusts her—not just her honesty, but her judgment. You already know the points she's told us have to be addressed. The fact that she singled those points out suggests to me, at least, that everything *else* is truly negotiable. Or, at least, that Manticore's position on those other points isn't set in stone ahead of time. That whole matter of our prewar correspondence is going to be a bear, for reasons all of us understand perfectly well, but outside of those two specific areas, I think she's perfectly willing to hear our proposals and repond to them."

"But she hasn't made any suggestions at all about protocol?" Montreau pressed. It was clear to Pritchart that the Secretary of State was seeking clarification, not objecting, and she shook her head.

"No. She hasn't said a word about protocol, delegation sizes, or anything else. Not yet, anway. Mind you, I don't doubt for a minute that if we came up with a suggestion she didn't like, she wouldn't hesitate to let us know. Somehow, I have the impression she's not exactly timid."

Something like a cross between a snort and a laugh sounded from Thomas Theisman's general direction, and LePic raised one hand to hide a smile.

"I don't think I'd choose just that adjective to describe her, either, Madam President," Montreau said dryly. "But the reason I asked the question doesn't really have that much to do with her."

"No?" Pritchart gazed at her for a moment, then nodded. "I see where you're going, I think. But to be honest, I'm not certain I agree with you." One or two of the others looked puzzled, while others were slowly nodding in understanding of their own. "I'd like to keep this as small and nonadversarial as we can manage, Leslie. The last thing we need is to turn this into some sort of dog and pony show that bogs down. I don't think for a minute that Alexander-Harrington was blowing smoke when she said Elizabeth's unwilling to let negotiations stretch out forever."

"Neither do I," Montreau acknowledged, but her expression never wavered. "And, like you, I'd like to keep the negotiating teams small enough and sufficiently focused to move quickly. In fact, I'd really like to handle as much of this as possible one-on-one between her and myself, as Secretary of State. Or, failing that, between her and you, as the Republic's head of state. But if we do that, getting any agreement or treaty we manage to come up with approved by Congress is going to be a lot harder."

The puzzled expressions were changing into something else, and frowns were breaking out here and there. Somewhat to Pritchart's surprise, one of the darkest and least happy frowns belonged to Tony Nesbitt.

"I take your point, Leslie," he said, "but inviting the Administration's political opponents to sit in on this—and that is what you had in mind, isn't it?" Montreau nodded, and he shrugged. "As I say, inviting the opposition to sit in on, even participate in, the negotiating process strikes me as a recipe for disaster, in a lot of ways."

Despite herself, one of Pritchart's eyebrows rose. Nesbitt saw it and barked a laugh which contained very few traces of anything someone might have called humor.

"Oh, don't get me wrong, Madam President! I'm probably as close to an outright member of the opposition as you've got sitting in this Cabinet, and I think you're well aware of exactly how little trust I'm prepared to place in anyone from Manticore. But compared to some of the other operators out there, I might as well be your blood brother! I don't like to admit it, but a lot of them are probably as self-serving as Arnold turned out to be... and about as trustworthy."

A flicker of genuine pain, the pain of someone who'd been betrayed and used by someone he'd trusted, flashed across the commerce secretary's expression, but his voice never wavered.

"However I might feel about Manticore, you and Admiral Theisman are right about how desperate our military position is. And if this is the one chance we've got to survive on anything approaching acceptable terms, I don't want some political grand-stander—or, even worse, someone who'd prefer to see negotiations fail because he thinks he can improve his personal position or deep-six the Constitution in the aftermath of military defeat—to screw it up. And if we get far enough to actually start dealing with the matter of who did what to whose mail before the war, it's likely to be just a bit awkward tiptoeing around someone who'd be perfectly willing to leak it to the newsies for any advantage it might give him!"

"I find myself in agreement with Tony," Rachel Hanriot said after a moment. "But even so, I'm afraid Leslie has a point. There's got to be someone involved in these negotiations who isn't 'one of us.' I'd prefer for it to be someone who's opposed to us as a matter of principle, assuming we can find anyone like that, but the bottom line is that we've got to include someone from out-side the Administration or its supporters, whatever their motives for being there might be. Someone to play the role of watchdog for all those people, especially in Congress, who don't like us, or oppose us, or who simply question our competence after the collapse of the summit talks and what happened at the Battle of Manticore. This can't be the work of a single party, or a single clique—not anything anyone could portray as having been negoti-ated in a dark little room somewhere—if we expect congressional approval. And, to be honest, I think we have a moral obligation to give our opponents at least some input into negotiating what we hope will be a treaty with enormous implications for every man, woman, and child in the Republic. It's not just *our* Repub-lic, whatever offices we hold. I don't think we can afford to let ourselves forget that."

"Wonderful." Walter Sanderson shook his head. "I can see this is going to turn into a perfectly delightful exercise in statesman-ship. I can hardly think of anything I'd rather do. Except possibly donate one of my testicles to science. Without anesthetic."

Pritchart chuckled. One or two of Sanderson's colleagues found his occasional descents into indelicacy inappropriate in a cabinet secretary. The President, on the other hand, rather treasured them. They had a way of bringing people firmly back to earth.

"Given what you've just said," she told him with a smile, "I think we'll all be just as happy if we keep you personally as far away as possible from the negotiating table, Walter."

"Thank God," he said feelingly.

"Nonetheless," Pritchart went on in a voice tinged with more than a little regret, "I think you and Rachel have a point, Leslie. Tony, I'm as reluctant as you are to include any 'negotiators' whose motivations are...suspect. And your point about the correspondence issue's particularly well taken. In fact, it's the part of this which makes me the most nervous, if I'm going to be honest. But they're still right. If we don't include someone from outside the Administration, we're going to have a hell of a fight in Congress afterward, even if Rachel didn't have a point of her own about that moral responsibility of ours. And to the brutally frank, I think we'll have a better chance of surviving even if we end up having to air some of our political dirty linen in front of Admiral Alexander-Harrington, if it lets us move forward with a least a modicum of multiparty support, than we will if we find ourselves in a protracted struggle to get whatever terms we work out ratified. The last thing we need is to have any of those people in Manticore who already don't trust us decide that this time around *we're* being High Ridge and deliberately stringing things out rather than acting in good faith."

Chapter Nine

"WHAT'S THE CURRENT STATUS of Bogey Two, Utako?"

"No change in course or heading, Sir," Lieutenant Commander Utako Schreiber, operations officer of Task Group 2.2, Mesan Alignment Navy, replied. She looked over her shoulder at Commodore Roderick Sung, the task group's CO, who'd just stepped back onto MANS *Apparition*'s tiny flag bridge, and raised one eyebrow very slightly.

Sung noted the eyebrow and suppressed an uncharacteristic urge to snap at her for it. He managed to conquer the temptation without ever allowing it to show in his own expression, and the fact that Schreiber was probably the best ops officer he'd ever worked with, despite her junior rank, helped. Her willingness to think for herself was the reason he'd hand-picked her from a sizable pool of candidates when Benjamin Detweiler handed him this prong of Oyster Bay, after all. And the fact that he'd worked hard to establish the relationship of mutual trust and respect which let a subordinate ask that sort of silent question helped even more.

All the same, a tiny part of him did want to rip her head off. Not because of anything *she'd* done, but because of the tension building steadily in the vicinity of his stomach.

"Thank you," he said out loud instead as he crossed to his own command chair and settled back into it.

At least I've demonstrated my imperturbability by taking a break

124

to hit the head, he reflected mordantly. *Unless, of course, Utako and the others decide I only went because the damned Graysons are worrying the piss out of me!*

That second thought surprised a quiet snort of amusement out of him, and he was amazed how much better that made him feel. Of course, there was a galaxy of difference between "better" and anything he would describe as "good."

Up until the past twelve hours or so, Sung's part of Operation Oyster Bay had gone without a hitch, so he supposed he really shouldn't complain too loudly, even in the privacy of his own mind, when Murphy put in his inevitable appearance. The advantages of technology and heredity were all well and good, but the universe remained a slave to probability theory. The Alignment's strategists had made a conscientious effort to keep that point in mind from the very beginning, as had the planners of this particular mission. In fact, both Sung's orders and every pre-op briefing had stressed that concern, yet he doubted his superiors would look kindly on the man who blew Oyster Bay, whatever the circumstances.

He frowned down at his small repeater plot, watching the red icons of the Grayson Space Navy cruiser squadron.

Just my luck to wander into the middle of some kind of training exercise, he thought glumly. *Although I'd like to know what the hell they think they're doing exercising clear up here. Damned untidy of them.*

Oyster Bay's operational planners had taken advantage of the tendency for local shipping to restrict itself largely to the plane of a star system's ecliptic. Virtually all the real estate in which human beings were interested lay along the ecliptic, after all. Local traffic was seldom concerned with anything much above or below it, and ships arriving out of hyper almost invariably arrived in the same plane, since that generally offered the shortest normal-space flightpath to whatever destination had brought them to the system, as well, not to mention imposing a small but significantly lower amount of wear and tear on their alpha nodes. So even though defensive planners routinely placed surveillance platforms to cover the polar regions, there wasn't usually very much *shipping* in those areas.

In this instance, however, for reasons best known to itself—and, of course, Murphy—the GSN had elected to send an entire squadron of what looked like their version of the Manties' *Saganami-C*-class heavy cruisers out to play halfway to the hyper limit and due north of Yeltsin's Star.

It wouldn't have pissed Sung off so much if they hadn't decided to do it at this particular moment. Well, and in this particular spot. The other five ships of his task group were headed to meet *Apparition* for their last scheduled rendezvous, and unless Bogey Two changed vector, it was going to pass within less than five light-minutes of the rendezvous point.

And considerably closer than that to *Apparition*'s course as she headed towards that rendezvous.

He propped his elbows on his command chair's armrests and leaned back, lips pursed as he considered the situation. One of the problems the mission planners had been forced to address was the simple fact that a star system was an enormous volume for only six ships to scout, however sophisticated their sensors or their remote platforms were and however stealthy they themselves might be. At least it was if the objective was to keep anyone on the other side from suspecting the scouting was in progress.

He'd studied every available scrap about the Manties' operations against Haven, and he'd been impressed by their reconnaissance platforms' apparent ability to operate virtually at will without being intercepted by the Havenites. Unfortunately, if Sung's presence was ever noted at all, whether anyone managed to actually *intercept* him or not, Oyster Bay was probably blown, which meant the Manties' task had been rather easier than his own. He never doubted that he could have evaded the local sensor net well enough to prevent it from pinning down the actual locations of any of his units even if it managed to detect their simple presence. Unfortunately, the object was for the Graysons to never even know he was here in the first place. The Manties' scout forces, by and large, hadn't been particularly concerned about the possibility that the Havenites might realize they were being scouted, since there was nothing they could have done to prevent it and it wasn't exactly as if they didn't already know someone was at war with them. But if the Graysons figured out that someone—anyone—was roaming about *their* star system before the very last moment, they could probably substantially blunt Oyster Bay's success. They'd still get hurt, probably badly, but Oyster Bay was supposed to be decisive, not just painful.

Bearing all of that in mind, the operational planners had ruled out any extensive com transmissions between the widely dispersed units of Sung's task group. Even the most tightly focused transmissions were much more likely to be detected than the scout ships themselves, which was why the ops plan included periodic rendezvous points for the scouts to exchange information at very short range using low powered whisker lasers. Once all their sensor data had been collected, organized, and analyzed, *Apparition* would know what to tell the guidance platforms. But without those rendezvous, Sung's flagship wouldn't have the data in the first place, and that would be unacceptable.

Unlike some of the more fiery of the Alignment's zealots, Roderick Sung felt no personal animosity towards any of the normals who were about to discover they were outmoded. However naïve and foolish he might find their faith in the random combination of genes, and however committed he might be to overcoming the obstacles that foolishness created, he didn't blame any of them personally for it. Well, aside from those sanctimonious prigs on Beowulf, of course. But his lack of personal animus didn't lessen his determination to succeed, and at this particular moment all he really wanted was for a spontaneous black hole to appear out of nowhere and eat every one of those blasted cruisers.

"Should we alter course, Sir?"

The commodore looked up at the quiet question. Commander Travis Tsau, his chief of staff, stood at his shoulder and nodded towards the plot by Sung's right knee.

"Bogey Two's going to pass within two light-minutes of our base course at closest approach," Tsau pointed out, still in that quiet voice.

"A point, Travis," Sung replied with a thin smile, "of which I was already aware."

"I know that, Sir." Tsau was normally a bit stiffer than Schreiber, but he'd known Sung even longer, and he returned the commodore's smile wryly. "On the other hand, part of my job is to bring little things like that to your attention. Just in case, you understand."

"True." Sung nodded, glanced back down at the plot, then drew a deep breath.

"We'll hold our course," he said then. "Without even the spider up, we should be nothing but a nice, quiet hole in space as far as they're concerned. And, frankly, they're already so close I'd just as soon leave the spider down. I know they're not *supposed* to be able to detect it, but . . ."

He let his voice trail off, and Tsau nodded. At the moment, *Apparition* was moving on a purely ballistic course, with every active sensor shut down. And, as Sung had just pointed out, that, coupled with all the manifold stealth features built into the scout ship, ought to make her more than simply invisible. The only real problem with that analysis hung on the single word "ought," since if that assumption turned out to be inaccurate, *Apparition* would stand precisely zero probability of surviving.

The *Ghost*-class ships had no offensive armament at all. They were designed to do precisely what *Apparition* was doing at this moment, and there was no point pretending they'd be able to fight their way out of trouble if the other side managed to find them in the first place. So they'd been equipped with every stealth system the fertile imaginations of Anastasia Chernevsky and the rest of the MAN's R&D establishment had been able to devise, packed into the smallest possible platform, and if that meant sacrificing armament, so be it. Even their antimissile defenses represented little more than a token gesture, and everyone aboard *Apparition* was thoroughly aware of that fact.

On the other hand, Chernevsky and her people are very, very good at their jobs, Sung reminded himself.

A huge chunk of *Apparition*'s available tonnage had been eaten up by the spider's triple "keels," and another sizable chunk had been dedicated to her enormously capable sensor suite. Habitability had also loomed as a major factor in her designers' minds, since the *Ghosts* were going to be deployed on long-endurance missions, but the architects had accepted some significant compromises even in that regard in favor of knitting the most effective possible cloak of invisibility.

Unlike the starships of most navies, the MAN's scouts hadn't settled for simple smart paint. Other ships could control and reconfigure their "paint" at will, transforming their hulls—or portions of those hulls—into whatever they needed at any given moment, from nearly perfectly reflective surfaces to black bodies. The *Ghosts*' capabilities, however, went much further than that. Instead of the relatively simpleminded nanotech of most ships' "paint," the surface of *Apparition*'s hull was capable of mimicking effectively any portion of the electromagnetic spectrum. Her passive sensors detected any incoming radiation, from infrared through cosmic rays, and her computers mapped the data onto her hull, where her extraordinarily capable nannies reproduced it. In effect, anyone looking at *Apparition* when her stealth was fully engaged would "see" whatever the sensors exactly opposite his viewpoint "saw," as if the entire ship were a single sheet of crystoplast.

That was the theory, at least, and in this case, what theory predicted and reality achieved were remarkably close together.

It wasn't perfect, of course. The system's greatest weakness was that it couldn't give complete coverage. Like any stealth system, it still had to deal with things like waste heat, for example. Current technology could recapture and use an enormous percentage of that heat, but not all of it, and what they couldn't capture still had to go somewhere. And, like other navies' stealth systems, the MAN's dealt with that by radiating that heat away from known enemy sensors. Modern stealth fields could do a lot to minimize even heat signatures, but nothing could completely eliminate them, and stealth fields *themselves* were detectable at extremely short ranges, so any ship remained vulnerable to detection by a sufficiently sensitive sensor on exactly the right (or wrong) bearing.

In this instance, though, they knew right where the Graysons were. That meant they could adjust for maximum stealthiness against that particular threat bearing, and as part of his training, Sung had personally tried to detect a *Ghost* with the MAN's very best passive sensors. Even knowing exactly where the ship was, it had been all but impossible to pick her out of the background radiation of space, so he wasn't unduly concerned that Bogey Two would detect *Apparition* with shipboard systems as long as she remained completely covert. He was less confident that the spider drive would pass unnoticed at such an absurdly short range, however. Chernevsky's people assured him detection was exceedingly unlikely—that it had taken them the better part of two T-years to develop their own detectors, even knowing what they were looking for, and that those detectors were still far from anything anyone would ever call reliable—but Sung had no desire to be the one who proved their optimism had been misplaced. Even the spider had a footprint, after all, even if it wasn't something anyone else would have associated with a drive system. All it would take was for someone to notice an anomalous reading and be conscientious enough—or, for that matter, *bored* enough—to spend a little time trying to figure out what it was.

And the fact that the spider's signature flares as it comes up only makes that more likely, he reflected. *The odds against anyone spotting it would still be enormous, but even so, they'd be a hell of a lot worse than the chance of anyone aboard Bogey Two noticing us if we just keep quietly coasting along.*

At the same time, he knew exactly why Tsau had asked his question. However difficult a sensor target they might be for Bogey Two's shipboard systems, the rules would change abruptly if the Grayson cruiser decided to deploy her own recon platforms. If she were to do that, and if the platforms got a good, close-range look at the aspect *Apparition* was keeping turned away from their mothership, the chance of detection went from abysmally low to terrifyingly high in very short order. Which meant what Sung was really doing was betting that the odds of the Grayson's choosing to deploy recon platforms were lower than the odds of her shipboard systems detecting the spider's activation flare if he maneuvered to avoid her.

Of course, even if we did try to crab away from her, it wouldn't help a whole hell of a lot if she decided to launch platforms. All we'd really manage to do would be to move her target a bit farther away from her, and there's a reason they call remote platforms remote, Rod.

No. He'd play the odds, and he knew it was the right decision, however little comfort that might be if Murphy did decide to take an even more active hand.

I wonder if Østby and Omelchenko are having this much fun wandering around Manticore? he thought dryly. *I know no one ever promised it would be easy, and I've always enjoyed a hand of poker as much as the next man, but* this *is getting ridiculous.*

Roderick Sung settled himself even more comfortably in his command chair and waited to see exactly what sort of cards Murphy had chosen to deal this time.

Chapter Ten

HONOR ALEXANDER-HARRINGTON hoped she looked less nervous than she felt as she and the rest of the Manticoran delegation followed Alicia Hampton, Secretary of State Montreau's personal aide, down the short hallway on the two hundredth floor of the Nouveau Paris Plaza Falls Hotel.

The Plaza Falls had been the showplace hotel of the Republic of Haven's capital city for almost two T-centuries, and the Legislaturalists had been careful to preserve it intact when they created the *People's* Republic of Haven. It had served to house important visitors—Solarian diplomats (and, of course, newsies being presented with the Office of Public Information's view of the galaxy), businessmen being wooed as potential investors, off-world black marketeers supplying the needs of those same Legislaturalists, heads of state who were being "invited" to "request Havenite protection" as a cheaper alternative to outright conquest, or various high-priced courtesans being kept in the style to which they had become accustomed.

The Committee of Public Safety, for all its other faults, had been far less inclined towards that particular sort of personal corruption. Rob Pierre, Cordelia Ransom, and their fellows had hardly been immune to their own forms of empire building and hypocrisy, but they'd seen no reason to follow in the Legislaturalists' footsteps where the Plaza Falls was concerned. Indeed, the hotel had been regarded by the Mob as a concrete symbol of the Legislaturalists' regime, which explained why it had been thoroughly vandalized during the early days of Rob Pierre's coup. Nor was that the only indignity it had suffered, since the Committee had actually encouraged its progressive looting, using it as a sort of whipping boy whenever the Mob threatened to become dangerously rowdy. The sheer size of the hotel had meant looting it wasn't a simple afternoon's work, so it had made a useful diversion for quite some time.

In the end, even something with two hundred and twenty floors had eventually run out of things to steal, break, or deface, and (fortunately, perhaps) a ceramacrete tower was remarkably non-flammable. Several individual rooms, and one complete floor, had been burned out by particularly persistent arsonists, but by and large, the Plaza Falls had survived...more or less. The picked-clean carcass had been allowed to molder away, ignored by any of the Committee's public works projects. It had sat empty and completely ignored, and most people had written it off as something to be eventually demolished and replaced.

But demolishing a tower that size was no trivial task, even for a counter-gravity civilization, and to everyone's considerable surprise, the privatization incentives Tony Nesbit and Rachel Hanriot had put together after Theisman's coup had attracted a pool of investors who were actually interested in salvaging the structure, instead. More than that, they'd honestly believed the Plaza Falls could be restored to its former glory as a piece of living history—*and* a profit-making enterprise—that underscored the rebirth of the Republic as a whole.

Despite their enthusiasm, the project had been bound to run into more difficulties than any sane person would have willingly confronted, but they'd been thoroughly committed by the time they figured that out. In fact, failure of the project would have spelled complete and total ruin for most of the backers by that point. And so they'd dug in, tackled each difficulty as it arose, and to everyone's surprise (quite probably their own more than anyone else's), they'd actually succeeded. It hadn't been easy, but the result of their labors really had turned into an emblem of the Republic's economic renaissance, and even though Haven remained a relatively poor star nation (by Manticoran standards, at least), its resurgent entrepreneurial class was robust enough to turn the Plaza Falls into a genuine moneymaker. Not at the levels its renovators had hoped for, perhaps, but with enough cash flow to show a modest—Honor suspected a *very* modest—profit after covering the various loan payments and operating expenses.

At the rates they're charging, it certainly wouldn't show much of a profit in the Star Empire, she thought, following their guide, *but the cost of living's a lot lower here in the Republic, even now. I hate to think what kind of trouble they'd have hiring a staff this devoted back in* Landing *at the sort of salaries they're paying here! For that matter, these days they couldn't get a staff this qualified back on Grayson this cheaply, either.*

Fortunately for the Plaza Falls' owners, they weren't on Manticore or Grayson, however, and she had to admit that they—and Eloise Pritchart's government—had done the visiting Manticoran delegation proud.

She stepped into the combination conference room and suite Pritchart had designated for their "informal talks," and the President rose from her place at one end of the hand polished, genuine wood conference table. The rest of the Havenite delegation followed suit, and Pritchart smiled at Honor.

"Good morning, Admiral."

"Madam President," Honor responded, with a small half-bow. "Please allow me to introduce my colleagues."

"Of course, Madam President."

"Thank you." Pritchart smiled exactly as if someone in that room might actually have no idea who somebody—anybody—else was. In fact, Honor knew, every member of Pritchart's delegation had been as carefully briefed on every member of *her* delegation as her delegation had been about *Pritchart's* delegation.

Formal protocol and polite pretenses, she thought, reaching up to touch Nimitz's ears as she felt his shared amusement in the back of her brain. *You've just gotta just love 'em. Or somebody must, at least. After all, if people weren't addicted to this kind of horse manure, it would have been junkpiled centuries ago! But let's be fair, Honor. It does serve a purpose sometimes—and the Navy's just as bad. Maybe even worse.*

"Of course, you've already met Secretary of State Montreau," Pritchart told her. "And you already know Secretary of War Theisman. I don't believe, however, that you've actually been introduced to Mr. Nesbitt, my Secretary of Commerce."

"No, I haven't," Honor acknowledged, reaching out to shake Nesbitt's hand.

She'd been sampling the Havenites' emotions from the moment she stepped through the door, and Nesbitt's were . . . interesting. She'd already concluded that Pritchart was as determined as she was to reach some sort of negotiated settlement. Leslie Montreau's mind-glow tasted as determined as Pritchart's, although there was more caution and less optimism to keep that determination company. Thomas Theisman was a solid, unflappable presence, with a granite tenacity and a solid integrity that reminded Honor almost painfully of Alastair McKeon. She wasn't surprised by that, even though she'd never really had the opportunity before to taste his emotions. The first time they'd met, after the Battle of Blackbird, she hadn't yet developed her own empathic capabilities. And the second time they'd met, she'd been a little too preoccupied with her own imminent death to pay his mind-glow a great deal of attention. Now she finally had the opportunity to repair that omission, and the confirmation that he, at least, truly was the man she'd hoped and believed he was reinforced her own optimism . . . slightly, at least.

But Nesbitt was different. Although he smiled pleasantly, his dislike hit her like a hammer. The good news was that it wasn't personally directed at her; unfortunately, the good news was also the *bad* news in his case. In many ways, she would have preferred to have him take her in personal dislike rather than radiate his anger at and profound distrust of anything Manticoran so strongly. Of course, he was about her own age, so everything she'd said to Pritchart about her own life-long experience of mutual hostility between their star nations held true for him, as well. And however unhappy he might have been to see her, and however clearly he resented the fact that the Republic *needed* to negotiate an end to hostilities, he also radiated his own version of Pritchart's determination to succeed. And there was something else, as well. An odd little something she couldn't quite lay a mental finger on. It was almost as though he were *ashamed* of something. That wasn't exactly the right word, but she didn't know what the right word was. Yet whatever it was, or wherever it came from, it actually reinforced both his anger and his determination to achieve some sort of settlement.

"Admiral Alexander-Harrington," he said, just a bit gruffly, but he also returned her handshake firmly.

"Mr. Nesbitt," she murmured in reply.

"Leslie and Tony are here not only as representatives of the Cabinet but as representatives of two of our larger political parties," Pritchart explained. "When I organized my Cabinet originally, it seemed pretty clear we were going to need the support of all parties if we were going to make the Constitution work. Because of that, I deliberately chose secretaries from several different parties, and Leslie is a New Democrat, while Tony's a Corporate Conservative." She smiled dryly. "I'm quite certain you've been sufficiently well briefed on our political calculus here Paris to understand just how lively meetings can be when these two sit in on them."

Montreau and Nesbitt both smiled, and Honor smiled back, although she suspected Pritchart was actually understating things.

"As I explained in my memo," the President continued, "I've decided, with your consent, to invite some additional representatives from Congress to participate in these talks, as well."

"Of course, Madam President." Honor nodded, despite the fact that she really wished Pritchart hadn't done anything of the sort. She would have much preferred to keep these talks as small and private, as close to one-on-one with Pritchart, as she could. At the same time, she was pretty sure she understood the President's logic. And given the fractiousness of Havenite politics—and the fact that selling anything short of victory to Congress and the Havenite people was likely to prove a challenging task—she couldn't really disagree with Pritchart, either.

It's an imperfect galaxy, Honor, she told herself tartly. *Deal with it.*

"Allow me to introduce Senator Samson McGwire," Pritchart said, indicating the man next to Nesbitt.

McGwire was a smallish, wiry man, a good twenty centimeters shorter than Honor. In fact, he was shorter than Pritchart or Leslie Montreau, for that matter. He also had gunmetal-gray hair, a great beak of a nose, blue eyes, bushy eyebrows, and a powerful chin. They were sharp, those eyes, and they glittered with a sort of perpetual challenge. From the way they narrowed as he shook her hand, she wasn't able to decide whether in her case the challenge was because she was a Manticoran, and therefore the enemy, or simply because she was so much taller than he was. For that matter, it could have been both. According to the best briefing Sir Anthony Langtry's staff in the Foreign Office had been able to provide, McGwire was not one of the Star Empire's greater admirers. For that matter, his New Conservative Party was widely regarded as one of the natural homes for Havenite firebrands with personal axes to grind with the Star Empire.

Which is one reason we're so happy to have Montreau as Secretary of State instead of that jackass Giancola, she thought dryly. *I'm sorry anyone had to get killed in a traffic accident, but the truth is that dropping him out of the equation has to be a good thing for everyone concerned. In fact, I have to wonder what a smart cookie like Pritchart was thinking putting a New Conservative into that Cabinet post in the first place!*

Not, she admitted, *that our ending up with High Ridge as Prime Minister and Descroix as Foreign Secretary was any better. But it least Elizabeth didn't have much choice about it.*

"Senator McGwire's the chairman of the Senate Foreign Affairs Committee," Pritchart continued. She tilted her head to one side, watching Honor's expression closely, as if trying to determine how much Honor already knew about the senator. "He's here in his capacity as chairman, but also as a representative of the New Conservative Party."

"Senator," Honor said, reaching out to shake his hand.

"Admiral." He made no particular effort to inject any warmth into the single word, and his handshake was more than a little perfunctory. Still, if Honor was parsing his emotions correctly, he had no more illusions about the Republic's disastrous military position than anyone else did.

"And this," Pritchart said, turning to a dark-haired, green-eyed woman about thirty T-years younger than Honor, "is Senator Ninon Bourchier. She's the senior ranking Constitutional Progressive member of Senator McGwire's committee."

"Senator Bourchier," Honor acknowledged, and tried not to smile. Bourchier was quite attractive, although nowhere near as striking as Pritchart herself, and she had a bright, almost girlish smile. A smile, in fact, which went rather poorly with the coolly watchful brain behind those guileless jade eyes. There was more than a touch of the predator to Bourchier, although it wasn't in any sense as if she had an active taste for cruelty or violence. No. This was simply someone who was perpetually poised to note and respond to any threat—or opportunity—with instant, decisive action. *And* of someone who thought very directly in terms of clearly recognized priorities and responsibilities. As a matter of fact, her mind-glow tasted a lot like that of a treecat, Honor decided, which wasn't especially surprising, since like Pritchart, Bourchier had been a dedicated member of the Aprilist movement. In fact, ONI had confirmed that she'd been personally responsible for at least seven assassinations, and she'd also been one of the civilian cell leaders who'd not only somehow survived Oscar Saint-Just's best efforts to root out dissidents but also rallied in support of Theisman's coup in the critical hours immediately after the SS commander's date with mortality. And these days she was an influential member of Pritchart's own Constitutional Progressive Party, as well.

"I've been looking forward to meeting you, Admiral," Bourchier said, gripping Honor's hand firmly, and Honor's urge to smile threatened to break free for just a moment. Bourchier's greeting sounded almost gushy, but behind its surface froth, that needle-clawed treecat was watching, measuring, evaluating Honor with that predator's poise.

"Really?" Honor said. "I hope our efforts won't be disappointing."

"So do I," Bourchier said.

"As do we all," Pritchart cut in smoothly, and gestured to a moderately tall—he was only five or six centimeters shorter than Honor—fair-haired, brown-eyed man who was clearly the youngest person present. He was also the most elegantly tailored, and she felt Nimitz resisting the urge to sneeze as he smelled the fair-haired man's expensive cologne.

"The Honorable Gerald Younger, Admiral Alexander-Harrington," Pritchart said, and Honor nodded to him. "Mr. Younger is a member of our House of Representatives," Pritchart continued. "Like Senator McGwire, he's also a New Conservative, and while he's not its chariman, he sits on the *House* Foreign Affairs Committee."

"Admiral Alexander-Harrington," Younger said with a white-toothed smile.

"Representative Younger," she replied, and carefully did not wipe the palm of her hand on her trousers when Younger released it. Despite his sleek grooming, he radiated a sort of arrogant ambition and predatory narcissism that made even McGwire seem positively philanthropic.

"And this, Admiral Alexander-Harrington," Pritchart said, turning to the final Havenite representative present, "is Chief Justice Jeffrey Tullingham. He's here more in an advisory role than anything else, but I felt it would probably be a good idea to have him available if any legal issues or precedents should happen to raise their heads during our talks."

"That strikes me as an excellent idea, Madam President," Honor said, at least partly truthfully, extending her hand to Tullingham. "It's an honor to meet you, Chief Justice."

"Thank you, Admiral."

He smiled at her, and she smiled back, fully aware—though it was possible he wasn't—that both those smiles were equally false. He wasn't at all pleased to see her here. Which was fair enough, perhaps, or at least reciprocal, since even though Honor agreed with Pritchart that having a legal expert's perspective on the talks was probably a good idea, she wished this *particular* "legal expert" were far, far away from them. Technically, as the senior member of the Havenite Supreme Court, Tullingham was supposed to be above partisan issues. In fact, although Manti-coran intelligence still knew little about his history prior to his appointment to the Court, his mind-glow strongly suggested that he was even more closely aligned with McGwire's and Younger's New Conservatives than the analysts had suspected. And despite a carefully cultivated air of nonpartisan detachment, the taste of his personal ambition—and basic untrustworthiness—came through her empathic sensitivity even more clearly than Younger's had.

And isn't he just a lovely choice to head the court that has the power of judicial review over every law their Congress passes? She managed not to shake her head, but it wasn't easy. *From Pritchart's emotions when she introduced him, she obviously has a pretty fair idea what's going on inside him. So how many dead bodies did he have to threaten to exhume—or personally plant—to get named to the Supreme Court in the first place?*

Well, his impact on Havenite law wasn't her problem, thank God. On the other hand, his impact on the negotiations very well could be. Unless she could talk Senator Bourchier into carrying out just one last little assassination....

She shook free of that thought (although from the taste of Bourchier's mind-glow when she looked at Tullingham, she'd prob-ably agree in a heartbeat) and waved at the other three members of her own delegation.

"As you can see, Madam President, Foreign Secretary Langtry decided it would be a good idea to send along at least a few professionals to keep me out of trouble, as well. Allow me to introduce Permanent Undersecretary Sir Barnabas Kew; Special Envoy Carissa Mulcahey, Baroness Selleck; and Assistant Under-secretary the Honorable Voitto Tuominen. And this is my personal aide, Lieutenant Waldemar Tümmel."

Polite murmurs of recognition came back from the Havenite side of the table, although Honor sensed a few spikes of irritation when she used Mulcahy's title. Well, that was too bad. She didn't intend to rub anyone's nose in the fact that Manticore had an hereditary aristocracy and rewarded merit with admission into it, but she wasn't going to spend all of her time here pussyfooting around tender Havenite sensibilities, either.

Even with her three assistants, her delegation was considerably smaller than Pritchart's, but it ought to be big enough. And it was a darn good thing they were here. She'd spent most of the voyage between Manticore and Haven discovering just how grateful she was for the three seasoned professionals Langtry had sent along.

Kew was the oldest of the trio—with silver hair, sharp brown eyes, a ruddy complexion, and a nose almost as powerful as McGwire's. Tuominen was shortish, but very broad shouldered. He'd always been known as something of a maverick within the ranks of the Foreign Office, and he was as aggressively "com-moner" as Klaus Hauptman. Actually, despite the fact that he'd been born on Sphinx, not Gryphon, his personality reminded her strongly of Anton Zilwicki's in many ways, although he was a considerably more driven sort, without Zilwicki's granite, methodical patience. Countess Selleck was the youngest of the three. Blond-haired, blue-eyed, and attractive in an understated sort of way, she was the intelligence specialist of the Manticoran delegation. She reminded Honor rather strongly of Alice Truman, and not just in a physical sense.

Lieutenant Tümmel was actually the one she'd found most difficult to fit smoothly into place, although that wasn't even remotely *his* fault. The brown-haired, brown eyed lieutenant was an extraordinarily competent young man, with enormous potential, yet she felt a lingering guilt at having accepted him as Timothy Meares' replacement. Even now, she knew, she continued to hold him more or less at arm's length, as if really accepting him would somehow be a betrayal of Meares' memory. Or as if she were afraid letting him get too close to her would lead to his death, as well.

No one, she noticed, offered to introduce the members of Pritchart's security detachment or her own armsmen. Not that anyone was unaware of their presence. In fact, Honor was more than a little amused by the fact that Pritchart's detachment was all but invisible to the Havenites, from long familiarity, while the same thing was true for her armsmen from the Manticoran side of the room, yet both sides were acutely aware of the presence of the *other* side's armed retainers.

And then there was Nimitz... quite possibly the deadliest "armed retainer" of them all. Certainly he was on a kilo-for-kilo basis, at any rate! And it was obvious from the taste of the Havenites' mind-glows that every one of these people had been briefed on the reports of the treecats' intelligence, telempathic abilities, and lethality.

Just as it was equally obvious that several of them—who rejoiced in names like McGwire, Younger, and Tullingham—cherished profound reservations about allowing him within a kilometer of this conference room. In fact, McGwire was so unhappy that Honor had to wonder how Pritchart had managed to twist his arm hard enough to get him here at all.

With the formal greetings and introductions disposed of, Pritchart waved at the conference table, with its neatly arranged data ports, old-fashioned blotters, and carafes of ice water. The chairs around it, in keeping with the Plaza Falls's venerable lineage, were unpowered, but that didn't prevent them from being almost sinfully comfortable as the delegates settled into them.

Pritchart had seated her own delegation with its back to the suite's outer wall of windows, and Honor felt a flicker of gratitude for the President's thoughtfulness as she parked Nimitz on the back of her own chair. Then she seated herself and gazed out through the crystoplast behind Pritchart and her colleagues while the other members of her own team plugged personal minicomps into the data ports and unobtrusively tested their firewalls and security fences.

Nouveau Paris had been built in the foothills of the Limoges Mountains, the coastal range that marked the southwest edge of the continent of Rochambeau where it met the Veyret Ocean. The city's pastel colored towers rose high into the heavens, but despite their height—and, for that matter, the sheer size and population of the city itself—the towering peaks of the Limoges Range still managed to put them into proportion. To remind the people living in them that a planet was a very large place.

Like most cities designed and planned by a gravitic civilization's engineers, Nouveau Paris incorporated green belts, parks, and tree-shaded pedestrian plazas. It also boasted spectacular beaches along its westernmost suburbs, but the heart of the original city been built around the confluence of the Garronne River and the Rhône River, and from her place at the table, she looked almost directly down to where those two broad streams merged less than half a kilometer before they plunged over the eighty-meter, horseshoe-shaped drop of Frontenac Falls in a boiling smother of foam, spray, and mist. Below the falls which had given the Plaza Falls' its name, the imposing width of the Frontenac Estuary rolled far more tranquilly to the Veyret, dotted with pleasure boats which were themselves yet another emblem of the Republic of Haven's renaissance. It was impressive, even from the suite's imposing height.

She gazed at the city, the rivers, and the falls for several seconds, then turned her attention politely to Pritchart.

The President looked around the table, obviously checking to be certain everyone was settled, then squared her own shoulders and looked back at Honor.

"It's occurred to me, Admiral Alexander-Harrington, that this is probably a case of the less formality, the better. We've already tried the formal diplomatic waltz, with position papers and diplomatic notes moving back and forth, before we started shooting at each other again, and we're all only too well aware of where *that* ended up. Since your Queen's been willing to send you to us under such . . . untrammeled conditions, I'd like to maintain as much *in*formality as possible this time around, in hopes of achieving a somewhat more satisfactory outcome. I do have a certain structure in mind, but with your agreement, I'd prefer to allow frank discussion among all the participants, instead of the standard procedure where you and I—or you and Leslie—simply repeat our formal positions to one another over and over while everyone else sits back, watches, and tries valiantly to stay awake."

"I think I could live with that, Madam President," Honor replied, feeling the slight smile she couldn't totally suppress dance around her lips.

"Good. In that case, I thought that since you've come all this way to deliver Queen Elizabeth's message, I'd ask you to repeat it for all of us. And after you've done that, I would appreciate it if you would sketch out for us—in broad and general strokes, of course—a preliminary presentation of the Star Kingdom—I'm sorry, the Star *Empire's*—view of what might constitute the terms of a sensible peace settlement."

"That sounds reasonable," Honor agreed, sternly telling the butterflies in her stomach to stop fluttering. Odd how much more unnerving *this* was than the mere prospect of facing an enemy wall of battle.

She settled further back into her chair, feeling Nimitz's warm, silken presence against the back of her head, and drew a deep breath.

"Madam President, ladies and gentlemen," she began, "I'll begin by being blunt, and I hope no one will be offended by my candor. Please remember that despite any titles I may have acquired, or any diplomatic accreditation Queen Elizabeth may have trusted me with, I'm basically a yeoman-born naval officer, not a trained diplomat. If I seem to be overly direct, please understand no discourtesy is intended."

They gazed back at her, all of them from behind the impassive façades of experienced politicians, and she considered inviting them to just relax and check their poker faces at the door. It wasn't as if those well-trained expressions were doing them any good against someone as capable of reading the emotions behind them as any treecat. And anything she missed, Nimitz wouldn't when they compared notes later.

Still, judging by the way they taste, Pritchart, Theisman, and Montreau—at the very least—already know that as well as McGwire and Tullingham do. Interesting that none of them've made a point of their knowledge, though.

"As I've already told President Pritchart, both my Queen and I are fully aware that the view of who's truly responsible for the conflict between our two star nations isn't the same from Manticore and Haven. I've also already conceded to President Pritchart that the High Ridge Government must bear its share of blame for the diplomatic failure which led to the resumption of hostilities between our star nations. I think, however, that no one in Nouveau Paris, anymore than anyone in Landing, can deny that the Republic of Haven actually fired the first shots of this round when it launched Operation Thunderbolt. I'm confident the decision to do so was not lightly taken, and I don't doubt for a moment that you felt, rightly or wrongly, both that you were justified and that it was the best of the several bad options available to you. But the fact remains that Manticore didn't start the shooting in *any* of our conflicts with Haven.

"Nonetheless, ladies and gentlemen, we've come to a cross-roads. I know some of you blame the Star Empire for all that's happened. I assure you, there are more than sufficient people in the Star Empire who blame the *Republic* for all that's happened. And the truth, of course, is that both sides must bear their own share of the responsibility. Yet at this moment, the Star Empire's military advantage is, quite frankly, overwhelming."

They weren't liking what they were hearing; that much was painfully obvious to her empathic sense, despite their impressive control of their faces. But she also tasted the bleak awareness that what she'd just said was self-evidently true. It was strongest from Pritchart and Theisman, but she tasted a surprisingly strong flare of the same awareness from Nesbitt. Montreau and Bourchier clearly recognized the same unpalatable truth, but there was something different, less personal about their recognition than Honor tasted in Nesbitt's.

Younger, on the other hand, seemed to be one of those people who were constitutionally incapable of accepting the very possibility of failure. It was as if he was able to intellectually recognize that Apollo gave the Manticoran Alliance a huge military advantage yet *unable* to accept the corollary that he could no longer "game" his way to the outcome *he* wanted.

McGwire and Tullingham, unlike Younger, clearly did recognize how severely the tectonic shift in military power limited their options, but that didn't mean they were prepared to give up. She suspected they'd be willing to bow to the inevitable, in the end, but only after they'd cut the best personal deals they could.

Well, they're welcome to cut all of the domestic political deals they want to, she thought grimly.

"The simple truth," she continued, "is that it's now within the power of the Royal Manticoran Navy to systematically reduce the orbital infrastructure of every star system of the Republic to rubble." Her voice was quiet, yet she felt them flinching from her words as if they'd been fists. "You can't stop us, however courageous or determined Admiral Theisman's men and women may be, even with the advantages of the missile defense system—Moriarity, I believe you call it—Admiral Foraker devised before the Battle of Solon, as we demonstrated at Lovat."

A fresh stab of pain ripped through Pritchart, and it was Honor's turn to flinch internally, in combined sympathy and guilt. Guilt not so much for having *killed* Javier Giscard, as for the way in which killing him had wounded Eloise Pritchart, as well.

"There are those in the Star Empire," she went on, allowing no trace of her awareness of Pritchart's pain to color her own expression or tone, "who would prefer to do just that. Who think it's time for us to use our advantage to completely destroy your fleet, along with all the casualties that would entail, and then to turn the entire Republic into one huge junkyard unless you surrender unconditionally to the Star Empire and the Manticoran Alliance. And, if you do surrender, to impose whatever domestic changes and limitations may be necessary to prevent you from ever again threatening the Star Empire or Queen Elizabeth's subjects."

She paused, letting her words sink home, tasting their anger, their apprehension, their resentment and frustration. Yet even now, hope continued to flicker, made even stronger in many ways by simple desperation. By the fact that there *had* to be some end less terrible than the total destruction of all they'd fought and struggled to build and accomplish.

"I would be lying to you, ladies and gentlemen," she resumed finally, "if I didn't admit that the Manticorans who would prefer to see the final and permanent destruction of the Republic of Haven probably outnumber those who would prefer any other outcome. And I'm sure there are any number of Havenites who feel exactly the same way about the Star Empire after so many years of warfare and destruction.

"But vengeance begets vengeance." Her voice was soft, her brown, almond-shaped eyes very level as they swept the faces of the Havenites. "Destruction can be a 'final solution' only when that destruction is complete and total. When there's no one left on the other side—will *never* be anyone left on the other side—to seek their own vengeance. Surely history offers endless examples of that basic, unpalatable truth. Rome had 'peace' with Carthage back on Old Terra in the end, but only when Carthage had been not simply defeated, but totally destroyed. And no one in the Star

Empire is foolish enough to believe we can 'totally destroy' the Republic of Haven. Whatever we do, wherever the Star Empire and the Republic go from this point, there will still be people on both sides who identify themselves as Manticoran or Havenite and *remember* what the other side did to them, and no military advantage lasts forever. Admiral Theisman and Admiral Foraker demonstrated that quite clearly two or three T-years ago, and I assure you that we in the Star Empire learned the lesson well."

Something like an echo of bleak satisfaction quivered around the Havenite side of the table at her admission, and she met Theisman's gaze, then nodded very slightly to him.

"So the position of the Star Empire, ladies and gentlemen," she told them, "is that it's ultimately in the best interests of both Manticore and Haven to *end* this. To end it *now*, with as little additional bloodshed, as little additional destruction, as little additional grounds for us to hate one another and seek vengeance upon one another, as possible. My Queen doesn't expect that to be easy. She doesn't expect it to happen quickly. But the truth is that it's a simple problem. *Solving* it may not be simple, yet if we can agree on the unacceptability of failure, it's a solution we can achieve. One we *must* achieve. Because if we fail to, then all that will remain are more of those 'bad options' that have brought us to this pass in the first place. And if all that remain are bad options, then Her Majesty's Government and military forces will choose the option most likely to preclude Haven's threatening the Star Empire again for as many decades as possible."

She looked around the conference table again, sampling the whirlwind emotions behind those outwardly calm and attentive faces, and shook her head slowly.

"I personally believe, both as an officer in Her Majesty's service and as a private citizen, that that would be a disaster. That it would only sow the seeds of still another cycle of bloodshed and killing in the fullness of time. None of which means it won't happen anyway, if we fail to find some other solution. That I won't carry out my own orders to *make* it happen. So it's up to us—all of us, Manticoran and Havenite—to decide which outcome we can achieve. And my own belief, ladies and gentlemen, is that we owe it not only to all the people who may die in the future but to those who have already died—to *all* our dead, Manticoran, Grayson, Andermani, and Havenite—to choose the *right* outcome."

Chapter Eleven

"GOOD MORNING, MICHAEL," the very black-skinned woman said from Rear Admiral Michael Oversteegen's com display.

"Mornin', Milady," Oversteegen drawled, and smiled slightly as her eyes narrowed. His chosen form of address was perfectly appropriate, even courteous...no matter how much he knew it irritated Vice Admiral Gloria Michelle Samantha Evelyn Henke, Countess Gold Peak. Especially in that upper-crust, languid accent. Of course, the fact that she knew *he* knew it irritated her only made it even more amusing.

Serves her right, he thought. *All those years she managed t' avoid admittin' she was only half-a-dozen or so heartbeats away from th' Throne. Not anymore, Milady Countess.*

It wasn't that Oversteegen had anything other than the highest respect for Michelle Henke. It was just that she'd always been so aggressive in stamping on anything that even looked like the operation of nepotism on her behalf. Oh, if she'd been incompetent, or even only *marginally* competent, he'd have agreed with her. The use of family influence in support of self-interest and mediocrity (or worse) was the single greatest weakness of an aristocratic system, and Oversteegen had studied more than enough history to admit it. But *every* social system had weaknesses of one sort or another, and the Manticoran system was an aristocratic one. Making that system work required a recognition of social responsibility on the part of those at its apex, and Oversteegen had no patience with those—like his own miserable excuse for an uncle, Michael Janvier, the Baron of High Ridge—who saw their lofty births solely in terms of their own advantage. But it also required the effective use of the advantages of birth and position to promote merit. To see to it that those who were capable of discharging their responsibilities, and willing to do so, received the preference to let them get on with it.

He was willing to concede that the entire system disproportionately favored those who enjoyed the patronage and family influence in question, and that was unfortunate. One of those weaknesses every system had. But he wasn't going to pretend he didn't see those advantages as a rightful possession of those who met their obligations under it . . . including, especially, the enormous obligation to see to it that those advantages were employed on behalf of others, in support of the entire society which provided them, not simply for their own personal benefit or the sort of shortsighted class selfishness of which aristocrats like his uncle (or, for that matter, his own father) were altogether too often guilty. In particular, one of the responsibilities of any naval officer was to identify and groom his own successors, and Oversteegen saw no reason he shouldn't use his influence to nurture the careers of capable subordinates, be they ever so commonly born. It wasn't as if being born into the aristocracy magically guaranteed some sort of innate superiority, and one of the greater strengths of the Manticoran system from its inception had been the relative ease with which capable commoners could find themselves elevated to its aristocracy.

Mike ought t' recognize that if anyone does, he reflected, *given that her best friend in th' galaxy is also th' most spectacular example I can think of of how it works. When it works, of course. Be fair, Michael—it doesn't always, and you know it as well as Mike does.*

"What can I do for you this fine mornin'?" he inquired genially, and she shook her head at him.

"I was going to invite you to observe a little command simulation over here aboard *Artic* in a couple of days," she said, using the nickname which had been bestowed upon HMS *Artemis* by her flagship's crew. "But given how feisty you're obviously feeling, I've changed my mind. Instead"—she smiled nastily—"I think you'd better join me for lunch so we can discuss the defenders' role. You've just inspired me to let *you* play system-defense force CO in our little exercise instead of Shulamit."

"I'd hate t' be quoted on this, Milady, but that sounds just a mite . . . I don't know . . . *vengeful*, perhaps?"

"Why, yes, I believe it does, Admiral Oversteegen. And, speaking as one decadent, effete aristocrat to another, isn't vengefulness one of our hallmark traits?"

"I believe it is," he agreed with a chuckle.

"I'm glad it amuses you, Admiral," she said cheerfully. "And I hope you'll go right on feeling equally amused when it turns out the other side has Mark 23s, too, this time."

"Why do I have th' impression you just this minute decided t' add that particular wrinkle t' th' sim, Milady?"

"Because you have a nasty, suspicious mind and know me entirely too well. But look at it this way. It's bound to be a very *enlightening* experience for you." She smiled sweetly at him. "I'll expect you at oh-one-thirty, Admiral. Don't be late!"

Michelle terminated the connection and tipped back in her flag bridge chair, shaking her head wryly.

"Are you really going to give the aggressor force Mark 23s, Ma'am?" a voice asked, and Michelle looked over her shoulder at Captain Cynthia Lecter, Tenth Fleet's chief of staff.

"I'm not only going to give the op force Mark 23s, Cindy," she said with a wicked smile. "I'm probably going to give it Apollo, too."

Lecter winced. The current iteration of the Mark 23 multidrive missile carried the most destructive warhead in service with any navy, and it carried it farther and faster than any missile in service with any navy outside what was still called the Haven Sector. That was a sufficiently significant advantage for most people to be going on with, she supposed, but when the faster-than-light command and control link of the Apollo system was incorporated into the mix, the combination went far beyond simply devastating.

"You don't think that might be a little bit of overkill, Ma'am?" the chief of staff asked after a moment.

"I certainly *hope* it will!" Michelle replied tartly. "He deserves worse, actually. Well, maybe not *deserves*, but I can't think of a word that comes closer. Besides, it'll be good for him. Put a little hiccup in that unbroken string of four-oh simulations he's reeled off since he got here. After all," she finished, lifting her nose with a slight but audible sniff, "it's one of a commanding officer's responsibilities to remind her subordinates from time to time of their own mortality."

"You manage to sound so virtuous when you say that, Ma'am," Lecter observed. "And you can actually keep a straight face, too. I think that's even more remarkable."

"Why, thank you, Captain Lecter!" Michelle beamed benignly and raised one hand in a gesture of blessing which would have done her distant cousin Robert Telmachi, the Archbishop of Manticore, proud. "And now, why don't you sit down with Dominica, Max, and Bill to see just how devious the three of you can be in putting all of those unfair advantages into effect?"

"Aye, aye, Ma'am," Lecter acknowledged, and headed off towards the tactical section, where Commander Dominica Adenauer was discussing something with Lieutenant Commander Maxwell Tersteeg, Michelle's staff electronic warfare officer.

Michelle watched her go and wondered if Cindy had figured out the other reason she was thinking about giving the op force Apollo. They weren't going to find a more capable system-defense CO than Michael Oversteegen, and she badly wanted to see how well the Royal Manticoran Navy's Apollo— in the hands of one Vice Admiral Gold Peak and her staff—could do while someone with all the Royal Manticoran Navy's war-fighting technology *short* of Apollo pulled out all the stops against her.

Her own smile faded at the thought. None of her ships currently had Apollo, nor did they have the Keyhole-Two platforms to make use of the FTL telemetry link even if they'd had the Apollo birds themselves. But unless she missed her guess, that was going to change very soon now.

I hope to hell *it is, anyway,* she reflected grimly. *And when it does, we'd damned well better have figured out how to use it as effectively as possible. That bastard Byng may have been a complete and utter incompetent—as well as an asshole—but not all Sollies can be that idiotic.*

She settled back, contemplating the main plot with eyes that didn't see it at all while she reflected on the last three T-months.

Somehow, when she'd just been setting out on her naval career, it had never occurred to her she might find herself in a situation like this one. Even now, it seemed impossible that so much could have happened in so short a period, and she wished she knew more about what was going on back home.

Be glad of what you do *know, girl,* she told herself sternly. *At least Beth approved of your actions. Cousin or not, she could've recalled you as the sacrificial goat. In fact, I'm sure a lot of people think that's exactly what she* should've *done.*

The four-week communications loop between the Spindle System, the capital of the newly organized Talbott Quadrant of the Star Empire of Manticore, and the Manticoran Binary System was the kind of communications delay any interstellar naval officer had to learn to live with. It was also the reason most successful navies simply assumed flag officers on distant stations were going to have to make their own decisions. There just wasn't time for them to communicate with their governments, even though everyone recognized that the decisions they made might have significant consequences for their star nations' foreign policy. But however well established that state of affairs might be, the potential consequences for Michelle Henke this time around were rather more significant than usual.

"More significant than usual." My, what a fine euphemistic turn of phrase, Mike! she thought sourly.

It didn't seem possible that it was one day short of two months since she'd destroyed a Solarian League battlecruiser with all hands. She hadn't wanted to do it, but Admiral Josef Byng hadn't left her much in the way of options. And, if she was going to be honest, a part of her was intensely satisfied that the drooling idiot hadn't. If he'd been reasonable, if he'd had a single functioning brain cell and he'd stood-down his ships as she'd demanded until the events of the so-called *First* Battle of New Tuscany could be adequately investigated, he and his flaship's entire crew would still be alive, and that satisfied part of her would have considered that a suboptimal outcome. The arrogant bastard had slaughtered every man and woman aboard three of Michelle's destroyers without so much as calling on them to surrender first, and she wasn't going to pretend, especially to herself, that she was sorry he'd paid the price for all those murders. The disciplined, professional flag officer in her would have preferred for him (and his flagship's crew) to be alive, and she'd tried hard to achieve that outcome, but only because no sane Queen's officer wanted to contemplate the prospect of a genuine war against the Solarian League. Especially not while the war against Haven was still unresolved.

But Elizabeth, Baron Grantville, Earl White Haven, and Sir Thomas Caparelli had all approved her actions in the strongest possible language. She suspected that at least some of that approval's firmness had been intended for public consumption, both at home in Manticore and in the Solarian League. Word of the battle—accompanied by at least excerpts of Elizabeth's official dispatch to her, approving her actions—had reached Old Terra herself via the Beowulf terminus of the Manticoran Wormhole Junction a month ago now. Michelle had no doubt Elizabeth, William Alexander, and Sir Anthony Langtry had given careful thought to how best to break the news to the Sollies; unfortunately, "best" didn't necessarily equate to "a *good* way to tell them."

In fact, Michelle had direct evidence that they weren't even remotely the same thing. The first wave of Solarian newsies had reached Spindle via the Junction nine days earlier, and they'd arrived in a feeding frenzy. although Michelle herself had managed to avoid them by taking refuge in her genuine responsibilities as Tenth Fleet's commanding officer. She'd retreated to her orbiting flagship and hidden behind operational security and several hundred kilometers of airless vacuum—and *Artemis'* Marine detachment—to keep the pack from pursuing her.

Agustus Khumalo, Baroness Medusa, Prime Minister Alquezar, and Minister of War Krietzmann had been less fortunate in that regard. Michelle might have been forced to put in appearances at no less than four formal news conferences, but her military and political superiors found themselves under continual siege by Solarian reporters who verged from the incredulous to the indignant to the outraged and didn't seem particularly concerned about who knew it. From her own daily briefings, it was evident that the flow of newsies—Manticoran, as well as Solarian—was only growing. And just to make her happiness complete, the insufferable gadflies were bringing their own reports of the Solarian League's reaction to what had happened along with them. Well, the *Old Terran* reaction, at least, she corrected herself. But the version of the "truth" expounded on Old Terra—and the reaction *to* it on Old Terra—always played a hugely disproportionate part in the League's policies.

And it was evident that Old Terra and the deeply entrenched bureaucracies headquartered there were not reacting well.

She reminded herself that all of her information about events on the League's capital world was at least three T-weeks old. She supposed it was remotely possible something resembling sanity had actually reared its ugly head by now and she just hadn't heard about it yet. But as of the last statements by Prime Minister Gyulay, Foreign Minister Roelas y Valiente, and Defense Minister Taketomo which had so far reached Spindle, the League's official position was that it was "awaiting independent confirmation of the Star Empire of Manticore's very serious allegations" and considering "appropriate responses to the Royal Manticoran Navy's destruction of SLNS *Jean Bart* and her entire crew."

While Roelas y Valiente *had* "deeply deplored" any loss of life suffered in the first "alleged incident" between units of the Solarian League Navy and the Royal Manticoran Navy in the neutral system of New Tuscany, his government had, of course, been unable to make any formal response to the Star Empire's protest and demand for explanations at that time. The Solarian League would, equally of course, "respond appropriately" as soon as there'd been time for "reliable and impartial" reports of *both* the "alleged incidents" to reach Old Terra. In the meantime, the Solarian League "sincerely regretted" its inability to respond directly to the "purported facts" of the "alleged incidents." And however deeply the foreign minister might have "deplored" any loss of life, he'd been very careful to point out that even by Manticoran accounts, the Solarian League had lost far more lives than Manticore had. And that that *Solarian* loss of life had occurred only after "what would appear to be the hasty response of a perhaps overly aggressive Manticoran flag officer to initial reports of a purported incident which had not at that time been independently confirmed for her."

All of which had clearly amounted to telling the Star Empire to run along and play until the grown-ups in the League had had an opportunity to find out what had *really* happened and decided upon appropriate penalties for the rambunctious children whose "overly aggressive" response was actually responsible for it.

On the surface, "waiting for independent confirmation" sounded very judicial and correct, but Michelle—unlike the vast number of Solarians listening to the public statements of the men and women who theoretically governed them—knew the League government already had Evelyn Sigbee's official report on what had happened in both the "New Tuscany Incidents." The fact that the people who supposedly ran that government were still referring to what they knew from their own flag officer's report was the truth as "allegations" was scarcely encouraging. And the fact that they were considering "appropriate responses" to *Jean*

Bart's destruction by an "overly aggressive Manticoran flag officer" and not addressing even the possibility of appropriate responses to Josef Byng's murder of three Manticoran destroyers and their entire ships' companies struck her as even less promising. At the very least, as far as she could see, all of that was a depressing indication that the idiots calling the shots behind the smokescreen of their elected superiors were still treating this all as business as usual. And if that really *was* their attitude…

At least the fact that Manticore was inside the Sollies' communications loop meant Old Terra had found out about Admiral Byng's unexpected demise even before Lorcan Verrochio had. In theory, at least, Verrochio—as the Office of Frontier Security's commissioner in the Madras Sector—was Byng's superior, but pinning down exactly who was really in charge of what could get a bit slippery once the Sollies' dueling bureaucracies got into the act. That was always true, especially out here in the Verge, and from her own experience with Josef Byng, it might be even truer than usual this time around. It was entirely possible that everything which had happened in New Tuscany, and even his decision to move his command there in the first place, had been his own half-assed idea.

Which doesn't mean Verrochio was exactly an innocent bystander, she reminded herself. *He sure as hell wasn't last time around, anyway. And even if it was all Byng's idea—this time—Verrochio had to sign off on it under the Sollies' own regulations, officially, at least. And then there's always the Manpower connection, isn't there?*

She frowned and suppressed an almost overpowering temptation to gnaw on her fingernails. Her mother had always told her that was a particularly unbecoming nervous mannerism. More to the point, though, as far as Michelle was concerned, she doubted her staff and her flagship's officers would be especially reassured by the sight of their commanding officer's sitting around chewing on her fingernails while she worried.

That thought elicited a quiet snort of amusement, and she ran back through the timing. It was obvious Elizabeth had reacted as promptly (and forcefully) as Michelle had expected. Additional dispatches had arrived since her initial approval of Michelle's actions—along with the influx of journalists of every stripe and inclination—and it was evident to Michelle that very few people back home had appreciated the patronizing tone Roelas y Valiente and Gyulay had adopted in the Solarians' so-called responses to Elizabeth's notes. She also doubted it had *surprised* anyone, however, since it was so infuriatingly typical of the League's arrogance.

When the first of the Solarian news crews reached Spindle, it had been obvious there was already plenty of blood in the water as far as *they* were concerned, even though they'd headed out for the Talbott Quadrant before the League had gotten around to issuing a formal press release about what had happened to *Jean Bart*. They'd arrived armed with the Manticoran reports of events, but that wasn't the same thing, by a long chalk. And the Solarian accounts and editorials which had accompanied the follow-on wave that had departed *after* the official League statements (such as they were and what there was of them) were filled with mingled indignation, anger, outrage, and alarm, but didn't seem to contain very much in the way of reasoned response.

Michelle knew it wasn't fair to expect anything else out of them, given the fact that all of this had come at them cold. Not yet, at any rate. And so far, none of the 'fax stories from the League which had reached Spindle had contained a single solid fact provided by any official Solarian source. Every *official* statement the Solly newsies had to go on was coming from Manticore, and even without the ingrained arrogance the League's reporters shared in full with their fellow citizens, it wouldn't have been reasonable for them to accept the Manticoran version without a healthy dose of skepticism. At the same time, though, it seemed glaringly evident that the majority of the Solly media's talking heads and pundits were being fed carefully crafted leaks from inside the League bureaucracy and the SLN. Manticore's competing talking heads and pundits weren't being leaked additional information, but that was mainly because there was no need to. They were basing their analyses on the facts available in the public record courtesy of the Star Empire of Manticore which, unlike the Solly leaks, had the at least theoretical advantage of actually being the truth, as well. Not that many of Old Terra's journalists and editorialists seemed aware of that minor distinction.

It was all looking even messier than Michelle had feared it might, but at least the Manticoran version was being thoroughly aired. And, for that matter, she knew the Manticoran version was actually spreading throughout the League faster than the so-called response emerging from Old Chicago. The Star Empire's commanding position in the wormhole networks could move things other than cargo ships, she thought grimly.

At the same time Elizabeth had dispatched her second diplomatic note to Old Terra, the Admiralty had issued an advisory to all Manticoran shipping, alerting the Star Empire's innumerable merchant skippers to the suddenly looming crisis. It would take weeks for that advisory to reach all of them, but given the geometry of the wormhole network, it was still likely it would reach almost all of them before any instructions from the League reached the majority of its local naval commanders. And along with the open advisory for the merchies, the same dispatch boats had carried secret instructions to every RMN station commander and the senior officer of every RMN escort force...and those instructions had been a formal war warning.

Michelle devoutly hoped it was a warning about a war which would never move beyond the realm of unrealized possibility, but if it did, the Royal Manticoran Navy's officers' orders were clear. If they or any Manticoran merchant ship in their areas of responsibility were attacked, they were to respond with any level of force necessary to defeat that attack, no matter who the attackers might be. In the meantime, they were also instructed to expedite the return of Manticoran merchant shipping to Manticore-dominated space, despite the fact that the withdrawal of those merchant ships from their customary runs might well escalate the sense of crisis and confrontation.

And, Michelle felt unhappily certain, office lights were burning late at Admiralty House while Thomas Caparelli and his colleagues worked on contingency plans just in case the entire situation went straight to hell.

For that matter, little though she cared for the thought, it was entirely possible the penny had officially dropped back home by now. But even if the Star Empire had received a formal response from the League—even if the League had announced it would pursue the military option instead of negotiating—*Michelle* hadn't heard anything about it yet.

All of which meant she was still very much on her own, despite all the government's approval of her previous actions and assurances of its future support. She'd received at least some reinforcements, she'd shortstopped the four CLACs of Carrier Division 7.1 on her own authority when Rear Admiral Stephen

Enderby turned up in Spindle. Enderby had expected to deliver his LACs to Prairie, Celebrant, and Nuncio, then head home for another load, and the LAC *crews* had expected nothing more challenging than a little piracy suppression. That, obviously, had changed. Enderby had been more than willing to accept his new orders, and his embarked LACs had been busy practicing for a somewhat more demanding role. She expected her decision to retain them for Tenth Fleet to be approved, as soon as the official paperwork could catch up, and the arrival of another division of *Saganami-Cs* had been a pleasant surprise—in more ways than one, given its commanding officer. For that matter, still more weight of metal was in the pipeline, although the original plans for the Talbott Quadrant were still recovering from the shock of the Battle of Manticore.

In a lot of ways, given Enderby's diversion, she was better off at the moment than she would have been under the initial plan, but that might turn out to be remarkably cold comfort if there was any truth to the New Tuscans' reports that major Solarian reinforcements had already been deployed to the Madras Sector, as well. . . .

Well, you've got orders for dealing with that, too, don't you? she asked herself. *Of course, they're basically to "use your own discretion." It's nice to know the folks back home think so highly of your judgment, I suppose, but still . . .*

She inhaled deeply. Baroness Medusa, the Talbott Quadrant's Imperial Governor, had dispatched her own note directly to Meyers at the same time Michelle had departed for New Tuscany and Josef Byng's date with several hundred laser heads. It must have reached Verrochio two T-weeks ago, and she wondered what sort of response *he'd* made.

You'll be finding out soon enough, girl, she told herself grimly. *But even if he dashed off a response the instant* Reprise *got there with O'Shaughnessy, it couldn't get back here for another T-week. And one thing Solly bureaucrats aren't is impetuous about putting their necks on any potential chopping blocks. So even if he didn't have a thing to do with anything that's happened—however unlikely that* is—*I doubt he's going to have been a lot faster out of the blocks than Roelas y Valiente was.*

She remembered the old proverb that said "Sufficient unto the day is the evil thereof." It was remarkably little comfort at the moment. She had absolute confidence in her command's ability to defeat any attack Frontier Fleet might launch against Spindle. They'd have to transfer in scores of additional battlecruisers if they hoped to have any chance against her own *Nikes, Saganami-Cs,* Enderby's CLACs, and the flatpack missile pods aboard her ammunition ships. In fact, she doubted Frontier Fleet had enough battlecruisers anywhere this side of Sol itself to take Spindle, even if they could send every one of them to call on her, and battlecruisers were the heaviest ships Frontier Fleet had. But *Battle Fleet* was another matter, and if the New Tuscans had been right about Solly *superdreadnoughts* at McIntosh...

She gave an internal headshake and scolded herself once again. If there were Solly ships-of-the-wall in the vicinity, she'd just have to deal with that when she got confirmation. Which, of course, was one reason she'd assigned Oversteegen to defend against Mark 23s. She might relent and pull Apollo back out of the equation, but she doubted it, because the purpose wasn't really to smack Michael, no matter how much he deserved it for being such a smartass. And no matter how much she would enjoy doing exactly that, for that matter.

No, the purpose was to force one of the best tacticians she knew to pull out all the stops in defense of the Spindle System. Seeing how well her own staff did against a truly capable Mark 23-equipped opponent would have been desirable enough in its own right, yet that was actually secondary, as far as she was concerned. She was confident of her own tactical ability, but there was always something new for even the best tactician to learn, and Michelle Henke had never been too proud to admit that. She'd be watching Rear Admiral Oversteegen closely, and not just to evaluate his performance. If he came up with something that suggested tactical wrinkles to her, she'd pounce on them in a heartbeat, because she might need them altogether too soon... and badly.

Chapter Twelve

"MAY I HELP YOU, Lieutenant?"

The exquisitely tailored *maître d'* didn't sound as if he really expected to be able to assist two such junior officers, who'd undoubtedly strayed into his establishment by mistake.

"Oh, yes—please! We're here to join Lieutenant Archer," Abigail Hearns told him. "Um, we may be a few minutes early, I'm afraid."

She managed, Ensign Helen Zilwicki observed, to sound very . . . earnest. Possibly even a little nervous at intruding into such elegant surroundings, but *very* determined. And the fact that her father could have bought the entire Sigourney's Fine Restaurants chain out of pocket change wasn't particularly in evidence, either. The fact that she was third-generation prolong and looked considerably younger than her already very young ag e, especially to eyes not yet accustomed to the latest generations of prolong, undoubtedly helped, yet she clearly possessed a fair degree of thespian talent, as well. The *maître d'* was obviously convinced she'd escaped from a high school—probably a *lower-class* high school, given her soft, slow Grayson accent—for the afternoon, at least. His expression of politely sophisticated attentiveness didn't actually change a millimeter, but Helen had the distinct impression of an internal wince.

"Ah, Lieutenant Archer," he repeated. "Of course. If you'll come this way, please?"

He set sail across the intimately lit main dining room's sea of linen-draped tables, and Abigail and Helen bobbed along in his wake like a pair of dinghies. They crossed to a low archway on the opposite side of the big room, then followed him down two shallow steps into a dining room with quite a different (though no less expensive) flavor. The floor had turned into artfully worn bricks, the walls—also of brick—had a rough, deliberately unfinished look, and the ceiling was supported by heavy wooden beams.

Well, by what *looked* like wooden beams, Helen thought, although they probably weren't all that impressive to someone like Abigail who'd grown up in a (thoroughly renovated) medieval pile of stone over six hundred years old. One which really *did* have massive, age-blackened beams, a front gate fit to sneer at battering rams, converted firing slits for windows, and fireplaces the size of a destroyer's boat bay.

Two people were seated at one of the dark wooden tables. One of them—a snubnosed, green-eyed officer in the uniform of a Royal Manticoran Navy lieutenant—looked up and waved as he saw them. His companion—a stunningly attractive blonde—turned her head when he waved, and smiled as she, too, saw the newcomers.

"Thank you," Abigail told the *maître d'* politely, and that worthy murmured something back, then turned and departed with what in a less eminent personage might have been described as relieved haste.

"You know," Abigail said as she and Helen crossed to the table, "you really should be ashamed of the way you deliberately offend that poor man's sensibilities, Gwen."

Personally, Helen was reminded rather forcefully of the old saying about pots and kettles, given Abigail's simpering performance for the same *maître d'*, but she nobly forbore saying so.

"Me?" Lieutenant Gervais Winton Erwin Neville Archer's expression was one of utter innocence. "How could you possibly suggest such a thing, Miss Owens?"

"Because I know you?"

"Is it my fault nobody on this restaurant's entire staff has bothered to inquire into the exalted pedigrees of its patrons?" Gervais demanded. "If you're going to blame anyone, blame *her*."

He pointed across the table at the blonde, who promptly smacked the offending hand.

"It's not polite to point," she told him in a buzz saw-like accent. "Even we brutish, lower-class Dresdeners know that much!"

"Maybe not, but that doesn't make it untrue, does it?" he shot back.

"I didn't say it did," Helga Boltitz, Defense Minister Henri Krietzmann's personal aide, replied, and smiled at the newcomers. "Hello, Abigail. And you too, Helen."

"Hi, Helga," Abigail responded, and Helen nodded her own acknowledgment of the greeting as she seated herself beside Helga. Abigail settled into the remaining chair, facing Helen across the table, and looked up as their waiter appeared.

He took their drink orders, handed them menus, and disappeared, and she cocked her head at Gervais as she opened the elegant, two centimeter-thick binder.

"Helga may have put you up to it, and I can't say I blame her," she said. "This has to be the snootiest restaurant I've ever eaten in, and trust me, Daddy's taken me to some *really* snooty places. Not to mention the way they fawn over a steadholder or his family. But *you're* the one who's taking such a perverse enjoyment over thinking about how these people are going to react when they find out the truth."

"What truth would that be?" Gervais inquired more innocently yet. "You mean the fact that I'm a cousin—of some sort, anyway— of the Queen? Or that Helen here's *sister* is the Queen of Torch? Or that your own humble father is Steadholder Owens?"

"That's exactly what she means, you twit," Helga told him, blue eyes glinting with amusement, and leaned across the table to whack him gently on the head. "And much as I'm going to enjoy it when they do find out, don't think I don't remember how you did exactly the same thing to *me!*"

"I never misled you in any way," he said virtuously.

"Oh, no? If I hadn't looked you up in *Clarke's Peerage*, you never would've told me, would you?"

"Oh, I imagine I'd have gotten around to it eventually," he said, and his voice was considerably softer than it had been. He smiled at her, and she smiled back, gave his right hand a pat where it lay on the table between them, then settled back in her chair.

If anyone had suggested to Helga Boltitz eight months ago that she might find herself comfortable with, or actually *liking*, someone from a background of wealth and privilege, she would have laughed. The idea that someone from *Dresden*, that sinkhole of hardscrabble, lower-class, grub-for-a-living poverty could have anything in common with someone from such stratospheric origins would have been ludicrous. And, if she were going to be honest, that was still true where the majority of the Talbott Quadrant's homegrown oligarchs were concerned. More than that, she felt entirely confident she was going to run into Manticorans who were just as arrogant and supercilious as she'd always imagined they'd be.

But Gervais Archer had challenged her preconceptions—gently, but also firmly—and, in the process, convinced her that there were at least some exceptions to the rule. Which explained how she found herself sitting at this table in such monumentally well-connected company.

"Personally," Helen said, "my only regret is that I probably won't be here when they do find out."

At twenty-one, she was the youngest of the quartet, as well as the most junior in rank. And she was also the non-Dresdener who came closest to sharing Helga's attitudes where aristocrats and oligarchs were concerned. Not surprisingly, given the fact that she'd been born on Gryphon and raised by a Gryphon highlander who'd proceeded to take up with the closest thing to a rabble-rousing anarchist the Manticoran peerage had ever produced when Helen was barely thirteen years old.

"If you really want to see their reaction, I suppose you could tell them yourself this afternoon," Abigail pointed out.

"Oh, no way!" Helen chuckled. "I might want to be here to see it, but the longer it takes them to figure it out, the more irritated they're going to be when they finally do!"

Abigail shook her head. She'd spent more time on Manticore than she had back home on Grayson, over the last nine or ten T-years, but despite the undeniable, mischievous enjoyment she'd felt when dissembling for the *maître d'*, there were times when she still found her Manticoran friends' attitude towards their own aristocracy peculiar. As Gervais had pointed out, her father was a steadholder, and the deepest longings of the most hard-boiled member of Manticore's Conservative Association were but pale shadows of the reality of a steadholder's authority within his steadling. The term "absolute monarch" fell comfortably short of that reality, although "supreme autocrat" was probably headed in the right direction.

As a result of her own birth and childhood, she had remarkably few illusions about the foibles and shortcomings of the "nobly born." Yet she was also the product of a harsh and unforgiving planet and a profoundly traditional society, one whose deference and rules of behavior were based deep in the bedrock of survival's imperatives. She still found the irreverent, almost fondly mocking attitude of so many Manticorans towards their own aristocracy unsettling. In that respect, she was even more like Helga than Helen was, she thought. *Hostility*, antagonism, even hatred—those she could understand, when those born to positions of power abused that power rather than meeting its responsibilities. The sort of self-deprecating amusement someone like Gwen Archer displayed, on the other hand, didn't fit itself comfortably into her own core concepts, even though she'd seen exactly the same attitude out of dozens of other Manticorans who were at least as well born as he was.

I guess you can take the girl off of Grayson, but you can't take Grayson out of the girl, she thought. It wasn't the first time that thought had crossed her mind. *And it won't be the* last, *either,* she reflected tartly.

She started to say something else, then paused as their drinks arrived and the waiter took their orders. He disappeared once more, and she sipped iced tea (something she'd had trouble finding in Manticoran restaurants), then lowered her glass.

"Leaving aside the ignoble, although I'll grant you *entertaining*, contemplation of the coronaries certain to follow the discovery of our despicable charade, I shall now turn this conversation in a more sober minded and serious direction."

"Good luck with *that*," Helen murmured.

"*As* I was about to ask," Abigail continued, giving her younger friend a ferocious glare, "how are things going dirtside, Helga?"

"As frantically as ever." Helga grimaced, took a sip from her own beer stein, then sighed. "I guess it's inevitable. Unfortunately, it's only going to get worse. I don't think anyone in the entire Quadrant's ever seen this many dispatch boats in orbit around a single planet before!"

All three of her listeners grimaced back at her in understanding.

"I don't suppose we can really blame them," she went on, "even if I do want to shoot the next newsy I see on sight! But exactly how they expect Minister Krietzmann to get anything done when they keep hounding him for 'statements' and 'background interviews' is more than I can imagine."

"One of the less pleasant consequences of an open society," Gervais said, rather more philosophically than he felt.

"Exactly," Abigail agreed, then smiled unpleasantly. "Although I'd like to see the newsy back home on Grayson who thought he could get away with 'hounding' Daddy!"

"Well, fair's fair," Helen said judiciously. They all looked at her, and she shrugged. "Maybe it's because I've spent so much time watching Cathy Montaigne maneuver back home, but it occurs to me that having Thimble crawling with newsies may be the best thing that could happen."

"Just how do you mean that?" Gervais asked. In the wrong tone, the question could have been dismissive, especially given the difference in their ages and relative senority. As it was, he sounded genuinely curious, and she shrugged again.

"Politics is all about perceptions and understandings. I realize Cathy's mainly involved in *domestic* politics right now, but the same basic principle applies in interstellar diplomacy. If you control the terms of the debate, the advantage is all on your side. You can't *make* somebody on the other side make the decision you want, but you've got a much better chance of getting her to do that if she's got to defend *her* position in the public mind instead of you having to defend *your* position. Controlling the information—and especially the public perception of that information—is one of the best ways to limit her options to the ones most favorable to your own needs. Don't forget, if the Sollies want a formal declaration of war, all it takes is one veto by a full member star system to stop them. That's a pretty significant prize for a PR campaign to go after. And, at the moment, the way we want to control the debate is simply to tell the truth about what happened at New Tuscany, right?"

Gervais nodded, and she shrugged a third time.

"Well, if all the newsies in the universe are here in Spindle getting *our* side of the story, looking at the sensor data *we've* released, and interviewing *our* people, that's what's going to be being reported back on Old Terra. They can try to spin it any way they want, but the basic message getting sent back to all those Sollies—even by their own newsies—is going to be built on what they're finding out *here,* from us."

"That's more or less what Minister Krietzmann says," Helga admitted, "although he's prone to use some pretty colorful adjectives to describe the newsies in question."

"I think Lady Gold Peak would agree, too, even if she is doing her dead level best to stay as far away from them as possible,"

Gervais said, and Abigail and Helen nodded. As Michelle Henke's flag lieutenant, he was in a far better position to form that kind of judgment than either of them were.

"What about Sir Aivars?" Helga asked. Helen, who was Sir Aivars Terekhov's flag lieutenant, raised both eyebrows at her, and Helga snorted. "He may be only a commodore, Helen, but everybody in the Quadrant knows how long he spent in the dip- lomatic service before he went back into uniform. Besides, Mr. Van Dort and the rest of the Prime Minister's cabinet all have enormous respect for him."

"We haven't actually discussed it," Helen replied after a moment. "On the other hand, he's passed up at least half a dozen oppor- tunities I can think of to hide aboard the *Jimmy Boy* to avoid interviews, so I'd say he was doing his bit to shape public opinion."

Gervais grinned as she used the crew's nickname for HMS *Quentin Saint-James*. The brand-new *Saganami-C*-class heavy cruiser had been in commission for barely five months, yet she'd had her official nickname almost before the commissioning cer- emonies concluded. Most ships wouldn't have managed the transi- tion that quickly, but in *Quentin Saint-James'* case things were a bit different. Her name was on the RMN's List of Honor, to be kept in permanent commission, and the nickname was the same one which had been applied to the first *Quentin Saint-James* the better part of two T-centuries ago.

And if "*Jimmy Boy*" was a youngster, she was scarcely alone in that. In fact, aside from Admiral Khumalo's ancient superdread- nought flagship *Hercules*, there wasn't a single ship heavier than a light cruiser in Admiral Gold Peak's Tenth Fleet which was even a full year old yet. Indeed, most of the *destroyers* were no older than *Quentin Saint-James* and her sisters.

"Well," Helga said after a moment, "I imagine the Minister will go right on 'doing his bit,' too. Don't expect him to like it, though."

"Some things are more likely than others," Helen agreed. Then she snorted.

"What?" Abigail asked.

"Nothing." Abigail looked skeptical, and Helen chuckled. "All right, I was just thinking about how the first newsy to shove his microphone in Daddy's face would make out. I'm sure Daddy would be sorry afterwards. He'd probably even insist on paying the medical bills himself."

"I wondered where you got that physically violent disposition of yours," Gervais said blandly.

"I am not physically violent!"

"Oh, no?" He did his best to look down his longitude-challenged nose at her. "You may recall that I was sent over to *Quentin Saint-James* with that note from Lady Gold Peak to the Commodore last week?" She looked at him suspiciously, then nodded. "Well, I just happened to wander by the gym while I was there and I saw you throwing people around the mat with gay abandon."

"I wasn't!" she protested with a gurgle of laughter.

"You most certainly *were*. One of your henchmen told me you were using something called the 'Flying Marc's Warhammer of Doom, Destruction, and Despair.'"

"Called the *what*?" Helga looked at Helen in disbelief.

"It's not called any such thing, and you know it!" Helen accused, doing her best to glare at Gervais.

"I don't know about that," he said virtuously. "That's what I was *told* it was called."

"Okay," Abigail said. "Now you've got to tell us what it's really called, Helen!"

"The way he's mangled it, even *I* don't know which one it was!"

"Well, try to sort it out."

"I'm guessing—and that's all it is, you understand—that it was probably a combination of the Flying Mare, the Hand Hammer, and—maybe—the Scythe of Destruction."

"And that's supposed to be *better* than what he just said?" Abigail looked at her in disbelief. Abigail herself had become proficient in *coup de vitesse*, but she'd never trained in Helen's chosen *Neue-Stil Handgemenge*. "*Coup de vitesse* doesn't even have names for most of its moves, but if it did, it wouldn't have *those*!"

"Look, don't blame me," Helen replied. "The people who worked this stuff out in the first place named the moves, not me! According to Master Tye, they were influenced by some old entertainment recordings. Something called 'movies.'"

"Oh, Tester!" Abigail shook her head. "Forget I said a thing!"

"What?" Helen looked confused, and Abigail snorted.

"Up until Lady Harrington did some research back home in Manticore—I think she even queried the library computers in Beowulf and on Old Terra, as a matter of fact—nobody on Grayson had ever actually seen the movies our ancestors apparently based their notions of swordplay on. Now, unfortunately, we have. And fairness requires that I admit most of the 'samurai movies' were at least as silly as anything the *Neue-Stil* people could have been watching."

"Well, *my* ancestors certainly never indulged in anything that foolish," Gervais said with an air of unbearable superiority.

"Want to bet?" Abigail inquired with a dangerous smile.

"Why?" he asked distrustfully.

"Because if I remember correctly, your ancestors came from Old North America—from the Western Hemisphere, at least—just like mine did."

"And?"

"And while Lady Harrington was doing her research on samurai movies, she got some cross hits to something called 'cowboy movies.' So she brought them along, too. In fact, she got her uncle and his friends in the SCA involved in putting together a 'movie festival' in Harrington Steading. Quite a few of those movies were made in a place called Hollywood, which also happens to have been in Old North America. Some of them were actually darned good, but others—" She shuddered. "Trust me, your ancestors and mine apparently had . . . erratic artistic standards, let's say."

"That's all very interesting, I'm sure," Gervais said briskly, "but it's leading us astray from the truly important focus we ought to be maintaining on current events."

"In other words," Helga told Abigail, "he's losing the argument, so he's changing the rules."

"Maybe he is," Helen said. "No, scratch that—he *definitely* is. Still, he may have a point. It's not like any of us are going to be in a position to make any earth shattering decisions, but between us, we're working for several people who will be. Under the circumstances, I don't think it would hurt a bit for us to share notes. Nothing confidential, but the kind of general background stuff that might let me answer one of the Commodore's questions without his having to get hold of someone in Minister Krietzmann's office or someone on Lady Gold Peak's staff, for instance."

"That's actually a very good point," Gervais said much more seriously, nodding at her in approval, and she felt a glow of satisfaction. She was preposterously young and junior for her current assignment, but at least she seemed to be figuring out how to make herself useful.

"I agree," Abigail said, although as the tactical officer aboard one of the new *Roland*-class destroyers she was the only person at the table who wasn't a flag lieutenant or someone's personal aide, and gave Helen a smile.

"Well, in that case," Gervais said, "have you guys heard about what Lady Gold Peak is planning to do to Admiral Oversteegen?"

✧   ✧   ✧

"It's time, Admiral," Felicidad Kolstad said.

"I know," Admiral Topolev of the Mesan Alignment Navy replied.

He sat once more upon MANS *Mako*'s flag bridge. Beyond the flagship's hull, fourteen more ships of Task Group 1.1, kept perfect formation upon her, and the brilliant beacon of Manticore-A blazed before them. They were only one light-week from that star, now, and they'd decelerated to only twenty percent of light-speed. This was the point for which they'd been headed ever since leaving Mesa four T-months before. Now it was time to do what they'd come here to do.

"Begin deployment," he said, and the enormous hatches opened and the pods began to spill free.

The six units of Task Group 1.2 were elsewhere, under Rear Admiral Lydia Papnikitas, closing on Manticore-B. They wouldn't be deploying their pods just yet, not until they'd reached their own preselected launch point. Topolev wished he'd had more ships to commit to that prong of the attack, but the decision to move up Oyster Bay had dictated the available resources, and *this* prong had to be decisive. Besides, there were fewer targets in the Manticore-B subsystem, anyway, and the planners had had to come up with the eight additional *Shark*-class ships for Admiral Colenso's Task Group 2.1's Grayson operation from somewhere.

It'll be enough, he told himself, watching as the pods disappeared steadily behind his decelerating starships, vanishing into the endless dark between the stars. *It'll be enough. And in about five weeks, the Manties are going to get a late Christmas present they'll never forget.*

Chapter Thirteen

AUDREY O'HANRAHAN reached for the acceptance key as her com played the 1812 Overture. She especially liked the version she'd used for her attention signal, which had been recorded using real (if exceedingly archaic) cannon. She had a fondness for archaisms—in fact, she was a member of the Society for Creative Anachronisms here in Old Chicago. Besides, the exuberance of her chosen attention signal suited her persona as one of the Solarian League's foremost muckraking journalists.

Investigative journalism of the bareknuckled, no-holds-barred, take-no-prisoners style O'Hanrahan practiced was considerably less lucrative than other possible media careers. Or, at least, it was for *serious* journalists; there was always a market for the sensationalist "investigative reporter" who was willing to shoulder the task of providing an incredibly jaded public with fresh, outrageous titillation. O'Hanrahan, however, had always avoided that particular branch of the human race's third oldest profession. The daughter and granddaughter of respected journalists, she'd proven she took her own reportorial responsibilities seriously from the very beginning, and she'd quickly gained a reputation as one of those rare birds: a newsy whose sources were always rock solid, who genuinely attempted to cover her stories fairly...and who never backed away from a fight.

She'd picked a lot of those fights with the cheerfulness of a David singling out Goliaths, and she'd always been an equal opportunity stone-slinger. Her pieces had skewered the bureaucratic reality behind the representative façade of the Solarian League for years, and she'd never hesitated to denounce the sweetheart deals the Office of Frontier Security was fond of cutting with Solarian transstellars. Just to be fair, she'd done more than a few stories about the close (and lucrative) connections so many senior members of the Renaissance Association maintained with the very power structure it was officially so devoted to reforming from the ground up, as well. And she'd done a series on the supposedly outlawed genetic slave trade which was so devastating —and had named enough specific names—that there were persistent rumors Manpower had put a sizable bounty on her head.

She'd also been one of the first Solarian journalists to report the Manticoran allegations of what had happened at Monica, and although she was no Manticoran apologist, she'd made it clear to her viewers and readers that the waters in Monica were very murky indeed. And as Amandine Corvisart showed the Solarian news media the overwhelming evidence of Manpower's and Technodyne's involvement, she'd reported that, too.

The Solarian establishment hadn't exactly lined up to thank her for her efforts, but that was all right with O'Hanrahan and her producers. She was only fifty-three T-years old, a mere babe in a prolong society, and if the market for old-fashioned investigative reporting was limited, it still existed. In fact, even a relatively small niche market in the League's media amounted to literally billions of subscribers, and O'Hanrahan's hard-earned reputation for integrity meant that despite her relative youth, she stood at the very apex of her particular niche. Not only that, but even those members of the establishment who most disliked her habit of turning over rocks they'd prefer remained safely mired in the mud paid attention to what she said. They knew as well as anyone else that if they read it in an O'Hanrahan article or viewed it in an O'Hanrahan 'cast, it was going to be as accurate, and as thoroughly verified, as was humanly possible. She'd made occasional mistakes, but they could have been easily counted on the fingers of one hand, and she'd always been quick to admit them and to correct them as promptly as possible.

Now, as she touched the acceptance key, the image of a man sprang into life in the holo display above her desk, and she frowned. Baltasar Juppé was scarcely one of her muckraking colleagues. He was nine or ten T-years older than she was, and influential, in his own way, as a financial analyst and reporter. It was a specialist's beat—in many ways, as specialized a niche as O'Hanrahan's, if larger—and it was just as well Juppé's audience was so focused. Human prejudice was still human prejudice, which meant people automatically extended more respect and benefit of the doubt to those fortunate souls who were physically attractive, especially when they had intelligence and charisma to go with that attractiveness. And where O'Hanrahan was auburn-haired, with crystal-blue eyes, elegant bone structure, a graceful carriage, and an understated but rich figure, Juppé's brown hair always hovered on the edge of going out of control, his brown eyes were muddy, and he was (at best) pleasantly ugly.

Although they ran into one another occasionally, they were hardly what one could have called boon companions. They belonged to many of the same professional organizations, and they often found themselves covering the same story—if from very different perspectives—given the corruption and graft which gathered like cesspool silt wherever the League's financial structure intersected with the permanent bureaucracies. For example, they'd both covered the Monica story, although Juppé had scarcely shared O'Hanrahan's take on the incident. Of course, he'd always been a vocal critic of the extent to which Manticore and its merchant marine had penetrated the League's economy, so it was probably inevitable that he'd be more skeptical of the Manticoran claims and evidence.

"Hi, Audrey!" he said brightly, and her frown deepened.

"To what do I owe the putative pleasure of this conversation?" she responded with a marked lack of enthusiasm.

"I'm hurt." He placed one hand on his chest, in the approximate region where most non-newsies kept their hearts, and concentrated on looking as innocent as he could. "In fact, I'm devastated! I can't believe you're that unhappy to see me when I come bearing gifts."

"Isn't there a proverb about being wary of newsies bearing gifts?"

"There probably is, except where you're concerned," he agreed cheerfully. "And if there isn't one, there ought to be. But in this case, I really thought you'd like to know."

"Know what?" she asked suspiciously.

"That I've finally gotten my hands on an independent account of what happened in New Tuscany," he replied, and his voice and expression alike were suddenly much more serious.

"You have?" O'Hanrahan sat up straighter in her chair, blue eyes narrowing with undisguised suspicion. "From where? From who? And why are you calling *me* about it?"

"You really are a muckraker, aren't you?" Juppé smiled crookedly. "It hasn't hit the public channels yet, and it probably won't for at least another day or so, but as you know, I've got plenty of contacts in the business community."

He paused, one eyebrow raised, until she nodded impatiently.

"Well," he continued then, "those sources include one of the VPs for Operations over at Brinks Fargo. And he just happened to mention to me that one of his dispatch boats, just in from Visigoth, had a somewhat different version of events in New Tuscany."

"From Visigoth?" she repeated, then grimaced. "You mean *Mesa*, don't you?"

"Well, yeah, in a way," he acknowledged. "Not in the way *you* mean, though."

"The way *I* mean?"

"In the 'the miserable minions of those wretched Mesan outlaw corporations' deliberately slanted and twisted' sort of way."

"I don't automatically discount every single news report that comes out of Mesa, Baltasar."

"Maybe not *automatically*, but with remarkable consistency," he shot back.

"Which owes more to the self-serving, highly creative version of events the so-called Mesan journalistic community presents with such depressing frequency than it does to any inherent unreasonableness on my part."

"I notice you're not all over the Green Pines story, and there's independent corroboration of *that* one," Juppé pointed out a bit nastily, and her blue eyes narrowed.

"There's been corroboration of the *explosions* for months," she retorted, "and if you followed my stories, you'd know I covered them then. And, for that matter, I suggested at the time that it was likely there was Ballroom involvement. I still think that's probably the case. But I find it highly suspect—and convenient, for certain parties—that the Mesans' 'in-depth investigation' has revealed—surprise, surprise!—that a 'notorious' Manticoran operative was involved." She rolled her eyes. "Give me a break, Baltasar!"

"Well, Zilwicki may be from Manticore, but he's been in bed with the Ballroom for years—literally, since he took up with that looney-tune rabble-rouser Montaigne," Juppé riposted. "And don't forget, his daughter's 'Queen of Torch'! Plenty of room for him to've gone completely rogue there."

"Maybe, if he was a complete lunatic. Or just plain *stupid* enough to pull something like that," O'Hanrahan retorted. "I checked his available public bio, including that in-depth report what's-his-name—Underwood—did on him, as soon as Mesa's version hit the data channels. I'll admit the man's scary as hell if you go after someone he cares about, but he's no homicidal maniac. In fact, his more spectacular accomplishments all seem to've been *defensive*, not offensive. You come after him or his, and all bets are off; otherwise, he's not especially bloodthirsty. And he's for damned sure smart enough to know what nuking a public park full of kids would do to public support for his daughter's new kingdom. For that matter, the whole damned galaxy knows what he'll do if someone goes after one of *his* kids. You really think someone with that kind of resume would sign off on killing hundreds or thousands of someone *else's* kids?" She shook her head again. "Which am I supposed to believe? The public record of someone like Zilwicki? Or the kind of self-serving, fabricated, made-up-out-of-whole-cloth kind of 'independent journalism' that comes out of Mendel?"

From the look in her eye, it was evident which side of that contradiction *she* favored, even if a huge segment of the Solarian media had chosen the other one. While it was true the Solarian League's official position, as enunciated by Education and Information, refused to rush to judgment on the spectacular Mesan claims that Manticore—or, at least, Manticoran proxies—had been behind the Green Pines atrocity, "unnamed sources" within the League bureaucracy had been far less circumspect, and O'Hanrahan and Juppé both knew exactly who those "unnamed sources" were. So did the rest of the League's media, which had been obediently baying on the appropriate trail of Manticoran involvement from day one.

Which, as Juppé knew full well, had absolutely no bearing on O'Hanrahan's categorization of the original story.

"Much as I hate to admit it, given how much impact Mesa sometimes has on the business community here in the League," he said, "I can't really argue with that characterization of a lot of what comes out of their newsies. Mind you, I really am less convinced than you seem to be that Anton Zilwicki's such a choir boy that he wouldn't be involved in something like Green Pines. But that's beside the point, this time." He made a brushing-aside gesture. "*This* story isn't from Mesa; it's straight from New Tuscany. It only came through Mesa because that was the shortest route to Old Terra that didn't go through Manty-controlled space."

O'Hanrahan cocked her head, her eyes boring into his.

"Are you seriously suggesting that whoever dispatched this mysterious story from New Tuscany was actually frightened of what the Manticorans might do if they found out about it?" she demanded in obvious disbelief.

"As to that, I'm not the best witness." Juppé shrugged. "I don't cover politics and the military and Frontier Security the way you do, except where they impinge on the financial markets. You and I both know a lot of the financial biggies are major players in OFS' private little preserves out in the Verge, but my personal focus is a lot more on banking and the stock exchange. So I don't really have the background to evaluate this whole thing. But I do know that according to my friend, and to the courier, they really, really wanted to avoid going through any Manty wormholes."

"Why?" Her eyes were narrower than ever, burning with intensity, and he shrugged again.

"Probably because this isn't really a *story*, at all. It's a dispatch from someone in the New Tuscan government to one of his contacts here on Old Terra. And it's not for public release—not immediately, at any rate."

"Then why send it?"

"I tracked the courier down and asked that very question, as a matter of fact. Got the answer, too—for a price." He grimaced. "Cost me the next best thing to five months' street money, too, and I hope like hell my editor's going to decide it was worth it instead of sticking my personal account for the charges. And to be honest, I don't think I'd've gotten it even then if the man hadn't been so unhappy with his bosses' instructions."

"And why was he so unhappy?" Her tone was skeptical.

"Because the person he's supposed to deliver it to is over at the Office of Naval Intelligence, but his immediate boss—somebody in the New Tuscan government; I couldn't get him to tell me who, but I figure it's got to be somebody from their security services—doesn't want the Navy to go public with it," Juppé said. "They want it in official hands, because it doesn't track with the *Manties'* version of the story, but they're asking the Navy to keep things quiet until Frontier Fleet can get reinforcements deployed to protect them from the Manties."

"According to the Manties, they don't have any big quarrel with *New Tuscany*," O'Hanrahan pointed out. "They've never accused the New Tuscans of firing on their ships."

"I know. But, like I say, this stuff doesn't match what Manticore's been saying. In fact, the courier let me copy what's supposed to be the New Tuscan Navy's raw sensor records of the initial incident. And according to those records, the Manty ships were not only light cruisers, instead of destroyers, but *they* fired first, before Admiral Byng opened fire on them."

"What?"

O'Hanrahan stared at Juppé, and the financial reporter looked back at her as she frowned in concentration.

"That's ridiculous," she said finally. "The Manties wouldn't be that stupid. Besides, what would be the point? Is this mysterious 'courier' claiming the Manties are crazy enough to deliberately provoke an incident with the *Solarian Navy*?"

"As far as I know, he's not claiming anything, one way or the other," Juppé replied. "He's just delivering the dispatch and the scan records, and as I understand it, they're certified copies of the official data." He grimaced. "Hell, maybe the Manties've known all along that it was their man who screwed up, and they've been working on 'proving' it was the League because they figure the only way to avoid getting hammered is to put the blame on the other side."

"Oh, *sure*." O'Hanrahan's irony was withering. "I can just see someone in the Manty government being stupid enough to think they'd get away with something like *that*!"

"I was just offering one possible theory," he pointed out. "Still, I have to say that if there's any truth to Mesa's allegations about Zilwicki and Green Pines, the Manties don't seem to be playing with a full deck these days. In fact, I think 'out of control' might not be a bad way to describe them. And, for that matter, weren't you one of the people who pointed out just how stupid what's-his-name—Highbridge?—was in the lead up to this fresh war of theirs?"

"That was *High Ridge*," she corrected, but her tone was almost absent. She frowned again, clearly thinking hard, and then her eyes refocused, boring into his once more.

"I'm not about to jump at the first set of counter allegations to come along, especially when they're coming from—*through*, at least—someplace like Mesa. So why bring this red hot scoop to me?"

Her suspicion clearly hadn't abated in the least, and he shrugged yet again.

"Because I trust you," he said, and she blinked.

"Come again?"

"Look," he said. "You know me, and you know how it works. If this is an accurate report, if it's *true*, the Manties' position is going to go belly-up as soon as it's verified, especially given what Mesa's already saying about Green Pines. And if that happens, the markets are going to go crazy—or maybe I should say *crazier*—as soon as the implications for the Star Empire and its domination of the wormhole net sink in. I mean, let's face it. If the Manties *did* fake the sensor data they sent with their diplomatic note—if this is another instance of what the Havenites say they were doing all along under what's-his-name—and they've killed the entire crew of a Solarian battlecruiser when they *know* the original 'incident' was their own fault, all hell's going to be out for noon, and Green Pines is only going to squirt more hydrogen into the fire. The SLN's going to pound their miserable little star nation into wreckage, and that's going to have enormous consequences where the wormholes are concerned. There'll be fortunes—*large* fortunes—to be made if something like that happens."

"And?" she encouraged when he paused.

"And I'm an analyst, not just a reporter. If I peg this one right, if I'm the first one—or one of the first two or three—on the Net to advise investors to dump Manty-backed securities and stock issues, to reevaluate their positions in shipping, I'll make a killing. I'll admit it; that's what I'm thinking about. Well, that and the fact that it won't hurt my stature as a reporter one bit if people remember I'm the one who broke *the* story on the financial side."

"And?" she demanded again.

"And I'm not equipped to evaluate it!" he admitted, displaying frustration of his own at last. "Especially not given the fact that this one's got a strictly limited shelf life. Frontier Fleet's going to want to run its own evaluations and check it against what it got from the Manties, we both know that. And then, if it holds up, the guys at the top are going to need to get together, decide whether or not they want to release it right away or confront the Manties with it privately. I guess they could go either way, but I'm willing to bet that as soon as they're confident the data's accurate, they'll go public, whatever the New Tuscans want. That doesn't give me a very wide window if I want to break it first.

"But in the meantime, *I* don't know whether or not to trust the info, either, and if I do, and I'm *wrong*, I'll be finished. You've got the background and the contacts to verify this one hell of a lot better than I can, and you've worked with most of them long enough that they'll keep their mouths shut until *you* break the story if they know you're working on it. So what I'm offering here is a *quid pro quo*. I've got my copy of the original message, and of the sensor data. I'm prepared to hand it over to you—to share it with you—and to share credit for breaking the story if it turns out there's something to it. What do you say?"

Audrey O'Hanrahan regarded him intently for several endless seconds, and it was obvious what she was thinking behind her frown. As he himself had said, it wasn't as if either of them didn't know how the game was played. The old saw about scratching one another's backs was well known among journalists, and Juppé's offer actually made a lot of sense. As he said, he didn't begin to have the sources she did when it came to verifying something like this....

"All right," she said finally. "I'm not going to make any commitments before I've actually seen the stuff. Send it over, and I'll take a look, and if it looks to me like there might be something to it, I'll run it by some people I know and get back to you."

"Get back to me before you go *public* with it you mean, right?"

"You've got my word I won't break the story—assuming there *is* a story—without talking to you first. And," she added in a more grudging tone, "I'll coordinate with you. Do you want a shared byline, or just simultaneous reports?"

"Actually," he smiled crookedly, "I think I'd prefer simultaneous reports instead of looking like either of us is riding on the other's coattails. After all, how often does a columns-of-numbers guy like me get to something this big independently as quickly as someone like you?"

"If that's the way you want it, it'll work for me—assuming, as I say, there's something to it. And assuming you don't want me to sit on it for more than a couple of hours after I get verification?"

"No problem there." He shook his head. "I'm already working up two different versions of the story—one version that breaks the exposé of the Manties' chicanery, and one version that warns everyone not to be taken in by this obviously fraudulent attempt to discredit them. I'll have both of them ready to go by the time you can get back to me."

"Fine. Then have that stuff hand-delivered to me ASAP."

"Done," Juppé agreed. "Clear."

He killed the connection, then leaned back in his own chair, clasped his hands behind his head, and smiled up at the ceiling.

The truth was, he thought, the "official New Tuscan scan records" were going to pass any test anyone cared to perform. He didn't know who'd obtained the authentication codes, but he could make a pretty fair guess that it had been the same person who'd coordinated the entire operation. Of course, they could have been grabbed considerably earlier. That might even explain why New Tuscany had been used in the first place. Cracking that kind of authentication from the outside was always a horrific chore, even when the hackers in charge of it were up against purely homegrown Verge-level computer security. The best way to obtain it was good old-fashioned bribery, which had been a Mesan specialty for centuries.

It didn't really matter, though. What *mattered* was that they had the "records," which didn't show what the Manties' records showed. And those records were about to be authenticated by no less than Audrey O'Hanrahan. He could have gone to any of half a dozen of her colleagues, many of whom had hard won reputations of almost equal stature and almost equally good sources. Any one of them could have broken the story, and he was quite positive every one of them would have, assuming the records proved out. But there were several reasons to hand it to O'Hanrahan, as his instructions had made perfectly clear, and only one of them— though an important one—was the fact that she was probably the most respected single investigative reporter in the entire Solarian League. Certainly the most respected on Old Terra.

It's all been worth it, he thought, still smiling at the ceiling above him. *Every minute of it, for this moment.*

There'd been many times when Baltasar Juppé had longed for a different assignment—*any* different assignment. Building his personal, professional cover had been no challenge at all for the product of a Mesan gamma line, but that very fact had been part of the problem. His greatest enemy, the worst threat to his security, had been his own boredom. He'd known since adolescence that he had a far greater chance of being activated than either of his parents, and definitely more than his grandparents had had when they first moved to Old Terra to begin building his in-depth cover. But even though recent events suggested that the purpose for which the Juppé family had been planted here so long ago was approaching fruitition, he hadn't really anticipated being activated this way for at least another several T-years.

Now he had been, and he thought fondly of the recording he'd made of his conversation with O'Hanrahan. It probably wasn't the only record of it, of course. He *knew* she had one, and despite all of the guarantees of privacy built into the League Constitution, an enormous amount of public and private surveillance went on, especially here in Old Chicago. It was entirely possible—even probable—that somewhere in the bowels of the Gendarmerie someone had decided keeping tabs on Audrey O'Hanrahan's com traffic would be a good idea. It would certainly make plenty of sense from their perspective, given how often and how deeply she'd embarrassed the Solly bureaucracies with her reporting. But that was fine with Juppé. In this case, the more records the better, since they would make it abundantly clear to any impartial observer that he'd done his very best to verify the story which had come so unexpectedly into his hands. And they would make it equally abundantly clear that O'Hanrahan hadn't known a thing about it until he'd brought it to her attention. Not to mention the fact that she was no knee-jerk anti-Manty...and that she'd been suspicious as hell when she heard about his scoop.

And establishing those points was, after all, the exact reason he'd screened her in the first place instead of simply very quietly delivering the information to her in person.

Just as Juppé had frequently longed for something more exciting to do, he'd experienced more than a few pangs of jealousy where reporters like O'Hanrahan were concerned. The public admiration she received would have been reason enough for that, he supposed, but her life had also been so much more *exciting* than his. She'd traveled all over the League in pursuit of her investigations, and her admirers respected her as much for her sheer brilliance and force of will, her ability to burrow through even the most impenetrable smokescreens and most carefully crafted cover stories, as for her integrity. Even more, perhaps, he'd envied how much she'd obviously *enjoyed* her work. But what he hadn't known until this very day—because he'd had no need to know—was that just as his own career and public persona, hers, too, had been a mask she showed the rest of the galaxy. And now that he knew the truth, and despite the envy that still lingered, Juppé admitted to himself that he doubted he could have matched her bravura performance. Gamma line or no, there was no way he could have equaled the performance of an *alpha* line like the O'Hanrahan genotype.

Chapter Fourteen

"MS. MONTAIGNE HAS ARRIVED, Your Majesty."

Elizabeth Winton looked up from the HD she'd been watching and suppressed a flare of severe—and irrational—irritation. After all, Mount Royal Palace chamberlains were chosen for their positions in no small part because of their ability to radiate calm in the midst of crisis, so it was scarcely fair of her to want to throttle this one for sounding precisely that way, she thought. The reflection was very little comfort on a morning like this, however, when all she wanted was someone—*anyone*—upon whom to work out her frustrations. She heard Ariel's soft sound of mingled amusement, agreement, and echoes of her own anger and (she admitted) dismay from his perch beside her desk.

"Thank you, Martin." Her own voice sounded just as calm and prosaic as the chamberlain's, she noted. "Show her in, please."

"Of course, Your Majesty." The chamberlain bowed and withdrew, and Elizabeth darted a glance of combined affection and exasperation at the 'cat, then looked back down at the patently outraged talking head on the recorded Solarian newscast playing on her HD.

I cannot believe *this crap, even out of those Mesa bastards,* she thought. *Oh, we were already afraid the Ballroom* was *involved. And I guess I'm no different from anyone else about having… mixed feelings about that. I mean, hell, all the civilian fatalities combined aren't a spit in the wind compared to what Manpower's*

180

done to its slaves over the centuries. For that matter, you could nuke half the damned planet and not catch up with Manpower's kill numbers! But nuclear weapons on a civilian target? Even low-yield civilian demo charges?

She shuddered internally. Intellectually, she knew, the distinction between nuclear weapons and other, equally destructive attacks was not only logically flawed but downright silly. And it wasn't as if nukes hadn't been used against plenty of other civilian targets over the last couple of millennia. For that matter, Honor Alexander-Harrington, her own cousin Michelle, and other naval officers just like them routinely detonated multimegaton nuclear devices in combat. But emotionally, Green Pines still represented a tremendous escalation, the crossing of a line the Ballroom, for all its ferocity, had always avoided in the past.

Which is what's going to make the new Mesan line so damnably effective with Sollies who already distrust or despise the Ballroom . . . or don't like the Star Empire very much.

For herself, she would have been more likely to buy a used air car from Michael Janvier—or Oscar Saint-Just's ghost!—than to believe a single word that came out of the Mesa System. Still, she was forced to concede, the Mesan version of their "impartial investigation's" conclusions hung together, if one could only ignore the source. There might be a few problems with the timing when it came to selling Green Pines as an act of bloody vengeance, but the Solarian public had become accustomed to editing unfortunate little continuity errors out of the propaganda stream. Besides, Mesa had actually found a way to make the timing work for it!

The attack on Green Pines had occurred five days *before* the abortive attack on Torch by what everyone (with a working brain, at least) realized had been Mesan proxies. Torch, Erewhon, and Governor Oravil Barregos's Maya Sector administration were still playing the details of exactly how that attack had been stopped close to their collective vest, but there wasn't much doubt the attackers had been the mercenary StateSec remnants Manpower had recruited since the Theisman coup. Judging from Admiral Luis Roszak's losses (and according to Elizabeth's classified Office of Naval Intelligence reports, those losses had been *far* higher than Roszak or Barregos had publicly admitted) those merce-naries must have been substantially reinforced. They'd certainly turned up with several times the firepower anyone at ONI had anticipated they might possess.

I wonder whether that assumption on our part comes under the heading of reasonable, complacent, or downright stupid? she thought. *After Monica, we damned well ought to've realized Manpower—or Mesa, or whoever's really orchestrating things—had more military resources than we'd ever thought before. On the other hand, I don't suppose the analysts ought to be too severely faulted for not expecting them to provide presumably traceable ex-Solly battlecruisers to StateSec lunatics who'd been recruited in the first place as disposable—and* deniable—*cat's-paws. Worse, Pat Givens' people at ONI have a pretty solid count on how many StateSec starships actually ran for it after the coup. Admiral Caparelli based his threat assessment on the numbers we knew about, or we'd never have expected Roszak and Torch to deal with it on their own. We're all just damned lucky they managed to pull it off, after all.*

She thought about her niece Ruth, and what would have happened to *her* if Luis Roszak's men and women had been unwilling to pay the price demanded of them, and shuddered.

Obviously, there's at least one batch of Sollies who cut against the stereotype, isn't there, Beth? she thought. *On the other hand, if Pat and Hamish are right, maybe they aren't going to be "Sollies" all that much longer. And Torch's and Erewhon's willingness to help cover exactly whose navy lost what stopping the attack suggests all sorts of interesting possibilities about* their *relationships with Barregos, too, when you think about it. I wonder if that idiot Kolokoltsov even suspects what may be cooking away in that direction?*

But whatever might or might not transpire in the Maya Sector, and despite any threat assessment errors which might have come home to roost for Admiral Roszak and his people, the fact remained that Mesa had neatly factored its own failed attack on Torch into its new propaganda offensive.

After all, its mouthpieces had pointed out, the Kingdom of Torch had declared war on the Mesa System, and a huge chunk of the Kingdom of Torch's military and government leadership had long-standing personal ties to the Audubon Ballroom. Obviously, Torch had figured out the Mesan attack was coming well in advance, since it had formally requested Roszak's assistance under the provisions of its treaty with the Solarian League. (It hadn't, but no one outside the immediate vicinity knew that . . . or was likely to believe it.) So the Mesan argument that Torch had orchestrated the Green Pines attack through the direct Ballroom links it had officially severed as an act of government-sponsored terrorism in retaliation for a legitimate attack by conventional military forces on a belligerent star nation had a dangerous, dangerous plausibility. Especially for anyone who was already inclined to distrust an outlaw regime midwifed in blood and massacre by that same "terrorist" organization.

Which also explains why the Ballroom finally crossed the line into using "weapons of mass destruction" against civilian targets, at least according to the Gospel according to Mesa, Elizabeth thought grimly. *Torch's formal declaration of war represents a whole new level in the genetic slaves' battle with Manpower and Mesa. Effectively, it's a major escalation in* kind, *so why shouldn't they have escalated the* weapons *they're willing to use, as well? Especially if they truly believed (wrongly, of course!) Manpower intended to genocide their own home world? Never mind the fact that they're supposed to have killed thousands of their fellow genetic slaves and Mesan seccies at the same time. And never mind the fact that if they could get to Green Pines, they could almost certainly have gotten to dozens of far more militarily and industrially significant targets, instead. Every right-thinking, process-oriented, comfortably insulated, moralistic cretin of a Solly knows they're terrorists, they think in terroristic terms, and they'd far* rather kill civilians in a blind, frenzied orgy of vengeance than actually *accomplish* anything. *God forbid anyone should think of them as human beings trying to survive with some tattered fragment of dignity and freedom!*

She realized she was grinding her teeth and stopped herself. And, she reminded herself again, the fabrication Mesa had woven really did have a damning plausibility. For that matter, Elizabeth couldn't shake her own strong suspicion that—

Her thoughts hiccuped as her office door opened once more.

"Ms. Montaigne, Your Majesty," the chamberlain announced.

"Thank you, Martin," Elizabeth said once more and rose behind her desk as Catherine Montaigne crossed the carpet towards her.

Montaigne had changed even less than Elizabeth—physically, at least—over the decades since their close adolescent friendship foundered on the rocks of Montaigne's strident principles. Even now, despite the way their relationship had cooled over those same decades, Elizabeth Winton the woman continued to regard

Montaigne as a friend, even though Montaigne's involvement with a legally proscribed terrorist organization continued to prevent Elizabeth Winton the Queen from officially acknowledging that friendship. It couldn't have been any other way, given all the thorny difficulties Montaigne's effective endorsement of the aforesaid legally proscribed terrorist organization created where the Manticoran political calculus was concerned. Especially since the ex-Countess of the Tor had become the leader of what remained of the Manticoran Liberal Party.

And those difficulties just got one hell of a lot "thornier," Elizabeth thought sourly. *Not just where domestic politics are concerned, either.*

"Cathy," the Queen said, extending her hand across the desk.

"Your Majesty," Montaigne replied as she shook the proffered hand, and Elizabeth snorted mentally. No one had ever accused Catherine Montaigne of a chutzpah deficiency, but she was clearly on her best behavior this morning. Despite the other woman's lifetime of experience in the public eye, Elizabeth could see wariness and worry in her eyes, and the formality of her greeting suggested Montaigne was aware of just how thin the ice underfoot had become.

Well, of course she is. She may be a lunatic, and it's for damned sure God forgot to install anything remotely resembling reverse gear when He assembled her, but she's also one of the smartest people in the Old Star Kingdom. Even if she does take a perverse pleasure in pretending otherwise.

"I'm sorry my invitation didn't come under more pleasant circumstances," Elizabeth said out loud, pointing at a waiting armchair when Montaigne released her hand, and the ex-countess' lips twitched ever so slightly.

"So am I," she said.

"Unfortunately," Elizabeth continued, sitting back down in her own chair, "I didn't have much choice. As I'm sure you'd already deduced."

"Oh, you might say that." Montaigne's expression was sour. "I've been under siege by newsies of every possible description since this broke."

"Of course you have. And it's going to get one hell of a lot worse before it gets better ... assuming it ever *does* get better," Elizabeth said. She waited until Montaigne settled into the armchair then shook her head.

"Cathy, what the *hell* were you people *thinking*?"

The Queen didn't need a treecat's empathic sense to recognize Montaigne's sudden flash of anger. Part of Elizabeth sympathized with the other woman; most of her didn't give much of a damn, though. Whatever else, Montaigne had *voluntarily* associated herself with some of the bloodiest terrorists (or "freedom fighters," depending upon one's perspective) in the history of mankind. Choosing to do something like that was bound to result in the occasional minor social unpleasantness, Elizabeth thought trenchantly.

The good news was that Montaigne had always understood that. And it was evident she'd anticipated that question—or one very much like it—from the moment she received Elizabeth's "invitation."

"I assume you're talking about Green Pines," she said.

"No, I'm talking about Jack's decision to assault the beanstalk," Elizabeth said caustically. "Of *course* I'm talking about Green Pines!"

"I'm afraid," Montaigne replied with a degree of calm remarkable even in a politician of her experience, "that at this moment you know just as much about what actually happened in Green Pines as I do."

"Oh, cut the *crap*, Cathy!" Elizabeth snorted disgustedly. "According to Mesa, not only was the Ballroom up to its ass in this entire thing, but so was one Anton Zilwicki. You *do* remember him, don't you?"

"Yes, I do." Montaigne's calm slipped for a moment, and the three words came out flat, hard, and challenging. Then she shook herself. "Yes, I do," she repeated in a more normal tone, "but all I can tell you is that to the best of my knowledge he wasn't involved in this at all."

Elizabeth looked at her incredulously, and Montaigne shrugged.

"It's the truth, Beth."

"And I suppose you're going to tell me the Ballroom wasn't involved 'to the best of your knowledge,' either?"

"I don't know. That's the truth," Montaigne insisted more forcefully as Elizabeth rolled her eyes. "I'm not telling you they weren't; I'm only saying I don't know one way or the other."

"Well, would you like to propose another villain for the piece?" Elizabeth demanded. "Somebody else who hates Mesa enough to set off multiple nuclear explosions in one of its capital's suburbs?"

"Personally, I think the idea would appeal to most people who've ever had to deal with the sick bastards," Montaigne returned levelly, her eyes as unflinching as her voice. "In answer to what you're actually asking, however, I have to admit the Ballroom— or possibly some seccy Ballroom wannabe—has to be the most likely culprit. Beyond that, I genuinely can't tell you anything about who actually did it. I can say, though, that the last time I was on Torch—and, for that matter, the last time Anton and I spoke—no one on Torch, and sure as hell not Anton, was even *contemplating* anything like this."

"And you're confident your good friend and general all-around philanthropist Jeremy X would've *told* you if he'd been planning this kind of operation?"

"Actually, yes," Montaigne shrugged. "I won't pretend my having plausible deniability about Ballroom ops hasn't come in handy from time to time. For that matter, I won't pretend I haven't outright lied about whether or not the Ballroom was behind something . . . or whether or not I had prior knowledge of the 'atrocity' du jour. But now that he and Web Du Havel—and your own niece, for that matter—have finally given the galaxy's genetic slaves a genuine home world of their own? You think he'd be crazy enough to plan something like this—something that *had* to play into Mesa's hands this way? Don't be stupid, Beth! If he'd had even a clue something like this might happen, he'd've stopped it if he'd had to personally shoot the people planning it! And if he *couldn't* stop it, he'd sure as hell have discussed it with me if only because he'd recognize what kind of damage control was going to be necessary."

The ex-countess looked disgusted by her monarch's obtuseness, and Elizabeth gritted her teeth. Then she made herself sit back.

"Look," she said, "I know the Ballroom's never been as monolithic as the public thinks. Or, for that matter, as monolithic as people like Jeremy—and you—like to pretend. I know it's riddled with splinter factions and no one ever knows when a charismatic leader's going to take some chunk of the official organization with him on his own little crusade. But the bottom line is that *someone* nuked Green Pines, and the way it was done is sure as hell consistent with the Ballroom's modus operandi. Aside from the nuclear element, at least!"

"Assuming the reports out of Mesa are accurate, then, yes, I'd have to agree with that," Montaigne acknowledged in that same unflinching tone. "But you're right about the Ballroom's occasional internal divisions. For that matter, I'd have to admit some of the action leaders who'd accepted Jeremy's leadership before Torch became independent are royally pissed off with him now for 'betraying the armed struggle' when he 'went legit.' At least some of them think he's sold out in return for open political power; most of them just think he's *wrong*." She shrugged. "Either way, though, they're hardly likely to run potential operations by him for approval."

"Or material support?"

"Torch has made its position on actively supporting strikes like this crystal clear, Elizabeth. You've heard what they've said as well as I have, and I promise you, they mean it. Like I say, Jeremy's not stupid enough not to see all the downsides of something like this."

Elizabeth tipped back her chair, regarding her "guest" with narrow eyes and scant cheerfulness. There was a certain brittleness to the office's silence, then the Queen raised an eyebrow and pointed an index finger at Montaigne.

"You've been talking in generalities, Cathy," she said shrewdly. "Why aren't you being more specific about how you know Captain Zilwicki wasn't involved in this?"

"Because—" Montaigne began firmly, then paused. To Elizabeth's astonishment, the other woman's face crumpled suddenly, and Montaigne drew a deep, ragged breath.

"Because," she resumed, "they've specifically linked Anton with this, and I don't think they just picked his name at random. Oh, I know how vulnerable our relationship makes me—and, by extension, the Liberal Party and the entire Star Empire—where something like this is concerned. But making that link in their propaganda is more sophisticated than Mesa's ever bothered to be before. I'm not saying it doesn't make sense from their perspective, because both of us know it does. I'm just afraid that . . . it didn't occur to them out of the clear blue sky."

She had her voice under iron control, but Elizabeth had known her for far too long to be fooled. There was more than simple pain in her eyes; there was something very like terror, and the Queen of Manticore felt the personal concern of friendship go to war with the cold-blooded detachment her position as a head of state demanded of her.

"Tell me, Cathy," she said, and her own voice was softer.

"Beth," Montaigne looked her squarely in the eye, "I swear to you on my own immortal soul that Anton Zilwicki would never—*never*—sign off on nuking a public park full of kids—*anybody's* kids, for God's sake!—in the middle of a town. He'd die, first. Ask anyone who knows him. But having said that...he was on Mesa. And I'm afraid the Mesans know he was. That that's the reason they decided to pin this on him, by name, and not just on Torch and the Ballroom in general. And—"

Her voice broke off, and Elizabeth felt her own eyes widen.

"You think they caught him," she said gently.

"Yes. No!" Montaigne shook her head, her expression showing an uncertainty and misery she would never have allowed herself to display in public.

"I don't know," she admitted after a moment. "I haven't spoken to him in almost six T-months—not since June. He and...someone else were headed for Mesa. I know they got there, because we got a report from them through a secure conduit in late August. But we haven't heard a word from them since."

"He was *on* Mesa?" Elizabeth stared at her, stunned by the notion that Zilwicki had voluntarily walked into that snake pit. "What in God's name was he *thinking*?"

Montaigne drew a deep breath, visibly forcing herself back under control. Then she sat for several seconds, considering the Queen with an edge of calculation.

"All right, Elizabeth—truth time," she said finally. "Six months ago, you weren't exactly...rational about the possibility that anyone besides Haven could have been behind Admiral Webster's assassination or the attack on Torch. I'm sorry, but it's true, and you know it. Don't you?"

Brown eyes locked with blue, tension hovering between them for a dozen heartbeats. Then Elizabeth nodded grudgingly.

"As a matter of fact, I'm still not convinced—not by a long chalk—that Haven *wasn't* involved," she acknowledged. "At the same time, I've been forced to admit there are are other possibilities. For that matter, I've even been forced to concede my own anti-Haven prejudices probably help account for at least some of my suspicion where Pritchart is concerned."

"Thank you." Montaigne's eyes softened. "I know you, Beth, so I know how hard it was for you to admit that. But at the

time, Torch and the Ballroom had pretty compelling evidence
that whatever might have been the case with Admiral Webster,
Haven *wasn't* involved in the attack on Berry and Torch. Which
suggested someone else had to be, and that led in turn to their
taking a very hard look at Mesa.

"You just admitted your 'anti-Haven prejudices' might predispose you to assume Pritchart was behind it. Well, fair's fair, and
I'll admit that *our* prejudices naturally predispose us to feel the
same way about Manpower. But there was more to it, and a lot
of that 'more' came from Anton and Ruth, not the Ballroom."

"What kind of 'more'?" Elizabeth asked, frowning intently.

"Well, the first thing was that we knew—and I mean *knew*, Beth,
with absolute, goldplated certainty—Haven hadn't been involved
in the Torch operation. And the more Ruth and Anton modeled
Manpower's behavior in Monica, the less its actions looked like
those of any plausible transstellar—even of a renegade, outlaw
transstellar. They were more like something a star nation would
have been doing."

Elizabeth nodded slowly, her eyes narrow. She recalled Michelle
Henke's suggestion to the same effect after she'd broken Josef
Byng's New Tuscany operation. It had seemed preposterous, but
both ONI and SIS had come, at least tentatively, to the conclusion Michelle was onto something. As of yet, no one had any
idea exactly *what* she was onto, unfortunately.

"Assuming it was Manpower—or Mesa, assuming there's even
as much difference between the two as we thought there was—the
attacks seemed to fit in neatly with Manpower's obvious ambitions
in Talbott. In fact, they seemed to imply that everyone was still
just scratching the surface of what those ambitions might really
be. And, frankly, Torch's position as an at least semi-official ally
of the Star Empire, the Republic, Erewhon, and the Solarian
League—or the Maya Sector, at least—had Anton and... Jeremy
wondering just how many birds Manpower was trying to hit with
a single stone."

Now whose name, I wonder, did she just substitute Jeremy's for?
Elizabeth thought. She considered pressing the point, but not
very hard.

"Under the circumstances, they decided someone needed to
take a good, hard look at Manpower from inside the belly of the
beast, as it were. They didn't have a specific action plan, beyond

getting inside Mesa's reach. They wanted to be close enough to
be hands-on, able to follow up leads directly instead of being
weeks or even months of communications time from the investigation. I think they were probably thinking in terms of setting
up a permanent surveillance op, if they could figure out a way to
pull it off, but, mostly, they were looking for proof of Manpower's
involvement in Webster's assassination and the attack on Berry."

She paused, with the look of a woman deciding against mentioning something else, and despite her focused intensity, Elizabeth
smiled ever so slightly.

*Unwontedly tactful of you, Cathy. Don't want to come right
out and say "And they wanted that proof to be good enough it
could convince even* you *to think logically about other candidates,
Elizabeth," now do you?*

"At any rate," Montaigne went on more briskly, "the one thing
they *weren't* going to do was link up with any 'official' Ballroom
cells on Mesa. We have reason to believe, especially in light of a
few recent discoveries, that any Ballroom cell on the planet is likely
to be compromised. So there's zero possibility Anton or ... any of
his people were involved in any Ballroom operation against Green
Pines. They were there expressly to keep a low profile; the information they were after—especially if it confirmed their suspicions—was
far more important than any attack could have been; and they were
avoiding contact with any known Ballroom operative."

Elizabeth's eyes had narrowed again. Now she leaned back and
cocked her head to one side.

"Would it make this any simpler for you, Cathy," she asked
almost whimsically, "if you just went ahead and said 'Anton and
Agent Cachat' instead of being so diplomatic?"

It was Montaigne's eyes' turn to narrow, and the Queen chuckled, albeit a bit sourly.

"I assure you, I've read the reports on just exactly how Torch
came into being with a certain closeness. And I've had direct reports
from Ruth, too, you know. She's done her best to be ... tactful, let's
say, but it's been obvious Agent Cachat's still something of a fixture
on Torch. And, for that matter, that he and Captain Zilwicki have
formed some sort of at least semi-permanent partnership."

"It *would* make it simpler, as a matter of fact," Montaigne said
slowly. "And since this seems to be cards-on-the-table time, I
suppose I should go ahead and admit that the reason I hadn't

already brought Victor up is that I wasn't certain it wouldn't prejudice you against anything I had to say."

"I'm a good and expert hater, Cathy," Elizabeth said dryly. "Reports to the contrary notwithstanding, however, I'm not really clinically insane. I won't pretend I'm *happy* to hear about shared skulduggery, hobnobbing, and mutual admiration societies between someone who used to be one of my own spies and someone who's still currently spying for a star nation I happen to be at war with. But if politics makes strange bedfellows, I suppose it's only reasonable wars should do the same. In fact, one of my closer associates made that point to me—a bit forcefully—not so long ago."

"Really?" Montaigne's eyebrows arched, and Elizabeth could almost see the wheels and the gears going around in her brain. But then the ex-countess gave herself a visible shake.

"Anyway," she said, "Victor was the reason we *knew* Haven hadn't ordered the Torch attack. Or, at least, that no official Havenite intelligence organ was behind it, since he would have been the one tasked to carry it out if Pritchart had sanctioned it. And you're right about the kind of partnership he and Anton have evolved. As a matter of fact, the way their abilities complement one another makes both of them even more effective. Victor has an absolute gift for improvisation, whereas Anton has a matching gift for methodical analysis and forethought. If anyone was going to be able to pry the truth out of that fucking cesspool, it was going to be them."

Her nostrils flared. Then she paused again, lips tightening.

"But you haven't heard from them in almost five months," Elizabeth said gently.

"No," Montaigne admitted softly. "We haven't heard from them, we haven't heard from the people responsible for transporting them in and out, and we haven't heard from the Biological Survey Corps, either."

"Whoa!" Elizabeth straightened suddenly in her chair. "*Beowulf* was involved in this, too?" She half-glared at Montaigne. "Tell me, was there anybody in the entire *galaxy* who wasn't sneaking around behind my back to keep me from getting my dander up?"

"Well," Montaigne admitted, smiling crookedly despite her own obvious deep concern, "actually, beyond a certain amount of Erewhonese assistance, that's just about everybody. I think."

"Oh, you *think*, do you?"

"I can't be absolutely *certain*, of course. I mean, what with Torch and all the others, it *was* something of a . . . multinational effort."

"I see." Elizabeth sat back once more, then shook her head. "You don't think having so many cooks stirring the soup could have anything to do with whatever obviously went wrong, do you?"

"I think it's possible," Montaigne acknowledged. "On the other hand, the way Anton and Victor normally operate, it's unlikely anybody but them really knew enough to seriously compromise the operation. Still," she drooped visibly again, "you're right— something *did* obviously go wrong. I can't believe Mesa just decided to include Anton in their version of what happened, and that means something blew, somewhere. What we don't know is exactly what blew and how serious the consequences were. But—"

"But this long without any word suggests the consequences could have been pretty damned serious," Elizabeth finished softly for her.

"Exactly." Montaigne drew a deep breath. "On the other hand, Mesa hasn't produced his body, or mentioned Victor or Haven, or taken the opportunity to take a swipe at Beowulf for *its* involvement. That suggests it didn't blow completely. I know"—despite her best efforts, her voice wavered—"there can be advantages to simply 'disappearing' someone and letting her side sweat the potential consequences in ignorance. And given how we seem to have been underestimating, or at least misreading, Mesa's role in this, and its possible sophistication, it's possible they recognized that accusing Haven and Beowulf of involvement, as well, would be too much of a good thing. Too much for even Solly public opinion to swallow. But I keep coming back to the fact that if they could actually *prove* Anton was on Mesa, it would have been the absolute clincher for this fairy tale about his being involved in the attack. So if they didn't offer that proof—"

"It seems unlikely they had it in the first place," Elizabeth said.

"Exactly," Montaigne said again, then chuckled.

"What?"

"I was just thinking," the ex-countess said. "You always did have that habit of finishing thoughts for me when we were kids."

"Mostly because someone as scatterbrained as you *needed* someone to tidy up around the edges," Elizabeth retorted.

"Maybe." Montaigne's humor faded. "Anyway, that's where we are. Anton was on Mesa about the time the nukes went off. I can't *prove* he wasn't involved, but if Mesa could prove he *was*, the bastards would have done it by now. So either he's on his way home, and his transportation arrangements have hit a bump, or else..."

Her voice trailed off, and this time Elizabeth felt no temptation at all to complete her thought for her.

"I understand," the Queen said, instead.

She tipped her chair back, rocking it slightly while she thought hard for the better part of a minute. Then she let it come back upright.

"I understand," she repeated. "Unfortunately, nothing you've just told me really helps, does it? As you say, we can't prove Captain Zilwicki—and, by implication, Torch and the Star Empire—weren't involved. In fact, going public with the fact that he was on Mesa at all would be the worst thing we could possibly do at this point. But I'm afraid that's going to make things rough on you, Cathy."

"I know." Montaigne grimaced. "You're going to have to take the position that the Star Empire wasn't involved, and along the way, you're going to have to point out that even assuming Anton was involved, he's no longer an ONI agent. Ever since he took up with that notorious incendiary and public shill for terrorism Montaigne, he's been establishing his own links to the abolitionist movement and, yes, probably to those Ballroom terrorists. Under those circumstances, clearly neither you, personally, nor the Star Empire is in any position to comment one way or the other on what he may have been responsible for since going rogue that way."

"I'm afraid that's exactly what we're going to have to do," Elizabeth acknowledged. "And when some frigging newsy pounces on his personal relationship with you, the very best I'm going to be able to do is 'no comment' and a recommendation they discuss that with *you*, not me."

"And they're going to come after the firebrand rabble-rouser with everything they've got." Montaigne sighed. "Well, it won't be the first time. And, with just a little luck, they'll give me the opportunity to get in a few solid counterpunches of my own. The idiots usually do."

"But it's going to make problems for your Liberals, too," Elizabeth pointed out. "If—*when*—this turns as ugly as I think it's going to do, Willie and I are both going to find ourselves forced to hold you at arm's length... at best. And that doesn't even consider the fact that at least someone inside the party's going to see this as an opportunity to boot you out of the leader's position."

"If that happens, it happens." Montaigne's tone was philosophical; the flinty light in her eyes suggested that anyone who wanted a fight was going to get one. In fact, Elizabeth thought, the other woman was probably looking forward to it as a distraction from her personal fears.

"I'm sorry," the Queen said quietly. Their eyes met once more, and this time Elizabeth's sad smile was that of an old friend, not a monarch.

"I've always been ambivalent about the Ballroom," she continued. "For personal reasons, in part. I understand all about 'asymmetrical warfare,' but assassinations and terrorist attacks cut just a little too close to home for me. I'm not hypocritical enough to condemn the Ballroom for fighting back in the only way it's ever been able to, but I'm afraid that's not the same thing as saying I approve of it. But whether I approve or not, I've always admired the sheer guts it takes to get down into the blood and the mud with something like Manpower. And despite our own political differences, Cathy, I've always actually admired you for being willing to openly acknowledge *your* support for the people willing to fight back the only way they can, whatever the rest of the galaxy may think about it."

"That...means quite a bit to me, Beth." Montaigne's voice was as quiet as Elizabeth's had been. "Mind you, I know it's not going to change anything about our political stances, but it does mean a lot."

"Good." Elizabeth's smile grew broader. "And now, if I could ask you for a personal favor in my persona as Queen of Manticore?"

"What sort of favor?"

Montaigne's tone and expression were both wary, and Elizabeth chuckled.

"Don't worry! I wasn't setting you up for a sucker punch by telling you what a wonderful, fearless person you are, Cathy." She shook her head. "No. What I was thinking about is that this news is going to hit the Haven System in about a week and a half, and I shudder to think about the impact it's going to have on Duchess Harrington's negotiations with the Pritchart Administration. I'm sure it's going to have repercussions with all of our allies, of course, and thank *God* we at least consulted with them—unlike a certain ex-prime minister—before we opened negotiations this time around, but I'm more concerned about Haven's reaction. So what I would deeply appreciate your doing would be writing up what you've just told me, or as much of it as you feel you could share with Duchess Harrington, at least, for me to send her as deep background."

"You want me to tell the Duchess Anton was actually on Mesa?"

There was something a bit odd about Montaigne's tone, Elizabeth thought, but the Queen simply shrugged and nodded.

"Among other things. It would help a lot if she had that kind of information in the back of her brain. And I believe the two of you know one another, don't you?"

"Fairly well, actually," Montaigne acknowledged. "Since I came home to Manticore, that is."

"Well, in that case, I probably don't have to tell you she has an ironclad sense of honor," Elizabeth said. "In fact, sometimes I think her parents must have had precognition or something when they picked her first name! At any rate, I assure you she'd never even consider divulging anything you may tell her without your specific permission."

"If *you're* confident of her discretion," Montaigne said in that same peculiar tone, "that's good enough for me." She smiled. "I'll go ahead and write it up for you, and I'm sure she won't say a word about it to anyone."

Chapter Fifteen

"ALPHA TRANSLATION in two hours, Sir."

"Thank you, Simon."

Lieutenant Commander Lewis Denton had been perfectly aware of that fact, but procedure mandated the astrogator's report just in case he'd somehow failed to notice. He smiled at the familiar thought, but the smile was brief, and it vanished quickly as he glanced at the civilian in the assistant tactical officer's chair.

Gregor O'Shaughnessy was doing a less than perfect job of concealing his tension, but Denton didn't blame him for that. Besides, it wasn't as if his own surface appearance of calm was fooling anyone, even if the rules of the game required everyone—including him—to pretend it was.

He glanced at the date/time display. Seventy-four T-days had passed, by the clocks of the universe at large, since HMS *Reprise* had departed from Spindle for the Meyers System, the headquarters of the Office of Frontier Security in the Madras Sector. Of course, it hadn't been that long for *Reprise*'s crew, given that they'd spent virtually all of it hurtling through hyper-space at seventy percent of light-speed. But they'd still been gone for just over fifty-three T-days even by their own clocks, and the return leg of their lengthy voyage had seemed far, far longer than the outbound leg.

✧　　✧　　✧

"More coffee, Ma'am?"

Michelle Henke looked up at the murmured question and nodded agreement. Master Steward Billingsley filled her cup, checked quickly around the table, topped off Michael Oversteegen's cup, and withdrew. Michelle watched him go with a smile, then returned her attention to the officers around the conference table in HMS *Artemis*' flag briefing room.

"You were saying, Michael?"

"I was sayin', Milady, that findin' myself up against Apollo seemed like just a tiny bit of overkill."

He smiled at her, and although it would have taken someone who knew him very well, Michelle recognized the twinkle deep in his eyes. Not every subordinate flag officer who'd been so thoroughly (one might almost, she admitted, say *shamelessly*) blindsided by a weapons system the other side shouldn't have possessed would have found the experience amusing. Fortunately, Oversteegen at least had a sense of humor.

"To be honest, it seemed that way to me, too." She quirked a smile of her own at him. "I didn't do it just to be nasty, though. I mean, I *did* do it to be nasty, but that wasn't the *only* reason I did it."

This time there was a general mutter of laughter, and Oversteegen's hand twitched in the gesture of a fencing master acknowledging a touch.

"The other reason I did it, though," she continued more seriously, "was that I wanted an opportunity to see someone—a live, flesh-and-blood someone, not an AI-administered simulation— respond to Apollo. I couldn't find anyone here in Tenth Fleet who wouldn't realize what was happening as soon as she saw it, but I could at least set up a situation in which she—or, in this case, *he*—didn't know it was coming ahead of time."

"And is your lab rat permitted t' ask how he performed?" he inquired genially.

"Not bad at all for someone who lost eighty-five percent of his total command," she reassured him, and another chuckle ran around the squadron and division commanders seated at the table with them.

"Actually, Sir," Sir Aivars Terekhov said, "I thought it was even more impressive that you managed to take out three of the *op force's* superdreadnoughts in return."

More than one head nodded in agreement, and Oversteegen shrugged.

"I remembered readin' your report from Monica," he said. "You might say I had a proprietary interest in your actin' tac officer's performance. I was impressed by th' way you used your Ghost Rider platforms t' reduce th' telemetry lag for your Mark 16s. Didn't seem t' me there was any reason I couldn't do th' same thing with Mark 23s." He shrugged. "It's not as good as Apollo, but it's a lot better than nothin'."

"You're right about that," Michelle agreed. "And, by the way, the dispatch boat which arrived this morning had several interesting items aboard. The latest newsfaxes from home—and from Old Terra—among other things." She made a face, and Oversteegen snorted harshly. "In addition to that inspiring reading and viewing material, however, there were two additional items which I think you'll all find interesting."

One or two people sat up straighter, and she saw several sets of eyes narrow in speculation.

"The first is that we should be receiving an entire battle squadron of Apollo-capable *Imperators* in about three weeks." The reaction of almost explosive relief which swept around the table was all she could have asked for. "There was a bit of a glitch in the deployment order, and their ammunition ships will be here a week or so before they are."

There were quite a few smiles, now, and she smiled back.

"Actually, the missile ships were originally scheduled to arrive two weeks *after* the wallers," she continued, "but the squadrons we were supposed to get under that deployment plan wound up going somewhere else, so we had to wait until their replacements finished working up."

She paused again, and Commodore Shulamit Onasis, the CO of Battlecruiser Division 106.2, frowned thoughtfully.

"I know that 'cat-in-the-celery-patch look, Ma'am," she said after a moment. "Why do I sense there's another shoe hanging in midair somewhere?"

"Well, I guess it might be because there is," Michelle admitted cheerfully. She had everyone's full attention again, she observed, and glanced at Cruiser Division 96.1's commanding officer from the corner of one eye. "It seems that although somehow the newsies haven't picked up on it yet, the reason our original reinforcing squadrons went somewhere else is that Duchess Harrington and Eighth Fleet have gone somewhere else, as well. To the Haven System, as a matter of fact."

The youthful senior-grade captain she'd been watching stiffened, and there was a sudden and complete silence. Her own smile slid into something much more serious, but she shook her head.

"No," she said. "She wasn't planning on attacking the system. In fact, unless something went very wrong, about three weeks ago she delivered a personal message from the Queen to President Pritchart. Apparently our discoveries about Manpower's involvement out here in New Tuscany have inspired a certain rethinking of who might actually have been behind Admiral Webster's assassination and the attack on Queen Berry. On that basis," she drew a deep breath and looked around the table, "and in light of the worsening situation with the Solarian League, Her Majesty has decided to pursue a negotiated settlement with the Republic after all, and she's chosen Duchess Harrington as her lead negotiator."

"My God," Captain (SG) Prescott Tremaine, CruDiv 96.1's CO, murmured. Michelle turned her head to look at him fully, and he shook his head, like a man shaking off a stiff right cross, then gave her a crooked smile. "You were certainly right when you said you had a couple of things we might be interested in, Ma'am!"

"I thought that would probably be true, Scotty," she said with a grin. "In fact, I should probably go ahead and admit I saved that particular little tidbit until I could watch *your* expression."

Most of the others chuckled at that one. Scotty Tremaine had been one of Honor Alexander-Harrington's protégés ever since her deployment to Basilisk Station aboard the old light cruiser *Fearless*. Michelle wondered if he'd been as surprised as she was when she discovered that the Admiralty, in its infinite wisdom, hadn't merely transferred him from the LAC community (where he'd not only made a considerable name for himself but actually survived the Battle of Manticore) but chosen to give a new-minted captain of the list such a plum assignment. Once she'd had time to think about it, however, she'd realized exactly why they'd done it. Even in a navy expanding as rapidly as the RMN, a flag officer had to have at least some experience in command of conventional starships, and aside from a brief stint in the "Elysian Space Navy" during the escape from Cerberus (where, admittedly, he'd performed extremely well), Scotty didn't have any. Obviously, Lucien Cortez had decided to rectify that situation, even if giving him a division of *Saganami-Cs* had to have stepped on the toes of quite a few captains—or even commodores—with considerably more seniority.

And they damned well gave him the right flagship, too, she reflected, remembering how tears had prickled at the backs of her eyes when she first saw the name HMS *Alistair McKeon* listed in the Admiralty dispatch announcing CruDiv 96.1's assignment to Tenth Fleet. She didn't know what the ship's original name had been supposed to be, but she understood exactly why she'd been renamed after the Battle of Manticore.

And why Tremaine had chosen her as his flagship.

"Well, I hope my reaction was up to your expectations, Ma'am," he told her now, his smile less crooked than it had been.

"Oh, I suppose it was... if you really like that stunned ox look," Michelle allowed. Then it was her turn to shake her own head. "Not, I ought to admit, that you looked any more stunned than *I* felt when the dispatch got here. I imagine that's pretty much true for all of us."

"Amen," Rear Admiral Nathalie Manning said softly.

Manning commanded the second division of Oversteegen's Battlecruiser Squadron 108. She had a narrow, intense face, brown eyes, and close-cropped hair, and the Admiralty wasn't picking *Nike*-class divisional COs at random. In fact, aside from the shape of her face and her height, she reminded Michelle of a younger, harder-edged Honor Alexander-Harrington in a great many ways. Now Manning smiled briefly at her, but there was a hint of alum behind that smile, and Michelle arched an inquiring eyebrow.

"I was just thinking, Ma'am," Manning said. "After the last few months, I can't help feeling just a bit apprehensive when things suddenly start going so well."

"I know what you mean," Michelle acknowledged. "At the same time, let's not get too carried away with doom and gloom. Mind you, I'd rather be a little bit overly pessimistic than too *optimistic*, but it's always possible things really are about to get better, you know."

✧   ✧   ✧

Maybe I shouldn't have been quite so quick to discourage Manning's pessimism, Michelle thought thirty-seven hours later.

She was back in the same briefing room, but this time accompanied only by Oversteegen; Terekhov; Cynthia Lecter; Commander

Tom Pope, Terekhov's chief of staff; and Commander Martin Culpepper, Oversteegen's chief of staff. It was not only a considerably smaller gathering, but a much less cheerful one. Terekhov and Oversteegen had come aboard *Artemis* for supper and to discuss the most recent news from Manticore, and their after-dinner coffee and brandy had been rudely interrupted by the burst-transmitted message they'd just finished viewing.

"I really, really hate finding out how many alligators are still in that swamp we're trying to drain," she said, and Oversteegen chuckled harshly.

"I've always admired your gift with words, Milady. In this case, however, I can't help wonderin' if it's not really a question of how many hexapumas there are in th' underbrush."

As usual, he had a point, Michelle reflected, wishing she could recapture some of the confidence she'd felt after the post-exercise debrief. Unfortunately, she couldn't, and she shuddered internally as she considered the one-two punch which had just landed here in the Spindle System.

Personally, Michelle Henke wouldn't have believed water was wet if the information had come from Mesa, but she was unhappily aware that quite a few Solarians failed to share her feelings in that regard. Those people probably *were* going to believe Mesa's version of the Green Pines affair . . . and the linkage between the "calculated Ballroom atrocity and a known Manticoran spy" was going to resonate painfully with the people who already hated the Star Empire. That much was evident just from the Solly newsies' strident questioning. News of the Mesan "shocked discovery" of Manicoran involvement in the attack had reached Spindle less than fourteen hours ago, and Tenth Fleet's public information officers had already been deluged with literally scores of requests—and demands—for an interview with one Admiral Countess Gold Peak.

As if I could possibly know one damned thing they don't know. Jesus! Is a lobotomy a requirement for a job in the Solly media?

She realized she was trying to grind her teeth together and stopped herself. Actually, she reminded herself, the newsy feeding frenzy was probably understandable, however stupid. They *had* to be frantic for any official Manticoran response. In fact, she hated to think what it must be like for Baroness Medusa's and Prime Minister Alquezar's official spokesmen right now. And she had to admit Mesa's fabrication really did have a certain damning plausibility. Until, that was, they inserted Anton Zilwicki into the mix. Michelle had met Anton Zilwicki. More than that, she'd known him and his wife well before Helen Zilwicki's death, back when they'd both been serving officers of the Royal Manticoran Navy. She never doubted Zilwicki possessed the ruthlessness to accept collateral civilian casualties to take out a critical target, but the man she knew would never—not in a thousand years—have set out deliberately to execute a terrorist attack and kill thousands of civilians purely to make a statement. Even if he'd become afflicted with the sort of moral gangrene which could have accepted such an act in the first place, he was far too smart for that. The man who was effectively Cathy Montaigne's husband had to be only too well aware of how politically suicidal it would have been.

Gilded the lily just a bit too richly there, you bastards, she thought now. *For anyone who knows Anton or Montaigne, at least. Which, unfortunately, is an awfully small sample of the human race compared to the people who* don't *know either of them.*

She grimaced, then made herself draw a deep breath and step back. There wasn't a damned thing she or anyone else in the Talbott Quadrant could do on that front. For that matter, any-thing that needed to be done about it fell legitimately to Prime Minister Alquezar and Governor Medusa. What Michelle had to worry about, as the commander of Tenth Fleet, was the *second* thunderbolt which had come slicing out of the cloudless heavens exactly thirteen hours and twelve minutes after the dispatch boat from Manticore delivered *its* bad news.

"It would seem," she said dryly, "that our worst-case estimate was too optimistic. I could have sworn the New Tuscans said Anisimovna told them Admiral Crandall only had about *sixty* ships-of-the-wall."

"Well, we already knew Anisimovna wasn't the most honest person in the universe," Terekhov pointed out dryly.

"Granted, but if she was going to lie, I would have expected her to overstate the numbers, not *under*state them."

"I think that's what all of us would have expected, Ma'am," Lecter said. Michelle's chief of staff was still functioning as her staff intelligence officer, as well, and now she grimaced sourly. "*I* certainly didn't expect them to have this many ships, and neither did Ambrose Chandler or anyone in Defense Minister Krietzmann's office. And none of us expected them to already be in Meyers before *Reprise* even got there with Baroness Medusa's and Prime Minister Alquezar's note!"

Michelle nodded in glum agreement and looked back at Lieutenant Commander Denton's strength estimate. Seventy-one superdreadnoughts, sixteen battlecruisers, twelve heavy cruisers, twenty-three light cruisers, and eighteen destroyers. A total of a hundred and forty warships, accompanied by at least twenty-nine supply and support ships. Upwards of half a billion tons of combat ships, deployed all the way forward to a podunk Frontier Security sector on the backside of nowhere. Until this very moment, she realized, even as she'd dutifully made plans to deal with the possible threat of Solarian ships-of-the-wall, she hadn't truly believed a corporation like Manpower could possibly have the capacity to get that sort of combat power moved around like checkers on a board. Now she knew it did, and the thought sent an icy chill through her veins, because if they could pull off something like this, what *couldn't* they pull off if they put their mind to it?

She drew a deep breath and ran her mind over her own order of battle. Fourteen *Nike*-class battlecruisers, eight *Saganami-C*-class heavy cruisers, four *Hydra*-class CLACs, five *Roland*-class destroyers, and a handful of obsolescent starships like Denton's *Reprise* and Victoria Saunders' *Hercules*. Of course, she also had right on four hundred LACs, but they'd have to go deep into the Sollies' weapons envelope to engage. So what it really came down to was her twenty-seven hyper-capable warships—the *Hydras* had no business at all in ship-to-ship combat—against Crandall's hundred and forty. She was outnumbered by better than five-to-one in hulls, and despite the fact that Manticoran ship types were bigger and more powerful on a class-for-class basis, the tonnage differential was almost thirteen-to-one. Of course, if she counted the LACs, she had another twelve million or so tons, but even that only brought it down to around ten-to-one. And as far as anyone in Meyers knew, she had only the ships she'd taken to New Tuscany, without Oversteegen's eight *Nikes*.

"If the people who set this up picked Crandall for her role as carefully as they picked Byng for his, she's bound to believe she's got an overwhelming force advantage. Especially if she assumes we haven't reinforced since New Tuscany," she said out loud.

"T' my way of thinkin', it'd take an uncommonly stupid flag

officer, even for a Solly, t' make *that* kind of assumption," Oversteegen replied.

"And what, may I ask, have the Sollies done lately to make you think they haven't hand-picked the flag officers out here for stupidity?" Michelle asked tartly.

"Nothin'," he conceded disgustedly. "It just offends my sense of th' way things are supposed t' be, I suppose. I'd expect better thinkin' than *that* out of a plate of cottage cheese!"

"I can't say I disagree," Terekhov said, "but fair's fair. There might actually be a little logic on her side." Michelle and Oversteegen both looked at him, and he chuckled sourly. "I did say 'a *little* logic,'" he pointed out.

"And that logic would be?" Michelle asked.

"If she assumes all of this came at us as cold as it came at her—although assuming it *did* come at her cold could constitute an unwarranted supposition; she could have been involved in this thing up to her eyebrows from the very beginning—then she probably assumes we didn't have any idea she might even be in the area. After all, when was the last time any of us can remember seeing *Battle Fleet* ships-of-the-wall putting time on their nodes clear out here in the Verge?"

"That's true enough, Ma'am," Lecter put in. "And, for that matter, as far as we know, *Byng* didn't know she was out here. There was nothing in any of the databases we captured to suggest she might be. So if she wasn't aware Anisimovna had mentioned her to the New Tuscans, she could very well believe that the first we knew about even the possibility of her presence is *Reprise's* scouting report."

"And she also can't have any way of knowing what's going on in the 'faxes back on Old Terra or in Manticore," Terekhov continued. "So whatever she does—assuming she does anything—she's going to be acting on her own, in the dark, with no hard information at all on enemy ship strengths or the diplomatic situation."

"Are you suggesting a Solly admiral's going to just sit in Meyers, waiting for orders from home, after what happened in New Tuscany?" Michelle asked skeptically.

"I'm suggesting that any reasonably prudent, rational flag officer in that situation would proceed cautiously," Terekhov replied, then bared his teeth in something which bore only a passing relationship to a smile. "Of course, what we're actually talking about is a

Solly flag officer, so, no, I don't think that's what she's likely to do. Besides, we've all read their contingency plans from Byng's files."

Michelle's mouth tightened.

It wasn't as if the SLN's "contingency planning" had come as a surprise, although she suspected the League would be most unhappy if the Star Empire chose to publicize some of its jucier details. There was "Case Fabius," for example, which authorized Frontier Security commissioners to arrange Frontier Fleet "peacekeeping operations" which "accidentally" destroyed any locally owned orbital infrastructure within any protectorate star system whose local authorities proved unable to "maintain order"—meaning they'd been unable to induce the owners in question to sell to the transstellars OFS had decided would control their economies henceforth. Or "Case Buccaneer," which actually authorized Frontier Security to use Frontier Fleet units—suitably disguised, of course—as "pirates," complete with vanished merchant ships whose crews were never seen again, to provoke crises in targeted Verge systems in order to justify OFS intervention "to preserve order and public safety."

All that was sufficiently interesting reading, but she knew what Terekhov was referring to. Byng's files had also confirmed something ONI had suspected for a long time. In the almost inconceivable event that some neobarb star nation, or possibly some rogue OFS sector governor, attacked the Solarian League (or chose to forcibly resist OFS aggression, although that wasn't specifically spelled out, of course), the SLN had evolved a simple, straightforward strategy. Frontier Fleet, which possessed nothing heavier than a battlecruiser, would screen the frontiers and attempt to slow down any invaders or commerce raiders, while Battle Fleet assembled an overwhelmingly powerful force and headed directly towards the home system of the troublemaker...which it would then proceed to reduce to wreckage and transform into yet another OFS protectorate.

"I see where you're going with that, Sir," Commander Pope said. "At the same time, not even a Solly admiral could think she'd get through the Lynx Terminus with less than eighty of the wall. For that matter, we've had a couple of squadrons based there ever since Monica, and there's been enough Solly traffic through the terminus by now that they have to know the forts are virtually all online by now."

"I wasn't actually thinking about her trying to go directly after the home system," Terekhov said.

"No, you're thinkin' she's likely t' see Spindle as th' *Talbott Quadrant's* 'home system,'" Oversteegen said.

"That's exactly what I'm thinking," Terekhov agreed, and Michelle nodded.

"We can always hope something resembling sanity could break out in Meyers," she said. "There's no way we can *count* on that, though. And I think that's especially true given how carefully the people who planned all this seem to have chosen their cat's-paws. So, starting right now, we're going to plan for the worst."

She drew a deep breath and sat back in her chair.

"Gwen," she said, looking at Lieutenant Archer, "I want you to have Bill make certain Admiral Khumalo and Baroness Medusa have both seen Commander Denton's report. I'm sure they'll want to sit down with him and Mr. O'Shaughnessy as soon as they're within a reasonable two-way FTL range of Thimble, but see to it that they have all the information *we* have ahead of time."

"Yes, Ma'am."

"As soon as you've done that, tell Vicki I'll want dispatch boats sent to every system in the Quadrant. Ask her to contact Captain Shoupe and start looking at the boats' availability. First priority is Captain Conner at Tillerman, then Montana. He gets a complete copy of Denton's report and data, and I'll want to put together a personal message for him before the dispatch boat pulls out."

"Yes, Ma'am." Gervais nodded, although he knew as well as she did that if Admiral Crandall had decided to respond forcefully, Jerome Conner's pair of *Nikes* at Tillerman had probably already found out the hard way.

Michelle knew exactly what he was thinking, and smiled tightly at him. The fact that he was right didn't change her responsibility to warn Conner as quickly as possible.

"In addition," she went on, "when Bill makes sure Admiral Khumalo and Baroness Medusa are up to speed, tell the admiral that unless he disagrees, I propose to send *Reprise* direct to Manticore to inform the Admiralty both of what she discovered at Meyers and that I am presently anticipating an attack in force on Spindle."

An almost physical chill went through the briefing room as she said the words out loud, and she straightened her shoulders.

"Inform the Admiral that I intend to get *Reprise* on her way within thirty minutes of her arrival in Thimble planetary orbit." Even Terekhov looked a little startled at that, and she bared her teeth. "If Crandall thinks *Reprise* got a good look at her task force, and if she is inclined to launch an attack, she's going to move as quickly as she can. We have to assume she could be here literally within hours, and if she's decided to head directly for the Lynx Terminus instead, it'll take her only one more T-day to get there than it would to get *here*.

"We may all agree that would be a stupid thing for her to do, but that doesn't mean she won't do it. For that matter, we can't really afford to assume the ships *Reprise* saw are the only ones they have. What if she's got a squadron or two sitting in reserve at McIntosh? We're already looking at more than Anisimovna told the New Tuscans about, so I don't think it would be a very good idea to think small."

Terekhov and Oversteegen nodded soberly, and she turned back to Gervais.

"Go ahead and get Bill started on that, Gwen. Then come straight back here. I think it's going to be a long night."

"Yes, Ma'am," Gervais said for the third time, and headed for the door.

"In the meantime, gentlemen," Michelle resumed, "I believe it's time the three of us started thinking as deviously as possible. If I were Crandall, and if I meant to go stomp on a bunch of neobarbs, I'd have my wall in motion within twenty-four hours, max. She may not feel that way, though. She may figure she's got enough of a firepower advantage she can afford to take a little longer, make sure she's dotted all the i's and crossed all the t's in her ops plan before she breaks orbit."

"Personally, given that the passage time is over a T-month, I'd do my operational planning en route, Ma'am," Terekhov said.

"So would I," she agreed. "And that's what I'm going to assume she's done. But even though we're going to plan for the worst, I can at least *hope* for the best, and the best in this case would be her taking long enough for our *Imperator* battle squadrons to get here before she does. Or for their Apollo pods to get here, at least. No?"

"I could certainly agree with that," Oversteegen acknowledged with a small smile.

"And when she does get here—assuming, of course, that she's coming—I want to accomplish four things.

"First, I want her to underestimate our actual combat power as badly as possible. I realize she's almost certainly already doing that, but let's encourage the tendency in every way we can.

"Second, I'd like to push her, to . . . keep her as much off-balance mentally as possible. In a lot of ways, the madder she is, the less likely she is to be thinking very clearly, and that's probably about the best we can hope for. She's not going to head for Spindle in strength unless she's already got blood in her eye, which means it's unlikely—hell, the next best thing to it, impossible!—that she's planning on presenting any sort of terms or demands Baroness Medusa and Prime Minister Alquezar are remotely likely to accept. So if push is going to come to shove anyway, I'd just as soon have her making *angry* decisions instead of good ones."

She looked at her two subordinate flag officers, and Oversteegen cocked his head and pursed his lips thoughtfully, then nodded.

"Third," she continued after a moment, "and although I realize it's going to sound a little strange after what I just said about pushing her, I'd be just as happy to stall for as long as possible. If Baroness Medusa can get her to burn a day or two in 'negotiations' before anyone actually pulls a trigger, so much the better."

"Is that really very likely, Ma'am?" Commander Culpepper asked dubiously. "Especially if she's *underestimating* the odds and we've managed to piss her off on top of it?

"If I may, Ma'am?" Terekhov said. Michelle nodded, and Terekhov looked at Oversteegen's chief of staff. "What it comes down to, Marty," he said, "is how much Crandall thinks she can get for nothing. If the baroness can convince her there's even a possibility she might surrender the system without firing a shot, she's likely to be willing to spend at least a little while talking before she starts shooting. And I'm pretty sure that with a little thought, we ought to be able to . . . irritate her significantly, let's say, while simultaneously reminding her that sooner or later she's going to have to justify her actions to her military and civilian superiors. However belligerent she may be feeling, and however angry she may be, she's got to know it'll look a lot better in the 'faxes if she can report she's 'controlled the situation' without any more fighting."

"And she's more likely t' feel that way if she does decide she's got a crushin' tactical superiority," Oversteegen added. "She's already goin' t' be assumin' exactly that, whatever we do, so there's no point tryin' t' convince her she should just turn around and go home while she's still in one piece. Which suggests th' admiral here has a point. No matter how pissed off she is, there's probably a damned good chance we can keep her talkin' long enough t' convince her superiors—or th' *newsies*, at least—that she tried *real hard* t' talk us into surrenderin' like nice, timid little neobarbs before she had no choice but t' blow us all t' kingdom come."

"That's what I hope, but Marty's got a point that it could also work the other way," Michelle pointed out. "If she feels confident she can punch right through anything in front of her, that may actually make her more impatient. Especially if she was already feeling the need to inflict a little punishment as revenge for what happened to *Jean Bart* even before we started pushing back at her." Her expression was grim. "Don't overlook that probability. We've bloodied the SLN's nose, and we've done it very publicly. I'd say it's a lot more likely than not that what she really wants is to hammer us so hard no other neobarb navy is ever going to dare to follow our example."

"Wonderful," Lecter muttered, and Michelle surprised herself with a bark of laughter.

"Trust me, Cindy. If that *is* the way she's thinking, she's in for a rude awakening. I'd really prefer to stall, as I said, in the hope the Admiralty's managed to expedite our reinforcements and they come over the alpha wall in the proverbial nick of time. I'm not going to hold my breath counting on that, though, and I'm not going to delay a single minute if it looks like they mean to keep right on coming. Which brings me to the *fourth* thing I want to be certain we accomplish."

She paused, and silence hovered for a second or two until Oversteegen broke it.

"And that fourth thing would be what, Milady?" he asked.

"The instant any Solly warship crosses the Spindle hyper limit inbound," Michelle Henke said flatly, "the gloves come off. There won't be any preliminary surrender demands *this* time, and despite whatever Admiral Crandall may be thinking, *we're* not going to be thinking in terms of a fighting retreat, either. I think it's about time we find out just how accurate our assumptions about Battle Fleet's combat capability really are."

Chapter Sixteen

"I SUPPOSE THE FIRST THING to worry about is whether or not it's true," Sir Barnabas Kew said.

Kew sat with Baroness Selleck and Voitto Tuominen at the conference table behind Honor as she stood gazing out over the thundering cataract of Frontenac Falls. She stood with her hands clasped behind her, Nimitz sitting very still on her shoulder, and her brown eyes were bleak.

"It isn't," she said flatly.

Her Foreign Office advisors glanced at one another, then turned as one to look at that ramrod-straight spine, those calmly clasped hands.

"Your Grace, I'll be the first to admit that neither Manpower nor Mesa have ever been noted for truth in advertising," Tuominen said after a moment. "This seems a little audacious even for them to be manufacturing out of whole cloth, though, and—"

"It isn't true," she repeated in that same flat tone.

She turned away from the window, facing them. But for Nimitz's slightly flattened ears and slowly twitching tail, the civilians might have made the mistake of assuming she was as calm as she looked, and she smiled sardonically as she tasted their emotions, sensed the way they were settling back into their chairs. Kew, especially, seemed to be searching for the most diplomatic possible way to point out that she couldn't know that, and she looked directly at him.

"A lot of things could happen in the galaxy, Sir Barnabas," she told him. "A lot of things I never would have expected. But one thing that isn't going to happen—that *couldn't* happen—would be for Anton Zilwicki to deliberately nuke a park full of kids in some sort of demented terrorist attack. Trust me. I know the man. *Nimitz* knows the man." She reached up to caress the treecat's ears gently. "And that man is utterly incapable of doing something like that."

"But—" Baroness Selleck began, then stopped, and Honor snorted harshly.

"I don't doubt he was on Mesa," she said. "In fact, I have reason to believe he was. What it looks like to me—and I'd really like to be wrong about it—is that Mesa figured out he'd been on-planet and decided to add him to the mix when they came up with their cover story for whatever actually happened."

She decided, again, not to mention the personal message from Catherine Montaigne which had accompanied the official dispatch from Mount Royal Palace. Or, even more to the point, that she'd already known Zilwicki and Victor Cachat were bound for Mesa even before the Battle of Lovat.

The other three glanced at one another, considering what she'd just said, then looked back at her.

"You think they captured him when he was there, Your Grace?" Selleck asked quietly, and Honor shook her head.

"No," she said softly. "They didn't capture him. If they had, they'd have produced him—or at least his body—to substantiate their charges instead of claiming he was 'caught in his own explosions.' But I don't like the fact that no one's heard from him since Green Pines. If he got off-planet at all, he should have been home, long since. So I *am* afraid they may finally have managed to kill him."

Nimitz made a soft, protesting sound of pain, and she stroked his ears again. As she'd said, unlike the civilians sitting around the table, she'd known Anton Zilwicki. In fact, she'd come to know him and Cathy Montaigne very well, indeed, since their return to the Old Star Kingdom following the Manpower Affair in Old Chicago. She and George Reynolds, her staff intelligence officer, had worked closely—if very much under the table—with both of them, and her own credentials with the Audubon ballroom had been part of the reason Zilwicki had been so prepared to share information with her.

"Excuse me, Your Grace, but would you happen to know *why* he was on Mesa?" Tuominen asked.

She cocked her head at him, and he shrugged.

"I don't really expect Pritchart or most of the members of her Cabinet to be lining up to take Mesa's word for what happened," he said. "I can think of a few of her congressional 'negotiators' who'd be likely to believe *anything*—officially, at least—if they thought it would strengthen their bargaining position, though. Even without that, there's the media to worry about, and Havenite newsies aren't all that fond of the Star Empire to begin with. So if there's another side to this, something we could lay out to buttress the notion that it wasn't Zilwicki or Torch..."

He let his voice trail off, and Honor snorted again, even more harshly than before.

"First," she said, "how I know he was on Mesa is privileged information. Information that has operational intelligence implications, for that matter. So, no, I don't intend to whisper it into a newsy's ear. Second, I'd think that if I suddenly announced to the media that I 'just happen' to know why Captain Zilwicki was on Mesa and that I *promise* it wasn't to set off a nuclear device in a public park on Saturday morning, it's going to sound just a little suspicious. Like the sort of thing someone trying desperately to discredit the truth might come up with on an especially stupid day. And, third, Voitto, I don't think anyone willing to believe something like this coming from a source like Mesa in the first place is going to change her mind whatever anyone says. Or not, at least, without irrefutable physical *proof* that Mesa lied."

"I can see that," Tuominen acknowledged with a grimace. "Sorry, Your Grace. I guess I'm just looking for a straw to grasp."

"I don't blame you." Honor turned back to the window, looking down on the boat-dotted estuary, wishing she were down there in one of her sloops herself. "And I don't doubt this is going to complicate our job here in Nouveau Paris, as well. To be honest, though, I'm a lot more worried about its potential impact on *Solly* public opinion and what it may encourage Kolokoltsov and those other idiots in Old Chicago to do."

Tuominen nodded unhappily behind her and wondered if one reason he himself was focusing so intensely on the situation here in the Republic of Haven was expressly to *avoid* thinking about how Old Chicago might have reacted to the same news. It was ironic that Manticore had received the reportage of the Mesan allegations about Green Pines before anyone on Old Earth had.

By now, though, the sensational charges were racing outward to all the interstellar community of man, and God only knew how that was likely to impact on the Solarian public's view of the Star Empire. The one thing Tuominen was prepared to bet on was that it wasn't going to help.

"I agree that the way the League reacts to this is ultimately likely to be a lot more significant as far as the Star Empire's concerned, Your Grace," Selleck said. "Unfortunately, there's not anything we can do about that. So I think Barnabas and Voitto are right to be considering anything we might be able to do to mitigate the impact here, in the Republic."

She shrugged.

"Voitto's right about people like Younger and McGwire. I've been quietly developing some additional information sources since we got here, and the more I find out about Younger, the more revolting he turns out to be. I'm still not sure exactly how the internal dynamics of the New Conservatives lay out, but I'm coming to the conclusion he's a much more important player than we'd assumed before we left Manticore. If there's anyone on Pritchart's side of the table who's likely to try to use something like this, it's Younger."

"But how *can* he use it, Carissa?" Kew asked. "I realize the media's going to have a field day, whatever we do. And God knows there's enough 'anti-Manty' sentiment here in the Republic already for these allegations to generate even more public unhappiness with the fact that their government's negotiating with us at all. But having said all of that, it's the only game in town. The bottom line is that Pritchart and her people have to be even more determined than we are to keep us from blowing up their capital star system!"

"Really?" Honor turned her head, looking over her shoulder at him. "In that case, why don't we already have an agreement?" she asked reasonably. "Carissa's exactly right about Younger, and I wouldn't be too sure McGwire doesn't fall into the same category. But everything about Younger's mind-glow"—she reached up to Nimitz again, suggesting (not entirely accurately) where her certainty about the Havenite's emotions came from—"suggests that he really doesn't care what happens to the rest of the universe, as long as he gets what *he* wants. Or, to put it another way, he's absolutely convinced he's going to be able to *make* things come out the way he wants them to, and he's prepared to do whatever it takes to accomplish that." She grimaced. "His and McGwire's obstructionism isn't just about getting the best terms they possibly can for the *Republic*. They're looking to cut their own domestic deals, improve their *own* positions here in Nouveau Paris, and Younger would blow up the negotiations in a heartbeat if he believed it would further his own political ambitions."

"I'm less afraid of his managing to completely sabotage the talks, Your Grace," Selleck said, "than I am about his stretching them out. Or trying to, at any rate. From what I've seen of him, I think he's calculating that the worse things get between us and the Sollies, the more likely we are to accept his terms in order to get some kind of a treaty so we can deal with the League without worrying about having the Republic on our back."

"That would be . . . fatally stupid of him," Kew said.

"I don't think he really believes the Queen—I mean, the Empress— is willing to pull the trigger on the entire Republic if we don't get a formal treaty in time, Barnabas," Tuominen said heavily.

"And even if he does believe we'll do that in the end, he doesn't think it's going to happen tomorrow," Honor agreed. "As far as he's concerned, he's still playing for time and the time's still there to be played for. And let's face it—to some extent, he's right. Her Majesty's not going to turn the Navy lose on Haven's infrastructure any sooner than she thinks she absolutely has to. If she were going to do that, she wouldn't have sent us to negotiate in the first place."

And I think I just won't mention how hard it was to bring her to that position, Honor added mentally.

"The problem is that no matter how much time he thinks he has, *we* don't have an unlimited supply of it, and this is only going to make that worse. So what I'm really worried about is that he's going to miscalculate with . . . unhappy consequences for everyone involved."

"I agree." Selleck nodded firmly. "The question is how we keep him from doing that."

"I don't know we can do anything directly with him," Honor replied. "On the other hand, President Pritchart's obviously had a lot of experience dealing with him domestically. So I think the logical move is for me to have a private little conversation with her to make her aware of our concerns."

✧   ✧   ✧

"Good afternoon, Admiral Alexander-Harrington."

Eloise Pritchart stood, reaching across her desk to shake Honor's hand as Angela Rousseau escorted her into the presidential office.

"Good afternoon, Madam President," Honor replied, and suppressed a smile as Sheila Thiessen nodded a bit brusquely to Spencer Hawke. After two a half weeks, the two bodyguards and paranoiacs-in-chief had achieved a firm mutual respect. In fact, they were actually beginning to *like* one another—a little, at least—although neither of them would have been willing to admit it to a living soul.

"Thank you for making time for me so promptly," she continued out loud as she settled into what had become her customary chair here in Pritchart's office. Nimitz flowed down into her lap and curled up there, grass-green eyes watching the President alertly, and Pritchart smiled.

"Right off the top of my head, Admiral, I can't think of anyone who has a higher priority where 'making time' is concerned," she said dryly.

"I suppose not," Honor acknowledged with a faint, answering smile.

"Now that you're here, can I offer you some refreshment?" the President inquired. "Mr. Belardinelli has some more of those chocolate chip cookies you like so much hidden away in his desk drawer, you know."

She smiled conspiratorially, and Honor chuckled. But she also shook her head, smile fading, and Pritchart let her chair come fully back upright.

"Well, in that case," the President said, "I believe you said you had something confidential you needed to discuss?"

"That's true, Madam President." Honor glanced at Thiessen, then back at the Pritchart. "I'm going to assume Ms. Thiessen is as deeply in your confidence as Captain Hawke is in mine."

Her tone made the statement a polite question, and Pritchart nodded.

"I thought so," Honor said. "On the other hand, you might want to switch off the recorders for this conversation." She smiled again, thinly. "I'm sure your office has to be at least as thoroughly wired for sound as Queen Elizabeth's. Normally, that wouldn't bother me, but what I'm here to discuss has intelligence operational implications. Implications for *your* operations, not Manticore's."

Pritchart's eyebrows arched. Then she glanced at Thiessen. Her senior bodyguard looked less than enthralled by Honor's request, but she made no overt objection.

"Leave your personal recorder on, Sheila," the President directed. "If it turns out we need to make this part of the official record after the fact, we can download it from yours." She looked back at Honor. "Would that be satisfactory, Admiral?"

"Perfectly satisfactory from *my* perspective, Madam President." Honor shrugged. "I doubt very much that anything I'm about to tell you is going to have repercussions for the *Star Empire's* intel operations."

"I have to admit you've managed to pique my interest," Pritchart said as Thiessen quietly shut down all of the other pickups in her office.

"And I suppose I should admit that piquing your interest was at least partly what I was after," Honor acknowledged.

"So now that you've done it, what was it you wanted to say?"

The President's mind-glow was tinged with rather more wariness than was evident in her expression or her tone, Honor noted.

"I wanted to address the allegations coming out of Mesa about the Green Pines atrocity," Honor said, and tasted Pritchart's surprise. Obviously, the President hadn't expected her to go there.

"Specifically," Honor continued, "the charges that Captain Zilwicki was on Mesa as a Ballroom operative specifically to set up the explosions as an act of terrorism. Or, at least, as an act of what they call 'asymmetrical warfare' against someone he and the Kingdom of Torch believed were planning a genocidal attack on Congo. I realize there's a certain surface persuasiveness to their version of what happened, especially given the captain's long-term relationship with Catherine Montaigne, his daughter's status as Queen of Torch, and the fact that he's made very little secret of his sympathy for the Ballroom. Despite that, I'm absolutely confident that Mesa's version of what happened is a complete fabrication."

She paused, and Pritchart frowned.

"I'm no more likely than the next woman to believe anything Mesa says, Admiral," the President said. "Nonetheless, I'm a little at a loss as to how this has operational implications for *our* intelligence."

"In that case, Madam President, I think you should probably sit down with Director Trajan and ask him where Special Officer Cachat is right now."

Despite decades of political and clandestine experience, Pritchart stiffened visibly, and Honor tasted the spike of surprise tinged with apprehension (and what tasted for all the world like a hint of *exasperation*) which went through the President.

"Special Officer...Cachat, did you say?" From Pritchart's tone, it was clear she was simply playing the game as the rules required, rather than that she actually expected Honor to be diverted.

"Yes, Madam President. Special Officer Cachat. You know—the Havenite agent who's probably more responsible than anyone else for the fact of Torch's independence in the first place? The fellow who's been hobnobbing with Captain Zilwicki, Queen Berry, and Ruth Winton for the last couple of years? The one who's your agent in charge for the Erewhon sector? *That* Special Officer Cachat."

Pritchart winced ever so slightly, then sighed.

"I suppose I should be getting used to having you trot out things like that, Admiral," she said resignedly. "On the other hand, aside from the evidence that you know far more about our intelligence community than I really wish you did, I still don't see exactly how this ties in with Green Pines."

"Actually, it's fairly simple," Honor replied. "According to Mesa, Captain Zilwicki went to Green Pines as a Ballroom operative for the specific purpose of using nuclear explosives against civilian targets. I'm sure your own analysts can tell you that Anton Zilwicki was probably the last person in the galaxy who would have signed off on that sort of operation, no matter what justification he thought he had. In addition, however, you should be aware that before Captain Zilwicki departed for Mesa—and, yes, he *was* on-planet—he stopped by my flagship at Trevor's Star to discuss the Webster assassination and the attack on Torch with me. At which time"—her eyes bored suddenly into Pritchart's across the President's desk—"he was accompanied by Special Officer Cachat."

"*What?*"

This time astonishment startled the question out of Pritchart, and Sheila Thiessen stiffened in shock behind the President. Both women stared at Honor for several seconds before Pritchart shook herself.

"Let me get this straight," she said in an odd, half-exasperated, half-resigned tone, raising her right hand, index finger extended. "You're telling me the intelligence officer in charge of all of my spying operations in the Erewhon sector entered a closed

Manticoran star system and actually went aboard a Manticoran admiral's *flagship*?"

"Yes." Honor smiled. "I had the impression Special Officer Cachat's methods are just a bit...unorthodox, perhaps."

"A *bit*?" Pritchart snorted and rolled her eyes. "Since you've had the dubious pleasure of meeting him, Admiral, I might as well admit I'm usually undecided between pinning a medal on him and *shooting* him. And I see I *am* going to have to have a little discussion with Director Trajan about his current whereabouts. Although, to be fair to the Director, I doubt very much that Cachat bothered to inform him about his agenda before he went haring off to Trevor's Star. Not, mind you, that anyone's disapproval of his travel plans would have slowed him down for a minute."

"I see you *have* met him personally," Honor observed dryly.

"Oh, yes, Admiral. Oh, yes! I have indeed had that...pleasure."

"I'm glad, since that probably means you're going to be readier to believe what I'm about to tell you."

"Where *Victor Cachat* is concerned? Please, Admiral! I'm prepared to believe just about anything when he's involved!"

"Well," Honor said, suppressing an urge to chuckle, "as I say, he and Captain Zilwicki came to visit me back in April. In fact, they came for the specific purpose of assuring me that they—*both* of them—were certain the Republic was *not* involved in the attack on Queen Berry and Princess Ruth."

Her tone had become far more serious, and Pritchart's nostrils flared.

"Given the flavor of Special Officer Cachat's mind-glow," Honor continued, stroking Nimitz, "I had no choice but to accept that he genuinely believed that. In fact, I have to admit I was deeply impressed by his personal courage in coming to tell me so." She looked into Pritchart's eyes again. "He was fully prepared to suicide, Madam President. Indeed, he *expected* to suicide after delivering his message to me, because he was pretty sure I wasn't going to allow him off my flagship afterward."

"But you did," Pritchart said softly, and it wasn't a question.

"Yes, I did," Honor acknowledged, and gave her head a little toss. "To be honest, it never occurred to me not to. He...deserved better. And, even more importantly, perhaps, I not only believed he was telling me the truth, I agreed with his analysis of what had probably happened."

Thiessen's eyes narrowed, but Pritchart only cocked her head. "And that analysis was—?"

"That, barring the possibility of some sort of unauthorized rogue operation, the Republic had had nothing to do with the Torch attack," Honor said flatly. "And, by extension, that Admiral Webster's assassination almost certainly hadn't been sanctioned by your Administration, either. Which, in my opinion, made Manpower the most likely culprit."

"Then why didn't you—" Pritchart began with an obviously involuntary flash of anger.

"I did." Honor's voice was even flatter. "I discussed my meeting, and my conclusions, with—well, let's say at the highest level of the Government. Unfortunately, by then events were already in motion. And, frankly, all I could really tell anyone was that *Special Officer Cachat* believed the Republic hadn't been involved. I think you'll agree that despite my own belief that he was right, that scarcely constituted *proof.*"

Pritchart settled back, gazing at Honor for several seconds, then drew a deep breath.

"No," she acknowledged. "No, I don't suppose it did. But, oh, Admiral, how I *wish* someone had listened to you!"

"I do, too, Madam President," Honor said softly. Brown eyes met topaz, both dark with sorrow for all the men and women who had died after that meeting.

"I do, too," Honor repeated, more briskly, after a moment. "But the real reason I've brought this up at this point is that Captain Zilwicki and Special Officer Cachat did believe Manpower—and possibly even the Mesan system government—were directly implicated in the attacks. In addition, our own intelligence agencies have been steadily turning up evidence that there's more going on where Manpower and Mesa are concerned than anyone's previously assumed. Captain Zilwicki and Special Officer Cachat intended to find out what that something 'more' was, and according to what I believe to be an unimpeachable source—Catherine Montaigne, in point of fact—the two of them, *jointly,* were headed for Mesa."

"Together?" Pritchart, Honor noted, didn't sound particularly incredulous.

"Together." Honor nodded. "Which means that while Captain Zilwicki was on Mesa, a point of which the Mesans obviously became aware, he was definitely *not* there on a Ballroom terrorist operation. Given the various . . . peculiarities where Torch is concerned, I think it's very likely the Ballroom was involved in getting them onto Mesa in the first place. And it's entirely possible that what happened in Green Pines was actually a Ballroom operation, or the result of one. The last thing Captain Zilwicki or Special Officer Cachat would have wanted would have been to compromise their own mission by becoming involved in a major terrorist strike, however, so any involvement they may have had must have been peripheral. Accidental, really."

"I can see that." Pritchart nodded slowly, and Honor reminded herself that, unlike most heads of state, the President had once been a senior commander in a clandestine resistance movement. That undoubtedly helped when it came to grasping the underlying logic of covert operations.

"I don't know for certain why Mesa's made no mention of Special Officer Cachat," Honor said. "It may be they aren't aware he was even present. More probably, the Star Empire's who they really want to damage with this at the moment. Explaining that intelligence operatives of two star nations who've been at war with one another for over twenty years just decided on a whim to join forces with the Ballroom would probably be a bit much even for the Solly public's credulity. The best-case possibility, of course, would be that they *weren't* aware of his presence and that he actually managed, somehow, to escape."

"And Captain Zilwicki?" Pritchart asked gently.

"And I very much doubt Captain Zilwicki did." Honor made no effort to hide her pain at that thought. "They wouldn't have handed this to the media—especially not with the assertion that he was killed in one of 'his own' explosions—unless they *knew* he was dead."

"I'm deeply and sincerely sorry to hear that," Pritchart said, and Honor tasted the truth of her statement in her mind-glow.

"The important point, Madam President," Honor said, "is that I think you can see from what I've just told you that everything Mesa's claiming is a fabrication. There are probably nuggets of truth buried in it, but I doubt we'll ever know what they actually were. From my perspective, the immediate and critical point is to keep this from sidetracking our negotiations. I don't doubt it presents opportunities for self-interested parties to go fishing in troubled waters," she carefully did not mention any specific names, "but it would be very unfortunate if someone managed to derail these talks. In particular, if Mesa's allegations play into the situation between the Star Empire and the Solarian League in a way that heightens tensions still further or even leads to additional military action, Queen Elizabeth's flexibility where a negotiated settlement is concerned is likely to be compromised."

She saw the understanding in Pritchart's eyes, tasted it in the President's mind-glow, but she knew it had to be said out loud, as well.

"It may well be that at least part of Mesa's objective is to do just that, Madam President. Manpower certainly has as much reason to hate the Republic as it does to hate the Star Empire. I could readily believe that someone in Mendel saw this as an opportunity to force the Star Empire's hand where military operations against the Republic are concerned as well as a means to provoke an open war between us and the League. And I think"—she gazed into Pritchart's eyes again—"that it would be a tragedy if they succeeded."

Chapter Seventeen

"I HAVE TO AGREE with Duchess Harrington," Thomas Theisman said as the imagery from Sheila Thiessen's personal recorder came to an end. He tipped back in his chair, eyes pensive. "It *would* be a tragedy."

"Especially if she's telling the truth," Leslie Montreau agreed. "Of course, that's one of the major rubs, isn't it? *Is* she telling the truth?" The Secretary of State shrugged. "It all hangs together, and I'm inclined to think she is, but you have to admit, Tom. It would be very convenient from her perspective if we bought into this notion that Mesa's version of Green Pines is a completely fabricated effort at disinformation."

"You're right," Pritchart acknowledged, and looked at Denis LePic. The Attorney General had been sitting there with a peculiar expression while the imagery replayed, and now she crooked an eyebrow at him.

"Why is it, Denis," she asked shrewdly, "that you don't seem any more astonished than you do to hear Duchess Harrington's version of one of your senior intelligence officer's perambulations about the galaxy?"

"Because I'm not," LePic admitted in tones of profound resignation.

"Wait a minute." Theisman looked at the Attorney General—who also ran the Republic's civilian intelligence services—in obvious surprise. "You're telling me you really didn't even know where

Cachat was? I mean, he really did take himself off to a Manty flagship in the middle of a war without even *mentioning* the possibility he might do something like that? Forgive me, but isn't he the man in charge of all FIS operations in Erewhon *and* Congo?"

"Yes." LePic sighed. "And, no, he didn't mention anything of the sort to me. Of course, I didn't *know* we didn't know where he was until this afternoon. Not until Eloise asked me to verify Duchess Harrington's story, at any rate. For all I know—or all I can prove, anyway—he might've been ambushed and devoured by space hamsters!" The Attorney General's expression was that of a man whose patience had been profoundly tried. "And I'm fairly confident no one in Wilhelm's shop's been covering up for him, either. *No one* knew where he'd gone—not even Kevin."

Montreau had joined the Secretary of War in looking at LePic in disbelief. Pritchart, on the other hand, only sat back in her chair with the air of a woman confronting the inevitable.

"And how long has this state of affairs obtained?" Theisman asked politely. "I mean, in the Navy, we like to have our station commanders and our task force commanders report in occasionally. Just so we've got some notion of what they're up to, you understand."

"Very funny," LePic said sourly. Then he looked at Pritchart. "You know Kevin's been rubbing off on Cachat from the very beginning. By now, I don't know which of them's the bigger loose warhead! If it weren't for the fact the two of them keep producing miracles, I'd fire both of them, if only to get rid of the anxiety quotient."

"I often felt that way about Kevin when we were in the Resistance," Pritchart admitted. "But, as you say, both our pet lunatics have that annoying habit of coming through in the crunch. On the other hand, I believe you were about to tell Tom how long Cachat's been incommunicado?"

"Actually, I was trying to *avoid* telling him," LePic admitted, and smiled even more sourly. "The truth is that it tracks entirely too well with what Alexander-Harrington's had to say. Our last report from him is over six T-months old."

"*What?*" Montrose sat abruptly upright. "One of your station chiefs has been missing for *six months*, and you don't have a clue where he's gone?"

"I know it sounds ridiculous," LePic said more than a little defensively. "In fact, I asked Wilhelm very much that same question this afternoon. He *says* he hadn't mentioned it to me because he couldn't have told me anything very much, since *he* didn't know very much. I'm inclined to believe that's the truth, mostly. Actually, though, I think a lot of the reason he kept his mouth shut was that he was hoping Cachat would turn back up again before anyone asked where he was." The Attorney General shrugged. "In a lot of ways, I can't fault Wilhelm's thinking. After all, he's the FIS's director. Cachat reports to him, not me, and as a general rule, I don't even try to keep up with Wilhelm's operations unless they develop specific, important intelligence that's brought to my attention. And as Wilhelm pointed out, it's not as if this were the first time Cachat's just dropped off the radar, and he's always produced results when it's happened in the past."

"But if someone else has gotten their hands on him, Denis, isn't he in a position to do enormous damage?" Theisman asked very seriously.

"Yes and no," LePic replied. "First of all, I think—as Duchess Harrington's description of *her* conversation with him indicates—it would be extraordinarily difficult for someone to take him alive to start with. And, second, I doubt anyone would get anything out of Victor Cachat under duress even if they did manage to capture him. I don't know if you've ever met the man, Tom, but, believe me, he's about as scary as they come. Think of Kevin Usher with less of a sense of humor, just as much principle a *lot* closer to the surface, and even more focus."

Theisman obviously found that description more than a little disturbing, and this time LePic's smile held a glimmer of amusement.

"On the other hand, no one's going to rely on even Cachat's ability to resist rigorous interrogation forever. His assistant station chief in Erewhon is Special Officer Sharon Justice. She's acting as special-officer-in-charge until Cachat gets back, and Wilhelm tells me that on Cachat's specific instructions, one of her first acts as SOIC was to change all communication protocols. Somebody might be able to get the identities of at least some of his sources out of him—I doubt it, frankly, but anything is possible—but I don't think anyone's likely to be able to compromise his entire network with Justice in charge."

"Justice. She was one of the StateSec officers involved in that business at La Martine, wasn't she?" Pritchart said thoughtfully.

"She was," LePic agreed.

"Which means she's going to feel a powerful sense of personal loyalty to Cachat," Pritchart pointed out.

"She does." LePic nodded. "On the other hand, everything Cachat's accomplished out there's been done on the basis of personal relationships." The Attorney General shrugged. "I won't pretend I don't wish the man could operate at least a *little* more by The Book, but no one can argue with his results. Or the fact that he's probably got more penetration—at second hand, perhaps, but still penetration—into the Manties than anyone else we've got, given his relationship with Ruth Winton and Anton Zilwicki. Not to mention the fact that he's damned near personally responsible for the *existence* of Torch."

"I know. That's why I took him away from Kevin and gave him to Wilhelm," Pritchart said. "On the other hand, it does sound like what little we *do* know corroborates Duchess Harrington's version of events."

"I think so." LePic agreed with the air of a man who didn't really want to admit any such thing. "At any rate, Cachat's last report did say he'd concluded that since *we* weren't involved in the attempt on Queen Berry, it had to have been someone else, and that the someone else in question had motives which were obviously inimical to the Republic. He'd reached that conclusion, I might add, even before we'd learned here in Nouveau Paris that the attempt had been made. By the time his report reached Wilhelm, he'd already pulled the plug, handed over to Justice, and disappeared."

"As in disappeared aboard a Manticoran flagship at Trevor's Star with a suicide device in his pocket just in case, you mean? That sort of 'disappeared'?"

"Yes, Madam President," LePic said a bit more formally than was his wont.

Pritchart gazed at him for several seconds, swinging her chair gently from side to side. Then she snorted.

"My, my, my," she murmured with a crooked smile. "Only Victor Cachat. Now that Kevin's out of the field, anyway."

"You're telling us," Montreau said, speaking with the careful precision of someone determined to make certain they really had heard correctly, "that one of FIS's *station chiefs* really went, with a known Manticoran intelligence operative, to a star system the

Manties have declared a closed military reservation, for a personal conversation with the *commanding officer* of their Eighth Fleet *before* the Battle of Lovat? And then went off on a completely unauthorized operation to Mesa? Which apparently ran right into the middle of whatever really happened at Green Pines?"

LePic only nodded, and Montreau sat back in her chair with an expression of utter disbelief.

"Actually, it makes sense, you know," Theisman said thoughtfully after a moment.

"Makes *sense*?" Montreau repeated incredulously.

"From what I know of Cachat—although I hasten to admit it's all second- or thirdhand, since I've never met him personally—he spends a lot of time operating by intuition. In fact, any way you look at it, a huge part of those successes Denis was just talking about have resulted from a combination of that intuition with the personal contacts and relationships he's established. And you've met Alexander-Harrington now, Leslie. If you were going to reach out to a highly placed member of an enemy star nation's political and military establishment because you were convinced someone was trying to sabotage peace talks between us and them, could *you* think of a better person to risk contacting?"

Montreau started to reply, then stopped, visibly thought for a moment or two, and shook her head, almost against her will.

"I'm willing to bet that was pretty much Cachat's analysis," LePic agreed with a nod. "And, if it was, it obviously worked, given Duchess Harrington's evident attitude towards the negotiations. Not only that, but it set up the situation in which she brought us her version of what really happened on Mesa."

His three listeners looked at one another with suddenly thoughtful expressions.

"You know, Denis," Theisman said in a gentler tone, "if he's been out of contact this long, the most likely reason is that he and Zilwicki were both killed on Mesa."

"I do know," LePic admitted. "On the other hand, this is Victor Cachat we're talking about. And he and Zilwicki are both—or at least *were* both—very competent operators. They almost certainly built firebreaks into and between their covers, whatever they were, on Mesa, not to mention multiple escape strategies. So it really is possible Zilwicki could have gone down without Mesa's ever realizing Cachat was there. And if the two of them were deep enough under, especially somewhere as far away as the Mesa System, three or four months—or even longer—isn't all that long a lag in communications. Not from a covert viewpoint, at least. I don't know about Manticore or the Ballroom, but *we* don't have any established conduits between here and Mesa, so his communications would have been circuitous at the very least, and probably a lot less than secure. And don't forget—it's been less than four months since Green Pines. If he did avoid capture, he might have been forced to lie low on the planet for quite a while before he could work out a way to get back out again. And if that's the case, he damned well wouldn't have trusted any conduit he could jury-rig to get reports back to us just so we wouldn't worry about him! For all I know, he's on his way home right this minute!"

Theisman looked doubtful, and Montreau looked downright skeptical. Pritchart, on the other hand, had considerably more hands-on experience in the worlds of espionage and covert operations than either of them did. Besides, she thought, LePic had a point. It *was* Victor Cachat they were talking about, and that young man had demonstrated a remarkable talent for survival even under the most unpromising circumstances.

"All right," she said, leaning forward and folding her forearms on her desk, "I'm with you, Denis, in wishing we knew something about what happened to Cachat. There's nothing we can do about that, though, and I think we're pretty much in agreement that what we do know from our end effectively confirms what Duchess Harrington's told us?"

She looked around at her advisers' faces, and, one by one, they nodded.

"In that case," the President continued, "I think it behooves us to pay close attention to her warning about Elizabeth's patience and the...how did she put it? The *'flexibility'* of Manticore's options. I don't know that I buy into the notion that this was deliberately aimed at Manticore and Haven alike, that Mesa wants Manticore to trash the Republic before the League trashes *Manticore*. I think it's at least remotely possible, though. More to the point, it doesn't matter if that's what they're trying to do if that's what they end up doing, anyway. So I think it's up to us to make sure our own problem children at the negotiating table don't decide to try to take advantage of this."

"And exactly how do you propose to do that, Madam President?" Theisman asked skeptically.

"Actually," Pritchart said with a chilling smile, "*I* don't plan to say a word to them about it."

"No?" There was no disguising the anxiety in Denis LePic's voice...nor any indication that the Attorney General had tried very hard to disguise it.

"It's called 'plausible deniability,' Denis," she replied with that same sharklike smile. "I'd love to simply march all of them in at pulser point to sign on the dotted line, but I'm afraid if I tried that, Younger, at least, would call my bluff. So I can't just shut him up every time he starts throwing up those roadblocks of his. That's part of the political process, unfortunately, and we don't need to be setting any iron-fist precedents for repressing political opponents. Despite that, however, I think I can bring myself to compromise my sense of political moral responsibility far enough to keep him from using *this* roadblock, at least."

"How?" This time the question came from Theisman.

"By using our lunatic who *hasn't* gone missing." Pritchart chuckled coldly. "Everyone knows Kevin Usher is a total loose cannon. I'm pretty sure that if he called Younger and McGwire, let's say, in for confidential in-depth briefings and was very careful to speak to both of them off the record, with no embarrassing recordings, and no inconvenient witnesses to misconstrue anything he might say, he could convince them it would be...unwise to use these unfortunate and obviously groundless allegations out of Mesa for partisan political advantage."

"Threaten them with, ah, *direct action*, you mean?" Unlike LePic, Theisman seemed to have no particular qualms with the notion, and Pritchart's smile turned almost seraphic.

"Oh, *no*, Tom!" She shook her head and clucked her tongue reprovingly. "Kevin *never* threatens. He only *predicts* probable outcomes from time to time." The humor disappeared from her smile as the shark surfaced once more. "He doesn't do it all that often, but when he does," the President of the Republic of Haven finished, "he's *never* wrong."

FEBRUARY 1922 POST DIASPORA

"The Solarian League can't accept something like this—not out of some frigging little pissant navy out beyond the Verge—no matter what kind of provocation they may think they have! If we let them get away with this, God only knows who's going to try something stupid next!"

—Fleet Admiral Sandra Crandall, SLN

Chapter Eighteen

"WELL, THIS IS A fine kettle of fish. Excuse me—*another* fine kettle of fish."

Elizabeth Winton's tone was almost whimsical; her expression was anything but. Her brown eyes were dark, radiating anger, determination, and not a little bit of fear, and the treecat stretched across her lap, instead of the back of her chair this time, was very, very still.

"It's not exactly a complete surprise," Hamish Alexander-Harrington, the Earl of White Haven, pointed out.

"No," the Queen agreed, "although the confirmation that this Anisimovna *understated* the number of superdreadnoughts rattling around the Verge probably comes under that heading."

"I doubt anyone's likely to disagree with that, Your Majesty," Sir Anthony Langtry said dryly.

"And I doubt anyone in this room thinks discovering they're really out there's going to make things any better," William Alexander, Baron Grantville, pointed out.

"That depends entirely on what sort of officer's in command of them," Admiral Sir Thomas Caparelli, the First Space Lord of the Royal Manticoran Navy, told the Prime Minister. "If this Crandall has the brains of a fruit fly, she'll stay where she is and try to keep things from spinning any further out of control until she knows exactly what happened at New Tuscany and she's had time to seek guidance from home."

"And just what leads you to assume any Solarian flag officer sent to the Madras Sector is going to have two brain cells to rub together, Sir Thomas?" Elizabeth asked acidly. "I'm willing to concede that there might be one or two Frontier Fleet commodores who were already in the area who could seal their own shoes without printed instructions. But if the officer in command of those ships was sent out under the same master plan that sent Byng, she's either a complete and total idiot who needs help wiping drool off her chin—and God knows the Solarian League's got enough of *them* to go around!—or else she's in Manpower's pocket. In the first case, she's going to react as if Mike's fleet is a nail and she's a hammer out of blind, unthinking spinal reflex. In the *second* case, she's going to react as if Mike's fleet is a nail and she's a hammer because that's what Manpower's paying her to do. From the perspective of the nail, I don't think it makes a lot of difference."

White Haven winced mentally at the Queen's succinct, biting analysis. Less because of the tone in which it was delivered than because of its accuracy. Of course, there *was* one little problem with her analogy.

"In this case, though," he pointed out aloud, "the hammer doesn't have a clue what it's about to let itself in for. Or, at least, if it does, it's going to be a lot less eager to start banging away."

"How realistic *is* it to hope this Crandall realizes how big her disadvantage really is?" Grantville asked.

"If I knew the answer to that one, Willie, we wouldn't need all of Pat Givens' boys and girls over at ONI," his brother replied. "Anyone who looks at what Mike did at New Tuscany with an open, unprejudiced mind is going to realize just how outclassed he and his ships were. Unfortunately, if she moved out immediately after *Reprise* spotted her at in Meyers, she won't have had time to hear anything about Second New Tuscany. And even if she waited long enough to hear from the dispatch boat that got away from Mike, she'd have to be able to make the leap from what happened to a single battlecruiser to what could happen to an entire fleet of superdreadnoughts. As Her Majesty has just pointed out, it's unlikely anyone Manpower's recruited for this command is going to be all that interested in looking at the data. And even if she is, I suspect she's still too likely to figure her superdreadnoughts are a hell of a lot tougher than any battlecruiser ever built."

"And that they're *enough* tougher she doesn't have to worry about any slick little tricks mere battlecruisers might try against them?" Grantville finished the thought for him with a question.

"Pretty much," Caparelli agreed. "More than that, she may hope we haven't been able to reinforce. In that case, she's going to want to move quickly, before we do send in additional units."

"Do you agree with Mike's assessment about their probable targeting priorities, Sir Thomas?" Elizabeth asked, her fingers caressing Ariel's ears.

"Judging from what we've seen of their contingency planning from the databases she captured at New Tuscany, I'd say yes, Your Majesty." The first space lord grimaced. "If it weren't for the wormhole, I'd be positive they were going to jump straight at Spindle. Given the importance of the Lynx Terminus, though, it's pretty much a coin toss. I don't see them splitting up and going after individual star systems in the Quadrant until after they've nailed Tenth Fleet. Not assuming Crandall knows what happened at New Tuscany, at any rate. But the idea of seizing the terminus, holding it to keep us from reinforcing while simultaneously forcing Admiral Gold Peak to come to them if she wants to reopen her line of communications, would have to appeal to a Solly strategist."

"I wish it *would*," White Haven muttered, and Caparelli barked a laugh of harsh agreement.

"Hamish is right about that, Your Majesty," he said. "We've got all but one of the forts fully online now. *And* we've got Apollo system-defense birds deployed in depth to cover them. In fact, we were planning on recalling Jessup Blaine from Lynx to refit his pod-layers with Keyhole-Two and Apollo."

"So you and Hamish are both confident the Lynx Terminus could hold off seventy-one superdreadnoughts if it had to?"

"Your Majesty, at the risk of sounding immodest, the only real question would be how long it took us to blow all seventy-one of them out of space. Those forts were designed to hold that terminus without any outside support against the attack of two hundred and fifty of our own pre-Apollo podnoughts. Now that they have Apollo, their defensive capability's been multiplied many times. We still aren't sure by exactly how much, but it's got to be at least a factor of four."

"Then Admiral Blaine could—" Elizabeth began.

"Admiral Blaine already has, Your Majesty," Caparelli interrupted.

"I sent his new orders before I started over to the Palace. If he hasn't already departed for Spindle, he'll be underway within the hour. And even though he doesn't have Apollo, his command would still eat those Solly superdreadnoughts for lunch. And there's one other bit of good news to go with that one—Admiral Gold Peak's Apollo ammunition ships are almost forty-eight hours ahead of the last schedule update she's received."

Elizabeth relaxed visibly, but Ariel raised his head and glanced at White Haven a moment before the earl cleared his throat. The quiet sound drew the Queen's attention, too, and an eyebrow rose.

"What Tom just said is completely accurate, Your Majesty," he said, "and I unreservedly support both his analysis and his instructions to Admiral Blaine. The problem is that it's unlikely Blaine could arrive at Spindle before the Sollies do, assuming they come straight from Meyers. So, if they do decide to move against Mike, she's going to have to take them on with what she has, and even if the Apollo pods get there in time, she doesn't have Keyhole-Two or pod-layers."

"And if they hit Mike without Blaine and before the ammunition ships get there, what are her chances?" Elizabeth asked quietly.

"From what I've seen of the tech readouts from their battlecruisers' databases," Caparelli replied for the earl after a moment, "and assuming the count on Crandall's SDs is accurate and Admiral Gold Peak fights as smart as she's always fought before, I'd say her chances range from about even to fairly good. There's no way she could survive in energy range of that many superdreadnoughts—I don't care what class they are—but I very seriously doubt that any Solarian superdreadnought's going to survive to close to energy range. Their missile armaments are light, even by our pre-pod standards, and from our examination of the battlecruisers' counter-missiles and those 'Halo' decoy platforms of theirs, they still don't have a clue what the new missile threat environment really is. For that matter, assuming the stats we've pulled out of the computers are really accurate—which, to be honest, in some instances I find a little difficult to believe—at least two thirds of their reserve fleet's still equipped with autocannon point defense, not lasers."

"You're joking," Langtry said, his expression eloquent of disbelief.

"No, I'm not." Caparelli shook his head for added emphasis. "As I say, it's hard to believe, but that's what the data says. In fact, it looks to Pat's analysts as if they've only just recently really started to become aware of the increased missile threat. From the reports we've had from Second Congo, at least *someone* in the League's been experimenting with extended-range shipkillers, but whatever Mesa may've told Luft and his lunatics, there's no evidence the one doing the experimenting is the *SLN*. They're upgrading their current-generation anti-ship missiles, but only marginally, and according to our captured data from Byng, the improvements are to seekers and EW capabilities, not range.

"Defensively, there's some information in the data about something called 'Aegis,' which is supposed to be a major advance in missile defense. As nearly as we can tell, though, what it really amounts to is ripping out a couple of broadside energy mounts, replacing them with additional counter-missile fire control and telemetry links, and then using main missile tubes to launch additional canisters of counter-missiles. It's going to thicken their counter-missile fire, but only at the expense of taking several shipkiller missiles out of an already light broadside. And to make things worse from their perspective, their counter-missiles themselves aren't as good as ours; the fire control software we've been looking at was several generations out of date, by our standards, at the start of the *last* war with Haven; and even on the ships where they've converted the autocannon to laser clusters, they don't appear to have increased the *number* of point defense stations appreciably."

He shook his head again, his eyes bleak with satisfaction.

"I don't doubt that they've increased their antimissile capability from what it used to be, Tony," he said. "And it's going to take more missiles to kill their ships than it would have before they did it. But the end result's going to be the same, and if Admiral Gold Peak doesn't have Apollo, she's got at least four missile colliers stuffed full of Mark 23 flatpacks, her shipboard magazines are full of Mark 16s, mostly with the new laserheads, and every one of her *Nikes* has Keyhole One. Trust me. If this Solly admiral's stupid enough to ram her head into Spindle, Admiral Gold Peak will give her the mother of all migraines. She may not be able to keep Crandall from taking control of the planet's orbitals if she's willing to suck up the losses involved, but she'll be damned lucky if she has ten percent of her ships left when Tenth Fleet runs out of ammo."

"Which will only make this mess even messier from a diplomatic standpoint," Langtry pointed out. "Especially with this new story O'Hanrahan broke."

"Oh, thank you, Tony!" Grantville snorted. "I could have gone all week without thinking about *that* one!"

"It *was* a master stroke, wasn't it?" Elizabeth said sourly. "If there's one newsy in the entire Solarian League no one could ever accuse of being in Manpower's pocket, it's Audrey O'Hanrahan. In fact, the way she was beating up on Frontier Security, Manpower, and Technodyne over Monica only gives this new 'scoop' of hers even more impact."

"I still don't understand how they did it." White Haven shook his head. "It's obvious from her past accomplishments that she's got contacts that should have spotted any forged data, no matter how well it was done. So how did they manage to fool her this time around?"

"Well, Pat's own analysts have all confirmed that the data she's using in her reports carries what appear to be genuine New Tuscan Navy security and ID codes," Caparelli said. "It may've been doctored—in fact, we know what parts of it were, and we're trying to figure out how to demonstrate that fact—but it certainly looks like the official record of what happened. And to be fair to O'Hanrahan, she's never claimed that she's been able to confirm the accuracy of the *data* on the chips—only that all of her 'informed sources' agree it came directly from the New Tuscans and that it's been certified by the New Tuscan Navy... unlike the data *we've* supplied."

"Which only makes it worse, in a lot of ways," Langtry observed. "She's not the one beating the drums, just the one who handed them the drumsticks. In fact, in the last 'faxes I've seen from Old Terra, she's actually protesting—pretty vehemently—that other newsies and talking heads are reading a lot more into her story than she ever meant for them to."

"So she's got good intentions. Great!" White Haven said dourly. "If I recall correctly, Pandora wasn't all that successful at stuffing things back into the box, either."

"Fair enough," Langtry agreed. "On the other hand, I detect Malachai Abruzzi's hand in all this, as well."

"But there's no way this is going to stand up in the end," Elizabeth protested. "Too many people in New Tuscany know what really happened. Not to mention the fact that we've already got the New Tuscan Navy's sensor records for the period involved, complete with all the same security and ID codes—and time chops—and the real records don't begin to match the ones someone handed *her*."

"With all due respect, your Majesty," Langtry said, "we have exactly the same kind of evidence and substantiation where our prewar diplomatic correspondence with Haven is concerned. In fact, I have to wonder if our little disagreement with the Peeps isn't what suggested this particular ploy to Manpower. Or to Mesa, for that matter." The Foreign Secretary grimaced. "It's almost like some kind of 'perfect storm,' isn't it? First Mesa drops Green Pines on us, and then O'Hanrahan, of all people, gives us the follow-up punch with this cock-and-bull story from New Tuscany."

"I think it was deliberately orchestrated," White Haven said grimly. "Both stories came out of —or at least *through* Mesa—after all. I'll lay you any odds you like that the whole business about dispatches from New Tuscany's a complete fabrication. Somebody in Mesa planned this very carefully, and I'll also bet you they deliberately set O'Hanrahan up to front for them exactly because she's always been so careful to be as accurate as possible. And the fact that she was one of the few Solly newsies questioning their version of Green Pines and demanding hard evidence to back up their claims only makes her even more damaging on *this* story, since no one in the galaxy could possibly accuse her of carrying water for Mesa in the past." The earl shook his head. "Playing *her* this way was probably a little risky from their perspective, but look at how it's paid off for them.

"And even if the truth is staring them right in the eye, people like Abruzzi and Quartermain and Kolokoltsov are capable of projecting perfect candor while they look the other way," Grantville added. "They'll swear the version that suits their purposes is the truth, despite any evidence to the contrary, and figure that when the smoke clears and it turns out they were wrong, they'll get away with it by saying 'oops.' After all, it was an honest mistake, wasn't it?"

He grinned savagely, and his tone was viciously scarcastic as he went on.

"I can hear them now. 'We're *so* sorry that our very best efforts to sort out the facts went awry, but in the meantime we just happen to have conquered a small, insignificant star nation called Manticore. It's all very unfortunate, but there it is, and you can't pour the spilled milk back into the glass, you know. So we'll just have to set up an interim government under the auspices of Frontier Security—only until the Manties get back on their feet and can elect a properly democratic government on the best Solarian pattern, so that misunderstandings like this don't arise in the future, of course. We'd never *dream* of interfering with their right of self-determination beyond that! Cross our hearts!'"

"I suppose you're right," Elizabeth said drearily. "And if Sir Anthony's right about Abruzzi and their Ministry of Information's involvement in pushing this story, it sounds as if that's exactly what they're deciding to do."

"It's what they're preparing the groundwork to do, at any rate, Your Majesty," Langtry agreed quietly.

"And if those superdreadnoughts at Meyers actually do attack Spindle, then, especially against this backdrop of O'Hanrahan's story, they're almost certainly going to decide they're in too deep to back out," White Haven added.

"In that case, it's probably a good thing I finally listened to Honor." Elizabeth drew a sharp breath, then shook herself and smiled. It was a tense smile, and no one would ever have described it as a happy one, but there was no panic in it. "It looks like we're about to get a chance to see how sound her strategic prescription for fighting the Solarian League really is. And if we are, then it'll be a damned good idea to get the Republic of Haven off our backs while we do it. Do you suppose I ought to make that point to her when we send her her copy of Mike's dispatch?"

The smile turned almost whimsical with the last sentence, and White Haven chuckled.

"Trust me, Your Majesty. My wife's actually quite a bright woman. I'm pretty sure she'll figure that out on her own."

✧   ✧   ✧

Fleet Admiral Sandra Crandall had never been a good woman to disappoint. She was a big woman, with a hard, determined face and what one thankfully anonymous subordinate had once described as the disposition of a grizzly bear with hemorrhoids trying to pass pinecones. In fact, Commander Hago Shavarshyan thought, that had been a gross libel against grizzly bears.

Shavarshyan was in a better position than most to appreciate that, since he had the dubious good fortune of having been added to Crandall's staff as a last moment afterthought. Apparently, it had occurred to her only *after* she'd decided to go to war against the Royal Manticoran Navy that it might, perhaps, be a good idea to have a staff intelligence officer who actually knew something about local conditions. Which was how Commander Shavarshyan found himself the single Frontier Fleet officer attached to a fleet whose staff, like every one of its senior squadron and division commanders, consisted otherwise solely of Battle Fleet officers, all of whom outranked him, and all of whom seemed to be competing to see who could agree most vehemently with their admiral.

Those thoughts floated through the back of Shavarshyan's brain as he stood behind the briefing officer's podium while Crandall and the other members of her staff settled down around the long briefing room table aboard SLNS *Joseph Buckley*.

"All right," Crandall growled once they were seated. "Let's get to it."

"Yes, Ma'am."

Shavarshyan squared his shoulders and put on his best professional expression, although everyone in the briefing room knew he'd received no fresh data in the thirty-five days since they'd left Meyers. That, unfortunately, wasn't what Crandall wanted to hear about.

"As you know, Ma'am," he continued briskly, "Admiral Ouyang's people and I have continued our study of Admiral Sigbee's New Tuscany dispatches. We've combined their contents with all the information available to Frontier Fleet's analysts, as well, of course, and I've compiled a report of all our observations and conclusions. I've mailed copies of it to all of you, which should be waiting in your in-baskets, but for the most part, unfortunately, I'm forced to say we really don't have any startling new insights since my last report. I'm afraid we've pretty much mined out the available ore, Admiral. I wish I could offer you something more than that, but anything else would be pure speculation, at best."

"But you stand by this nonsense about the Manties' missile ranges?" Vice Admiral Pépé Bautista, Crandall's chief of staff, asked skeptically. Bautista's manner was more often than not caustic even with his fellow Battle Fleet officers, if they were junior to him. He clearly saw no reason to restrain his natural abrasiveness where a mere Frontier Fleet commander was concerned.

"Exactly which nonsense would that be, Sir?" Shavarshyan inquired as politely as possible.

"I find it hard enough to credit Gruner's report that the Manties opened fire on *Jean Bart* from forty million kilometers out." He grimaced. "I'd like to see at least some reliable sensor data before I jump onto *that* bandwagon! But even granting that's correct, are you seriously suggesting they may have even *more* range?"

"Sir, I'd like to have better data myself," Shavarshyan acknowledged, and that much was completely sincere. Lieutenant Aloysius Gruner was the commanding officer of *Dispatch Boat 17702*, the only unit of Josef Byng's ill-fated command to escape before Byng's death and Sigbee's surrender. Gruner had been sent off very early in the confrontation, which explained how he'd evaded the Manties to bring back news of the catastrophe in the first place. Apparently, Admiral Byng, in yet another dazzling display of incompetence, had seen no reason even to order his other courier boats to bring up their nodes, which meant they'd all still been sitting in orbit when Sigbee surrendered. They were fortunate the one boat he *had* ordered to get underway had still been close enough to receive Sigbee's burst-transmitted final dispatch—the one which had announced *Jean Bart's* destruction and her own surrender—but there'd been no time for her to send *DB 17702* detailed tactical reports or sensor data on the Manties' weapons. And, through no fault of Gruner's, he couldn't provide that information either, since courier boats' sensor suites weren't what anyone might call sophisticated. Although he'd been able to tell them *what* had happened, more or less, they had virtually no hard information on how the Manties had *made* it happen. Additional information might well have been sent to Meyers by now, but if so, it was still somewhere in the pipeline astern of Task Force 496.

Of course it is, Shavarshyan thought bitingly. *Anything else would actually have suggested there was at least a smidgeon of* competence *somewhere among the people running this cluster-fuck.*

"At the same time, Lieutenant Gruner *was* there," he continued out loud. "He saw what actually happened, and even if we don't have the kind of data I'd prefer, he was very emphatic about the engagement range. Nothing in Sigbee's dispatch suggests he was wrong, either. And given the geometry of the engagement, forty million kilometers at launch equates to something on the order of twenty-nine or thirty million kilometers from rest. Now, nothing we have—not even those big, system-defense missiles Technodyne deployed to Monica—have that kind of range, that kind of powered endurance, but thirty million klicks from rest would work out pretty close to the consecutive endurance for two missile drives at the observed acceleration. So, the only conclusion I can come up with is that they must really have gone ahead and put multiple drives into their missiles. And if they've put in enough drives to give them a powered envelope of *thirty* million kilometers, I just think it might be wiser to consider the possibility that they might have even more range than that."

His tone could not have been more respectful or nonconfrontational, but he'd seen Bautista's jaw tighten at the reference to Monica. Not, Shavarshyan felt confident, so much at the reminder of the Technodyne missiles' enhanced range as at the fact that the Manties' missiles had out-ranged even them. Which, of course, was the reason Shavarshyan had mentioned it.

Bautista started to open his mouth angrily, but Vice Admiral Ou-Yang Zhing-wei, Crandall's operations officer, spoke up before he could.

"I'm disinclined to think they could have a *great* deal more range, Pépé, but Commander Shavarshyan is right. It's a possibility we have to bear in mind."

"Yes, it is," Crandall agreed, although she manifestly didn't like doing so. "All the same," she continued, "it really doesn't matter in the long run. Assuming Gruner's observations and Sigbee's report were accurate at all, we already knew we were going to be out-ranged by at least some of these people's missiles. On the other hand, I agree with Sigbee—and with you, Commander—that no missile big enough to do that could be fired from missile tubes the size of the ones we've actually observed aboard even those big-assed Manty battlecruisers. So they had to come from pods."

She shrugged. Like the woman herself, it was a ponderous movement, without grace yet imbued with a self-aware sense of power.

"But whether they came from pods or missile tubes, they can't have the fire control links to coordinate enough of them to swamp the task force's point defense, and their accuracy at such extended ranges—assuming they actually have even more range—has to be poor. I know some of them will get through. We'll take damage—hell, we may even lose a ship or two!—but there's no way they're going to stop a solid wall of battle this size by just chucking *missiles* at it. And I'm not going to let them bluff me into going easy on them because of some kind of imagined 'super weapon' they've got!"

She snorted in contempt, and her eyes were harder than ever.

"By now that damned destroyer of theirs must've gotten back to Spindle. I imagine that once they all got done crapping their skinsuits, they sent home for reinforcements. But after the reaming they got from the Havenites, they can't have much left to reinforce *with*. So we're just going to turn up and be their worst nightmare, and we're going to do it right now."

"I understand your thinking, Ma'am," Ou-yang said. "And I agree we need to move quickly. But it's one of my responsibilities to see to it that we don't get hurt any worse than we can help while we pin their ears back the way they've got coming. And just between you and me, I'm not all that fond of surprises, even from neobarbs."

Ou-yang rolled her eyes drolly with the last phrase, and Crandall chuckled. At least, that was what Shavarshyan thought the sound was. It was difficult, sometimes, to differentiate between the admiral's snorts of contempt and snorts of amusement. In fact, the commander wasn't certain there *was* a difference.

At the same time, he had to admire Ou-yang's technique. The operations officer was the closest thing to an ally he had on Crandall's staff, and he rather thought she shared some of the suspicions which kept him awake at night. For example, there was that nagging question of exactly how someone like Josef Byng, a Battle Fleet officer with limitless contempt for Frontier Fleet, had ended up in command of the *Frontier Fleet* task force he'd led so disastrously to New Tuscany. Given the involvement of Manpower and Technodyne in what had happened in Monica, and knowing some of the dirty little secrets he wasn't supposed to know about Commissioner Verrochio and Vice Commissioner Hongbo, Shavarshyan had a pretty fair idea of who'd been pulling strings behind the scenes to bring that about.

Which brought him to the even more nagging question of exactly how Admiral Crandall had chosen the remote hinterlands of the Madras Sector for her "Exercise Winter Forage." He was willing to admit the distance from any of Battle Fleet's lavish bases in the Core and Shell made the sector a reasonable place to evaluate the logistic train's ability to sustain a force of Battle Fleet wallers for the duration of an extended campaign. On the other hand, they could have done the same thing within a couple of dozen light-years of the Sol System itself, if they'd wanted to pick one of the thoroughly useless, unsettled star systems in the vicinity and just park there.

But even granting that Battle Fleet had decided it just had to actually deploy its evaluation fleet hundreds of light-years from anywhere in particular in the first Battle Fleet deployment to the Verge in more than division strength in the better part of a century, it still struck him as peculiar that Sandra Crandall should have chosen this particular spot, at this particular time, to carry out an exercise which had been discussed off and on for decades. And one possible explanation for the peculiarity lay in the fact that *someone* had obviously had the juice to get Byng assigned out here *and* get him to agree to the assignment. If they could accomplish that outright impossibility, Hago Shavarshyan didn't see any reason they couldn't accomplish the mere implausibility of getting Crandall out here for "Winter Forage."

He didn't care for that explanation at all, which unfortunately made it no less likely. But it did leave him with another burning question.

How deep inside Manpower's pocket *was* Sandra Crandall? Shavarshyan hadn't been a Frontier Fleet intelligence officer for the last fifteen T-years without learning how things happened here in the Verge. So the fact that Manpower had an "understanding" with Verrochio and Hongbo had come as no surprise. He *was* surprised by Manpower's apparent reach inside Battle Fleet and the SLN in general, but it wasn't that much of a stretch from the arrangements he'd already known about. So he could more or less handle the concept of individual Battle Fleet admirals taking marching orders from Manpower.

He'd come to the conclusion that Byng, at least, had been more in the nature of a ballistic projectile than a guided missile, however. Certainly no one with any sense would have relied upon his competence to accomplish any task more complicated than robbing a candy store. If *he'd* been running an operation that sent Josef Byng out here, it would have been only because he anticipated that the man's sheer stupidity and bigotry would steer him into doing pretty much exactly what he'd actually done. He certainly wouldn't have taken the chance of explaining his real objectives to him, and he would never have relied upon the man's nonexistent competence when it came to achieving those objectives.

At first, Shavarshyan had assumed Manpower had been as

confident of Byng's ability to smash the Manties as Byng himself had been. On that basis, his initial conclusion had been that New Tuscany represented the failure of their plans. But then he'd started thinking about *Crandall's* presence. If they'd been confident Byng could handle the job, why go to the undoubted expense (and probably the risk) of getting seventy-plus ships-of-the-wall assigned for backup? That sounded more as if they'd expected Byng to get reamed ... which, after all, was precisely what had happened.

Assuming all of that was true, the question which had taken on a certain pressing significance for Hago Shavarshyan since his unexpected staff reassignment was what they expected to happen to *Crandall's* command. Was Byng supposed to provide the pretext while Crandall provided the club? Or was Crandall simply Byng written larger? Was *she* supposed to get reamed, as well? And was she aware of how her—call them "patrons"—expected and wanted things to turn out? Or was she another ballistic projectile, launched on her way in the confident expectation that she would follow her preordained trajectory to whatever end they had in mind?

If, in fact, Crandall was intentionally cooperating with Manpower, it seemed pretty clear Ou-yang Zhing-wei wasn't part of the program. Bautista was basically another Byng, as far as Shavarshyan could tell, but Ou-yang obviously had functioning synapses and a forebrain larger than an olive. In fact, it was the operations officer who'd convinced Crandall that she had to at least attempt a negotiated outcome instead of simply opening fire the minute she crossed the hyper limit. Bautista had all but accused Ou-yang of cowardice, and Crandall clearly hadn't cared for the note of moderation, but Ou-yang was at least as good at managing her admiral as she was at carrying out training simulations.

And the fact that it took this fat-assed task force a solid week *to get underway probably helped,* the commander thought sourly from behind his expressionless face. *Not even* Crandall *can argue that we're going to have the advantage of surprise when we arrive!*

He'd heard about Crandall's tirade in Verrochio's office, complete with her vow to be underway for Spindle within forty-eight hours. Unfortunately, the real life lethargy of Battle Fleet's stimulus-and-response cycle had gotten in her way.

Welcome to reality, Admiral Crandall, he thought even more sourly. *I hope it doesn't bite your ass as hard as I'm afraid it will, given that* my *ass is likely to get bitten right along with yours.*

Chapter Nineteen

"ALL RIGHT, DARRYL," Sandra Crandall said grimly. "I suppose it's time. Let's go ahead and talk to these people."

"Yes, Ma'am," Captain Darryl Chatfield, her staff communications officer replied, and turned to the attention light at his flag deck station which had been blinking for a studiously ignored forty-five minutes.

Task Force 496, Solarian League Navy, lay just outside the twenty-two light-minute hyper limit of the G0 star known as Spindle. The planet of Flax—the capital of both the star system and the Talbott Quadrant itself—lay nine light-minutes inside the limit, well beyond the range of any shipboard weapon. Which didn't change the fact that TF 496 was in flagrant violation of the territorial limit recognized by centuries of interstellar law. No government could have expected to actually police every cubic light-second of a sphere twelve light-hours across, yet warships were still legally required to respond to the challenges and requests for identification of any star nation once they crossed its "twelve-hour" limit. They were also legally required to acknowledge and obey any lawful instructions they received *from* that star nation, even if the star nation in question were some dinky little single-system in the back of beyond. They were normally granted at least some leeway in exactly how quickly they responded, but they were still supposed to honor their legal obligations in a reasonably timely fashion.

Which was precisely the reason Sandra Crandall had waited a carefully considered three-quarters of an hour before deigning to respond to the Manticorans' challenges, Commander Shavarshyan reflected. Not to mention the reason she'd decided to conduct her first contact with them from such an extended range. She could say all she wanted in her official report about remaining far enough out to respect the Spindle hyper limit in order to preclude any avoidable incidents, but the real reason was to make the Manties sweat during the nine-minute transmission lag each way. Conducting any sort of official conversation with that kind of delay built in between exchanges came under the heading of calculated insult—*additional* calculated insult, given her refusal even to identify herself as legally required—and she hadn't bothered to hide her enjoyment of the thought, at least in her private meetings with her senior staffers.

After all, he thought, *it would never do to have these neobarbs thinking we take them* seriously, *would it?* He shook his head mentally. *I think she'll take it as a personal failure if she misses a single opportunity to piss one of them off. And if she finds out she* has *missed one, I'm sure she'll go back and—*

His thoughts broke off rather abruptly, and his lips twitched with a sudden and utterly inappropriate desire to grin as a shortish, slender man with thinning gray hair appeared on the master com display. Instead of the cringing, perspiring poor devil Crandall had expected to discover bending anxiously over his com, imploring her to respond to his terrified communications pleas while he waited for the looming Solarian juggernaut to take note of his wretched existence, the man on the display wasn't even looking into his own pickup. Instead, he was angled two-thirds of the way away from his terminal, tipped back in his chair, heels propped on the seat of another chair which had been turned to face him, while he gazed calmly at the book reader in his lap. A book reader which was aligned—not, Shavarshyan suspected, just coincidentally—so that a sharp eyed observer could look over his shoulder and recognize a novel about the psychically gifted detective Garrett Randall by the highly popular Darcy Lord.

The man on the display went right on looking at his book reader, hit the page advance, then twitched as somebody outside the field of his own pickup hissed something in what had to be a carefully audible stage whisper. He glanced over his shoulder at his own display, then straightened, bookmarked his place, turned to face the com, pressed a button to terminate what had obviously been a purely automated repeating challenge, and smiled brightly.

"Well, *there* you are!" he said cheerfully.

For a moment, Shavarshyan cherished the hope apoplexy might carry Crandall off. Her demise would have to improve the situation. Although, he reminded himself conscientiously, that might be wishful thinking on his part. Admiral Dunichi Lazlo, BatRon 196's CO, her second-in-command, was no great prize... and no mental giant, either. Still, watching Crandall froth at the mouth and collapse in convulsions would have afforded the Frontier Fleet commander no end of personal satisfaction.

His hopes were disappointed, however.

"I am Admiral Sandra Crandall, Solarian League Navy," she grated.

"I see." The man on the display nodded politely, eighteen minutes later. "And I'm Gregor O'Shaughnessy, of Governor Medusa's staff. What can I do for you this afternoon, Admiral?"

He asked the question cheerfully enough, but as soon as he had, he nodded equally cheerfully to the pickup, turned back to the other chair, put his feet back up in it, and switched his book reader back on. Which made a sort of sense, if not exactly *polite* sense, given the two-way lag. After all, he had to do *something* while he waited. Unfortunately, Crandall didn't seem to feel that way about it. For just a moment she resembled an Old Earth bulldog who couldn't understand why the house cat draped along the sunny window sill was completely unfazed by her own threatening presence on the other side of the crystoplast, and her blood pressure had to be attaining interesting levels as O'Shaughnessy did to *her* precisely what she'd intended to do to *him*. Then she gave herself an almost visible mental shake and leaned closer to her own terminal.

"I'm here in response to your Navy's unprovoked aggression against the Solarian League," she told O'Shaughnessy icily.

"There must be some mistake, Admiral," he replied in a calm reasonable tone, looking back up from his novel again after the inevitable delay. Which did not, Shavarshyn thought, add to Admiral Crandall's sunny cheerfulness. "There hasn't been any unprovoked aggression against any Solarian citizens of which I'm aware."

"I'm referring, as you know perfectly well, to the deliberate and unprovoked destruction of the battlecruiser *Jean Bart*, with all hands, in the New Tuscany System two and a half months ago," she half-snapped, then slashed one finger at Chatfield. The com officer cut the visual from her end, and she turned her chair to face Bautista.

"This bastard's just *asking* for it, Pépé!" she snarled, still watching the Manticoran perusing his novel.

"Which will only make it even more satisfying when he finally gets it," the chief of staff replied. Crandall grunted and looked at Ou-yang.

"I don't think this brainstorm about 'negotiating' is going to work out very well, Zhing-wei." It wasn't quite a snarl, this time, although it remained closer to that than to a mere growl.

"Probably not, Ma'am," the operations officer acknowledged. "On the other hand, it was never for *their* benefit, was it?"

"No, but that doesn't make it any more enjoyable."

"Well, Ma'am, at least it's giving us plenty of time to take a look at what they've got in orbit around the planet," Ou-yang pointed out. "That's worthwhile in its own right, I think."

"I suppose so," Crandall admitted irritably.

"What *do* they have, Zhing-wei?" Bautista inquired, and Shavarshyan wondered—briefly—if the chief of staff was deliberately trying to divert Crandall's ire from the Manticorans. But the question flitted through his brain and away again as quickly as it had come. If anyone aboard *Joseph Buckley* was even more pissed off at the Manties than Crandall, that person was Vice Admiral Pépé Bautista.

"Unless we want to take the remotes in close enough the Manties may pick them up and nail them, we're not going to get really good resolution," Ou-yang replied. "We are picking up a superdreadnought and a squadron—well, eight, anyway—of those big heavy cruisers or small battlecruisers or whatever of theirs, but I'm pretty sure that isn't everything they've got."

"Why?" Crandall sounded at least a bit calmer as she focused on Ou-yang's report.

"We've got some fairly persistent 'sensor ghosts,'" the ops officer told her. "They're just a bit too localized and just a shade too strong for me to believe the platforms are manufacturing them. The Manties' EW capabilities are supposed to be quite good, so I'm willing to bet at least some of those 'sensor ghosts' are actually stealthed units."

"Makes sense, Ma'am," Bautista offered. "They probably want to keep us guessing about their actual strength." He snorted harshly. "Maybe they think they can pull off some sort of 'ambush!'"

"On the other hand, they might just be trying to make us worry about where the rest of their ships are," Ou-yang pointed out. The chief of staff frowned, and she shrugged. "Until we actually turned up, they couldn't have been confident about what kind of strength we'd have. They may have expected a considerably smaller force and figured we'd be leery of pressing on when the rest of their fleet might turn up behind us at any moment."

Shavarshyan started to open his mouth, then closed it, then drew a deep breath and opened it again.

"Is it possible," he asked in a carefully neutral tone, "that what they're really trying to do is to convince us they're even weaker than they actually are in order to make us overconfident?"

He knew, even before the question was out of his mouth, that the majority of his audience was going to find the very idea preposterous. For that matter, he didn't really expect it to be true himself. Unfortunately, suggesting possibly overlooked answers to questions was one of an intelligence officer's functions.

Crandall and Bautista, however, didn't seem to appreciate that minor fact. In fact, they both looked at him in obvious disbelief that even a Frontier Fleet officer could have offered such a ludicrous suggestion.

"We've got seventy-one *ships-of-the-wall*, Commander," the chief of staff said after a moment in an elaborately patient tone. "The last thing these people want to do is actually *fight* us! They know as well as we do that any 'battle' would be a very short, very unhappy experience for them. Under the circumstances, the *last* thing they'd want would be to make us even more confident than we already are. Don't you think they'd be more interested in encouraging us to feel *cautious*?"

Shavarshyan's jaw tightened. It was hardly a surprise, however; he'd known how Bautista would react before he ever spoke. That, unfortunately, hadn't relieved him of his responsibility to do the speaking in question. But then, to his surprise, someone else spoke up.

"Actually, Pépé," Ou-yang Zhing-wei said, "Commander Shavarshyan may have a point." The chief of staff looked at her incredulously, and she shrugged. "Not in the way you're thinking. As you say, they can't *want* to fight us, but they may have orders to do just that. And I suggest all of us bear in mind that this particular batch of neobarbs has been fighting a war for the better part of twenty T-years."

"And that experience is somehow supposed to make battlecruisers and heavy cruisers capable of taking on superdreadnoughts?" Bautista demanded.

"I didn't say that," Ou-yang replied coolly. "What I'm suggesting is that whether they want to fight us or not, there probably aren't a whole lot of shy and retiring Manty flag officers these days. Hell, look at what this Gold Peak's already done! So if they've got orders to fight, I expect they'll follow them. And in that case, it's entirely possible they'd want us to underestimate their strength. It might not help them a *lot*, but when the odds are this bad, I'd play for any edge I could find, if I were in their place."

"I see your point, Zhing-wei," Crandall acknowledged, "but—"

"Excuse me, Ma'am," Captain Chatfield said. "Two minutes to the Manties' response."

"Thank you, Darryl." Crandall nodded to him, then looked back at Bautista and Ou-yang. "There may be something to this, Pépé. At any rate, let's not automatically assume there *isn't*. I want you and Zhing-wei to give me an analysis based on the possibility that all of her sensor ghosts are those big-assed battlecruisers. And another based on the possibility that all of them are superdreadnoughts that managed to get here from Manticore faster than we got here from Meyers. Understood?"

"Yes, Ma'am," Bautista acknowledged, although it was evident to Shavarshyan that he continued to put very little credence in the suggestion.

Crandall turned back to face the com display and composed her features just as O'Shaughnessy nodded from it.

"Oh, I'm perfectly well aware of what happened in New Tuscany, of course, Admiral," O'Shaughnessy said with an affable smile. Then his eyes narrowed, and his voice hardened ever so slightly. "I'm just not aware of any unprovoked aggression on the *Star Empire's* part."

He looked out of the display at her for another heartbeat, then deliberately cocked his chair back and returned his attention to his novel.

Crandall seemed to swell visibly, and Shavarshyan closed his eyes. He wasn't especially fond of Manties himself, but he had to admire the skill with which O'Shaughnessy had planted his picador's dart. On the other hand, he also had to wonder what the lunatic thought he was doing, baiting the CO of such a powerful force.

"Unless you wish me to move immediately upon your pathetic little planet, I advise you to stop splitting semantic hairs, Mr. O'Shaughnessy," Crandall said, as if underlining Shavarshyan's last thought, and her expression was as ugly as her tone. "You know damned well why I'm here!"

"I'm afraid that since I'm not a mind reader, and since you haven't bothered to respond to any of our earlier communication attempts, I really don't have a clue as to the reasons for this visit," O'Shaughnessy told her coolly eighteen minutes later, looking up from his reader once more. "Perhaps the Foreign Ministry proto-colists back in Old Chicago will be able to figure it out for me when they play back the recording of your edifying conversation which will undoubtedly be attached to Her Majesty's next note to Prime Minister Gyulay."

Crandall twitched as if he'd tossed a glass of ice water over her, and her face turned a full shade darker at his none too subtle reminder that whatever her ultimate intentions might be, this was at least theoretically an exchange between official representatives of two sovereign star nations.

"Very well, Mr. O'Shaughnessy," she said with icy precision. "In order to avoid any misunderstandings—any *additional* misunder-standings, I should say—I would like to speak to . . . 'Governor Medusa' personally."

She slashed her finger at Chatfield again, bringing up *Joseph Buckley*'s wallpaper in place of her own image. Then she went a step further, pressing the stud that cut off the Manticorans' video feed as well, and glared at the blank display.

No one offered any theories this time as the admiral sat stol-idly and silently in her command chair. Bautista, Ou-yang, and Ou-yang's assistants were poring over the take from the remote reconnaissance platforms, and Shavarshyan suspected they were just as happy to have something else to do while their admiral fulminated. He wished *he* did. In fact, he punched up his own threat analysis files and sat earnestly—and obviously—studying the already thoroughly studied and over-studied data. The minutes dragged by until Chatfield cleared his throat.

"One minute to the Manties' response, Ma'am," he said in an extraordinarily neutral tone.

"Turn it back on," Crandall growled, and the display came back to life.

O'Shaughnessy had been reading his book again until Crandall's demand to speak to Medusa actually reached him nine minutes earlier. Now he looked up.

"I see." He gazed at her for a moment, then nodded. "I'll see if the governor's available," he said, and his image was replaced by the Star Empire of Manticore's coat of arms.

The silence on *Joseph Buckley's* flag bridge was intense as this time the Manties turned on *their* wallpaper. As the single Frontier Fleet outsider present, what Shavarshyan felt was mainly dark, bitter amusement as he sensed the conflicting tides within Crandall's staffers. They were only too well aware of her fury, and most of them obviously wanted to express their own anger to show how deeply they agreed with her. But at the same time, a counter-vailing survival instinct left them hesitant to launch into a flood of vituperation at O'Shaughnessy's arrogance for fear of drawing Crandall's ire down upon themselves when her frustration lashed out at the nearest target of opportunity. It was an interesting dilemma, he reflected, since their silence might also be construed as an effort to avoid any suggestion that O'Shaughnessy had just humiliated Crandall by putting her in her place.

He was just making a mental bet with himself that Bautista would be driven to speak before Ou-yang when the Manticoran wallpaper disappeared and a smallish woman with dark, alert, almond-shaped eyes appeared on the master display in its place. He recognized Dame Estelle Matsuko, Baroness Medusa, from his file imagery, and she looked remarkably composed. But there was something about the glitter in those dark eyes...

Not a woman to take lightly, Shavarshyan decided. Particularly not after the exchanges between O'Shaugnessy and Crandall. In fact, her obvious self-control only made her more dangerous. And if anger sparkled in the depth of those eyes, there was no more sign of fear than there'd been in O'Shaughnessy's, as far as *he* could see. Indeed, she looked much too much like the matador, advancing into the ring only after her picadores had well and truly galled the bull. Which, given that she was clearly not an idiot and *had* to be aware of the minor fact that she had nine obviously hostile squadrons of ships-of-the-wall deliberately violating her star system's territoriality, made Hago Shavarshyan extremely nervous.

"Good afternoon, Admiral Crandall," she said frostily. "What can I do for the Solarian League Navy?"

"You can begin by surrendering the person of the flag officer who murdered Admiral Josef Byng and three thousand other Solarian military personnel," Crandall said flatly. "After that, we can discuss the surrender of every warship involved in that incident, and the matter of reparations to both the Solarian League and to the survivors of our murdered spacers."

This time, neither party was prepared to retreat behind its wallpaper. Personally, Shavarshyan thought that was fairly foolish, given that they couldn't reduce the awkward intervals between exchanges even if they'd wanted to. Yet if it was arguably foolish for Medusa, it was much more obviously foolish for Crandall. She was an admiral in the Solarian League Navy—a Battle Fleet admiral—on what she'd intended from the beginning to be a punitive expedition, and there she sat, locking eyes—uselessly—with a com image which was nine minutes old by the time she even saw it. The image of the official representative of the star nation of neo-barbarians she'd set out to chastise.

"I see," Medusa said finally. "And you think I'm going to submit to your demands because—?"

She cocked her head slightly and raised polite eyebrows.

"Unless you're considerably more foolish than I believe," Crandall's tone made it obvious *no one* could be more foolish than she believed Medusa was, "the nine squadrons of ships-of-the-wall just outside your hyper limit should suggest at least one reason."

Yet another endless interval dragged past; then Medusa nodded calmly.

"Which means I should assume this enumeration of warships is intended to communicate the threat that you're prepared to commit yet more acts of deliberate aggression against the Star Empire of Manticore?"

"Which means I am prepared to embrace whatever means are necessary to safeguard the sovereignty of the Solarian League, as every Solarian flag officer's standing orders require," Crandall retorted.

It was remarkable, Shavarshyan thought, still studiously pondering the facts and figures on his own display, how an eighteen-minute wait between exchanges undeniably robbed threats of immediacy and power while simultaneously distilling the pure essence of anger behind them.

"First of all, Admiral Crandall," Medusa said calmly after the inevitable delay, "no one's transgressed against the sovereignty of the Solarian League. We've simply taken exception to the massacre of our ships and our personnel and insisted that the man responsible for that massacre answer to the applicable provisions of interstellar law. Interstellar law, I might add, which has been formally recognized and codified by the Solarian League in several solemn treaties.

"Admiral Gold Peak gave Admiral Byng every opportunity to avoid any additional violence, and when he refused to take any of them, she fired on only one of his ships—the one he happened to be aboard at the moment, to be precise—when she could just as easily have fired on all of them. She also *ceased* fire and extended yet another opportunity to avoid bloodshed—*further* bloodshed—after Admiral Byng's . . . demise."

Crandall's expression was livid, but Medusa continued in that same tone of deadly calm.

"Secondly," she said, "we happen to be in possession of the file copies from Admiral Sigbee's flagship of both her own and *Admiral Byng's* standing orders, which I presume must have been at least generally similar to your own. Oddly enough, there's nothing in them about committing blatant acts of war against sovereign star nations. Aside from little things like 'Case Buccaneer,' that is, but we won't go into that particular 'contingency plan' at this point. Unless you insist on discussing Frontier Fleet, OFS, piracy, and 'disappeared' merchant ships officially and on the record, of course."

Her dark eyes glittered, and Shavarshyan inhaled sharply as the Manticoran's steely smile challenged Crandall to press her on that point in an official exchange both sides knew was being recorded.

"I make this point only to clarify the fact that we're well aware you're acting at the present moment on your own authority," Medusa continued after a moment. "Mind you, I'm equally well aware that one of the functions of a flag officer this far from her star nation's capital is to do precisely that in moments of crisis. However, you would do well to consider that in this instance the Star Empire of Manticore has already communicated formally with the Solarian League on Old Terra about both New Tuscan incidents. I am in receipt of copies of the League's official responses to those communiques, should you care to view them. And if you would care to avail yourself of the Lynx Terminus, we would be quite happy to send your own dispatches directly to Old Chicago, should you wish to seek guidance from your superiors before we have another of those...misunderstandings, I believe you called them? I suspect those superiors might not be entirely pleased if some avoidable 'misunderstanding' on your own part leads to a further regrettable escalation of the tensions between the Solarian League and the Star Empire."

From the corner of his eye, Shavarshyan saw Ou-yang Zhing-wei purse her lips as that salvo went home. Medusa's confirmation that Manticore had not simply captured Sigbee's databases but hacked their most secure files was bad enough. The Manticoran's pointed suggestion that she knew far more about the League's official reaction to New Tuscany than Crandall possibly could had been even worse. Whether Bautista and Crandall were prepared to face the implications or not, Ou-yang clearly recognized the diplomatic minefield Task Force 496 was about to enter. And, just as clearly, she understood that no naval officer's connections were so good she couldn't be thrown to the wolves if she screwed up too egregiously. Crandall, fortunately for her blood pressure, if not for anything else, was too busy glaring at Medusa to notice the ops officer's expression. It was, perhaps, less fortunate that she was so totally infuriated that she also completely ignored Medusa's offer to put her into direct communication with her superiors on Old Terra. Clearly, the baroness was telling her it wasn't too late to take a deep breath and back down under cover of the diplomatic smokescreen of seeking guidance from above.

It was a pity Crandall wasn't paying attention.

"I have no intention of sitting here for a solid T-month while you and your 'Star Empire' redeploy your own warships, Madame Governor," the admiral said coldly. "My standing orders require what I believe my standing orders require, and the terms I've already stated are the minimum I'm prepared to accept."

And then she sat there again, glaring at Medusa's image, while rage and fury fermented inside her.

"And if I should happen to reject your 'minimum terms'?"

Shavarshyan couldn't decide whether the ever so slight curl of Medusa's lip was deliberate or an involuntary response which had escaped her formidable self-control. In either case, the unstated contempt came through quite nicely.

"In that case, *Governor*," Crandall responded, "I will advance upon the inhabited planet of your star system. I will engage and destroy every military starship in the system. And after I've done that, I'll land Marines on your planet and secure control of it in the name of the Solarian League until an appropriate civilian administration can be set up by the Office of Frontier Security. And, I feel confident, Frontier Security will continue to administer this world—and every other planet of your so-called Talbott Quadrant—until such time as the Solarian League's just requirements for accountability and redress are fully satisfied."

She paused very briefly, her smile thin and cold, as she deliberately raised the stakes. Then she continued in that same, cold voice.

"I'm prepared to to give you the opportunity to comply with my reasonable demands without further loss of life or destruction, but the Solarian League Navy doesn't intend to permit an act of war against the League to pass unanswered. I have no doubt you have indeed been in communication with the League. I also have no doubt of where my own duty lies, however. Because I have no desire to see additional avoidable bloodshed, I will give you precisely three T-days from the moment my ships made their alpha translations to accept my terms. If you do not do so within that time, I *will* cross the limit and proceed exactly as I've described, and the consequences of that will rest upon *your* shoulders. In the meantime, I'm uninterested in any further communication of yours, unless it is for the purpose of accepting my terms. Good day, Governor."

She stabbed a button, and the display went blank.

"All right, Clement," Karol Østby said quietly, "let's not stub our toes at this point, okay?"

"Yes, Sir." Commander Clement Foreman, Østby's operations officer, smiled tautly at him on MANS *Chameleon*'s cramped flag bridge.

The scout ship had reached her rendezvous with *Ghost* and *Wraith* as all three of them crept ever so cautiously towards the final deployment point. This was, in many ways, the riskiest moment of their entire mission—and the tension on the flag bridge could have been carved with a blade.

Foreman considered his displays for a moment, then keyed his mike.

"All emplacement teams, this is Control," he said. "Proceed."

Absolutely nothing changed on the flag bridge itself, yet Østby felt an almost tangible release as the order was finally given. Which was about as irrational as responses came, he supposed. The scout ships themselves were extraordinarily stealthy, and the arrays they were about to emplace were equally so. Which meant they were actually entering the moment of maximum danger as they deployed their work parties with the tools and equipment necessary for their task, since those tools and that equipment, while still very hard to detect, were considerably *less* stealthy. And still, however unreasonable it might be, there was that sense of relief—not relaxation, only *relief*—as they actually set about it at last.

He watched his own displays, listening over his earbug as progress reports flowed into flag bridge. He knew perfectly well that it wasn't really taking as long as it felt like it was taking, just as he knew how critical it was that they take the time to be sure it was done right, but whatever he might know intellectually, it didn't *feel* that way.

He looked at the date/time display, and a fresh sense of confidence swept through him. His people had trained far too hard, mastered their duties far too completely, to screw up now. They would fail neither him nor the Alignment . . . and in another fifteen days, the entire galaxy would know that as well as *he* did.

Chapter Twenty

"ALL RIGHT, JACOMINA," Sandra Crandall said flatly. "These people have just run out of time."

"Yes, Ma'am." Captain Jacomina van Heutz, SLNS *Joseph Buckley*'s commanding officer, nodded from the small display on Crandall's flag bridge. The admiral looked over her shoulder at Bautista and Ou-yang, and both of them nodded, as well. Shavarshyan thought Ou-yang's nod seemed less cheerful than Bautista's, although that could have been his imagination.

But whatever the ops officer might be feeling, it didn't matter. Not anymore. As Crandall had just observed, the Manties' time had run out, and she wasn't wasting any effort on additional attempts to communicate. Nor was she demonstrating a great deal of finesse, although the intelligence officer supposed there wasn't much point being fancy when you were a sledgehammer and your target was an egg.

He'd helped Ou-yang work on her analysis of the sensor ghosts her recon platforms had been picking up, and he'd come to the conclusion that the operations officer was correct. Those "ghosts" really were there, although it had proven impossible to wring any details out of the frustratingly vague data. Apparently the reports about the efficacy of Manticoran stealth systems had actually understated the case, which didn't make Shavarshyan a lot happier when he reflected on all the *other* reports which had been so confidently dismissed by naval intelligence at the same time.

And to add insult to injury, it seemed the ops officer's fears about the Manties' ability to pick up *their* recon platforms had been well founded. They'd tried getting in close enough for a better look, and each time their platforms had been detected, localized, and killed before they could get close enough to penetrate their targets' stealth. He wasn't at all certain Solarian sensors could have locked them up that well, but from Ou-yang's reaction, he suspected it would have been at best a toss-up.

On the other hand, there were only ten of those ghosts. Even if every one of them was a superdreadnought, Crandall's force still outnumbered the enemy by a margin of almost seven-to-one, and even if every single story about Manticoran capabilities proved accurate, those were still crushing odds. And if, as seemed much more likely, they were simply more of those outsized battlecruisers, Bautista's confident expectation of a rapid, devastating victory was amply justified.

Shavarshyan wondered if he was the only one who felt dismay at that prospect. He'd continued to hope the Manties might recognize the insanity of taking on the entire Solarian League. Both sides had painted themselves thoroughly into corners, yet he'd hoped—almost prayed—that Medusa would recognize she was dealing with a maniac. That Crandall really would destroy every single Manticoran ship in the star system unless the Manticoran governor gave her what she wanted.

But it would appear Medusa was just as done talking as Crandall. Despite the horrific odds, she'd declined to take the only escape available to her uniformed men and women, and now Hago Shavarshyan was going to be an unwilling party to their massacre. That was bad enough, yet what was going to happen when word of this reached the capital system of the Star Empire of Manticore would be even worse. When the SLN did come face-to-face with a true Manticoran battle fleet—when Manty superdreadnoughts squared off against their Solarian counterparts in anything remotely resembling even numbers—the carnage was going to be incredible. Whatever Crandall and Bautista thought, *he* knew better, and so did Ou-yang Zhing-wei. And the inevitability of the League's final victory was going to be very cold consolation to the mothers and fathers and wives and husbands and children of the thousands of people who were going to be killed first.

It was like watching helplessly from an orbiting satellite as an airbus loaded with schoolchildren plummeted directly towards a mountainside, and even though none of it had been his decision, he felt contaminated—unclean—as the eagerness of Crandall, Bautista, and the others like them flowed about him.

At least it should be fairly quick, he thought grimly as the battle boards at Ou-yang's station flickered from the amber of standby to the unblinking blood-red of readiness. Then he grimaced at his own reflection. *Sure it'll be "quick"; and isn't it a hell of a thing when that's the best I can think of?*

"So much for any last-minue outbreak of sanity on their side."

Captain Loretta Shoupe looked up from her displays and wondered if Augustus Khumalo was as aware as she was of how calm his voice sounded. She glanced at his profile as he studied the icons in HMS *Hercules'* flag bridge master plot, and the calmness of his expression, the steadiness of his eyes, were not the surprise they once would have been.

He's grown, she thought, with a possessive pride whose fierceness *did* surprise her a bit, even now. *He's no happier about this than anyone else, but if there's a gram of hesitation anywhere in him, I can't see it.*

"Well," Khumalo said with more than a little regret, "I suppose it's time." He raised his voice slightly. "Communications, pass the word to *Tristram.* Instruct Commander Kaplan to execute Paul Revere. Then contact Commodore Terekhov and inform him that Code Yankee is now in effect. Captain Saunders," he looked down at the command chair com display tied into *Hercules'* command deck, "tactical command is passing to Commodore Terekhov at this time."

"Yes, Sir," Victoria Saunders replied, and he sat back in his chair. Much as it galled him to admit it, *Quentin Saint-James'* fire control was far better suited to manage modern missile fire than his aged flagship's antiquated systems. He'd actually considered shifting his flag in order to exercise tactical command himself, and a part of him wished he had, even now. But efficiency was more important than getting his own combat command ticket punched. And Augustus Khumalo was too self-honest to pretend he was in Aivars Terekhov's league as a combat commander.

"Signal from *Hercules*, Ma'am," Lieutenant Wanda O'Reilly announced. "Execute Paul Revere."

"Acknowledged," Naomi Kaplan replied. O'Reilly was the closest thing HMS *Tristram*'s officer complement had to a genuine problem child, but there was no trace of her occasional petulance in that crisp report. Kaplan gave her a nod of approval, then looked at Abigail Hearns.

"Is your sensor data fully updated, Guns?"

"We're just finishing an update from Commodore Terekhov now, Ma'am," Abigail replied, watching the waterfall graphic rising steadily on one of her side displays. "Estimate fifteen seconds to complete the upload."

"Very well." Kaplan turned to Lieutenant Hosea Simpkins, her astrogator and, like Abigail, one of her Grayson officers. "Astro, unless Tactical's update hits a glitch, execute Paul Revere in twenty-five seconds."

"Aye, aye, Ma'am. Execute Paul Revere in twenty-five seconds from . . . now."

✧   ✧   ✧

Tristram disappeared from normal-space forty light-minutes outside the Spindle hyper limit without fuss or bother. Unlike the translation from hyper-space into normal-space, a stationary *upward* translation left no betraying footprint behind, and she materialized almost exactly where she was supposed to be in the alpha bands.

"Fleet challenge, Ma'am!" O'Reilly announced.

"Reply," Kaplan ordered calmly.

"Replying, aye, Ma'am," the com officer acknowledged, and triggered *Tristram*'s transponder code.

That transponder had been locked down, for fairly obvious reasons, while the destroyer hid outside Crandall's massive task force. And while Kaplan didn't really anticipate any itchy trigger fingers among the rest of Tenth Fleet's tactical officers, she still felt a profound sense of relief when HMS *Artemis* acknowledged her identity. Unlike Sandra Crandall, Naomi Kaplan had an excellent appreciation of just how much firepower was waiting for her.

"Very well, Guns," she said, once *Tristram*'s right to be there had been confirmed. "Send the data."

"Aye, aye, Ma'am. Sending now."

"Lord, what an *arrogant* bitch," Michelle Henke said quietly, standing between Dominica Adenauer and Cynthia Lecter as the three of them studied the data *Tristram* had just transmitted to *Artemis*.

"And this is a surprise because—?" Lecter asked equally quietly, and Michelle snorted in bitter amusement.

"More a case of a confirmation I didn't really want," she acknowledged. "I did think she might at least inform the governor her time limit had officially expired, though."

"With all due respect, Ma'am, I don't see where it makes much difference." Lecter twitched her shoulders slightly. "It's obvious the same people who picked Byng also picked her, and whether she's here as a knowing cat's-paw or got selected because she's just as stupid as he was, we all knew what she was here *for* from the outset."

Michelle nodded. And Cindy was right. She *had* known why Crandall was here, and all of her own planning had been predicated on that knowledge. Yet that didn't diminish the undeniable flicker of fury she felt as she contemplated Crandall's dismissive arrogance.

No, that's not being quite fair to yourself, girl, she thought. *Sure, part of you is pissed off because even though the overconfident idiot is doing exactly what you predicted when you made your own plans—exactly what you* want *her to do, if she's stupid enough to attack in the first place—you resent being taken so lightly. Because it's part and parcel of the kind of arrogance you've seen out of so many Sollies. But what* really *pisses you off is that she doesn't give a single solitary damn about all the people she's about to get killed. Of course—*her lips skinned back in a hexapuma's hunting snarl—*at the moment she's thoroughly convinced that none of the people in question are going to be* hers. *And she doesn't know she took long enough getting here for the Apollo pods to beat her, either.*

Her smile turned even thinner and colder for a moment as she contemplated how the arrival of those pods had changed her initial defensive planning. But then she put that reflection aside and concentrated on the data in front of her. There hadn't been any changes she could see, although a few additional details had been added to the initial report HMS *Ivanhoe* had delivered three days ago. Mostly little stuff, like additional data on individual ships' electronic and gravitic emissions.

As she'd expected, the various destroyers' emissions signatures varied widely, which wasn't surprising given how much the *Rampart* and *War Harvest* classes had been refitted over their lifetimes. The heavier ships' emissions were much closer to their "book" profiles, though. *Hercules'* CIC had easily tagged the individual units of Rear Admiral Gordon Nelson's battlecruiser squadron, since they'd lifted his ships' electronic fingerprints out of the data they'd captured from Byng's task force. And although they didn't have hard individual IDs on the other battlecruiser squadron, it was obvious all of them were *Nevadas*.

There was an impressive uniformity among the superdreadnoughts, as well. All but seven of them were *Scientist*-class ships, and all seven of the others were members of the *Vega* class, which were basically only repeat *Scientists* with a couple of additional missile tubes in each broadside. By the standards of the prewar Royal Manticoran Navy, they weren't that bad a design, although the first of the *Scientists* had been built long enough ago that they'd still been equipped with projectile-firing point defense systems. At least all of these ships seemed to have been upgraded to laser clusters since, judging from the detailed passive scans Augustus Khumalo's Ghost Rider platforms had pulled in. And it was painfully obvious that even now the Sollies didn't begin to grasp just how capable—and stealthy—the Ghost Rider recon drones actually were. To be sure, the really close passes had been purely ballistic, with no active emissions to betray their presence, but even so they shouldn't have been able to get in close enough to literally read ships' names off their hulls without someone noticing *something*.

Don't complain, she told herself firmly, and considered the armament readouts on Crandall's ships.

The *Scientists* were 6.8 million-ton units with thirty-two missile tubes, twenty-four lasers, and twenty-six grasers in each broadside. That was a heavier—or, at least, more numerous—energy broadside than any modern Manticoran or Grayson superdreadnought would have mounted. On the other hand, they had only sixteen counter-missile tubes and thirty-two point defense stations in each broadside, whereas *Artemis*, although technically only a battlecruiser, had thirty-two CM tubes and thirty much heavier and much more capable point defense clusters. Even the *Saganami-Cs* had twenty tubes and twenty-four clusters in each broadside, and given the fact that Michelle Henke had absolutely no intention of straying into energy range of her opponents, that imbalance was just likely to prove fatal for Admiral Sandra Crandall.

Stay out of energy range, hell, Michelle thought astringently. *I'm going to stay clear out of her missile envelope, too!*

"I wonder if Crandall's superstitious?" she mused. Adenauer looked up from the plot and raised one eyebrow, and Michelle chuckled coldly.

"You didn't recognize her flagship's name, Dominica?"

The ops officer shook her head, and it was Lecter's turn to chuckle.

"This is the sixth *Joseph Buckley* they've built," she said, "and I've got to wonder why even Sollies haven't learned from that much history. It hasn't been exactly the luckiest name in the SLN's history."

"Well, fair's fair, Cindy," Michelle pointed out. "They didn't name any of them for the luckiest *scientist* in history, either."

"Is that your understatement for the day, Ma'am?" Lecter asked, and this time Adenauer chuckled, too, as the name finally clicked for her, as well.

Dr. Joseph Buckley had been a major figure in the development of the original impeller drive on Beowulf in the thirteenth century. Unhappily, he hadn't been one of the more fortunate figures. He'd been a critical part of the original developmental team in 1246, but he'd had a reputation among his peers even then for being as erratic as he was brilliant, and he'd been determined to prove it was accurate. Although Adrienne Warshawski was to develop the Warshawski sail only twenty-seven years later, Buckley had been too impatient to wait around. Instead, he'd insisted that with the proper adjustment, the impeller wedge itself could be safely inserted into a hyper-space gravity wave.

Although several of his contemporaries had acknowledged the theoretical brilliance of his work, none had been prepared to endorse his conclusions. Unfazed by his peers' lack of confidence, Buckley—whose considerable store of patents had made him a wealthy man—had designed and built his own test vessel, the *Dahak*, named for a figure out of Babylonian mythology. With a volunteer crew embarked, he'd set out to demonstrate the validity of his work.

The attempt, while spectacular, had not been a success. In fact, the imagery which had been recorded by the *Dahak*'s escorts still turned up in slow motion in HD compilations of the most awe-inspiring disaster footage in galactic history.

While Buckley undeniably deserved to be commemorated alongside such other greats as Warshawski and Radhakrishnan, and despite the huge body of other work he'd left behind, it was the dramatic nature of his demise for which he was best remembered. And his various namesakes in SLN service had fared little better than he himself had. Of the current ship's predecessors, only one had survived to be withdrawn from service and decommissioned.

"Actually, only three of them were lost on active service, Cindy," Michelle pointed out.

"Four, if you count the battlecruiser, Ma'am," Lecter argued respectfully.

"Well, all right. I'd forgotten about her." Michelle shrugged. "Still, I don't think it's exactly fair to blame the 'Buckley Curse' for a ship lost 'to causes unknown,' though."

"Why? Because having witnesses makes it more final? Or because faulty fusion bottles and wedge-on-wedge collisions are more spectacular?"

"They're certainly more in keeping with the original's final voyage," Michelle pointed out.

"All right, I'll grant that much," Lecter agreed. "And, actually, I suppose losing only four of them—or three, if we go with your list—in the better part of seven hundred T-years probably isn't really *proof* the Curse exists. And I'm not an especially superstitious gal myself. But having said all that, *I* wouldn't care to serve aboard one of them! And especially not"—her smile disappeared and her eyes darkened—"if I was sailing into what promised to be the ugliest war my navy'd ever fought."

"Neither would I," Michelle acknowledged. "On the other hand, she doesn't think that's what she's doing, now does she?"

✧   ✧   ✧

Sir Aivars Terekhov sat in his command chair on HMS *Quentin Saint-James'* flag bridge and thought about the last time he'd taken a *Saganami-C*-class heavy cruiser into combat. By most navies' standards, the odds he faced were even worse this time, but he wasn't really interested in most navies' standards. Unlike Ou-yang Zhing-wei and Hago Shavarshyan, he knew precisely what those ten "sensor ghosts" they'd been picking up actually were.

Four of them were the CLACs *Pegasus*, *Hippogriff*, *Troll*, and *Goblin*, with the next best thing to four hundred LACs embarked. As stealthy as the Manticoran Alliance's light attack craft were, four CLACs were much smaller sensor targets than all those LACs would have been if they'd been deployed, which meant they could be more readily concealed or, at least, that their natures could be more readily disguised, while they remained in their shipboard bays.

Two more of the "ghosts" were ammunition ships, stuffed to the deckhead with Apollo missile pods crammed full of fusion-powered Mark 23 and Mark 23-E MDMs. And the other four were Scotty Tremaine's cruisers: *Alistair McKeon*, *Madelyn Hoffman*, *Canopus*, and *Trebuchet*.

You just keep right on coming, Admiral Crandall, Terekhov thought coldly. *You don't even begin to realize just how much you've got us exactly where we want you . . . but you're about to find out.*

"Sir, Admiral Khumalo would like to speak to you," Lieutenant Atalante Montella, his communications officer, said quietly.

"Put him on my display, Atalante."

"Yes, Sir."

A moment later, Augustus Khumalo's face appeared on the tiny com screen deployed from Terekhov's command chair.

"Good afternoon, Sir," he said.

"Good afternoon, Aivars," Khumalo acknowledged. The admiral looked considerably calmer than Terekhov suspected he actually was, and there was little sign of tension in his deep voice.

"As you can see," Khumalo continued, "our friend Crandall at least has the virtue of punctuality."

"I suppose anyone has to have at least *some* positive qualities, Sir."

"You may have been disabused of that supposition by the time you're my age," Khumalo replied with a thin smile. "At any rate, assuming she maintains her current acceleration and heads for a zero/zero intercept with the planet, she probably expects to be joining us here in about four hours. Of course, she doesn't expect any of us to still be *alive* when she gets here."

"Life is full of disappointments, Sir."

"My own thought exactly." Khumalo's teeth showed briefly. Then he twitched his shoulders in a sort of abbreviated shrug. "Admiral Enderby is launching his birds now. As soon as they're all clear of the bays, he'll pull the carriers further back in-system to keep them out from underfoot, and Commander Badmachin is rolling pods. Unless Admiral Gold Peak decides differently, it looks like we'll be going with Agincourt."

"Understood, Sir."

"In that case, I'll leave you to it," Khumalo said with a nod. "Khumalo, clear."

He disappeared from Terekhov's com screen, and Terekhov returned his attention to *Quentin Saint-James'* master plot. In many ways, he supposed, Oversteegen's *Nikes* might have been a better choice than his own heavy cruisers, given that the *Nike* was equipped with Keyhole, and the *Saganami-C* wasn't. In fact, before the ammunition ships *Aetna* and *Vesuvius* had arrived with their massive loads of Apollo pods, the *Nikes* would have been in orbit around Flax while the *Saganami-Cs* played the part of the beaters coming along behind the quarry. The cruisers still had a lot of control links, however. Almost certainly enough of them, coupled with Apollo, to show Crandall the error of her ways.

And if there isn't, he thought grimly, *there's always Admiral Gold Peak, isn't there?*

✧　　✧　　✧

"Captain?"

"Yes, Nicolette?" Captain Jacomina van Heutz looked across *Joseph Buckley's* command deck at Commander Nicolette Sambroth.

"Ma'am, I'm still picking up those grav pulses," Sambroth said, and van Heutz frowned.

Sambroth was one of the better tac officers with whom she'd served, but the commander appeared to have been badly spooked by the implications of the Manties' apparent FTL com ability. Not that van Heutz really blamed her, assuming the report of the single dispatch boat to escape the New Tuscan debacle was accurate. Not only that, but she knew Vice Admiral Ou-yang shared Sambroth's concerns.

And I'm not too damned happy over them myself. Especially when I think about what's going to happen two or three engagements down the road, when we run into a real Manty wall of battle. But for right now . . .

"You're passing your observations along to Admiral Ou-yang?" Her tone made the question a statement, and Sambroth nodded.

"Of course, Ma'am."

"Then we're just going to have to assume Admiral Crandall has that information as well," van Heutz pointed out rather gently.

Sambroth looked up from her displays. Their eyes met for a moment. Then the tactical officer nodded again, with a rather different emphasis.

Van Heutz nodded back, returned her own attention to her plot, and settled back in her command chair.

Josef Byng always was a frigging idiot, she thought. *I'm not even going to pretend I miss him, either. But this—*

She shook her head, eyes hardening on the plot, and wondered how many other members of the SLN officer corps secretly recognized that Byng's demise could only improve that officer corps' overall efficiency. Probably more than she was prepared to believe, actually. She certainly *hoped* so, at any rate, given what the ability to deny that reality implied. Yet as she contemplated what his removal was about to cost the Star Empire of Manticore—and ultimately cost the Solarian League Navy—the price tag seemed exorbitantly high.

And it's only going to get worse. No matter how bad I think it's going to be, it's only going to get worse.

✧　　✧　　✧

Captain Alice Levinsky, commanding officer of LAC Group 711, watched the *Shrikes* and *Katanas* of Carrier Division 7.1 forming up around Her Majesty's Light Attack Craft *Typhoon*. She was aware of a certain queasiness as she contemplated the juggernaut of superdreadnoughts rumbling steadily towards Flax. Against a Havenite wall of battle, even the Manticoran Alliance's newest-generation LACs no longer possessed anywhere near the survivability they'd boasted when the *Shrike-A* was first introduced all of nine T-years ago. And even if they had, superdreadnoughts—even Solly superdreadnoughts—were normally too heavily armored for even a *Shrike*'s enormous graser to damage significantly. Of course, the *Shrike-B*, like her own *Typhoon*, had significantly improved its graser's grav lensing when the newest generation of bow wall came in. The *Bravos* really could blast their way through SD armor, assuming they could get close enough.

Despite that, two-thirds of her LACs were *Katana*-class space-superiority fighters with magazines packed with Viper dual-purpose missiles, because Manticoran LAC doctrine had changed—especially after the hideous losses of the Battle of Manticore—to emphasize the missile defense role rather than the strike role. LACs were smaller and much more elusive targets than any hyper-capable ship and, especially with the new Mark 33 counter-missiles (or the Vipers based on the same missile body and drive), one of them could provide very nearly as much screening capacity as an all up destroyer. Which meant a LAC group had become the most effective (and least costly) means of bolstering a wall of battle's missile defenses, which also freed up the perpetually insufficient number of lighter starships for deployment elsewhere.

But, Levinsky reminded herself coldly, these weren't Havenite superdreadnoughts. They were *Sollies*, and that was an entirely different kettle of fish. Like the rest of Tenth Fleet's officers, Levinsky had studied the technical data from the captured Solarian battlecruisers attentively, and unless that data was grossly inaccurate, the Sollies' anti-LAC capabilities were even more primitive—a *lot* more primitive—than the Havenites' had been during Operation Buttercup.

Which suggested all sorts of interesting tactical possibilities to one Alice Levinsky.

"Commodore Terekhov confirms Agincourt, Sir," Lieutenant Stilson MacDonald said.

"Thank you," Scotty Tremaine acknowledged. There was no need for his communications officer to know just how much calmer his voice was than *he* was.

Had Captain Levinsky only known, a part of Tremaine—a rather large part, as a matter of fact—would have preferred to be sitting where she was rather than in his palatial command chair on the flag deck of a brand spanking new heavy cruiser. It wasn't so much that he doubted his competence in his present role as that he'd become so *comfortable* in his previous role.

How did a nice boy who only wanted to be a shuttle pilot end up sitting here, *of all places?* he thought wryly.

He'd really assumed that when he finally got starship command it would be of a carrier, not a cruiser. But he'd also long since concluded that BuPers worked in mysterious and inscrutable ways. True, this one seemed a bit more inscrutable than most, but when the Navy offered you a command slot like *this* one, you took it. He couldn't imagine anyone who wouldn't, and if anyone *had* turned it down, the idiot in question would have signed the death warrant for any hope of future promotion. The Navy wasn't in the habit of entrusting its starships to people whose own actions demonstrated they lacked the confidence for that sort of responsibility.

And if they really insist on prying me out of the LACs, this is one hell of a lot better than a kick in the head, he admitted. *Not only that, but at least they let me have the EWO I wanted.*

He glanced at the battered and bedamned-looking chief warrant officer sitting at the electronic warfare officer's station. Aboard any other starship he could think of, that position would have been held by a commissioned officer. Aboard a unit as powerful as a *Saganami-C,* especially on a division flagship's staff, the officer in question would have been at least a senior-grade lieutenant, and more probably a lieutenant commander. But CWO Sir Horace Harkness was pretty much a law unto himself within the RMN.

"Of course you can have Harkness!" Captain Shaw, Admiral Cortez's chief of staff, had snorted when he'd made the unusual request. "There's a note somewhere in your personnel jacket that says we're not supposed to break up Beauty and the Beast." The captain's lips had twitched at Tremaine's expression. "Oh, you hadn't heard that particular nickname, Captain Tremaine? I hadn't realized it had escaped your attention."

Then Shaw had sobered, tipping back in his chair and regarding Tremaine with thoughtful eyes.

"I don't say it's the sort of habit we really want to get into, Captain, but one thing Admiral Cortez has always recognized is that there are exceptions to every rule. Mind you, if it were just a case of favoritism, he wouldn't sign off on it for a minute. Fortunately, however, the two of you have demonstrated a remarkable and consistently high level of performance—not to mention the fact that between you, you and his wife seem to have permanently reformed him. So unless we have to, no one's interested in breaking up that particular team. Besides"—he'd snorted in sudden amusement—"even if we were, I'm quite sure Sir Horace would be more than willing to massage the computers in your favor."

Tremaine had opened his mouth, but Shaw had waved his hand before he could speak.

"I'm perfectly well aware that he's promised not to do that sort of thing anymore, Captain Tremaine. Even the best-intentioned can backslide, however, and we'd prefer not to expose him to *too* much temptation."

Tremaine's own lips twitched in remembered amusement, and he was astonished how much better the memory made him feel.

"All right, Adam," he said, turning to Lieutenant Commander Adam Golbatsi, his operations officer. "You heard Stilson."

"Yes, Sir. I'm on it," Golbatsi acknowledged.

"Good." Tremaine looked at Harkness. "Any change in their EW, Chief?"

"No, Sir. Not so's you'd notice." Harkness shrugged. "I know we didn't get complete stats on their wallers at New Tuscany, Skipper, but so far, these guys don't look to have anything better than Byng had. Or, if they do, they haven't bothered to bring it to the party yet."

"I have t' agree with Chief Harkness, Sir," Commander Francine Klusener, Tremaine's chief of staff said, looking up from her own console.

If there'd been anyone on his staff who might have had his or her nose put out of joint by finding a mere warrant officer in the staff electronic warfare officer's slot, Tremaine would have bet on Klusener. Not because the fair-haired, gray-eyed commander was anything but highly intelligent and competent in her own right. She was, however, by far the most nobly born of any of his staffers, with an accent that was almost as languid and drawling as Michael Oversteegen's. Fortunately, that was the *only* thing about her anyone could have accused of languor, and she and Harkness had actually hit it off very well from the beginning.

"I've been lookin' at th' take from th' platforms," she continued now. "They ought t' be pullin' out all th' stops after what happened t' Byng. Better safe than sorry, after all." She shrugged. "If they are, then I don't think th' attack birds are going t' have much problem lockin' up th' real targets."

"Compared to *Peep* EW?" Harkness shook his head with an evil smile. "Not hardly, Ma'am! These people're *toast*, if that's the best they've got."

"Let's not get carried away with our own enthusiasm, Chief," Tremaine said mildly.

"No, Sir," Harkness agreed dutifully.

Chapter Twenty-One

"COMING UP ON TURNOVER in two minutes, Ma'am."

Sandra Crandall looked up from a conversation with Pépé Bautista as her astrogator, Captain Berend Haarhuis, made the announcement, one hundred and fourteen minutes after her task force had started in-system. Its velocity relative to the planet Flax had increased to just over twenty-three thousand kilometers per second, and the range was down to a bit over eighty-one million kilometers, and Crandall nodded in satisfaction. Then she looked at Ou-yang Zhing-wei.

"Any more movement out of them?"

"No, Ma'am," Ou-yang replied. "We're picking up more of those grav pulses, though. And I'm still a bit concerned about this volume here."

She indicated a large-scale display of the space immediately about Flax. A zone directly on the far side of the planet was highlighted in amber, and Crandall glanced at the indicated area, then grimaced.

"The pulses have to be from that damned FTL com of theirs," she said with an impatient shrug. Her tone was irritated, perhaps even a bit petulant, as if she still didn't much care for admitting the Manties really had developed a practical faster-than-light means of communication. Unfortunately, even she had been forced to admit that what had happened at New Tuscany demonstrated that they had.

"At the moment, though," she continued, "all it really means is that they may be getting recon information on us a little quicker than we're getting it on them. It's not going to change the odds any. And unless they've magically teleported in reinforcements directly from Manticore, I'm not especially worried about what they may be hiding in that uncertainty volume of yours, either, Zhing-wei. There wasn't anything particularly scary in there before we started in, after all."

"No, Ma'am," Ou-yang concurred. An outside observer might have detected a smidgeon less than total agreement in her tone, however, Hago Shavarshyan thought. "On the other hand," she continued a bit diffidently, "we never did get a resolution on those sensor ghosts. And we've got these other impeller sources over here."

She dropped a cursor onto the master display, indicating the sextet of impeller wedges their remotes had picked up thirty-six minutes earlier. They hadn't been able to get a solid read on whatever was generating those impeller signatures, but from the wedge strength, whatever they were, they were well up into the multimillion-ton range ... despite the ridiculously high acceleration numbers they were putting out.

"Freighters," Bautista said dismissively. Ou-yang looked at the chief of staff, and he shrugged. "That's all they *can* be, Zhing-wei. Oh, I'll grant you they're fast. They must be fleet auxiliaries to pull that accel—probably supply ships; maybe repair ships—but they sure as hell aren't *warships*! With their assumed masses, they'd have to be superdreadnoughts, and with us bearing down on them this way, why run with six of them and leave number seven behind with nothing but cruisers to support it?"

"What I'm worried about is why they waited this long to run in the first place," Ou-yang said rather more sharply than she normally spoke to Bautista.

"Waiting until they figured out we really weren't bluffing, probably," he replied with another, slightly more impatient shrug. "Or maybe just waiting until they were sure all our units were headed in-system, without leaving any light units outside the limit to micro jump around the hyper sphere and pounce when they come out the other side."

"Or maybe until they'd finished offloading their cargo," Ou-yang said pointedly. Bautista arched an eyebrow, and the ops officer inhaled deeply.

"We've all agreed the missiles they used on *Jean Bart* had to come from *pods*, Pépé," she pointed out. "To get that kind of range, they have to be bigger than their battlecruisers' tubes can manage, right?" Bautista nodded, and it was her turn to shrug. "Well, I don't know about you, but *I* have to wonder how many pods six 'freighters' that size can transport. And I also have to wonder why it is that all of a sudden any recon drone we steer into a position to take a look at the planet's shadow is getting blown right out of space."

"You think they've stockpiled pods in that volume?" Crandall asked, intervening before Bautista could respond to Ou-yang's "God-give-me-strength" tone.

"I think there's *some* reason they don't want us seeing in there, Ma'am." The ops officer shook her head. "And I agree with Pépé that they wouldn't be sending away six ships-of-the-wall when we'll be into missile range of the planet in another hour and a half—not unless they were going to pull *all* of their ships out, at least. On the other hand, whatever these things are, their stealth and EW are good enough we couldn't get firm resolution on them—not even confirmation they were really there—until they lit off their impellers. So I think we have to look very carefully at the possibility that our departing bogies hung around, using EW to play hide and seek with our platforms until we actually started in-system, then pulled out after unloading some cargo that didn't have the same kind of stealth capability. Something we might've picked up if they'd just dumped it into orbit earlier. And if they've left something on the far side of the planet that they don't want us getting a good look at, missile pods are certainly the first possibility that leaps to my mind when I start thinking about that."

Bautista had flushed in obvious irritation, but Crandall nodded thoughtfully.

"Makes sense," she acknowledged. "Or as much sense as anything someone stupid enough not to surrender is likely to be doing, anyway. And you're right, six freighters that size could dump a hell of a lot of pods."

Bautista's expression smoothed quickly as Crandall took Ou-yang's suggestion seriously. It wasn't the first time something like that had happened, and Shavarshyan wished he could believe Crandall had deliberately chosen Ou-yang for her staff in hopes the ops officer's ability (for a Battle Fleet officer, at least) to think outside the box might offset Bautista's inclination towards sycophancy and his habit of automatically dismissing any opinion that didn't agree with his own. Much as the Frontier Fleet officer might have wanted to believe Crandall had done it on purpose, he wouldn't have wagered anything on the probability. Still, now that Crandall had endorsed at least the possibility that Ou-yang had a point, Bautista's expression, after a moment of blankness, had become intently—one might almost have said theatrically—thoughtful.

He may not do subtle very well, Shavarshyan thought dryly, *but he does have an awesome ability to spot the glaringly obvious, especially when someone rubs his nose in it. No, siree! No one's going to hide any flare-lit Old Earth elephants from Pépé Bautista in any dark rooms, no matter* how *hard they try!*

"All the same," Crandall continued, "whatever they've got stockpiled is still going to be bottlenecked by their available fire control."

"Agreed, Ma'am," Ou-yang acknowledged without even glancing in the chief of staff's direction. "On the other hand, as Commander Shavarshyan and I have both pointed out, we don't really know how good their fire control is." She shrugged. "There's no way a heavy cruiser, even one the size the Manties seem to be building these days, could match a waller where control links are concerned, but I think it's entirely possible they can throw bigger salvos than we'd anticipated."

"Maybe." Bautista's tone, like his expression, was much more thoughtful than it had been, and he pursed his lips. "I still don't see any way they could throw salvos big enough to saturate our defenses, though."

"I'm not saying they can," Ou-yang said. "But they may not have to *saturate* our defenses to get at least a few leakers through. The fact that they won't get a lot of concentrated hits doesn't mean we're not going to get hurt, and one way they might degrade our defenses would be to simply fire off huge numbers of missiles. Most of them might be basically blind-fired, but if they buried their real fire in that kind of background hash, it would take at least a little while for missile defense to sort out which were the genuine threats and engage them. It'd be wasteful as hell, and I'm not saying that's what they're going to do. I'm only saying they *could* do it, and that's why I'd feel a lot more comfortable knowing what they're so busy hiding."

"Well, I'm sure we'll be finding out shortly." Crandall smiled tightly. "And when we do, *they're* going to find out that—"

An alarm sounded, and Ou-yang stiffened in her chair.

"Status change!" she announced sharply. "We have hyper footprints directly astern of the task force, Ma'am!"

Crandall snapped around to the master plot as twenty-one fresh icons flared into existence four and a half light-minutes behind her own ships. Whatever they were, they'd popped out of hyper-space in an exhibition of pinpoint-precise astrogation. Their tightly grouped crash translation put them right on the limit, approaching it at almost five thousand kilometers per second, and everyone on *Joseph Buckley*'s flag bridge seemed to hold his or her breath while they waited for the sensor platforms Ou-yang had left behind to identify the newcomers.

Or *almost* everyone, at least.

"Turnover in fifteen seconds, Ma'am," Haarhuis announced.

Crandall's eyes flicked to the astrogator, then back to the plot, and her expression was grim. Whatever else those new icons might be, they had to be Manticoran warships—warships which had been waiting in hyper until her own force was deeply mired inside the star's hyper limit. And if it should happen that they were superdreadnoughts, her potential losses had just climbed drastically....

"The platforms make it fourteen of those big battlecruisers, what look like four light cruisers, and three ships in the four to five million-ton range," Ou-yang finally announced. The icons in the master plot blinked, changing color and shape to reflect the IDs CIC had assigned to each of them as lightspeed data on their emissions came in. "From their formation and emissions, it looks like the three biggies are probably freighters. Ammunition ships, I'd guess."

Her voice was taut, but it also carried an undeniable note of relief, and Hago Shavarshyan felt his own clenched stomach muscles relax. Crandall said nothing for a moment or two, but then she gave a sharp bark of a laugh.

"Well, I'll give them credit for audacity," she said as Bautista and Ou-yang looked at her. "This Gold Peak's obviously an *ambitious* bitch, isn't she?" The admiral jutted her chin at the icons beginning to accelerate in-system after her own forces. "And she must've used quite a bit of ingenuity arranging her ambush. But ingenious or not, she's no mental giant!"

Crandall gazed at the plot for a few more seconds, then glanced at Haarhuis.

"Go ahead and make turnover, Berend. Kick our decel to get us back on profile, then drop back to eighty percent."

"Yes, Ma'am," the astrogator acknowledged, and began passing orders as she turned back to Bautista and Ou-yang.

"Like I say, I'll give them marks for audacity," she said with a grim smile, "but falling in love with your own ingenuity can be painful sometimes." Her chuckle was harsh. "Bad enough for them to even think about 'ambushing' someone our size—reminds me of the story about the kid who tried to catch a house cat and wound up catching a tiger!—but they fucked up their timing, too. I don't care how much acceleration advantage they've got, they can't possibly overtake us until well after we've reached the planet and dealt with their friends in orbit."

"*Did* they screw up their timing, Ma'am?" Ou-yang asked. The admiral gave her a sharp look, and the ops officer shrugged. "I agree with what you just said about their ability to overtake us, but it strikes me as a bit of a coincidence that they should just happen to come in at almost *exactly* the same time we were scheduled to make turnover."

Crandall considered that for several moments, then grimaced.

"You may be right that the timing was deliberate. I can't imagine what kind of an advantage they'd think it would give them, though. And I don't think we should completely rule out the possibility that it really was a coincidence they hit so close to our turnover point. In fact, I'm still inclined to think that's exactly what it was. We know they've got a range advantage, at least as long as they stick to their missile pods, and we also know from what they did at New Tuscany that they can obviously tow at least a fair number of pods inside their wedges without compromising their acceleration. So what they probably wanted to do was to catch us in-system of them, stuck inside the hyper limit, with them outside us but close enough they could get into their range of us well before we reached the planet. There's no way we could match their acceleration rate, so as long as they were careful about it, they could probably get into their range of us while staying outside *our* missile range of *them*, and use their accel advantage to cut back out across the limit and escape into hyper if we reversed course to come after them. That's why I'm

pretty sure they screwed the pooch with their timing, because even
with the accel rates Gruner reported, they *can't* catch us with the
geometry they've actually got. And they damn sure can't do it
before we get to the planet, pound every warship in orbit around
it out of space, and bring the entire system's infrastructure—such
as it is and what there is of it—into our own range. At which
point they've got three options: surrender to keep us from trash-
ing all that infrastructure; go ahead and fight us on our terms,
in which case we still wreck their infrastructure and they all get
dead; or turn around and run away with their tails between their
legs when they run out of missiles."

Ou-yang nodded slowly, although Shavarshyan wasn't at all
sure the ops officer shared Crandall's conclusions. Or, at least,
that she shared her admiral's confidence. It was fairly obvious to
the Frontier Fleet officer that Ou-yang expected Task Force 496
to get hurt a lot worse than Crandall did, yet even the operations officer had to admit that two widely separated forces, each
massively inferior to the single enemy force between them, were
unlikely (to say the very least) to achieve victory.

✧　　✧　　✧

"Well," Michelle Henke said, gazing into the master plot on
HMS *Artemis'* flag bridge, "at least we know what she's going to
do now."

"Yes, Ma'am," Dominica Adenauer said. "Our arrival doesn't
seem to have fazed her, does it?"

"Fair's fair." Michelle shrugged. "There's not a lot else she could
do, really."

Adenauer nodded, although Michelle sensed her continuing
disgruntlement. It wasn't so much that Adenauer disagreed with
anything Michelle had just said as that the ops officer was accustomed to dealing with Havenite opponents, and no Havenite admiral
would ever have ambled this confidently towards a Manticoran
foe. The fact that Sandra Crandall was doing just that did not give
Dominica Adenauer a flattering estimate of the Solly's IQ.

Michelle shared that opinion, but she also stood by her observation about Crandall's alternatives. Her superdreadnoughts were
holding their acceleration to just over three hundred and thirty-
seven gravities, in strict accordance with the "eighty percent of
maximum power" which was the galactic naval standard inertial
compensator safety margin. At maximum military power, they

could have managed almost four hundred and twenty-two gravities, but that was it. At eighty percent power, Michelle's trio of four million-ton milspec ammunition ships—HMS *Mauna Loa*, *New Popocatépetl*, and *Nova Kilimanjaro*—could manage a hundred gravities more than the Solly SDs' maximum *military* acceleration; running flat out they could manage over six hundred and fifty gravities, while her *Nikes* could top six hundred and seventy.

What that meant was that Crandall's ships-of-the-wall could neither run away from her nor catch her if they tried to go in pursuit. And with Michelle outside Crandall's position, coming up her ships' wakes, there was really no way she could dodge, either. Nor could she possibly make it all the way across the hyper sphere to the opposite edge of the limit without being brought to action. And however confident Crandall might be of her task force's *defensive* capabilities, the Solarian admiral had to know her missiles were substantially out-ranged. In fact, just on the basis of what Michelle had done at New Tuscany before that first dispatch boat translated out, Crandall damned well ought to know her own anti-ship missiles' maximum powered envelope from rest was *at best* less than a quarter of that of the missiles which had killed *Jean Bart*. So, given her unpalatable menu of maneuver options, the one she was pursuing actually made the most sense. However nimble Michelle's *ships* might be, the planet couldn't dodge, and it was what Michelle had to defend. So if Crandall could get into her own range of Flax with what she no doubt believed to be her crushing superiority in missile tubes, she could compel Michelle to either come to her or concede *strategic* defeat regardless of any *tactical* advantages the RMN might possess.

And if we're wrong about our ability to penetrate their defenses, it could still work for her, Michelle conceded grimly.

She gazed into the plot for several more seconds, then turned and crossed to her command station. She settled into the chair, looking down at the com which was kept permanently tied in to *Artemis'* command deck.

"Captain Armstrong, please," she told the com rating monitoring the link.

"Yes, Ma'am!"

The rating disappeared. The crossed arrows of *Artemis'* wallpaper replaced her image for a moment, then disappeared in turn as Captain Victoria Armstrong appeared on Michelle's display.

"You called, Admiral?" she inquired. Her dark green eyes were guileless, but Michelle had long since discovered the wicked sense of humor which was just as much a part of Armstrong as the chestnut-haired flag captain's confidence and rock-steady competence.

"I believe I did," she replied. "Now, let me see...There was *something* I wanted to discuss with you, but..."

Her voice trailed off, and Armstrong grinned appreciatively at her.

"Could it have had something to do with that unpleasant person headed for Flax, Ma'am?" the captain suggested in a politely helpful tone, and Michelle snapped her fingers.

"That *was* what I wanted to talk about!" she said wonderingly, and heard someone behind her chuckling. Then own expression sobered. "So far, it looks pretty much like the alpha plan right down the line, Vicki."

"Yes, Ma'am," Armstrong replied, equally seriously. "Wilton and Ron and I were just discussing that. I have to wonder what's going through this Crandall's mind at the moment, though."

"I'd guess we gave her a bad few minutes when we turned up, judging by the way she delayed her turnover, but I imagine she got over it once she figured out we don't have any superdread-noughts. At any rate, I don't expect her to be screening us with any surrender offers anytime soon."

"That *would* make it simpler, wouldn't it, Ma'am?"

"Probably. But it looks like it's going to take Admiral Khumalo and Commodore Terekhov to convince her of that, after all. In the meantime, go ahead with the Agincourt Alpha variant. We'll just quietly follow along behind until—and unless—we're needed."

"Yes, Ma'am."

Michelle nodded to the captain, then turned back to the plot, tipping back her chair and crossing her legs as she considered the imagery.

At this scale, even Crandall's task force seemed to crawl across the display, and her own ships' motion was barely perceptible as they began building on the vector they'd carried across the alpha wall with them. Given the steady, consistent improvements in compensator design over the last ten or fifteen T-years, Man-ticoran captains—and admirals, she thought wryly—no longer fretted anywhere near as much as the officers of other navies over compensator safety margins. The fact that they'd been operating on a wartime basis for twenty T-years or so, rather than the *peacetime* basis of the rest of the galaxy had something to do with that, as well. The RMN had discovered that even with old-style compensators, "Book" safety margins had been excessively cautious, and Michelle's current acceleration rate was 6.5 KPS². She'd thought about restricting her accel, but there wasn't really much point. Even if the acceleration she'd displayed at New Tuscany hadn't been reported to Crandall, it must have already been reported to the SLN back on Old Earth in Sigbee's official report. And if Crandall hadn't already been aware of it, perhaps seeing it now might rattle the Solly.

Not that Michelle really expected it to have any impact on what was about to happen, and her mouth tightened as she recognized an all-too-familiar awareness deep down inside herself. She'd seen too many tactical plots like this one not to know what was coming, not to sense the inevitability.

She remembered the first time she'd seen a plot like this and known it wasn't a simulation. She'd trained for that moment her entire professional life, and yet, deep inside, she hadn't quite believed it was real. Or that it couldn't somehow be averted at the very last moment, at least. She'd done her best to prepare herself, and she'd thought, in her inexperience, that she'd succeeded.

She'd been wrong. Despite the most realistic exercises the Royal Manticoran Navy had been able to provide, she hadn't been ready—not truly—for mortality. Still hadn't come face-to-face with the reality that *she* could die as easily as anyone else. That the universe could survive her personal extinction and go right on. And, even worse perhaps, she hadn't really recognized that all the weapons and targeting systems would do precisely—and inevitably—what they'd been designed to do. That once those missiles were fired in earnest, other people *were* going to die in shocking, horrifying numbers, whether *she* did or not.

And now it was the turn of Sandra Crandall and all of the officers and enlisted personnel aboard *her* starships to face that recognition. She wondered how many would survive the experience.

❖   ❖   ❖

Gervais Archer watched his admiral and wondered what was going through her mind. As a rule, he felt generally confident of his ability to read her moods. She wasn't the most inscrutable person he'd ever met, after all. She could be as tactically sneaky and subtle as anyone he'd ever seen, but her personality was open and direct, not to mention stubborn, with a distinct tendency to come at things head on.

Yet at this moment, he couldn't read her body language. Not clearly. There was no sign of hesitance or uncertainty, no indication of second guessing herself, no sign any concern over future consequences would be permitted to erode present determination. But there *was* something. Something he wasn't accustomed to seeing from her, and he wondered why the word he kept thinking of was "sorrow."

Michelle Henke drew a deep breath and squared her shoulders, unaware of her flag lieutenant's thoughts as she ordered her own to attend to the business at hand.

Whatever's going to happen, it's going to happen. Too late to change that, and the decision wasn't really yours to begin with, girl. So instead of thinking about what Crandall's too damned stupid to see coming, think about what she is *doing right this moment.*

Actually, she rather suspected Crandall was doing exactly the same thing she was—staring at icons in a plot. Of course, her own data was far better than anything Crandall could have. Michelle had seeded the entire star system with FTL sensor platforms, and she'd paid special attention to the volume inside the hyper limit, particularly along the plane of the ecliptic. At the moment, her plot was being driven by a highly stealthy platform less than one light-second from Crandall's flagship, and the directional transmissions from the platform were less than five seconds old by the time she saw them on the display. Aside from the actual impeller signatures of Tenth Fleet's ships, any data *Crandall* had was almost five *minutes* old. At the moment, that meant little, but when the missiles started to fly, it was going to mean a great deal, indeed.

Thank you, Michael and Sir Aivars, she thought sardonically. *And thank* you, *Admiral Hemphill.*

She glanced at the time display. Five minutes had passed since her battlecruiser squadrons reentered normal-space. Crandall clearly had no idea she was already in Michelle's powered range, assuming Michelle was prepared to accept a two-and-a-half-minute ballistic phase between her second and third missile drives. Powered range wasn't necessarily the same thing as *accurate* range, though, and she wasn't about to waste birds from this far out unless she had to.

The range from Crandall to Khumalo and Terekhov was shrinking steadily, however. And when it fell to three light-minutes...

About another seventeen minutes, Admiral Crandall, Vice Admiral Gloria Michelle Samantha Evelyn Henke thought grimly. *Another seventeen minutes.*

✧   ✧   ✧

"I make it another seventeen minutes, Sir," Commander Pope said quietly, and Aivars Terekhov nodded, then looked at Commander Stillwell Lewis.

"Let's go ahead and spot the alpha launch, Stillwell."

"Yes, Sir."

Commander Lewis began inputting commands, and as those commands reached the shoals of pods the withdrawing ammunition ships had left behind, onboard tractors began reaching out from clusters of them. They locked onto the ships designated to control them, moving out of the planetary shadow, settling into launch position. And as if that had been a signal—which it had—the LACs which had been left behind by the CLACs began jockeying into position. If everything went as planned, those LACs wouldn't be needed, except to sweep up the pieces. Neither would Gold Peak's battlecruisers, for that matter. In fact, if *everything* went as planned, those battlecruisers would represent no more than an insurance policy which hadn't been needed after all. And, possibly, an additional threat to shape the thinking of the Solly CO.

Of course, everything seldom went "as planned," Terekhov thought, remembering his battle plans at Monica and a star called Hyacinth.

He watched Lewis, then glanced over his shoulder at Ensign Zilwicki and his somber mood lightened suddenly. In fact, he found it difficult not to smile, despite the approaching Solarian juggernaut. The eyes of his extraordinarily youthful flag lieutenant were bright with concentration, watching everything on *Quentin Saint-James'* flag deck. If she'd been a cat, the lashing of her tail would have presented a serious safety hazard.

"Calmly, Helen," he said softly, barely loud enough for her to hear, and she looked at him quickly. Their eyes met, and then she grinned crookedly.

"That obvious, was I, Sir?"

"Let's just say it's reasonably apparent that what you'd really like to be doing just now is Commander Lewis' job."

"Sorry, Sir." She grimaced. "It's just—"

"Just that the last time, you and Abigail were sitting in the hot seats," he acknowledged. "And you will be again, someday. Promise."

"Yes, Sir."

He gave her another smile, then turned back to his own displays and his own thoughts.

Despite the best efforts of both BuWeaps and BuShips, the Royal Manticoran Navy's missile pods kept obstinately proliferating, spinning off one new variant after another, and of late, pod capacity had trended steadily downward. The original "flatpack" pods, which had come in with the final generation of superconductor capacitors, had carried twelve MDMs each. Then along had come the next-generation flatpacks, with internal tractor systems. They'd still managed to keep capacity up to a dozen birds, but only until they'd shifted to the fusion-powered Mark 23. At that point, the designers had been forced to figure out how to cram in the pod's own fusion plant, since its new power budget had to be able to spin up the Mark 23s' plants at launch. The Bureau of Weapons had opted to hold the pod's dimensions constant in order to simplify handling and manufacturing constraints, despite the fact that it had dropped its capacity to only ten Mark 23s.

The reduction in throw weight hadn't been universally popular, particularly since the number of pods each ship carried hadn't magically increased, which left them with a sixteen percent overall reduction in magazine capacity. BuWeaps had argued, however, that the advantages of the new fusion-powered missiles—especially the advantages that kind of power supply made possible for the electronic warfare platforms—and of the new pods' vastly extended capacity for independent deployment more than compensated for the reduction in missiles per pod, especially coupled with the introduction of the Keyhole platforms. Although each pod might carry fewer missiles, Keyhole-based tactics were going to emphasize stacked patterns, anyway. The number of control links the new platforms made available would have required that even with the older style pods, if salvo density was going to be maximized.

But then Apollo had come along, and the Apollo control missile—the Mark 23-E. The Echo was the heart of the Apollo system . . . and big enough that a single Mark 23-E displaced two standard Mark 23s. That had pushed the maximum capacity of a same-dimension pod down to just *nine* missiles, only eight of which were attack birds. No one had objected to that, given the incredible increase in lethality Apollo made possible, but it had constituted yet another reduction in over all ammunition stowage, so BuWeaps had gone back to work and come up with yet another in the flatpack pod series—the Mark 19.

The Mark 19 was the same size as the Mark 15 and Mark 17 pods, and it contained no more missiles, but its surface contours had been changed significantly. Whereas earlier marks of pods had been symmetrical, the Mark 19 was *asymmetrical*. Its surface contours had been deliberately designed so that flipping alternate layers of pods allowed them to pack even more flatly into the available volume of the RMN's SD(P)s' missile cores. As a consequence, although the total number of missiles which could be deployed using a single pattern of pods was no greater, the total missile stowage of the existing SD(P) classes had been restored to pre-fusion levels. In fact, it had actually *increased* by just under four percent.

None of which had any particular relevance to Tenth Fleet at this particular moment, since it had no SD(P)s currently on its order of battle. But the fact that the reserve missile pods for the podnoughts Tenth Fleet was supposed to receive had already arrived had quite a bit of relevance. And despite the fact that not a single one of Michelle Henke's heavy cruisers mounted Keyhole, and certainly none of them had Keyhole-Two capability, Aivars Terekhov was very happy to settle for only nine missiles per pod.

And wasn't it nice of BuWeaps to leave the Echo's sub-light telemetry links in place, too? he thought coldly, watching the icons of Sandra Crandall's ships sweeping closer and closer.

Chapter Twenty-Two

SLNS *JOSEPH BUCKLEY* plowed implacably closer to the planet Flax, decelerating steadily. Task Force 496's approach velocity dropped towards nineteen thousand KPS, and the tension on Sandra Crandall's flag deck ratcheted steadily upward.

No one was going to admit that, of course. But as Hago Shavarshyan watched the men and women around him, he'd realized that quite a few more of them were more aware of the implications of what was about to happen than they cared to reveal. Or than he himself had suspected.

Part of the tension was an odd mix of apprehension and anticipation. For some, it represented eagerly sought retribution for the destruction of *Jean Bart*, but for the majority it was something far less welcome: the anticipation of launching the first real war the Solarian League had ever fought. Because that was what this really was. Crandall could present it any way she wanted, but this no simple "police action." For the first time in its history, the Solarian Navy faced an adversary which had a genuine battle fleet, a true wall of battle, even if that wall was far smaller than the SLN's. And little though any Solarian officer wanted to admit it, most of the men and women around Shavarshyan were clearly aware that they were about to go up against an *experienced* adversary. Confident in their own equipment and doctrine or not, however contemptuous of "neobarbs" they might be, they were far from immune to the anxious butterflies which always affected the novice when he looked across the field of battle at a grimly prepared veteran foe in battered, well-used armor.

And this particular bunch of novices is suddenly realizing just how grateful it is that it's not up against ships-of-the-wall this time, he reflected with grim humor.

"Range five-six-point-seven-five million kilometers," Lieutenant Commander Golbatsi announced, and his eyes flitted from the icons on his plot to the time-to-range display ticking steadily down to one side. "Closing velocity one-nine-point-three-eight thousand KPS. Point Longbow in three minutes from...now."

"Thank you, Adam," Scotty Tremaine acknowledged, and quirked an eyebrow at Lieutenant MacDonald. "May I assume you would have mentioned anything we'd heard from Commodore Terekhov, Stilson?"

"You may, Sir," the com officer replied, and Tremaine smiled.

Every member of his staff, with the exception of Lieutenant Yelland, had seen combat before. None of the others had seen as much of it as he and Horace Harkness, but none were showing any signs of panic, either. Which, given the sheer tonnage rumbling towards them, was a not insignificant accomplishment, technical superiority or no technical superiority, he supposed.

"Any changes in their EW, Chief?" he asked.

"No, Sir." Harkness shook his head, his eyes intent as he studied his own displays. "We're picking up a little activity on those 'Halo' platforms of theirs, but nobody's bringing them online just yet. We should see them pretty soon, though—this looks like pre-battle systems tests to me."

Sandra Crandall crossed her arms and chewed her lower lip thoughtfully as she gazed into the tactical plot.

"Halo system test completed, Ma'am," Ou-yang Zhing-wei told her. "EW appears nominal."

The admiral nodded curtly, and her frown deepened. Assuming the range numbers from the New Tuscany dispatch boat were accurate, her task force was little more than ten million kilometers outside the maximum powered missile envelope of those ships orbiting Flax. It still seemed likely the Manties would wait to open fire at their maximum *effective* range, however. The longer the range, the less accurate their fire control would be under any circumstances, and when she cranked in her task force's better EW ability and active defenses, "effective range" got a *lot* shorter against an alert fleet of superdreadnoughts than it would have been against Josef Byng's surprised battlecruisers. Still, if Ou-yang was right about what those fleeing impeller wedges had dropped off, the Manties probably had far more missiles than they could possibly control, and no special reason to conserve ammunition. Under *those* circumstances, they'd want to start whittling away at her as soon as possible, even at relatively poor hit probabilities. She was committed to close combat with them now, which meant *they* were committed to close combat with *her*, as well, and they'd want to reduce her offensive power as much as possible before that happened. And they might always get lucky. Even unlikely things sometimes happened.

But there were also those grav pulses Ou-yang had reported, and some of them seemed to be originating from surprisingly short ranges. If they really were from FTL recon platforms, the fact that they could get that close and survive said unhappy things about how stealthy they were. That was bad enough, but it also meant the Manties were getting disgustingly good looks at her SDs, and she felt no inclination to start showing them an active Halo system any sooner than she had to. There was no point giving their computers additional time to analyze her EW. Still . . .

"Activate Halo at forty million kilometers," she said.

"Point Longbow in one minute, Ma'am."

"Thank you, Dominica."

Michelle Henke's acknowledgment of Dominica Adenauer's report sounded preposterously calm. Particularly, Michelle realized a moment later, because that was exactly how she felt. This moment lacked the vengefulness of New Tuscany. Instead, there was a balanced, singing tension at her core. A sense of something almost but not quite like detachment. A poised, catlike something, she realized, that she'd seen more than once in Honor Alexander-Harrington but never expected to experience herself.

God, I refuse to turn into another Honor! The thought sent a ripple of amusement through her, a flicker of welcome warmth. *Lord knows I love her, and we all need her, but I flat out* refuse *to grow up* that *much!*

She shook her head, unaware of the way her staff was looking at her, or the way her sudden smile swept across her flag deck like a calming breeze.

"Point Longbow, Sir."

Stillwell Lewis' taut-voiced announcement cut through the disciplined silence of *Quentin Saint-James'* flag deck, and Sir Aivars Terekhov nodded.

"Engage," he said simply.

"Missile launch!"

Jacomina van Heutz twitched as Commander Sambroth's warning rapped out sharply, and her eyes flicked to the fountain of fresh icons which suddenly speckled the plot.

"Range at launch five-three-point-niner-six million kilometers." Sambroth sounded as if she couldn't really believe her own numbers. "Assuming constant accelerations, time of flight seven-point-five minutes!"

"Stand by missile defense," van Heutz heard her own voice say, but it seemed to come from someone else, far away, as she saw the impossible number of missiles screaming towards her ship.

The *Saganami-C*-class heavy cruiser massed four hundred and eighty thousand tons. It mounted twenty missile launchers in each broadside, and it was capable of "off-bore" fire with both broadsides simultaneously. More, it had been designed from the outset around the Mark 16 dual-drive missile. Although it was no pod-layer, it did have the capability to "stack" two double broadsides simultaneously, and the designers had provided it with a sixty percent redundancy in control links as a reserve against battle damage. Tuning in all of that redundancy gave each of Aivars Terekhov's cruisers one hundred and twenty-eight telemetry links, and each of those links was assigned to one Mark 23-E missile, which, in turn, controlled eight standard Mark 23s.

The twelve ships of Cruiser Squadron 94 and Cruiser Division 96.1 fired just over fifteen hundred missile pods at Task Force 496, Solarian League Navy.

"Estimate twelve thousand—repeat, twelve *thousand*—incoming!"

Sandra Crandall's head snapped around at Ou-yang Zhing-wei's hard, flat announcement. She stared at her ops officer, eyes huge, too shocked by the numbers to register even disbelief. At that, she was doing better than Pépé Bautista. Her chief of staff's expression was that of someone infuriated by a lie rather than someone stupefied by astonishment.

"Halo active," Ou-yang continued. "Missile Defense Plan Able activated."

✧   ✧   ✧

"Commodore Terekhov's opened fire, Ma'am."

Dominica Adenauer's report was one of the least necessary ones Michelle Henke had ever heard. The thousands upon thousands of icons streaking across the master plot were painfully evident. None of which absolved Adenauer of her formal responsibility to tell her admiral about it.

"Acknowledged," Michelle said softly.

✧   ✧   ✧

Scotty Tremaine watched the hurricane racing toward the Sollies with something very like a sense of awe. He'd seen larger salvos— not once, but many times. For that matter, the mutual holocausts Home Fleet and Lester Tourville's Second Fleet had inflicted upon one another at the Battle of Manticore dwarfed even this. But a full third of *these* missiles had come from ships under *his* command, and that realization sent an icy chill through his blood.

He glanced for just a moment at Horace Harkness' profile and felt an obscure, irrational flicker of reassurance. Harkness' elemental solidity, his unflappable sense of who and what he was, was like a touchstone. It was a reminder of all the challenges Tremaine had met and surmounted in the twenty T-years since he'd first set eyes on that battered, competent face, and in the wake of finding himself cast in the role of Juggernaut, Scotty Tremaine took a warm and very human comfort from it.

✧   ✧   ✧

Helen Zilwicki stood at Terekhov's side, watching the same plot, and thought about how different this was from the Battle of Monica.

As Terekhov's flag lieutenant, she'd been there when he and Admiral Gold Peak and Admiral Oversteegen and their ops officers threshed out their plans for Operation Agincourt. Fire distribution had been one of the critical points, and no one had been prepared to make any unwarranted assumptions about the ease with which Solly missile defenses might be penetrated. They'd all been

aware that Solarian antimissile doctrine and capabilities were...
seriously flawed compared to those of the Republican Navy, but
they'd forced themselves to adopt the most pessimistic estimates
of their ability to capitalize on those flaws.

Of the 12,288 standard Mark 23s in that stupendous initial launch,
fully one quarter—just over three thousand—were EW platforms.
The remaining nine thousand plus were distributed over twenty-three
of Sandra Crandall's seventy-one superdreadnoughts. Experience
against the Republic of Haven indicated that two hundred to two
hundred and fifty Mark 23 hits would destroy—or mission-kill, at
least—even the latest Havenite SD(P)...which was why Fire Plan
Alpha had allocated *four* hundred missiles to each of its targets.

"Spot and allocate the Bravo launch," Sir Aivars Terekhov said.

The wavefront of destruction roared towards Sandra Crandall's
superdreadnoughts from far, far beyond the Solarians' own range
of Aivars Terekhov's command. There was no fear-pumped adrenaline surging through the minds of the tactical officers behind that
stupendous missile launch. Despite the pygmy size of their own
vessels, compared to those of their opponents, they recognized
the full, deadly depth of their advantages. Knew the men and
women aboard those superdreadnoughts could not effectively
threaten them in any way.

Knowing that, those minds ticked with cool, merciless precision, watching their displays, monitoring their missiles and the
EW environment with hawklike attentiveness.

There was no matching coolness aboard *Joseph Buckley* or the
other units of Task Force 496.

No one in the entire task force, in his darkest nightmare, could
have anticipated the sheer weight of fire streaking towards them.
By any meterstick of the Solarian League Navy, it was simply and
starkly impossible. The surprise and disbelief that generated were
total, yet for all of the SLN's institutional arrogance and com-
placency, all of their own shock, the men and women of Sandra
Crandall's command were professionals. Astonishment, even terror,
might reach out to paralyze them, but training slotted into place,
like a bulwark between them and panic's palsy.

Jacomina van Heutz heard the quick, purposeful flow of orders
and responses around her, and even in the midst of her own

shock, she felt a glow of pride. Fear might flatten her people's voices, incredulity might echo in their tones, but they were doing their jobs. They were *responding*, doing their best, not simply gaping in horror.

Yet behind that pride, there was another emotion—sorrow. Because however well they did their jobs, it wasn't going to matter in the end.

Hago Shavarshyan watched Ou-yang Zhing-wei and her assistants grapple with the horrifying surprise of that massive missile launch.

Shavarshyan was no tac officer, but he'd had enough tactical training to know that what was coming at them was *not* the blind-fired covering barrage Ou-yang had suggested to Crandall and Bautista. The most cursory analysis of those missile signatures showed that every one of them was maneuvering as part of a coherent, carefully managed whole. The fact that that was flatly impossible didn't mean it wasn't happening, and the ops officer was totally focused on her displays, on her earbug, on the reports flowing in to her from the task force's huge array of sensor platforms.

The intelligence officer envied her. At least she had something to distract her.

"It's got to be some kind of EW!" Bautista protested hoarsely. The chief of staff was staring at the plot, shaking his head again and again.

"That's no ECM, Pépé," Crandall grated. She jabbed her chin at the secondary displays showing *Joseph Buckley*'s combat information center's analysis of the incoming impeller signatures. "They're there."

"But...but they can't possibly *control* them." Bautista turned his head to stare at Crandall. "They can't have the control links! And...and even if they *did*, at this range their accuracy has to suck!"

"I doubt even Manties would have fired missiles they can't control." Despite her own shock, despite her truculence and undeniable arrogance, Sandra Crandall's eyes were dark with a refusal to hide behind simple denial. "You may be right about the accuracy penalty, but if they can throw enough salvos this size, even crappy accuracy's going to rip our ass off."

Bautista's eyes went even wider at her harsh-voiced admission.

He opened his mouth once more, as if to say something, but no words came, and he closed it again.

Crandall never even noticed.

"Good telemetry from the advanced platforms, Sir." Stillwell Lewis sounded almost jubilant. "They're bringing up their Halo platforms, but their shipboard systems show very little change. No surprises so far."

"Let's not get overconfident, Stillwell," Terekhov replied calmly.

"No, Sir."

Helen suppressed an inappropriate urge to smile. Lewis' tone was chastened as he acknowledged Terekhov's admonition, and she knew the commodore was right. Yet at the same time, she understood exactly where the ops officer's confidence came from.

The Ghost Rider platforms watching the Solarians were three light-minutes from *Quentin Saint-James*. But those three light-minutes equated to less than three *seconds* of transmission lag for their FTL transmitters. For all intents and purposes, Lewis was watching Crandall's ships in real time. Without Keyhole-Two platforms, there was no FTL telemetry link between Terekhov's cruisers and their missiles, yet the time lag built into their fire control and EW loop was still only half that of any navy without Ghost Rider.

That would have been bad enough from the Sollies' perspective even if there'd been no Apollo birds driving along behind the attack missiles. But the Mark 23-Es *were* there, and each of them represented a far more sophisticated and capable advanced control node than the SLN had ever imagined. The Echoes had been preloaded with dozens of alternative attack profiles, based on every permutation of Solarian defensive measures Tenth Fleet's tactical officers and the simulators had been able to come up, and their extraordinarily competent onboard AIs were far more capable of adjusting and reshaping those profiles on the fly than any previous attack missile would have been. Of course, even with those stored profiles and AIs, Lewis' fire wouldn't be remotely as effective as it would have been if he'd had the all up Keyhole-Two systems, instead.

It was simply incomparably better than anything anyone *else* had.

"Halo active." Horace Harkness gazed at his displays, hands moving with the precision of a pianist as he refined the data. "Looks like about a twenty percent increase on their battlecruisers' efficiency, but the filters should be solid unless it gets a lot worse. We're seeing a lot of lidar lighting off, too, though. I think we'll be looking at the first counter-missiles pretty soon."

Scotty Tremaine nodded. Twenty percent was a lower increase than the ops plan had allowed for, and he wasn't about to assume it wasn't going to go up over the next couple of minutes. But even if it did . . .

"Bravo pods in position," Commander Golbatsi said, and a fresh wave of missile pod icons blinked with the red data codes of readiness on Tremaine's plot. "Launch codes receipted and acknowledged by all pods."

"Thank you, Guns."

"Profile Alpha-Québec-One-Seven," Stilson MacDonald announced suddenly.

"Execute," Tremaine said sharply.

"Executing Alpha-Québec-One-Seven, aye!" Adam Golbatsi responded, and sent the command that locked the entire division's first wave missiles into the final attack profile Aivars Terekhov had just ordered.

A strange spike—almost a sense of relief, or perhaps of commitment—swept *Alistair McKeon*'s flag bridge, as if everyone on it had inhaled simultaneously.

The same awareness flickered across *Quentin Saint-James'* flag deck, but Terekhov didn't seem to notice. His eyes, like his thoughts, were on the master tactical plot, and those eyes were blue ice.

"Launch the Bravo birds," he said, and a second salvo, as massive as the first, roared out of the pods.

Thirty seconds and 14,177,748 kilometers short of their targets, the Mark 23-Es of Operation Agincourt's Alpha launch receipted their final instructions and switched to attack profile AQ-17. Their closing velocity was up to 207,412 KPS, just over sixty-nine percent of the speed of light, which was over four and a half times the maximum any Solarian missile could have generated, given the same geometry, and the differential would only increase over the last half-minute of their existence.

The Apollo missiles' AIs didn't really care about that, or about their own rapidly approaching destruction, except inasmuch as it simplified their task. They simply obeyed their instructions, considering the information transmitted to them from their slaved attack missiles' sensors and comparing the warp and woof of the Solarian defenses to the requirements of AQ-17. Certain minor adjustments were in order; the AIs made them, then sent out fresh instructions.

The EW platforms and penetration aids seeded throughout the salvo responded.

Solarian counter-missile doctrine had never envisioned a salvo density like this. Traditional missile defense planning focused on identifying the attack missiles most likely to achieve hits and then targeting each of them with multiple counter-missile launches. But there wasn't going to be time for that in the face of such a ferocious closing velocity. In fact, there would be time for only a single CM launch before the MDMs screamed completely across their engagement envelope, and even taking full advantage of the additional fire control of the Aegis refits a third of Crandall's ships had received, her superdreadnoughts could produce less than two thousand counter-missiles per launch. That was approximately one CM for every 6.5 Mark 23s slicing towards them, which would have been hopelessly inadequate under any circumstances.

Now "inadequate" became "futile" as the control missiles activated their slaved electronic warfare platforms.

Missile defense officers stared in disbelief as their displays went berserk. Dragon's Teeth blossomed like seductive flowers, flooding Task Force 496's fire control with false targets. The number of threat sources doubled, then doubled yet again, and *again*, hopelessly swamping the Solarian systems' ability to discriminate the true threats from the counterfeit. The computers driving those systems, and the men and women behind those computers, did their best, but their best wasn't good enough.

The incredible horde of false signatures guaranteed the limited number of counter-missiles the Solarians could bring to bear would be effectively useless, but Michelle Henke and her officers had been unwilling to settle for that. Even as the Dragon's Teeth spawned, the Dazzler platforms spread across the front of the attack salvo activated in a carefully sequenced chain, ripping huge, blinding holes in Task Force 496's sensor coverage. The Dazzlers' exquisitely choreographed chaos reduced even the last ditch laser clusters of their targets' point defense systems to impotence.

Of the ninety-two hundred Mark 23 attack birds in Aivars Terekhov's Alpha launch, Sandra Crandall's task force managed to stop exactly one thousand and seven. The other 8,209 got through.

✧   ✧   ✧

SLNS *Joseph Buckley* lurched indescribably as the Manticoran missiles detonated and X-ray lasers ripped at her massive armor.

Thick as that armor was, it was no match for the stilettos of focused radiation punching into it like brimstone awls. It shattered under the transfer energy as the lasers ripped deeper and deeper, and the huge ship bucked in agony.

Jacomina van Heutz clung to the arms of her command chair as her shock frame hammered her. The fleeting instant in which the Manticoran missiles could bring their lasers to bear against her ship's sidewalls as they penetrated the Solarian formation with a closing velocity which had climbed to seventy-three percent of light-speed was far too brief for any of *Joseph Buckley*'s damage to register on merely human senses as individual hits. It was all delivered in one stroboscopic lightning bolt of devastation, too sudden and intense for even the ship's computers to register or sort out.

Those missile-born talons gouged and tore. Energy mounts and missile tubes, counter-missile launchers, radar arrays, point defense clusters, boat bays, gravitic sensors, impeller nodes—all of them shattered, exploding into tattered ruin in a single catastrophic moment, faster than a man could have blinked. In less time than it would have taken to cough, Sandra Crandall's flagship was transformed into a broken wreck, a splintered hulk, coasting onward under momentum alone, with three quarters of her crew wiped out of existence.

Nor did van Heutz's ship die alone. Her squadron mates *Joseph Lister*, *Max Planck*, and *Joseph Hutton* died with her. Like *Buckley*, *Hutton* at least avoided immediate and total destruction, but *Lister* and *Planck* were less fortunate. *Lister* shattered, breaking into three distinct pieces; *Planck* simply disappeared in a flash of white-hot fury.

Archimedes, *Andreas Vesalius*, *Hipparchus*, *Leonardo da Vinci*, *Gregor Mendel*, *Marie Curie*, *Wilhelm Roëntgen*, *Alfred Wegener*, *Avicenna*, *al-Kawarizmi*...every one of the Alpha launch's twenty-three targets—thirty-two percent of Crandall's total wall of battle—was reduced to splinters and wreckage in that single inconceivable, exquisitely synchronized explosion.

Sir Aivars Terekhov watched a third of the superdreadnought icons on his plot blink virtually simultaneously from the glaring crimson of hostile units into the purple crosses of dead ships... or into nothing at all. His arctic blue eyes didn't even flicker at the proof of how utterly outclassed the Solarian League Navy truly was, but his nostrils flared. He gazed at the display for almost a full minute, absorbing the results, watching the sudden disintegration of the Solarian wall's formation as individual captains tried to avoid the debris of slaughtered consorts or swerved in frantic, independent evasion patterns as the Bravo launch swept towards them. Then he turned to look at Stillwell Lewis.

"Execute Exclamation Point," he said.

"Executing Exclamation Point, aye, Sir!"

Lewis' finger stabbed a key at his console, and twenty seconds later, every one of the Bravo launch missiles detonated as one, millions of kilometers short of their targets.

"Spot the Charlie pods but hold launch," Terekhov said.

"Holding Charlie launch, aye, Sir," Lewis replied, and Terekhov sat back in his chair, waiting.

Forty-five more seconds ticked past. A minute. Ninety seconds. Then, abruptly, every surviving Solarian starship's wedge went down simultaneously.

Another two and a half minutes oozed into eternity while light-speed limited transmissions sped towards HMS *Hercules* and *Quentin Saint-James*. Then—

"Sir," Captain Loretta Shoupe told Augustus Khumalo quietly, "Communications is picking up an all-ships transmission from an Admiral Keeley O'Cleary. She wants to surrender, Sir."

Chapter Twenty-Three

AND NOW, MICHELLE HENKE thought dryly as she stood on *Artemis'* flag bridge, hands clasped behind her, and watched the icons of Admiral Enderby's LACs move steadily towards their destinations, *for the fun part. I know I shouldn't, but I can't help thinking everything would've been a bunch simpler if O'Cleary just hadn't surrendered for another salvo or two. As it is, we've got a hell of an interesting little problem here.*

She snorted, grimacing at her own thoughts, but it was true. And, ironically, the direct consequence of one of the Royal Manticoran Navy's greater advantages.

The one huge problem with the RMN's decision to adopt increased automation in order to reduce its warships' manpower requirements was that it worked even better than anyone had expected. There were very few warm bodies aboard modern Manticoran or Grayson cruisers or destroyers, and even superdreadnoughts had crews smaller than prewar battlecruisers. That was an enormous advantage in Fifth Space Lord Cortez's Sisyphean task of manning the navy's ships, but it also meant the smaller companies of the ships in question found it much more difficult to generate detachments for little things like, oh, boarding parties, for example.

Solarian ships' companies, conversely, were even larger and more manpower-intensive than prewar Manticoran designs had been, and Sandra Crandall had entered the Spindle System with seventy-one superdreadnoughts, each with a ship's company of over six thousand. Even completely ignoring the rest of her task force, that had amounted to the next best thing to a half-million personnel. Tenth Fleet, on the other hand, had nowhere near that many people. A *Roland*-class destroyer like Naomi Kaplan's *Tristram* had a total company of less than seventy, and not a single one of them was a Marine. A *Saganami-C*, like Aivars Terekhov's *Quentin Saint-James*, was somewhat better off—at least each of them had a hundred and forty Marines available, but that was out of a total crew of only three hundred and fifty-five. For that matter, even one of the lordly *Nikes*, like her own *Artemis*, had a company of barely seven hundred and fifty. Which meant the total personnel of all Michelle's warships—including Khumalo's superdreadnought flagship and the four carriers of Stephen Enderby's CLAC squadron *and* their LAC groups—amounted to barely thirty-two thousand. Crandall's surviving forty-eight superdreadnoughts, alone, carried ten times that many men and women, and that didn't even consider the fifty thousand or so aboard her battlecruisers and destroyers.

Nor did it consider the need to provide search and rescue parties for the nine crippled superdreadnoughts which had not been totally destroyed.

All of which meant she was incredibly shorthanded for dealing with such a stupendous haul of POWs, and she frankly didn't know what she was going to do with all of them. She had nowhere near the hyper-capable personnel lift to transfer them back to the prison camps in the Star Empire currently populated by the personnel of Lester Tourville's Second Fleet. For that matter, she wasn't at all certain those camps, despite their frenetic expansion following the Battle of Manticore, would have had sufficient space for her current catch even if she'd been able to get them there!

Baroness Medusa was scrambling to find someplace to store them, at least temporarily. Unfortunately, no one on Flax had ever contemplated the absurd notion that the planet might suddenly have to absorb the better part of four hundred thousand "visitors" like these, and the governor's options were limited. At the moment, Michelle knew, Medusa was inclining towards the same solution Michelle herself had experienced during her brief stint as a prisoner of war on Haven. Flax possessed several large, uninhabited tropical islands, many with the sorts of climates that evoked Pavlovian salivation from vacation resort developers. There was no housing on them at the moment, but food and water could be transported in, emergency sanitation arrangements could be made, and more permanent housing could be built once the immediate crisis had been dealt with.

No matter what we do, the Sollies're going to scream we've "abused" their personnel by "refusing" to house them properly and deliberately leaving them "exposed to the elements," she thought glumly. *But all we can do is the best we can do, and hope the Admiralty can find someplace back home to keep them... not to mention the shipping to get them "someplace back home"!*

From the perspective of pure combat power, Crandall's task force wasn't even in the same league as Tenth Fleet. In fact, Michelle and her senior tacticians had been shocked by the totality of their own success. They'd deliberately adopted pessimistic assumptions about their ability to penetrate Solarian missile defenses, only to find their most *optimistic* estimations had fallen short of the reality. Despite everything, she'd been convinced it would take at least several salvos to inflict the sort of damage required to extort a surrender from someone as belligerent and obviously arrogant as Sandra Crandall. She'd certainly never anticipated that Terekhov's opening salvo would shatter its targets so completely.

She was fully aware of the scale of her victory, and that her firepower advantage was overwhelming. Yet from the perspective of securing its prizes, Tenth Fleet was in the position of someone who'd chartered a small boat to fish for near-tuna and landed a twelve-meter fluke-shark, instead. An impressive achievement, yes, but what did you *do* with the thing?

Well, I guess we're about to find out, aren't we? she thought.

At the moment, Terekhov's cruisers and Khumalo's superdreadnought flagship maintained their positions in orbit around Flax, just over eight hundred thousand kilometers from what remained of Crandall's wall of battle. The undamaged Solarian ships, plus their lighter consorts, were motionless relative to the planet, sidewalls and impeller wedges down in obedience to Michelle's orders, and all of her battlecruisers lay seven hundred and fifty thousand kilometers outside their current positions. That geometry put every hyper-capable Manticoran combatant beyond effective energy range of the Solarian SDs—a not so minor consideration, given the fact that any one of those superdreadnoughts could have annihilated Michelle's entire fleet if she'd been foolish enough to stray into the effective envelope of their massive energy batteries.

Which was the reason she had absolutely no intention of doing any such thing. It was also the reason both the *Saganami-Cs* and the *Nikes* were surrounded by veritable shoals of missile pods. Even if these superdreadnoughts' wedges had been active, it would have taken them six minutes at their maximum acceleration to reach energy range even of the battlecruisers, much less Terekhov's cruisers. Flight time for a Mark 23 over the same range would have been only twenty-four seconds. Based on what had already happened to Task Force 496, Michelle rather doubted it would survive the fifteen far larger salvos it would have received during those six minutes. More importantly, she felt confident the Sollies could do the same sums.

But even as she held her starships at a discreet distance, her LACs had maneuvered into position "above" and "below" the surviving Solarian warships. Since it had seemed likely the Sollies would have underestimated the capabilities of new-generation Manticoran light attack craft at least as badly as they'd underestimated those of current-generation Manticoran missiles, she'd arranged demonstration firings of the *Shrike-Bs'* massive grasers. She wanted no misconceptions about what those capital ship-weight energy weapons could do to the unarmored topsides and bottoms of the Solarian ships-of-the-wall.

And while all that was being arranged, her destroyers—all five of them—had accelerated off in pursuit of the nine hulked SDs. Five *old-style* destroyers could easily have found the boarding parties for search-and-rescue operations aboard nine superdreadnoughts. Whether or not her five *Rolands* were up to the task was another question.

Now it was time to find out if they were . . . and if her *other* arrangements were going to work, after all.

For the Sollies' sake, she hoped they did.

"Put me through to O'Cleary, Bill," she said without looking over her shoulder.

"Yes, Ma'am," Lieutenant Commander Edwards replied.

Michelle gazed into the plot for another few seconds, then turned to face the master com display as a fair-haired, dark-eyed woman in the white uniform of the Solarian League Navy appeared upon it.

"Admiral O'Cleary," Michelle said, and at this piddling range the light-speed transmission lag was barely two seconds.

"Admiral Gold Peak," the other woman responded. Originally TF 496's third in command, she'd become it's second in command when Admiral Dunichi Lazlo's flagship, *Andreas Vesalius*, blew up with all hands. With what remained of *Joseph Buckley* currently unable to communicate with anyone (assuming there was anyone aboard to do be communicated *with*), O'Cleary had become the task force's acting CO. Her voice was a little gravelly, but Michelle suspected that was normal, not something—like the stunned anger glowing at the backs of O'Cleary's eyes—produced by the shocking outcome of the Solarian attack on Spindle.

"My boarding parties are now prepared to take possession of your superdreadnoughts, Admiral," Michelle said levelly, "and I fully realize emotions are going to be running high among your personnel. *My* personnel have been instructed to exercise as much restraint as possible, but they've also been instructed to remember that their own security and the discharge of their orders takes precedence over all other considerations. I sincerely hope no one on either side will cause any avoidable incidents, but I remind you formally, for the record, that under the Deneb Accords, the legal responsibility to avoid such incidents by prompt compliance with my instructions and those of my designated prize crews rests with your personnel, as the ones who have been permitted to surrender."

O'Cleary's jaw tightened visibly, but despite her anger, she had herself firmly under control.

"I assure you, Admiral, that I've made all my personnel aware of that fact," she grated. "As you say, emotions are . . . running high among them. And as you, I hope there will be no 'avoidable incidents.' "

"Good." Michelle inclined her head in a brief, courteous half-bow of agreement, then cleared her throat.

"I'm sure you realize, Admiral O'Cleary, that no one here in the Quadrant has made any provision for quartering such a large number of prisoners of war."

Michelle saw O'Cleary's eyes flash at the term "prisoners of war," but she didn't especially care. In point of fact, she was conceding them a status she wasn't required to under interstellar law, and O'Cleary knew it. There'd been no formal declaration of war when

Crandall attacked the sovereign territory of another star nation. Technically, her actions amounted to piracy on the grand scale, and Michelle was under no legal obligation to accord her officers and crews the courtesies normally due regular POWs. The fact that she'd allowed them to surrender under the provisions of the Deneb Accords meant she'd *chosen* to extend that status to them, but whether or not she was legally required to continue to extend it was what the lawyers like to call "a gray area."

"Governor Medusa is currently making arrangements to provide food, shelter, and any necessary medical attention," she continued levelly. "We'll do everything in our power to ensure that no one suffers any hardship. Despite that, however, it's very likely—inevitable, to be honest—that housing and services are going to be jury-rigged, at best, at least initially. As I say, we'll try to avoid imposing hardship conditions, but, again, I remind you that the Deneb Accords specifically recognize the right of any belligerent to use whatever means are necessary, up to and including lethal force, to maintain order among POWs. We have no intention of attempting to pressure any of your personnel into collaborating, and we recognize the Deneb Accords' stipulation that it's the duty of captured personnel to attempt to escape. However, it would be well for you to remind your personnel that that stipulation does not grant immunity from the use of force to stop them from escaping or to maintain order among them."

"Is that an order, Admiral?" O'Cleary asked coldly.

"No, it is not," Michelle replied, equally coldly, enunciating each word carefully. "It is, however, a very strong *suggestion*, and I remind you our current conversation is being recorded. It can—and will be—produced at any inquiry which may result from your personnel's conduct—or ours—while your people are in our custody."

Their eyes locked for several seconds. Then O'Cleary inhaled deeply.

"Very well. Your 'suggestion' is noted, and I'll speak to my people. Is there anything else?"

"Yes," Michelle said, "there is. As I'm sure you've already deduced for yourself, the combined manpower of my fleet is far inferior, numerically, to that of your own task force." *Not that I have any intention of admitting just* how *inferior,* she added silently. "That poses some obvious difficulties for my boarding parties—difficulties which might well provoke the sort of incident we've both just agreed should be avoided—and I've been giving some thought to ways those difficulties might be alleviated. By my staff's calculations, the combined small craft and escape pod capacity of your superdreadnoughts should suffice to remove approximately five thousand of your personnel from each ship."

O'Cleary's face stiffened, and she began to open her mouth indignantly, but Michelle continued coldly.

"Before you say a word, Admiral. I advise you to consider your position carefully. As you've just acknowledged, interstellar law requires you to obey my lawful commands. I, on the other hand, am obligated to provide for the reasonable safety of your personnel as long as you and they *do* obey my lawful commands. The planet Flax is less than one million kilometers from your present position. That's well within the powered range of your life pods, even allowing a two hundred percent reserve for an unassisted landing. In short, removing your personnel from your vessels in the manner I've indicated poses no threat to life or limb, assuming you've properly maintained the equipment in question. As a consequence, I'm formally informing you that failure to comply with this instruction will be interpreted as a decision on your part to resume hostilities."

She held the Solarian's eyes with her own, daring O'Cleary to call her bluff while silently praying the other woman was smart enough to realize it was no bluff at all. After a handful of tense heartbeats, it was O'Cleary's eyes which fell.

"I understand," she grated.

"I'm glad to hear that." Michelle gave her a tight smile. "Once your small craft and life pods have separated from your starships, they'll proceed to Flax. There, they will enter orbit as Admiral Khumalo directs and comply with any additional instructions he may issue. They will *not* land except as he or I specifically order. We'll make every effort to get them planet-side as promptly as possible, consonant with Governor Medusa's ability to arrange accommodations. I'll guarantee that, under any circumstances, your life pods will be allowed to make planetfall well within their life-support endurance. If, however, any of your small craft or life pods fail to comply with instructions from myself, Admiral Khumalo, or our designated subordinates, they *will* be destroyed. I realize these arrangements are unusual, but so are our present circumstances. I've attempted to reach the best compromise I can between the security of my own people and the proper treatment of yours. I expect you to make it clear to all your personnel that we intend to treat them as decently and honorably as circumstances permit, but that any disobedience to our lawful instructions will be met promptly with whatever level of force—up to and including deadly force—we feel is required. Is that understood, as well?"

"Yes," O'Cleary got out.

"Good. You may not believe this, Admiral, but I take no pleasure in issuing instructions I know must seem humiliating. Unfortunately, I have no choice. In fact, I'd be derelict in my responsibility to ensure the safety of *your* personnel if I failed to take the measures necessary to control the present situation and prevent the sort of escalation which would require me to use force to enforce the terms of your surrender."

Michelle gazed into O'Cleary's eyes for another moment, hoping the Solarian could recognize the sincerity in her own expression. Then she nodded courteously.

"Gold Peak, clear," she said, and turned back to the master plot with an inner sigh.

Truth be told, O'Cleary's attitude had been less belligerent than she'd feared. Unfortunately, that didn't mean it made Michelle happy. Nor, for that matter, did it mean the *other* officers and enlisted personnel aboard those surrendered ships were going to share O'Cleary's attitude.

"ETA three minutes, Ma'am," the pinnace's flight engineer said.

"Thank you, PO Pettigrew," Abigail Hearns replied, then stood and turned to face the armed, skinsuited men and women of her boarding party. Given the nature of their mission, there weren't a great many of them. In fact, there were a lot *less* of them than she wished she had.

"Three minutes, people," she said, and saw expressions and shoulders tighten. "Remember your briefings, and watch yourselves. We don't want any accidents—or incidents—and this sort of thing can be risky enough even aboard a friendly ship. So while we'd like to avoid any unpleasantness, we'd really like to have all of you back on board safe and sound, too."

One or two people chuckled, and Abigail allowed herself an answering smile. Then she looked at the youthful midshipman in the seat beside hers. In some ways, young Walter Corbett reminded her of Gwen Archer, with the same red hair and green eyes. But Corbett had a truly monumental nose, compared to Archer's, and he was only nineteen and skinny as a rail, to boot. He was also possessed of a nervous energy that found the onerous task of sitting still difficult under normal conditions.

Today's conditions were anything but normal, however, and Corbett had sat almost unbreathing for the last ten minutes, his nose two centimeters from the viewport as he stared out it at the shattered behemoth waiting for them.

Abigail didn't blame him. Corbett's snotty cruise might have been less personally and directly terrifying (so far, at least) than her own aboard then-Captain Oversteegen's *Gauntlet*, but there'd been terror and cataclysm enough to go around. And, she thought, any temptation to smile fading as she remembered how the other ships of HMS *Tristram*'s division had been slaughtered by Josef Byng, he'd had ample demonstration of the risks attendant upon his chosen profession.

And he's about to get more, she reminded herself grimly. Unlike young Corbett, she'd seen the insides of butchered starships before. *Let's try to see to it he gets back aboard* Tristram *in one piece so he can at least profit from the experience that's about to provide so much nightmare fodder.*

"Remember, Walt," she hadn't spoken loudly, but Corbett's head twitched around like a startled rabbit's, "you're a Queen's officer. I know you never expected to be doing anything like this on your snotty cruise. Well, I didn't expect everything that happened on *my* snotty cruise, either, as Lieutenant Gutierrez here could testify."

She twitched her own head at the massive lieutenant sitting in the row of seats immediately behind the two of them. His Marine-style armored skinsuit was badged with the shoulder flash of the Owens Steadholder's Guard, not the Royal Manticoran Marines, and a well-used flechette gun rode the cargo rack above his head. A sound which might have been an understatement-spawned snort came from the general direction of the lieutenant in question, and a quick grin danced across Corbett's face in response. Clearly he'd heard all about then-Sergeant Mateo Gutierrez and Midshipwoman Hearns' adventures on the planet Refuge.

"You need to remember three things," Abigail continued in a rather sterner tone. "First, you *are* a Queen's officer. Second, any

Sollies still alive in there"—she nodded towards the forward bulk-head, beyond which the wreck of SLNS *Charles Babbage*, one-time flagship of Battle Squadron 371, Solarian League Navy, waited for them—"have spent their entire careers thinking of themselves as the most powerful navy in the galaxy and of the Star Empire of Manticore—and its navy—as an upstart little pipsqueak with delusions of grandeur. Third, we have no idea how many Solly personnel may still be alive aboard the *Babbage* or what kind of shape they may be in, but there are fewer than thirty people in our boarding party."

She looked into his eyes steadily until he nodded, then continued.

"Right this minute, most of *Babbage's* surviving crew are prob-ably still in a state of shock. I don't know how long that's going to last, and from our perspective, it could be either a good thing or a bad thing... or possibly even both at once. On the one hand, most of them are probably too stunned and too focused on hoping someone's going to come and find them to be thinking about any organized, effective resistance. On the other hand, even if ninety percent of her company is dead, there are still ten times as many survivors aboard her as in *Tristram's* entire complement. A lot of them are going to be too happy to see anybody coming to pull them out of the wreckage to give us any trouble, but I'll be astonished if any of them are thinking very clearly. For the ones who aren't, the shock and humiliation—and the *anger*—of being hammered so badly by a bunch of 'neobarbs' may push some of them into open defiance. And, frankly, the fact that you're only a midshipman's going to piss off a lot of the people you're about to run into. They'd probably resent taking orders from you under any circumstances; under *these* circumstances, what they feel is going to be a lot worse than simple resentment.

"That leaves you with two problems you're going to have to balance off. First, be aware of their resentment and make what allowance for it you can, but, second, remember you are an officer, that they *are* subject to your orders, and that an appearance of weakness may well lead to some kind of incident."

She paused once more, and Corbett nodded again.

"Yes, Ma'am," he said, and despite her grim awareness of what awaited them inside that broken ship, Abigail's lips twitched. It would have been unfair to call his tone plaintive, but that was headed in the right direction.

"It probably won't be *that* bad, Walt. Not where the survivors are concerned, at least. Yes, you have to be aware of all the things I've just said. But that's why I've attached the Bosun to your group. I wouldn't go so far as saying I'm sending him along to 'look after you,' but I *will* say I expect you to remember he's been in the Navy since *you* were five T-years old. Use his experience accordingly."

"Yes, Ma'am," Corbett said more firmly, and Abigail glanced over his shoulder at Gutierrez. The lieutenant's eyes met hers with the memory of another middy who'd desperately needed the experience of another veteran noncom, and his reassuring nod was a vast relief. Obviously, Mateo had had a few words of his own with Senior Chief Petty Officer Franklin Musgrave, *Tristram*'s bosun.

"Then all I'm going to add," she told the youngster, "is that you're going to see some terrible things in the next few hours." She held his gaze steadily and felt a glow of approval when it didn't waver. "No matter what you think you can imagine, it's going to be worse. I know. I've seen it before, and there's no way to really prepare someone for it until they've experienced it for themselves. It's all right to feel shocked, nauseated. In fact, there'd be something wrong with you if you didn't. But whatever we feel, we still have our responsibilities, and I think if you focus *on* your responsibilities, on getting the job done, you'll find it helps. That's another thing I found out the hard way."

"Yes, Ma'am," he repeated.

"Good."

She looked up into her personal armsman's eyes again for a moment, gave him a tiny nod of acknowledgment, then patted Corbett lightly on the shoulder and—as she'd just advised the midshipman to do—turned her thoughts to her own duties.

Rear Admiral Michael Oversteegen watched his plot aboard HMS *Rigel*. Despite his relaxed, comfortable, loose-limbed sprawl in his command chair, his eyes were alert, sharply focused on the display's icons.

"Anythin' from Major Markiewicz or Sebastián, Irena?" he asked.

"No, Sir," Lieutenant Irena Thomas' tone could not have been more respectful, but Oversteegen's lips twitched in a slight smile. Respectful or not, it was the tone a subordinate used to inform a superior officer that he should tend to his own knitting, secure in the knowledge she would somehow remember to inform him if anyone asked to speak to him.

Showin' more worry than you want to, aren't you, Michael? he asked himself sardonically. *Still, I s'pose you're not th' only one that's true of just now.*

His smile faded, and he glanced at the tactical board at Commander Steren Retallack's station. His ops officer sat tipped back, arms folded, but Oversteegen knew Retallack was watching the "surrendered" Solarian SDs like the proverbial hawk. And well he should be.

Like everyone else in Tenth Fleet, Oversteegen devoutly hoped Michelle Henke's elaborate precautions would prove unnecessary, but he fervently agreed with his CO's disinclination to be proven wrong about that sort of assumption. At the moment, none of the Solarian SDs had more than fifteen hundred personnel still aboard, which—given their old-fashioned manpower-intensive design philosophy—was too few people for them to effectively move or fight. That, unfortunately, wasn't quite the same thing as saying they didn't have enough people to fire their weapons. To be sure, their active targeting systems were down, as were their wedges and defensive sidewalls, but the hugely redundant passive sensors any ship-of-the-wall mounted would be more than capable of providing accurate target data on anything inside energy range.

The Deneb Accords and interstellar law were very clear on the mutual responsibilities of victor and vanquished. When O'Cleary dropped her impeller wedges in the universal FTL signal that she surrendered, Tenth Fleet had been legally obligated to grant quarter rather than continuing the attack while it waited for her formal, light-speed surrender offer to arrive. (Assuming, of course, that Michelle Henke had chosen to regard them as anything besides pirates.) By the same token, O'Cleary's ships were legally required to *stay* surrendered, with their crews obedient to the lawful orders of any boarding party, if they didn't want the other side to renew the action. There was, however, a bit of a gray area in that the crew of any captured ship had a legal right to attempt to retake their vessel, and one could argue that ambushing a boarding party when it first came onboard constituted a sort of preemptive retaking. Whether or not the argument held up in court would depend upon whose court it was, but that would be cold comfort to anyone—on either side—who got killed in the course of the attempt.

And although at the moment, Michael Oversteegen admitted with a cold lack of apology, he didn't really much care what might happen to any Sollies who tried something like that, he *did* care—very much—what happened to any Manticoran personnel who might be involved.

So just remember we're watchin' you, Admiral O'Cleary. And it's perfectly all right with me for you t' go right on sweatin' all those missile pods. Because th' first time one of those superdreadnoughts even twitches, we are goin' t' blow the son-of-a-bitch straight t' hell.

✧   ✧   ✧

This, Major Evgeny Markiewicz reflected sourly, *is the kind of story you really like to kick back over a good beer and bullshit about later. Preferably,* much *later. It's not the kind of story you enjoy while the damned thing is happening.*

He'd collected quite a few stories like that over the eighteen-T-years since he'd enlisted in Her Manticoran Majesty's Marine Corps, and he'd just as soon have avoided adding this one to his collection.

Well, if I can't take a joke, I shouldn't have joined, he told himself, and turned his attention to the task at hand.

The good news was that a *Nike*-class battlecruiser carried a three hundred-man Marine detachment, twice the size of a *Saganami-C*'s. The bad news was that that still gave HMS *Rigel* only two companies. And the even worse news, as far as he was concerned, was that he'd been tasked to provide Marine support for two separate naval boarding parties.

Which wouldn't be all that bad, I suppose, if we weren't going to be outnumbered ten-to-one by the Sollies still aboard the damned ships.

He glanced at lieutenant Sebastián Fariñas, Admiral Oversteegen's San Martin-born flag lieutenant, standing at his shoulder, then across the pinnace's troop compartment at Captain Luciana Ingebrigtsen, the commander of his Alpha Company. He'd more or less flipped a coin to decide whether he should accompany her or Motoyuki MacDerment, Bravo Company's CO. Since he was going with Ingebrigtsen, he'd sent Gunny Danko (otherwise known as Sergeant Major Evelyn Danko) along with MacDerment to keep an eye on him. Both Ingebrigtsen and MacDerment were good, solid officers, but they were undeniably still a bit young for their rank. There was a lot of that going around, and while he was confident in their competence, there was no harm providing a little adult supervision. By the same token, he was equally confident that whichever one of them he chose to accompany, it was the *other* one Murphy would choose to drop straight into the crapper. (Both of those beliefs, he supposed, might owe a little something to his eleven years' enlisted experienced before the Corps sent him off to OTC.)

Of course, the fact that he'd assigned himself to Alpha Company also meant that Alpha Company had been assigned to board SLNS *Anton von Leeuwenhoek*, which happened to be the flagship of one Admiral Keeley O'Cleary. Which also explained Fariñas' presence.

At the moment, Ingebrigtsen was involved in a quiet conversation with Master Sergeant Clifton Palmarocchi, Alpha Company's senior noncom. Palmarocchi had been around the block and back again, and the chunky, muscular master sergeant, with his thinning fair hair and pronounced Gryphon accent, would have made an admirable illustration for the term "grizzled veteran." That was just fine with Markiewicz, especially when he contemplated the absurd youthfulness of the junior officer standing at Ingebrigtsen's elbow and nodding sagely at whatever she was saying. The captain might be young, but Lieutenant Hector Lindsay looked like he ought to be playing mumblety-peg in a schoolyard somewhere. Well, maybe it wasn't quite that bad, but it was bad enough. In fact, Lindsay was still a few months shy of his twentieth birthday, standard, fresh out of OCS, which made him even younger than Lieutenant Fariñas (no ancient graybeard himself), and he'd had "his" platoon for just under two months, having come aboard literally as *Rigel* was pulling out for Talbott.

There was a reason, the major suspected, Ingebrigtsen and Palmarocchi had both ended up accompanying First Platoon instead of either of her other platoons. And, he admitted to himself, if he'd thought about it, *he* would have picked this pinnace to help keep an eye on Lindsay. The boy was smart enough, and motivated as hell, but he was so shiny and new that it hurt.

Well, Markiewicz decided, glancing at his armor's HUD, where the pinnace's flight engineer was feeding him a duplicate of the pilot's HUD, *we'll be finding out shortly how well this is all going to work.*

❖   ❖   ❖

"Good seal, Ma'am," Petty Officer 2/c John Pettigrew announced as a green light indicated a solid mating with *Charles Babbage*'s

Emergency Airlock Number 117. "According to the diagnostic ping, the lock's operable, but it looks like it's running on emergency local power."

"Thank you, PO," Abigail acknowledged, then glanced at Gutierrez.

"Let's get them moving, Lieutenant," she said far more formally than she normally spoke to him.

"Yes, Ma'am."

Gutierrez took time to salute before sealing his helmet, which, Abigail knew, was his equivalent, under the circumstances, of pitching a tantrum. He hadn't liked the decision to place him in tactical command of the boarding party instead of staying where he was supposed to be, watching *her* back, one little bit. Unfortunately the fact that *Tristram* carried no Marine detachment made ex-Sergeant Gutierrez the closest thing to a Marine CO Naomi Kaplan had available. That, coupled with the fact that Abigail was the only one of her Navy officers with any experience in ground combat was what had determined who would command *Tristram*'s boarding party.

Everyone, including (perhaps even especially) Lieutenant Abigail Hearns hoped combat experience would be completely irrelevant to their present mission. The entire reason *Tristram* had been assigned responsibility for *Charles Babbage* was the sheer extent of the superdreadnought's devastating damage. Although Abigail's little command was technically a boarding party, their real function was search and rescue, and any Solly with a functional brain was going to be simply delighted to see them.

Unfortunately, as she'd pointed out to Corbett, they couldn't rely on the functionality of any survivors' brains. In fact, it was entirely possible that what they'd been through could have thoroughly unhinged some of them, in which case all bets were off and all of Mateo Gutierrez's experience might be required, after all.

He understood that as well as she did, but he also understood that it meant he was going to be concentrating on running the boarding party's entire security element instead of solely watching over one Abigail Hearns. And while he was far too professional to object, it was obvious he didn't see any reason to pretend—with Abigail, at least—that he was at all amused.

Well, you're just going to have to deal with it, Mateo, she thought, smiling affectionately at his broad back.

Chapter Twenty-Four

EVGENY MARKIEWICZ had never thought much of officers who fretted over details which should have been left in the hands of their noncoms. He'd seen entirely too many examples of that from the noncom's perspective, which meant he knew exactly how much it pissed off the noncoms in question. What was worse, it represented a misuse of the officer's time and attention. He was supposed to be in charge of *managing* his command, however big or small it might be, not allowing himself to become absorbed in the sorts of details which could all too easily distract him from that management function.

At the moment, he found that somewhat more difficult than usual to remember.

The boat bay aboard SLNS *Anton von Leeuwenhoek*, Admiral Keeley O'Cleary's flagship, was larger than it would have been aboard a Manticoran superdreadnought. Partly that was because Solarian ships carried greater numbers of small craft. That had been true even before Manticoran crews had been downsized, although the difference was even more marked these days. For another thing, Solarian small craft tended to be larger than their Manticoran counterparts. According to his briefing, they didn't carry any more personnel or cargo—in fact, they carried slightly less—but they had a longer designed operating radius, and their basic designs were much older and hadn't profited from the RMN's wartime emphasis on greater operational efficiency and component reduction.

At the moment, all those small craft, aside from two purely reaction-drive cutters, were absent, however. By this time, they were sitting obediently in orbit around Flax, under the watchful eyes—and weapons—of Commodore Terekhov's cruisers, and the boat bay was a huge, gaping cavern in their absence. A cavern which looked even larger with only a trio of Manticoran pinnaces docked in it like lonely interlopers.

Captain Ingebrigtsen had Lieutenant Lindsay and Platoon Sergeant Frances Harper handle First Platoon's debarkation, and Markiewicz had been pleased by the way Ingebrigtsen managed not to hover. For that matter, he'd been pleased by the way Lindsay had let Harper get on with it. But now, as the platoon's forty-four men and women formed up in *Leeuwenhoek*'s boat bay gallery, he recognized Ingebrigtsen's itchy expression. He ought to, given that he shared the same ignoble temptation to start fooling around with those details he was supposed to stay clear of.

Fortunately, young Lindsay seemed unaware of the pair of incipient backseat drivers somehow managing to restrain themselves. The lieutenant glanced around, then looked at Sergeant Harper.

"Let's get a squad on each of the lift banks, Frankie," he said.

"Aye, Sir!" Harper replied, and barked a few crisp commands. The platoon quickly and smoothly unraveled into its constituent squads, and Markiewicz gave a mental nod of approval. It was a simple evolution, but the confidence in Lindsay's voice and the briskness with which he'd acted were both good signs.

And, unlike one Major Markiewicz, Lindsay appeared completely immune to the temptation to micromanage his platoon sergeant.

"Bay secure, Ma'am," Lindsay reported a moment later to Ingebrigtsen.

"Thank you, Hector," the captain replied gravely, and keyed her battle armor's com. "Bay secure," she announced. "Second Platoon, come ahead."

"Aye, aye, Ma'am," Lieutenant Sylvester Jackson responded almost instantly. "On our way."

The second pinnace's hatch cycled open, and Jackson's platoon swam briskly down the personnel tube. They fell in just inside the gallery, and Jackson—four years older than Lindsay, with sandy hair and a pronounced Sphinxian accent—reported to Ingebrigtsen.

"You know what to do, Sly," Ingebrigtsen told him.

"Aye, aye, Ma'am." Jackson saluted her and Markiewicz, then

turned to his own platoon sergeant and passed through Lindsay's people into the central shaft of each bank of lifts. They did not enter the lift *cars*, however. Instead, they sent the cars upward, overriding the automatic command to close the shaft doors behind them, and, as per their pre-mission orders, followed the cars up the shaft in their armor. Markiewicz didn't really expect anyone aboard *Leeuwenhoek* to be stupid enough to try anything, but if anyone was so suicidally inclined, he had no intention of offering his people up in neatly packaged, easily bushwhacked lots.

"All right, Aldonza," Ingebrigtsen said over her com. "Your turn."

"Understood, Ma'am."

Lieutenant Aldonza Navarro, Third Platoon's CO, had a more pronounced San Martin accent than Fariñas'. At a hundred and seventy-two centimeters, she was on the short side for most of the San Martinos Markiewicz had met, but there was nothing wrong with her efficiency, and Third Platoon quickly assembled in the boat bay.

Markiewicz, meanwhile, was monitoring his HUD, watching the icons of Jackson's Marines as they ascended the lift shafts. Jackson's second squad left its shaft at the 03 Deck lift doors. The lieutenant himself stayed with his first squad, leaving the shaft at the 02 Deck level. His second squad continued to the 01 Deck, and Markiewicz gave another mental nod as all three squads settled into position.

"Take the banks, Aldonza," Ingebrigtsen instructed, and Third Platoon relieved Lindsay's people as the anchoring security element on the lift banks here in the boat bay. At the same time, First Platoon fell back in, and Ingebrigtsen nodded—in her case, physically—in approval.

"Ready to proceed, Sir," she said formally, turning to Markiewicz.

"Very good, Captain." Markiewicz smiled. "Let's get this show on the road, then."

"Aye, aye, Sir. Head them up-shaft, Hector."

"Aye, aye, Ma'am!" Lindsay acknowledged, and First Platoon started climbing into the shaft Jackson had used, with Ingebrigtsen, Fariñas, and Markiewicz trailing along behind.

This time, Markiewicz noted, Lieutenant Lindsay hadn't quite managed to keep his excitement out of his voice, but the major was inclined to cut the youngster a little slack. After all, his platoon had been chosen to accompany Markiewicz to *Leeuwenhoek*'s flag bridge to formally accept Admiral O'Cleary's personal surrender before the rest of his Marines began moving through the rest of the core hull to secure it. Which meant young Hector Lindsay was about to go into the Corps' history books as the first junior officer—*very* junior officer, in his case—of any star nation to command the squad which took a Solarian League Navy's flag officer's surrender on the flag deck of an SLN superdreadnought. Markiewicz wasn't exactly immune to the same awareness, which was one reason he couldn't justify taking Lindsay to task for it. At the same time, though, he wondered if Lindsay had figured out he'd drawn this particular assignment because he was the least experienced of Ingebrigtsen's platoon commanders? Navarro, with the most combat experience of all, had taken over the boat bay detachment because it constituted Markiewicz's reserve. If something went wrong and dropped them all into the crapper after all, he wanted somebody who'd been there and done that in charge of the force assigned to pull them all back out again.

I wonder if Luciana had the heart to explain that to Lindsay? he wondered. *I know* I *didn't!*

Abigail Hearns took one more look around. The passageway immediately inboard from the emergency airlock was longer and a bit wider than it would have been in a Manticoran or Grayson-designed warship, but it looked rather cramped at the moment, with her entire boarding party and six counter-grav sleds of salvage and rescue gear packed into it. Other than that, about the best she could say was that it was still atmosphere tight. Only the emergency lights were up, and close to a third of the lighting elements were dead. One of her engineering ratings had already determined that the backup hardwired emergency com system was down, but from the looks of things, that could just as easily have been due to lack of maintenance as to the damage *Charles Babbage* had suffered at Manticoran hands.

The ship—or, rather, the battered hulk which had once been a ship—was under an apparent gravity of about 1.2 *g*. The wreckage had been rotated perpendicular to its line of flight, putting the decks and deckheads back where they ought to be, and *Tristram* was playing tugboat to slow what was left of the *Babbage* down. In many ways, Abigail would have preferred to remain in microgravity. It would have made getting about faster and simpler, not to mention avoiding the stress the deceleration was putting on damaged structural members. And she was well aware that the deceleration might actually be life-threatening for survivors under some circumstances. Unfortunately, the wreck's velocity of almost eighteen thousand kilometers per second had already carried it past Flax. It was now hurtling across the inner system at roughly six percent of light-speed, bound for a fatal encounter with the gas giant Everest in just under twenty hours. It was extraordinarily unlikely, given Tenth Fleet's limited manpower, that the SAR parties would be able to completely search ships as mangled and torn as *Babbage* and her consorts in that time. Which meant they had to be slowed down somehow.

Tristram looked like a guppy tethered to a whale as she worked to decelerate *Babbage*'s wreckage, but there wouldn't have been any point using a larger, more powerful vessel. *Tristram* could brake them at the current rate indefinitely, and they dared not apply any greater deceleration, for a lot of reasons. At this rate, it would take over fifteen T-days (and the next best thing to twelve light-hours) to actually stop them relative to the system primary, but it would also divert them well clear of any collisions with odds and ends of system real estate, which would be a very good thing from the SAR perspective.

Assuming anyone who maintained their internal systems as poorly as these people appeared to have had managed to survive to be rescued in the first place, of course.

Don't rush to conclusions, Abby, she reminded herself. *This is strictly an emergency access way, and the lock's the only thing it leads to. Let's not decide all of their maintenance is as half-assed as it looks right here until we've actually seen it.*

She told herself that rather firmly, and she knew she had a point. But she couldn't help reflecting on how any Manticoran or Grayson executive officer would react to something like this, even if it was "only" an emergency access way. In fact, *especially* if it was "only" an emergency access way. There was a reason things like that were provided when a ship was designed, after all, and when an emergency finally came along and bit your posterior, it was a little late to think about catching up on that overdue maintenance you'd really been meaning to get to sometime real soon now.

At least we're in, we're in one piece, and we're in solid com contact with the pinnace. Which means—

"All right, Mateo, let's go," she said.

"Yes, Ma'am," Lieutenant Gutierrez replied, then nodded to PO 1/c William MacFarlane, one of the noncoms to whom he'd issued another flechette gun. "Lead 'em out, Bill."

"Yes, Sir," MacFarlane acknowledged in turn, and started cautiously down the poorly lit passage.

Three more ratings with flechette guns followed him, with Gutierrez behind them. The lieutenant and Bosun Musgrave had spent the better part of half an hour deciding which naval personnel should be trusted with things that went bang. MacFarlane and the other flechette-armed ratings—there were three more bringing up the rear—were the ones with actual combat experience or who had most recently qualified with the weapons. Everyone else carried at least a sidearm as regulations required, but Gutierrez had been bloodthirstily explicit when he explained what would happen to anyone other than his designated flechette gunners who dared to switch any weapon from "safe" to "fire" without his specific instructions to do so. Given the profoundly stupid things Abigail had seen people do with firearms, she heartily approved of her armsman's attitude.

Now the rest of the party followed MacFarlane to the airtight door at the end of the airlock access way, and Selma Wilkie, one of Lieutenant Fonzarelli's engineering techs, examined the controls.

"Power's down, Ma'am," she reported to Abigail over the general net, then continued in a carefully expressionless voice. "According to the telltales, there's standard pressure on the other side, though."

Abigail heard someone snort contemptuously and shook her own head. They were inside the superdreadnought's outer armor but still well outside the big ship's core hull. Passages like this one were specifically designed and intended to be depressurized when the ship went to action stations as a means of limiting blast damage when the armor was breached. The fact that *Charles Babbage* hadn't bothered to do that said an enormous amount about the Solarian League Navy's readiness states. Or about Task Force 496's pre-battle appreciation of the threat levels it faced, at least.

"Well, it's nice we'll have air, Selma," Abigail responded mildly. "On the other hand, who knows? They may actually have depressurized the next lateral. Besides, I understand Sollies don't like to take showers or wash their socks. So if it's all the same to you, I think we'll just keep our helmets sealed, anyway."

"Suits me just fine, Ma'am," Wilkie replied with a chuckle, and someone else laughed out loud. That laugh sounded just a bit nervous, perhaps, but Abigail wasn't going to fault anyone for that.

"Open it up," she said.

"Aye, aye, Ma'am."

Wilkie engaged the manual unlocking system and gripped the old-fashioned wheel. It took her a second longer—and a lot more effort—than it ought to have to get it moving, and the squealing sound it made set Abigail's teeth on edge. Not just because of the fingernails on a blackboard effect, either. There was no excuse at all for not properly maintaining the manual override mechanism on an emergency escape hatch!

Once Wilkie managed to undog the pressure door, it swung smoothly open. Macfarlane stepped quickly through it, turning to his left, up-ship, and one of the other flechette gunners stepped through it to the right.

"Clear port," MacFarlane reported.

"Clear starboard," the other man said.

"Go," Gutierrez responded, and the rest of the boarding party flowed quickly through the opening under his critical eye. Fortunately, everyone remembered how he'd briefed them and no one fell over his or her feet in the process. In fact, although Abigail knew he'd never admit it, his "vacuum-sucker" spacers moved with commendable caution and speed.

She herself paused and bent to examine the emergency hatch more closely. The passageway to which it had granted access was also illuminated only by emergency lighting, but at least all of the lighting units seemed to be up this time. And as she examined the hatch, she found that the normal power-assisted unlocking system appeared to have been far better maintained than the manual system had. Of course, there was the minor problem that at the moment it didn't *have* power, wasn't there?

A shadow fell over her, and when she looked up, she found that Musgrave had been looking over her shoulder.

"Ain't that a kicker, Ma'am?" the bosun muttered in tones of profound disgust. Over, she noticed, his dedicated link, not the general net.

"It does seem just a bit slipshod, Bosun," she acknowledged over the same link. "But not a lot more than leaving pressure in here."

"Someone needs his butt kicked up between his ears, begging your pardon, Ma'am," Musgrave concurred.

"Oh, I couldn't agree with you more. On the other hand, the SLN's a peacetime navy. Or it *was*, anyway. I imagine they put up with quite of bit of sloppiness."

"Peacetime or not, they should've had the brains to at least pump the air! And even allowing for that, this here's an example of piss-poor maintenance discipline," Musgrave growled, glowering at the neglected manual unlocking system. "'Less I'm mistaken, accidents've been known to happen in peacetime, too, Ma'am."

"That they have," Abigail agreed more grimly. "Even aboard Solarian ships-of-the-wall, I suppose."

She straightened and consulted the schematic which had been loaded into her electronic memo board. Theoretically, at least, she had the deck plans for the entire ship—or for the *Scientist* class as originally designed, at least—supplied specifically for SAR by Admiral O'Cleary. She hoped the schematics really were complete, without any surprises, intentional or unintentional, but she wasn't prepared to trust them fully. Still, they offered at least general guidance, and she'd marked them with the damage *Tristram*'s sensors had been able to map before she download them to the board.

"All right, Walt," she said to Midshipman Corbett, who carried an identical memo board. "This is where we split up. According to our damage map, this passage should extend another hundred meters forward before you hit a breach. It's got to be good for at least fifty meters, since that's the closest set of blast doors in that direction. You take your people and head forward."

She tapped her own memo board with a stylus, and a lift bank flashed amber on both boards simultaneously.

"Make sure your com link doesn't get compromised, and stop at this lift bank," she continued, indicating the flashing section of the schematic. "Meantime, I'll head aft to Lift Nineteen. Whether there's power to the lifts or not, we can use the shafts to move inboard."

"Aye, aye, Ma'am," Corbett acknowledged. "Bosun?"

"I'm on it, Sir," Musgrave said with just a hint of reassuring gruffness, nodded to Abigail, and started down the passage in the indicated direction with his extraordinarily youthful superior officer in tow.

Abigail watched half of the boarding party moving off with them, then turned to grin at Gutierrez.

"Let's go, Mateo."

✧   ✧   ✧

Major Markiewicz followed Captain Ingebrigtsen and Master Sergeant Palmarocchi out of the lift doors at the 00 Deck level. According to the schematic in his battle armor's memory, he was approximately sixty meters aft of *Leeuwenhoek*'s command deck, and one hundred meters forward of her flag bridge. The 00 Deck corresponded to the Royal Manticoran Navy's Axial-One, the central—and best protected—deck of a warship's core hull, and *Leeuwenhoek*'s was both broader and higher than the other decks stacked above and below it. The passage before Markiewicz was well lit, yet he felt uneasily aware of its vastness, as if he couldn't quite make out details.

Don't be stupid, Evgeny. You can see just fine. It's just that you shouldn't be seeing this much empty space aboard any warship.

He snorted mentally, then turned to the dark-haired SLN lieutenant who'd been waiting at the lift doors. Allowing for prolong, she was probably somewhere in her thirties, he estimated—old for her rank in the RMN. Then again, the Sollies hadn't had as many vacancies created for promotion over the last couple of decades as Manticore had.

The name "PABST, V." was stenciled on the breast of her skinsuit, and she wore no helmet. She was of slightly above average height, although she looked like a stripling standing in front of his looming battle armor.

"Major Markiewicz, Royal Manticoran Marines," he said crisply over his armor's external speakers.

"Lieutenant Pabst—Valencia Pabst," she responded. "I'm Admiral O'Cleary's flag lieutenant."

"Excuse me, Lieutenant," Ingebrigtsen put in a bit sharply, "but don't Solarian officers salute *superior* officers?"

Pabst looked at her for a moment, as if Ingebrigtsen had spoken in some foreign tongue. Then she shook herself visibly, flushed, came to a reasonably correct position of attention, and saluted Markiewicz.

"I beg your pardon, Major."

There was more than a little anger in her voice, but Markiewicz figured she was entitled to that.

"I realize this has all come as something of a shock, Lieutenant Pabst," he replied, charitably ascribing her lapse in military courtesy to the aforesaid shock as he returned her belated salute.

"Yes, Sir. It has," she agreed, still with that core of cold anger and resentment. "If you'll follow me, please?"

"Lead on, Lieutenant," Markiewicz replied.

"Top?" Ingebrigtsen said quietly to Palmarocchi.

"On it, Ma'am," the master sergeant replied, and dropped back beside Lieutenant Lindsay.

He spoke very quietly to the young man for a moment, and then Lindsay and his platoon's first squad arranged themselves unobtrusively at Ingebrigtsen and Markiewicz's heels. The second and third squads stayed put, keeping an eye on the lift banks while Master Sergeant Palmarocchi and Platoon Sergeant Wilkie kept an eye on them. Markiewicz really wished Palmarocchi was along to watch his back, but he supposed that between them a grass-green lieutenant, an experienced captain, and a weary old major who'd once upon a time been a battalion sergeant major ought to be able to manage a single squad of Marines.

The hike from the lift to *Leeuwenhoek*'s flag bridge seemed to take far longer than it ought to, and Markiewicz suspected he wasn't the only person who found the silent emptiness of the deck eerie. Pabst obviously didn't feel much like making small talk, for which he scarcely blamed her, but no one had much to say over the Marines' com net, either.

Good communications discipline, the major thought wryly. *Maybe we should try boarding surrendered Solly superdreadnoughts more often as a training technique.*

Lengthy as the walk seemed while they were making it, it ended abruptly at an open pressure door. Pabst glanced at Markiewicz, then stepped through the door.

He followed her, and found himself on the SD's flag deck.

Like the passageway outside it, *Leeuwenhoek*'s flag deck was considerably more spacious than a Manticoran flag deck would have been. That was interesting, Markiewicz thought, given the far larger number of people crammed aboard the Solarian ship. A Manticoran designer, with considerably more volume to play with, would have fitted the command stations into no more than two thirds of the volume *Leeuwenhoek*'s architect had assigned to them.

The various displays and consoles had a sleek, aesthetically pleasant grace to them. Their shapes and spacing seemed to flow into one another, almost as if they'd been designed to do just that, although, he thought as he glanced over them, they didn't seem to be arranged quite as well from the viewpoint of *information flow.* The ops officer on a Manticoran admiral's staff, for example, was placed so that he could see the astrogator's display by looking in one direction and the master tactical plot by looking in the other, all without moving out of his bridge chair. The way *Leeuwenhoek's* command stations were arranged, however, the ops officer would have to stand up, take at least two steps, and crane his neck awkwardly to see the astro display. And one of the reasons he'd have to was that he had at least twice as many assistants as a Manticoran ops officer would have required, and he would have had to walk around one of them to see it.

Obviously, they figure the guy who does the shooting doesn't have to see where the guy who's steering is headed, he thought dryly. *Not to mention the minor fact that they're* way *over-manned.*

He noted those details out of the corner of one eye. Most of his attention was focused on identifying Admiral Keeley O'Cleary. In one way, it wasn't very difficult, since his armor's memory had been loaded with her picture. But what he hadn't counted on was the sheer number of stars stenciled on various people's skinsuits.

He was still registering the fact that the compartment seemed to be filled with an extraordinary number of flag officers when O'Cleary stepped forward. She looked at him, dark eyes stony, and he saluted.

"Major Evgeny Markiewicz, Royal Manticoran Marines, Ma'am," he said.

"Admiral O'Cleary," she replied, acknowledging his salute with frigid correctness. "I trust you'll forgive me if I don't add 'Welcome aboard,' Major?"

Silence, Markiewicz decided, was golden, and he contented himself with a courteous little half-nod from behind his armor's visor.

"Vice Admiral Hansen Chamberlain, my chief of staff," O'Cleary continued, indicating a short, squared-off officer to her right. "My operations officer, Rear Admiral Tang Dzung-ming. My staff intelligence officer, Rear Admiral Lavinia Fairfax. And my staff communications officer, Captain Kalidasa Omprakash."

At last, someone who isn't *an admiral!* Markiewicz thought as he acknowledged each introduction in turn. Then he indicated his own officers.

"Captain Ingebrigtsen," he said, "Lieutenant Fariñas, Rear Admiral Oversteegen's flag lieutenant, and Lieutenant Lindsay."

All three of them saluted, and O'Cleary returned the courtesy. Then she looked back at Markiewicz.

"I suppose I should be handing you a sword or something, Major," she said tartly. "Unfortunately, I'm afraid the Solarian League Navy isn't very *practiced* at this sort of thing."

It could have come out with an edge of humor, but it didn't. Nor was there any humor in the cold smile which accompanied it.

"If I've discovered one thing over the last twenty years or so, Admiral," Markiewicz replied, meeting her eyes steadily, "it's that we don't get much of a chance to practice a lot of the more important things until it's too late."

O'Cleary's lips tightened, but then, visibly, she made herself stop and draw a deep breath.

"I imagine that's something we should all bear in mind," she said then. "In the meantime, however, how does your Admiral Gold Peak wish to handle this, Major?"

"Ma'am, as soon as I have formally received your surrender, and that of Captain Lister, I will so notify Admiral Gold Peak's staff. At that time, I will place one of my squads on the command deck, one in Central Engineering, and another in each of your boat bays to provide traffic control and security. As soon as that's been accomplished, a naval boarding party will come aboard *Leeuwenhoek* and complete the task of securing the vessel. I am to extend Admiral Gold Peak's compliments to you, and invite you to return aboard *Rigel*, Admiral Oversteegen's flagship with Lieutenant Fariñas. My understanding is that Admiral Gold Peak will be arriving aboard *Rigel* shortly herself."

"I see."

O'Cleary gazed at him for several moments, her face expressionless, then nodded.

"Very well, Major. It would seem that I, like the rest of this task force, find myself in Admiral Gold Peak's hands at the moment. I will, of course, comply with her wishes."

"Thank you, Admiral."

"Would you prefer to receive Captain Lister's surrender here, or on his command deck?"

"Since my orders are to secure the bridge, as well, Ma'am, I think it would probably be more convenient for the Captain if he simply waited there for me."

Markowitz kept his voice as politely, militarily impersonal as he could, and O'Cleary nodded again. There might actually have been a trace of awareness of his efforts not to step any more heavily on her toes—or Lister's—than he had to.

Of course, there might not have, too.

"Kalidasa, please be good enough to inform the Captain that Major Markiewicz will meet him on his bridge," she said, without looking over her shoulder at Captain Omprakash.

"Yes, Ma'am."

"Well, I suppose that concludes the formalities—here, at least," she said, and gave Sebastián Fariñas a thin smile. "Should the other members of my staff accompany us, Lieutenant?"

"If you so desire, Ma'am," Fariñas said, "I feel certain Rear Admiral Oversteegen would be pleased to offer them the hospitality of his ship. The decision, however, is yours."

"In that case, I'd like Vice Admiral Chamberlain to accompany us."

"Of course, Ma'am."

"Iwasaki," Lindsay said over the platoon net, and Corporal Dunstan Iwasaki and his section of three stepped forward, arranging themselves as an honor guard around O'Cleary, Chamberlain, and Fariñas.

Well, the kid got that right, Markiewicz decided after glancing at Ingebrigtsen. From the captain's expression, it was obvious she hadn't set that up ahead of time. And that she was as as pleased to see it as Markiewicz was.

O'Cleary cocked her head, smiling slightly, as if she were trying to decide whether it was an honor guard or a security detail to keep her from making some kind of break for it. Then she snorted quietly, a bit less bitterly, somehow, and nodded to Markiewicz.

"If I don't see you again, Major," she said, "allow me to thank you for your courtesy in a difficult situation."

"Thank you, Ma'am," he acknowledged, and he and his officers saluted her again. She and Chamberlain returned the salute, then followed Fariñas out of the compartment.

"We've got a pair survivors, Ma'am."

Abigail stopped in midstride, raising one hand to stop the rest of her party, as Midshipman Corbett's voice came over the com. There was something about his tone . . .

"Are you all right, Walt?" she asked quietly over her private link.

"Yes, Ma'am," he replied over the same link. "It's just—" He

paused, and she heard a distinct swallowing sound. "It's just...
kind of bad in here."

Abigail looked down at her memo board and checked the icons
representing Corbett and his party. Her own party had already
encountered over seventy dead and only six survivors—all of
whom had been in skinsuits and trapped in compartments they
could not escape. They'd also counted twenty-three lifepod hatches
which showed vacuum on the other side, which presumably meant
whoever had been close enough to them had already escaped
the ship. Her six survivors had been sent back to the pinnace,
escorted by a single one of her spacers, and all of them had seemed
too dazed by the scope of the disaster—and too grateful to be
alive—to offer anything resembling resistance. Yet so far, Corbett
hadn't located a single survivor and only a scattering of bodies.

But that, she realized as she punched up the scale on the board,
had obviously just changed. He and his party were one passageway
farther in than her own, and he'd just entered the core hull. In
fact, if the schematic was accurate, he was in one of the nodal
damage control compartments.

Which, she thought coldly, *is supposed to have upwards of forty
people in it when the ship's at Action Stations. So if he's only got
two survivors...*

"Do you need any more hands?" She kept her voice impersonal.

"No, Ma'am. Not yet, anyway." Corbett might have swallowed
again, but his voice was a little stronger when he resumed speaking. "The Bosun and my sick berth attendant have them stabilized
in life support stretchers. I'm detaching two of my people to take
them back to the pinnace, then return here. Uh, if that's all right
with you, I mean, Ma'am."

"Walt, it's your call," she told him. *And, of course, you've got
the Bosun there to make sure you don't step on your sword,* she
added silently.

"Thank you, Ma'am."

His voice was definitely stronger this time, and she smiled
crookedly.

"You're welcome," she said. "Now, let's be about it."

Chapter Twenty-Five

"—AFRAID IT'S NOT QUITE so simple as all that, Admiral. The consensus of my House committee is quite firm on this point. Before the Administration could possibly get Congress to sign off on any formal treaty, especially one in which the Republic accepts some sort of 'war guilt' clause, the futures of these star systems have to be settled. That, after all, was the reason we voted to support the resumption of hostilities in the first place."

Honor Alexander-Harrington bit her tongue rather firmly. It was an exercise with which she'd had an unfortunate amount of experience over the last five or six weeks. In fact, she'd gotten to practice at it almost every time Gerald Younger opened his mouth.

She drew a deep, unobtrusive breath and thought longingly of public dueling grounds and ten-millimeter pistols as the representative sat back in his chair, jaw clenched with manly fortitude and brown eyes hard with steely determination. It wasn't so much that she was unwilling to believe his committee members felt— or could be brought to feel—exactly as he'd just said they did, although she doubted they were nearly so adamant (or united) as he was suggesting. No, the problem was that she could taste the real emotions behind his argument, which meant she knew he personally didn't give a single solitary damn about the future of the disputed star systems and never had. He'd been harping on this point for a full half-day now, but what he really wanted was something else entirely. It was unfortunate that she couldn't pluck exactly what that "something else" was out of his mind, but she'd come to the conclusion that he was probably after one of two things.

Either he intended to give in eventually on the unstated understanding that his concession on this point would earn a matching concession from her on another point—probably the amount of reparations the Republic was going to ante up eventually, given the way he kept harping on linking the issue to "war guilt"—or else he didn't want anything out of *her* at all. In fact, the way he kept referring to the reasons the Havenite Congress had voted to support the Pritchart Administration's resumption of hostilities suggested to Honor that the latter possibility was more probably the correct one. He'd been just a little bit too careful, just a tad too obvious, about *not* saying explicitly that the real reason the Republic was in its current dire predicament was due to missteps by that same administration. Which strongly suggested that the real target of his extortion was Eloise Pritchart. Honor had no idea what sort of domestic concession he might want to squeeze out of the Pritchart Administration, but it was at least equally probable that there was one and that he knew Pritchart would eventually promise it to him if he'd only shut up.

The fact that he hadn't said one single word about the Green Pines allegations might be another indicator pointing in that direction. They would have made a much more suitable stick for beating the Star Empire directly, at any rate. Of course, from what Honor had come to know of Pritchart, it was entirely possible there were other reasons he'd chosen not to reach for that particular club.

However that might be, though, he was clearly after *something*, and from the taste of Pritchart's mind-glow, she was clearly of the same opinion . . . and probably thinking about the Havenite equivalent of dueling grounds, too.

"Mr. Younger," Honor said, once she was reasonably certain she had her temper under control, "I don't really think it's very practical for us to sit here and dispose of the political futures of entire star systems without actually consulting the people who live in them. As I'm sure you're well aware, the majority of the star systems which were still in Manticoran possession at the time hostilities were resumed were militarily strategic ones which had been retained only for their military value. Pending the conclusion of a formal peace treaty, those star systems would have been granted their independence or returned to Havenite control, depending on local conditions and desires. Certain other systems, admittedly, were still in our possession mainly because they were so far in our rear and had been occupied for so long. Those systems which had indicated their desire to remain independent of the Republic would have been permitted to so do by the Star Empire pending the conclusion of that same treaty. Some of them, as you're well aware, had already expressed a desire to remain independent before the resumption of our current hostilities, and I strongly doubt that Her Majesty would be willing to force them back into the Republic's welcoming arms at bayonet point if that's not where they want to go.

"At the moment, however, if it's escaped your attention, *none* of those star systems are currently in Manticoran possession at all. Given that fact, and the past history I've just summarized, I fail to see precisely why you expect Her Majesty's Government to countersign some sort of blank check for the *Republic* to determine their futures at this conference table instead of consulting with them after the cessation of hostilities."

"I'm not asking you to 'countersign' anything, Admiral," Younger replied. "I'm asking you, as Queen Elizabeth's representative, to acknowledge the validity of the results of the plebiscites conducted in those 'strategic' star systems following their liberation from Manticorian occupation by Republican armed forces. And to pledge to abide by plebiscites to be conducted on any other planet which was previously part of the People's Republic of Haven and which is currently occupied by Republican forces."

"And I'm telling you, Sir," Honor replied in a tone whose patience would have made anyone who knew her well extremely nervous, "that Her Majesty is not prepared to acknowledge anything, anywhere, in any star system, without first having had the opportunity to examine the evidence and the results to be sure the processes were free, open, and legitimate."

"Are you suggesting the results of the plebiscites the Republic has already conducted might not represent the true desires of the systems' inhabitants?"

Younger's eyes had narrowed, and there was an edge of ice in his voice. All in all, no one could possibly have misinterpreted the offense he'd taken at the mere suggestion of electoral chicanery. Honor, however, was fully aware of the actual emotions behind that bristling façade, and she felt Nimitz stir on the perch beside her chair as he tasted her almost overwhelming desire to punch Younger squarely in the nose. From the feel of the treecat's emotions, he was entirely in favor of the notion. He knew as well as Honor that the Havenite legislator understood perfectly well that she was suggesting nothing of the sort. In fact, what Younger felt at the moment was a powerful sense of satisfaction, undoubtedly at his ability to burn time on such a minor issue.

And speaking of time, she decided, it was time for a certain amount of candor.

"Mr. Younger," she said calmly, "you and I are both perfectly well aware I'm suggesting nothing of the sort."

His eyes widened, and she tasted his surprise at her head-on approach. Well, that was too bad, wasn't it? After all, she was an admiral, not a diplomat, and he could either like that fact or lump it. At the moment, she didn't much care which, either.

"I haven't said Manticore won't acknowledge the validity of the plebiscite results. What I've said is that Manticore won't acknowledge their validity without the opportunity to evaluate their reliability, accuracy, openness, and honesty for ourselves. You're as aware as I am of the distinction between those two positions, and you're also as aware as I am that this is a point on which I, as the Star Empire's representative to these talks, am not going to make the concession you're demanding. I can only assume, therefore, that your purpose in demanding it is to use up time. Which, I observe, you are doing despite the fact that I informed you perfectly straightforwardly at the beginning of these negotiations that there was a limit to how long I was authorized to continue talking before the Star Empire resumes active operations against the Republic."

He started to open his mouth, his expression indignant, but she raised her right hand between them, index finger extended vertically in an unspoken command to be silent, and continued in the same measured tone.

"There could be many reasons for your desire to 'run out the clock,' including the belief—mistaken, I assure you—that Manticore is so desperate for a settlement with the Republic, in light of the potential for conflict with the Solarian League, that if these talks can simply be strung out long enough, we'll accept revisions to our more substantive demands, such as the . . . clarification of our differences over our prewar diplomatic correspondence. If that is what you're hoping for, I'm quite certain President Pritchart doesn't share your belief."

She didn't so much as glance in Pritchart's direction, but she could feel the President stiffening ever so slightly in her chair. Not because Honor was wrong, but because Pritchart was surprised by just how *correct* she was.

"I suspect you're well aware that the President believes—accurately, as it happens—that my instructions are to return to Manticore with *no* treaty rather than with a *bad* treaty, time limit or not. Which suggests to me, Sir, that you're bringing a domestic agenda to this table in the belief the President will give you whatever it is you want from her here in the Republic in order to convince you to stop wasting time. Whether or not that belief of yours is accurate is, of course, more than I could say. I would suggest, however, that signing up for fiddle lessons when the house is already on fire is scarcely the most profitable use of your time. Bearing that in mind, I think that rather than sitting here wasting valuable time, we should take a short recess, during which you may discuss with President Pritchart just what it is you want and stop trying to get it out of her by using my mission as your prybar."

Younger's face had darkened steadily, and the power of his anger pulsed in Honor's awareness like a blow torch. He had himself sufficiently under control to glower at her in hot-eyed silence rather than open his mouth and let his fury betray how accurately she'd read him, however. She met his glare steadily for a moment, then looked at Pritchart at last.

The President's topaz eyes met hers with commendable steadiness, although the firm lips below them might have quivered ever so slightly. Honor wasn't prepared to swear to that either way, but she could taste the other woman's mingled irritation, frustration, and—overwhelming, this last emotion—entertainment.

"I believe, under the circumstances, that a recess probably *is* in order," Pritchart said after taking a moment to be certain she had her own voice under control. "I see it's very nearly lunchtime, anyway. If I may, Admiral, I'd suggest we take a couple of hours for lunch, during which Representative Younger can contact the

members of his committee and canvas their response to your...
forthright statement of the Star Empire's position on this point."

She smiled pleasantly at Honor, then turned to Younger.

"If you desire, Gerald," she continued pleasantly, "I'm sure Leslie and Walter and I could also make the time available before
our next session with Admiral Alexander-Harrington and her
delegation to discuss the *Administration's* view on this point. I'm
always happy to hear Congress' views and advice, as you're well
aware, and if the members of your committee have pronounced
reservations on this point, I'd like to be made aware of them. I
would never seek to dictate to the consciences of the Republic's
elected representatives, but I must confess that at this moment,
I'm unaware of any general groundswell of opinion on this point.
If it's going to present serious difficulties, I'd appreciate a briefing on it."

The expression Younger turned on her was even closer to a
glare than the one he'd bewstowed on Honor, but he kept a firm
leash on his anger and nodded with at least a pretense of courtesy.

"Well then," Pritchart said just a tad brightly, smiling at Honor.
"In that case, Admiral, we'll meet back here in two hours. Will
that be convenient for your delegation?"

"Well, that was certainly entertaining, wasn't it?" Honor observed
with an edge of whimsy as the members of her delegation—herded
along by the alert sheepdogs of her armsmen—filed through the
door into their suite's dining room. Like the conference room
Pritchart had provided for their negotiations, the dining room's
windows looked out over the boiling foam of Frontenac Falls,
and she crossed the floor to gaze out at the spectacular scenery.

"I'm not sure 'entertaining' is exactly the word I'd choose, Your
Grace," Tuominen said dryly. "Your approach to the rarefied and
refined world of diplomacy seems just a trifle...*direct*, shall we say?"

"Oh, come now, Voitto!" Sir Barnabas Kew shook his head,
smiling broadly. "You know you enjoyed seeing that insufferable
young bugger taken down a notch just as much as *I* did! Talk
about poisonous little vipers." The permanent undersecretary shook
his head and glanced at Honor. "I don't know what the specifics
of his agenda may be, Your Grace, but I'm convinced you nailed
what he's up to."

"Nimitz and I have been discussing him for a while," Honor

said, which was true enough, as far as it went, and Kew, Tuominen, and Baroness Selleck all nodded. She'd shared her—and
Nimitz's, of course—impressions of all of the Havenite negotiators,
although she'd been a bit less explicit about Pritchart, Theisman,
and Nesbitt for various reasons.

"Of their entire delegation," she continued, "Younger and Tullingham are undoubtedly the most cynical and self-seeking. McGwire's
no prize, you understand, but I think he's at least aware that in
the Republic's current circumstances, a certain pragmatic resignation is in order. Tullingham could scarcely care less what happens
to Pritchart's and Theisman's Constitution—which, personally, I
don't think is the most desirable possible trait in a Supreme Court
justice—but my impression is that while he's the sort who thinks
it's a perfectly wonderful idea to put legal opinions up for sale to
the highest bidder, he's definitely *not* the sort who'd risk riding
something like this down in flames just to satisfy his personal
ambitions. His approach is more a case of 'business is business,'
you might say. Younger, on the other hand..."

She shook her head, not trying to hide her own disgust.

"What about him, Your Grace?" Selleck asked, regarding her
narrowly, and Honor tasted her speculation. Of course, the baroness
had been included among her advisers in no small part because
of her familiarity with the various opposition groups which had
emerged to resurrect the Republic after Saint-Just's death.

"I'm more than a little surprised he hasn't tried to use Green
Pines, actually," Honor admitted. "I know that was what we hoped
for when I had my little chat with the President, but I honestly
didn't expect him to keep his mouth *completely* shut about it."
Nor, she thought, had she anticipated the shiver of fear which
went through the representative's mind-glow whenever it looked
like someone *else* might be about to bring it up. "But the more
we see of him, the more convinced I am that he'd been fishing
in some very murky waters long before we ever turned up in
Nouveau Paris."

"You may well be right," Selleck said. "As I've said, I still don't
have a good feel for how the internal dynamics of his party fit
together, but my sources are suggesting more and more strongly
that he's a more prominent player than we thought before. Are
you suggesting he's a more important player than we've realized
even now?"

"That's hard to say, Carissa," Honor replied thoughtfully, turning away from the windows and moving towards the table as James MacGuiness appeared in the doorway on the other side of the room, keeping an eagle eye on the Navy stewards who'd been sent down from Eighth Fleet to provide him with a reliable, security-screened support group.

"I don't know how important a player he actually is," she continued, seating herself at the head of the table. "For that matter, I don't know that he's really as important a player as *he* thinks he is. Obviously, he's got some stature, or he wouldn't have been included in Pritchart's delegation in the first place. The problem is that he's one of those people who just *knows* he's smarter, sneakier, and just generally all around better than anyone else. I have no idea what it is he wants out of Pritchart, but whatever it is, it never crossed his mind that he wasn't going to get it in the end. Or not until she asked him for that 'briefing,' anyway."

She chuckled, and most of the others joined her. Then she looked up at MacGuiness.

"And just what are you planning on feeding us this afternoon, Mac?"

"I trust you'll find it palatable, Your Grace," MacGuiness said with a small bow and a lurking smile.

"But you're not going to tell me what it is until you put it on the table in front of me, are you?"

"I do treasure my little surprises," he acknowledged with a broader smile, and she shook her head fondly.

"All right, bring it on!" she challenged, and he chuckled as the stewards whipped away covers and set bowls of rich-smelling she crab soup in front of the diners.

"Excuse me, Your Grace."

Honor looked up from her second serving of cherry pie as Lieutenant Tümmel appeared apparently by magic at her shoulder. It was obvious to her that he'd been taking teleportation lessons from MacGuiness, and she'd come to realize she valued his gift for unobtrusiveness even more because Tim Meares hadn't had it. Meares had been just as efficient as Tümmel, but he'd never had Tümmel's ability to blend into the background and pop out of it again at exactly the right moment. Which meant it was at least one way in which Tümmel didn't constantly remind her of her last flag lieutenant and what had happened to him.

"Yes, Waldemar?" she said, allowing no trace of the familiar pain the thought of Meares caused her to show in her eyes or voice.

"We've just received a dispatch from Manticore, relayed from *Imperator*. It's a personal to you, from Her Majesty, and I'm afraid it's flagged as urgent."

"I see."

Honor laid down her fork, wiped her lips on her napkin, and rose. Anxious—or at least intensely speculative—eyes followed her, and she smiled slightly.

"Don't mind me, people," she said. "Go ahead and enjoy your dessert."

Twenty minutes later, Honor sat back from the display in her own suite's sitting room, and her expression was much less amused than it had been. She tipped back her chair and crossed her legs, and Nimitz flowed up into her lap and sat upright, facing her.

"Not so good, is it, Stinker?" she asked, reaching out to stroke his ears. Actually, she realized, "not so good" might be putting it entirely too optimistically. The news was over three weeks old, after all. By this time, it was only too probable that Michelle Henke had already had the opportunity to prove—or disprove—the more optimistic estimates of the superiority of Manticoran military hardware. She felt Nimitz's concern mirroring her own, but then he twitched his upper pelvis in imitation of a human shrug.

<Mike is strong,> his fingers flickered. <She can deal with this.>

For just a moment, Honor was tempted to ask what made him an expert on the subject of battle fleets. Fortunately, the temptation disappeared as quickly as it had come. Treecat understanding of advanced technology and weaponry was still for all intents and purposes nonexistent, but those who'd adopted humans had been sufficiently exposed to it to understand *what* it did, even if they didn't grasp *how* it did it. And Nimitz had seen more naval combat than the majority of professional naval personnel ever saw in an entire lifetime. Some of that combat had come uncomfortably close to killing both him and Honor. In fact, ever since Paul Tankersley had designed his first treecat skinsuit, he'd seen exactly the same combat *she* had from exactly the same command bridges.

And he knows Mike *better than almost anyone else does, too,* she reflected. *So, yes, he definitely* is *entitled to an opinion.*

"I hope you're right, Stinker," she said quietly, instead of what she'd started to say, and he bleeked in amusement as he felt her shift gears. She shook her head at him with a smile and gave his left ear a gentle yank. He smacked her hand with carefully retracted claws, and she chuckled, but then her smile faded and she folded her arms about him, hugging him while she thought.

"The question," she said aloud, using the 'cat as her sounding board once again, "is whether or not we tell Pritchart about this."

<You want to tell her,> Nimitz signed, and she snorted.

"Yes, actually. I do," she admitted. He flicked his ears in silent question, and she sighed.

"Beth hasn't made Mike's dispatches public yet—or she hadn't when she sent her message, at least. Sooner or later, though, that's going to change, which means Pritchart's going to find out eventually, whatever happens. I don't want her deciding I was so nervous about her possible reaction to the news that I tried to keep it from her. I don't think she's likely to get infected with whatever Younger has and start playing stalling games, but I could be wrong about that. And I've been as candid with her as I could from the very beginning, including leveling with her about Green Pines. I don't want to jeopardize whatever balance of trust I've built up with her."

Nimitz considered that for several moments, grass-green eyes thoughtful. Unlike any other member of Honor's delegation, he'd been able to sample Eloise Pritchart's mind-glow even more thoroughly than Honor had, and it was obvious to her he was considering what she'd said in the light of that insight. She wasn't about to rush him, either. Unlike the steadily decreasing number of Manticorans who continued to reject the evidence of treecat intelligence, Honor Alexander-Harrington had enormous respect both for the ability of 'cats in general to follow complex explanations and for Nimitz's judgment, in particular, where human nature was concerned.

Finally, his fingers began to move again, and her eyes widened.

<The real reason you want to tell her is you like her,> he told her.

"I—" she began, then stopped as she realized that, as usual, Nimitz had come unerringly to the point.

"You're right," she admitted out loud. "Which may not be a good thing." She smiled ruefully. "I don't think hard-nosed, professional diplomats are supposed to *like* the people they're trying to beat a treaty out of."

<So?> Nimitz signed. <Not what Soul of Steel sent you to be. She sent you to get agreement, not just talk and argue. Besides, I like Truth Seeker, too.>

"'Truth Seeker?'" Honor repeated, leaning back and looking deep into his eyes. "Is that what you've decided her treecat name should be?"

Nimitz nodded, and Honor's eyes narrowed. As a general rule, the names treecats assigned to humans usually turned out to be extraordinarily accurate. Some of them were more evocative than truly descriptive—her own, for example, "Dances on Clouds"—but even those were insightful encapsulations of the humans involved. And now that she thought about it, "Truth Seeker" summed up her own feel for Pritchart's personality.

Slow down, Honor, she told herself firmly. *That's certainly the personality you* want *her to have, and so does Nimitz. So maybe you're both reading more into what you're picking up from her than is really justified.*

And maybe you're not, too.

"And have you come up with a name for Thomas Theisman, too?" she asked.

His right true-hand closed into the letter "S" and "nodded" up and down in the sign for "Yes," but it seemed to Honor to be moving a little slower than usual. He looked up at her for a second or two, and her eyebrows rose. She could literally feel him hesitating. It wasn't because he was concerned about how she might react to it, but more as if...as if he didn't quite expect her to believe it.

Then he raised his right hand, palm-in, touched his forehead with his index finger, then moved it up and to the right. As his hand rose, his forefinger alternated back and forth between the straight extended position indicating the number "1" and the crooked position indicating the letter "X" before the hand turned palm-out and closed into the letter "S" once more. Then both hands came together in front of him, thumbs and index fingers linked, before they rose to his chin, left in front of right, thumb and first two fingers of each hand signing the letter "P." They

paused for a moment, then separated downward, and Honor felt
her eyebrows rising even higher.

"'Dreams of Peace?'" she said, speaking very carefully, as if
she couldn't quite believe what she heard herself saying. "*That's
his treecat name?*"

Nimitz nodded his head very firmly, and Honor tasted his
confidence—his assurance—about the name he'd assigned. No
wonder he'd been hesitant to share it with her! If anyone in the
galaxy had demonstrated his unflinching, tough-as-nails readiness
to do whatever duty required of him, however grim that duty
might be, it was Thomas Theisman! He was the one who'd rebuilt
the Republican Navy into a war machine that could actually face
the RMN in combat. The man who'd planned and executed Operation Thunderbolt. The man who'd planned Operation Beatrice!
The man—

Her thoughts paused, and Nimitz stared up into her eyes with an
intensity which was rare, even for the two of them. They sat that
way for several, endless seconds, and then Honor inhaled deeply.

Yes, Theisman had always done his duty. *Would* always do his
duty, without flinching or hesitating, whatever its demands. But
she supposed the same thing could be said of her, and what was
she doing here on this planet, of all planets in the universe, if
she didn't "dream of peace"? And the more she thought about
it, about what it must have been like to spend all those years
trying to defend his star nation against an external enemy even
while he saw State Security making "examples" out of men and
women he'd known for years—out of *friends*—the more clearly
she realized just how longingly a man like Thomas Theisman
might dream of peace.

I wish Elizabeth were here, she thought. *Maybe she can't taste
Ariel's emotions the way I can taste Nimitz's, but she trusts Ariel.
And if he told her he agreed with what Nimitz has named Pritchart
and Theisman . . .*

"You do realize that what you just told me doesn't make my
decision any easier, don't you, Stinker?" she asked him with a
crooked smile.

He blinked once, slowly, then bleeked in agreement, radiating his love for her . . . and his simultaneous deep amusement.
Nimitz understood perfectly well that they'd come to Haven on
serious business. He even understood exactly what stakes they

were playing for. Yet when it came down to it, this whole business of "negotiating" was a two-leg concept which had very little meaning for a race of telepaths who couldn't have engaged in diplomatic subterfuge even if they'd ever had any desire to do so in the first place. He knew Honor had to play by two-leg rules, but he found the entire process incredibly roundabout, cumbersome, and just plain silly.

"Yeah, sure," she said, hugging him once more. "Easy for *you*, Bub!"

✧　　✧　　✧

"Yes, Admiral?"

Eloise Pritchart's expression was politely curious as she gazed out of Honor's com display. Even without the physical proximity which would have permitted Honor to physically sample the President's emotions, it was obvious Pritchart wondered why she'd screened when their delegations were due to sit down together again in less than half an hour.

Well, she's about to find out, Honor thought. *And it'll be interesting to see if she and Theisman react the way someone with Stinker's notion of their treecat names ought to.*

"I'm sorry to disturb you, Madam President," she said out loud, "but I've just received a dispatch from home. It doesn't require any immediate action on our part," she assured Pritchart as the other woman's eyebrows rose, "but I thought I'd share it with you. As part of the deep background for the Star Empire's negotiating stance, as it were."

"By all means, Admiral, if you think that's appropriate." Pritchart sat back in her chair, shoulders squared, and looking into those topaz eyes, Honor could see the other woman's memories of the *last* time she'd provided her with "deep background."

"'Appropriate' can be such an interesting word," Honor observed wryly. "I hope it applies in this case, but I suppose we'll just have to see, won't we?

"At any rate, Madam President, it would appear that just over three T-weeks ago, one of our destroyers, HMS *Reprise*, returned to the Spindle System from Meyers with what I suppose could be called interesting news. It would appear that notwithstanding all of the historical evidence to the contrary, it really is genuinely possible for a Solarian ship of the wall to make it all the way out into the Verge under its own power. In fact—"

Chapter Twenty-Six

"WELL," ELIZABETH WINTON said dryly, "I suppose the question presently before us is '*Now* what the hell do we do?'"

"I suppose so, Your Majesty," William Alexander replied. "On the other hand, our decision trees have just been rather brutally simplified. Once you're on the hexapuma's back, your only *real* options are to hang on or get eaten!"

"Not necessarily, Willie," his brother said. Baron Grantville looked at him, eyebrows rising, and Hamish Alexander-Harrington barked a laugh. There was no humor in the cold sound, and his blue eyes were even colder.

"You really think there's another option, Hamish?" the Prime Minister asked skeptically.

"Of course there is! If you can reach your pulser, you put a dart through the six-legged bastard's brain, instead," the Earl of White Haven replied harshly.

Grantville's face tightened as he heard the combined anger, vengefulness, and confidence in his brother's voice. The Alexander temper was famous throughout the Royal Manticoran Navy, and Grantville had enjoyed even more experience with it than most of White Haven's fellow officers. For that matter, he had it himself, in full measure. And he knew his brother well enough to understand exactly how a man who'd commanded the men and women of the Royal Navy in battle would feel about someone who'd cold-bloodedly set out to annihilate a handful of battlecruisers

340

and heavy cruisers with an entire fleet of superdreadnoughts. The fact that things hadn't worked out the way Sandra Crandall had expected wasn't likely to do a thing to make White Haven any less angry, either. Nor, for that matter, *should* it.

After all, "it's the thought that counts," isn't it? Grantville reflected. *On the other hand...*

"You know, Ham, I've been doing a little historical research of my own since Mike's first reports about New Tuscany got back to us," he said. "You were right when you suggested Lincoln to me, but there are some other interesting tidbits in Old Earth history, too. For example, I assume you're familiar with the term 'victory disease,' aren't you?"

"As a matter of fact, I am." White Haven's teeth flashed in something which bore a certain vague resemblance to a smile, and Samantha flattened her ears as she lay stretched tense and angry along the back of his chair. "On the other hand, we're the ones who were supposed to be the recipient of a Pearl Harbor attack this time around, not the ones stupid enough to *launch* it. And I'm not proposing any of us underestimate the scale of the threat, either. What I am pointing out is that there's no point pretending none of this has happened, or that the League's going to accept the outright destruction of twenty-three superdreadnoughts and the capture of forty-eight more—not to mention all Crandall's escorts, screening elements, and supply ships—without doing its damnedest to turn the entire Star Empire into rubble. In my opinion, Mike did exactly what she should've done under the circumstances, given an opposition force commander who obviously couldn't have poured piss out of a boot even if it did have instructions on the heel. But the fact that she chose the *right* option doesn't mean she chose a *good* one, since there weren't any good ones available to her."

He paused, inviting anyone to disagree with anything he'd just said. Queen Elizabeth clearly didn't, and as much as Grantville would have liked to, he couldn't. Sir Anthony Langtry seemed torn between a diplomat's responsibility to find an option short of war and an ex-Marine's bloodthirsty belligerence. Sir Thomas Caparelli and Admiral Patricia Givens, on the other hand, were in obvious agreement with White Haven.

"All right," the earl continued when no one accepted his invitation. "Since the Sollies're going to decide, as the Queen put it before Crandall actually showed up, that the Star Empire's a nail and the thing for them to do is reach for the biggest damned hammer they've got, there's not much point kowtowing to that jackass Kolokoltsov and his pain-in-the-ass, equally arrogant buddies. The way they've been viewing that Green Pines crap with alarm and calling for 'an impartial interstellar investigation'—by *Frontier Security*, of all people!—into 'the Star Empire's apparent involvement in terroristic actions' is a pretty fair indicator of where *their* brains—such as they have, and what there is of them—were headed even before Mike kicked Crandall's arse! So I think our best option is to tell them flat out that the entire mess is the result of the way their people have fu— ah, *screwed* up by the numbers, and that we're all done putting up with it. Send them the tac recordings from Spindle and ask them how many more superdreadnoughts they want our cruisers to kill before we even bring up our battlecruisers—much less our own *wallers*—and get down to the main event. And while we're doing that, we go ahead and activate Case Lacoön, too."

Faces tightened around the table with his last sentence. Case Lacoön was the Royal Manticoran Navy's plan to close all wormhole nexii under its control to Solarian traffic. Or, rather, that was the *first* phase of Lacoön. The *second* phase included active commerce raiding and the extension of *de facto* Manticoran control to every wormhole nexus within its reach, regardless of who that nexus nominally belonged to.

"I realize what we're talking about here," White Haven said grimly, "and I know the Sollies're going to scream bloody murder about our 'interference with free trade' even before we decide to move to Lacoön Two. But the realization of just how much we can hurt them economically, coupled with what happened at Spindle, may actually be a big enough clue stick to get through even to Sollies. It's the biggest one we've got short of launching a general offensive, at any rate, so I think we have to see whether or not it's big enough to do the trick. It's not like we've got all that much to lose, anyway. Worst case, the League goes ahead and does what it was going to do anyway and we get to find out whether or not Honor's right about how fragile it is. Best case—though I'm not going to suggest anyone hold his breath waiting for it—*somebody* in Old Chicago suddenly sprouts an IQ higher than his body temperature and they decide it just might not be a good idea after all to get a couple or three million of their spacers killed."

He shrugged.

"I'm not saying it's a good idea. But I am saying that, just like Mike, we're fresh out of *good* alternatives. So it's time we stop trying to avoid the inevitable and position ourselves to fight the League as effectively as humanly possible if—*when*—it comes to that."

The silence in the Mount Royal Palace conference room was intense, and White Haven leaned back in his chair, his face hard.

"I don't really like saying it," Langtry said finally, "but I think Hamish has a point. Nobody's ever captured a Solarian ship-of-the-wall before, far less blown twenty-three of them out of space. And unless I'm mistaken, no one's ever killed *anyone's* superdreadnought using nothing but heavy cruisers. Talk about rubbing salt into the wound!"

He shook his head, contemplating the way Solarian arrogance was likely to react to the insult of being that casually—and totally—trounced by someone who hadn't even used a capital ship in the process.

"We're in uncharted territory," he continued, "and, unfortunately, the one thing I think we can all agree on is that the League isn't going to...take the news well, shall we say? That being so, the only modest change to Hamish's proposal I'd suggest would be to include a diplomatic note which basically tells Kolokoltsov we consider Crandall's actions at Spindle yet another act of war and that if they're not repudiated—publicly, and in the strongest possible terms—within two standard T-days of the receipt of our note, Her Majesty's Government will assume it represents the Solarian League' chosen policy vis-à-vis the Star Empire. In that case, given the existence of a state of war of the League's choosing between it and us, we will immediately close all nexii under our control to all Solarian traffic and inform all our station commanders that we're at war with the League and that they're to act accordingly."

"I don't have a problem with that," White Haven said. "I don't expect it to do any good, but at least there won't be any questions about our prewar diplomacy *this* time around."

"Wait." Elizabeth raised one hand, and her expression was rueful. "I don't believe *I'm* about to say this, but here goes. Don't you think it might be a good idea to find out whether or not we're going to get a treaty out of Pritchart before we go sending any ultimatums to the Solarian League?"

"With all due respect, Your Majesty," Langtry said, "the ultimatum's already been delivered—by the League, not us. It arrived in Spindle about two weeks ago. That's Hamish's entire point. Fortunately, judging from Duchess Harrington's dispatches, the chance of our getting a treaty out of Nouveau Paris is actually pretty good. I'm not counting any chickens before the eggs hatch, you understand, but we can't allow our policy towards the League to be dictated by concerns over our relations with the Republic. Obviously, we've got to bear both concerns in mind, and they're going to influence one another heavily, but we can't afford to couple them *too* closely together when we start formulating policy and military strategy."

"All right, I can see that," Elizabeth said. "But let's pursue this notion of sending them the tactical recordings a little farther. Is there really much chance they'll draw the proper conclusions from them? Pat?"

She looked at Admiral Givens, and the woman who headed the Office of Naval Intelligence flashed an unhappy smile that was almost a grimace.

"Your Majesty, I'm afraid that comes under the heading of 'nobody knows.' There's simply no way to predict the answer. Crandall obviously didn't draw the right conclusions from what happened to Byng, but I think we'd all agree she wasn't the sharpest stylus in the box. And, for that matter, the Battle of Spindle's a rather larger exclamation point than what happened at New Tuscany. On the other hand, Old Chicago's a lot further from Spindle than Meyers is from New Tuscany. And the truth probably is that their so-called intelligence analysts have been so insulated from reality for so long that no one's telling the bureaucrats who're actually calling the shots just how bad the balance of military capabilities really is from the SLN's perspective. Assuming, of course, any of the aforesaid analysts *want* to tell them in the first place."

"Why shouldn't they want to?" Elizabeth asked. "That's their job, isn't it? And it's *their* navy that's going to get reamed if they screw up!"

"Why didn't High Ridge's and Janacek's analysts tell *them* what was really happening, Your Majesty?" Givens countered sadly, almost gently. "After studying what we've recovered from the databases Admiral Gold Peak captured at New Tuscany, I'm even more of the opinion that everyone in the League's been telling their superiors what those superiors wanted to hear for so long that it's unlikely any of them remember *how* to tell someone an unpalatable truth. And, truth to tell, I actually sympathize with them. A little, anyway."

"Excuse me?"

Elizabeth's eyebrows rose, and Givens shook her head.

"Your Majesty, there's always a temptation, for any analyst, to choose the hypothesis she knows her superiors, or her government, or the people responsible for shaping policy want to hear. Telling them something else isn't the way to make herself popular, after all. But it's not necessarily even a matter of a self-serving refusal to rock the boat, either. Sometimes it's even a case of recognizing what their superiors are *willing* to hear—of avoiding truths that will simply get them disregarded or fired, because they know that if *they* go, they'll only be replaced by someone even less willing to risk flouting the party line. Of course, it can be a case of simple mental laziness, too. In fact, that happens a lot more frequently than most of us in the intelligence community like to admit. But even more often than that, probably, perfectly honest, hard-working analysts screw up by the numbers simply because they've gotten into a habit of thought. Because someone's allowed herself to become so firmly wedded to one view of the evidence—often without even realizing she's done so—that her own internal filters screen out anything that would challenge the existing interpretation.

"Frankly, that's a huge part of what's happened to the League, and it's happened because the League's been able to survive anyway. It hasn't bitten them on the butt the way Jurgensen's failures at ONI bit us when Theisman launched Thunderbolt. The League is so big and so powerful that to some extent, at least, the Sollies really have been able to make reality be what they *wanted* it to be. After all, who was big or nasty enough to pound them if they were wrong? So they've gone happily along, seeing themselves as the lords of all creation, literally for centuries. Of course it's going to be hard for any doomsayers to get through to the real decision-makers!"

"Even with the tactical records from Spindle in front of them?"

"Assuming the analysts themselves believe the records in question are genuine, they'd still have to get them past their own superiors, Your Majesty, and that's not likely to be as simple as it would be in an ideal galaxy. I'd say it's possible—even probable—someone higher than them in the food chain's going to be suppressing any unfortunate little evidence that she helped create the current fubar. I mean, the current situation. And even if that isn't the case, those superiors are going to have preconception filters of their own. And I'd estimate it's at least equally probable that someone's going to tone down the analysts' reports in the interests of cool reason and avoiding 'hysterical alarmism.'"

"Pat's raised a couple of good points, Your Majesty," White Haven said, and Elizabeth returned her attention to him. "For one thing, she's absolutely right about the inertia quotient, the way the currently accepted wisdom—whatever it happens to be—has a tendency to throttle anything that challenges it." He snorted acerbically and shook his head. "I've had a little personal experience with that, if you remember that minor disagreement Sonja Hemphill and I had going on for so long. That much can happen to anybody, even someone who's making a genuine effort to be intellectually honest and fair, if he's not aware that he's investing too much confidence in what he already 'knows' is true without making enough allowance for the fact that things might have changed. But she's also right about the attitude we're likely to see out of the SLN's senior officers, too, because they're not going to be anywhere near as interested in intellectual honesty as they are in covering their arses. I never thought I'd say this about anyone, but compared to quite a few of the Sollies' most senior officers, Edward Janacek was competent, farsighted, and thoughtful."

"I wouldn't go quite *that* far, Hamish," Caparelli interjected dryly. "Almost, and I'll grant you the Sollies are probably even worse, but nobody could actually make Janacek look *good.*"

"All right." White Haven nodded, accepting the correction. "But my point stands. These people have been gaming the system for so long, without believing for a moment there could possibly be any realistic threat *to* the system, that their very first thoughts are going to focus on making sure nothing threatens their personal positions *within* the system. Some of them will be stupid enough to try to make it all go away by suppressing—what was it you called it, Pat? 'Any unfortunate little evidence'?—that could possibly implicate them when it comes time to play the blame game. And others are simply going to be so unaccustomed to thinking about external threats they literally don't recognize one when they actually see it. Or not until it's too late, at least."

"We do have Admiral O'Cleary's official report to support the data," Langtry pointed out, and it was Givens' turn to snort.

"Yes, we do, Mr. Secretary," she agreed when he raised an eyebrow at her. "But, first, the very fact that O'Cleary surrendered is going to be a severe blow to her credibility as far as the people back on Old Earth are concerned. Not only are they going to be thinking in terms of personal cowardice on her part, but I guarantee you someone's going to suggest she has a powerful interest in overstating the effectiveness of our weapons technology. After all, if we really have 'super weapons' at our disposal, then her cowardly decision to surrender looks a lot better, doesn't it?

"That's not the only thing that's going to help people who want to undercut her credibility, either. There's also the matter of our willingness to transmit her report to them. That's suspicious in its own right, isn't it? We undoubtedly have our own sinister motives for getting it to them as quickly as possible, don't we? And, for that matter, there's the little question of why it was left up to *her* to do the surrendering and report-writing, isn't there?"

The brief silence which answered her was thoughtful, to say the least.

"I take it you don't incline to the theory that it was suicide after all?" Elizabeth said after a moment.

"At this point, I don't have a strong feeling either way, Your Majesty," Givens replied. "I'd have to say that if *I* were a Solarian admiral who'd managed to make the absolutely wrong call on every single decision and gotten twenty-plus ships-of-the-wall destroyed as an obvious consequence of my own abject stupidity, the temptation to just go on and shoot myself in the head would definitely be there. On the other hand, most people who decide to shoot themselves in the head, don't shoot themselves in the *back* of the head. For that matter, she could've used the overrides of her skinsuit's med panel to administer a lethal dose that would have put her painlessly to sleep. We don't like to talk about it, but every spacer knows how to do that, given all the nasty, lingering ends we can wind up facing."

"That sounds to me like you *don't* think it was suicide."

"Well, there's no question it was her pulser, Your Majesty, and it was in *her* hand when Admiral Gold Peak's Marines recovered her body. Judging from the admiral's report, there's no forensic evidence to suggest anyone else fired the fatal dart, for that matter. Unfortunately, there aren't any witnesses who actually saw her do it, either, which is pretty suspicious in its own right. And given the fact that everyone on her flag bridge was skinsuited, there probably wouldn't *be* any forensic evidence, even under ideal conditions."

"But if it wasn't suicide, who killed her?" Grantville asked, frowning intently.

"From our perspective, that question's wide open," Givens said. "I don't want to sound too Byzantine, but one possibility that's occurred to me is that someone else on her flag bridge—probably one of her own staffers—was also working for Manpower and had orders to see to it she didn't have an opportunity to discuss her decisions and the reasons for them with us.

"The problem, though, is that our perspective isn't the important one at the moment. The *important* one is the one from Old Chicago, and it's likely to occur to someone back on Old Earth that Admiral Crandall's demise was arranged by some nefarious Manty."

"But . . . why?" the Prime Minister asked almost plaintively.

"Why, in order to make sure *O'Cleary* wrote the official dispatch, Mr. Prime Minister! Obviously, she's either turned her coat in return for some bribe on our part, or else we delicately informed her that the same thing that happened to Crandall could happen to *her* if her report didn't say what we wanted it to say. The fact that despite all the damage the *Buckley* took, Crandall was the only fatality on her flag bridge would be suspicious enough for some people, even without the possible irregularities of her 'self-inflicted wound' or the mysterious lack of witnesses."

"Wonderful."

Elizabeth reached up and lifted Ariel down into her lap. She sat stroking the 'cat for several seconds, then drew a deep breath.

"All right. We're basically spinning our wheels. That's not a criticism, either—only a reflection of how little chance we have of guessing how the Solly bureaucracy's going to spin this for its own internal consumption, much less the media. But I do have one other question I'd like all of you bright people to consider with me."

"Yes, Your Majesty?" Grantville asked just the least bit warily when she paused.

"I think we're all in agreement that, preposterous as it seems, the real prime mover in all of this has been Manpower and/or Mesa." The Queen shook her head, as if even now she couldn't quite believe what her own voice was saying. "I know we don't have any direct evidence linking Crandall to what happened at New Tuscany, or, for that matter, proving Byng *knew* he was working for Manpower. We *do* know Manpower was behind Monica, and this Anisimovna's involvement at New Tuscany, as well, clearly demonstrates they were pulling the strings, whether he realized it or not. And the official Mesan version of what happened at Green Pines pretty clearly indicates that the system government itself is carrying water for Manpower where we're concerned.

"My point is that it seems to me we'd be just as guilty of filtering out 'inconvenient evidence' as we're accusing the Sollies of being if we didn't face the fact that all of our threat analyses have fallen seriously short of the mark where Manpower *and* Mesa are concerned. So, given that we have so much evidence of Manpower's involvement in both Monica and New Tuscany, do we go directly after Mesa?"

"As in taking direct military action against the system, Your Majesty?" Caparelli sounded like a man who wanted to be positive he was interpreting her correctly.

"That's one possibility," Elizabeth said grimly. "Frankly, it has a certain definite appeal, too. If Eighth Fleet can take out the Haven System's defenses and infrastructure, a couple of battle squadrons ought to be more than enough to do the same job on Mesa. But I was also thinking about making the point to the Sollies and demanding that *they* investigate the extent to which Manpower's been manipulating their military forces."

"From a purely military perspective, taking out Mesa wouldn't be that difficult, assuming they don't have a surprise for us even more fundamental than our surprises for the Sollies, Your Majesty," Caparelli said. "Of course, *getting* there could be a bit difficult, not to mention time-consuming. And if we took action unilaterally, I'd say there'd have to be at least a pretty fair chance some of Mesa's proxies in the League would point to it as yet another example of mindless Manticoran military aggression—this time directed at a star system well inside the Shell, even if it isn't formally a member of the League."

"I wouldn't have any fundamental objections to carrying out

the strike, Tom," White Haven said thoughtfully. "Not if we have
the situation with Haven under control, at least. Frankly, I don't
see where it could make our relations with the League any worse,
at any rate!"

"I think I'm inclined to be a little more cautious about that,
Your Majesty," Langtry said. "I'm not going to shed any tears for
anything we do to those Manpower bastards, and I could see a
lot of pluses to pointedly suggesting to others who might wish
the Star Empire ill that every action produces a *reaction*. At the
same time, the propaganda version of Green Pines is still playing to the hilt with the mainstream Solly newsies. Except for
O'Hanrahan and a couple of other muckrakers, no one seems to
be choking on Mesa's version, and Abruzzi's working it for all he's
worth over at Education and Information. If we act precipitously
against Mesa, the people buying into that version are going to
see it as an escalation of our 'earlier attacks' on the system and,
probably, an effort to shut them up before they turn up something
still more damaging about what 'really happened' at Green Pines."

"So are you suggesting that their cock-and-bull story should
paralyze us militarily?" White Haven asked, a bit more caustically
than he usually spoke to his old friend, and Langtry frowned.

"No, Ham, I'm not," the Foreign Secretary said. "But I am
suggesting that Mesa isn't going anywhere. There's time to get
around to dealing with Manpower—and Mesa—later, if we decide
to, and I'd prefer not to complicate things with the League any
more than we have to at this point."

"But our hitting Mesa might actually give the League an out,
Tony," Elizabeth countered. He looked a question at her, and
she shrugged. "If we were willing to commit to active military
operations against Mesa, it would be pretty convincing evidence
we really think they're responsible for what's been going on in
Talbott. It's possible even Sollies would recognize the opportunity
to back away from a direct confrontation with us at least long
enough to find out whether or not our suspicions were justified."

"Possible, Your Majesty," Langtry conceded. "Frankly, though,
I think 'likely' would be another matter entirely. Especially not
with that damned Green Pines story clouding the issue. At least
some of the talking heads are going to argue that backing the
Ballroom in Green Pines is an example of our already conducting
active operations against Manpower in what we hoped would be

an untraceable fashion. Under that interpretation, open military action would only be more of the same. And since we've resorted to backing terrorist attacks, we're tarred with the same brush, aren't we? I mean, isn't there a moral equivalence between Anisimovna's blowing up the New Tuscan space station and *our* nuking a city full of civilians? Where do we get off trying to claim some sort of moral superiority over our enemies in that case?"

"Let's not reject the notion out of hand, Tony," Grantville said, then chuckled harshly at Langtry's evident surprise.

"I know I'm the one who's been most nervous about expanding our current unpleasantness with Haven into an even broader conflict," the Prime Minister continued. "But I think the Queen may have a point here, and it's not as if we have to make up our minds about it this afternoon. We've provided the Sollies— and their newsies, for that matter—with all our evidence about Manpower's involvement in both Monica and New Tuscany. If we go ahead and send them the tac data from Spindle as Hamish is suggesting—and which I think is a very good idea, by the way—we can also remind them about our belief that Manpower's at the bottom of what's been going on in Talbott.

"I don't imagine even Kolokoltsov and the others are going to decide overnight to formally declare war. First, because I have to think it's at least possible simple disbelief and shock over what happened to Crandall is going to make even Sollies hesitate at least briefly while they try to find out what really happened. And, second, because even if *that* doesn't happen, getting a formal war declaration out of the Assembly's going to be the next best thing to impossible, Green Pines or not, given how their Constitution's written. So even if they decide to throw the League Navy at us anyway, it's going to be a *de facto* state of war, not a *de jure* one. Which means that if we continue to insist Manpower's really to blame, and if we act consistently with that belief down the road, they'll still be able to pull in their horns if and when they finally figure out—or decide to admit, at any rate—that we've been right about Manpower all along and that they've been had over Green Pines. In fact, if they get chewed up even remotely this badly in a couple of more battles, they may find themselves looking desperately for some sort of 'statesmanlike' way to climb out of the hole they've dug for themselves. And much as what I'd really like to do is start shoveling dirt in on top of them, the *smart* thing to do would be to reach down and give them a boost when they start trying to climb. *If* they start trying to climb.

"In the short term, though, Tony, I'm inclined to agree with you. We can always decide to pursue the military option with Mesa later. There's no reason we have to add it to the pot right this instant and risk complicating our relations with the League even further."

"All right," Elizabeth decided. "I agree with both of you, so we'll set aside any immediate direct military action against Mesa. At the same time, though, Sir Thomas, I want the Admiralty to be working on the operational planning to do exactly that if and when the moment seems appropriate."

"Yes, Your Majesty."

"And in the meantime," the Queen continued more grimly, "you and Hamish are formally instructed that the Crown has determined that an effective state of war exists between the Star Empire and the Solarian League. You are authorized and directed to transmit the appropriate activation orders for Lacoön One and to make any military movements you deem appropriate in its support. I want to avoid any additional provocations, if at all possible, but that desire takes secondary priority. The security of our ships, personnel, and citizens, and the accomplishment of Lacoön's objectives are to be your primary consideration. And you are also instructed to take all necessary and prudent steps to prepare for the execution of Lacoön Two, as well. Is that clearly understood?"

"It is, Your Majesty," White Haven replied quietly, and she met his eyes steadily for a handful of heartbeats, then nodded.

"Good."

Chapter Twenty-Seven

FLEET ADMIRAL ALLEN HIGGINS felt a familiar mix of leftover surprise, regret, apprehension, and amusement as he stepped out of the lift car onto the flag bridge of his superdreadnought flagship. He was accustomed to all those feelings, but they'd grown sharper in the weeks since Duchess Harrington had resumed command of Eighth Fleet and headed off for the Haven System.

The surprise stemmed from the fact that he, of all people, held his current position. Allen Higgins had been one of the flag officers Edward Janacek had appointed to a major fleet command. Not only that, he was connected by marriage to the Janacek family. Under the circumstances, he was amazed he'd been retained on active duty at all, and he supposed the fact that he still had a flag bridge to call his own said interesting things about Earl White Haven, since one of Janacek's very first moves on reassuming the post of First Lord of Admiralty had been to purge the Navy of every single White Haven protégé and ally. He hadn't even pretended the purge wasn't largely inspired by his personal hatred for the earl, either. Frankly, Higgins had expected White Haven—with whom he himself had never gotten along very well, having once fallen afoul of the infamous Alexander temper—to wield an equally thorough retaliatory broom. And if he were going to be honest about it, he also had to admit that, based on the Navy's performance in the face of the Havenites' Operation Thunderbolt, White Haven would have been completely justified.

Yet the White Haven Admiralty had shown a surprising degree
of tolerance. Possibly because it didn't have much choice. It
could hardly have fired *every* serving (and surviving) flag officer, after all, given the frantic need to expand the Navy once
more and the demand for experienced admirals that entailed.
Higgins didn't think that was the real explanation, though.
Instead, to his considerable surprise, the new Admiralty had
contented itself with removing the more outrageously political
Janacek appointees and those whose demonstrated performance
had proven conclusively that they weren't suitable material for
combat commands.

Given the minor fact that Allen Higgins had been the commanding officer on Grendelsbane Station when the Peep offensive
rolled over it, he'd expected to find himself on that list of "less
than suitable material" officers. After all, he was the one who'd
lost several hundred LACs and seven SD(P)s discovering the
Peeps did, indeed, have LACs and MDMs of their own. And the
one who'd abandoned the system in the face of the overwhelming attack—and, just incidentally, destroyed the nineteen CLACs
and no less than seventy-three modern ships-of-the-wall lying
helpless in the station's building slips to keep them from falling
into Peep hands. And, of course, there was the minor matter of
the forty thousand yard workers he'd been unable to take with
him, as well. It was the memory of that cataclysmic day which
accounted for the strand of regret which wove itself through his
emotions at moments like this.

And yet, he hadn't been beached by White Haven after all,
despite Grendelsbane. He wondered, sometimes, how much of
that was due to the fact that even though he'd been a Janacek
appointee, he'd never pretended to be an admirer of Edward
Janacek. Or to the fact that he'd been summarily placed on
half-pay by Janacek "pending the determination of a full and
impartial board of inquiry" as soon as he got back to Manticore.
The truth was that the main reason he'd been retained on active
duty under Janacek in the first place was that he happened to
be married to one of Janacek's cousins. Janacek hadn't kept him
on because he valued his services or trusted his cronyism; he'd
kept him on as a combined sop to his critics and a way to
keep peace in the family.

Higgins had actually felt uncomfortable about serving under

Janacek, especially since he knew the reasons the opportunity had been offered to him. He'd silenced his own conscience by arguing that at least *some* competent flag officers had to remain on duty, but he felt confident Janacek had never really trusted him. Which was probably why he'd found himself assigned to Grendelsbane, when he thought about it, since it had been far enough away to keep him safely out of sight, out of mind.

And which was also why Janacek had decided his cousin-in-law had made an admirable choice when he needed someone to throw under the ground car after Thunderbolt blew Grendelsbane (among other things) into dust bunnies on Janacek's watch.

In his more cynical moments, Higgins was confident Janacek's obvious decision to scapegoat him was a major factor in White Haven's decision to *rehabilitate* him. A sort of tit-for-tat way to plant one right in Janacek's eye. On the other hand, White Haven had left him dirtside until the board of inquiry reported on Grendelsbane, and the board's conclusions had been that no one could have done better than Higgins given the numerical odds and the knowledge he'd possessed about Havenite weapons capabilities. So it was certainly arguable that White Haven, Sir Thomas Caparelli, and Sir Lucien Cortez had decided to offer him a command solely on the basis of that report.

In his *less* cynical moments, Higgins didn't find that difficult to accept. Yet he was still more than a bit bemused by the quirk of fate which had put *him* in command of Home Fleet and, in the process, converted him into the only "Admiral of the Fleet" currently in Manticoran service.

Of course, he wouldn't have been where he was if not for the massive losses the Royal Manticoran Navy had suffered in the Battle of Manticore. To his considerable astonishment, Allen Higgins had become one of the dozen or so most senior flag officers in the entire Navy in the wake of that brutal winnowing. When Duchess Harrington had relinquished command of Home Fleet to resume command of Eighth Fleet—or, rather, when there'd been enough Manticoran and Alliance ships-of-the-wall to rebuild a Home Fleet in *addition* to Eighth Fleet—Allen Higgins had found himself replacing her. Well, stepping into her position, since it was unlikely anyone could actually *replace* her.

Although Higgins respected Alexander-Harrington's accomplishments, he was also one of those officers who was well aware of the role the media had played in creating the legend of "the Salamander." To her credit, she seemed to genuinely attempt to avoid that sort of media adulation, but coupled with her stature on Grayson and her political status as one of the main leaders of the Opposition to the High Ridge Government, it had turned her into the next best thing to a physical avatar of the goddess of war as far as the Manticoran public was concerned. And, for that matter, as far as most of the *Navy* was concerned. Which had made stepping into her shoes an interesting experience.

It also accounted for some of his current apprehension. After all, no matter how well he did, he was going to find himself being compared to the memory of Sebastian D'Orville, who'd died leading the previous Home Fleet into headlong battle, or of Duchess Harrington, whom Higgins had relieved as Home Fleet's CO, and whose Eighth Fleet had saved the home system from Operation Beatrice. And, if he were going to continue to be honest, part of that apprehension also stemmed from what had happened in Grendelsbane. There was no point trying to pretend the experience hadn't scarred him. He didn't think it had left him doubting his judgment, but it *had* left him dreading a repeat performance. He would have felt much more comfortable if he'd been able to convince himself lightning didn't really strike twice in the same place. Unfortunately, it did. So instead, he spent his time telling himself disasters like Grendelsbane weren't really lightning bolts, so he didn't have to worry about stupid proverbs.

Which, he reflected, *makes me feel* ever *so much better when I think about it.*

His lips twitched as that brought him almost full circle through the cycle of thoughts which always ran through his mind at moments like this. It was fortunate his sense of humor, at least, had survived Grendelsbane and the Battle of Manticore, he supposed. It was a dryer and sometimes more biting sense of humor than it once had been, but it was still there, and he suspected he was going to need it, now that Lacoön One was in effect. The League wasn't going to be happy when it discovered Manticore had closed the Junction to all Solly traffic. Or that nondiscretionary recall orders had been issued to every Manticoran merchantman in Solarian space. Or, now that he thought about it, that orders had been dispatched to every station commander to take whatever steps seemed necessary to protect Manticoran ships, property, and lives from Solarian action.

No, they weren't going to be very happy about that at all, he thought. In fact, he reflected, as he looked at his flagship's crest, mounted on the flag bridge bulkhead beside the lift doors, a lot of them were going to be taking his flagship's name in vain when they heard about it.

HMS *Inconceivable*. He wasn't sure what he thought of "inconceivable" as the name for one of Her Majesty's starships, but it was certainly a fitting appellation for *his* flagship, under the circumstances.

"I don't suppose you've got that flight schedule for me yet," a patient, long-suffering voice said as Colonel Andrew LaFollet of the Harrington Steadholders Guard stepped through the office door, and he looked at the speaker with an artfully innocent expression.

"Flight schedule?" he inquired blankly. "Which flight schedule would that be?"

His sister glared at him, and the treecat on the end of Miranda LaFollet's desk bleeked a laugh.

"The one," she said with a ferocious glower, "for the trip to Sphinx. You *do* remember the trip to Sphinx? The one for Clarissa's birthday?"

"Oh, *that* schedule!" He smiled at her. "What makes you think I might have it? You're the one in charge of things around here when the Steadholder and Mac are away, not me!"

Miranda glowered some more, but the smile twitching at the corners of her mouth gave her away. After a moment, she gave up. There was no point trying to change her big brother at this point. Besides, she'd be disappointed if she succeeded . . . she thought.

"All right," she said. "You win. *I'll* make the flight arrangements, but I can't do that until you hand me the security plan. So where is it?"

"Oh, well, I've got *that* right here," he told her with a chuckle and tossed the chip folio across to her. She missed the catch, but Farragut reached up a long-fingered true-hand and plucked it neatly out of the air.

"Thanks," she told the 'cat as he handed it across to her. "Nice to see that at least some male members of some species are capable of showing a modicum of courtesy," she added, looking rather pointedly at Andrew.

"Ha! He's just sucking up to his celery source!"

Miranda laughed, and Andrew winked at her, then waved casually and headed back out of her office. She smiled after him for a few moments, then shook her head and inserted to the data chip into her reader. A file header appeared on her display, and her smile faded into a frown of intensity as she studied the file's contents.

She supposed it was entirely possible—even likely—that a great many Manticorans would find it more than mildly ridiculous for someone to file a security plan that ran to better than fifty pages just for a day trip to take a ten-month-old baby and his grandmother to his aunt's birthday party. Miranda LaFollet, on the other hand, did not, because the grandmother in question was her Steadholder's mother, and the ten-month-old was Raoul Alfred Alastair Alexander-Harrington, who would someday, Tester willing, *be* her Steadholder.

Not that she'd be around to see that day. At least, she hoped she wouldn't, she thought with a familiar edge of bittersweetness. She'd been just too old for prolong when the treaty of alliance with Manticore brought it to the planet Grayson. At fifty, she was thirteen years younger than Lady Harrington, but if anyone had simply looked at the two of them, they would have thought the interval was twice as great...and in the opposite direction. Miranda would have been more than human if there hadn't been times she resented the extended lifespans Manticorans took for granted, but she'd truly come to terms with it. Or she thought she had, at least. And if neither she nor Andrew would ever be able to receive the prolong treatments, their younger siblings, like her brother Micah, certainly had.

She sat gazing sightlessly at the display for a couple of seconds, then shook her head with a snort. She had more important things to do than sit around brooding, she told herself tartly, and returned her attention to Andrew's plan.

"—*stupidest* damned idea I've ever heard of! It's not like we don't have other things—*worthwhile* things—we could be doing instead, after all! And if anything ever *really* happens to the station, who the hell's going to have *time* to run for a frigging life pod in the first place?"

Ensign Paulo d'Arezzo felt a very strong desire to throttle Lieutenant Anthony Berkeley. Unfortunately, he lacked Helen Zilwicki's aptitude for hand-to-hand mayhem. Or perhaps fortunately, given the fact that Berkeley was a full senior-grade lieutenant, which would have brought up all sorts of sticky things about "striking a superior officer, the Star Empire then being in a state of war." He rather doubted a court-martial would feel "because the deceased was such a loudmouthed moron" constituted sufficient justification for violating Article Nine. Although if the members of the court actually *knew* Berkeley...

"And *another* thing," the lieutenant went on, waving his right hand, index finger extended to emphasize his point as he shared his insights, "how the hell much did this little brain fart *cost*? I mean, launching every single pod the station *has*? Jesus! Just recertifying all of them is gonna take weeks, and you *know* they're gonna downcheck at least some of them!"

You know, Paulo thought, *it was a lot more fun aboard* Hexa-puma *even when people were shooting at us! If Helen had to get herself sent back off to Talbott without me, why couldn't I have at least stayed aboard the ship, like Aikawa? For that matter, why couldn't I have stayed* anywhere *that would have kept me away from a klutz like Berkeley?*

Deep inside, he rather suspected he would have been grumpy anyplace they sent him if Helen wasn't around. That thought was one he tried not to examine too closely, though. It still made him... uncomfortable after he'd spent so many years running away from any sort of serious emotional entanglement. But the truth was that her absence left an empty place down inside him—one he'd never realized was there when all he'd been able to think about was the attractive physical "packaging" Manpower Incorporated had designed into someone it had intended to sell as a pleasure slave. A sex toy, really.

But, be that as it might, assigning him to work directly under Anthony Berkeley had to come under the heading of cruel and unusual punishment. If there'd been any real justice in the galaxy, he'd have been assigned to Admiral Yeager's Research and Development Division, with Captain Lewis. *That* would have been interesting, especially for someone with Paulo's natural bent for the electronic warfare officer's career track. But, no. In their infinite wisdom, the powers-that-were at the Bureau of Personnel had decided he and Senior Chief Wanderman should get a little hands-on time with the fabrication side. Which, little though he cared to admit it, might actually contain at least a modicum of rationality. It never hurt for an EWO to have at least some familiarity with the nuts and bolts of his hardware, after all. But there *had* to be some way for him to get that familiarity without putting up with Berkeley!

If only there were some way he could quietly and discreetly leave the small classroom in which their party of evacuees had been instructed to wait. Unfortunately, there wasn't one, and Berkeley happened to be the senior officer present, which put him in charge of their small detachment. If Paulo tried to sneak out, the lieutenant would demand to know where he was going, and somehow "anywhere *you* aren't" didn't seem the most diplomatic possible response. *Truthful*, yes; diplomatic, no.

"And if we just *had* to do something this stupid," Berkeley continued, "at least we could have done it when we weren't—"

"Excuse me, Lieutenant," a contralto voice said from the doorway, "but exactly what 'stupid' something did you have in mind?"

Berkeley's mouth shut with an almost audible click, and he spun towards the slender, dark-haired commander standing in the open door with her head cocked to one side.

"I, uh, didn't see you there, Commander McGillicuddy," he said.

"No," Commander Anastasia McGillicuddy agreed pleasantly. "I don't suppose you did. However, I was just passing through when I heard what sounded remarkably like a raised voice. I was down at the end of the hall, you understand, so I wasn't completely certain that was what I was hearing. I decided to find out."

Her smile was as pleasant as her tone, but her brown eyes were cold, and the much taller and bulkier Berkeley seemed to shrink slightly.

"As I drew closer, I realized you were availing yourself of this opportunity to continue the instruction of the junior officers entrusted to your care," she went on. "I was impressed by your apparent vigor. Obviously, you'd been discussing a subject you felt strongly about. So I thought I'd take this opportunity to find out what it was."

"Ma'am, I was just—that is, well . . ." Berkeley's abortive response trailed off, and despite himself, Paulo actually felt a feeble—*very* feeble—flicker of sympathy.

He throttled it without difficulty.

"Should I assume, Lieutenant, that you question Vice Admiral Faraday's priorities?" McGillicuddy asked softly.

Berkeley said nothing at all, and her nostrils flared. Then she looked past Berkeley to the junior officers and enlisted waiting in the classroom. She considered them briefly, then returned her attention to Berkeley.

"Since you feel qualified to critique this exercise, Lieutenant," she told him, "I'll arrange for you to present your view of it directly to Captain Sugihara." Berkeley's fair complexion turned considerably fairer at the mention of Captain Brian Sugihara, Rear Admiral Trammell's XO. "In the meantime, I strongly suggest you give some consideration to the appropriateness of your present forum. Especially considering that you happen to be the senior officer present. You might want to spend the time more profitably doing something like... oh, I don't know. Considering your report to Captain Sugihara, perhaps. In fact, you might want to give a little thought to whether or not Article Ten figures into your thinking, as well."

Paulo felt his lips trying to purse in a silent whistle as that last salvo landed. Obviously McGillicuddy had heard even more—and was even more pissed off—than he'd thought. From the little Paulo had seen of her, she didn't seem like the sort who normally screamed at a subordinate—even a *stupid* subordinate—in front of that subordinate's juniors. The fact that Berkeley had ticked her off enough to do that was sufficiently significant on its own, but her last sentence had been so pointed not even Berkeley could miss the implication. Article Ten was the article which forbade actions or speech prejudicial to discipline and the chain of command. If Berkeley was brought up on that charge and it went into his personnel record...

McGillicuddy held Berkeley's eyes for another few seconds, then nodded, glanced once at the breathlessly watching group of JGs, ensigns, and enlisted, and left without another word.

"Well, *I'm* undoubtedly the most unpopular officer in *Weylund*," Claudio Faraday said with an air of satisfaction. "For that matter, I might well be the most unpopular officer in the entire Beta subsystem!"

"I think that might be going just a *bit* far, Sir," Marcus Howell replied. "At least as far as the entire subsystem's concerned. Although, now that I think about it, they probably *aren't* too fond of you down on Gryphon at the moment, either."

"Nope. And I imagine I may be hearing a little something from the bean-counters back at Admiralty House, too." Faraday sounded a bit more serious, but his air of contentment was unabated. "We've probably just written off—what? ten percent?—of the station's life pods, after all."

"Not to mention shutting down the entire R&D section until we get the pods recertified, Sir," Howell pointed out respectfully.

"Oh, thank you for recalling that little detail to my attention, Marcus!"

"One of the things chiefs of staff are for, Sir."

Faraday glowered at him, but the vice admiral didn't seem able to work up much wattage. Then he allowed his chair to come upright, planted his elbows on his desk, and leaned forward over his folded forearms.

"Actually," he said much more seriously, "the downtime bothers me most. But I don't expect Admiral Hemphill to kick up much dust over it. I know most people think of her as the tech weenies' tech weenie, but she's got a lot better understanding of the realities than some of her research people out here do." He shook his head. "Frankly, I think quite a few of *them* haven't figured out they're actually in the Navy and hence subject to the Service's little foibles, like making sure they're up to date on relevant emergency procedures. And even for most of the others, the thought that anyone might possibly want to hurt *them* never enters their minds! Which doesn't even consider the fact that genuine accidents can happen even aboard the most modern space station."

Howell nodded. He wasn't sure he agreed with Faraday's decision to actually evacuate the space station and send all but a tiny caretaker detachment down to the planet Gryphon. He was perfectly ready to admit that the readiness state of *Weyland*'s disaster and evacuation planning had been, well, disastrous, though. And Faraday was certainly correct about the possibility of accidents. There hadn't been a major catastrophe aboard any of the Star Empire's main industrial platforms in decades, but there'd been several moderately severe accidents, and catastrophe was always possible, however improbable it might seem. If that had happened aboard *Weyland* a few weeks earlier, personnel losses might have been cataclysmic.

The series of of simulations Faraday had ordered had created a great deal of anger and frustration. At the same time, his grumpy subordinates had finally been forced to accept that he was serious about trying to get them off the station alive if something went wrong. They might not have been happy about it, but they'd at least started going through the motions with something resembling efficiency.

Of course, they'd known it was only going to be *simulations*, which would let them get back to work on more serious concerns after a half-hour or so of nonsense. Until this morning, that was, when the exercise had concluded with the words "this is no sim."

Which was basically all the warning they'd gotten before their life pods blasted out of the station and headed for Gryphon... whose authorities had had no more notion they might be coming than *they'd* had that they might be *going*. The planetary authorities' disaster and evacuation planning for *Weyland* had come up a little short, as well, with the station's personnel jammed into whatever improvised holding stations they could come up with while they tried to figure out what to do with them. Since they were *supposed* to already have detailed plans for doing just that, the current planetary fubar probably wasn't going to make Vice Admiral Faraday very popular with them when their efficiency reports—or their civilian equivalents—got written.

"All in all, a good day's work," Faraday concluded. "I figure we should be able to start re-docking the fabrication section's pods in a couple of days. I want to *start* there, at any rate."

"May I ask why, Sir?" Howell asked with a slight sense of trepidation.

"Indeed you may," Faraday replied with a sharklike smile. "While we're re-docking Fabrication's pods and recertifying Research's pods, you and I, and Admiral Yeager, and a security team from ONI which just *happens* to've been in-system when I called this little exercise, are going to do a walk-through. We'll be sending an updated backup down to Gryphon for storage just in case. And we're *also* going to see just how many of Yeager's worker bees remembered to secure their classified data properly before heading for their pods."

"Ouch!" Howell's wince wasn't entirely feigned, and Faraday chuckled nastily.

"I'm already unpopular with them, Marcus. I might as well go whole hog and kill as many birds as possible while I'm chucking stones. And I already warned Yaeger this was coming. I won't say she's looking forward to it, but she understands why I'm doing it and that I'm not going to deliberately collect any more heads than I have to.

"Which, unfortunately, doesn't mean some aren't going to roll anyway, of course."

Howell nodded again. Some people never seemed to understand that military efficiency demanded a certain degree of ruthlessness. Military commanders weren't—or shouldn't be, at any rate—in the business of winning popularity contests. They should be in the business of promoting the efficiency, which definitely included the survivability, of the units under their command. Not only was it a CO's duty to prune away deadwood, but it was also his responsibility to make all the personnel under his command aware of the fact that he'd *do* that pruning, with ruthless dispatch, whenever it was required. Punishing those who screwed up in order "to encourage the others" had been an axiom of military discipline for so many centuries because, whether it was nice or not, it worked.

Punishment may not be the best possible motivator, but it's one that works, Howell thought. *And it's one any effective officer has to have in his toolbox for the times when it's the only one that will. And at least Claudio understands the nuts and bolts of positive motivation, as well. Now that he's got their attention, at least.*

The chief of staff's lips twitched on the brink of a smile, but he suppressed it and paged to the next item on his electronic notepad.

"All right, Sir. I'm going to assume from what you've just said that you want us to give the immediate priority to getting the fabrication section's life pods back aboard. Having said that, though, there's the question of Engineering. In particular—"

Millions upon millions of kilometers from Vice Admiral Claudio's day cabin, shoals of missile pods continued to bore through space at twenty percent of the speed of light, and the visible disks of the stars called Manticore-A and Manticore-B grew steadily larger before them.

Chapter Twenty-Eight

WHAT HAPPENED WASN'T anyone's fault.

Unlike the High Ridge Government's abysmal intelligence failure (in more than one sense of the word) during the run-up to Operation Thunderbolt, no one had ignored any warning signs. Perimeter Security and Home Fleet had maintained their unceasing watch for any threat, despite the negotiations with Haven. Neither Admiral Givens' ONI nor any other of the Star Empire's intelligence services had misinterpreted, disregarded, or even overlooked a single scrap of relevant evidence that was hidden in their files. True, none of the analysts involved had been looking in the right direction, but they were scarcely alone in that, since no one outside the innermost core of the Mesan Alignment even knew the Mesan Alignment Navy existed. So it wasn't surprising Manticoran intelligence's attention had been focused elsewhere, given all the other "distractions" the Alignment had arranged to keep the Star Empire occupied.

But because no one had been aware of the Alignment's existence, or had even a clue as to its ultimate objectives, no one had ever heard of something called the spider drive, either. Or suspected for a single moment that it might actually be not only possible but practical to launch something like Oyster Bay without its intended victims' elaborate, exquisitely sensitive, carefully maintained early warning systems detecting the attack with plenty of time to prepare for it.

Indeed, it might have been argued, although with debatable justice, that if there *was* a failure on the Manticorans' part, it was one of hubris. After all, the Royal Manticoran Navy had just been given overwhelming proof of its technological superiority to the vaunted SLN. Coupled with Manticore's persistent ability to stay ahead of Havenite R&D efforts, there was a certain confidence in the prowess of the RMN's hardware. To their credit, the Admiralty's strategists had conscientiously maintained their awareness that—as Thomas Theisman had demonstrated in Operation Thunderbolt—any technological advantage was transitory. Despite that, however, they were convinced that right now, at this particular moment, their overall advantage was overwhelming. And so, in most respects, it was.

The ships which had mounted Oyster Bay, however, represented a radical departure from anything the galaxy had previously seen which was just as impressive, in its own way, as anything Manticore had accomplished. They weren't a particularly *graceful* departure, of course. In fact, compared to any impeller-drive ship, they were squat, stumpy, and downright peculiar looking because, unlike the gravitic drives everyone else used, the spider generated no impeller wedge. Instead of using two inclined planes of focused gravity to create bands of stressed space around the pocket of normal-space which surrounded a ship, the spider used literally dozens of nodes to project spurs or spikes of intensely focused gravity. For all intents and purposes, each of those spurs was almost like generating a tractor or a presser beam, except that no one in his right mind had ever imagined tractors or pressers *that* powerful. In fact, at a sufficiently short range, they would have made quite serviceable energy weapons, because *these* focused, directional beams were powerful enough to create their own tiny foci—effectively, holes in the "real" universe—in which space itself was so highly stressed that the beams punched clear through to the alpha wall, the interface between normal-space and hyper-space.

No single beam would have been of any particular use. Powerful as it might be, it was less than a shadow compared to the output of even a single one of any starship's beta nodes, far less an alpha node. It wasn't even enough to produce the "ripple" along the hyper-space wall which Manticore used for its FTL communications technology. But it did lock *onto* the wall, and that provided the ship which mounted it a purchase point in deep space—one which was always available, anywhere, in any direction. And when dozens of those beams were combined, reaching out, locking onto the alpha wall and *pulling* in micro-spaced bursts, they produced something that was very useful, indeed.

The maximum acceleration the new technology could theoretically have attained was vastly lower than the acceleration theoretically attainable under impeller drive. After all, *in theory* an impeller wedge could be accelerated instantaneously to the speed of light. There were, however, a few shortcomings to that sort of acceleration, which was why theoretical acceleration rates had always been of far less interest to practical ship designers than the maximum rates which could be compensated for with sufficient efficiency to allow mere humans to survive without being turned into extremely thin layers of paste on the bulkheads.

And in that respect, even the spider drive's lower theoretical maximum acceleration presented a definite challenge, given the fact that it produced no impeller wedge. Without a wedge, it also produced no convenient "sump" for an inertial compensator, and that meant the maximum survivable normal-space acceleration for a spider drive-equipped ship was limited by the ability of currently available grav plate technology to offset the consequences of acceleration. Unfortunately, grav plates were far less capable in that respect than inertial compensators, which had an inevitable effect on the maximum accleration a spider-drive ship could attain. It also meant that unlike impeller-drive vessels, a spider-drive ship's decks had to be aligned perpendicular to its axis of movement rather than parallel, which was a large part of what produced its shorter, "squatter" hull form, not to mention requiring some significant rethinks about the way spacecraft designers had been arranging ship interiors literally for centuries.

Although the Alignment's physicists had been inspired to push grav plate technology harder than anyone else, there were still limits. Up to an actual acceleration of one hundred and fifty gravities, it could achieve an efficiency of over ninety-nine percent, producing a "felt" acceleration of only one gravity. Above that level, however, the plates' efficiency fell off dramatically. The physical plant itself grew larger and more massive on a steeply climbing curve, which cut into internal volume, and even then, each additional gravity of actual acceleration produced a "felt" increase of approximately .05 *g*. That didn't sound too terrible, but what it meant was that fifty additional gravities produced an apparent increase of two and a half gravities, which raised the ship's internal gravity to 3.5 *g*, at which point the crew's ability to move about and perform even routine duties began to become... impaired. And it also meant that grav plates powerful enough to produce that effect required almost twice the volume required to produce the 150:1 ratio.

After considering the situation carefully, the architects had designed and stressed the ship structures and control stations to permit effective maneuvering and combat at up to four gravities, but combat *efficiency* began to decline noticeably at that rate of acceleration due to the physiological limitations of the crew. Moreover, that still equated to an *actual* acceleration of only two hundred and ten gravities, which was pathetic by the standards of any impeller-drive warship. Actual acceleration could be pushed—in emergencies, and briefly, at least—to almost three hundred and ten gravities, but that produced a "felt" gravity of 9 *g*. Crew acceleration couches were provided for just that contingency, yet three hundred and ten gravities was still barely half of the acceleration which the RMN's biggest superdreadnought could currently attain, and even with the best acceleration couches in the universe, no one could stand nine gravities for long. Worse, smaller spider-drive ships had no acceleration advantage over larger ones. And the need to stabilize the ship relative to the hyper wall required at least three sets of "spider legs," which led directly to the "triple skeg" hull form which had been adopted. Which, in turn, meant that instead of two broadsides, a spider-drive ship had *three*... none of which could be protected by the impenetrable barrier of an impeller wedge. That meant both that areas no impeller-drive ship had to armor did require massive armor protection aboard a spider-drive warship and that there was no wedge floor and roof for a side wall to stitch together. And just to make matters even more interesting, the spider drive could not be used through a spherical sidewall like the ones fortresses generated.

All of that was true, and all of it constituted indisputably significant disadvantages. But the spider also had one overwhelming *ad*vantage: it was effectively undetectable by any sensor system deployed by any navy (including the MAN itself) at any range much beyond a single light-second. Even for the MAN, it was damnably hard to detect; for someone who didn't even know what to look for, the task was about as close to outright impossible as challenges came. For all intents and purposes, a spider-drive ship's drive field was invisible, and it was actually the *drive signature* of a ship for which virtually all long-range passive sensors searched.

Which explained how Admiral Frederick Topolev's and Rear Admiral Lydia Papnikitas' strike forces had been able to deploy their missile pods without anyone's ever noticing they were there. And it also explained how Commodore Karol Østby's and Commodore Milena Omelchenko's scouting forces had been able to prowl undetected about both components of the Manticore Binary System for over two months, while Commodore Roderick Sung's scouts and Admiral Jennifer Colenso's strike ships had done exactly the same things at Yeltsin's Star.

And no one knew a thing about it or even suspected what was about to happen.

Now the Mesan attack came sweeping in out of the darkness. The incoming weapons had extraordinarily low radar signatures, and they were coming in at barely 60,000 KPS. Even if some of them had been detected, their velocity was so low it was unlikely to pop through the defenders' threat filters. As it happened, however, none of them *were* picked up as they sliced deeper and deeper in-system, unseen and undetected, like the talons of some huge, lethal, invisible bird of prey.

There were actually six separate attacks on the Manticore Binary System itself, one for each inhabited planet's infrastructure and each divided into two separate waves, although they'd been carefully synchronized to form a single, devastating sledgehammer of a blow.

The first wave of each attack consisted of a weapon which was as much a fundamental breakthrough, in its own way, as the Manticoran introduction of the multidrive missile: a graser torpedo which used its own variant of the spider drive. It was a large and cumbersome weapon, with the same trilateral symmetry as the *Shark*-class ships which had launched it, and for the same reasons.

The torpedo's size made fitting it into magazines and actually firing it awkward, to say the least, and the *Sharks* had never been intended to deploy it operationally. For that matter, the *Sharks* themselves had never been supposed to be deployed "operation-ally." The *Leonard Detweiler* class, which had been *intended* to carry out this operation, had been designed with magazines and launch tubes which would make it possible to stow and fire torpedoes internally, but none of the *Detweilers* were even close to completion, and it had required the development of an ingenious external rack system to allow the *Sharks* to use it for Oyster Bay.

For all its size, it was also a slow weapon. It was simply impossible to fit a spider drive capable of more than a few hundred gravities' acceleration into something small enough to make a practical weapon. As compensation, however, its drive had almost as much endurance as most of the galaxy's recon drones, which gave it an impressive absolute range. And a large percentage of the torpedo's volume had been reserved for systems which had nothing at all to do with propulsion. Whereas the Royal Manticoran Navy had concentrated on improving the efficiency of its standard laser heads, Daniel Detweiler's R&D staff had taken another approach. They'd figured out how to squeeze what amounted to a cruiser-grade graser projector into something small enough to deploy independently.

The power of the torpedo's graser wasn't remotely comparable to that of the weapon mounted by current-generation *Shrikes*, yet it was more powerful than any single bomb-pumped laser head. Of course, there was only one of it in each torpedo, but R&D had decided the new weapon could sacrifice the laser head's multi-shot capability, because it offered three highly significant advantages of its own. First, it was just as hard to pick up as a spider-drive *ship*, and the best antimissile defense in the universe couldn't hit something it didn't know was coming. Second, the torpedo carried extraordinarily capable sensors and targeting systems and an AI which approached the capability of the one Sonja Hemphill's people had fitted into the Apollo control missile. As a consequence, its long-range hit probability was significantly higher on a per-beam basis than anything short of Apollo itself. And, third, a bomb-pulsed laser had a burst endurance of barely five thousandths of a second; a laser torpedo's graser's endurance was a full *three seconds*...and it had a burn-through range against most sidewalls of over fifty thousand kilometers.

Fitting all that into something the size of a torpedo had required some drastic engineering compromises, and there'd never been any possibility of squeezing in the power supply for more than a single shot. Even if there had been, no one could build a graser that small and that powerful which could survive the power bleed and waste heat of actually firing. But that was fine with the MAN's designers and tacticians. In fact, they were just as happy every graser torpedo would irrevocably and totally destroy itself in the moment it fired, since they weren't looking forward to the day one of their enemies finally captured one intact and figured out how to duplicate it.

Now the the time had come to find out just how profitably they'd invested their R&D time.

The torpedoes had begun accelerating well before they or any of the missile pods accompanying them reached the range at which any transmission from the communications platforms the *Ghost*-class scout ships had emplaced could have reached them. On the other hand, they had less need for any additional information than the missiles did. They already knew where to find their targets, and they pulled steadily away from their purely ballistic pod companions.

"That's funny," Sensor Tech 1/c Franklin Sands murmured. He reached out and tapped a command into his display, then frowned as the more detailed readout appeared.

"Ma'am," he said, looking over his shoulder, "I'm picking up something funny over here."

Lieutenant (JG) Tabatha Dombroski, HMS *Star Witch*'s junior tactical officer, had the heavy cruiser's combat information center watch, and she quirked one eyebrow as she looked in Sands' direction. "Something funny" wasn't how the competent and experienced tech normally reported his findings.

"What is it?" Dombroski asked, walking across CIC's relatively spacious compartment towards him. Then she snorted. "Forget I asked that. I imagine that if you already knew what it was, you'd have told me, wouldn't you?"

"I believe the Lieutenant might reasonably assume that, Ma'am," Sands replied gravely, but his eyes twinkled. Lieutenant Dombroski had made fewer mistakes than quite a few JGs he'd known over the years, and she was more than willing to admit that even her enlisted personnel could probably teach her a thing or two.

"All right, I will," she told him as she reached his command station and looked over his shoulder. "So what is it we haven't been able to ID?"

"This, Ma'am," Sands said more seriously. He indicated his readouts, and Dombroski gazed thoughtfully at them.

There wasn't much to see. *Star Witch*'s division of obsolescent *Star Knight*-class heavy cruisers were conducting routine training exercises in preparation for deployment to Silesia. They'd been listed for disposal when the Battle of Manticore burst upon the RMN, at which point they'd been pulled back out of reserve and refitted for service, so they had more training to worry about than most. It might be argued that, since they were headed for what had become an admittedly important but still strategically secondary assignment—and weren't even scheduled to leave for another two and a half weeks—there was no tearing urgency to the process, but Commodore James Tanner, CruDiv 114.1's commanding officer, didn't believe in letting last-minute details pile up. He'd gotten permission to conduct formation exercises in a conveniently empty area well inside the hyper limit but above the ecliptic, which was what he'd been doing for the last three days. Between maneuvering and tactical exercises, each ship had been tasked with completing her own system tests while there would still be time for the techs aboard *Hephaestus* to correct any faults before their scheduled departure, as well. As part of her own tests, *Star Witch* had deployed half a dozen Ghost Rider recon platforms, and Sands was currently in charge of monitoring their telemetry, not that he'd really expected to find anything. All he was doing was to make certain CIC's computers and the drones were talking to each other properly, and a less experienced or conscientious rating probably would never have noticed the tiny scrap of transmission he'd picked up.

"Any idea who it's from?" Dombroski asked after a moment. "I mean, who's out there on that bearing?"

"That's what's funny about it, Ma'am." Sands shrugged. "It's directional as hell, and it originated from even further above the ecliptic than we are. As far as I can tell, there's *nobody* out there. No one according to any of our shipping logs, anyway."

"What do the computers make of it?" Dombroski's frown deepened.

"That's just coming up," Sands said as another display blinked. They both looked at it, and he pursed his lips in a silent whistle.

"That's one damned big burst packet, Ma'am," he said.

"Yeah," Dombroski agreed. "More to the point, though, we don't even recognize the encryption."

"Internal Andermani or something, Ma'am?" Sands sounded puzzled, but not yet really concerned, and Dombroski shook her head grimly.

"Even if it's Andermani, whoever sent it wouldn't have used that encryption unless they wanted to keep anyone who happened to detect it from understanding it. And like you say, it's a *big* packet. And one coming from somewhere none of our people are supposed to be."

"But—" Sands began, then shut his mouth rather firmly.

"I know what you're thinking," the lieutenant told him, "and you've got a point. *I* don't know how anyone who's not supposed to be here could have gotten in, either. Not how she could've gotten past Perimeter Security without being detected on the way in, anyway. And I may be jumping at shadows. All the same, though, this is something to be passed on to older and wiser heads, I think."

She rested one approving hand lightly on Sands' shoulder for a moment, then keyed her headset.

"Commander Neukirch," she requested.

"Neukirch," a deep, slightly sleepy voice responded after a brief pause.

"Drombroski, Sir, in CIC. I'm sorry to disturb you, but we've just picked up something down here that makes me a little nervous."

"Nervous?" Lieutenant Commander Gilderoy Neukirch's voice sharpened. As *Star Witch*'s tactical officer, he was Dombroski's immediate superior. She hadn't been aboard all that long, but he'd formed a positive opinion of her judgment.

"Yes, Sir. It's a burst transmission. It's a big one—it looks like our platform crossed its path before we caught all of it, despite its compression. According to our shipping logs, there shouldn't be anyone at its apparent origination point, either. And, Sir, it's encrypted, and we don't even recognize the encryption."

Neukirch sat abruptly upright in bed.

"Inform the bridge immediately," he said sharply. "Then screen Captain McMahon. Tell him I suggest he get up, get dressed, and meet me in CIC as soon as possible."

✧　　✧　　✧

"Ah, excuse me, My Lady," Andrew LaFollet said with infinite politeness, "but unless I'm mistaken, isn't Lady Clarissa's birthday *today*?"

Doctor Allison Chou Harrington, one of the Star Empire of Manticore's premier geneticists, looked up from the unhappy youngster on the changing table and gave Lord Raoul Alexander-Harrington's personal armsman the sort of look which had been known to level tall mountains and reduce glaciers to steaming swamps.

"If *you* would like to shoulder your responsibilities as this young monster's guardian and change his diaper yourself, Colonel Andrew LaFollet, I'm sure we could facilitate things," she told him.

"Assassins, blades, bullets, and bombs come with the job, My Lady," he replied solemnly. "Diapers—and the surprises they so often contain—weren't listed anywhere when I signed up."

"Well, they *should* have been," she said, reaching for the cleansing tissue he extended to her.

In fact, as both of them knew perfectly well, Allison had volunteered to change Raoul. It was, she said, a grandmother's duty. Besides, she liked babies, especially her own personal grandbabies. Of which, as she had pointed out to her daughter upon occasion, she still had only one. Well, two counting Katherine, of course.

"There, baby!" she said, sealing the clean diaper in place and scooping him up for tickling and an enthusiastic hug before she tucked him back into his onesie. "All clean and fresh smelling... for now, at least."

He gurgled happily, and she laughed. Despite the volume of which he was capable, he was actually an extraordinarily even-tempered baby. He took particularly vocal exception to having his diapers changed, for some reason, yet other than that he spent a lot more time being delighted with the universe than he did complaining about it. It had been sixty-two T-years and some change since Raoul's mother had been his age, but Allison didn't remember young Honor Harrington being quite as cheerful as he was. Then again, Honor hadn't met Nimitz until she was twelve, and Raoul was for all intents and purposes being raised by treecats, as well as humans. God only knew where *that* was going to end up!

"I'll go give Jeremiah the heads up," LaFollet told her, and she nodded. Sergeant Jeremiah Tennard was actually her daughter Faith's personal armsman, but the twins' armsmen frequently doubled up watching the kids so that one of them could keep an eye on her or Alfred. Which was how he'd come to be assigned to Allison when she came ahead to Sphinx to reopen the Copper Walls house. And how he'd become her limo pilot for this little junket, as well.

And they're so damned well meaning and eager about it I can't even work up a good mad, she thought. *Even if it does sometimes make me feel like they think I'm another nine-year-old they have to keep track of!*

"Lindsey!" she called.

"Yes, Milady?" Lindsey Phillips, Raoul's nanny, poked her head into the nursery.

"I think we're ready," Allison told her. "He smells better, anyway."

"Milady, *I* could have done that, you know," Lindsey told her. "Unless I'm mistaken, it's listed somewhere in my job description."

"No, is it?" Allison smiled at the young woman who was also Katherine Alexander-Harrington's nanny, as she'd been for Faith and James Harrington, as well. "You mean that, all these years, I could actually have had *you* changing *diapers*?"

"As a matter of fact, you could have," Lindsey told her gravely.

"Ah, if only I'd known!"

Lindsey chuckled and took Raoul, balancing him against her shoulder, and the two women walked out the nursery door and down the short hallway in the comfortable, centuries-old house high in the Copper Wall Mountains. They paused on the veranda, gazing out across the dense green trees of Sphinx and the just visible blue flashes of the Tannerman Ocean far beyond and below them.

A customized armored air limousine in the green livery of Harrington Steading sat on the parking circle, with LaFollet and Sergeant Tennard talking beside it. Overhead, a pair of heavily armed sting ships circled patiently, and Allison shook her head. It was at moments like this, especially when all the security was focused here, on the Harrington freehold which had been in her husband's family since the Plague Years and which had been her own home since she returned with him to Manticore from Beowulf so many decades before, that the absurdity of the changes in her life snapped into crisp, unambiguous clarity. And it was also at moments like this that she found herself most wistfully wishing things hadn't gotten quite so complicated.

But there's no point wishing, she reminded herself once again. *And however "complicated" things may seem sometimes, you couldn't change any of it without changing* all *of it, and then where would you be? Somehow I don't see you giving up Raoul or Katherine just to avoid having to put up with other people's schedules!*

"Here we are, Andrew," she said, and Raoul's armsman turned and smiled at her. "I hope we haven't really made you late," she said.

"Actually, we *are* running a little late, My Lady," he said, "but that's all right. Miranda just screened. It seems Faith had a little accident when they were leaving the Landing House. Something to do with sliding down the grand staircase banister again."

"Oh, Lord!" Allison rolled her eyes, and Lindsey chuckled. Honor's younger sister was almost nine T-years old, and she'd developed a veritable obsession for banisters after watching half a dozen treecats go tobogganing gleefully down them. Thankfully, her twin brother James seemed to have avoided that particular mental aberration.

"It's all right, My Lady," Andrew assured her. "At least she didn't break anything, this time."

"Would that be that she didn't break any portion of her own person, or that she didn't break anything *else*?" Allison inquired, and the armsman chuckled.

"Neither, in this case," he said. "But she did manage to bloody her nose, with predictable consequences for her clothes. So what with picking her up, stopping the nosebleed, her father's discussion of questionable decisions, and then getting her changed, they missed their flight out of Landing and had to re-book. They're in transit now, but Miranda says Lady Clarissa's pushed her party back an hour to give them time."

"I see." Allison shook her head. "Well, by the time they get here, I'm sure Raoul will have come up with another delay of his own. But until then, let's get your show on the road."

"Of course, My Lady."

The torpedoes were unaware that anyone had overheard their e-mail. Not that they would have cared if they had known, of course. Nor were they particularly impressed by the meticulous precision, planning, and execution by their merely human masters which had gotten the transmitting platforms into position to send it to them without any Manticoran ever spotting the MAN at it. They simply receipted the portion of it which was addressed to them and ignored the rest.

Special caps fitted to protect their sensors from particle erosion and micrometeorites during their long ballistic run in to attack range were blown free while onboard artificial intelligences considered the updated targeting information and concluded that none of it required significant modification of their pre-launch instructions. Their targets were rather large, after all, and they'd already known exactly where to find them.

The tricky part had been synchronizing the attack waves. Manticore-A and Manticore-B were far enough apart that even if the Manticorans' FTL station's range was great enough for transmissions between them (which seemed, to say the least, unlikely), it would take the better part of thirteen minutes for word of what happened around one component of the binary system to reach the other. Because of that, Oyster Bay's planners had been willing to settle for only approximate coordination between those separate parts of the operation.

Within the Manticore-A subsystem, however, timing was far more critical. Although the planets Manticore and Sphinx were well over twenty-five light-minutes apart at the moment, it was imperative that all the attacks be executed in a time window too narrow to allow for any effective reaction by the system's defenders. And unlike certain members of the Solarian League Navy, the MAN had a very powerful respect for the Royal Manticoran Navy. Not only that, but as they'd studied and updated Oyster Bay's planning requirements, they'd become painfully aware that the Manticorans' reaction was going to be even faster and better coordinated than they'd originally allowed for, given the existence of their grav-pulse communicators and how they'd undoubtedly upgraded their routine readiness postures in the wake of the Battle of Manticore. No doubt they'd based any changes on the need to defeat a repeat of any attack using known weapon systems, since one didn't normally make plans on the basis of threats one *didn't* know about, but the MAN had found that reflection less than completely reassuring. In the Alignment strategists' opinion, it was generally a good idea to proceed with caution when one decided to march into a napping tigress' cave to steal her young, and so the initial deployment of Oyster Bay's weapons had been painstakingly planned and calculated, then carried out with meticulously rehearsed precision.

None of which mattered at all to the weapons in question themselves.

The eighteen torpedoes heading the Mike Attack wave bound for the planet Manticore simply adjusted their courses very slightly, while those leading the Sierra Attack, bound for the planet Sphinx, didn't even have to do that. Onboard passive sensors located the unmistakable emission signatures of their targets and pre-attack testing signals began cascading through their systems.

❖   ❖   ❖

"No, Sir," Lieutenant Commander Neukirch said. "I don't have any more idea what this could be or who it could have come from than Lieutenant Dombroski has. But I think she did exactly the right thing by reporting it up the line."

"I agree entirely," Commodore Tanner replied. "And I've already kicked a flash report up to Perimeter Security, but even with the grav com it's going to be another couple of minutes before we hear anything back. If anyone has any powerful insights, I want to hear them now."

The silence, Tanner reflected, was deafening. His com display was divided into four quadrants which were occupied, respectively, by the faces of Captain Matheson Marcos, the commanding officer of HMS *Star Dance* (which also made him Tanner's flag captain); Captain Vince McMahon, *Star Witch*'s CO; and both cruisers' senior tactical officers. Commander Alexandros Adriopoulos, Tanner's chief of staff, was physically present, still holding the mug of coffee he'd been sipping when *Star Witch*'s emergency transmission came in three hundred and seventy seconds previously. And none of them, obviously, had any insights at all, powerful or not.

Fair's fair, Jim, he admonished himself. *You know just as much as they do, and you don't have any brilliant analysis to offer, either. Except for the blindingly obvious point Neukirch already made, of course. So don't go taking your grumpy out on them.*

"All right," he said out loud. "A few things we can do on our own while we wait for Perimeter Security to get back to us. Commander Neukirch, your request to deploy additional Ghost Rider platforms is approved. Use however many you think you need, but try to find me whoever sent that transmission."

Neukirch started to open his mouth, but Tanner's raised hand preempted anything the lieutenant commander had been about to say.

"I know I'm asking you to find a very small needle in a very large haystack, Commander. But we've got at least an approximate bearing, and I don't want that datum getting any older before we start trying to chase it down. Do your best. No one expects miracles."

"Yes, Sir."

"Alexandros," the commodore turned to his chief of staff, "I think it's time we woke up the division's other skippers and tac officers. The more people we have looking for this, the better. And while I'm thinking about it, get a flash directly off to Home Fleet, as well. I'm sure Perimeter Security will be keeping Admiral Higgins in the loop, but let's see if we can't cut the transmission time as much as possible."

"Yes, Sir."

"In the meantime," Tanner continued, turning his attention to Marcos and McMahon, "I think we shou—"

"Excuse me, Sir!"

Tanner's eyes darted to Neukirch's image as the tactical officer's suddenly hoarse voice cut him off in mid-syllable. Neukirch looked as if he'd just been punched in the belly. The lieutenant commander was staring at something outside his com pickup's field of view, and Tanner could actually see the color draining out of the younger man's face. Then Neukirch inhaled deeply and looked back at the commodore.

"I think I know what it was about, Sir," he said in a voice like crushed gravel.

The Mike Attack torpedoes reached the proper point in space. They aligned themselves with finicky precision, doublechecked and triple-checked their targeting, then fired.

Every one of them activated in the space of a single second, and three seconds later, not one of them still existed. But their closing speed on their target was well over seventy thousand kilometers per second; the target in question was completely unprotected by impeller wedge or side wall, which increased their standoff range to the next best thing to a half-million kilometers; and their approach vectors had been carefully calculated.

One moment, the Manticore Binary System was going about its routine business, peacefully and calmly. The next moment, eighteen powerful grasers ripped through Her Majesty's Space Station *Hephaestus* like demons. There was absolutely no warning. No time to bring up the station's spherical sidewall, or to evacuate, or don skinsuits, or set internal pressure security. There was no time *at all* as that devastating wave of destruction struck like a chainsaw hitting an egg.

Despite the provision of her sidewall generators, *Hephaestus* had never truly been intended or designed to survive that sort of attack. Even if its builders had ever dreamed in their worst nightmares that something like it was a real possibility, it would have been physically impossible to structure and armor the station to face it. But none of those builders had ever really imagined something like this getting past Perimeter Security and Home Fleet, actually reaching attack range of the Star Empire's capital planet without so much as being challenged, and so no one had even tried. For that matter, there'd never been a single, comprehensive construction or expansion plan of any sort for *Hephaestus*. The station had simply grown, steadily and inevitably, adding additional lobes and habitats—cargo platforms, personnel sections, heavy fabrication modules, shipyards—as they were required. Taking advantage of the flexibility microgravity made possible. Expanding into a huge, lumpy agglomeration of raw industrial power which had its own peculiar beauty as it floated in orbit, by far the brightest single object in the planet Manticore's night skies. It stretched over a hundred and ten kilometers along its central spine, and tentacles reached out in every direction, some of them the better part of forty or even fifty kilometers long in their own right. It boasted a permanent population of over nine hundred and fifty thousand. By the time transients, ship crews, field trips by visiting school children, and other visitors were added, the station's total population on any given day was certainly upward of a million, and probably close to twice that on most days.

Yet for all its sheer size, all the industrial processes churning away in and about it, *Hephaestus* was a fragile structure—a fairy tale construct which could never have survived its own weight inside a planetary gravity field.

And which was certainly far too frail to survive holocaust when it came.

✧ Chapter Twenty-Nine

NO ONE EVER MANAGED to accurately reconstruct exactly what happened during the first few seconds of the attack. There was simply too much mayhem, too much chaos, and despite the multitude of sensor systems—civilian, as well as military—operating throughout the inner system, no one was looking in the right direction when it all began.

Had anyone been in a position to chart the damage, however, they would have known that the very first hit—first by almost an entire tenth of a second—struck compartment HF/1-17-1336-T-1219 of HMSS *Hephaestus*. HF/1-17-1336-T-1219 was the control section of module GM-HF/1-17-13, a general manufacturing module attached to the Royal Manticoran Navy's Shipyard HF/1-16 and Shipyard HF/1-17, which were currently assigned to BuShips' Refit and Repair Command (*Hephaestus*). HF/1-16 happened to be empty, awaiting the arrival of the brand new *Nike*-class battlecruiser HMS *Truculent* later that afternoon. HF/1-17, on the other hand, was occupied by the *Roland*-class destroyers HMS *Barbarossa*, HMS *Saladin*, and HMS *Yamamoto Date*, all three of which were completing their final fitting out, with almost their full complements embarked.

The thirty-two technicians manning HF/1-17-1336-T-1219 never even realized the station was under attack. Working in a shirtsleeve environment, concentrating on routine tasks and the hectic pace at which *Hephaestus* always operated, they were totally

381

unprepared for the ravening blast of focused gamma radiation which killed them instantly, splintered the compartment around them, and ripped open one entire flank of GM-HF/1-17-13.

At the instant it fired, the torpedo which struck the control section was moving at the next best thing to 70,000 KPS and deliberately yawing on its axis, sweeping its graser in a spiraling cone to traverse the entire volume of the station. The beam itself moved *away* from GM-HF/1-17-13, but the lethal overpressure of the explosion's shock front—followed by equally explosive decompression—killed the sixteen techs working directly in the twenty thousand-ton fabrication module almost as quickly as the control room techs had died. Splinters of HF/1-17-1336-T-1219 blew into and through GM-HF/1-17-13, carried all the way across the module compartment, and opened the far bulkhead into the vacuum of HF/1-17.

The second breach of the fabrication module could scarcely have mattered less to the people who'd been working inside it, since they were all already dead or dying by the time it occurred. It mattered a great deal, however, to the forty-eight space station personnel moving through the outsized boarding tubes connecting the three destroyers' main airlocks to the space dock gallery and the station proper. None of them were in skinsuits when the flying battle axes which had once been part of GM-HF/1-17-13 shredded the tubes and spilled them into the enormous docking bay's merciless vacuum.

As the boarding tubes were torn apart, atmosphere vented from them in a hurricane. GM-HF/1-17-13 had already decompressed almost entirely, but the vacuum around the station sucked greedily at the wounds, and at least a quarter of the equally unprepared crewmen aboard the three destroyers found themselves in death pressure before emergency blast doors slammed shut under computer control.

As it happened, the blast doors made no difference at all, however. Even as the graser which had ripped HF/1-17-1336-T-1219 moved away, cutting deeper towards the station's central spine, another graser moved *towards* HF/1-17 and HF/1-16. It sliced across both shipyards in a searing eyeblink, and if it was less powerful than a *Shrike*'s weapon, its power was more than ample for the minor task of cutting an unarmored destroyer, unprotected by impeller wedge or sidewalls, cleanly in half.

It did precisely that to HMS *Saladin*... whose fusion plant abruptly lost containment with absolutely no warning to the engineering safety systems. Not even cybernetic reflexes were equal to that sort of cataclysmic failure, and the resulting fireball made whatever other damage the torpedoes might have done to that section of HMSS *Hephaestus* totally superfluous.

HMS *Longshoreman*, one of *Hephaestus'* ready-duty tugs, was headed away from the station, towing the brand new *Saganami-C*-class cruiser *Jessica Rice* towards Traffic Control's impeller limit, when the attack came in. The two ships were accelerating at the piddling rate of barely ten gravities out of deference to the fact that *Jessica Rice* was on internal grav plates only, since her inertial compensator was inoperable without the impeller wedge traffic regulations forbade her in such close proximity to the station. They were well clear of the slip in which *Jessica Rice* had been berthed, but that didn't matter.

One of the Mesan torpedoes scored a direct hit on the station's spine, slashing outward and across successive secondary axes in a horrendous bow wave of secondary blasts and explosive decompressions. It reached the outer edge of the station and kept right on going until it ripped lengthwise across *Jessica Rice's* unarmored topsides, shattering the big, powerful ship. And then she, like *Saladin*, blew up. The explosion disabled *Longshoreman's* after impeller ring, sending her wedge into automatic shutdown... and leaving her unprotected as a chunk of what had once been HMSS *Hephaestus* which out-massed the tug by at least fifty percent slammed into her and destroyed her completely.

"Jesus Christ!"

Lieutenant Édouard Boisvin, executive officer of HMS *Stevedore*, looked up in surprise at Senior Chief Petty Officer Oxana Karpova's exclamation. The senior chief had primary helm control for the powerful tug's approach to *Hephaestus*, and that sort of outburst from her was unheard of.

Boisvin opened his mouth to demand an explanation, but nothing came out. As he looked up, he saw the same visual display Karpova and her backup helmsman had been watching, and his vocal cords froze.

He felt himself sitting there, unable to look away, unable even to speak, as the entire space station blew apart before him. It was impossible for his stunned brain to pick individual explosions out of the chaos of devastation ripping across the station. Bits and pieces of it registered with horrifying clarity—not then, but for later replay in the nightmares which would plague him for years. Individual modules, blown loose from their moorings, spraying across the backdrop of incandescent explosions like fragile, backlit beads before the wavefront of destruction reached out and engulfed them, as well. The pieces of a heavy cruiser, her spine broken, spinning end-over-end and breaking up into smaller bits as they spun. A construction ship, underway on reaction thrusters, vanishing into the fiery vortex's maw.

Those tiny vignettes, snapshot images of catastrophe's outriders, would come back to him in those nightmares. But all that registered at the moment was the sheer impossibility of what he was seeing. There wasn't even room for horror—not in those first, fleeting seconds. The *unbelievability* of it would be the first and forever most overwhelming impression of any of the surviving witnesses. Their sheer incredulity.

Yet even though Édouard Boisvin couldn't look away, the ingrained, acquired reflexes of relentless training moved the thumb of his right hand to a button on his command chair's armrest and *Stevedore*'s emergency signal blared from speakers throughout the ship.

◇　　◇　　◇

"—not really a problem, Admiral. Oh, it sounded like it was going to be a bear, but once I started looking into it, it was only a scheduling snafu," Captain Karaamat Fonzarelli, Refit & Repair's senior officer aboard *Hephaestus* said.

Rear Admiral Margaret Truman, *Hephaestus*' CO, nodded. She'd suspected it was something like that, but it was a relief to hear she'd been right.

"I've been on the screen to Logistics about it," Fonzarelli continued from his end of the com link. "According to them, it's mostly a question of when and where we want the spares delivered. So I told them t—"

Truman's display went abruptly blank.

Her eyebrows were still only beginning to rise in surprise when another torpedo's graser sawed directly through her quarters... and her.

"Look, Daddy! What's that?"

John Cabeçadas was struggling with his carry-on bag. The damned thing's strap *insisted* on twisting, especially when he was carrying Serafina. The sixteen-month-old was usually as good as gold, but, of course, whenever he was having trouble with the carry-on bag, she was inevitably fretful. He'd just decided he was going to have to hand her to his wife, Laura, when his older daughter Jennifer asked the question.

"I don't know," he told her, unable to entirely keep the irritation out of his voice. The girl was incredibly bright and even more curious than most nine-year-olds, and she'd been one question after another ever since their shuttle delivered them to *Hephaestus*. To be honest, much as he loved her and as happy as her keen wittedness normally made him, John was looking forward to getting her settled aboard the ship to Beowulf, where there'd be no convenient windows and she could ask her questions of the ship's library.

"What are you talking a—" he began, turning and looking through the transparent wall of the personnel tube which had been provided to give tourists a panoramic view of the station's huge bulk.

He never finished the question. There wasn't time. There was barely enough time for him to begin to reach for Jennifer, to feel Laura and twelve-year-old Miguel at his back, to experience the first terrible flicker of a father's utter helplessness, and then the explosion tore the tube apart around them.

"I am so frigging *tired* of worrying about the Manties' tender damned sensibilities!" Jacqueline Rivera groused.

Rivera had never been a great admirer of the "Star Empire of Manticore's" pretensions to grandeur even before this latest crisis had blown up, and she'd deeply resented the front office's insistence that she tone down her usual commentary. It wasn't simply that she'd disagreed with Corporate editorial policy—she had, in this case, but that hadn't been the real cause of her current ire. No, what she'd resented was being *reminded* of editorial policy by some executive assistant producer (who probably owed her position solely to the fact that she was someone's cousin-in-law or current live-in lover) as if Jacqueline were some unknown newbie and not one of Solarian News Services' senior reporters.

So, all right, she might have been hitting just a little harder

at questions about the credibility of the Manty version of events
in Talbott than Corporate might have preferred once the great
Audrey O'Hanrahan herself backed off. Sure, it was true "Saint
Audrey" had urged everyone to "reserve judgment," especially
now that the authenticity of the "official New Tuscany" report
to which she'd gained access had been called into question by
Solarian reporters actually in Talbott. And of *course* she might
have a point when she'd argued that the Manties' enemies might
have fed it to her as part of a clever, deliberate disinformation
campaign. It was even *possible* the Mesan System authorities'
claims about the Green Pines terrorist attack were fabrications,
although Rivera damned well knew better than that. She'd filed
three good 'casts on that very point, as a matter of fact, which was
why Corporate had sent her out to Manticore...and told her to
make nice while she was here, the stinking bastards. "More flies
with honey," indeed! The damned Manties had finally come out
into the open, proving they'd always funded and supported those
murdering Ballroom bastards—just as Rivera had always known
they were doing—and this was the time to go for the jugular, not
"demonstrate journalistic impartiality and detachment"!

"Calm down, Jackie," Manfred O'Neill, her longtime recording
tech, said pacifically. "It's hardly the end of the world. After all,
this is *the* story at the moment."

"Oh, yeah?" Rivera glared at him. "Look, you may think they
sent us out here to do us some kind of favor, but I know better!
We could've been covering Green Pines instead, damn it!"

"Never said anyone did it to do us a favor," O'Neill replied
cheerfully. "I only said it's going to turn out to be the hot corner,
and it is. Hotter'n Green Pines, for that matter, especially if there's
anything to these new rumors from Spindle. Everybody's already
pretty much mined Green Pines out, and it's not like the system
authorities're handing out any fresh info, anyway. But there's going
to be *lots* of stuff coming through here if things really are going
to hell for the Manties in Talbott, and when it does, I don't think
anyone back home is going to be worrying a lot about reminding
us to watch our Ps and Qs when we report it."

Rivera looked at him for a moment, then felt at least a little of
her resentment easing away. Manny had a way of cutting to the
heart of things, and maybe he had a point. Not that it changed
the fact that—

The Mesan graser which incinerated Passenger Concourse Green-317 terminated Jacqueline Rivera's reflections upon her career prospects along with her, Manfred O'Neill, and four hundred and nineteen other arriving passengers from the Hauptman Lines starship *Starlight*.

Approximately three-hundredths of a second later, *Starlight*, her crew of twenty-eight, and the two hundred through-passengers to Sphinx who hadn't disembarked followed them into destruction.

"Is Aikawa back aboard yet, Ben?" Ansten FitzGerald asked as his steward poured him a second cup of coffee.

"No, sir," Steward 1/c Benjamin Frankel replied with a smile. "He's not due back until this afternoon, I believe."

"Um." FitzGerald frowned thoughtfully. *Hexapuma* would be in the yard dogs' hands for at least another three or four weeks, but she'd just been assigned a trio of bright, shiny new midshipmen. Frightening as the concept seemed in some ways, he'd decided to ask Aikawa Kagiyama to take them under his wing. He was confident Aikawa would rise to his responsibilities and set them a *good* example.

Of course he was.

He snorted in amusement at his own thoughts, but he couldn't really deny that a part of him was actually a little relieved at having at least another few hours before he found out whether or not his "confidence" was justified.

"Well, in that case—"

HMS *Hexapuma* blew up with all hands as the Mesan graser ripped across her fusion plant.

The destruction of HMSS *Hephaestus* was for all intents and purposes total in the first three seconds of the Mesan attack.

Some of the surviving fragments of the station were large enough and sufficiently intact to hold pressure, and a handful of the ships which had been docked survived more or less in one piece. Three of them—the destroyer *Horatius*, the Grayson freighter *Foxglove*, and the tug *Bollard*—actually came through the holocaust virtually undamaged. *Horatius'* paint wasn't even scratched.

But they were the exception to the rule, tiny pockets of survival in a hurricane of devastation . . . and the attack on HMSS *Vulcan* was equally successful.

The MAN's Sierra Attack wasn't quite perfectly synchronized with the Mike Attack's assault on *Hephaestus*, but the delay was less than four seconds. By the time visual evidence of what had happened to *Hephaestus* could have reached *Vulcan* moving at the limited velocity of light, Sphinx's space station had been just as completely demolished.

Between the two space stations, alone, the first ten seconds of Oyster Bay had already cost the Old Star Kingdom over four million dead.

Allen Higgins' face was parchment-pale as he stared at the FTL platform-driven flag bridge master plot. It was only chance he'd been on the flag bridge at all, but that coincidence wasn't much help as CIC's computers emotionlessly updated the plot. Home Fleet was much too far away from either space station to have offered any sort of protection even if it had realized the attack was coming... or been able to see it when it did. Because it was, it was also too far away to be *attacked*, and in some ways, that made it far worse. The people who were supposed to protect the Star Empire—who were supposed to die to prevent something like this from ever *happening*—were perfectly placed to see exactly how totally they'd failed in that purpose, and the fact that it wasn't even remotely their fault meant nothing at all beside that terrible sense of failure.

And for Allen Higgins, their CO, it was even worse than it was for the rest of them.

For a moment, he was paralyzed, his mind replaying the memories of Grendelsbane with merciless clarity. Yet that lasted *only* for a moment. Only until he realized how infinitely much worse *this* disaster was.

And then the conventional Mesan missiles began their attack runs.

Daniel Detweiler's researchers hadn't yet figured out how to fit multiple full-size, sustainable drives into a single missile of manageable dimensions. They had, however, realized what the RMN must have done, and they were working industriously to duplicate the Manticoran advantage. In the meantime, they'd come up with Cataphract, a variant of their own based on taking the standard missile bodies for the SLN's new-generation anti-ship missiles and adding what amounted to a separate final stage carrying a standard laser head and a counter-missile's drive system. For Oyster Bay, they'd brought out the longest-ranged, heaviest version of their new weapon, fitted the birds into out-sized pods, then launched them behind other, specialized pods which carried nothing but low-powered particle screens and the power supplies to maintain them for the ballistic run in-system to their targets. The missile-laden pods had followed in the zone swept by the shield-equipped platforms; now they completed their own system checks and began to launch.

A version of the new weapon had been used with lethal effectiveness against Luis Rozsak's ships at the Second Battle of Congo. Unfortunately, the full report on that wasn't available to the RMN. They knew *something* had improved the range of the missiles which had been provided to the "People's Navy in Exile," and they'd managed to deduce approximately how it had been done, but that was about it. And even if they'd had access to Rozsak's report, it wouldn't have fully prepared them for this. Rozsak had faced the Cataphract-A, based on the SLN's new cruiser/destroyer Spatha shipkiller; the pod-launched missiles of Oyster Bay were Cataphract-Cs, based on the capital-ship Trebucht, with much heavier and more powerful laserheads. The combined package had a powered range from rest of over sixteen million kilometers and a terminal velocity of better than .49 *c*. That attack envelope would have made it formidable enough by itself, but installing the high-speed drive as the *last* stage also gave it far more agility when it came to penetrating the target's defenses during its terminal maneuvers.

That agility, however, was scarcely required today. There *were* no active defenses, just as their targets made no attempt at evasive maneuvers, because no one knew they were coming in time to react.

There was time for their targets—or some of them, at least—to realize they were under attack. To see the impossible impeller signatures of missile drives swarming away from the pods' ballistic tracks. Some of those missiles were effectively wasted because of targeting decisions made by officers who hadn't felt justified in relying solely upon the efficacy of the as yet untested torpedoes. Those laser heads either never fired at all or else used themselves up picking off chunks of wreckage large enough to satisfy their targeting criteria.

But the vast majority of them had other concerns. There really weren't many of them, given the number of targets they had to cover, but it didn't *take* very many to kill targets as naked as these. They roared in on the carefully plotted positions of the totally unprotected orbital shipyards floating around Manticore and Sphinx with devastating effectiveness.

Bomb-pumped lasers ripped deep, mangling and shattering, spewing bits and pieces of the Star Empire of Manticore's industrial might across the heavens. And behind them came the old-fashioned nuclear warheads—warheads which detonated only if they were unable to obtain a hard kinetic kill. Fireballs glared like brief-lived, intolerably bright stars, flashing in stroboscopic spikes of devastation, and more thousands of highly skilled workers and highly trained naval personal died in those cataclysmic bubbles of plasma and radiation.

Within a total space of barely eleven minutes, both of the Star Empire's major orbital industrial nodes and well over ninety percent of its dispersed shipyards, along with the better part of five and a half million trained technicians and naval personnel—and, all too often, their families—had been wiped out of existence.

By any yardstick anyone cared to use, it was the most devastating surprise attack in the history of the human race, and it wasn't over yet.

✧   ✧   ✧

"Bring her hard to port, Chief! Fifty degrees *now!*"

"Fifty degrees, aye, Sir!" Chief Petty Officer Manitoba Jackson acknowledged, and HMS *Quay* turned sharply.

"Bring her to"—Lieutenant Commander Andrew Sugimatsu, *Quay*'s CO, stabbed a look at his maneuvering plot—"five hundred and ten gravities and lay her on her side. Put our belly towards any wreckage with our name on it!"

"Rolling ship and coming to five-one-zero gravities, aye, Sir." Jackson's voice was flattened and stunned, as if actual awareness was seeping past the sheer shock effect of such unmitigated disaster.

Sugimatsu gave him a sharp look. The CPO had been in the Navy almost as long as Sugimatsu had been alive, but he'd spent his entire service as one of the highly skilled specialists assigned to the management of the home system's tugs. He'd never actually seen combat, unlike Sugimatsu, and what he *was* seeing at this moment was the massacre of people he'd known and worked with for decades. The lieutenant commander would have trusted Jackson's nerve and composure in the face of any conceivable *natural* disaster, but there was nothing "natural" about *this*, and Sugimatsu spent a brief moment being grateful that CPO Leslie Myerson, *Quay's* second helmswoman, *was* a combat vet.

"Sir," another voice said from the other side of *Quay's* small bridge, "there's going to be a lot of wreckage coming this way pretty darn soon."

"I'm well aware of that, Truida," Sugimatsu said. He looked across at Lieutenant Truida Verstappen, his executive officer.

"The problem," he continued, "is that anything coming *our* way is also coming the planet's way. And unless I'm really badly mistaken, we're all that's in a position to intercept it."

Verstappen looked at him for a moment, then nodded as he confirmed what she'd already realized must be his intentions.

"Get ready with the tractors," Sugimatsu told her. "No way can we catch all this crap with the wedge, so we're going to have to roll back down and grab the bigger pieces that get past us before they hit atmosphere."

"We've only got six tractors," Verstappen pointed out quietly.

"Then we're just going to have to hope there are only six pieces big enough to survive reentry," Sugimatsu said grimly.

Even as he said it, he knew they would never be that lucky. Not after something like this.

Quay drove sideways, accelerating hard to put herself directly between the wreckage of HMSS *Vulcan* and the planet Sphinx. As Sugimatsu had observed, she was the only ship in a position to intercept the avalanche about to come crashing down on the planet. Most of the station's wreckage might be small enough to be completely destroyed when it hit atmosphere, but some of it definitely *wasn't* going to be. In fact, *some* of it was going to be solid hunks of battle steel armor, specifically designed and manufactured to resist direct hits by capital ship-range energy weapons.

The good news—such as it was, and what there was of it—was that at least half the wreckage which had been blasted out of *Vulcan's* orbit had been blown *outward*, not inward. There'd be plenty of time for someone to deal with it before it became a threat to anyone. And most of the planet-bound wreckage was clustered in a fairly tight pattern, which gave Sugimatsu the chance to put *Quay* directly in the center of the debris' track, using the tug's impeller wedge as a huge broom, or shield. Anything that hit the wedge would no longer be a problem. That, in fact, had been one of the unspoken reasons there were always ready-duty tugs on call at each of the space stations. If necessary, they were supposed to interpose their wedges to protect the stations against collision or attack.

Well, that *part of the plan didn't work out so well, did it?* Sugimatsu thought grimly. *But maybe we can still do a little something for the planet.*

The problem was that the wedge wasn't big enough. "Fairly tight pattern" was a purely relative term, unfortunately, especially when one used it in relation to something the size of HMSS *Vulcan* and a planet, and while his present course would take *Quay* directly through the central, densest portion of the wreckage stream, he couldn't possibly intercept all of it. Nor could he come around in time for a second pass, even with the tug's enormous acceleration rate. He simply couldn't kill speed fast enough. So one pass was all he got—that and his ship's half-dozen powerful tractors—and a lot of those chunks of debris were bigger—*much* bigger, in some cases—than *Quay* herself.

He punched a button on his command chair's arm.

"Engineering," a voice rasped in his earbug.

"It's going to be ugly, Harland," he told his engineer quietly. "No way in hell are we going to be able to catch all of it on the wedge. So make damned sure the tractors are up and ready."

"Understood," Lieutenant Harland Wingate acknowledged. As *Quay*'s engineer, he was also the tug's tow master. "You do realize, though," he continued, "that my instrumentation down here isn't designed to grab ships that aren't trying to *help* me grab them."

"I understand," Sugimatsu told him. "We're just going to have to do our best. I'm putting Truida in charge of tracking and evaluation. She'll tell you which ones to grab and where they are."

"I can use all the help I can get," Wingate said grimly. Then he paused for a moment. "Should I try emergency overpower?" he asked.

Sugimatsu started to reply, then paused. He knew what Wingate was asking. The tug's tractors were powerful enough that they had to be handled with great care under normal circumstances. Too much power, too much torque, and they could rip chunks right out of the ship they were supposed to be towing. In fact, under the wrong circumstances, they could destroy a ship outright. So what Wingate was really asking was whether or not he should deliberately red-line the tractors and *try* to shred the wreckage into pieces too small to survive atmospheric entry. He might or might not succeed in any given case—a lot depended on the exact composition and structural strength of any piece of debris. But if he did succeed, that would be one more piece of wreckage, one more kinetic projectile, *Quay* could try to stop.

And if he pushes the tractors that hard, there's a damn good chance he'll burn them out and we'll lose *something we might have stopped.*

Andrew Sugimatsu's jaw muscles clenched. He'd seen combat. He'd expected to see it again. But he'd never expected to find himself having to make *this* kind of call in the very skies of one of his star nation's inhabited planets.

He thought for an eternity all of three or four seconds long. Then—

"Crank the bastards to max," he said harshly.

The people who'd planned Oyster Bay had carefully arranged their attack to avoid anything that could be construed as a direct attack on the planetary populations of Manticore or Sphinx. Given the nature of the war they were planning to fight, it wasn't because the MAN had any particular objection to killing as many Manticorans as possible. But there was that bothersome little matter of the Eridani Edict, and while it was probably going to take a while for anyone to figure out who'd carried out the attack, and how, that anonymity wasn't going to last forever. Eventually, the fact that the MAN and its allies were the only people who'd had the technical capability to do it was going to become obvious. There were plans in place to prevent the Manticorans from returning the compliment once they figured out who was to blame, but the Mesan Alignment's *diplomatic* strategies could be very seriously damaged if anyone figured out too soon how little the Eridani Edict truly meant to it.

That was the real reason the primary destruction of the space stations had been left to the torpedoes, which had overflown the planets, well clear of them. The follow up laser heads had come in on a similar trajectory, but some of the planners had argued against using any of them. Despite all the safeguards built into their guidance systems, there was always the chance, however remote, that one of them was going to ram into the planet at relativistic speeds. And, the critics had pointed out, if that happened, the Alignment's opponents would inevitably claim it had been deliberate.

The final distribution of fire had been a compromise between those who distrusted the torpedoes' ability to do the job and those who wanted no missiles anywhere near either of the inhabited planets. And as was the definition of any compromise, neither side had been completely satisfied.

But however careful they'd been to avoid direct attacks on the planets, none of them had lost any sleep over the possibility of *indirect* damage from the bits and pieces of wreckage raining down into the planets' gravity wells. That was something totally beyond any attacker's ability to control, and no one could possibly question the fact that the space stations had been legitimate military targets. Under those circumstances, the Eridani Edict's prohibition against *deliberate* attacks on planetary populations had no bearing. So if a few thousand—or a few hundred thousand—Manties were unfortunate enough to get vaporized when a fifty-thousand-ton chunk of wreckage landed on top of their town, well, making omelettes was always hard on a few eggs.

✧   ✧   ✧

"*What?*"

Andrew LaFollet snapped upright in his seat, one hand pressed to his earbug. Allison Harrington had been concentrating on her grandson and the bottle he was industriously draining, but the sharp incredulity of the colonel's tone whipped her head around towards him.

He was listening intently, and she thought she could actually see the color draining out of his face. Then he stabbed the button that connected him to the pilot's position.

"Get us on the ground, Jeremiah—*now!*" He listened for a moment, then nodded. "All right. If we're that close to town. But get us there fast!"

He let go of the button, and as he turned to face Allison, she felt the limo's sudden acceleration pushing her back in her seat.

"What is it, Andrew?" she asked, arms tightening instinctively around Raoul.

"I'm not sure, My Lady—not yet. There's a lot of confusion

on the emergency channels. But—" He paused, visibly gathering himself. "But it sounds like the system is under attack."

"What?" Allison looked at him blankly, which, as anyone who knew her could have attested, was not her customary response.

"Someone's attacked *Hephaestus* and *Vulcan*, My Lady," he said flatly. "I don't know how, but it sounds like the damage is going to be heavy, and I want you out of the air and on the ground somewhere safe."

"Alfred and the kids!" she said suddenly, her face tightening, but he shook his head quickly.

"They ought to be almost exactly halfway between Manticore and Sphinx, My Lady, and it sounds like this has to be an attack on our orbital infrastructure. It's not another fleet battle, anyway. And I don't think anyone's going to be wasting firepower on a local puddle jumper that isn't even particularly close to either planet."

Allison stared at him, then swallowed harshly as she realized he was almost certainly correct.

"Thank you," she said quietly.

Quay hurtled across the wreckage stream spilling down from orbit. Her sensors' view was restricted, but she had more than enough coverage out the sides of her wedge for Truida Verstappen to know the belly band wasn't getting it all. She'd set up her computers to tag everything that crossed the sensors' field of view, and *Quay*'s cybernetic brain began plotting descent curves. They could only be approximate until the tug turned and brought her powerful forward radar and lidar into action, but at least Lieutenant Verstappen would know where to start looking.

Had anyone been in a position to actually watch, they would have seen HMS *Quay* slash into the heart of the wreckage. Despite the impenetrability of the wedge itself, it was still a high risk move. Sugimatsu had to get deep enough into the stream to intercept the most dangerous chunks of it, and that meant intersecting its path late enough that quite a few major pieces of debris were actually swept into the open throat of *Quay*'s wedge. He'd counted on that, since he couldn't avoid it anyway. And it didn't matter whether a piece of wreckage hit an impeller wedge on its way in or on its way out. What did matter was the distinct possibility that *Quay* might strike one of those pieces on its way *through*. The odds were against it—on the scale of the tug's overpowered wedge, both she and even a very large piece of wreckage were actually rather small objects in a relatively large volume—but the odds weren't as *much* against it as he could have wished, and he realized he was holding his breath.

Something large, jagged, and broken—it looked, in the fleeting glimpse he had, as if it were probably at least half of a heavy fabrication module, which must have massed the better part of thirty-five thousand tons—went screaming past *Quay's* prow and impacted on the inner surface of her wedge's roof. Or, rather, was ripped into very, very, *very* tiny bits and pieces in the instant it entered the zone in which local gravity went from effectively zero to several hundred thousand gravities in a space of barely five meters.

The ship shuddered and bucked as other multiton chunks of *Vulcan's* shattered bones slammed into her wedge. Not even her inertial compensator could completely damp the consequences of that much transferred momentum without shaking her crew like a terrier with a rat. But she'd been built with generous stress margins for a moment just like this one, and she came out the other side intact, already turning to bring tracking systems and tractors to bear on whatever had gotten past her.

Verstappen's hands flew over her console. If she'd only had more time, time to really evaluate the wreckage before they physically intercepted it, she would have been far better placed to prioritize threats. As it was, she had to do it on the fly, and perspiration beaded her forehead. At their velocity, even with the range of a tug's tractors, they had only seconds—no more than a minute or two, maximum—before their velocity would carry them too far from the debris to do any good.

"Take the queue, Harland!" she barked, pressing the key that locked in her best estimate of threat potentials, and down in Engineering, Harland Wingate and his two assistants went frantically to work.

Quay's tractors stabbed out, no longer powerful, carefully modulated hands making gentle contact with other ships but deliberately overpowered demons, ripping and rending, striking with so much transfer energy that even enormous pieces of debris shattered.

In the one hundred and three seconds they had to work, those tractors destroyed eighteen potentially deadly shards of Her Majesty's Space Station *Vulcan*. Four more looming projectiles were dragged bodily after *Quay* as she went streaking away from her intercept. There would have been more, but two of her tractors had burned out under the abuse.

Given how little time *Quay* had been given, she and her crew did a magnificent job. But magnificent isn't always enough.

Several large pieces got past her, including three at least the size of cruisers, accompanied by a trailing shower of smaller bits and pieces, trailing a de-orbiting arc across the daylight side of Sphinx.

Sphinx's gravity produced an atmosphere which was shallower—"flatter"—than that of most planets humanity had settled, and the wreckage of what had once been HMSS *Vulcan*, some with personnel still trapped aboard, hit the boundary of that atmosphere at an altitude of ninety-five kilometers.

The first impactor struck the planetary surface twenty seconds later. Even closing at a paltry eight kilometers per second—barely twenty-five times the speed of sound at local sea level—the fragments were wrapped in a sheath of plasma as they shrieked downward. Not all the debris *Quay* had missed reached the surface, of course, but even those chunks that never struck the ground transferred their kinetic energy to the atmosphere, creating bow waves of plasma, and then a sequence of air bursts along the entire length of their descent paths, sparking forest fires and flattening anything beneath them.

Twenty seconds, it took. Twenty seconds of shrieking, incandescent fury. Of superheated air exploding outwards in demonic shockwaves. Twenty seconds of seething violence howling its way down the heavens.

There was no one to backstop *Quay*. The only armed aircraft which could possibly have reached any of those pieces in time were the sting ships flying escort on Allison Harrington's air limo, and there was too much confusion for anyone to get word to them quickly enough. Even if there hadn't been, they carried no weapons powerful enough to have destroyed such massive kinetic hammers.

Multiple fragments, two of them massing between two hundred and three hundred thousand tons each, slammed into the icy waters of the Tannerman Ocean. The resulting impact surge would kill over ten thousand people in dozens of small coastal towns and inflict billions of dollars worth of damage.

But that was the *good* news.

Twenty seconds was far too little warning to do any good, too little time for anyone to react. Alarms were only beginning to sound in the city of Yawata Crossing, emergency messages only starting to hit the public information channels, when an even larger impactor—three hundred thousand tons of wreckage, the size of one of the old *Star Knight*-class heavy cruisers—struck approximately five and a half kilometers from the exact center of the city of one and a quarter million people...with an effective yield of better than two megatons.

The three follow-on strikes by fragments in the forty thousand-ton range were barely even noticeable.

Andrew LaFollet moved suddenly.

Allison had been staring out the limo's window, her brain whirling as she tried to process the impossible information. She wasn't even looking in LaFollet's direction—in fact, her attention had been drawn by a brilliant flash somewhere out to sea, ahead of the limo—and so she was taken completely by surprise when he snatched Raoul out of her arms.

She started to turn her head, but LaFollet hadn't even paused. Raoul began a howl of protest, but it was cut off abruptly as LaFollet shoved the baby into the special carrier affixed to the mounting pedestal of Allison's chair—the one which would normally have been Honor's, if Honor had been present. The internal tractor net locked down around the infant instantly, gentle and yet implacably powerful, and LaFollet slammed the lid.

That carrier had been designed and built by the same firm that built and designed life support modules for treecats, and every safety feature human ingenuity could come up with had been designed into it. Allison was just starting to come upright in her own chair, her eyes wide, when LaFollet stepped back and hit a button.

Allison's shoulder harness yanked tight with brutal, bruising force, and battle steel panels snapped out of the limo's bulkheads and overhead, sealing her and the baby in a heavily armored shell. A fraction of a second later, the blast panel blew out, and the shell went spinning away from the limo under its built-in emergency counter-grav.

LaFollet hit a second button, and Lindsey Phillips' chair followed

Allison's. Then he jumped for his own chair and reached for the third emergency ejection button.

Black Rock Clan was one of the older treecat clans. Not so old as Bright Water Clan from whence it had originally sprung, perhaps, but certainly of respectable antiquity. It was a large clan, too—one which had been growing steadily over the last double-hand of turnings. The hunting was good, here in the western picket-wood of the mountains the two-legs called the Copper Walls. The "gardening" tricks the two-legs had taught the People helped, as well, and Black Rock had learned to look forward to the regular visits of the Forestry Service's doctors, which had kept so many of their young from dying in kittenhood.

But for all that, Black Rock Clan, like most treecat clans, kept largely to itself. There were no two-legs living in Black Rock's immediate vicinity, and so there was no one to tell the People what had happened in the black emptiness so far beyond their sky.

And perhaps that was just as well. At least none of the People realized what was about to happen.

Chapter Thirty

THE MEN AND WOMEN in the conference room rose in a spontaneous gesture of respect as Queen Elizabeth III came through the door.

The Queen normally had little use for such formalities. In fact, they usually irritated her, since it was her opinion that all of them—including her—had better things to be doing with their time. But today she simply nodded back to them and crossed without speaking to her own chair. She carried Ariel in her arms, and Prince Consort Justin walked at her side. Justin's own treecat, Monroe, rode on his shoulder, and the 'cats' flattened ears, the way Monroe's tail wrapped around his person's throat, reflected the dark emotional aura of the room entirely too well.

Justin pulled back the Queen's chair and seated her before he sat at his own place. Their treecats arranged themselves along the backs of their chairs, settling with tightly-coiled tension, and then the standing officers and civilians followed the prince consort's example.

For a small eternity the silence was total, and Elizabeth surveyed the faces of her most senior advisers and ministers. She didn't need Honor's empathic sense to know what all those people were feeling. None were the sort to panic, yet in many ways, the horrifying impact of what happened had hit them even harder than the general public. For the public as a whole, the shocked

disbelief, the stunned incomprehension, was its own anesthesia...
for now, at least. That was going to change, and, given human
nature, all too many of the Old Star Kingdom's subjects were going
to blame her and, even more, the men and women sitting around
this conference table with her. Rational or not, it was *going* to
happen. Elizabeth knew that... just as she knew that entirely too
many of those advisers and ministers already blamed *themselves*.

And just as she knew the shock of the totally unanticipated
cataclysm which had descended upon them had been made
incomparably worse by coming so closely on the heels of the
news from Spindle. In her worst nightmares, she would never have
believed Manticore's prospects could be so catastrophically shifted
in barely three T-days. She knew how mentally and emotionally
paralyzing that body blow had been for her; she suspected that
even she couldn't imagine how stunning and traumatizing it had
been for the men and women directly responsible for the Star
Empire's defense.

"All right," she said finally, her voice level. "I already know it's
bad. Tell me *how* bad." She looked around the circle of faces, and
her brown eyes settled inevitably upon one of them. "Hamish,"
she said quietly.

"Your Majesty," Hamish Alexander-Harrington said in a flat,
unflinching, yet curiously deadened voice, "I think the short
answer is *very* bad. I'm not qualified to speak to the civilian
aspects. I'm sure Tyler"—he nodded across the table to Sir Tyler
Abercrombie, the Home Secretary—"has better information on
the civilian casualty toll than I do. But from the purely military
perspective, it would be extraordinarily difficult, if not outright
impossible, to exaggerate the damage this has done to us."

The Earl of White Haven looked away from Abercrombie, sitting very upright in his chair and turning it slightly to face the
Queen directly.

"*Hephaestus*, *Vulcan*, and *Weyland* are gone, Your Majesty.
There's been some talk about recovering some of the modules and
repairing them, but my staff's current estimate, based on input
from both BuShips and BuWeaps, as well as from Construction
and Repair, is that it would be faster and more efficient to start
over from scratch.

"That means we've just lost every 'hard yard' we had. I don't
as yet have a complete count of the numbers and classes of ships

lost with them, but I already know it represents a significant loss of combat power. In addition, we've lost better than ninety-nine percent of the labor force of all three stations. For all intents and purposes, the only real survivors we have are people who, for one reason or another, were off-station when the attack hit. Most of *them*," he added heavily, "also lived aboard the stations, which means virtually all of them have lost their entire immediate families. That means it's going to be quite some time—and rightly so—before their morale recovers to a point at which they can really be considered part of the labor force again."

His face showed his distaste at having to make that observation. Grief and bereavement, especially on such a horrific scale, weren't supposed to be reduced to mere production factors, but whether they were supposed to be or not, they were something which had to be taken into consideration this time, and he continued unflinchingly.

"The damage to the dispersed orbital yards is almost as bad. At this moment, my best figures are that fifteen of them—none of which had units under construction—are undamaged, and another eight are probably repairable, although the ships under construction have been so badly damaged we're probably going to have to break them up and start over rather than trying to repair and complete them.

"In effect, we've lost every ship under construction, the labor force which was building them, and the physical plant in which they were being built—and which was fabricating almost all the components the dispersed yards were assembling. That means that what we have in commission and working up at Trevor's Star now is all we're going to have for at least two T-years. For any capital ships, the delay will be more like four T-years. Minimum."

Despite all the disastrous reports the other people in that conference room had already received, people winced all around the table and one or two faces turned perceptibly paler at the First Space Lord's flat, unvarnished admission.

"What about the repair facilities in Trevor's Star, Ham?" Prime Minister Grantville asked quietly, and White Haven looked at his brother.

"That's still intact," he admitted, "and it's going to play a huge part in regenerating yard capacity within the time frame I just mentioned, Willie. But it's primarily *repair* capacity. It was never intended for sustained, high-volume component *production*, so it's going to require a lot of modification before it can really make its presence felt. And, more importantly, we're going to have to divert a hell of a lot of its potential capacity to something we're going to need even worse."

William Alexander's face tightened at his brother's last sentence. He started to open his mouth, then shook his head and waved his right hand in a small arc, inviting White Haven to continue with his report. No doubt there'd be time for even more bad news soon enough.

"Before we can begin any new construction projects, we're going to have to replace our yard capacity, Your Majesty," the first lord went on, turning back to the Queen. "We're fortunate in that our extraction and refining platforms are untouched—probably because they're so dispersed and they were too far from the building platforms for convenient targeting—but raw materials have never been a significant bottleneck for us. *Fabrication* has been, however, and any of our previous problems pale beside what we're looking at now. Before we can replace our yard capacity, we have to replace the core industrial capacity the space stations represented. BuShips is working on a complete listing of our repair and fabrication ships. Obviously, we'll be recalling them from most of our foreign stations—we're going to need them here, at home, too badly to leave them anywhere else.

"Given our situation where the League is concerned, the fact that we're going to be unable to increase the size of our wall of battle is obviously a huge problem. However, we actually have one that's worse."

He inhaled deeply, like a man steeling himself for the first touch of a surgeon's scalpel.

"Whoever planned this operation obviously knew exactly how to hurt us. Not only did they take out our building capacity, but when they destroyed *Hephaestus* and *Vulcan*, they also destroyed our missile production lines. I remain confident that the missiles we have deployed are superior to those of any probable enemy, but the ones we already have aboard ship, or aboard ammunition ships assigned to our fleet formations, are *all* the missiles we have. All we're *going* to have until we can rebuild our production facilities...which is why I said we'd need the Trevor's Star facilities for something else even more than for rebuilding our Manticoran yards. At this time, I have no firm estimate for how long it's going to take to get Trevor's Star up for missile production—we're still inventorying our mobile repair and construction capabilities, and I'm sure some of them will help—but I'll be extraordinarily surprised if we can get new missile lines into production in less than ten T-months. And even then, it's going to take us a long time to ramp back up to anywhere near the production levels we had yesterday. Given the fact that our tactical advantages are so hugely bound up with our missile superiority, and given the numbers of missiles required to destroy or mission-kill even a Solarian ship-of-the-wall, that means our ability to take the war to the League has just evaporated. In fact, while it's likely we have enough Apollos already in inventory to finish off the Republic if it comes to that, doing so would leave us with essentially *none* for use against the League for almost an entire T-year."

The silence in the conference room was even deeper and darker, and White Haven seemed to give himself a little shake.

"The solitary bright spot I've so far been able to find—aside from the fact that Trevor's Star is still intact—is that *Weyland* was virtually empty when the attack went in." Several people blinked in surprise, and White Haven's lips twitched in something which might one day become a smile once more. "Vice Admiral Faraday had scheduled a surprise emergency evacuation exercise. Given the interruption in the station's operations—not to mention the expense and the disruption of government services on Gryphon when all those life pods dropped in so unexpectedly—I imagine Faraday probably anticipated taking more than a little flak over his exercise." The ghost of a smile disappeared. "As it happens, he doesn't have to worry about that anymore. He and his staff *were* aboard when the station was destroyed. All of them were lost, as was almost all of the station's senior command crew and a quarter of its engineering staff. But because of his exercise, the entire R&D staff and over ninety-five percent of the station's manufacturing workforce—and, thank God, their families—were on the planet and survived. That workforce will be literally invaluable when we start trying to rebuild."

"And how much research did we lose with the station, Hamish?" Prince Consort Justin asked quietly.

"None, Your Highness," White Haven replied, and gave Justin a hint of a nod. The prince consort, the earl knew, had already known the answer to his question. He'd asked it to make certain *everyone else* in the conference room knew.

"All research notes and reports were automatically backed up at a secure location on Gryphon every twelve hours," White Haven continued, still addressing the prince consort even though he was actually talking to the entire conference room. "They were downloaded by the ground station and backed up after the evacuation, so they're literally up-to-the-minute. We've lost some experimental hardware and prototypes, but we have all the data and all the minds which created the hardware in the first place."

"Which is, unfortunately, of limited utility for the immediate future," Grantville observed. He smiled sadly. "Until we've got someplace to build things again, it doesn't really matter how many more wonder weapons they might be able to come up with, does it, Ham?"

"No, I don't suppose it does," White Haven agreed.

"All right," Elizabeth said again. "I'm sure none of us enjoyed hearing any of that—except the bit about *Weyland*, of course. But I imagine we're going to hear still more things we don't really want to know about. So let's start with you, Tyler." The Queen visibly steeled herself. "What are the latest casualty figures?"

Sir Tyler Abercrombie was tall, broad shouldered, and distinguished looking. He was only a T-year younger than White Haven, and his dark hair had silvered at the temples, adding to his air of distinction. The aura he usually projected was one of calm, competent confidence; today, his brown eyes were haunted, and his hands trembled visibly as he adjusted his memo pad's display.

"First, Your Majesty," he said, in a voice that was steadier than his hands, as he looked up from the pad at her, "I'm sure everyone present will understand that any numbers I offer at this point have to be considered purely preliminary. And I'm sure everyone else hopes as much as I do that we're going to find our initial projections are wrong—that a lot of the people who are currently missing are simply that—missing in the confusion, not dead—and that they'll turn up later. Unfortunately, I don't expect that to happen. In fact, I believe the current figures are probably going to climb at least somewhat."

Several sets of shoulders seemed to tighten, and expressions which had already been grim became set in stone.

"The loss of life aboard the space stations themselves is currently estimated at five-point-four million," the Home Secretary said levelly, looking back down at the pad. "That number includes only those we know were onboard at the time. It does not include arriving transients who hadn't yet passed through immigration or those who were still in the concourses waiting to transship without ever entering customs in the first place because they weren't entering Manticoran sovereignty. We don't think that latter number's going to be very high, since most interstellar through passengers make— *made*—their connections at the Junction, not *Hephaestus* or *Vulcan*. It also doesn't include military personnel aboard the vessels docked at the stations at the time of the attack.

"Additional loss of life from the attacks on the orbital shipyards amounts so far to three hundred and ninety-six thousand. We estimate that another thousand or so were probably killed aboard small craft and private vessels that found themselves caught in the crossfire."

He paused again, then cleared his throat.

"In the case of Gryphon, we were extraordinarily lucky. *Weyland* was less than half the size of *Vulcan*, so there was less debris to begin with. In addition, Gryphon's population is still much sparser than that of our other planets, and it's concentrated closer to the equatorial zone. There were several major debris strikes on the planetary surface, but they were concentrated in the high northern latitudes. The most serious consequences would appear to be the damage to the local ecosystems and the consequences of one major ocean strike. Human casualties, however, were nil, so far as we now know, and the estimates from my biosciences people are that the ecological damage is all well within recoverable ranges.

"In the case of Manticore itself, we were once again fortunate— in this case, in that there were a larger than usual number of tugs moving vessels and freight in and around the volume of *Hephaestus*. Two of them were destroyed along with the station, but the others survived, and we were also fortunate that Lieutenant Commander Strickland, the captain of one of those surviving tugs—*Stevedore*, I believe—reacted quickly enough to organize her fellow skippers. Between them, they managed to intercept all but a half dozen significant pieces of wreckage. The Mount Royal Palace defenses destroyed the two of those pieces which might have threatened Landing, and the other four struck either uninhabited or only sparsely inhabited areas of the planet. None struck water, either. We don't have anything like definitive numbers yet, but I doubt the total casualty count from debris strikes on the planet will exceed two hundred.

"We were less fortunate on Sphinx."

He shook his head slowly, and his eyes, darker than ever, flicked briefly to an iron-faced Hamish Alexander-Harrington before they returned to his memo pad.

"There was only a single tug in position to intervene. My impression is that its crew performed far better than anyone could possibly have expected. Nonetheless, the city of Yawata Crossing was effectively destroyed by a major debris strike. The city of Tanners Port wasn't directly impacted, but there was a major ocean strike. It would almost certainly have destroyed Yawata Crossing even without the direct hit on that city, and it did destroy at least three-quarters of Tanners Port, and three other, smaller cities, were very severely damaged. There was too little time for significant evacuation before the first impact waves came ashore, and loss of life was heavy, especially in Tanners Port. Local authorities had more warning, further away from the actual strikes, and emergency evacuation efforts thankfully reduced human losses, although property damage is certainly going to run into the high billions of dollars. The town of Evans Mountain was also badly damaged—by a cascade of smaller pieces of debris in its case—although the casualty count there seems to have been much lighter. And according to the Sphinx Forestry Service"—Abercrombie's eyes flitted to the treecats on the backs of Elizabeth and Justin's chairs—"it would appear at least one treecat clan was completely destroyed."

A soft sound came from all three of the treecats in the room. White Haven opened his arms as Samantha flowed down from his chair back and buried her muzzle against him, and Ariel and Monroe joined their voices to her own soft lament.

"Counting the known casualties on the planetary surfaces," Abercrombie concluded softly, "the civilian human death toll so far is approximately seven million, four hundred and forty-eight thousand. I've asked the Forestry Service to give us a definitive figure for treecat fatalities as soon as possible." The Home Secretary met Ariel's eyes, not the Queen's. "They're working on that. At the moment, the best estimate from their search and rescue teams is approximately eighty-five hundred."

White Haven winced. Seven and a half million human dead was even worse than he'd anticipated. True, it was less than a third of the population of the city of Nouveau Paris. For that matter, it was about a million and a half less than the population of the city of Landing. And the permanent population of the Manticore Binary System had grown to just over 3.6 billion, an increase of almost twenty percent in just the past thirty T-years or so, so the percentage of deaths was still barely more than two-tenths of a percent of the total. But the people who'd been killed represented a horrendous percentage of the labor force which had been the backbone and the sinews of the Star Empire's industrial might. And from his own service's perspective, the naval personnel lost, combined with the casualties already suffered during the Battle of Manticore, came close to equaling the total manpower of the entire Royal Manticoran Navy at the beginning of the First Havenite War. The consequences for fleet experience, training, and morale were going to be bad enough—especially given the whipsaw effect on the heels of the surge in confidence which had followed the Battle of Spindle—but working around the casualty total might very well be enough to bring Lucian Cortez's BuPers to the breaking point this time, after all.

Against all that, less than nine thousand treecats might not seem so terrible. But there were many planets occupied by human beings, while by the Sphinx Forestry Service's best estimate, the total treecat population was probably less than twelve million, which meant those nine thousand lives represented almost a full percent of them. Not one percent of the treecats living on the planet Sphinx; one percent—one out of every hundred—of every treecat in the entire universe.

And the 'cats were telempaths.

Elizabeth had reached up to gather Ariel back into her arms, and Monroe had leaned forward, pressing his wedge-shaped chin into the top of Justin's shoulder while the prince consort caressed his ears. They sat that way for several seconds, then Elizabeth bent and kissed the top of Ariel's head gently, straightened once more, and cleared her throat.

"Thank you, Tyler," she said quietly, then looked around the table again.

"I'm sure it's going to take a while for Tyler's numbers to soak in, for all of us. In the meantime, however, and however painful we may find it, it's our responsibility to look beyond the immediacy of the human—and treecat—cost and consider the future. Specifically, the extent—and speed—with which we can recover from the damage to our military, industrial, and economic power. We've already heard from the Navy. So I suppose it's your turn, Charlotte."

"Of course, Your Majesty," Dame Charlotte FitzCummings, Countess Maiden Hill, replied. Maiden Hill was the Star Empire's Minister of Industry, and her expression was every bit as grim as White Haven's or Abercrombie's.

"Basically, all I can do is confirm Hamish's summation." The dark-haired countess' normally pleasant voice was harsh, hard-edged. "We've already begun an emergency mobilization of all civilian repair and service ships assigned to both the Junction's central nexus and Basilisk. We're also making plans to tow the Junction industrial platforms back into the inner system, but, to be honest, like the Trevor's Star platforms, they're really designed for repair and routine service work, not heavy fabrication. We can increase their construction capacity, but what they have now is too small to have any immediate effect. My people are working on their own inventories of capabilities, and we've already arranged to coordinate as closely as possible with the Navy. Personally, I suspect we're going to find we have more capacity than we believe we do right this minute. The natural reaction to something like this has to be pessimism. But even if that's true, I very much doubt we're going to be able to significantly reduce the time constraints Hamish described.

"To be honest, what's going to hurt at least as badly as the hit our physical plant's taken is the workforce we've lost." She nodded her head slightly in Abercrombie's direction. "No one ever contemplated the catastrophic destruction of an entire space station without *any* opportunity to evacuate personnel. Even if Haven's attack had succeeded, there would've been time to evacuate, but this . . . bolt from the blue didn't give us any warning at all. For all intents and purposes, we've just lost our orbital infrastructure's entire skilled labor force—aside from the *Weyland* survivors—which completely disrupts our existing emergency plans. Not that any of those plans ever contemplated an emergency on this scale, anyway. Somehow we're going to have to prioritize the workers we have left between essential construction tasks and training an entirely *new* workforce."

She shook her head heavily.

"Our three biggest advantages, the ones that have kept us intact for the last twenty or thirty T-years, have been our R&D, the quality of our educational system and workforce, and the strength of our economy. As Hamish just pointed out, we still have the research capability, and we still have the educational system. But we no longer have the workforce, and with our industrial capacity this brutally cut back, the strength of our economy has to be doubtful, at best."

"Bruce?" Elizabeth said quietly, looking at the elegantly groomed, slightly portly man sitting between Maiden Hill and Francine Maurier, Baroness Morncreek, the Chancellor of the Exchequer.

Bruce Wijenberg was one of the minority of the Cabinet's members without even a simple "Sir" in front of his name. Which wasn't because titles hadn't been offered, however. Like Klaus Hauptman, Wijenberg was aggressively proud of his yeoman ancestry. Besides, he was from Gryphon. Despite his sophistication and polish, he retained at least a trace of the traditional Gryphon antipathy towards the aristocracy. He much preferred the House of Commons, and he'd been the Centrist Party's leader there before he'd accepted his Cabinet appointment. He'd really been happier in that role and he hoped to return to it sometime in the next few years, which would become impossible if he accepted a patent of nobility.

He was also the Star Empire's Minister of Trade.

"There's no point pretending we haven't just taken an enormous hit, Your Majesty," he said now, meeting her eyes squarely, his Gryphon burr more pronounced than usual. "Our carrying trade isn't going to be directly affected, and our Junction fees probably aren't going to fall too significantly—not immediately, at least. The *indirect* effect on our carrying trade *is* going to make itself felt pretty quickly, though. As Charlotte's just pointed out, for all intents and purposes we've lost our industrial sector completely. That means an awful lot of manufactured goods we used to be exporting aren't going to be available now. That accounts for a significant percentage of our total carrying trade—not to mention an enormous chunk of the Old Star Kingdom's Gross System Product. And as our industrial exports drop, the resultant drop in shipping's also going to have at least some effect on our Junction fees.

"Most of the rest of our GSP comes out of the financial sector, and I can't even begin to predict how the markets are going to react. There hasn't been an example of something like this happening to a major economic power since Old Earth's Final War, and even that's not really comparable, given how interstellar trade's increased since then. On the one hand, a huge percentage of our financial transactions have always consisted of servicing and brokering interstellar transactions between other parties, and the wormholes and shipping routes which made that possible are still there. What *isn't* there, and won't be for quite some time, is the dynamo of our own economy. People who were invested in the Star Kingdom—foreigners, as well as our own people—have just taken a devastating hit. How well anyone's going to recover from it, how quickly that's going to happen, and what's going to happen to investor confidence in the meanwhile is more than anyone except Nostradamus would even try to predict."

"Bruce has an excellent point, Your Majesty," Morncreek put in. The small, dark baroness looked almost like a child sitting beside the taller, bulkier, fair-haired Wijenberg, but her voice was crisp.

"At the moment, we've suspended the markets," she continued. "We can probably get away with that for a few more days, but we can't just freeze them forever, so we're going to have to respond with some sort of coherent policy quickly. And as the first stage in doing that, I think the most important thing is for us to stop and take a deep breath. As Charlotte says, we still have our educational system, and as Bruce just pointed out, shipping routes aren't going to magically change. We *have* the ability to recover from this . . . assuming we can survive long enough. How bad things are going to get economically before they start getting better is more than I'm prepared to predict, and the price tag's going to be enormous, but I'm confident of our ultimate capacity to rebuild everything we've lost . . . if whoever did this to us gives us the time."

She looked directly at Hamish Alexander-Harrington, Sir Thomas Caparelli, and Admiral Patricia Givens, and her dark eyes were sharp. Francine Maurier had been First Lord of Admiralty herself, and that lent her unspoken question an even sharper edge.

"I don't know whether or not they will, My Lady," Givens admitted. She seemed to have aged at least a couple of decades in the last twenty hours, and her eyes were filled with bitter anguish. "At this point, we don't have the least idea *who* did it to us, much less *how.*"

Samantha made a soft, distressed sound in White Haven's arms as the bleeding wound of the second space lord's sense of personal failure reached out to her. The earl didn't need Honor's empathy to understand his companion's distress, and his right hand twitched in an automatic reflex to reach out to Givens.

"Your Majesty," the admiral continued, facing Elizabeth squarely, "what's just happened represents the worst intelligence failure in the history of the Star Empire. A *total* failure. And as the head of the Office of Naval Intelligence, that failure is mine."

Givens never physically moved, yet her shoulders seemed to hunch under the weight of her admission, and silence hovered. Then Elizabeth looked past her to White Haven. She started to speak, then stopped and shifted her eyes to Caparelli, instead.

"Sir Thomas?" the Queen said very softly.

"Your Majesty," the First Space Lord looked more granite-like than ever, yet he replied almost instantly, and his eyes were level and his voice—as granite-like as his face—was unflinching, "Admiral Givens is entirely correct in at least one sense. We never saw this coming. *None* of us saw it coming. And that does represent an enormous failure on the part of your armed forces and your intelligence services. We were supposed to keep something like this from happening, and we didn't."

The silence was deeper and darker than ever. He let it linger for a heartbeat, then inhaled deeply.

"You'll have my letter of resignation by the end of the day, Your Majesty. And the reason you'll have that letter is because the responsibility ultimately is mine. But in defense of my subordinates—including Admiral Givens—I don't think this was something any of them *could* have seen coming. I've already spoken with Admiral Hemphill. Her people have been systematically examining every recorded sensor reading from every surveillance platform and ship in the entire binary system. She began with the moment of the attack, and she proposes to go back for at least six T-months. While that's going to take a long time, she tells me her preliminary assessment is that we're looking at the result of a previously unsuspected technological capability that's probably at least as revolutionary in its own way as anything *we've* managed.

"But that kind of capability doesn't just happen overnight. Whoever did this to us didn't just wake up the day before yesterday, pick the Star Empire at random, and decide to hit us with something he just happened to have lying around. Whoever did this—and I have a few suspicions about who that 'whoever' might be—developed the capability he just used for the specific purpose, the exact sort of operation, he just used it to accomplish. And given what's been happening lately in Talbott and the League, I also very strongly suspect we were the primary target all along, from the moment he first set out to develop his new tech.

"So if there was an intelligence failure involved, it wasn't a failure to correctly interpret information. It didn't happen because someone overlooked something. I suppose it's remotely possible we're eventually going to discover there was some tiny clue *somewhere*, but if this attack was the work of who I think it was, then we've been trying to put their capabilities under a microscope ever since the Battle of Monica. If we didn't realize they'd managed to put together the technology and the resources to pull this off, it wasn't because we weren't looking. It was because we didn't know—because *nobody* knew—what to be looking *for*."

No one spoke for a moment, then Grantville cleared his throat.

"I'm very much inclined to endorse what you've just said, at least to the extent that it bears upon Admiral Givens' performance." The Prime Minister looked directly across the table at Givens. "I've known you too long, worked with you too closely, to believe for a single moment that what's just happened represents any 'failure' on your part, Pat. From what Sir Thomas just said, it's obvious no one over at BuWeaps had a hint the weapons used in this attack were even *possible*, much less that anyone was actually developing them. That wouldn't be the case if whoever did the research and developing hadn't exercised extraordinary care to keep anyone from realizing what he was up to. So in my view, barring some totally unexpected revelation, this doesn't represent an intelligence failure on any one person's part. I doubt very much that it represents a failure on the part of our intelligence community as a *whole*, for that matter. Yes, we were supposed to see something like this coming. But to use one of Hamish's charming phrases, when you're ass-deep in alligators, sometimes it's hard to remember your original purpose was to drain the swamp. With everything that's been coming at us over the last few years, how in the world were you supposed to realize someone was cooking up a totally new—and presumably unorthodox as hell—technology that could defeat the best sensor platforms and technology in existence?"

Givens looked back at him with those wounded eyes. She didn't speak, but at least she didn't disagree with him—not openly, at any rate. He held her gaze for a moment, then looked back at Caparelli.

"I said I think I agree with what you've said at least inasmuch as it bears on Patricia's performance at ONI," he said. "But it's clear you're suggesting Manpower might somehow be behind this." The Prime Minister shook his head. "I know we're in the process of radically reevaluating everything we thought we knew about Manpower and Mesa. But are you seriously suggesting *they* have this kind of capability? Look at our confrontation with the League. What makes you think *Manpower* is more likely to be behind this than that the SLN's just demonstrated it has previously unsuspected capabilities of its own?"

Caparelli started to reply, but White Haven laid a hand on his forearm, stopping him.

"If I may, Tom?" he said quietly. Caparelli glanced sideways at him, then nodded, and White Haven turned to his brother.

"On the face of it, Willie, it does seem more likely someone like the League should be able to develop and deploy something like this—whatever '*this*' is—than that an outlaw outfit like Manpower or even an entire single-system star nation like Mesa could. But I'm as certain as Tom that it *wasn't* the League, and not just because we've convinced outselves of our technological superiority to the SLN. If they'd had this sort of capability—and some way to get it to us this quickly—they wouldn't even have bothered to talk to us after what happened at New Tuscany. Think about the scale and the scope of what whoever it really was did here." He shook his head. "I suppose it's remotely possible Crandall could have been stupid enough to sail directly into a confrontation with us even knowing the League Navy had something like this in its locker. For that matter, if the development was kept 'black' enough, she might not even have known it existed. It could even have been developed by one of the system defense forces, not the SLN itself, although that seems unlikely. But none of those possibilities change the fact that someone like Kolokoltsov would for damned sure have told us to pound sand from the outset rather than playing diplomatic games if the League had had this capability and been busy moving it into position to hit us all along.

"I agree with Tom's assessment. Whoever developed this, developed it for exactly the sort of operation he just carried out, and, frankly, there was no *reason* for the League to develop it. When you're the biggest, baddest conventional navy in the history of humanity—which is exactly how the SLN's always thought of itself—you don't need something like this. For that matter, you don't *want* something like this, because it's going to fundamentally destabilize the equation that's *made* you the biggest, baddest navy in existence."

Grantville looked skeptical, and White Haven waved one hand in an impatient gesture, as if he were looking for the exact way to express what he was trying to say.

"This is like . . . like our development of the grav-pulse com and the multidrive missile, Willie, only more so. You may remember just how much trouble Sonja had convincing certain members of our naval establishment—myself included—to support her changes, despite the fact that even those of us who disagreed with her had an enormous incentive to figure out how somebody our size survived against someone the size of the People's Republic. It's human nature to stick with what you know works, and there's always something scary about cutting loose from known, quantifiable, predictable technologies and capabilities, *especially* when you know you're the best around, have a significant qualitative or quantitative advantage over your adversaries, under the existing rules. That's why we kicked and screamed at each other so much—and so loudly.

"But we did head out in those new directions. And we did it because we *had* to. Because of that enormous incentive. Someone back on Old Earth once said that when a man knows he's going to be hanged, it concentrates his thoughts, and that's exactly what happened to us. But the League's never worried about that. It's never had any reason to, and that's precisely why the SLN's always been the most *conservative* fleet in existence. I can't conceive of any reason for the Sollies to have changed that permanently ingrained a mindset so completely. Under the existing rules, they've always been the eight-hundred-kilo gorilla, and any fundamental change could only jeopardize their position, or at least require them to duplicate the new technology themselves, quite possibly at the expense of throwing away the huge numerical superiority they've spent literally centuries building up.

"But Manpower, on the other hand—" The earl shook his head again. "However uncomfortable the conclusion may be, I think just about all of us have decided Mike and Honor are right about Manpower's responsibility for everything that's happened in Talbott. Which means that whatever we may have thought Manpower was for the last few centuries, it *isn't* just 'an outlaw outfit.' I still don't have a clue in Hell what it *is*, but I know it's more than that. And, like Tom, I know it's managed to keep anyone from guessing it was. What I can't even begin to speculate meaningfully on is how *long* it's been more than that, but I'm sure as hell not prepared to assume the leopard just decided to change its spots the day before yesterday. So given that someone's already demonstrated that he's developed both the intent and the capability to maneuver us into open warfare with the Solarian League, I think *that* someone is a much more likely candidate to have orchestrated this attack. And I also think someone who's apparently spent a long time planning and building up capabilities he didn't want the rest of the galaxy to know about is a much more likely candidate to have very quietly embraced a brand-new, completely destabilizing military technology.

"If you know anyone that description fits better than Manpower, please tell me who it is."

Grantville gazed at his brother for several seconds, then sat back in his chair.

"I can't," he said quietly.

"Neither can I." Elizabeth's grim voice drew all eyes back to her. Her own attention was fixed on White Haven and Caparelli, however.

"Am I correct in assuming you and Sir Thomas believe Manpower—or whatever the hell we should start calling these people—wouldn't have hit us and left our allies alone?"

"I doubt very much that they would have," White Haven said heavily. "I suppose it's possible they left the Andermani out. They have to be aware the Emperor's more than a little unhappy about this confrontation of ours with the League, and the Andermani have always had that reputation for . . . pragmatism, let's say. And there's got to be a limit on their current capabilities—how far they could stretch their attack when they started planning it—as well. So they may well have figured Gustav would recognize a sinking ship when he saw one. For that matter, they may have figured he's smart enough and cautious enough to figure there's no reason they couldn't do the same thing to him later if he didn't decide to step aside.

"But anyone smart enough to put all of this together is going to understand Benjamin Mayhew better than that, Your Majesty. They're going to've had a page or two in their plans for him. I'm very much afraid our dispatch boat telling him about what's happened here is going to cross one from him telling us the same thing already happened at Yeltsin's Star."

"I agree entirely with Hamish, Your Majesty," Caparelli said. "And I'd add one other point. The Andermani still don't have their military hardware fully up to our standards. The Graysons do. I don't believe anyone would launch an attack like this on us without trying to make certain he took out the people most likely to help us rebuild, as well."

Elizabeth looked at him for several more seconds, then nodded.

"That was about the conclusion I'd reached myself, unfortunately, Sir Thomas."

"I would like to make one additional point if I may, however, Your Majesty," the first space lord said quietly.

"Of course."

"I realize that at this moment what we're all most aware of is the damage we've taken and the fact that we don't have a clue how the attack was pulled off. Frankly, from a military perspective, the most frightening thing is that none of our sensor systems saw a single thing coming.

"My own feeling, and Admiral Hemphill's tentative analysis supports the same conclusion, is that what we have to be looking at is some radically new propulsive system. The missiles used in this attack were essentially conventional weapons—variants on our own MDMs. Analysis of their maneuvers from the moment they brought their drives up further suggests they were delivered in pods, probably coasted ballistically in to their launch points at a velocity of about point-two cee. The weapons that were used on the space stations were another case entirely. At this point, it looks like they were probably some sort of throwaway, disposable version of our own *Shrikes*, although nobody in Admiral Hemphill's shop has the least clue how Manpower—excuse me, how whoever launched this attack—managed to cram a weapon that powerful into a remote platform. Or how they gave its graser that sort of pulse endurance. For all intents and purposes, though, it's basically only a longer-ranged version of our own Mistletoe, probably using whatever new drive technology their ships use instead of relying completely on stealth the way Mistletoe does.

"So, so far, the only *fundamentally* destabilizing thing we've seen—or, rather, *not* seen—is the drive technology itself. That's scary enough, but I suspect it's an advantage that's going to be considerably less valuable the second time it's used against someone who knows it's out there, even if he doesn't know how it's done. And whatever it may let them do in sublight maneuvering, unless the laws of physics have been repealed, they still have to radiate a hyper footprint when they leave hyper-space. Admiral Hemphill tells me she feels quite confident she'll eventually be able to identify whatever trace footprint or hyper ghost we failed to spot or identify properly at the time the ships which deployed this attack's weapons dropped in on us.

"My point is, Your Majesty, that it's going to be much more difficult for this adversary to launch a second attack on this star system—or, for that matter, on Grayson or New Potsdam—without our at least spotting their arrival from hyper. If we spot *any* unidentified hyper footprint or ghost, we'll immediately saturate the space around it with grav-pulse com-coordinated scout ships and deploy remote sensor platforms in a shell dense enough for someone to *walk* across. Even without our knowing exactly what we're looking for, it's extremely unlikely any significant force of starships could penetrate that kind of surveillance wall without our detecting *something*. And unless these people have been able to build an awfully large fleet of SD(P)s with Apollo capability of its own, 'something' is all Home Fleet or the system-defense Apollo pods are going to need."

"So a second, similar attack is unlikely to succeed?" Grantville asked.

"Obviously no one can absolutely guarantee it won't, Mr. Prime Minister," Caparelli said with unaccustomed formality. "I think 'unlikely to succeed' would be putting it mildly, however."

The first space lord shrugged, and looked back at Elizabeth.

"Your Majesty, I fully realize that what I'm talking about here is, at best, an argument that we can defend ourselves against similar attacks. I'm not even remotely trying to suggest that until we know how it was done, and until we're completely confident we know exactly who did it, we'll be in any position to take offensive action. And one thing we've learned against the Havenites is that the side which can't take effective offensive action ultimately loses. But barring the need to expend a large percentage of our limited missile supply against either the Republic or the League before we can get new production lines set up, I believe we ought to be able to protect ourselves against whoever this was until we do know what we need to know to go after them."

Elizabeth started to speak, but White Haven raised an index finger, requesting attention. She looked at him for a moment, then nodded.

"I'd just like to add something to what Tom's said, Your Majesty," he said. "First, I wouldn't be a bit surprised if the people who did this did it in hopes that either the League or the Republic *will* finish us off before we can recover. Frankly, I don't know how likely they are to succeed, if that was their intention; there are too many political and diplomatic elements tied up in that kind of decision tree for me to offer any kind of meaningful opinion. But, secondly, the one thing that's struck me about this—in addition to what Tom and Sonja have said about new drive technologies—is that the people behind it can't have a very large navy."

"What?" Grantville blinked at his brother, and most of the other people around the table looked either surprised or downright skeptical. Caparelli, on the other hand, nodded firmly.

"Think about it, Willie," White Haven said. "If someone had anything like the number of capital ships we have, and if all of them had this kind of technology, they wouldn't have had to raid our *infrastructure*. They could have simply arrived, demonstrated their invisibility, and demanded our surrender, and we wouldn't have had any choice but to give it to them. If they'd gotten a couple of dozen capital ships with this new drive of theirs as far in-system as they got their pods before launch, what other option would we have had? Even if we'd wanted to bring in Home Fleet— every single ship at Trevor's Star, for that matter—they'd already have control of the planetary orbitals long before we could get into position. For that matter, they'd've been into missile range of the planets before we could even bring the system-defense missiles online to nail them! And even under the Eridani Edict, they'd be fully justified in bombarding the planets if we refused to surrender under those circumstances. But instead of going for the jugular, they attacked our arms and legs.

"Not only that, but the nature and pattern of the attack strongly suggest that whoever planned and launched it was operating with strictly limited resources. Yes, it was extraordinarily well planned and executed. From a professional perspective, I have to admire the ability, imagination, and skill behind it. But successful as it was, it was essentially a hit-and-run raid, albeit on a massive scale, and its success—as Tom has just pointed out—derived entirely from the fact that it achieved *total* strategic and tactical surprise. If any significant percentage of the weapons committed to it—either those graser platforms or the missile pods—had failed, or been detected on their way in, or even if we'd only suspected something was coming in time to alert the stations and activate their sidewalls and get the tugs deployed to interpose their wedges against potential attacks, the damage would have been *much* less severe. Give us fifteen or twenty minutes' warning, and we'd've had a good ninety-five percent of our personnel off *Hephasteus* and *Vulcan*, for that matter, not to mention getting a lot of our ships out of the station docking slips! The people who put this together had to be as well aware of those possibilities as I am, and they have to know the axiom that anything which *can* go wrong, *will* go wrong. True, they seem to have pretty much avoided that this time around, but they damned well knew better than to *count* on that. So if they'd had more resources to commit to the attack, we'd have seen *overkill*, not just 'exactly enough to do the job if everything works perfectly.'"

He shook his head.

"All of it points to the same conclusion. They've got this revolutionary new drive technology, but they don't have it in large numbers. If they had the numbers, they'd either have been able to follow through with an outright knockout blow or have at least been able to deploy enough additional weapons to give them the sort of redundancy factor any competent planner would be looking for."

Grantville's expression turned thoughtful, and several of the faces which had looked dubious began to look if not more hopeful, at least less desperate.

The Queen looked around the conference table again, and her nostrils flared.

"I think you've all made very good points," she said. "I know information's going to change over the next several days—that we're going to find some things aren't quite as bad as we thought they were, and that others are even worse. But the bottom line is this. Hamish is probably right about how the people who did this—and I think we all know who that almost certainly was— were thinking when they planned the operation. And now, they undoubtedly think they've won. It may take a while, but between Haven and the Solarian League, with our industrial base smashed, it's obviously over, and they know it. We've lost."

The silence in the conference room could have been carved with a chisel. And then, despite everything, the woman the treecats called "Soul of Steel" smiled.

There was nothing humorous or whimsical about that smile. No amusement. It was a thing of chilled steel—the smile of a wolf in the door to her den, between her young and the world as the hunting hounds closed in upon it. It was grim, hard, and yet, in spite of everything she'd just said, there wasn't a gram of surrender in it. For better or for worse, it was the wolf-smile of a woman who would die on her feet in the defense of her people and her home before she surrendered or yielded.

"No doubt they *do* know that," Elizabeth Adrienne Samantha Annette Winton said very softly. "But there's one tiny flaw in their analysis, ladies and gentlemen. Because even if they do know it ... *we* don't."

MARCH 1922 POST DIASPORA

"History is filled with roadkills who *thought* they knew exactly where 'the inevitable' was headed."

—Hamish Alexander-Harrington,
Earl of White Haven

Chapter Thirty-One

INNOKENTIY KOLOKOLTSOV looked up with what he hoped was carefully hidden trepidation as Astrid Wang knocked once, lightly, on the frame of his office door, then stepped through it. She had what he'd come to think of as "The Look." If anyone had asked him to define the constituent parts of "The Look," he wouldn't have been able to. He knew it included worried eyes, tight lips, and a slightly furrowed brow, but there was a certain subtle something more, as well. Something which tied all the other components together and warned him she was the bearer of yet more bad news.

It was odd, really, how their definition of "bad news" had shifted. Once upon a time, it had meant "This is irritating, and it's going to be bothersome to deal with." Now it meant "Oh my God, what *now?*"

"Yes, Astrid?" His voice came out calmly enough, but a flicker in her green eyes told them she'd heard his wariness anyway. "What is it?"

"A courier from Admiral Rajampet just delivered this, Sir."

She held out the red-bordered folio of a high-security message chip, and Kolokoltsov gazed at it for a moment, his lips puckering slightly, like a man sucking on an underripe persimmon. What was it about Rajampet, he wondered, that had produced this mania for hand-delivered, officer-couriered memos rather than old-fashioned e-mail or a simple com conference over one of the innumerable secure channels available to the people who ran the Solarian League? Whatever it was, it was getting worse pretty much in tandem with the situation.

Which probably means that by next week sometime he'll be sending them written in invisible ink on even more old-fashioned paper—probably with an entire battalion of Marines providing security between his office and mine!

Somewhat to his surprise, the thought woke a flicker of genuine—and much needed—humor. Not much of one, but given what had been going on here on the League's capital planet for the past couple of days, he'd settle for any humor he could get.

After a moment, he sighed. "I suppose you'd better give it to me."

"Yes, Sir." Wang handed it over, then withdrew with just a little more haste than usual. It was almost as if she were afraid simple proximity to whatever fresh tidings of disaster had just arrived would somehow infect her with an incurable disease.

Kolokoltsov snorted at the thought, and the folio, dropped the chip into a reader, and sat back in his chair.

"What do you make of Rajani's latest brainstorm?" Kolokoltsov asked considerably later that evening.

He, Nathan MacArtney, Malachai Abruzzi, and Agatá Wodoslawski were sharing a quiet and very private supper at the moment. It was the third night in a row they'd done so, and Omosupe Quartermain had been present the first two times, as well. At the moment, though, she was off chairing a very hush-hush meeting with a dozen or so of the Sol System's most powerful industrialists. Kolokoltsov didn't expect much in the way of practical solutions out of her meeting, but at least it would be evidence that she and her colleagues were Doing Something. Precisely *what*—in the way of meaningful improvements, at least—eluded him, but he supposed her idea of producing an "industrial mobilization plan" couldn't hurt. At least it would be something they could show the newsies.

"Which brainstorm would that be?" The sourness in Wodoslawski's smile had nothing to do with the excellent wine which had accompanied supper.

"The one about redeploying every single Frontier Fleet battlecruiser to raid Manticoran infrastructure," Kolokoltsov said dryly.

"Actually, compared to some of the other ideas he's come up

with, that one sounds almost reasonable." MacArtney's tone was considerably more sour than Wodoslawski's smile had been.

"Fair's fair, Nathan," Abruzzi said. "None of us have come up with any better ones."

"Yes?" MacArtney growled. "Well, it wasn't *our* precious Navy that screwed the pooch either, now was it? And it wasn't one of *us* who 'forgot' to tell the rest of us that that idiot Crandall was already in the Talbott Cluster! Not to mention that he was the one who assured us no 'magical Manticoran missiles' were going to get through *his* defenses!"

MacArtney, Kolokoltsov reflected, was the angriest and arguably the most frightened of their quintet. That undoubtedly had a great deal to do with the fact that Frontier Security reported to him . . . and that of all of them, he was the most aware of just how catastrophic the blow to the Solarian League Navy's prestige was really likely to be out in the star systems of the Verge.

"And then there's the whole Green Pines thing," MacArtney continued in tones of profound disgust. Abruzzi seemed to stiffen, but the interior undersecretary waved a dismissive hand. "I'm not blaming you for that one, Malachai—" he did not, Kolokoltsov noticed, say what he *did* blame Abruzzi for, "—but even that's going to turn around and bite us on the ass if we're not careful, thanks to Rajani! You've got the reliable newsies behind us when it comes to demanding a Frontier Fleet investigation, all right. Fine. Great! Exactly what we wanted . . . when Rajani was telling us how unstoppable his damned fleet was. The problem is that we've whipped up too *much* fervor in some quarters. They want us to go ahead and make the Manties admit their involvement and pay Mesa a huge indemnity, and the Manties've just proved we can't *make* them do anything! Not if Rajani's superdreadnoughts keep getting popped like zits, anyway!"

"I think we can all agree that neither Rajani nor the rest of Battle Fleet have precisely covered themselves with glory," the foreign affairs undersecretary observed out loud. "On the other hand, much as I hate to admit it, the same thing could be said of all of us, whether as individuals or as a group." He looked around the table, and his level brown eyes were serious. "We all took the Manties much too lightly. We didn't really press Rajani, because—let's be honest here, now—none of us really thought it mattered. No matter what the Manties might have tucked away in the way of military surprises, it didn't matter, did it? Not compared to our basic tech capabilities and the size of Battle Fleet."

"I don't think that's entirely fair, Innokentiy," MacArtney protested. "We discussed the possibilities, and he—"

"Sure, we 'discussed' a whole range of possible responses," Kolokoltsov said bitingly. "But what we didn't for even one minute consider was simply going ahead and admitting Byng was a frigging idiot who'd fucked up, murdered the crews of three Manticoran warships with absolutely no justification, and then gotten himself and everyone else aboard his flagship killed doing something even stupider. And unless my memory fails me, Nathan, a great deal of the reason we didn't consider doing that was the fact that we agreed with Rajani that we couldn't afford to let a batch of neobarbs 'get away' with something like New Tuscany because of the way *Jean Bart*'s destruction would undermine the Navy's prestige."

MacArtney glared at him, but this time he kept his mouth shut, and Kolokoltsov smiled thinly.

"Well, unless I'm sadly mistaken, the destruction or capture of over seventy ships-of-the-wall, plus every single member of their screen, plus their entire supply group, by a force of Manticoran *cruisers*, has probably had at least some slight 'undermining' effect of its own, wouldn't you say?"

MacArtney's glare grew even more ferocious for a moment. Then it seemed to fold in on itself, and he sat back in his chair, shoulders slumping.

"Yes," he admitted heavily. "It has."

"Well," Abruzzi said a bit tartly, "I'm sure all that levelheaded admission of reality is very cathartic, and I suppose it's something we really do have to do. On the other hand, deciding who's to blame isn't going to have much impact on getting out of this damned hole. Unless, Innokentiy, you want to suggest we go ahead and acknowledge that this is all the League's fault and ask the Manties if they'd be so kind as to allow us to lick their boots while we make amends."

Kolokoltsov started a quick, hot retort. He managed to stop it before any of the syllables leaked out, but it wasn't easy. Especially when he recalled how airily Abruzzi had assured everyone the Manties were only posturing for their own purely domestic political ends. It wasn't as if they'd *really* been prepared to risk a direct confrontation with the might of the *Solarian League*! Oh, goodness, no!

"No, Malachai, that *isn't* exactly what I had in mind," he said after a moment, and the shutters which seemed to close behind Abruzzi's eyes told him the education and information undersecretary had recognized the careful—and hard held—restraint in his own coldly precise tone. "Mind you, in a lot of ways, I really would prefer to settle this diplomatically, even if we did end up having to eat crow. When I think of what this is going to cost, I'd be even be willing to substitute dead buzzard for the crow, if that offered us a way to avoid paying it. Unfortunately, I don't think we *can* avoid it."

"Not after pumping so much hydrogen into the Green Pines fire, anyway," Wodoslawski agreed glumly. "I'd say that's pretty much finished poisoning the well where diplomacy's concerned. And now that the newsies have hold of what happened to Crandall, as well, any suggestion on our part that we ought to be negotiating's only going to be seen as a sign of weakness. One that turns loose every damned thing we've been worrying about from the beginning."

"Exactly." Kolokoltsov looked around the supper table. "It's no use recognizing how much less expensive it would've been to treat the Manties' claims and accusations seriously."

In fact, Kolokoltsov couldn't think of another single event—or any *combination* of events, for that matter—in his entire lifetime which had come even close to having the impact this one had. The citizens of the Solarian League had been told so often, and so firmly, that their navy was the largest and most powerful not simply currently but in the entire history of mankind that they'd believed it. Which was fair enough—*Kolokoltsov* had believed it, too, hadn't he? But now that navy had been defeated. It wasn't a case of a single light unit somewhere, one whose loss might never even have been noted by the League's news establishment. It wasn't even a case of a Frontier Fleet squadron surrendering to avoid additional loss of life. Not anymore, anyway.

No. It was a case of an entire fleet of ships-of-the-wall—of Battle Fleet's most powerful and modern units—being not simply defeated but *crushed*. Humiliated. Dispatched with such offhand ease that its survivors were forced to surrender to mere *cruisers* of a neobarb navy from the backside of nowhere.

The newsies who'd charged off to the Talbott Cluster to cover the New Tuscany incidents had gotten far more than they'd bargained for, he thought grimly. They'd come flooding home in their dispatch boats, racing to beat the Royal Manticoran Navy dispatches bearing word of the battle—and of Admiral O'Cleary's surrender—back to Manticore. The first rumors of the catastrophe had actually reached the Old Earth media even before the latest Manticoran diplomatic note—this one accompanied by Admiral Keeley O'Cleary in person—reached Old Chicago.

The public hadn't taken it well.

The initial response had been to brush off the reports as yet more unfounded rumors. After all, the news was impossible on the face of things. Cruisers—even *battlecruisers*—simply didn't defeat ships-of-the-wall any more than antelopes hunted down tigers. The very suggestion was ludicrous.

But then it began to sink in. Ludicrous or not, it had happened. The greatest political, economic, and military power in the explored galaxy had been backhanded into submission by a handful of cruisers. Estimates of fatalities were still thankfully vague, but even the Solarian public was capable of figuring out that when a superdreadnought blew up in action, there weren't going to be a lot of survivors from its crew.

There was an edge of fear, almost of hysteria, in some of the commentary. And not just on the public bulletin boards, either. Theoretically well-informed and levelheaded military and political analysts were climbing up on the "the universe is ending" wagon, as well. After all, if the Manties could do *that*, then who knew what they *couldn't* do? Indeed, some of the most panic-stricken seemed to expect Manticore to dispatch an unstoppable armada directly through the Beowulf terminus of the Manticoran Wormhole Junction to attack Old Earth.

To be honest, there'd been moments, especially immediately after the news broke, when Kolokoltsov had worried about the same thing. But that was nonsense, of course. For a lot of reasons—not least because he figured the Manties had to be at least a *little* brighter than he and his colleagues had proven themselves. Which meant he very much doubted anyone in the Star Empire of Manticore was stupid enough to attack the home world of humanity and provide the League with such a wonderfully evocative emotional rallying point.

But if there was an undeniable element of fear, there was an even more undeniable—and overwhelming—feeling of outrage. Things like this weren't supposed to *happen* to the Solarian League. The League's invincibility was a physical law, like the law of gravity, and just as inevitable. Which meant that if it *had* happened, *someone* was to blame.

At the moment, much of that outraged anger was directed at the Manties. The way Abruzzi's propagandists had milked Mesa's Green Pines allegations had helped there, since they'd managed to get public opinion aimed at the Ballroom "baby killers" and their "Manticoran paymasters." Personally, Kolokoltzov figured there might have been as much as one actual fact in the Mesan reports. There sure as hell hadn't been *two* of them, as far as he could tell, but the spectacular charges had been useful grist for Abruzzi's mill.

Except, as MacArtney had suggested, inasmuch as they'd whipped up too *much* heat. The public anger against Manticore—here on Old Earth, at least—had attained near hysterical levels, and the fear bound up in it in the wake of New Tuscany only fanned its heat still higher. Yet there were already at least a few voices whose owners were looking for someone to blame closer to home than the Manticore Binary System. The ones who wondered how the people in charge of the League's security could have been so soundly asleep at the switch that they hadn't even seen this coming. And other voices which wanted to know just what those same people in charge had been doing to let a loose warhead like Sandra Crandall plunge the SLN into such a disastrous fiasco.

Those were the dangerous ones, and not simply because of the threat they posed to Innokentiy Kolokoltzov's personal power and prestige. He wasn't going to pretend personal considerations didn't play a major part in his own attitude and decision-making processes, but they weren't the end-all and be-all of his concerns. Not by a long chalk. The far more dangerous problem was that any thorough and open investigation of the disastrous decisions leading up to the Battle of Spindle would open some very nasty cans of worms. Any inquiry like that would lead directly to Kolokoltsov and his colleagues, and while the personal consequences were likely to be highly unpleasant, the *institutional* consequences might well prove fatal to the entire system which had governed the Solarian League for centuries.

He'd actually considered calling for an inquiry himself, anyway. There'd been enough blue-ribbon panels and "impartial investigatory boards" which had obediently produced the necessary conclusions to hand-wave away other embarrassing little problems over the years. This time, though, in the wake of such anger and such stunning and public disclosure of disaster, he wasn't at all confident any inquiry could be properly controlled. And one that *couldn't* be controlled would be even more catastrophic than what had happened at Spindle.

Like it or not, there *was* no political structure to replace the bureaucratic one which had evolved over so many years. The very language of the League's Constitution foreclosed the possibility of such a structure, especially in light of the centuries of unwritten constitutional law and traditions which had settled into place. Kolokoltsov strongly doubted that any *political* structure could ever be created, under any circumstances, to truly govern something the size of the League. But even if he were wrong about that, even if it had been possible to create such a structure under ideal circumstances and conditions, it most definitely would *not* be possible under the ones which actually obtained.

Which meant he and his colleagues *had* to come up with a response. They were squarely on the back of the tiger, and the best they could hope for was that the beast came equipped with some sort of saddle and reins.

So far, he hadn't seen any sign of them, unfortunately.

"Let's face it," he told the other three. "It's too late for any sort of diplomatic settlement, and the two things we absolutely can't afford are to have the League's ability to deal with something the size of Manticore or our own ability to control the situation called into question."

"I don't disagree with you, Innokentiy," Wodoslawski said after a moment. "Unfortunately, I'd say the League's ability to deal with Manticore's already been pretty thoroughly 'called into question.'"

"In the short term, you're right," Kolokoltsov agreed. "Rajani can dance around it all he wants to, but the truth is that until we figure out how the Manties did what they did—and how we can duplicate the same technology—we can't fight them."

"Then how—?" Abruzzi began.

"I said we can't *fight* them. That's why Rajani's idea of burying them under battlecruisers won't work."

"Actually, you know, it might," MacArtney said slowly. "Oh, we'd lose a hell of a lot of battlecruisers, but we could afford that more than the Manties could afford what would happen to their star systems."

"No," Kolokoltsov said firmly. "It *won't* work, Nathan. Even if it did 'work' in the sense of so thoroughly shooting up the Manties' industrial base and rear areas that they had to surrender, the cost would be catastrophic. What we'd be doing—and what there wouldn't be any way to keep people from figuring *out* we were doing—would be to use battlecruisers to run the Manties out of missiles. Do you really want to have someone like that bitch O'Hanrahan and her 'muckraking' friends baying at our heels over *that* once the smoke clears? Can't you just hear her now? Hear her explaining how we deliberately used warships—and their *crews*, Nathan—as missile sponges, as *targets* that couldn't even hope to shoot back effectively, until the Manties literally ran out of ammunition?"

MacArtney looked as if he wanted to argue, but the temptation faded quickly as he pictured exactly what Kolokoltsov was describing.

"And even if that weren't true," Kolokoltsov continued, "it would probably be even more disastrous in the long run than simply giving in to the Manties' demands right this minute. God only knows how many ships and how many people we'd lose, but despite everything Rajani's been saying, I strongly suspect casualties would only get worse, not better, and there comes a point when phrases like 'favorable rates of exchange' lose their meaning. If we managed to 'defeat' Manticore only at the expense of casualties ten times, or twenty times—or a hundred times—as great as theirs—and right now, the ratio is even *worse* than that, by a considerable margin—we'd've set exactly the precedent we wanted to avoid all along. Sure, Manticore would be history, but do you think the example of what they'd done to us first would just disappear in the minds of all those people out there in the Verge—or the Shell, for that matter—who don't like us very much? Not to mention the possibility that we'd take so much damage against Manticore that someone else—maybe someone who's not even on our radar horizon at the moment—saw an opportunity to come at us from behind. I don't know about you, but I can think of at least a couple of System Defense Forces whose loyalty might be just a tad less than totally reliable under those circumstances."

"So what *can* we do?" MacArtney demanded.

"At the moment, I think we don't have any choice but to play defense," Kolokoltsov said frankly. "The bottom line is that even if we can't afford to go after Manticore until we figure out how to match their weapons, they can't realistically come after *us*, either. They've got to worry about the Republic of Haven, and even if they manage to settle with Haven somehow, it's going to take time.

"What we have to do is use that time to accomplish two things. First, we have to make it clear to everyone here in the League that what's happening is the result of Manticoran decisions, not ours. The only way to stay ahead of the mob this time around is to run even faster and shout even louder, so I say we keep right on bearing down on Green Pines *and* endorse that recording someone sold O'Hanrahan as the real version of what happened at New Tuscany. As for what happened to Crandall at Spindle, we can't conceal our losses, but we don't have to confirm that the Manties did it to her with cruisers and battlecruisers."

"What about the newsies' reports?" Wodoslawski asked skeptically.

"We don't challenge them directly," Abruzzi said, his eyes narrowed in intense thought as he considered what Kolokoltsov had just said. "We point out that none of the newsies were aboard either side's ships during the actual battle. Oh, sure, some of them were allowed aboard a couple of the surrendered superdreadnoughts afterward, but none of them had access to the raw sensor data of the battle, and none of them have been allowed aboard *any* of the Manty ships to see firsthand whether they were *really* cruisers and not ships-of-the-wall. They're taking other people's word for what happened when you come right down to it, aren't they? So we take the position that our analysts 'strongly doubt' the Manticoran version—the only one that's been 'leaked' to the media—of what happened. We should be properly open to all possibilities, including the possibility the Manties are telling the truth, but insist the available evidence is far too sparse to confirm the truth either way at this point."

"Exactly." Kolokoltsov nodded, and Wodoslawski's skepticism eased visibly. After all, this was a game they'd played many times.

"In the meantime," Kolokoltsov went on, "we point out that everything that's happened in the Talbott Cluster is the result of Manticoran imperialism. We've had our concerns over their actions and intentions for some time, and what they did at New Tuscany, and their attack on Admiral Byng, have made us even more concerned. After all, the mere fact that they've changed their name officially to the Star *Empire* of Manticore is surely an indication of their expansionism and ambitions! And the reports of their backing for outright acts of terrorism and mass murder by the Audobon Ballroom—the fact that they're clearly *using* the Ballroom as a weapon against someone they've unilaterally decided is their enemy—only underscores the kind of lunatic excesses their territorial ambitions and arrogance produce.

"As for what happened at Spindle, there are a couple of ways we might come at it. We could always toss Crandall to the wolves, exactly the way she deserves, especially since she's not around to dispute anything we say. We could observe more in sorrow than in anger that while her intentions were good, and her suspicions about Manticoran imperialism were undoubtedly justified, she approached the situation far too impetuously. Or we could argue that the only records we have of her conversations with the Manties come from *Manticoran* sources...just like the falsified sensor recordings from New Tuscany. In reality, she was nowhere near as confrontational and bloody-minded as the Manties' version indicates. I'm sure someone over at Rajani's could create a much more reasonable version of her conversations with O'Shaughnessy and Medusa for domestic consumption. And the fact that she's so conveniently dead, under mysterious circumstances, would be only logical if the Manties were going to falsify the official record of what she'd said to them. After all, it would never do for them to have left her alive to tell the galaxy they were lying, would it?

"The first possibility—laying the blame off on Crandall—could blow up in our faces if it leads to a demand that we acknowledge her fault and more or less accept the Manties' demands in full. That would push us back into that unacceptable outcomes area. The second possibility has risks of its own, of course. The biggest one is that eventually, someone—like O'Hanrahan—is going to start screaming that we knew the truth all along and suppressed it. If that happens, we might be looking at exactly the sort of domestic witch hunts we most need to avoid. On the other hand, the majority of the public's so jaded where conspiracy theories are concerned that we could probably fob off any inquiry with a suitable cover story...unlike what would happen if the wrong people started nosing around our *actual* immediate post-New Tuscany decisions."

"And the reason we're doing all of this is—?" Wodoslawski asked.

"We're doing it because, in the end, we're going to have to go to war with Manticore, no matter what we want," Kolokoltsov said flatly. "And under the circumstances, given the fact that we can't go to war right *now*, the groundwork has to be set up carefully. We have to explain why the war is their fault and why we can't just go smack the hell out of them the way they deserve right this minute."

"Sounds like a tall order to me," she said dubiously, and he nodded.

"It is. But I think we've got at least a decent shot at it, if we handle things right. First, we go ahead and admit that, however many ships of whatever classes they deployed at Spindle, they've clearly demonstrated that at least some of their weaponry is, in fact, superior to anything we have currently *deployed*. Obviously, the Navy's been pursuing similar weapons developments for some time, but has declined to put them into service because the League was unwilling to take responsibility for such a dramatic escalation in the lethality of weapons of war. Which, by the way, also helps buy us a little time. Because of that unwillingness to pursue such an escalation, we didn't press the R&D on it, and there's going to be an inevitable delay before we can bring our own systems fully up to operational status and start getting them deployed.

"In the meantime, however, the Manties have become aware both of their current superiority and also of the fact that it's a fleeting one, and they've decided to push their imperialist agenda while they still have a decided edge in combat. Clearly, the way in which they've distorted what happened in both incidents at New Tuscany—and probably what happened at Monica, as well—is all part of an elaborate deception plan. It's intended to erect a façade of *Solarian* aggression in order to create a peace lobby here in the League which will agitate in favor of allowing their new 'Empire' to retain its ill-gotten gains rather than risk a lengthy, expensive war to force them to surrender those gains. That's probably why they're insisting on this nonsense about Manpower being behind it all, too."

"So you don't think there's anything to that?" Abruzzi asked.

"To the idea that a single corporation, no matter how rich and well-connected, could arrange to throw entire battle fleets around the galaxy? *Please!*" Kolokoltsov rolled his eyes. "Oh, I don't doubt for a minute that Manpower is involved in this thing up to its eyebrows, and everybody knows how all the Mesan transstellars scratch each other's backs. For that matter, all that nonsense about the Manties being involved in what happened in Green Pines is an obvious crock... that came out of the official Mesan 'system government.' So, sure, Manpower's involved, and we all know how much Manpower's hated Manticore—and vice-versa—for centuries. But there's no way a single corporation could be pulling the sorts of strings the Manties are insisting it is! On the other hand, Manpower is the poster child for corrupt transstellars, and thanks to people like O'Hanrahan, 'everybody knows' the transstellars are involved in corruption and sweetheart deals all over the Shell and the Verge. The Manties are trying to take advantage of that."

"You really believe that?" MacArtney sounded skeptical again, and Kolokoltsov shrugged.

"You probably know more about that sort of thing than I do, given what goes on with Frontier Security. I'm not casting any stones when I say that, either. I'm just saying you're probably better informed about conditions in the Shell and Verge than I am. But I'm pretty sure that's what the Manties are doing. It's what I'd be doing, in their place, at any rate. Whether they really have ambitions beyond the Talbott Cluster or not, and whoever's really to blame for what happened at Spindle, they really do have all sorts of powerful motivations to create exactly the kind of 'peace lobby' I'm talking about. I think they've decided to wave Manpower's involvement under the collective noses of our do-gooders here in the League—can anyone say 'Beowulf'?—to undercut public support for further military operations against them."

"And just how will we go about defeating this nefarious Manticoran plan?" Wodoslawski asked, frowning intently.

"One thing we're going to have to do is make sure there are no more Crandalls," Kolokoltsov said. "And I know Rajani's already begun activating units from the Reserve. In fact, I suspect he's already begun redeploying his active units, as well, under Article Seven. Mind you, he hasn't told us that, but I'll be damned surprised if he hasn't. So as part of our 'No More Crandalls' policy, one thing we're going to have to do is get him back under control, whatever happens."

"I think between us we can do that," MacArtney said. "Go on."

"All right. The most important thing is that we don't even try to seek a formal declaration of war. Especially with this bogus Manpower issue running around, someone would be certain to veto the declaration even if we asked for one, and any debate in the Assembly would have too much chance of triggering the sort of witch hunt the League can't afford. Besides, we don't want to find ourselves pushed into conducting some sort of offensive operations, and that could happen if we somehow managed to get a formal declaration after all. So instead, we go right on activating the Reserve while we push—hard—on R&D to figure out what the hell they've done with their missiles and how to duplicate it. Rajani isn't going to like it, but we settle into a defensive *military* posture while we work on the tech problems and take the offensive *diplomatically* and in the media. We take the position that despite the horrible provocation Manticore has offered us, we aren't going to charge forward into a bloodbath—ours or anyone else's. Instead, we make it clear we're pursuing the diplomatic option, trying to find a negotiated solution that will get Manticore back out of the Talbott Cluster, where it belongs and, ultimately, hold it responsible for its provocative actions at New Tuscany and Monica and, probably, Green Pines, too."

"Sort of an offensive short of war, you mean?" Wodoslawski asked.

"Exactly. What we're really doing is playing for time while we find a way to compensate for these new missiles of theirs. We keep up a barrage of diplomatic missions, news releases, that sort of thing, to keep things simmering along below the level of outright combat, until we've managed to equalize the hardware equation. We don't need to have weapons as *good* as theirs; we just need to have weapons *close* enough to theirs to make our quantitative advantage decisive again. Once we reach that point, we regretfully conclude that diplomacy isn't going to work and we have no choice but to pursue the military option after all. Which we then do under Article Seven, without seeking a formal declaration."

"And you really think this is going to work?" Wodoslawski asked.

"I think it's got a good chance," Kolokoltsov replied. "I don't say it's foolproof, by any stretch of the imagination. We're going to be juggling hand grenades whatever we do, though, and the fact remains that Manticore has to realize the League is simply too damned big for them to ultimately defeat, no matter how good their weapons are. So as long as we're willing to talk, *they'll* be willing to talk, because if they push military operations instead, especially while they have such an overwhelming tactical advantage, they'll be clearly perceived as the aggressors, not the 'plucky little neobarbs' defending themselves against the big, nasty Solarian League. They're already halfway in the doghouse over the Green Pines allegations, and they can't afford to lend those any credence by acting the part of swaggering military bullies. There's no way they could survive rallying a unified Solarian public opinion against them, so they're not going to come to us and inflict millions of additional casualties in what's clearly a war of aggression.

"In the meanwhile, it's going to be obvious to the entire League that we're Doing Something. However we got into this mess, we're taking a measured, mature position, doing our best to reverse Manticore's expansionism without anyone else's getting hurt. Ultimately, that's going to have a soothing effect on public opinion. It'll probably even get a bunch of the people who cry most loudly over how evil Manpower is—like those idiots in the Renaissance Association—on our side because of how hard we're working to avoid additional bloodshed. And the more we emphasize how we're seeking a diplomatic solution, the less likely anyone is to notice that we *can't* pursue a military solution. But at the same time, we keep the pot bubbling so that everyone's used to the notion that we have this ongoing conflict-short-of-outright-shooting with Manticore."

"So that when the time's right, we can turn the heat under the pot back up in a way that either pushes Manticore into shooting again or gives *us* a clear pretext for going after *them*," Abruzzi said. He was actually smiling now, and Kolokoltsov nodded.

"I'm not saying this is a perfect policy," he said. "I'm just saying that given what happened to Crandall, and the way the the public's reacting to it, I think it may be the best one we've got. And another—"

"Excuse me, Mr. Undersecretary."

Kolokoltsov turned in his chair, eyebrows rising in astonishment. His butler, Albert Howard—who'd been with him for over thirty years and knew better than to *ever* walk into the middle of one of Kolokoltsov's private strategy sessions—had just opened the dining room door. His expression was as apologetic as his tone, but he raised the small com unit in his hand slightly when Kolokoltsov started to open his mouth.

"I'm very sorry to intrude, Sir," Howard said quickly, "but Admiral Rajampet is on the com. He says it's urgent. I told him you were in conference, but he insisted I get you immediately."

Kolokoltsov shut his mouth again, and his eyes narrowed. After a moment, he nodded.

"All right, Albert. Under the circumstances, I'm sure you made the proper decision." He held out his hand, and Howard handed over the com, bowed slightly, and disappeared once more.

Kolokoltsov looked at the others for a few seconds, holding the com, then sighed slightly, shook his head, and activated it.

"Yes, Rajani?" he said as the small holo display materialized above his hand. "What can I do for you?"

Rajampet's image on the undersized display was tiny, but it was large enough for his odd expression to register. There was something wild and feral about it, and then the admiral grinned like a wolf.

"I'm glad to see the others are there with you, Innokentiy," he said in a harsh, exultant voice. "We just got an emergency dispatch over here in my office, and you'll never *guess* what's been happening with those bastards in Manticore!"

Chapter Thirty-Two

"I NEVER KNEW IDIOCY came in so many flavors!"

Irene Teague looked up from her display, eyebrows raised, as Daud ibn Mamoun al-Fanudahi stalked into her office. Powered doors weren't very suitable for slamming behind oneself, but al-Fanudahi did his best.

"I beg your pardon?" Teague said as he hammered the manual close button savagely with the heel of his hand. Her tone was only politely interested, but that fooled neither of them, and he glared at her.

His obvious disgust and ire weren't directed at her—that much was readily apparent, but it was also remarkably cold comfort at the moment. It had become obvious, over the past few days, that even his earlier concerns over possible Manticoran military hardware had fallen short of the reality, yet even that hadn't been enough to fray his habitual control this way. So if something finally had . . .

"I cannot *believe* that even those . . . those *cretins* could—!"

She'd been wrong, she realized. It wasn't disgust and ire; it was blind, naked fury.

"What is it, Daud?" she asked considerably more urgently.

"It's just—"

He broke off again, shaking his head, and then, abruptly, the power of his anger seemed to desert him. He sank into the chair facing her deck, legs stretched out before him, shaking his head

441

again, this time with an air of weariness, and Teague felt a tingle of something entirely too much like outright fear as she saw the darkness in his eyes.

She started to say something else, then stopped, got up, and poured a cup of coffee. She glanced at him speculatively for a moment, then added a healthy slug from the bottle of single-malt she kept in her credenza before she poured another cup, this one without the whiskey, for herself. She passed the first Navy-issue mug across to him, then perched on the edge of her deck, holding her own in both hands, and cocked her head at him.

"Drink first," she commanded. "Then talk to me."

"Yes, Ma'am," he replied and managed a wan smile. He sipped, and his smile turned more natural. "I think it's probably a bit early in the morning for this particular cup of coffee," he observed.

"It's *never* too early for coffee," she replied. "And somewhere on this planet, it's well past quitting time, so that means it's late enough for any little additions."

"Creative timekeeping has its uses, I see."

He drank more whiskey-laced coffee, then settled back into the chair, and she saw his shoulders finally beginning to relax.

The sight relieved her. The last thing he needed was for fury to betray him into saying something unfortunate to one of his superiors, and she didn't want that. In fact, she was a bit surprised by how genuinely fond of him she'd become over the last few months. The fact that he was Battle Fleet and she was Frontier Fleet had become completely irrelevant as she began to realize just how justified his anxiety over possible Manticoran weapons really was. His persistent refusal to allow her to endorse his more "alarmist" analyses left her feeling more than a little guilty, even though she followed his logic. Unfortunately, she'd also followed his tracks through the reports everyone else had systematically ignored, as well, and her own sense of anxiety had grown steadily sharper in the process. The number of *other* reports which had apparently been creatively misfiled—and they'd discovered and managed to hunt down—had only made things even worse.

Then had come news of the Battle of Spindle. Despite all her own concerns, despite al-Fanudahi's most pessimistic projections, the two of them had been shocked by the totality of the Manticoran victory. Not even they had anticipated that an entire fleet of superdreadnoughts could be casually defeated by a force whose heaviest unit was only a battlecruiser. That was like . . . like having a professional prizefighter dropped by a single punch from her own eight-year-old daughter, for God's sake!

But if the two of them had been shocked, the rest of the Navy had been stunned. The sheer impossibility of what had happened was literally too much for the Navy's officer corps to process.

The first reaction had been simple denial. It *couldn't* have happened, therefore, it *hadn't* happened. There had to be some mistake. Whatever the initial news reports might have seemed to indicate, the Manties had to have had a task force of their own ships-of-the-wall present!

Unfortunately for that line of logic (if it could be dignified by that description), the Manties appeared to have anticipated such a response. They'd sent Admiral O'Cleary herself home along with their diplomatic note, and they'd allowed her to bring along tactical recordings of the engagement.

At the moment, O'Cleary was a pariah, tainted with the same contamination as Evelyn Sigbee. Unlike Sigbee, of course, O'Cleary was home on Old Earth, where she could have her disgrace rubbed firmly in her face, and even though she was Battle Fleet, not Frontier Fleet, Teague found herself feeling a powerful sense of sympathy for the older woman. It was hardly O'Cleary's fault she'd found herself under the orders of a certifiable moron and then been left to do the surrendering after Crandall sailed her entire task force straight into the jaws of catastrophe.

Despite the convenience of the scapegoat O'Cleary offered, however, there was no getting around the preposterous acceleration numbers of the Manty missiles which had ravaged TF 496. The reports which had confidently been dismissed as ridiculous turned out to have been firmly based in fact, exactly as al-Fanudahi had been warning his superiors. Indeed, they'd actually *understated* the threat by a significant margin, and as fresh proof of the fundamental unfairness of the universe, Admiral Cheng had seized upon Al-Fanudahi's original estimates, based on the lower acceleration and accuracy numbers in the original reports, and sharply reprimanded him for not having "fully appreciated the scope of the threat" in the analyses Cheng had then proceeded to ignore.

Nonetheless, the fact that al-Fanudahi had been right all along couldn't be completely ignored. Not any longer. And so the despised prophet of doom and gloom had suddenly found himself presenting briefings flag officers actually listened to. Not only that, but the Office of Operational Analysis was finally being asked to do what it *should* have been doing all along. Of course, its efforts were a little handicapped by the fact that it had been systematically starved of funds for so long and that ninety percent of its efforts had gone into feel-good analyses of Battle Fleet's simulations and fleet problems instead of learning to actually think about possible external threats to the League. Of which, after all, there had been none. Which meant, preposterous and pathetic though it undoubtedly was, that the only two people it had who were actually familiar with those threats happened to be in Teague's office at that very moment.

To be fair, at least some of their colleagues were immersed in crash efforts to familiarize themselves with the same data, but most of them were still running about like beheaded chickens. They simply didn't know where to *look*—not yet—and Teague felt grimly confident that they wouldn't figure it out in time to avoid an entire succession of disasters.

Not, at least, if the idiots in charge of the Navy didn't start actually paying attention—*really* paying attention, as in processing the information, not simply acknowledging it—to al-Fanudahi. Which, even now, they seemed remarkably disinclined to do.

If there'd truly been such a thing as justice, Cheng Hai-shwun and Admiral Karl-Heinz Thimár would have been out of uniform and begging for handouts on a corner somewhere, Teague thought bitterly. In fact, if there'd been any such thing as *real* justice, they'd have been in prison! Unfortunately, both of them were far too well connected. In fact, it seemed unlikely either of them would even be relieved of his present assignment, despite the catastrophic intelligence failure represented by the Battle of Spindle. And, given the fact that al-Fanudahi had been the bearer of uniformly bad tidings in the briefings people were finally listening to, Teague had an unpleasant feeling that she knew exactly who would end up scapegoated to save Cheng and Thimár's well protected posteriors.

For the moment, though, people had finally been at least listening to what al-Fanudahi had been trying to tell them all along, which was why his present mixture of anger and despair was so frightening to her.

"Ready to talk about it now?" she asked gently after a moment.

"I suppose so," he replied. He took one more sip, then lowered the cup into his lap and looked at her.

"What have they done this time?" she prompted.

"It isn't so much what they've *done* as what they're getting ready to talk themselves into *doing*," he said, and shook his head. "They've decided that what's happened to the Manties offers them the perfect opening, and I think they're getting ready to take advantage of it."

"What?" Teague's tone was that of a woman who felt pretty sure she'd misheard something, and he snorted in harsh amusement.

"I've just come from a meeting with Kingsford, Jennings, and Bernard," he told her. "They're working on a brainstorm of Rajampet's."

Teague's stomach muscles tightened. Admiral Willis Jennings was Seth Kingsford's chief of staff, and Fleet Admiral Evangeline Bernard was the commanding officer of the Office of Strategy and Planning. Under most circumstances, the notion of the commanding officer of Battle Fleet meeting with his chief of staff and the Navy's chief strategic planner to consider the implications of combat reports might have been considered a good thing. Under the present circumstances, and given al-Fanudahi's near despair, she suspected that hadn't been the case this time around. Maybe it was his use of the word "brainstorm," she thought mordantly.

"What sort of brainstorm?" she asked out loud.

"As Rajampet sees it, what just happened to the Manties' home system offers what he calls a 'strategic window of opportunity.' He wants to mount an immediate operation to take advantage of the opening, and he proposes to use Admiral Filareta for the purpose."

"Filareta?" Teague repeated a bit blankly, and al-Fanudahi shrugged.

"He's Battle Fleet, so you probably don't know him. Trust me, you're not missing much. He's smarter than Crandall was. In fact, I'm willing to bet his IQ is at least equal to his shoe size. Aside from that, his only recommendation for command is that he has a pulse."

It was a mark of just how much he'd come to trust her—and vice-versa—she reflected, that he dared to show open contempt for such a monumentally senior officer in front of her.

"What makes Admiral Rajampet think this Filareta's in a position to do anything?"

"For some reason known only to God and, possibly, Admiral Kingsford, Filareta is swanning around in the Shell, halfway to Manticore, with a force even bigger than Crandall's was."

She looked at him sharply, and he looked back with a carefully expressionless face.

"And just what is this Admiral Filareta doing out in the Shell?" she asked.

"By the oddest coincidence, he, too, is conducting a training exercise." Al-Fanudahi smiled without any humor at all. "You might be interested to know—I checked myself, out of idle curiosity, you understand—that in the last thirty T-years Battle Fleet has conducted only three exercises which deployed more than fifty of the wall as far out as the Shell. But *this* year, for some reason, Crandall was authorized to conduct her training exercise in the Madras Sector and Fleet Admiral Massimo Filareta was *simultaneously* authorized to conduct 'wargames' in the Tasmania Sector. And, unlike Crandall, Filareta's exercise constitutes—and I quote—'a major fleet exercise.' Which is how he comes to be parked out in Tasmania with *three hundred* wallers, plus screen. Rajampet wants to reinforce him with another seventy or eighty of the wall which 'just happen' to have been deployed to various sector bases within a couple of weeks' hyper time from Tasmania, then send him off to attack Manticore directly."

"*What?*"

She stared at him in disbelief, and he grinned sourly, then extended his whiskey-laced coffee mug towards her.

"Care for a little belt?" he invited.

"I don't think an entire bottle would help a lot," she replied after a moment, and shook her head. "You're serious, aren't you?"

"Believe me, I wish I wasn't."

"What can he be *thinking*?"

"I'm not sure I'd apply that particular verb to whatever's going on inside his skull at the moment," al-Fanudahi said tartly. Then he sighed.

"As nearly as I could figure out from what Jennings and Bernard were saying to Kingsford, and the kinds of questions all three of them were asking me, Rajampet thinks that even if reports of what happened to them are grossly exaggerated, the Manties have to be reeling. As Jennings put it, the moment is 'psychologically ripe.' After a pounding like that, they aren't going to have the stomach for a standup fight against the SLN."

"Just like a handful of their cruisers didn't have the stomach for a standup fight against Crandall, you mean?" Teague said bitterly.

"I think they expect things to work out a little better this time."

"They think the Manty Home Fleet won't fight to defend their home system when a batch of *cruisers* were willing to go toe-to-toe with Crandall over the administrative center of a province they haven't even firmly integrated into their empire yet?"

Teague hadn't even tried to keep the incredulity out of her savage tone, and al-Fanudahi grinned with at least a trace of genuine humor.

"There you go using that verb again," he said. Then he sobered.

"It does tie in with existing strategic planning," he pointed out. "And, apparently, the theory is that getting hammered that way, completely out of the blue, is bound to have had a devastating effect on the Manties' morale and confidence, completely disregarding whatever effect it's had on their actual, physical capabilities. In fact, Jennings suggested that the psychological impact was probably even greater because it came so close on the heels of what happened at Spindle. And, of course, they can't be certain *we* weren't the ones who did it. So when a fresh Solarian fleet turns up on their doorstep in about half the time they can have expected anyone to take getting there, and when they realize we're willing to go at them again, this time on their home ground, despite Spindle, they'll realize they're screwed and throw in the towel. Especially if they do think we're the ones who just hit them and they're looking over their shoulder, waiting for us to do it again at the moment they're engaged against our conventional wallers."

Teague looked at him again, then sighed, walked back around her desk, and flopped into her own chair.

"Go on. I'm sure there's more and better still to come."

"Well, I did point out—diffidently, you understand—that even allowing for the fact that Filareta is a lot closer to Manticore than anyone would have expected, it's going to take around a month to get him reinforced the way they're talking about, and then *another* month and a half to get him to Manticore, by which point at least some of the shock effect should have dissipated. Bernard agreed that was a possibility, but her staff psychologists"—his eyes met Teague's and rolled—"estimate that would actually work in our behalf. Apparently they feel three months or so would be about right for the anesthetizing effect of the shock to wear off and give way to despair as 'a more sober evaluation of their situation' sinks in fully."

"I don't suppose any of these staff psychologists are planning on accompanying Admiral Filareta to Manticore?"

"Oddly enough, I don't believe they are."

"Neither would I," Teague muttered.

"After that concern of mine had been suitably allayed," al-Fanudahi continued, "I pointed out that our reports indicate the Manties probably have at least a hundred or so wallers of their own left in Home Fleet. Given the outcome of the Battle of Spindle, it seemed to me that perhaps a greater numerical advantage on our part would be in order. Admiral Jennings, however, informed me that Admiral Thimár's reports indicate the Manties took heavier losses than we'd originally assumed when Haven attacked their home system. You'll be interested to know that ONI's best estimate is that the Manties have no more than sixty or seventy of the wall left."

"I thought *we* were the Office of Naval Intelligence," Teague observed.

"No, we're the Office of *Operational Analysis*," al-Fanudahi corrected in a chiding tone of voice. "Admiral Kingsford was kind enough to point that out to me. Apparently, additional human intelligence reports you and I haven't had access to strongly support Admiral Thimár's conclusions about Manticoran losses."

"Fascinating."

"I thought so, too. But after I'd had the opportunity to digest that information for a few moments, I pointed out that even sixty or seventy of their wallers would presumably be more than enough to deal with three or four hundred of ours, given their newly revealed advantage in missile warfare. Which, I noted, didn't even consider any fixed defenses their capital system might have deployed after a couple of decades of active warfare with the Republic of Haven.

"Admiral Bernard agreed that that was certainly a reasonable cause for concern, but it's apparently the joint view of Admiral Rajampet and Admiral Kingsford that no one could have gotten in to hammer the Manties' shipyards and space stations that hard without blowing his way through the fixed defenses first. In other words, whoever it was must have already taken out a lot of the combat capability they might have used against us. And with the damage to their industrial sector, not to mention their losses in trained military manpower, they won't have been able to do very much to replace lost capability."

Teague realized she was shaking her head, slowly, again and again, and made herself stop.

"They're insane," she said flatly.

"Or a reasonable facsimile thereof," he agreed glumly.

"Haven't they even *considered* the implications of what happened to the Manties?" she demanded.

"The only implications they're interested in are the ones that have left Manticore vulnerable," al-Fanudahi replied flatly. "I pointed out to them that we don't have a clue how whoever it was did whatever the hell he did. All we have so far are *news* reports, for God's sake! It's obvious someone got in and blew the crap out of Manticore's infrastructure, but that's *all* we know."

"Bullshit it's all we know!" Teague snapped. "We know damned well that nothing *we* have could've done it! What happened to Crandall at Spindle's proof enough of *that*. I guarantee you that there's no way Spindle had anything like the depth of sensor coverage their home system has, and their Home Fleet is a hell of a lot more powerful than a handful of cruisers and battlecruisers. So if somebody got through all of that and got in close enough to do the kind of damage the newsies are reporting—or anything remotely *like* the damage they're reporting—they had to do it with some kind of hardware we've never even heard of. *Another* kind of hardware we've never even heard of!"

"My own thoughts exactly," al-Fanudahi agreed heavily.

The two of them sat looking at one another in silence for at least a couple of minutes. Then Teague leaned back and inhaled deeply.

"You realize who it was, of course," she said quietly.

"Well, we've just agreed it wasn't us," he replied. "And if Haven had anything like this—or if they'd even been close to getting something like this deployed—they never would've launched that do-or-die attack of theirs. So, from where I sit, that eliminates most of the usual suspects. And given what's been going on in Talbott, and the assassination of the Manty ambassador right here in Old Chicago, and that obvious nonsense about Manty sponsorship of that attack on Green Pines, and that attack on Congo, the name that pops to the top of my list begins with the letter 'M.'"

"Mine, too." Her eyes were as dark as his had been, and her expression was very, very grim. "Daoud, I'm starting to have a really bad feeling. The sort of feeling a person might get if she believed the Manties had been right all along about Manpower's involvement. It doesn't seem possible, but..."

Her voice trailed off, and al-Fanudahi nodded.

"I agree," he said. "And, frankly, the fact that no one—not Rajampet, not Kingsford, not Jennings or Bernard—seems to be so much as thinking about that worries me even more than the fact that they don't seem to be aware that our hardware has just been demonstrated to be the *third*-best—if that—in the galaxy. It's bad enough they aren't tearing their own commands apart trying to figure out just how the hell Manpower got so deep inside they can actually influence major deployment decisions, but even that pales beside the rather more pressing question of what could have inspired Manpower—or whoever—to hit Manticore so directly. To risk stepping that far out of the shadows."

"So you think this goes a lot farther than just getting Manticore out of the Talbott Cluster and away from Mesa."

"I wouldn't be a bit surprised if that was a big part of it, maybe even some kind of triggering event," al-Fanudahi said. "But anyone who could pull this entire sequence of events together—anyone who could get whole task forces and fleets of Solarian capital ships deployed where he wants them, *when* he wants them, then pull something like the attack on Manticore out of his ass—isn't just improvising as he goes along. Either of those operations must have required a massive organization and very careful—and lengthy—planning. Byng and Crandall—even Filareta—could *probably* have been steered into position by somebody with enough money and enough political clout to influence a handful of high-level strategic decisions. After all, as far as anyone knew, they were just routine *peacetime* deployments, so why not do a little favor for someone with deep enough pockets? But this direct assault on Manticore required serious industrial power, *military* planning, and almost certainly some sort of technological breakthrough that neither we nor the Manties know anything about. That's *way* outside the parameters for even the biggest and nastiest transstellar, Irene. It's an entirely different level of capabilities."

"And whoever it is—whether it's Manpower or someone else who's just been using Manpower as a front—there has to be a reason she's decided to go ahead and show us all she has that kind of capability," Teague said quietly.

"Precisely." Al-Fanudahi rubbed his forehead wearily. "Maybe at least part of it was opportunism. Maybe the real target's been Manticore all along, and the combination of the Manties' confrontation with us in Talbott and their losses in the Battle of Manticore was just too great a temptation, like Rajampet's 'strategic window of opportunity,' and the bad guys jumped before they were ready. But I don't think it's that simple. I don't think someone who was able to build up the capabilities we're talking about in the first place without anyone even noticing is going to just throw away all that careful concealment, however great the strategic temptation, before he was pretty much ready to move anyway."

"Move against Manticore, you mean." Teague frowned with a dissatisfied air. "I don't think you're wrong, Daoud, but at the same time, I don't see the point." She shook her head. "Oh, don't get me wrong. Obviously, if we didn't even know these people were planning whatever the hell it is they're planning, it's not very likely we're going to be able to magically discern what it is they're after. What their endgame is. And I know Manticore's richer than sin, for its size, at least, and its merchant marine is all over the damned galaxy, with its nose in everybody else's business. And I don't doubt for a minute that Manpower resents the hell out of the Manties' enforcement of the Cherwell Convention. I'll grant you all of that. But why go to such lengths to crush Manticore? God only knows how long they must've spent planning and building up their resources before they could pull something like this off. So why *do* it? Why make that kind of investment just to attack a relatively small star nation on the far side of the damned League from them? It doesn't make any sense!"

"No, it doesn't," al-Fanudahi agreed quietly. "That's why I'm so worried by the fact that no one else even seems to care about 'Manpower's' involvement in all this. Because I agree with you, Irene. Nobody's going to go to all this trouble and the huge expense which must've been involved just because they don't like the Star Empire of Manticore. There's got to be more to it, and the very unpleasant question that's been occurring to me over the last day or so is why they got *us* involved in the first place. If they already had the capability to carry off something like this attack of theirs, why run the risk of trying to manipulate *us* into squashing Manticore? They could've done this on their own any-time they wanted to without involving the League at all. And if their intelligence on Manty capabilities was as good as it must've been for them to have planned and executed this operation, they must've had a damned good idea of just how outclassed our Navy was going to be when it went up against the Manties. So they obviously weren't counting on us to do the job for them."

"You're sure about that?" Teague's question wasn't a challenge, but her eyes were troubled. "You don't think they might have resorted to doing the job themselves only because they'd realized *we* weren't going to be able to after all?"

"No way." He shook his head. "Just getting their strike forces into position would have taken a long time. Unless I'm sadly mistaken, they would have had to start moving them before the first New Tuscan incident. Certainly before the second one. So that means they had both wings of their plan in motion at the same time. No. They knew we wouldn't be able to take the Manties, but they maneuvered us into a war with them, anyway. And that suggests to me that maybe it wasn't so much that they wanted the Manties at war with us as they wanted *us* at war with the Manties."

"Why?" Teague's frown was deeper than ever, and al-Fanudahi shrugged unhappily.

"If I knew the answer to that question, I might be able to do something about it," he said. "But what I'm very much afraid of, Irene, is that we just *thought* this was all about using the League to crush Manticore. I think it goes a lot deeper than that, and as preposterous as it sounds, I can only see one other target on the range at the moment."

He looked across her desk at her, his dark eyes worried.

"Us," he said very, very softly.

Chapter Thirty-Three

"MADAM PRESIDENT, Secretary Theisman is on the com."

"Thank you, Antoine," Eloise Pritchart said, suppressing a familiar temptation to smile.

Antoine Belardinelli, her senior secretary, was probably the only member of her staff who persistently "forgot" to refer to Thomas Theisman as "Admiral Theisman." Everyone else was willing to accept that Theisman preferred his naval title (to which he was still entitled, since he was CNO, as well as Secretary of War), but Belardinelli was adamant. As far as he was concerned, one of the most important features of the restored Republic was that elected officials really were in charge again, and so he invariably used Thesiman's civilian title. If that irritated the Secretary, Belardinelli was quite prepared to live with it. In fact, he and Angelina Rousseau, the President's personal aide, had been sparring over that little omission on his part ever since the first post-coup elections. Of course, although the "Two A's," as Belardinelli and Rousseau were commonly referred to, were both highly efficient and both deeply devoted to Eloise Pritchart, they loathed one *another* with deep and reciprocal passion. Which might be the real reason Rousseau—never one to back away from a fight herself, especially with Belardinelli—was so adamantly on the military side. If they hadn't been squabbling over Theisman's proper title, they would have found something else to fight about, after all.

Personally, Pritchart was just as happy to have them use up at least some of their energy on something fairly harmless, and she knew Theisman found the entire situation amusing.

"You're welcome, Madam President," Belardinelli replied now, and disappeared from Pritchart's display to be replaced by Thomas Theisman.

"And how are you this fine morning, Mr. Secretary?" Pritchart inquired.

"Did it again, did he?" Theisman asked with a smile.

"Unless I miss my guess, Angelina was in the outer office when your call came in. He wasn't using his hush mike, anyway. My observation's been that when he 'forgets' to do that, it's usually on purpose."

"Have you ever considered just locking the two of them in a room with a pair of pulsers to let them settle this once and for all?"

"Often, as a matter of fact," she said gravely. "Unfortunately, Sheila won't let me play with guns anymore."

"Pity."

"Indeed. And now that we have that out of our systems, Admiral, to what do I owe the pleasure?"

"We've finished that study you requested," Theisman said in a much more serious tone, and Pritchart let her chair come upright.

"I see. And your conclusions were—?"

"Pretty much what I'm sure you expected." Theisman shrugged. "Frankly, Spindle doesn't make much difference as far as our own strategic situation vis-à-vis Manticore is concerned. We're still where we were—screwed, in other words, if they come after us. What we know now is that we're not alone in that predicament. In fact, it would appear the Sollies are even worse screwed than we are. Personally, I take at least a modicum of dog-in-the-manger satisfaction from that conclusion, given how the Sollies made us pay through the nose for their tech transfers right after the first war started."

Pritchart nodded. She knew Theisman would be sending her the actual report, along with a complete précis, but that wasn't what she wanted from him now, and as he said, his summary of the Octagon's conclusions were about what she'd expected.

"So Admiral Trenis' analysts are satisfied that the sensor data Duchess Harrington provided us with is genuine?" she asked.

"The missile performance wasn't quite as good as what we've

observed against our own units," Theisman said, "but I suspect that's because their heavy cruisers' fire control isn't sophisticated enough to take full advantage of the FTL link. It certainly wasn't because anything the Sollies did knocked them back, at any rate." He grimaced. "I can admire a professional job as much as the next man, but in this instance, those poor Solly bastards were even more outclassed than we were during Operation Buttercup. Which says really depressing things about how bad Solly intelligence must be, when you think about it. We and the Manties have been throwing multidrive missiles at each other for quite a while now, but it's obvious this Crandall didn't have a clue what that was going to mean. You'd think *someone* would've mentioned those unimportant little details to their Office of Naval Intelligence."

"Well, one thing I've never had any trouble agreeing with the Manties about is that the Sollies are the biggest, most arrogant pains in the posterior of anyone in the entire galaxy," Pritchart said tartly. "I don't like the thought of that many people getting killed, whoever they are. At the same time, though, I'd be lying if I said a nasty little part of me doesn't take a certain satisfaction in seeing the almighty Solarian League flat on its face in the mud while somebody tapdances on its spine."

"By and large, I can't disagree," Theisman replied. "Still, as your Secretary of War, it behooves me to point out that the Sollies' value as an additional threat to the Manticorans has just been... substantially devalued."

"So you don't agree with Younger's argument that the League's sheer size is still going to keep the Manties running scared of a confrontation with Old Chicago?"

"Madam President—Eloise—let's be serious here." Theisman shook his head. "Whatever else anyone might say about Manticorans, they don't 'run scared' worth a damn. If they'd had any inclinations in that direction, the Legislaturalists would still be running the People's Republic, and the Manticore Binary System would belong to us. Neither of which, you may have noticed, is the case."

"Now that you mention it, I had noticed," she replied with a slight smile.

"In the long term, I'm sure the Manties would vastly prefer to avoid a direct, large-scale confrontation with the League," Theisman continued soberly. "They've already had a graphic demonstration from us about the transitory nature of technological advantages, and the League's so damned big and so damned rich it could afford to scattergun a hundred separate research programs into each and every one of the Manties' current toys. Eventually, they'd manage to duplicate them, too, and when that happened, Manticore would almost certainly be history.

"But unless the Sollies' leadership consists solely of outright lunatics—which, unfortunately, no one over here at the Octagon is prepared to rule out—they're going to realize that for the next several years, any war against Manticore would be a one-sided massacre. It may be they're stupid enough to pull the trigger, anyway, but I seriously question whether even the Solly public would tolerate that sort of bloodbath for any lengthy period."

"So what?" Pritchart asked in her best devil's advocate tone. "Who cares about a little thing like angry voters? It's not as if there's any real political accountability or oversight in the League, you know."

"Not now, there isn't," Theisman said grimly. "But personally, I think the Sollies should be paying attention to more than just the operational aspects of events here in our corner of the galaxy. There's that little matter of what's been going in in the Maya Sector, for example. And then there's *us*. If you'll recall, Madam President, the citizens of the People's Republic didn't have any real political oversight, either. A situation which changed rather abruptly when the Manties' Eighth Fleet came calling and Saint-Just got distracted dealing with that minor threat."

Pritchart started to reply lightly, then stopped as she realized Theisman was serious. Had it been anyone else, she would have dismissed his suggestion out of hand. Corrupt though it might be, the Solarian League was still the *Solarian League*, and the notion that the system which had governed it literally for centuries could be changed was ludicrous. But Thomas Theisman had more firsthand experience than most in arranging exactly that sort of change, and although he disliked politics, he *understood* them well. Not to mention the fact that he was probably the best student of *history* she knew. So if *he* thought the League might be that fragile...

"Well, I suppose the point at the moment is that what's happened at Spindle's going to make the Star Empire more confident, not less," she said, putting thoughts of the League aside for future consideration. "Since they've just demonstrated they have a decisive military advantage over the SLN, McGwire and Younger's belief that they're going to be even more willing to make concessions would appear to be, ah, ill-founded."

"I believe you could say that, yes," Theisman agreed dryly. "Which, I might point out, is very probably the reason the duchess handed the sensor recordings over to us. I'm sure she thought about that pretty carefully, since it had the potential to give us so much more data on their systems, but unless I'm mistaken, she figured that letting us actually *see* how effective their weapons were against the Sollies would underscore the extent of—and the basis for—their confidence. And, to be fair, the tactical situation was such that they really didn't show us a lot more about their capabilities than we already knew. I'd really love to have seen how their *Nikes'* fire control would have done running the attack, for instance. At this point, we don't know whether or not *they* have the FTL fire control systems."

"In that case, I think it would be a good idea for you to personally brief McGwire and Younger. I know neither of them's on your list of favorite people, but I'd appreciate it if you'd take the opportunity to lean on them just a bit."

"You want me to do this wearing my military hat as CNO, or my civilian hat, as Secretary of War?"

"Both, I think. We need them to be *very* clear on this point, Tom."

Pritchart frowned and toyed with one lock of platinum hair.

"Duchess Harrington's been remarkably patient about not bringing up that matter of our correspondence—so far, at least—but she's never pretended it's not going to have to be addressed," the President continued after a moment. "Personally, I think that, given the fact that we've already acknowledged we were the ones who started shooting this time around, she's been willing to wait on that point. I think she's been letting us wrangle and argue about things like plebiscites and formulas for computing reparations as a way to clear away the underbrush before she tackles what she knows is going to be the thorniest issue of all. For that matter, she's probably been letting the negotiations build momentum, as well, to help carry us past any potholes farther down the road. Admiral or not, she's got good diplomatic instincts.

"Either way, though, we're going to have to approach that issue pretty damned soon. In one way, it's going to be a lot easier for Alexander-Harrington than she can possibly suspect, given what we think we know about Arnold's shenanigans. But it's going to be a nightmare for us, on the domestic side, and I want every member of our delegation to understand very clearly just how... bleak our military prospects would be if this thing goes belly-up on us."

"And you think our two 'colleagues' are stupid enough to have missed that already?" Theisman sounded just a bit skeptical.

"I...don't know." Pritchart's frown deepened. "I *do* know I don't trust either of them a single centimeter past his personal perception of his own best interests. That goes without saying, I suppose. But I'm not sure how good either of them is at recognizing the limits of those interests. Or their obtainability, at any rate. Frankly, Younger worries me more than McGwire. There's something about him, about his ability to believe he'll always come out on top, that makes me very nervous. McGwire's probably even more self-serving than Younger, if that's humanly possible, but I think he also has a more pragmatic grasp of the fact that reality sometimes has this unpleasant habit of being something besides what he'd like it to be. See if you can emphasize that to him in this case."

"Gosh, thanks," Theisman said.

"Consider it one of the perks of your position, Mr. Secretary. Yet another opportunity to meet the movers and shakers who control our political destiny."

"Sure. Will Sheila object if *I* take a gun?"

Much later that evening, the attention signal on Pritchart's desktop com warbled softly.

She looked up from the report she'd been reading—she was *always* reading some report, after all—and frowned as the signal warbled again. Then she bookmarked her place and pressed the acceptance key.

"Yes?"

"I'm sorry to disturb you, Madam President," Angelina Rousseau said almost before her image had appeared on the display. "I know you're working, but I think you'd better take this call."

"Angelina, I've got that reception in less than an hour," Pritchart reminded her.

"I know, Madam President," Rousseau repeated. "But it's Admiral Alexander-Harrington, Ma'am. She says it's urgent."

Pritchart stiffened, sitting upright in her chair.

"Did she tell you what she needs to speak to me about?"

"No, Ma'am. All I know is that a dispatch boat just came in from Manticore."

"'Just came in'?"

"Yes, Ma'am." Angelina Rousseau was an extraordinarily attractive woman, but Pritchart hadn't chosen her as her senior aide on the basis of her decorative qualities, and the younger woman's brown eyes were dark. "It made its alpha translation less than thirty minutes ago and burst-transmitted an FTL message to the Manticoran delegation."

"I see," Pritchart said slowly, even as her mind raced. Obviously, whatever was on Alexander-Harrington's mind, it had something to do with that dispatch boat. And if she was already on the com . . .

"Well, you'd better go ahead and put her through. Oh, and, Angelina?"

"Yes, Ma'am?"

"Give Sheila a heads-up." The President smiled thinly. "It's possible we're going to be a little late to that reception, after all."

"Yes, Ma'am."

Rousseau vanished from the display, and Pritchart found herself looking at Honor Alexander-Harrington, instead, with what she hoped was a carefully concealed sense of trepidation. At least Alexander-Harrington's treecat wasn't close enough to read right through her pretense of calm. That was something . . . but not all that much, under the circumstances.

The fact that Pritchart had discovered she really did like Alexander-Harrington—quite a lot, in fact—didn't make the Havenite President feel any calmer about having the duchess screen her so unexpectedly.

Mostly that was because she'd felt a cautious sense things were going well. Given the tortuous and so often disastrous history between the Republic of Haven and the Star Empire of Manticore, that feeling that things were actually starting to work out had produced an automatic fear that another shoe was waiting somewhere, ready to fall squarely on top of her head when she least expected it. All of which which made Alexander-Harrington's abrupt request more than a little ominous.

Sometimes it's hard to believe I first met the woman barely two T-months ago, Pritchart thought. *Still, I don't suppose it should be at all surprising I'd rather deal with her than some of my own "allies" right here in Nouveau Paris. That incredible jackass Younger, for one. If nothing else, at least she has a brain that works. And quite a lot of integrity to go along with it, too, which is even rarer. Unfortunately.*

Left to their own devices, Pritchart suspected, she and Alexander-Harrington could have hammered out a workable set of terms at least a month ago. On the other hand, she supposed that after the better part of a T-century of enmity and two decades of actual hostilities, they were moving with blinding speed to have come as close together as they had. In fact, the only points still dividing them were that the question of reparations and that matter of the forged diplomatic notes.

What galled her most was that it was Gerald Younger and Samson McGwire who were throwing almost all the grit into the gears. Neither one of them had been at all happy about being required to accept the "guilt" for resuming hostilities, which Pritchart found especially ironic, given the fact that they'd been two of Arnold Giancola's closest allies. And they were *still* trying to insist on settling the reparations question while the Manties were "still under Solarian pressure." Despite which, the President felt confident that agreement on that point—on Alexander-Harrington's proposed basis—was no more than a day or two away now.

Which, of course, would only mean they finally had to deal with the prewar diplomatic correspondence, and she didn't expect McGwire or Younger to magically get *more* cooperative when that happened. To be fair (which she found extremely difficult in their cases), neither of them knew Giancola had manipulated the correspondence in question (or, at least, if they *did* know, they'd buried their connection to Giancola's thoroughly illegal shenanigans so deep Kevin Usher's best investigators couldn't find it). And Pritchart still hadn't dared to tell them that their own Secretary of State—and close political ally—had betrayed his oath of office by forging the Star Empire's supposed diplomatic correspondence . . . exactly the way Manticore had been insisting someone had all along.

If she'd trusted the integrity of either of them as far as she could spit, she would have taken them into her confidence long ago. Now, despite the fact that she *didn't* trust their integrity, she was going to have to, and she dreaded putting that sort of weapon into the hands of men who wouldn't hesitate for an instant to wring any personal advantage they could out of it, regardless of the consequences for the Republic and the peace process.

Well, Eloise, she thought tartly, *it's not like you haven't known this was coming, now is it? That's the real reason you sicced Thomas on the two of them—to get them to understand that our collective position's far too precarious for anyone to be playing personal power games. Not that what happened at Spindle's likely to make either of them suddenly see the light if the Battle of Manticore didn't! Frankly, I wish Alexander-Harrington would just go ahead and strangle both of them. I'm sure she could do it without even breaking a sweat, and I'd be perfectly willing to write out a presidential pardon for murder on the spot. Preferably in their blood. For that matter, she's got diplomatic immunity, now that I think about it. I wouldn't even need the pardon!*

"Thank you for taking my call on such short notice, Madam President," Alexander-Harrington said. "I know how crowded your schedule is."

"You're quite welcome, Admiral." Pritchart smiled wryly. "There aren't many people on Haven who'd take precedence over you in my appointments book, you know. Besides, our conversations are always so . . . interesting."

Alexander-Harrington smiled back, but it was an almost perfunctory response, without the genuine humor she would normally have displayed, and Pritchart's mental antennae quivered.

"Well, I'm afraid this conversation is going to be brief," Alexander-Harrington said.

"It is?" Pritchard asked just a bit cautiously.

"Yes." Alexander-Harrington paused for a moment, then inhaled, as if visibly bracing herself, and Pritchart's trepidation turned into something much stronger. Honor Alexander-Harrington was one of the least hesitant people she'd ever met, yet she was visibly unhappy about whatever she was about to say. Indeed, as Pritchart thought about it, she realized the other woman was almost shaken looking.

"Madam President, I'm afraid we're going to have to suspend our negotiations, at least briefly."

"I beg your pardon?" Pritchart felt the bottom drop out of

her stomach as that long-awaited shoe came crashing down, and an emotion entirely too much like panic surged through her. If the negotiations failed, if Manticore resumed active operations—

"I assure you that it has nothing to do with anything that's occurred over the negotiating table," Alexander-Harrington said, almost as if she'd read Pritchart's mind. "I hope we'll be able to resume the talks sometime soon. In the meantime, however, I'm afraid I've just been recalled."

"I see," Pritchart said, although, in fact, she didn't see anything of the sort. "Do you have any idea when you might be returning?"

"I'm afraid not, Madam President. In fact, I'm not certain if *I'll* be returning at all."

"But...why not?" Anxiety—and not just over the negotiations, given the other woman's apparent unhappiness and the sense of kinship she'd developed where Alexander-Harrington was concerned—startled the undiplomatic question out of her.

"Madam President, I—" Alexander-Harrington began, then paused. She gazed at Pritchart for several seconds, then gave a little nod.

"Eloise," she said in a softer voice, using Pritchart's given name for the very first time, "it's not just me they're recalling. They've recalled Eighth Fleet, as well."

An icicle ran down Eloise Pritchart's spine. She'd actually become accustomed to having the Manties' Eighth Fleet hanging out there like some sort of infinitely polite Sword of Damocles. And at least as long as it was sitting there, like a spectator to the negotiations, she could be confident it wasn't off doing something else. Something neither she nor the Republic might care for at all. But—

Her eyes narrowed suddenly as Alexander-Harrington's expression registered fully. This was a woman who'd faced death not just once, but repeatedly. The thought that anything could cause *her* to look this shaken was just this side of terrifying. In fact, Pritchart couldn't imagine anything which could have produced this effect, unless...

"Is it the Sollies?" she asked.

Alexander-Harrington hesitated for a moment, then sighed.

"We don't know—not yet," she said. "Personally, I doubt it. But that only makes it worse."

She looked at Pritchart levelly.

"I'm sure you'll be hearing reports about what's happened soon enough, and when you do, I'm sure people here in the Republic are going to start thinking about how it's changed the diplomatic calculus. At the moment, to be honest, I don't have any idea which *way* it's going to change things. I hope—even more than I hoped before I had the opportunity to actually meet you, Thomas Theisman, and some of your colleagues—that it won't force Queen Elizabeth to stiffen her position where the Republic is concerned, but I can't promise that."

Pritchart felt an almost overwhelming urge to lick her lips, but she suppressed it sternly and made herself sit motionless, waiting, her expression as tranquil as she could make it.

"I don't have instructions to do this," Alexander-Harrington continued, "but before I leave, I'll have a copy of Elizabeth's official message to me made for you. In the meantime, I'll summarize."

She inhaled again, and squared her shoulders.

"Approximately one week ago, in Manticore..." she began.

Chapter Thirty-Four

"SO THAT'S WHAT HAPPENED, as best we can make out at this point."

Thomas Theisman looked around at the other members of Eloise Pritchart's Cabinet, and his expression was grim.

"At the moment, no one has any idea *how* it was done," he continued. "I'm sure our current damage estimates are going to change—whether they're going to get better or worse is more than I can say at this point, but they're so preliminary change is inevitable. What worries me more, however, is the fact that we don't have a clue about what whoever did it used or what his ultimate objectives are."

"I don't want to sound callous," Tony Nesbitt said after a moment, "but do we really *care* what their 'ultimate objectives' may be?" It was his turn to look around at his colleagues' faces. "From our perspective, isn't the most important thing that someone has just kicked the Manties' legs out from under them? Surely they'd find it a lot more difficult to bring the war to us the way Admiral Alexander-Harrington was prepared to now that their home system and most of their industry's been trashed behind them."

"I have to admit the same thought's been occurring to me." Rachel Hanriot looked almost regretful—or possibly a bit ashamed—as she admitted that.

"And me," Henrietta Barloi said. The Secretary of Technology shrugged. "At the very least, doesn't this put us in a much stronger negotiating position?"

Unlike Hanriot, Pritchart noted, Barloi didn't look a bit regretful.

464

In fact, she couldn't conceal a certain satisfaction at the thought...
assuming she was trying to in the first place.

"Allow me to point out that changes in negotiating postures are
two-edged swords," the President observed. "No one on Admiral
Alexander-Harrington's negotiating team ever tried to pretend
Elizabeth Winton's magically become one of the Republic's greater
admirers. She offered to resume negotiations from a *position of
strength*. In many ways, that was a statement of her confidence—
her faith in her ability to control the situation if we chose not to
be 'reasonable.' If she sees that margin of strength disappearing,
if she finds herself with her back against the wall and faced by
multiple threats, I'd say she's likely to ruthlessly destroy those
threats in the order she can reach them. And guess who she can
reach a lot sooner than she can reach the League or somebody
she hasn't even been able to identify yet?"

Barloi didn't look convinced, but Nesbitt's expression became
more thoughtful, and Hanriot nodded.

"My own feeling from the negotiations," Leslie Montreau offered,
"is that Manticore—assuming the admiral's attitude reflects the Star
Empire's true desires—would rather have a negotiated settlement.
I think they truly want one that comprehensively addresses the
differences between us as the first step in a genuinely stable relationship with us. I'd have to agree Queen Elizabeth still doesn't like
us very much, but despite her famous temper, she's also pragmatic
enough to recognize that having a peaceful neighbor at her back
is a lot safer than turning her back on someone she's beaten to
her knees. But I have to agree that you're right, Madam President.
Pragmatic or not, she's also demonstrated she can be as ruthless
as any head of state I can think of. If she can't have a peaceful
neighbor, she'll settle for an enemy she's thoroughly neutralized."

"And there's another aspect to this, too," Denis LePic observed.
"Obviously Tom and his people are a lot more qualified to speak
to the purely military implications of this attack, but Wilhelm
Trajan's people over at Foreign Intelligence have been kicking it
around, as well. They're looking less at what kind of hardware
might have been used and more at *why* it was used in the first
place...and by whom. They've come to the conclusion that it
couldn't have been the Sollies, for a lot of reasons, including the
timing. And we know it wasn't us. That leaves the famous 'parties
unknown,' and based on what's been happening in the Talbott

Cluster, suspicion's focusing on Manpower. Unfortunately, that raises at least as many questions as it may answer.

"For example, where did a transstellar corporation—or the Mesa System's official government, for that matter—get its hands on the military muscle to do something like this? And assuming it had the capability in the first place, why aim it at Manticore? And if Manticore is its target, and it had this sort of capability, why try to maneuver the Sollies into the mix? And if it turns out that Manpower—or whoever Manpower's fronting for—has ambitions where Manticore's concerned, how do we know those are the *only* ambitions it has out here in the 'Haven Quadrant'?"

He leaned back in his chair and looked around the table.

"We don't have answers to any of those questions. Given that, I'd be extraordinarily cautious about concluding that my enemy's enemy must be *my* friend."

"Those are all valid points, Denis," Nesbitt acknowledged after a moment. "Still, given the size of the Manty merchant fleet and the huge advantages the Manticoran Wormhole Junction provide to it, I can think of a lot of reasons that wouldn't have anything to do with us for someone to be interested in picking off Manticore."

"Maybe," Stan Gregory said. "On the other hand, don't forget the real reason the Manties and Manpower have been busting each other's chops for so long. They're probably the only people in the galaxy, outside of Beowulf, at least, who're every bit as serious as we are about enforcing the Cherwell Convention. In regard to which, let's all remember what happened in Congo five months ago. And Mesa's Green Pines fantasy. Not to mention who most probably tried to kill Queen Berry, since we know damned well it wasn't *us*."

"A very good point," Theisman agreed. "Of course, it raises another question. If Manpower has, or even just has access to, the hardware that let them get in and out of the Manticore Binary System without even being detected, why did they use a bunch of ex-StateSec 'mercenaries' against Torch? Why not just blitz the Congo System and then send in a couple of conventional cruisers and a brigade of Marines to sweep up the pieces?"

"To preserve secrecy until they were ready to pull the trigger on Manticore itself?" Nesbitt suggested. "To try to point the Manties' suspicion at us, because of the StateSec connection?"

"Either of those *might* make sense," Theisman acknowledged, "although, frankly, the first seems a lot more likely to me. After all, they know the Manties aren't idiots and that Admiral Givens has to've figured out *someone* was hiring and supporting SS refugees, so it seems a lot less plausible they'd think they could implicate us. Still, it's possible, I suppose. And the fact that we can't rule out even your second suggestion only emphasizes what the President and Denis are both saying. We don't *know* anything about the thinking behind this. My own view is that we can't afford to assume anything *about* anything at this point. Certainly, speaking as Secretary of War, I can't offer any assurances about our ability to prevent the same thing from happening to us. And given our abysmal ignorance about this entire episode, the fact that *I* can't think of any good reason for someone to do it to us as well doesn't exactly fill me with confidence."

"Well, what do you think?" Pritchart asked some time later.

Most of the cabinet secretaries had departed, leaving her with Theisman, LePic, and Montreau. Not only were they her key advisers on military affairs, intelligence, and foreign policy, but Montreau had joined the other two as one of her closest political allies.

The Secretary of State remained aware of her status as the newest member of Pritchart's inner circle, however, and she glanced at Theisman and LePic, as if waiting for one of them to respond. When neither of them spoke up immediately, she shrugged.

"I think we just spent the last hour and a half thrashing around and basically admitting to one another that we don't know a damned thing *about* a damned thing, at present," she said frankly. "I also think that between you, you, Tom, and Denis managed to at least cool Tony's ardor for suddenly getting more aggressive at the peace table, though—assuming there's any more peace table to get aggressive at. I wish I could feel more confident Henrietta's convinced that this isn't the time to start pushing back as well, though."

"*I* wish we knew more," Pritchart fretted, with an openness she would have risked with very few other people. "You're right, we *don't* know a damned thing." She looked at LePic. "Have Wilhelm's people got *any* leads, Denis?"

"None I haven't already shared with you." LePic grimaced. "I *wish* we had confirmation one way or the other about Cachat and Zilwicki! If anyone might be able to shed at least a little light on whatever the hell is going on in Mesa and with Manpower, it would be them."

"You don't think that whatever they got involved with led to this, do you?" Montrose asked. The others looked at her, and she shrugged. "I don't see how it could have, myself, but as Denis just implied, we don't have a clue what's going on inside Mesa, whatever we used to think we knew. Since that's true, we can't know if Officer Cachat and Captain Zilwicki didn't stumble across something that provoked whoever's really calling the shots into attacking Manticore."

"I think that's unlikely, Leslie," Theisman said. "This was obviously a carefully planned and prepared operation. I don't think it was a panic reaction, and given how long ago Zilwicki, at least, was killed on Mesa without anyone here or in Manticore making any huge new revelations, they're probably feeling pretty confident on that front."

"I'm still not prepared to write Cachat off," LePic said stubbornly. Theisman looked skeptical, and the Attorney General shrugged. "I'm not saying I *expect* him to make it home this time, just that he's managed to run between the raindrops so long that I'm not going to accept he's actually dead until someone delivers his body. And even then, I'll want proof it wasn't a clone!"

"Well," Pritchart said, "I'm going to hope you're right, Denis, and not just because lunatic or not, he's *our* lunatic. As you say, if he's been poking around Manpower, maybe he can give us at least some clue as to what the hell's going on. In fact, I've had a disturbing thought, one that occurred to me after Tom's briefing."

"I've had quite a few of those myself," Theisman observed. "Which one were you referring to?"

"You made the point that we don't know what whoever hit Manticore's ultimate objectives may be, but we have to suspect Manpower's involved, for all the reasons you enumerated. And then we have Cachat's suspicion that Manpower was involved in the attempt on Queen Berry from which it's only a short step to their being involved with Admiral Webster's assassination in Old Chicago. For which"—her eyes bored suddenly into Theisman's—"some form of suicidal compulsion appears to have been used. Very much, now that I think about it. Like what happened to a certain Yves Grosclaude."

It was suddenly very, very quiet.

"Are you suggesting *Manpower* was working with Giancola?" LePic asked very carefully.

"No, I'm suggesting Arnold was working with *Manpower*," Pritchart replied grimly. "If they're willing—and able—to manipulate the *Solarian League* into going to war with the Manties, why in the world wouldn't they figure they could do the same with us? I mean, look how much *easier* it would be, given the fact that we didn't even have a formal peace treaty from our last war!"

"My God." Montreau shook her head almost numbly, her face suddenly ashen."That never even occurred to me!"

"No reason it should have, before," Pritchart pointed out.

"It's possible we're seeing conspiracies where there aren't any," Theisman warned.

"I know. And the only thing more dangerous than not seeing conspiracies that *are* there is seeing ones that *aren't*," Pritchart acknowledged. "But talking about conspiracies and suicidal assassins, there's that attempt on Alexander-Harrington, too. We know we didn't do it, although I've never blamed the Manties for figuring we were the ones with the best motive. But if Manpower's been moving chess pieces around like this, and if they have the technology—or whatever—they used to control the assassin who killed Webster and that poor patsy who carried out the Torch attack, why shouldn't they have tried to pick off one of the Manties' best military commanders? Especially if the object of the exercise was for us to trash Manticore for them?"

"Oh, how I do hope you're engaging in flights of paranoia," Theisman said after a moment.

"So do I, I think." Pritchart frowned thoughtfully for several seconds, then gave herself a shake.

"Maybe I am indulging my paranoia, but maybe I'm not, too. You know, I *almost* went ahead and told Alexander-Harrington about Arnold."

The other three stared at her, visibly aghast, and she chuckled.

"I did say 'almost,'" she pointed out. "Frankly, does anyone in this room think she wouldn't have been more likely to respect my confidence than several members of Congress we could mention right off hand?"

"Put that way, I suppose she would have," Theisman admitted.

"There's no 'supposing' to it," LePic said sourly. "Younger? McGwire?" He shuddered.

"Now, I almost wish I'd gone ahead and told her," Pritchart continued thoughtfully. "Given the depth and murkiness of the water we're all floundering around in at the moment, I'd really like to know what *she'd* think about the possibility of a Giancola-Manpower connection."

Chapter Thirty-Five

HONOR ALEXANDER-HARRINGTON sat silently on her flag bridge as HMS *Imperator* decelerated steadily towards the planet of her birth. Nimitz was on the back of her command chair, but not lying stretched along it as he usually was. Instead, he sat bolt upright, gazing into the visual display with her. The two of them might have been carved out of stone, and the silence on the bridge was absolute.

Honor's expression was calm, almost serene, but inside, where thoughts and emotions ought to have been, there was only a vast, singing silence, as empty as the vacuum beyond her flagship's hull.

She no longer needed to look at the plot. Its icons had already told her how short of reality her dread had fallen. The space about the system's two inhabited planets was crowded with shipping, showing far greater numbers of impeller signatures than would have been permitted in such proximity when Eighth Fleet departed for the Haven System. But those ships weren't the evidence her fears might have been too dark—that the damage had actually been less severe than she'd dreaded. No, *those* ships were the proof it had been even worse, for they were still only sorting through the wreckage, better than two weeks after the actual attack, and warning beacons marked prodigious spills of debris—and bodies—which had once been the heart and bone of the Star Empire of Manticore's industrial might.

It's odd, a corner of her brain whispered. *There was wreckage*

470

after the Battle of Manticore, too, but not like this. Oh, no. Not like this. This time every single warship we lost was caught docked, *not destroyed in action. And most of the dead are* civilians *this time.*

A sense of failure flowed through her, steadily, with all the patience of an ocean, and with it came shame. A dark guilt that burned like chilled vitriol, for she had failed in the solemn promise she'd made when she was seventeen T-years old. The vow she'd kept for all the years between then and now—honored with a fidelity which only made her present failure infinitely worse. This was *exactly* what she'd joined the Navy all those years ago to prevent. This was the wreckage of *her* star nation, these were the bodies of *her* civilians, and all of it was the work of enemies *she* was supposed to have stopped before they ever got close enough to play atrocity's midwife.

Nimitz made a small, soft sound of protest, and she felt him leaning forward, pressing against the back of her neck. She knew, in the part of her brain where conscious thought lived, that he was right. She hadn't even been here. When this attack came sweeping through her star system like a tsunami, she'd been over a light-century away, doing her best to end a war. She wasn't the one who'd let it past her.

But however right he might have been, he was still wrong, she thought grimly. No, she hadn't been here. But she was a full admiral in her Queen's service. She was one of the Royal Navy's most senior officers, one of the people who planned and executed its strategy.

One of the people responsible for visualizing threats and stopping them.

Imperator settled into orbit, farther out than usual to clear the debris fields which had once been Her Majesty's Space Station *Vulcan*, and she gazed at the image of her home world, so far below.

"Excuse me, Your Grace," a voice said quietly.

Honor turned her head and looked at Lieutenant Commander Harper Brantley, her staff communications officer.

"Yes, Harper?"

It was wrong, she thought, that her voice should sound so ordinary, so normal.

"You have a communications request," Brantley told her. "It's from the Admiralty, Your Grace," he added when she arched an eyebrow. "The request is coded private."

"I see." She stood, held out her arms, and caught Nimitz as he leapt gracefully into them. "I'll take it in my briefing room," she continued, cradling the 'cat as she walked across the bridge.

"Yes, Ma'am."

Honor felt Waldemar Tümmel watching her. Her young flag lieutenant had been hit even harder than most of her personnel by the news from home, given that his parents and two of his four siblings had all lived aboard *Hephaestus*. Their deaths hadn't yet been confirmed—not as far as anyone aboard *Imperator* knew, at any rate—but there was no optimism in his bleak emotions. She'd done her best to reach out to him during the voyage back to Manticore by way of Trevor's Star, tried to help him through his anxious grief, but she'd failed. Worse, she didn't know if she'd failed because that grief was too deep or because her own mingled grief and guilt had kept her from trying hard enough.

Yet despite everything, he continued to do his duty. Partly because its familiar demands were comforting, something he could cling to and concentrate upon to distract himself from thoughts of his family. Even more, though, she knew, it was because it *was* his duty. Because he refused to allow what had happened to his universe to prevent him from discharging his responsibilities.

Now she felt him wondering if she would need him in the briefing room, and she looked at him long enough to shake her head. He gazed at her for an instant, then nodded and settled back into his bridge chair.

Spencer Hawke, on the other hand, never even hesitated. He simply followed his Steadholder across her flag bridge and into the briefing room, then arranged himself against the bulkhead behind her.

Honor felt him there, at her back. Technically, she supposed, she should have instructed him to wait outside the briefing room door, given the security code Brantley had said the message carried. That thought had crossed her mind more than once over the years, in similar situations, yet it had never even occurred to her to actually do it with Andrew LaFollet, and she knew she would never do it with Hawke, either. He was a Grayson armsman, and he would guard his steadholder's secrets with the same iron fidelity with which he guarded her life.

She seated herself, set Nimitz on the conference table to one side of her terminal, and brought up the display.

"Put it through, Harper," she told the com officer when his image appeared.

"Yes, Ma'am," he replied, and disappeared, to be replaced almost instantly by a brown-haired, brown-eyed man of average build in the uniform of a captain of the list. She recognized him immediately.

"Good afternoon, Jackson," she said.

"Good afternoon, Your Grace," Captain Jackson Fargo replied quietly. "It's good to see you home again, although I wish it were under other circumstances."

"I know." She smiled briefly at the man who headed Hamish Alexander-Harrington's Admiralty House staff. "It's good to see you again, too, with the same proviso."

"Thank you, Your Grace." Fargo gave her a small half-bow, then cleared his throat. "The First Lord asked me to screen you. He's actually on Sphinx at this moment. Well, more accurately, he's aboard a shuttle which happens to be headed in your direction at this moment. His ETA is about twelve minutes, and he asked me to tell you he would very much like to join you aboard your flagship when he arrives, if that would be convenient."

A tiny flicker of joy flashed like distant lightning across the horizon of the emptiness within her, and she felt herself smiling ever so slightly.

"I believe, Captain," Lady Dame Honor Alexander-Harrington told him, "that I'll be able to find the time somehow."

God, he looks terrible!

The thought flicked through Honor's mind the instant Hamish swung across the boarding tube's interface and into the internal gravity of *Imperator*'s boat bay.

She felt Nimitz's agreement and tasted a fresh stab of the treecat's own concern as Samantha looked across at them from her perch on Hamish's shoulder. Nimitz's mate looked worn, exhausted. Her normally immaculate pelt was almost disheveled, and her tail hung down Hamish's back like the banner of a defeated army.

Hamish looked almost as bad, Honor thought. But then she realized that wasn't really true. His shoulders were as square as always, his back as straight, his head unbowed. He carried himself with assurance, and only someone who knew him well might have noted the fresh lines on his face, the fresh silver at his temples, the shadows in his blue eyes. But Honor didn't need those physical signs. She could taste—share—his inner exhaustion, and beneath his duty to show the confident face the public—and his subordinates—needed to see, there was a bottomless, brooding grief. A sense of failure that fully matched her own, and something else, even darker and more personal. Less corrosive than her own guilt—though she knew he shared that, as well—but colder and even more crushing.

No sign of those emotions was permitted to show as he formally requested the boat bay officer of the deck's permission to board the ship. Then he was through the formalities, past the sideboys, past Captain Cardones, with Tobias Stimson, his own armsman at his heels. Sergeant Stimson was as alert and professional looking as always, the perfect example of a Grayson armsman, yet when she looked at him, she tasted his own dark night of the soul, like a mirror of Hamish's and Samantha's.

Concern for both of them—all three of them—flared through her, but then Hamish was there, holding out his hand to her.

She took it in the formal handshake to which they were always careful to restrict themselves on official occasions, and she felt a fresh stab of concern as she realized his fingers were actually trembling slightly with exhaustion and the terrible, midnight-black grief that rode his shoulders like some hunched, ravenous beast. She stood there, looking into his eyes for a heartbeat which seemed to last forever, seeing that beast's shadows in those blue depths, and then she let go of his hand. Before even she realized what she was doing, her arms went about him, instead, and she closed her own eyes, leaning forward to rest her cheek on his shoulder.

For just an instant, he stiffened as she abruptly abandoned formality. But only for an instant, and then his arms tightened around her, hugging her while Samantha and Nimitz crooned to one another.

"Welcome home," he whispered in her ear. "Oh, God—welcome *home*, Honor."

❖   ❖   ❖

"Well," Honor said in a determinedly light tone as the lift carried them towards her quarters, "we've just put naval discipline back a century or so."

"Frankly," Hamish said, one arm still around her, "I'm not too worried about the precedent. After all, how many fleet commanders are going to be married to first lords?"

"Not many, I suppose," she conceded, but she tasted the determination with which he sought to match her own light tone and knew how hard he found it.

The lift car stopped, the doors opened, and she, Hamish, Nimitz, Samantha, Hawke, and Stimson headed down the passage to her quarters. Clifford McGraw had the duty outside her door, and he came to attention, saluted her and Hamish, then nodded to Stimson and Hawke and hit the door button.

The panel slid aside, and Honor and Hamish stepped through it. Somewhat to her surprise, neither Hawke nor Stimson made any move to follow them. She stopped and looked back over her shoulder, and her eyebrows rose in even greater surprise, for Stimson had his hand on Hawke's shoulder. Even among the personal armsmen of a Garsyon steadholder, noncoms didn't usually physically stop one of their officers in the pursuit of his duty, and she looked a question at both of them. She more than half expected an explanation, but instead, Hawke only shook his head, nodded in Hamish's direction, and then closed the door behind them.

"My God," Honor said. "I can't believe all *three* of them are just going to stand out there in the hall without at least making sure there are no ruthless assassins hiding in the sleeping cabin! I don't suppose *you* had anything to do with Toby's little contribution to Spencer's decision?"

"Not me," Hamish replied, and shrugged with a strained smile. "They're probably just giving us a little privacy." There was something odd about his tone, she thought, but before she had time to consider it he went on. "And, frankly, if that's what Toby was thinking, it was a damned good idea. Lord knows we can use it."

"Amen to that," she said fervently, and walked back into his arms.

They stood that way for quite some time, with Nimitz leaning forward from Honor's shoulder to rub his cheek against Samantha's. Then Honor straightened and stepped back with a ghost of a smile.

"It's all right, Mac," she called out, raising her voice slightly. "You can come out now."

Hamish made a sound which might someday turn into a chuckle again as James MacGuiness poked his head through the hatch from his steward's pantry.

"Hello, Mac," the earl said.

"Good afternoon, Milord," MacGuiness replied with all of his customary aplomb. "Might I offer you a little something?"

"Actually, you can offer me a glass of whiskey," Hamish said. "A rather large one. Some of Her Grace's Glenlivet Grand Reserve. And don't contaminate it with ice."

"Of course, Milord. And for you, Your Grace?"

"I think it's still a little early for me to start in on the whiskey," Honor said, with a thoughtful glance at Hamish. "Make it an Old Tilman, please."

MacGuiness bowed slightly and vanished back into his pantry, but only for a few seconds. How he got the specified beverages into their glasses that quickly, with a perfect head on her stein of beer, was simply fresh proof of his magical abilities, in Honor's opinion.

She took the beer with a small smile of thanks, and he smiled back, handed Hamish his whiskey, and disappeared once more. This time, the door closed quietly behind him.

Honor looked at Hamish, then waved her beer at the couch facing her coffee table. Hamish nodded in silent agreement, then sat, and she settled herself beside him. His arm went back around her, and he took a deep swallow from his glass before he leaned back, closed his eyes, and exhaled in a long, ragged sound of weariness she knew he would never have let anyone else hear.

Nimitz and Samantha had flowed onto the other end of the couch, where they were curled tightly together with Samantha's muzzle buried against Nimitz while he crooned to her and his true-hands caressed her long, silken coat.

The four of them sat that way for a time which could not possibly have been as long as it seemed, simply absorbing the comfort of the others' presence. But for all her joy at seeing him again, the dark thunderhead of his mind-glow—and Samantha's—hammered at her empathic sense like a hurricane just beyond the horizon. The minutes stretched out, and then, finally, he took another pull at his drink and opened his eyes again.

"I need this," he said softly, and she knew he wasn't talking about the whiskey. "I can't believe how *badly* I need this. And Emily is going to need it, too, as soon as you can get dirtside on Manticore."

"I want to see her, too," Honor told him equally quietly. "But I don't think it's going to happen soon." He looked at her, and her smile was more crooked than usual. "Hamish, we're already taking advantage of our positions, just sitting here. I don't think anybody's going to complain, and I'm pretty sure we've got enough official business to discharge to keep us from feeling *too* guilty. But I'm not going to abuse my authority by cutting myself orders to Manticore or Sphinx to see *my* family when the rest of the people under my command can't do the same thing."

The darkness flared within him as she spoke. For a moment, she thought it was anger at her refusal to abuse the privileges of her rank, but its taste wasn't quite right for that. She was still trying to parse his emotions out when he shook his head.

"You won't have to cut yourself any orders, Honor," he said. "And it won't be a case of favoritism, either. Trust me, Elizabeth's going to want you on Manticore as fast as you can get there. She's going to want to hear how Pritchart and her people reacted to all this. And she's going to want *your* reaction to it, as well."

She started to object, then changed her mind. He was undoubtedly right, after all.

"I suppose that's fairly inevitable," she admitted instead, and he snorted.

"You can leave out the 'fairly,'" he told her, and she smiled briefly. But then her smile faded, and she set her untasted beer on the coffee table and reached out with her flesh-and-blood hand to touch the side of his face.

"All right," she said. "I take your point. And I won't even try to pretend I don't want to see Emily as badly as she wants to see me. Or as badly as I want to see the kids, for that matter. But I think you're forgetting I can taste mind-glows, Hamish."

His eyes darkened, as if shutters had just come down behind them, and her fingers stroked his cheek gently.

"Whatever it is, you can't protect me from it forever," she said very softly.

"I—"

He stopped, looking into her face, then exhaled.

"I know," he said, and she tasted the pain behind the words, the realization that despite how desperately important to him she was, she was also only one of literally millions of people who couldn't be "protected from it forever." Not that realizing that kept him from wishing with all his heart and soul that he could.

"So tell me," she said.

He looked at her a moment longer. She felt him steel himself, felt him gathering himself the way both of them had gathered themselves as missiles began to fly and people under their command began to die.

"Debris from the strike on *Vulcan* got through to the planet," he said, and his voice was flat, harsh, the words quick and unflinching, offering her the stark honesty of one professional officer to another, now that the moment had finally come. "One of the tugs—the *Quay*—did her damnedest, but she couldn't catch it all. One of the strikes, a big one, probably up in the multi-hundred thousand-ton range," he looked straight into her eyes, "took out Yawata Crossing, Honor. The entire city."

Someone punched Honor squarely in the chest. She stared at him, literally unable for several seconds to process the information. Then she sucked in a deep, agonized breath, and he reached out to take her face between both his hands and leaned forward until their foreheads touched.

"All three of your aunts," he said, and his voice was soft, now, the voice of her lover and husband, shadowed with his own grief at inflicting this upon her. "Your Uncle Al was away on business, but Jason and Owen were both at home. So"—he inhaled deeply again—"were all the kids. And your cousin Devon, and his wife, and two of the children. Matthias and Frieda. Holly and Eric. Martha." He closed his eyes. "Al is all right—or as close to it as a man can be when his wife and kids are...And Devon's daughter Sarah, and your cousin Benedict and cousin Leah, were all away. But the rest were all there. It was your Aunt Clarissa's birthday, and..."

His voice died, and tears trickled down Honor's cheeks as the list went on and on in her mind, adding the other names. All the names. The Harrington clan was a large one, but most of its members had always lived in and around Yawata Crossing, and family affairs—like birthdays—were important to them. They always gathered for moments like that, all of them who could, and she pictured them there, laughing and teasing the guest of honor as they always did. Her father's sisters, their husbands, their children—their *grand*children. Cousins and in-laws.

"I'm sorry, love," he whispered. "I'm *so* sorry."

She tasted his love, his shared grief, the pain he felt for her pain and the special guilt he felt for having inflicted it upon her.

She knew, now, what monster had ridden his shoulders...and why there'd been no mention of collateral damage to Sphinx in any of the official correspondence which had accompanied her recall. Hamish Alexander-Harrington was the First Lord of Admiralty, and whether it had been an abuse of his position or not hadn't really mattered to him. She was not going to learn about something like this through some cold letter or recorded message. No, he'd taken that crushing task upon himself, in person. She knew that now, just as she knew he wasn't done yet.

"Tell me the rest," she said, and her voice was just as harsh as his had been, ribbed with the steely self control fighting to hold back the darkness.

"Andrew and Miranda were taking Raoul to Clarissa's party," he said, and her heart seemed to stop. "Your dad and the twins were supposed to be there, too, but there'd been some kind of delay. They were in transit between Manticore and Sphinx when the attack hit. They came through it just fine, and Andrew, Raoul, and Lindsey had swung by your parents' place to pick up your mom. They hadn't gotten to Clarissa's yet, either, but Miranda—"

He shook his head, and she closed her eyes. *Not Miranda, too, God,* she prayed. *Not Miranda, too!*

She heard both 'cats keening their own lament, and a fresh spasm of anguish went through her.

Of course, she thought. *Of course Farragut was with her. And no wonder Toby saw to it that Hamish and I could be alone when he told me.*

"Andrew?" she heard her own voice ask. "Raoul and Mother?"

The look he gave her filled her with terror. Her own shocked grief and pain threatened to drown the universe, yet even through it, she tasted his mind-glow. Knew he would rather have had his own heart ripped out than bring her this news.

"Raoul and your mother are fine," he said quickly, then made a harsh, ugly sound deep in his throat. "Well, as fine as they can be. But they were too close to the Yawata strike. Andrew got the two of them—and Lindsey—punched out in time, and they're all fine, although Lindsey came out of it with a badly broken collarbone. But—"

His hands slid down from her face, and his arms went back around her.

"He ran out of time, love," he whispered. "He got the three of them out, but he and Jeremiah were still in the limo when the blast front hit it."

Honor Alexander-Harrington had forgotten there could be that much pain in the universe. She knew it was a miracle her mother and her son had survived, and she knew she would never be able to express how unspeakably grateful she was for that incredible gift.

Yet that gift came at the price of a dark and personal agony, for it was the last gift, the last miracle, Andrew LaFollet would ever give her. And now, the last—and the most beloved—of her original Grayson armsmen was gone.

I made him Raoul's armsman to keep him safe. *To keep him away from me, from the way people keep* dying *for me.* The thought trickled through the tearing anguish. *I tried. God, I tried to keep him safe.*

But she'd failed. Even then, she knew it wasn't truly her fault, just as she knew that if Andrew had known exactly what was going to happen, he would have done exactly the same thing. That her armsman had died knowing precisely what he was doing and knowing he'd succeeded. That was something. In time, it might actually help her deal with this numbing sense of devastation, but not now. Not yet.

"Your mother insisted that all of them—including your father—go to White Haven, to be with Emily," Hamish's voice went on after a moment from the dark void which surrounded her. "That was her official argument, anyway. Mostly, though . . . Mostly, I think, it was an excuse to get your father away from Yawata Crossing. It wasn't as if there was anything they could have done there, Honor. Not after something like that."

"Of course not." She felt the tears flowing, and the guilt she'd felt before, the sense of failure, was a knife in her heart. "Mother was right. She usually is."

"I know," he said quietly, changing position to pull her face down against his shoulder while Nimitz and Samantha cuddled tightly against her.

"Somehow," she heard herself say, and the steel had gone out of her voice, replaced by dead, defeated flatness, "I never thought about this. Never worried about it—not really. I *thought* I had, but I know better now. I never really let myself think that it could have happened. That I could have *let* it happen."

"You didn't!" he said softly, fiercely. "There wasn't one, solitary *damned* thing you could have done to stop this, Honor."

"But we should have. We were *supposed* to. It's our *job*, Hamish, and what *use* are we if we can't even do our jobs?"

Hamish Alexander-Harrington heard the grief, the pain, in that dead soprano voice, and he understood it. Better than he'd ever understood anything in his life, in that moment, he understood exactly what his wife was feeling, for he'd felt it himself. But his arms tightened around her, and he shook his head hard.

"You aren't thinking a single thing *I* haven't already thought," he told her. "If it was anyone's 'job,' Honor, it was the Admiralty's. So, trust me, love, there's not one single, ugly, hateful thing you can think about yourself that I haven't already thought about myself. But we're both wrong. Yes, keeping this from happening is what our lives have been about ever since we put on the uniform. But you weren't even *here* when it happened, and *nobody* saw it coming. Nobody was asleep at the switch, Honor. Nobody ignored anything. Every damned one of us did our jobs, exactly the way we were supposed to, and this time, it just wasn't enough. Somebody got past us because they came at us in a way no one could have predicted."

She stiffened in his embrace, and even without her own empathic ability, he could literally feel her effort to reject what he'd just said, to continue to punish herself. But he wouldn't let go—not with his arms, not with the fierce embrace of his heart. He held her ruthlessly, knowing she could feel what he felt, knowing she couldn't escape his love.

For a long, long moment the tension held, and then she sagged against him, and he felt the deep, almost silent sobs shuddering through her. He closed his eyes again, holding her against himself, cradling her in his arms and his love.

He never really knew, later, how long they sat there. It seemed to last forever, yet finally, she shifted slightly, pillowing her head on his shoulder, and he tugged a handkerchief from his pocket and dried her eyes.

"Better?" he asked very quietly.

"Some," she replied, although she wasn't at all certain that was actually the truth. "Some."

"I'm sorry, love," he said again, softly.

"I know." She patted the arm still around her gently. "I know."

There was another long moment of silence, and then she inhaled deeply and sat up straight.

"I'll miss them," she told her husband, and her voice remained soft, but her eyes were not. They glittered, still bright with tears, yet there was a darkness beneath that glitter, a hardness beneath those tears.

Hamish Alexander-Harrington knew his wife as only two humans who had both been adopted by a pair of mated treecats ever could. He'd seen her deal with joy and with sorrow, with happiness and with fury, with fear, and even with despair. Yet in all the years since their very first meeting at Yeltsin's Star, he suddenly realized, he had never actually met the woman the newsies called "the Salamander." It wasn't his fault, a corner of his brain told him, because he'd never been in the right *place* to meet her. Never at the right time. He'd never had the chance to stand by her side as she took a wounded heavy cruiser on an unflinching deathride into the broadside of the battlecruiser waiting to kill it, sailing to her own death, and her crew's, to protect a planet full of strangers while the rich beauty of Hammerwell's "Salute to Spring" spilled from her ship's com system. He hadn't stood beside her on the dew-soaked grass of the Landing City duelling grounds, with a pistol in her hand and vengeance in her heart as she faced the man who'd bought the murder of her first great love. Just as he hadn't stood on the floor of Steadholders' Hall when she faced a man with thirty times her fencing experience across the razor-edged steel of their swords, with the ghosts of Reverend Julius Hanks, the butchered children of Mueller Steading, and her own murdered steaders at her back.

But now, as he looked into the unyielding flint of his wife's beloved, almond eyes, he knew he'd met the Salamander at last. And he recognized her as only another warrior could. Yet he also knew in that moment that for all his own imposing record of victory in battle, he was not and never had been her equal. As a tactician and a strategist, yes. Even as a fleet commander. But not as the very embodiment of devastation. Not as the Salamander. Because for all the compassion and gentleness which were so much a part of her, there was something else inside Honor Alexander-Harrington, as well. Something he himself had never had. She'd told him, once, that her own temper frightened her. That she sometimes thought she could have been a monster under the wrong set of circumstances.

And now, as he realized he'd finally met the monster, his heart twisted with sympathy and love, for at last he understood what she'd been trying to tell him. Understood why she'd bound it with the chains of duty, and love, of compassion and honor, of pity, because, in a way, she'd been right. Under the wrong circumstances, she could have been the most terrifying person he had ever met.

In fact, at this moment, she *was*.

It was a merciless something, her "monster"—something that went far beyond military talent, or skills, or even courage. Those things, he knew without conceit, he, too, possessed in plenty. But not that deeply personal something at the core of her, as unstoppable as Juggernaut, merciless and colder than space itself, that no sane human being would ever willingly rouse. In that instant her husband knew, with an icy shiver which somehow, perversely, only made him love her even more deeply, that as he gazed into those agate-hard eyes, he looked into the gates of Hell itself. And whatever anyone else might think, he knew now that there was no fire in Hell. There was only the handmaiden of death, and ice, and purpose, and a determination which would not—*could not*—relent or rest.

"I'll miss them," she told him again, still with that dreadful softness, "but I won't forget. I'll *never* forget, and one day—*one day, Hamish*—we're going to find the people who did this, you and I. And when we do, the only thing I'll ask of God is that He let them live long enough to know who's killing them."

Chapter Thirty-Six

"THANK YOU FOR AGREEING to see me, My Lady. I realize this is a difficult time for you."

"Don't thank me, Judah," Honor replied, standing behind her Landing mansion's desk as James MacGuiness escorted Admiral Judah Yanakov into her office. MacGuiness' composed, professional expression might have fooled a lot of people, but not someone who knew him...and Yanakov did. Honor tasted the Grayson admiral's concern for her steward's grief, as well as her own, and she smiled sadly, almost wistfully, as she gripped Yanakov's extended hand. "It's 'a difficult time' for a lot of people right now."

"I understand, My Lady."

Yanakov looked at her searchingly, not trying to hide his concern, and she met his gaze squarely. She was fairly certain he was one of the handful of people who'd figured out she could actually sense the emotions of those about her, although she wasn't at all sure whether he realized she could do it on her own, without Nimitz's presence. In any case, he'd never made any attempt to hide his respect and his genuine affection for her from her, and there was a clean, caring flavor to his worry about her.

Of course, there was something else, as well. She'd expected that when he requested a face-to-face meeting on such short notice.

"Have a seat," she invited, and he settled into the indicated chair, looking out with her across the waters of Jason Bay through the crystoplast wall. "Can we offer you something?" she added, and he shook his head.

"I think we're all right then, Mac," she said, looking up at MacGuiness, and the steward managed an almost normal-looking smile before he bowed slightly and withdrew. She watched him go, then turned her own attention back to the crystoplast.

There was a storm coming in, she thought, gazing at the black clouds rolling towards the city across the angry whitecaps. A storm that mirrored the one in her own soul.

The final, official count of fatalities was still far from complete, but she knew only too well what it had been for her own family. Aside from her mother and father, the twins, and Hamish, Emily, Raoul, and Katherine, she had exactly five close surviving relatives in the Star Empire. That number would be reduced to four very soon now, because Allen Duncan—her Aunt Dominique's husband—had decided to return to Beowulf. There were too many memories on Sphinx, too much pain when he thought about his wife and all four of his children. Much as he'd come to love Manticore, he needed the comfort of his birth world and the family he had there.

Beyond him, her immediate family, her cousin Sarah, who'd suddenly become the second Countess Harrington, and Benedict and Leah Harrington, her Aunt Clarissa's surviving children, her closest living Manticoran relative was a fifth cousin. She knew how unspeakably lucky she was to still have her parents, her brother and sister, and her own children, but it was hard—*hard*—to feel grateful when all the rest of her family had been blotted away as brutally and completely as Black Rock Clan.

Nimitz stirred unhappily on his perch by the windows as that thought flickered across her mind, and she tasted his echo of the grief which had swept through every treecat clan on Sphinx. Honor knew, now, that Nimitz and Samantha's decision to move their own family to Grayson had been part of a deliberate, fundamental change in treecat thinking. She suspected that Samantha had played a greater role in pushing through that change than she was prepared to admit to the two-legs, but it had clearly been a reaction to the 'cats' awareness of the dangers human weaponry posed. Yet that awareness had been as close to purely intellectual as a treecat was likely to come. It had been a precaution against a threat they could theoretically envision, but not something the vast majority of them had ever *expected* to happen.

That had changed, now.

Frankly, Honor wouldn't have blamed the 'cats if they'd decided that what had happened to Black Rock Clan was proof their long ago ancestors had been right to have nothing to do with humans. If they'd blamed even their own humans for letting things come to such a pass in a war which was none of the treecats' affair and turned their backs on any future relationship with them.

They hadn't done that. Perhaps it was because they were so much like humans, in some ways. Or perhaps it was because they *weren't*—because they were such uncomplicated, straightforward people, without humanity's unfailing ability to seek someone close at hand to blame for disasters. Whatever the reason, their response had been not simply grief, not simply shock, but anger. Anger directed not at their own two-legs, but at whoever was really responsible. Cold, focused, *lethal* anger. Honor had always known, far better than the rest of humanity, just how dangerous a single treecat's anger could be. Now the bitter fury of the entire species was directed to a single end, and if some people might have found the thought that a race of small, furry, flint-knapping arboreals could pose any serious threat to someone who commanded superdreadnoughts was ludicrous, Honor Alexander-Harrington did not. Perhaps that was because *she* was too much like a 'cat, she thought. She knew, without question or doubt, where her own anger was going to lead in the end, and so she understood the treecats only too well.

She gave herself a mental shake. She'd been wandering down dark and dangerous side roads in her own thoughts over the past few days. She wasn't alone in that—she knew that perfectly well—but she forced herself to back away from the cold iron of her own icy hatred, from the distilled essence of her vengeful fury, and concentrate once again on the more natural storm moving in across Jason Bay.

The surf would be piling higher against the seawall of the marina where her sloop *Trafalgar* was currently moored, she thought after a moment, and made a mental note to have someone check the boat's security. She really ought to do that herself, but there was no way she'd have time for it, even assuming Spencer or any of her other armsmen would have been prepared to let her out of the house long enough to attend to it.

That thought leaked even through the cinders and ash of her

rage and twitched the corners of her mouth in a temptation to smile. Spencer hadn't been happy about her decision to take *Trafalgar* out all by herself immediately after she'd finished her face-to-face briefings with Elizabeth at Mount Royal Palace. He'd tried to insist she take at least one of her armsmen along, but she'd flatly refused. She hadn't been able to prevent him from flying top cover with no less than three sting ships, a tractor-equipped air car, and a standby SAR diver, but at least she'd been able to keep him high enough above her for her to find a shadow of the solitude she and Nimitz had needed so badly.

The weather had been blustery that day, too, if not as energetic as the Bay looked today, and it had been too long since she'd smelled saltwater and felt spray on her face. But *Trafalgar*'s familiar motion, the kick of the wheel against her hands, and the sluicing sound of water as the sloop heeled sharply, burying her lee rail in a smother of racing white foam, while seabirds cried plaintively overhead, had reconnected her to the sea. And with that, she'd been reconnected to the continuity of life, as well. The deaths of her family, of Miranda and Farragut, and of Andrew, were not going to leave her unscarred, just as no comfort short of vengeance could ever truly slake her fury. She knew that. But her soul had been scarred before, and she'd survived. She would survive this time, too, just as she would find that vengeance, and scars and retribution were not the only things in the universe. The iodine-smelling wind, the way the loose ends of her braid whipped on its strength, the surging motion of the deck, and the song of wind slicing around the stays and humming in the mast had swept through her like the tide of life itself.

She only wished she could get her father aboard *Trafalgar* for a weekend.

She shook that thought aside and returned her attention to Yanakov.

"I'm always happy to see you, Judah, but given how busy everyone is just now, I rather doubt this is purely a social occasion."

"As usual, My Lady, you're right," Yanakov admitted.

"Well then, Admiral Yanakov, let's be about it," she invited, and Yanakov smiled for a moment. Then he seemed to sober again.

"The main reason I'm here, My Lady, is to say goodbye."

"Goodbye?" Honor repeated a bit blankly.

"Yes, My Lady. I've been recalled. They need me back home."

"Oh?" Honor sat up straighter.

Reports of the attack which had hit Yeltsin's Star simultaneously with the one on the Manticore Binary System were still incomplete. Transit time was under four days for a dispatch boat, as compared to the roughly six and a half between the Junction's Trevor's Star terminus and the Haven System, so she'd known for days now that the Graysons had been pounded, as well. What she was short on were details. Which wasn't surprising, really. No doubt Grayson had enough wreckage of its own that needed sorting through before it could issue anything like definitive reports.

"You've gotten a more complete report from home?" she continued, and he nodded heavily.

"I have. In fact, I brought a copy of it for you."

He slipped a chip folio out of the inside pocket of his tunic and laid it on the corner of her desk. She wasn't surprised that it had been delivered directly to her instead of coming through the Admiralty, given that she was the second ranking officer of the Grayson Space Navy, even if she was on "detached duty" to her birth star nation.

"How bad is it?" she asked quietly.

"Bad," he said flatly. "In fact, it's worse than the original estimates. Blackbird is gone, My Lady, and it looks like we lost virtually a hundred percent of the workforce."

Honor's stomach muscles tightened. It wasn't a surprise, however much she might have wished the preliminary reports had been wrong. Given the dispersed architecture of the Blackbird yards, she'd at least dared to hope the attack might have been a little less effective than the one on the concentrated capacity of *Hephaestus* and *Vulcan*. At the same time, though, she'd realized that anyone who could put together an operation as conceptually daring and as brilliantly executed as the one which had cauterized the Star Empire would have recognized the differences between her targets and planned accordingly. Apparently, she had.

"They don't seem to have used as many of those graser-armed remote platforms of theirs," Yanakov continued, as if he'd heard her thoughts, "but they used a lot more missiles and kinetic strikes to compensate. According to the Office of Shipbuilding, at least ninety-six percent of the physical plant was destroyed outright or damaged beyond repair. And, as I say, personnel losses were near total."

Honor nodded, and fresh shadows gathered in her eyes. She'd

been one of the major investors when Blackbird was built, and the economic loss was going to be a severe blow in a financial sense. That was totally immaterial to her, however, beside the *human* cost. Almost a third of the total workforce had been from Harrington Steading itself or employed by Skydomes. And over eighteen percent of those employees had been women—a stupendous percentage for patriarchal Grayson, even now.

"The only good news is that Blackbird was far enough away from the planet that we didn't take any collateral damage to the orbital habitats or farms. Or"—his eyes met hers—"to the planet itself, of course."

"Thank God for that," Honor said with soft, intense sincerity.

"We had even more new construction caught in the yards," he went on, "but we didn't have many ships in for repairs or overhaul, so at least we were spared that."

"And they want you back home to take over the system defenses," Honor said, nodding. But Yanakov shook his head.

"I'm afraid not, My Lady," he said quietly. "The latest dispatch boat from Grayson brought me direct orders from the Protector. He sent a personal message for you, as well." The Grayson admiral took another chip folio from his tunic and laid it beside the first one. "I'm sure it will explain everything in greater detail, but I wanted to tell you personally."

"Tell me what, Judah?" Honor sat back in her chair. "You're beginning to make me a little nervous, you know."

"I'm sorry, My Lady. That wasn't my intention. But"—Yanakov inhaled deeply—"I wanted to tell you myself that I've been appointed High Admiral."

For a moment, it didn't register. Then Honor's eyes widened, and she felt her head shaking in futile, instinctive rejection.

They sat in silence for several seconds until, finally, it was her turn to draw a breath.

"Wesley was out at Blackbird?" she said softly.

"Yes, My Lady. I'm sorry. He was there for a stupid, routine conference." Yanakov shook his own head, his eyes bright with mingled sorrow and anger. "Just one of those things. But I know how close the two of you were. That's why I wanted to tell you in person. And," he managed an unhappy smile, "to assure you that if you should happen to want the assignment, it's yours. After all, you're senior to me."

"Not on a bet, Judah," she replied almost instantly. "I know how much Hamish hates being tied to the Admiralty, and I know how much Wesley hated having to give up a space-going command. I don't think I'd like it any more than either of them." She shook her head again, much more firmly. "They're not getting *me* off a flag deck that easily! Not now, especially."

Her voice turned harsher on the last sentence, and Yanakov nodded.

"I was afraid that was what you'd say," he admitted. "I thought it might be worth a try, at least, though."

"I'd do almost anything for you, Judah," she told him. "*Almost* anything."

Yanakov chuckled. It sounded a bit odd—perhaps because both of them had heard so few chuckles in the last few weeks—but it also sounded remarkably natural. As if they might actually get used to hearing it again, sometime. Then he stood and extended his hand again.

"I'm afraid they want me home in a hurry, My Lady. I'm headed back aboard the same dispatch boat and it's scheduled to break Manticore orbit in less than two hours. So I'm afraid I have to say goodbye now."

"Of course."

Honor stood, but instead of taking his hand, she walked around the deck and stood facing him for perhaps two seconds. Then she put her arms around him and hugged him tightly.

She felt him stiffen instinctively, even after all these years. Which, she supposed, showed you could take the boy out of Grayson, but you couldn't take the Grayson out of the boy. But then his automatic response to being touched so intimately by a woman who was neither his wife nor his mother or sister disappeared, and he hugged her back. A bit tentatively, perhaps, but firmly.

A moment later, she stepped back, both hands on his shoulders, and smiled at him.

"I'm going to miss Wesley," she told him softly. "We're both going to miss a lot of people. And I know you don't really want the job, Judah. But I think Benjamin made the right pick."

"I hope so, My Lady. But when I think about the monumental mess we've got to clean up..." He shook his head.

"I know. But you and I have done that before, haven't we?"

He nodded again, remembering the horrific damage he'd helped her put right after they'd beaten off Operation Stalking Horse's assault on his home star system.

"Well, then," she said, and squeezed his shoulders. "On your way, High Admiral. And"—she looked into his eyes once more—"God bless, Judah."

✧   ✧   ✧

"Ladies and gentlemen, please find your seats," Fleet Admiral Rajampet invited loudly and, Daoud al-Fanudahi thought, completely unnecessarily. As far as he could tell, not one of the astronomically senior flag officers in the briefing room was out of his or her seat, and he found Rajampet's instruction symptomatic. The Navy had been spending quite a bit of time passing lots of *other* totally unnecessary orders back and forth, after all. When it hadn't been too busy panicking, at least. Or, even worse, posturing.

He wasn't absolutely certain which of the latter this particular meeting was going to do, but he had a bad feeling about it.

He himself, along with Irene Teague, was seated well back from the main conference table, as befitted their junior rank. And that, too, he found symptomatic. They were probably the only two people in the entire room who actually had a clue what was going on, so *of course* they were seated as far from the decision-makers as the physical limits of the briefing room permitted.

You know, he told himself a bit severely, *this tendency of yours to perpetually look on the dark side of things may be one of the reasons certain of your superiors think of you as an incurable pessimist—not to mention just a bit of an alarmist.*

Maybe it is, another corner of his mind replied, *but the real reason is that this pack of idiots doesn't want to face the fact that they've gotten their collective asses in a crack—and all the rest of the League along with them—because none of them have the least idea what they're up against. They're not about to admit that by actually asking questions that might give them a glimmer of reality. Especially not when asking would only prove how monumentally they screwed up by not asking sooner!*

Rajampet's unnecessary order had at least one beneficial consequence; it brought the whispered side conversations to an abrupt halt. The CNO looked around the other officers, eyes bright in their nest of wrinkles, and let the silence linger for a moment, then cleared his throat.

"I'm sure none of us need to recapitulate the events of the last several weeks," he began. "Obviously, all of us are dismayed by what happened to Admiral Crandall's task force at Spindle. And I think it would be fair to say," he continued in a deliberately judicious, soberly thoughtful tone, "that the efficacy of the Manticoran Navy's weapons has come as a most unpleasant surprise to all of us."

He allowed himself to glance—briefly—at Karl-Heinz Thimár and Cheng Hai-shwun. Other eyes followed his, but Thimár and Cheng had obviously realized this, or something like it, had to be coming. They sat there calmly, apparently oblivious to the looks coming their way. The bureaucratic infighter's number one rule, "Never let them see your fear," was well known to everyone around the table, but the two men ostensibly responsible for the SLN's intelligence arms were giving a bravura demonstration of it, and with very little sign of strain. Which, al-Fanudahi reflected, said a great deal about how highly placed their various relatives and patrons actually were.

"It would appear, however, that we aren't the only ones the Manties have pissed off," Rajampet continued after a second. "Intelligence is still working on determining exactly who was responsible for the attack on their home system. I'm sure we'll see some progress on that front quite soon."

Precisely what prompted that confidence on his part eluded Daoud al-Fanudahi, who happened to be the person who was supposed to be doing the progressing and who still didn't have even a glimmer of proof, whatever he might know instinctively had to be the truth.

"In the meantime, however, we have to consider how to respond to the Manties' blatant imperialism and arrogance," the CNO went on in that same, measured tone. "I don't believe there can be much doubt—especially in light of the Manties' decision to close all wormholes under their control to Solarian shipping—that what we're really looking at here on their part is a comprehensive strategy which they've been contemplating for some time. On the one hand, they've revealed their new weapons' capabilities; on the other, they're threatening our trade and economic life's blood. Both of those, obviously, are pointed suggestions that the League should stay out of their way instead of objecting to their expansionism in and beyond the Talbott Cluster."

Lord, don't any *of these idiots read our reports?* al-Fanudahi wondered behind an impassive face. *"Imperialism"? "Expansionism"? I don't know what the Manties are up to in Silesia, but that's the* last *thing that was on their mind when they got involved in Talbott! But do any of our lords and masters want to hear about that? Of course not! After all, it would* never *do to dispute Kolokoltsov's and Abruzzi's version of reality, would it?*

"Given that attitude on their part," Rajampet said, "it's unlikely they'll be inclined to respond favorably to the government's diplomatic initiatives. At the same time, however, they have to be reeling from what's happened to them. Let's face it, ladies and gentlemen—we got reamed at Spindle. But compared to what's happened to the Manties' home system, what happened to Admiral Crandall's task force was only a minor inconvenience, as far as the Navy and the League are concerned. Even with her entire force off the table, we still have over two thousand of the wall in full commission, another three hundred in refit or overhaul status, and better than eight thousand in reserve. Task Force 496 represented less than half of one percent of our total wall of battle and our support structure is completely unscathed, whereas the Manties have just had their entire industrial base blown out from under them. There's no meaningful comparison between the relative weight of those losses. They represent totally different orders of magnitude, and it has to be psychologically even worse for the Manties because it happened so soon after Spindle. From what had to be an incredible peak of confidence, they've had their feet kicked out from under them. At the moment, no matter how much money they have in the bank, and no matter how big their merchant marine—or even their remaining navy—may be, they're effectively no more than a fourth-rate power in terms of sustained capabilities, and don't think for a moment that they don't know that as well as we do."

The briefing room was silent, and even al-Fanudahi had to admit that, looked at from the perspective Rajampet had adopted, there was something to be said for his analysis. While al-Fanudahi wasn't even tempted to assume the Manticorans were simply going to obediently lie down and die for the League, he was forced to concede that their position was ultimately hopeless. It had probably been that way from the beginning, given the difference in size between the potential opponents, but the catastrophic destruction of their industrial base was decisive. He wished he had some idea of how big their ammunition stockpiles had been before the mysterious attack, but however big they'd been, that was all the missiles the Manties were going to have for a long, long time. So, in the end, they *were* going to lose if the SLN chose to press home an offensive.

Unfortunately, al-Fanudahi was unhappily certain they had more than enough missiles to make the price of the League's final victory almost unbearable. And that price, as Rajampet seemed to be forgetting (or ignoring) would be paid in the lives and blood of men and women who wore the same uniform he and al-Fanudahi did, not just in millions upon millions of tons of warships.

"What most of you are not aware of, however," Rajampet continued, "is that we have heavy forces considerably closer to Manticore than you may have believed. And far closer than the Manties could ever have anticipated. In fact, Admiral Filareta is currently in the Tasmania System, conducting a major fleet training exercise—Operation East Wind—with just over three hundred of the wall. Which means, of course, that he's only a very little more than four hundred light-years from Manticore and that he could reach that star system within a little over six weeks from receiving his orders . . . or approximately two and a half months from the date we dispatch them. Which means he should be in position, barring unanticpated delays, by May twentieth."

From the sudden stir which ran through the audience, the news of Filareta's forward deployment had come as almost as much a surprise to them as it had to al-Fanudahi. But Rajampet wasn't quite finished.

"In addition to the forces already under Admiral Filareta's command," he said, "we have the equivalent of another ten squadrons within approximately two weeks of Tasmania, all of which could be ordered to join him and arrive within that same window. Concentrated with his present units, that would give him a strength of almost four hundred of the wall. He'd still be considerably understrength—by The Book, at least—in screening units, and he doesn't have the logistic support Admiral Crandall had as part of Operation Winter Forage, but he's far closer to the Manties' front doorstep than they could possibly be anticipating."

Al-Fanudahi's heart sank. He'd hoped—prayed—that Rajampet would abandon this notion after his own briefings to Kingsford, Jennings and Bernard.

"What the Strategy Board and I propose," Rajampet told the gathered officers, "is to concentrate the units I've mentioned under Filareta's command and send him to Manticore."

The room was hushed, and he paused long enough to survey the faces looking back at him, then shrugged ever so slightly.

"I fully realize—as does the Strategy Board—that there's a degree of risk in the action we're contemplating. In our opinion, however, the potential gain vastly outweighs the risk. First, the Manties are quite probably going to be so disheartened by what's happened to their home system that much of their truculence will have been hammered out of them before Filareta ever arrives. Second, even if they should be so foolish as to attempt to resist him, their capacity to do so must have been seriously damaged in the course of any attack capable of penetrating to their inner-system space stations as this one did. Third, having a second fleet, six times the size of the one they confronted at Spindle, arrive in their *home system* this promptly has to drive home the totality of our quantitative advantage in any protracted struggle. And, fourth, ladies and gentlemen, we are currently redeploying the remainder of our active wallers towards Manticore and simultaneously beginning the largest activation of the Reserve in the Navy's history."

Al-Fanudahi wouldn't have believed the silence could get even more intense, but he would have been wrong. He wondered if any of those assembled flag officers were thinking about the constitutional implications of what Rajampet had just said. Even the broadest interpretation of Article Seven's "self-defense" clause had never been construed to cover a general mobilization of the Reserve without formal authorization from the civilian government. Kolokoltsov and his cronies, however, clearly doubted they could get that authorization without touching off a political dogfight such as the League had never seen. So at the moment, he and his fellow bureaucrats were simply going to look the other way and carry on with their "diplomatic efforts to resolve the crisis" while Rajampet did the dirty work. Which meant that, ultimately, the Navy was going to carry the can if it all blew up even half as catastrophically as al-Fanudahi was afraid it might.

Not to mention the millions of more men and women in Navy uniform who were going to get killed along the way.

"My own belief, and that of the Strategy Board, is that the

Manties will realize we aren't going to be bluffed or blackmailed, even by something as painful as Spindle, into simply giving them the blank check they want. Faced with Filareta's squadrons as the proof of our determination that their actions are not going to be allowed to stand, it seems most likely to us that they'll surrender to the inevitable rather than risk suffering even more fatalities and damage to their home system.

"At the same time, however, we realize there's no way to be certain of that, and we're prepared for the possibility that the Manties may be insane enough not to surrender. We're even prepared for the possibility that they may have sufficient of their new missiles available from existing stores to beat off Filareta's attack, at least temporarily. Which is why the redeployment of our active wall is designed to concentrate no fewer than an additional five hundred wallers on Tasmania—this time with complete logistical support and a powerful Frontier Fleet screen—within two and a half months. In three months' time, that total will reach six hundred. Which means we'll be able to dispatch a *second* wave, substantially larger and even more powerfully supported, against Manticore within a maximum of five months—long before they will have been able to restore sufficient industrial capacity to reammunition their own ships."

He looked around the briefing room once more.

"One way or the other, ladies and gentlemen," he said very quietly after several moments, "what happened at Spindle is *not* going to be allowed to stand. And, for the Manties' own sake, I hope they realize how serious we are before they make things even worse."

Chris Billingsley poured the final cup of coffee, set the carafe on the small side table, and withdrew without a word. Michelle Henke watched him go, then picked up her cup and sipped. Other people were doing the same thing around the conference table, and she wondered how many of them were using it as a stage prop in their effort to project a sense that the universe hadn't gone mad around them.

If they are, they aren't doing a very good job of it, she thought grimly. *On the other hand, neither am I because as near as I can tell, the universe* has *gone crazy.*

"All right," she said finally, lowering her cup and glancing at

Captain Lecter. "I suppose we may as well get down to it." She smiled without any humor at all. "I don't expect any of you to be any happier to hear this than I am. Unfortunately, after we do, we've got to decide what we're going to do about it, and I'm going to want recommendations for Admiral Khumalo and Baroness Medusa. So if any of you—and I mean *any* of you—happen to be struck by any brilliant insights in the course of Cindy's briefing, make a note of them. We're going to need all of them we can get."

Heads nodded, and she gestured to Lecter.

"The floor is yours, Cindy," she said.

"Yes, Ma'am."

Lecter didn't look any happier about the briefing she was about to give than her audience looked about what they knew they were going to hear. She spent a second or two studying the notes she'd made before she looked up and let her blue eyes look around the conference table.

"We have confirmation of the original reports," she said, "and it's as bad as we thought it would be. In fact, it's worse."

She drew a deep breath, then activated the holo display above the conference table, bringing up the first graphic.

"Direct, immediate civilian loss of life," she began, "was much worse than any pre-attack worst-case analysis of damage to the space stations had ever suggested, because there was absolutely no warning. As you can see from the graphic, the initial strike on *Hephaestus*—"

"I never realized just how much worse a victory could make a defeat taste," Augustus Khumalo said much later that evening.

He, Michelle, Michael Oversteegen, and Aivars Terekhov sat with Khumalo and Baroness Medusa on the ocean-side balcony of the governor's official residence. The tide was in, and surf made a soothing, rhythmic sound in the darkness, but no one felt very soothed at the moment.

"I know," Michelle agreed. "It kind of makes everything we've accomplished out here look a lot less important, doesn't it?"

"No, Milady, it most definitely does *not*," Medusa said so sharply that Michelle twitched in her chair and looked at the smaller woman in surprise.

"Sorry," Medusa said after a moment. "I didn't mean to sound as if I were snapping at you. But you—and Augustus and Aivars and Michael—have accomplished an enormous amount 'out here.' Don't ever denigrate your accomplishments—or yourselves—just because of bad news from somewhere else!"

"You're right," Michelle acknowledged after a moment. "It's just—"

"Just that it feels like the end of the world," Medusa finished for her when she seemed unable to find the words she'd been looking for.

"Maybe not quite that bad, but close," Michelle agreed.

"Well, it damned well should!" Medusa told her tartly. "Undervaluing your own accomplishments doesn't necessarily make you wrong about how deep a crack we're all in right now."

Michelle nodded. The Admiralty dispatches had pulled no punches. With the devastation of the home system's industrial capacity, the Royal Manticoran Navy found itself—for the first time since the opening phases of the First Havenite War—facing an acute ammunition shortage. And that shortage was going to get worse—a *lot* worse—before it got any better. Which was the reason all of Michelle's remaining shipboard Apollo pods were to be returned to Manticore as soon as possible. Given the concentration of Mark 16-armed units under her command, the Admiralty would try to make up for the differential by supplying her with all of those they could find, and both her warships and her local ammunition ships currently had full magazines. Even so, however, she was going to have to be extraordinarily circumspect in how she expended the rounds available to her, because there weren't going to be any more for quite a while.

"At least I don't expect anyone to be eager to poke his nose back into this particular hornets' nest anytime soon," she said out loud.

"Unless, of course, whoever hit the home system wants to send his 'phantom raiders' our way," Khumalo pointed out sourly.

"Unlikely, if you'll forgive me for sayin' so, Sir," Oversteegen observed. Khumalo looked at him, and Oversteegen shrugged. "Th' Admiralty's estimate that whoever did this was operatin' on what they used t' call 'a shoestring' seems t' me t' be well taken. And, frankly, if they *were* t' decide t' carry out additional attacks of this sort, anything here in th' Quadrant would have t' be far less valuable t' them than a follow up, knock out attack on th' home system."

"I think Michael's probably right, Augustus," Michelle said. "I don't propose taking anything for granted, and I've got Cindy and Dominica busy working out the best way to generate massive redundancy in our sensor coverage, just in case, but I don't see us as the logical candidate for the next sneak attack. If they *do* go after anything in the Quadrant, I'd imagine it would be the Terminus itself, since I can't see anything else out this way that would have equal strategic value for anyone who obviously doesn't like us very much. And that, fortunately or unfortunately, we're just going to have to leave in other peoples' hands."

Her uniformed fellows nodded, and Baroness Medusa tilted back her chair.

"Should I assume that—for the moment, at least—you feel relatively secure here in the Quadrant, then?"

"I think we probably are," Khumalo answered, instead of Michelle. He was, after all, the station commander. "There's a great deal to be said for Admiral Oversteegen's analysis where these mysterious newcomers are concerned. And, frankly, at the moment, the League doesn't have anything to send our way even if it had the nerve to do it. That could change in a few months, but for now, at least, they can't pose any kind of credible threat even against ships armed 'only' with Mark 16s."

"Good." Medusa's nostrils flared. "I only hope that sanity leaks out somewhere in the League before anyone manages to get additional forces out our way. Or directed at the home system."

Chapter Thirty-Seven

"YOU SCREENED, PAT?" Sir Thomas Caparelli asked as his face appeared on Patricia Givens' com display. "I'm sorry I was out of the office, but Liesel told me you'd said it was urgent when I got back. And also that I wasn't to use my personal com?"

"That's right," Givens replied. "And I did tell her I needed you to screen back on a secure com."

She looked better than she had immediately after the disastrous attack, Caparelli thought, but "better" was a purely relative term. The shadows of guilt had retreated in her eyes, yet he was beginning to think they would never completely disappear, and the near hysteria of a certain portion of the Star Empire's news media hadn't helped. He doubted there was anything they could have said that she hadn't already said to herself—he *knew* that was true in his own case—but the angry, panic-driven sense of betrayal coming from that particular group of newsies and editorials had inspired them to hammer the "blatant intelligence failure" far harder than they'd hammered the rest of the Navy.

Realistically, neither he nor Givens could have expected anything else, Caparelli supposed. Public opinion had been wound tight enough with the combined euphoria of the Battle of Spindle and the looming threat of war against the Solarian League, and it was perfectly understandable why the psychological impact of the devastating onslaught had hit the Star Empire's subjects like an old-fashioned piledriver. And it was perfectly reasonable for those same subjects to want the heads of whoever had allowed it to happen. As a matter of fact, Caparelli *agreed* with them in many ways; that was why he'd submitted his resignation—twice. Unfortunately, in his opinion, it had been *rejected* twice, as well.

The first rejection had come from Hamish Alexander-Harrington, who'd pointed out—again—that no one could have seen something like this coming and that holding any individual or group of individuals responsible would be a blatant case of scapegoating.

Caparelli hadn't been able to logically dispute the first lord's analysis, but that didn't mean he'd agreed with it. Nor did it mean he was able to accept it, whatever logic might say. So he'd submitted his resignation a second time, this time directly to Queen Elizabeth . . . who'd returned it to him unread with the admonition "don't be silly." She'd accompanied that pithy bit of advice with a firm injunction to take his resignation back, to tear it up, and never to submit it to her again. First, because she agreed with Earl White Haven, and secondly (and, he suspected, even more pragmatically), because his abrupt departure from the Admiralty would *look* like a case of scapegoating. In the Queen's opinion, the hysterical segment of public opinion represented a distinct minority, and she had no intention of allowing herself or the Grantville Government to fan the hysteria by looking as if they were racing about in a panic of their own, looking for someone—*anyone*—to blame.

And so, out of a sense of duty more than anything else, he'd stayed. And he'd supported White Haven when the first lord rejected Givens' resignation, as well. Which was why the two of them were still sitting in their offices having this discussion three and a half T-weeks after the attack.

He realized he'd allowed a silence to settle while his thoughts rattled back around the newly worn ruts in his brain, and he gave himself a shake.

"Sorry, Pat. Woolgathering, I guess."

"There's a lot of that going around," she said with biting irony, then inhaled sharply. "Sorry," she said in turn.

"Don't worry about it." He smiled. "But now that we're both here, what was it you needed to tell me?"

"Actually, this may be something we need to take to the PM and Her Majesty," Givens said, her expression and her tone both suddenly much more serious. "One of my people just brought

me something from one of our 'black'—in this case, *very* black—
Beowulf conduits."

Caparelli stiffened very slightly. Beowulf was, by any measure,
Manticore's staunchest ally within the Solarian League. It was
also the home system's biggest single trading partner, and a lot of
Manticorans had married Beowulfers—and vice versa—over the
centuries since the Junction had been discovered. The Harrington
family was a case in point. Or, he corrected himself grimly, it had
been, at least. When there'd *been* a Harrington family.

Beowulf was also the only League member system which had
been kept routinely up to date on Manticoran military developments. The Beowulf System-Defense Force and the Royal Navy
had been quietly in agreement that it would be in both services'
best interests if Beowulf didn't suddenly begin introducing Manticore's new tech goodies into its own ships, where they might
find their way into the SLN's less than pristine hands, and the
BSDF had somehow mysteriously failed to provide any of those
"observers" the SLN had been so busily ignoring for so long. But
that didn't mean Beowulf didn't have a very good basic grasp of
what Manticore had been up to. Not only that, but Beowulf was
the only non-Manticoran star system which had been included
from the beginning in planning for Case Lacoön, and there were
all sorts of open channels of communication between the Beowulf
Planetary Board of Directors and Her Majesty's Government.

Which was all well and good, but one of those little secrets
polite people never mentioned was that even allies spied on one
another. There were lots of reasons for that, particularly if the
allies in question were less than totally confident about their
"ally's" long-term intentions. That wasn't the case here, but another
reason—and one which had operated in the case of Beowulf
more than once—was because "spies" could exchange information
that couldn't be exchanged openly. The sort of information that,
for one reason or another, one government couldn't risk openly
handing to another, no matter how friendly they were. And any
"black" Beowulf conduits which reported to Pat Givens and ONI
almost certainly came under that heading.

"All right," he told her. "I'm braced."

✧   ✧   ✧

"This," Hamish Alexander-Harrington said, "is not good."
It was probably the most unnecessary observation he'd ever

made, and he knew it. Still, someone had to break the ice of shocked dismay and get the conversation moving.

His wife glanced at him, her lips moving in a shadow of a smile as she sensed his thoughts, but his brother—seated across the conference table from them—snorted harshly.

"I suppose you could say it comes under that heading," he said. "Of course, it's had a lot of company there lately, hasn't it?"

"How much confidence do you have in this source, Admiral Givens?" Elizabeth Winton asked from her place at the head of the table.

"A high level, Your Majesty," Givens replied, and White Haven noticed that she looked more alive, more engaged, than he'd seen her since what everyone had come to think of as The Attack. "We haven't used this particular conduit very often. In fact, this is only the third message—aside from a handful of 'is this channel still open?' sort of exchanges—that's been passed through it, and it's been in existence for the better part of seventy T-years. Both of the other messages that came to us this way proved to be completely accurate, which is significant in its own right. More to the point, in my own mind, at least, that's a *long* time to maintain a back channel 'just in case.' Someone's invested a lot of effort in making sure it stayed open despite any changes in personnel—at either end. Which, to be honest, is the main reason I'm inclined to put so much trust in it now."

"If the information's as reliable as you believe it is, then I can see why they didn't want to pass it to us openly," William Alexander said.

"I suppose that technically it does come under the definition of treason against the Solarian League," Elizabeth agreed.

"That's arguable, Your Majesty," Sir Anthony Langtry said. The Queen looked at him, and he shrugged. "First, 'treason' is a particularly elusive term as defined—more or less—in the Solarian Constitution. Secondly, if the warning's accurate, someone could make a good case for *Rajampet's* plans being the real act of treason. He's bending Article Seven into a pretzel if that's what he's using to justify this."

"Not that anyone's going to call him on it, Tony," Honor Alexander-Harrington observed, and her soprano voice was almost as shadowed as Patricia Givens' eyes. "Or, not in time to do *us* any good, at any rate."

"I'm afraid that's entirely too likely," Elizabeth said, smiling at Honor in unhappy agreement.

"So, if we assume the information is accurate, what do we do with it?" Grantville asked.

"That depends in part on how serious the actual military threat is, Willie," the Queen replied, and looked at the first space lord. "Sir Thomas?"

"In some ways, that's harder to say than I'd like, Your Majesty," Caparelli told her. "If the numbers are correct—if they're really talking about throwing four hundred or so of the wall at us—then the initial attack is going to be toast, to use Hamish's favorite term. We've got almost that many wallers of our own, all of which are longer-ranged and far better protected in any missile duel than the wallers Admiral Gold Peak took out at Spindle, and that doesn't even include our system-defense pods. So I'm totally confident of our ability to defeat this force decisively. The only question, to be brutally honest, would be whether or not any of them survived long enough to strike their wedges."

He paused, looking around the conference table, and his steely confidence was plain to see.

"Unfortunately, a lot depends on what the thinking behind this is, and, frankly, we don't know that. One thing I *do* know is that if we defeat another Solarian task force—although this one is going to be big enough no one's going to be able to get away with calling it anything except a 'fleet,' which is going to present its own problems when it comes around to psychological impact time—it's going to have an enormous influence on Solarian public opinion where we're concerned. As I see it, there are two possible extremes to their potential reactions. First, they could be so horrified by the devastating nature of the SLN's defeats that they could turn completely against any future operations. Possibly even completely enough to present Kolokoltsov and the rest of them with a genuine challenge to their control of the League. Second, though, they could be so horrified and *infuriated* by the devastating nature of their defeats that they basically give Rajampet a blank check. There's room for all sorts of variations between those two extremes, of course, but I think that's what it really comes down to. And in some ways, unfortunately, I think it's a crapshoot which way they'll jump."

"Hamish? Honor?" Elizabeth looked at them, eyebrow arched.

Honor glanced at her husband for a moment, then squared her shoulders and faced Elizabeth with Nimitz pressing his cheek into the side of her neck from the back of her chair.

"I think Sir Thomas has it pretty much right, Elizabeth," she said. "To be honest, even if the League threw its entire active wall of battle at us in a single wave, we could be fairly confident of defeating it. Throwing in their wallers in dribs and drabs is simply going to make the job even easier from our perspective. The only real worry, in the short term, is the question of our ammunition supply, and judging from what happened at Spindle, I'm pretty sure we've got enough to deal with their entire active superdreadnought strength.

"Unfortunately, if we end up having to do that, it'll make a huge hole in our supply of missiles, which will present all kinds of potential problems if we can't work something out with Haven after all. Which, of course, doesn't even consider what we might need against Manpower."

Her voice turned harder and flatter on the last word, and the light glittering in her brown eyes for just a moment sent a shiver down Elizabeth Winton's spine. Most of the Star Empire's senior officers and political leaders were careful to emphasize—in public, at least—that they still didn't know exactly who'd attacked the home system. There was no doubt whatsoever in Honor Alexander-Harrington's mind, however.

And there was no doubt in Elizabeth's mind exactly what Honor intended to do about it. It wasn't that Elizabeth disagreed with her; it was only that even after all these years, the Queen still hadn't realized that when it came down to it, Honor Alexander-Harrington's granite determination was even more merciless than her own famed temper. Colder and less outwardly expressive, perhaps, and definitely slower to awaken, yet that made it only more deadly in the end.

"If we could count on facing only the League, I think we'd probably be pretty much okay for the first couple of years," Honor continued after a moment. "It's going to take them longer to get substantial numbers of the Reserve refitted, activated, and manned—and trained—than it's going to take us to get our missile production started up again. They've got enough battlecruisers and cruisers in Frontier Fleet to pose a significant threat to our commerce if they resort to a full bore *guerre de course* and use them as raiders, but thanks to the wormhole network, we actually have the 'interior lines,' so they'd be even more vulnerable to commerce raiding than we are.

"But the one thing we wouldn't be able to do is take the war to *them* until we got the missile supply back under control, and that means they'd have a lot more time to react to their technological inferiority. Without an adequate, reliable supply of missiles, we *can't* go after them. If they *choose* not to go after us while they look for answers to our hardware advantages, then by the time we've got our missile lines back in full production, they'll probably be well on their way to producing new designs that are a lot more survivable and a lot more dangerous. And, even worse, we've lost so much industry that there's no way in the galaxy we could hope to stay in shouting range of their production capability. If they turn out six times as many ships, we lose, even if their ships are individually only half as good as ours."

"And the fact that, as you say, we can't take the war to them means we can't exploit those fracture lines of the League's you pointed out to us," Elizabeth said, nodding her head in grim understanding and agreement.

"Exactly." Honor reached up to stroke Nimitz and met her Queen's eyes levelly. "If this information is accurate, if Rajampet really is planning on feeding another four hundred wallers into the furnace, it's going to get really, really ugly, no matter what happens. Worst-case scenario, frankly, is that in defeating them we inflict enough losses to provide the rallying point Sir Thomas was talking about. Assume each of those ships has a complement of sixty-five hundred, which is actually on the low side. That would still give us over two and a half million people aboard the wallers alone. Potentially, that's two and a half million *fatal* casualties, on top of the losses Crandall took at Spindle. More likely, we'd kill a lot less than that outright and take the rest prisoner, but I'm not sure that would be a lot better from a psychological perspective. To be honest, I'm inclined to think that's *exactly* what Rajampet has in mind."

White Haven stirred beside her, and she looked at him.

"I'm not one of the Sollies' greater admirers myself," he said, "but deliberately courting that kind of death toll purely as a political maneuver seems a bit too cynically calculating to me, even for a Solly."

"That's because deep down inside you're a straightforward, decent sort of person, Ham," his brother said grimly. White Haven's gaze moved to him, and Grantville shrugged. "You might want to remember Cordelia Ransom and Rob Pierre. The number of casualties Honor's talking about here are actually a lot lower than the casualties Pierre was willing to inflict just by launching his pogroms against the Legislaturalists, much less fighting *us*. Ransom wouldn't have turned a hair at sacrificing three or four times that many people if it suited her purposes, and let's not even get started on that sociopath Saint-Just!"

"But—" White Haven began, then stopped, and Grantville nodded.

"That's right, Ham." His voice was almost gentle now. "We're used to thinking of *Peeps* as political sociopaths. From what I've seen so far out of Kolokoltsov and his crew—and especially out of Rajampet, so far—they're at least as bad. Maybe even worse, because I don't think any of them have the personal involvement or the legitimate basis for outrage that Pierre, at least, definitely did have. To them, it's just a matter of gaming the system the way they've always gamed it."

"Which leaves us in one hell of a mess, doesn't it?" Queen Elizabeth summed up, and no one in that conference room disagreed with her.

◇   ◇   ◇

"Are you serious, Admiral Trenis?"

Eloise Pritchart tried to keep the disbelief out of her voice as she gazed at the director of the Republican Navy's Bureau of Planning. That position made Linda Trenis the Republic of Haven's equivalent of Patricia Givens, and, over the years, especially since the fall of the People's Republic, she'd become accustomed to presenting reports some of her superiors initially found... somewhat difficult to credit. Now she simply looked back at the President and nodded.

"Yes, Madam President, I'm quite serious."

"But, let me get this straight—you don't have any idea who *sent* you this particular information?"

"That's not precisely what I said, Madam President. I know exactly who handed it over to us. No, I don't know the identity of the person who actually provided it at the source, but I do know where it came from—in general terms, at least."

"But, excuse me, Linda," Thomas Theisman said, turning to

face her and the President, with his back towards the panoramic window of Pritchart's Péricard Tower office, "why in the world would somebody in *Beowulf* suddenly drop this kind of information on *us* of all people?"

"That's something I'm less prepared to theorize about," Trenis said. "I have some thoughts on the subject, but that's all they are at this point."

"Well, if you have *any* thoughts on this subject, you're well ahead of me," Pritchart said candidly, leaning back in her chair and crossing her legs. "So let's hear them, Admiral."

"Of course, Madam President."

Linda Trenis was a highly organized woman. One of her greatest strengths when it came to building tightly reasoned analyses was the way she carefully considered every snippet of information before fitting it in place. It was painfully evident that the thought of presenting what could be no more than her preliminary, off-the-cuff impressions to the Republic's head of state wasn't very high on her list of favorite things to do. But she'd known it would be coming, so she drew a deep breath and began.

"There could be a lot of reasons for someone in Beowulf to want us to know about this. Frankly, it's unlikely any of them would be because they like us so much, though. Mind you, I don't think they've ever *disliked* us as much as Manticore did, and I think that's been even more true since the restoration of the old Republic, but 'not as much as Manticore' doesn't mean they actually care for us all that much. Once upon a time, we were actually on pretty good terms with them, but that relationship started going down the tubes when the Legislaturalists came in. The Technical Conservation Act was the kiss of death as far as the Beowulfans were concerned, and they cut off military and intelligence cooperations with us a hundred and forty years ago… which, obviously, wasn't the case where Manticore's concerned. So there's never been much doubt that if they had to choose between the two of us, they'd choose Manticore in a heartbeat. And, to be honest, if I lived right on the other side of the Junction from Manticore, I'd probably make the same choice."

Pritchart and Theisman both nodded, and Trenis shrugged.

"I think, then, that we have to begin from the assumption that they told us about this because they thought it would *help* Manticore, not because they thought it would hurt them. At first, I couldn't see any reason they might think that. Then, as I considered it, it occurred to me that they might have a better appreciation of how we're thinking here in Nouveau Paris than we'd realized."

"I beg your pardon?" Pritchart blinked, and Theisman frowned.

"What I'm trying to say, Madam President, is that we've had a natural and understandable tendency to concentrate our counter-intelligence activities against Manticore. Now, though, I've started wondering just how thoroughly *Beowulf* might have penetrated the Republic."

"Beowulf, Linda?" Theisman sounded dubious, and Trenis looked at him. "We're an awful long way from Beowulf," the Secretary of War pointed out. "Why should they worry about penetrating *us*? And if they have, why haven't they been feeding any information they've gathered to the Manties?"

"To take your second question first, Sir, we don't know they *haven't* been feeding information to the Manties, do we?" Despite herself, Trenis smiled slightly at Theisman's expression. "As to why they should worry about penetrating us, we *are* the people who've happened to be at war with their next door neighbor—and friend—for the last twenty T-years. People don't talk about it a lot, but Beowulf's intelligence agencies are pretty good, and I think it would make sense for them to keep an eye on the people fighting a star system barely six hours away from their own home system."

Theisman's expression segued into a thoughtful frown, and Pritchart nodded.

"At the same time," Trenis continued, "I'm inclined to think they either haven't gotten very much from us, or else that they've chosen for reasons of their own not to share what they have gotten with Manticore. It may be that Manticore's been sharing information with Beowulf, and that, as a result, Beowulf's known Manticore already had almost everything Beowulf could have provided. Let's not underestimate what the Manties are capable of in this area all on their own. On the other hand, I'm inclined to wonder if the Beowulfers might not have stepped up their efforts after that assassination attempt on Alexander-Harrington and what happened to Webster and on Torch."

"Oh?" Pritchart tilted her head to one side, eyes narrowing. Trenis wasn't on the list of people who knew about Albert Giancola or Kevin Usher's suspicions about Yves Grosclaude's highly convenient—or *in*convenient, depending upon one's perspective—demise.

"Madam President, *we* didn't do it. And, frankly, something like this indicates a completely new capability on somebody's part. Given the way Beowulf feels about Mesa, and given the fact that Manpower wouldn't hesitate for a moment to rent out a new assassination tool, *and* that any analyst has to look very closely at the possibility that we're looking at some new bioscience technique, I think it's likely Beowulf's suspicion focused on Mesa well before anyone else's did. If that's the case, it would be logical for them to assume Manpower had rented it to *us*, especially in light of the attempt on Duchess Harrington. And if they did think that, one way to find the Mesa connection would have been to come at it from our end."

Pritchart realized she was nodding slowly. It was all purely speculative, of course, but it made a sort of sense. In fact, it might well make a *lot* of sense, especially—as Trenis had suggested—in light of Beowulf's hatred for and suspicion of all things Mesan.

"Assuming there's anything at all to what I've just said," the admiral continued, "I think it's possible, even probable, that after what happened at Monica, New Tuscany, and now Spindle, Beowulf's concluded that we really might have been innocent bystanders, at least where the assassinations were concerned. From which it follows that whoever *was* behind the Webster murder and the attack on Queen Berry was trying to sabotage the original summit talks between you and Queen Elizabeth. And from *that*, it's only a fairly short step to assuming we've genuinely wanted to end the fighting ever since you sent Countess Gold Peak back to Manticore with the summit offer. More than that, if they really have managed to get any sort of penetration here in Nouveau Paris, I'd say it's probable that they're aware of how favorably we reacted to Duchess Harrington's arrival and Elizabeth's offer to negotiate after all, as well."

"You're saying someone in Beowulf thinks we're likely to want a solid, reasonable treaty more than we'd want to take advantage of Manticore's possible distraction?" Pritchart said thoughtfully, although there was still a pronounced hint of skepticism in her tone.

"I think it's possible, Madam President."

"It may be possible, Linda, but it sounds sort of high-risk to me, coming from somebody who thinks of himself as Manticore's friend," Theisman remarked.

"It could be," Trenis acknowledged. "On the other hand, what have they really told us? That the Sollies are stupid enough to reach back into the sausage machine and go after Manticore again? Sure, if we're inclined to try to take advantage of the Manties' position after their home system's been hammered, and knowing the League is going for their throat from the front, we can start putting our plans together a little sooner. But that's really all this would do for us, and I don't think anyone in Beowulf would be stupid enough to think *we're* stupid enough to actually jump Manticore unless the Star Empire's already been pretty much pounded flat. So, in that sense, telling us about the Sollies' plans doesn't translate into any sort of meaningful *military* advantage."

"You're thinking somebody in Beowulf, probably someone fairly high up in the decision-making tree, is thinking in terms of the *diplomatic* implications of this news," Pritchart said slowly.

"I'm thinking that's a possibility, Madam President. Don't forget, though, that all of this came at me just as cold as it's coming at you. I may be completely out to lunch here. But whatever else is going on, never forget how long Beowulf and Manticore have been friends. And who handed this to me. To be honest, we'd always thought Beowulf's chief of station for their intelligence services here on Haven was their commercial attaché. Now, though, assuming the whole thing isn't some huge deception measure after all, they've effectively confirmed that it's actually been their *naval* attaché all this time . . . and she came out into the open on their ambassador's specific instructions. Bearing in mind the relationship between them and the Manties, I just don't see why Beowulf's *ambassador* would authorize someone to hand us anything they expected to *hurt* the Star Empire."

"I'm inclined to agree," Theisman said. "But the law of unintended consequences hasn't been repealed, as far as I'm aware."

"And, there's another side to this," Pritchart said. Theisman looked at her, and she shrugged. "McGwire, Younger, and Tullingham," she said flatly, and the Secretary of War grimaced.

Trenis looked puzzled. Pritchart saw the expression and, after a moment, decided to explain.

"You're right about the Administration's desire to conclude an equitable treaty with Manticore, Admiral Trenis. Unfortunately, not everyone agrees on exactly what the term 'equitable' implies. And, frankly, there are some fairly influential players outside the Administration who are going to regard this fresh threat to the Star Empire—especially after what happened to their home system—as grounds for us to harden our position. They're going to see all too clearly that the Manties' back is to the wall, and they're *not* going to see any reason at all why we shouldn't use that to force concessions out of Manticore, instead of the other way around."

"Which," Theisman said dryly, "might not be the most productive possible way to approach Elizabeth Winton at a moment like this."

Trenis winced slightly, and Pritchart chuckled.

"Frankly, I can't say I'm totally averse to the prospect of achieving better terms myself," the President admitted. "I'd particularly like to knock that notion of reparations on the head, even though I can't really say the Manties are unjustified in looking for them. What I'm concerned about, though, is that this fresh development is going to embolden the congressional critics of our decision to negotiate with Manticore in the first place. There wasn't a lot they could do to spoke our wheel while Eighth Fleet was right here in the Haven System as a pointed reminder of how little choice we had. Now they're going to decide the Solarian threat has just given us a club to hold over the *Manties'* head, and that's going to produce all kinds of...unfortunate repercussions."

Despite her chuckle of a moment before, there was absolutely no amusement on Eloise Pritchart's face as she shook her head.

"This Administration is still too badly wounded by what happened in the Battle of Manticore for me to ignore what the opposition is likely to do with this information in Congress. Put another way, at this moment I don't have the moral authority and public support numbers I had before Operation Beatrice, so I can't bully Congress into doing what I want without building a consensus first, and this is going to make it a lot easier for the opposition to keep me from doing that. And that means that whatever Beowulf may be thinking, and however badly *I* want to return to the negotiating table and get this war *ended*, this little revelation is a lot more likely to derail, or at least seriously impede, the negotiating process than it is to speed it up."

APRIL 1922 POST DIASPORA

"Whatever else anyone might say about Manticorans, they don't 'run scared' worth a damn."

—Admiral Thomas Theisman,
Republic of Haven Navy

Chapter Thirty-Eight

FLEET ADMIRAL MASSIMO FILARETA was tall, black-haired, and broad-shouldered, with a closely cropped beard and piercing dark eyes. In a service renowned for nepotism and family interest, he took second place to none in terms of his lofty connections. He was also well known for a tendency to party hard when the opportunity came his way, and among those who knew him particularly well there were rumors that he enjoyed certain pleasures even the most jaded Solly might call "esoteric." He was scarcely alone in that among the SLN's senior officers' ranks, however, and he'd also established a reputation for hard work, levelheadedness, and attention to detail that matched both his imposing physical presence and his expensive tastes.

At the moment, though, his levelheadedness appeared to be somewhat in abeyance, Admiral John Burrows, his chief of staff noted with undeniable unhappiness.

Burrows was the physical antithesis of his superior. Where Filareta stood a shade over a hundred and ninety centimeters, Burrows barely topped a hundred and sixty-two, and he was fair-haired, blue-eyed, and distinctly portly. Like Filareta, Burrows enjoyed a reputation for working hard, but he was actually more comfortable than his superior was when it came to improvising. And he'd also developed a certain talent for reading Filareta's mood and adroitly...managing him.

"And what do *you* think about this brainstorm, John?" Filareta demanded rather abruptly, wheeling from his contemplation of his enormous day cabin's smart wall, which currently displayed the central star of the Tasmania System.

"I assume you're referring to Admiral Rajampet's latest missive, Massimo?"

Burrows put an edge of drollness into his tone, but Filareta wasn't in the mood for their usual shared, more or less tolerant contempt for the CNO.

"And just what else did you think I might be referring to?" he asked rather nastily.

"Nothing," Burrows admitted, dropping the effort to defuse the other man's obvious unhappiness. His more sober expression was an unstated apology for his original attempt at humor, and Filareta grunted.

"Well, whatever," he said, waving one hand. "What *do* you think of it?"

"I haven't had time to fully examine the availability numbers," Burrows replied rather more formally. "Assuming that everyone who's supposed to get here actually does before we hyper out, it looks like we'll probably hit the specified force level. We might even have a few of the wall to spare. So, from the nuts-and-bolts perspective, it looks doable. I don't like how light we're going to be in screening elements, and I wish we had a lot better information than we do at this point on what happened at Spindle, though."

"The screen numbers could worry me less," Filareta said dismissively. "That point about Spindle, though—*that* one's well taken. Of course, Sandra Crandall always was too stupid to close the outer hatch first, but still..."

His unhappiness was even more pronounced, and Burrows discovered that he shared it.

"I think there's probably something to the theory that the Manties aren't going to want to go on pushing things, especially assuming ONI's estimate of the damage they took in this attack on their home system is remotely accurate," he offered after a moment. "If the Strategy Board's right about that, turning up with four hundred-plus of the wall ought to inspire them to see reason."

"And if the 'Strategy Board' is *wrong* about that," Filareta's withering irony made it perfectly clear who he thought had really come up with the notion, "then turning up with four hundred-plus of the wall is going to get a lot of people killed."

"Yes, it is," Burrows agreed. "On the other hand, I have to say I think the estimates about the damage the Manties' system defenses must've suffered are probably pretty well taken." Filareta looked at him sharply, and the chief of staff shrugged. "I'm not saying they've been hammered as completely flat as the ops plan seems to be suggesting, but nobody could get in close enough to inflict that kind of damage inside the limit without fighting his way through a shit pot of their inner system defenses, at least. And if the loss reports for the Battle of Manticore are remotely accurate, they couldn't have had more than a hundred or so wallers of their own left even before this latest attack."

"Which I might find rather more reassuring if they hadn't pinned Crandall's ears back with nothing heavier than *cruisers*," Filareta observed rather caustically.

"I know I just said myself that I wish we had more information about what happened at Spindle," Burrows said. "But from the way I read what data we do have, I think what she really ran into was a bunch of missile pods deployed in the system-defense role."

"And your point is?"

"My point is that they were probably system-defense *pods*—I mean a specialized design specifically optimized for that role. Sure, all they *showed* us was cruisers, but as you just pointed out, Admiral Crandall never was the sharpest stylus in the box, and Manty stealth systems seem to be better than anyone thought they were. It's entirely possible they managed to get an entire dispersed defensive array emplaced without her spotting it. And the minimum powered envelope estimates I've seen are a hell of a lot higher than the range at which they took out *Jean Bart*. So I'm inclined to think that what they'd really managed to do was to deploy a specialized area-defense version of their pods, probably with substantially larger missiles to get that extra range. Think of them as . . . oh, old-fashioned mines with three or four normal drives shoved up their asses. It's the only way I can think of that they could've gotten the range, but missiles that big simply wouldn't be practical for shipboard weapons." Burrows shrugged. "Where the hell would you put the magazines?"

Filareta started a quick reply, then paused at Burrows' last question. He thought for a moment or two, then nodded.

"I hadn't really thought about that," he admitted. "If they've gone to missile-dominated combat, then they have to have struck some kind of balance between missile ranges and missile *size,* don't they? They've got to have enough rounds onboard to do the job."

"Exactly." Burrows grimaced. "I'm willing to concede that even their shipboard weapons will have a substantial range advantage, but it's not going to be as great as the advantage they had over Crandall. And the second point about their being a specialized system-defense variant is that the only 'proof' they polished her off with 'nothing heavier than cruisers' comes from the *Manties.* If I were they, and what I'd really used was a sophisticated, integrated system-defense weapon—one that probably *did* have an FTL component—I'd do *my* best to convince the League I'd done it with a scratch force of light ships, too...if I thought I could get away with it. But everything I've seen from our own intelligence and R&D people says that any kind of broadband FTL is going to require humongous platforms. The *smallest* estimate I've seen suggests that nothing much smaller than a waller could carry the system and a worthwhile weapons load. So since they obviously were using FTL against Crandall, they sure as hell weren't doing it from something as small as a heavy cruiser. To be honest, that—coupled with the size requirements for the missiles themselves—is why I'm convinced it had to be a system-defense set up. Crandall crapped out because they managed to get the dispersed platforms in-system and up and running before *she* got there."

Filareta nodded slowly, his eyes intent, but there was something else behind those eyes. Burrows could see that, even though he didn't have a clue what else the fleet admiral was turning over in his mind.

"So what you're saying is that whoever"—that "something else" behind Filareta's eyes flickered more strongly for a moment—"blew the piss out of their system infrastructure has to've done it *through* that same kind of defensive system."

"That's what it sounds like to me," Burrows confirmed. "And to do that, they have to have either crippled the system, or else at least run it out of ammunition. Frankly, it seems more likely that whoever it was had better intel on the Manties than we do and figured out a way to go after the remote platforms, which probably means the Manties' command net has just been shot full of holes. Even if they did it just by running them out of ammunition, though, it seems more than a little unlikely that the Manties will have been able to replace their expended missiles with their industrial structure so trashed. And even assuming that they've been able to replace their expenditures this time around, there's no way in hell they'll be able to take *us* out and be able to reload again before the next wave arrives."

"I'm sure our ghosts will take great comfort from that fact," Filareta said rather dryly, and Burrows snorted.

"I agree it would be a . . . suboptimal outcome, Sir," he acknowledged. "My point, though, was that the Manties have to be aware of the same facts. So when we turn up so unexpectedly, even if they have the physical capability to repel our attack, I actually think the Strategy Board's right about whether or not they'll have the intestinal fortitude to actually try doing it. And if we point out to them that the next wave's already in the pipeline, and is going to be even more powerful, I think it really is likely they'll recognize the writing on the wall and give it up."

"Um."

Filareta frowned, obviously pondering what his chief of staff had just said. He still looked a far cry from anything Burrows would have called cheerful, but his expression was at least a little lighter than it had been.

"I hope to hell you're right," he said frankly at last. "If you're not, then we're going to get reamed, even if we wind up taking them out in the end."

He paused, as if inviting Burrows to respond, but the chief of staff only nodded. After all, Filareta was absolutely correct.

"All right," the fleet admiral said finally. "Go ahead and bring Bill and Yvonne inside on this." Admiral William Daniels was the task force's operations officer, and Admiral Yvonne Uruguay was the staff astrogator. "I want our movement planned by the time our reinforcements get here." It was Filareta's turn to grimace. "There's no way we're going to make our specified schedule, but let's see how close we can come."

"Yes, Sir," Burrows agreed. Frankly, he'd be surprised if they could hit within a T-week of the operations schedule included with their orders from Old Earth. On the other hand, allowances for that kind of slippage were built into any interstellar fleet movement orders. They had to be.

Filareta turned to look back at the smart wall again, contemplating it for several moments. Then he inhaled deeply and nodded to the distant solar furnace which dominated the view.

"All right, John," he said again, never turning away from the wall. "Go talk to Bill and Yvonne. I want their preliminary reactions in time for lunch. And go ahead and schedule a full dress staff meeting for tomorrow morning."

The "private yacht" was about the size of most navies' battlecruisers, and almost as heavily armed. Which didn't prevent it from being one of the most luxuriously appointed vessels in the galaxy . . . as well as one of the fastest. It had made the passage from the Mesa System forty percent more rapidly than anyone else's ship could have managed it.

Albrecht Detweiler reflected on exactly what that implied as he stood to one side on what would have been the flag deck aboard an actual warship and watched the enormous space station, gleaming in the reflected light of the F6 star called Darius, growing larger on the visual display as MANS *Genesis* approached it. The station—known officially as *Darius Prime*—orbited the planet Gamma, Darius' only habitable world, and at the moment, it was over Gamma's night side, just approaching the terminator. The planetary surface below it sparkled with lines and beads of light, and there were four other stations to keep it company, although none of them were remotely the same size as Manticore's *Hephaestus* or *Vulcan*.

Or the size they *had* been, at any rate.

His eyes moved to the ships taking form in the shipyards *Darius Prime* supported. Eventually, those ships would become the first units of the *Leonard Detweiler* class, he knew, although it wouldn't happen anywhere near as soon as he wished. The much smaller units of the *Shark* class in parking orbit beyond *Darius Prime* were visible evidence of why he wished that. Most of the still far from complete *Detweilers* were already larger than the *Sharks*—in many cases, *substantially* larger. When they were completed, they would be far, far tougher—and far more dangerous—than their smaller predecessors, and he was going to need the capability they represented as quickly as he could get it. Unfortunately, wishing couldn't change anything.

His lips twitched briefly at the thought, and he turned his attention to the *Sharks*. *Genesis* had arrived almost three hours before her scheduled ETA, yet it was evident the fleet was already home and waiting for him. Well, that was fine with him. No doubt the Mesan Alignment Navy would someday acquire the taste for formal reviews of the fleet—and the punctillious timing which went with them—which seemed to be a part of every *other* navy in space. So far, it hadn't, and given how little use he had for pomp, he'd prefer for that to take as long as possible.

Not that they don't deserve *a formal review*. His face hardened with mingled satisfaction and a degree of apprehension as he reflected upon the reports of Oyster Bay's effectiveness. *I don't think anyone else in history ever managed to pull off this successful an operation. Certainly not against someone as good as the Manties!*

The casualty count had been higher than projected, and part of him regretted that. He supposed that was foolish of him, given where all of this had to lead eventually, yet there it was. He couldn't quite avoid thinking about all the children who'd never even seen it coming. Funny how that bothered him when thinking about all of the other millions who were going to be killed eventually didn't. He wondered if that was because those other millions were still an abstraction for him, still only a potential, whereas the dead from the Manticoran space stations and in the city of Yawata Crossing weren't. He *hoped* that wasn't the reason. All of those additional deaths were coming—he couldn't have changed that at this point even if he'd tried—and he couldn't afford to brood over them this way when they finally arrived.

Well, you won't, he told himself. *By the time they come along, you'll have enough emotional scar tissue to keep you from losing any sleep. And, be honest with yourself, Albrecht—you'll be damned glad you do.*

"We'll be docking with the station in about thirty-five minutes, Sir," *Genesis'* captain told him.

"Thank you," Detweiler replied, suppressing the urge to smile. Hayden Milne had been his yacht's skipper for over three T-years, during which time he'd been firmly trained to never—ever—refer to him by name. He'd been simply "Sir" to every member of the crew for as long as anyone could remember, and Detweiler's temptation to smile faded as he thought about that. He was doomed to stay in the shadows for at least a while longer, after all.

At the same time, there was no point hiding from the men and women of the MAN. Every one of them knew Benjamin was their commander and that Albrecht stood behind Benjamin, although the fact that the two of them were *Detweilers* had been carefully concealed even from most of them. They knew Benjamin and Albrecht as their leaders, however. Which, after all, was the reason both he and those orbiting *Sharks* were in the same star system this afternoon.

"I suppose I should wander back to my quarters and tell my wife," he continued out loud.

"Of course, Sir."

Detweiler nodded to the captain, then turned and headed for the lift, followed even here by Heinrich Stabolis, his enhanced bodyguard.

They stepped into the lift car, and Stabolis pressed the proper destination code, then stood back with his hands folded behind him. Detweiler couldn't begin to count the number of times he'd seen Stabolis standing in exactly that posture over the years, and it was amazing how seeing that familiar sight always helped bolster his confidence.

"So far, so good, Heinrich," he said.

"As you say, Sir," Stabolis agreed, and Detweiler grinned.

"You know, Heinrich, you don't say a lot, do you?"

"I suppose not, Sir." There might have been the faintest glimmer of an answering smile on the bodyguard's face.

"But you're always there," Detweiler continued more seriously. "If I haven't mentioned it lately, I appreciate it."

Stabolis ducked his head in mute acknowledgment, and Detweiler reached out to rest one hand lightly on his shoulder for a moment. Then they reached their destination, the doors opened, and Stabolis stepped out into the passage, glancing both ways before he moved to allow his charge to leave the lift. They walked down the wide, tastefully decorated passageway to Detweiler's private suite, and he pressed the admittance buttoned himself.

"Yes?" a pleasant soprano voice said after a moment.

"It's me, Evie," he said. "Time to go in about thirty minutes."

"Then should I assume Heinrich's managed to get you down here without any gravy on your shirt?"

The door opened, and Evelina Detweiler looked out at her husband. Behind her, Albrecht saw Ericka Stabolis, Evelina's bodyguard, trying hard not to smile at *her* principal's comment. Ericka had been with Evelina almost as long as Heinrich had been looking after Albrecht, and she had the same black hair, blue eyes, and regular features—a bit more delicate in her case—as her brother. Indeed, people were often struck by the extraordinarily close physical resemblance between the Stabolis siblings. They shouldn't have been; Ericka and Heinrich were clone twins. She was every bit as deadly as her brother, and the only significant difference between them was that she had two X chromosomes.

"No," Albrecht said now, mildly, as his wife inspected him. "I not only managed not to spill the gravy, but I've actually had *two* cups of coffee without dribbling *any* of it down my chin."

"I *am* impressed," Evelina told him with a chuckle, then stood back to let him through the doorway. He smiled and touched her lightly on the cheek. The Long-Range Planning Board had known what it was doing when it paired the two of them, he thought. Sometimes the LRPB's choices resulted in pairings that couldn't stand each other. Officially, that didn't happen, of course, but *unofficially* everyone knew it did. Fortunately, mistakes like that could usually be fixed, and in the case of an alpha line pairing like any of the Detweilers, the Board's members put special effort into trying to pick compatibles.

"Just let me change my jacket," he told her.

"Fine. But not the *red* one," she said firmly.

"I *like* the red one," he protested.

"I know you do, dear." She shuddered. "On the other hand, I'm still hoping they can do something about your taste in clothing in our grandchildren."

✧   ✧   ✧

"Attention on deck!"

The command rapped out as Albrecht Detweiler, his wife, and his son Benjamin stepped out onto the stage at one end of the spacious compartment.

In one sense, there was no real pressing need for them to be here. Albrecht could have addressed the senior officers of the returning Oyster Bay fleet electronically, and he doubted they would have minded or felt slighted. But they deserved better, and whether they ever actually realized it or not, he knew they would never forget that he'd come all the way out to Darius to greet them on their return. It wasn't exactly a trivial trip from Mesa, even with the streak drive, but that wasn't what they were going to remember.

He walked across to the podium, flanked by Evelina and Benjamin, and stopped, looking out across the assembled faces of the men and women in the maroon and green uniforms of the MAN. He stood there for the better part of a full minute, taking the time to look at *each* of those faces, then, finally, he nodded.

"Please, be seated."

Feet scuffed on the space station deck as the naval officers obeyed his invitation, and he let them settle themselves once again.

"Ladies and gentlemen," he said after several seconds, his voice quiet, "I came out to Darius to greet you and to tell you how extraordinarily well each and every one of you have performed. I can tell you now that Oyster Bay was a complete success."

No one actually seemed to move, yet a stir went through his audience. Shoulders straightened almost imperceptibly, eyes brightened, and he nodded again.

"All three major Manticoran space stations were totally destroyed," he told them. "They've been less forthcoming about the damage to their dispersed yards, but there was no way they could conceal what had happened to *Hephaestus* and *Vulcan*, given how many witnesses there were. *Weyland*'s destruction has also been confirmed by official Manticoran sources. As I say, there's been no official word on damage to their dispersed yards, but all unofficial sources indicate near total destruction there, as well.

"The attack on Yeltsin's Star was equally successful. Their Blackbird Yard was totally destroyed, along with virtually its entire workforce. We have confirmation that *every* ship under construction at Yeltsin's Star was also destroyed or too heavily damaged to be repairable. Given that the Manties' missile production was concentrated in their space stations and that Grayson's missile production was concentrated at Blackbird, we've succeeded in destroying their ability to replace ammunition expenditures for the foreseeable future."

He could actually feel the satisfaction of the assembled officers, and they deserved it. Still—

"The only aspect of the entire operation which can be considered less than a hundred percent success was no one's fault," he said gravely, and the bodies shifted slightly. "We'd hoped to destroy the Manties' entire next generation of capital ships still in the yards. Unfortunately, it appears we'd underestimated their construction speeds. You did, indeed, destroy *an* entire generation of capital ships, but the one *before* it had already been launched, and the majority of their new construction was safely at Trevor's Star, working up, at the time of your attack."

The faces looking back at him were extraordinarily sober now, and he shrugged very slightly.

"As I say, you carried out your orders perfectly, ladies and gentlemen. The fault—if there was a fault—lies in our own original estimates of the Manties' building times. And, to be completely honest, we recognized at the time we sent you out that it was possible we were going to catch less of their new construction in the yards than we might have wished. So, while that portion of the operation was less successful than we'd hoped, the overwhelming effectiveness of the *rest* of Oyster Bay more than compensates. Given that virtually all of the Manticorans' combat advantages depend upon their advances in missile warfare, the fact that you've destroyed their missile production lines has dealt a much more significant blow to their war fighting capability than we would have achieved even if we'd caught the rest of their ships under construction. Once they've expended their existing *missiles*, it won't matter how many missile-armed *ships* they have."

Here and there a head nodded, although some of the expressions he could see remained less cheerful than they had been.

"In the meantime, however," he said more briskly, "the entire Alignment is in your debt. We're *proud* of you, and we owe you a debt no one could ever truly hope to repay. The first operation of the Mesan Alignment Navy has been, by any conceivable measure, the most successful attack by *any* navy in the history of space warfare. What you accomplished with a mere handful of ships is unparalleled, and you've dealt a deadly blow to both the capabilities and the confidence of our most dangerous enemies. I wish, more than I could ever tell you, that we could bring all of you back to Mesa for the public parades and celebrations you so richly deserve. For now, though, it's essential we continue to conceal our military capabilities. Especially the capabilities conferred upon us by the spider drive. At this time, no one else in the entire galaxy knows—whatever they may *suspect* in Manticore—who was behind Oyster Bay, or where a similar attack might be launched. It's imperative we maintain that ignorance, that uncertainty, for as long as possible. So much as I would prefer to tell everyone how proud I am of you, I can't. Not yet. I can only tell *you*, and even there, I lack the words to express the depth of that pride.

"Ladies and gentlemen of the fleet, for centuries our ancestors have worked and planned for this moment." He swept them with his eyes once more, seeing the shoulders come back once again, seeing the eyes brighten anew. "Those ancestors cannot be here today, and so I find myself forced to stand in their place. But if they *could* be here, if it were possible for them to speak to you, I know that they, as I, would say 'thank you.' Thank you for your courage, your dedication, your professionalism, and for the brilliant way in which you've finally begun the crusade for which all of us have hoped, planned, and waited for so very long."

✧   ✧   ✧

"Did I lay it on too thick, Ben?" Albrecht asked an hour or so later as he, Evelina, and their son sat down to a private supper. There was more than a hint of humor in his tone, but Benjamin wasn't fooled.

"Actually, Father," he said very seriously, "I think they understood you meant every word of it. *I* certainly did, at any rate."

Albrecht looked sharply at him across the table, and Benjamin returned his regard levelly. After a moment, Albrecht picked up his wineglass and sipped.

"Now you've gone and embarrassed your father," Evelina scolded with a small smile. "Don't you know the Chief Executive of the Mesan Alignment isn't supposed to come all over sentimental just because the Navy's officers have performed so superbly?"

"Oh, hush, Evie." Albrecht lowered his glass and shook his head at her. "I know perfectly well I can't fool you or Ben."

"No, and there's no reason you should try to fool the Navy over this one, either," she told him. "I agree with every word you said to them, Albrecht. And I hope they know exactly how deeply you meant it."

"So do I," Benjamin said.

"Well, I *do* wish we'd caught more of their construction in the yards," Albrecht said. "I know all the analysts agree that taking out their ability to resupply with missiles was even more important, but I'd really hoped we could get a bigger jump on them when the *Detweilers* begin commissioning."

Benjamin frowned, but he also nodded.

The Mesan Alignment had established the first colony on Gamma almost two hundred T-years ago, and it had grown steadily since, although the really exponential growth had begun only over the last seventy T-years or so. Exactly when to begin that particular side of the Alignment's preparations had always been a bit ticklish, since no matter how well it was hidden, there was always the possibility of someone's stumbling across it, which could have raised all sorts of questions. On the other hand, the capabilities Darius represented had always been central to the Alignment's strategy, and Albrecht's grandfather had authorized the first colonization flight as one of his last acts as the Alignment's chief executive.

By now, the Darius System's total population was in the very near vicinity of 3.9 billion, of whom just under two billion were representatives of one of the alpha, beta, or gamma genomes the Alignment had worked to improve for so long. The remainder of the system population were genetic slaves, but the conditions of their slavery were very unlike those which obtained elsewhere. For one thing, they were treated far better, without the often savage discipline slaves often received elsewhere. In fact, the Darius System was one of the very few places where the Mesan Constitution's official legal protections theoretically intended to protect slaves from gross mistreatment were actually enforced. For another, they had a much higher standard of living. And for yet another, they formed the backbone of a highly trained, highly skilled labor force which had earned the respect of its supervisors.

Every one of those slaves had been born here in Darius, and not one of them had ever left the system. Their knowledge of what was happening elsewhere in the galaxy, of the history of Mesa, or of *their* own history had been carefully controlled for generations. They'd been aware for those same generations that they and their parents and grandparents had been laboring to build first the basic industry and then the specialized infrastructure to support a massive navy, but they were convinced it was intended as a *defensive* fleet.

Yet for all the years which had been plowed into Darius, all the effort, all the generations of labor, the fact remained that its space stations and shipyards were significantly less capable than Manticore's had been prior to Oyster Bay. Benjamin Detweiler didn't like admitting that, but he agreed with his father; the day someone stopped admitting the truth was the day he could kiss any of his hopes for the future goodbye. And the truth was that, despite the accomplishments of the Alignment's R&D, and despite any tactical advantages which might accrue from the streak drive and the spider, very few star nations could have matched the industrial efficiency of the Star Empire of Manticore. Indeed,

Benjamin suspected that even Manticore had failed to grasp just how great an advantage it possessed in that regard.

Over the last five or six T-years, he and Daniel had been trying to introduce Manticoran practices here at Darius, only to discover that the task wasn't as simple and forthright as it ought to have been. If they'd really wanted to duplicate Manticore's *efficiency*, they would've had to duplicate Manticore's entire industrial base—and its society—and they simply couldn't do that. Their labor force was extraordinarily good at following orders, extremely well trained, and highly motivated, but the kind of independence of thought which characterized Manticoran workers wasn't exactly something which had been encouraged among the slave workers of Darius. Even if it had been, their basic techniques and technologies were simply *different* from Manticore's. Better than the majority of League star systems could have produced, if those other star systems had only realized it, yet still at least a full generation behind the Manties.

"I wish we'd taken out more of their wall, too, Father," he said finally. "On the other hand, the point about their missile supply is extremely well taken. Especially if we can get them to use up most of the ones they've got on the Sollies."

"I know."

Albrecht sipped more wine, then looked down into his glass.

"I know," he repeated, "but I've been thinking. I know they got away from us in the yards, but we know where they *are*, and—"

"No, Father."

The two words came out very firmly, and Albrecht looked up to see Benjamin sitting back from the table and folding his arms across his chest. For a moment, there was something almost comical about the father's wheedling expression and the stern light in the son's eyes.

"I know what you're about to say, Father," Benjamin continued. "In fact, Dan and Collin and I figured it might occur to you as soon as we realized we hadn't caught as many ships in the yards as we'd hoped."

"So the three of you sat down and discussed it behind my back, is that it?" Albrecht's voice could have been ominous, but instead, it was almost quizzical, and Benjamin shrugged.

"You're the one who put me in charge of the Navy, Daniel in charge of research, and Collin in charge of intel, Father. I don't think you did it because you expected us to sit on our brains."

"No, you're right about that," Albrecht acknowledged.

"Well, since we were using them as something besides cushions, it occurred to us to think the same thing you're thinking. If Topolev and Colenso could get into Manticore and Yeltsin's Star undetected, why not do the same thing to Trevor's Star? Pick off the warships we didn't get first time around?"

"That *is* what I was thinking," Albrecht said. "From your response, I'm assuming the three of you decided it wasn't such a great idea after all?"

"Oh, the *idea*'s just fine, Father. The problem is how likely it is that we wouldn't get away with it. Let's face it, Oyster Bay was in many ways a one-off operation. It succeeded because the Manties didn't have a clue about our capabilities. Well, now they do—have a clue, I mean. They still don't know how we did it, but they damned well know we *did* do it, and if nothing else, they're going to be pouncing on every 'ghost footprint' their hyper sensors pick up with everything they've got. And, frankly, the fact that *we* haven't been able to come up with an effective detector for the spider drive doesn't fill me with unbounded confidence that the Manties might not have something we don't even know about that could do the job. I think it's *unlikely*, but I'm not prepared to assume it's impossible.

"So looking at it from the perspective of getting in in the first place, things would be a lot more iffy a second time around—especially a second time around that came close on the heels of Oyster Bay."

Benjamin looked across the table at his father until Albrecht nodded to show he was following so far.

"Secondly," Benjamin continued then, "the force levels we'd require would actually be higher. Oyster Bay succeeded because we could plan on achieving total surprise and our targets were civilian installations. They weren't armored, they didn't have any active or passive defenses in operation, and they couldn't dodge. After what happened to their home system, I can guarantee you no one as experienced as the Manties is going to let us catch their *battle fleet* under circumstances like that. At the very minimum, their impellers are going to be permanently hot. Most likely, they'll have minimum station-keeping wedges up, for that matter, and they're going to have their damned FTL recon platforms deployed widely enough to give them plenty of time to get wedges and sidewalls fully up before *anything* gets close enough to attack. So we'd need a hell of a lot more firepower to achieve decisive results, and, unfortunately, the *Sharks* are too small—and we don't have enough of them—to provide that level of combat power. Worse, in a lot of ways, they're too fragile to survive the kind of damage Manty laserheads can hand out.

"And that brings me to the third point, which is—and, frankly, Father, I think this is probably the most important consideration—that we literally *cannot* afford to lose the *Sharks*. More specifically, we can't afford to lose their *crews*. The people aboard those ships right now are the seed corn for the crews of the ships we're building here in Darius. We've just blown an enormous hole in the Manties' trained manpower, one that's going to be a huge factor in how long it takes them to recover from Oyster Bay. Given the way things are proceeding, and given our own operational and strategic planning, we can't afford to have the same thing happen to us. We're going to be in the position of having to enormously expand our naval personnel no matter what happens, and we don't have the institutional base the Manties do. We *need* every single one of the men and women who carried out Oyster Bay. We need their skills and their experience, and we need them *here*—alive—not vaporized at Trevor's Star."

"Do you really think that would be a likely outcome?" Albrecht asked after several seconds. His tone was curious, not confrontational, and Benjamin shrugged again.

"Frankly? No. I don't think the attack would be anywhere near as successful as Oyster Bay was, and I think giving the Manties another look—or the *chance* for another look, anyway—at our new hardware would be risky, but I don't really think they'd be likely to detect, track, and kill the *Sharks* wholesale. Unfortunately, 'don't think they'd be likely to' isn't a very good basis for operational planning. One thing you taught all of us a long time ago was that we can't *make* the universe be what we want it to be, so we'd better figure out what it really *is* and factor that into our planning. And in this case, the potential return, even assuming everything went near perfectly, doesn't begin to compare to the potential damage we'll take if everything *doesn't* go near perfectly."

Albrecht sat in evident thought for a few moments, then finished the wine in his glass and set it back down on the table.

"You're right. I didn't put any of you boys where you are

just so you could watch me make mistakes. And I hadn't really thought about all the implications you've just pointed out. I still wish we could do it, but you're right. The last thing we need to do is to start making the kind of 'we're invincible' mistakes those jackasses in the League are making. As Isabel would have said, this isn't the time for us to be flying by the seat of our pants if we don't have to."

"Thank you, Father," Benjamin said quietly.

"In the meantime, though," his father said rather more briskly, "I want you and Daniel to come to Mannerheim with me."

"Excuse me?" Benjamin looked at him quizzically, and Albrecht snorted.

"Hurskainen and the others will all be there, and I want you two along to answer any questions—with due regard for operational security, of course—they may have about Oyster Bay."

"Are you sure that's a good idea? If you want us there, we'll come, of course. On the other hand, do we really want to be answering questions about the new systems and the new hardware?"

"That's a very well taken point," Albrecht acknowledged. "On the other hand, these people have all demonstrated their ability to maintain operational security, or we'd never have gotten as far as we have. I think a couple of them are feeling a bit nervous now, though. The way we accelerated Oyster Bay came at them cold, and while I wouldn't say any of them are experiencing what I'd call second thoughts, I do think the...anxiety quotient, let's say, is a bit higher than we might like."

He paused until Benjamin nodded, then he shrugged.

"In its own way, this meeting's going to be even more critical than Oyster Bay was. No one's going public, but we'll be very quietly activating the Alignment as an actual star nation. That's going to represent a huge step, and one we're not going to want to make public until the League's started to show a few surface fissures, at least. But once we begin the process, we're going to have to bring in successively lower levels in all of our member star systems' governments. The fact that we're up to *something* is, frankly, likely to leak out a lot sooner than we'd really prefer. I doubt very much that anyone on the outside is going to figure out what we're *really* up to, but that's not going to guarantee we won't have a few dicey moments in the not too distant future. And most of the people who're going to be in Mannerheim for our little meeting didn't get where they are by being stupid. It's going to occur to them, too, that we're looking at what's in many ways our greatest period of vulnerability over the next T-year or two. That being the case, I'd like them to feel as reassured as possible about the hardware we used in Oyster Bay."

"And if they ask me whether or not we have all that hardware really and truly *operational*?"

"If they ask you that, you admit the *Sharks* were originally intended primarily as prototypes and training vessels, and you don't pretend we have more of them than we do," Albrecht said promptly. "The last thing we need to do is to trip ourselves up by lying to these people—or to ourselves. But at the same time, I think you should point out to them that our plans always envisioned their 'system-defense forces' as the real basis of our joint naval strength, at least in the opening stages. There are *eleven* of them, for God's sake! None of them may be all that huge in isolation, but when you combine them, they get a hell of a lot more impressive. What the MAN represents at this stage is our hole card, the ace we have stuffed up our sleeve just in case we need it. I want them to be aware we have that card and that we can play it if we have to. And I'd like them to recognize that the fleet we're building will have exactly the same capabilities—only better—and be a hell of a lot bigger. I don't want them worrying about whether or not we'll be ready to take center stage as planned when the time comes just because we moved Oyster Bay ahead."

"I see."

It was Benjamin's turn to sit thinking for several seconds. At length, he looked up, met his father's eyes again, and nodded.

"All right, Father. I see what you're saying, and I think Dan and I can probably provide the...comfort quotient you're looking for. As long as they're not expecting us to sail our invincible fleet of invisible superdreadnoughts right into Old Earth orbit next week, at any rate!"

✧ Chapter Thirty-Nine

ALBRECHT DETWEILER sat back in his chair and contemplated the true crown jewels of the "onion" his ancestors had spent so long building.

The conference room in which he sat was probably, at that moment, the most carefully protected, eavesdropping-proof conference room in the entire explored galaxy. If it wasn't, he reflected wryly, it certainly wasn't for lack of trying. This meeting was just as important, and probably even more critical, than Oyster Bay had ever been.

For all its security, it was a large, comfortable chamber, decorated with light sculpture masterpieces carefully chosen from each of the star systems represented by the people in it. Each of the chairs around the enormous table at the center of the room had cost enough to put a student through college on most Fringe planets, and the console in front of each of them was equipped with every conceivable feature . . . including the very latest in security systems.

The people seated around the table looked right at home in the understated elegance and clean beauty of the conference room's decor, and for very good reason. Every one of the others was actually rather more physically attractive than Detweiler himself, offering a level of physical beauty that was really quite remarkable. In fact, it was even more remarkable when one saw them all gathered in one place, but that was inevitable. The advantage which physical attractiveness bestowed upon any politician, regardless of the political system in which he worked, appeared to be one of the unchanging verities of the human condition.

Counting Detweiler himself, there were an even dozen people seated at the table and, extraordinarily unusual though it was, none of the others was accompanied by a single attendant or aide. It was probably the first time that had been true for most of them in at least twenty T-years, Detweiler thought, which was fairly amusing. He himself had always been as hands-on as possible, and he actually treasured solitude in which to get on with his current project. Most of the others had succumbed, to one extent or another, to the desire to underscore their importance (if only to themselves) by surrounding themselves with at least a small core of assistants. Yet this time around, he was flanked by three of his sons—Benjamin, Collin, and Daniel—while the others sat unaccompanied.

On the other hand, it wasn't as if his sons were there to bolster his importance. There was no need for that, not in this room on this day, and all the others knew the younger Detweilers were present as working members of their council, not mere aides or go-fors. In fact, they were effectively cabinet officers in an extraordinarily powerful star nation...even if none of the rest of the galaxy happened to have heard of it.

Although that, of course, would be subject to change...at the right moment.

Which was approaching rapidly, he thought, and cleared his throat.

It wasn't a very loud sound, but the conference room's acoustics were as phenomenal as the rest of its design. Various small, quiet-voiced side conversations came to an abrupt end, and heads turned as their owners looked in his direction.

"Well," he said in a deliberately understated tone, "I suppose it's time we get down to business, isn't it?"

Every one of the nine men and two women seated around that table with him was the head of state of a star system-wide government, whereas Albrecht Detweiler had no official title. For that matter, the number of people who even knew he existed was minute. But there was no question, as they nodded in response to his comment, who was in charge in that conference room.

"I know all of you have heard preliminary reports on the

success of Oyster Bay," he continued. "Benjamin here"—he nodded sideways at his oldest son—"will give you the official report in a few minutes. I can tell you already, however, that the preliminary accounts have actually understated the damage we did to the Manties and the Graysons. I'm not prepared to call it a *total* success, but that's more because I always want that little bit higher level of accomplishment than because of any failure or shortcoming in the way this operation was planned and executed.

"Benjamin and Collin will also be briefing you on Kolokoltsov and the rest of the Quintet's decision to sign off on Rajampet's attack on the Manticoran home system." He smiled thinly. "Needless to say, that operation's going to be somewhat less successful than our own was."

A quiet chuckle ran around the table, and his smile grew broader for a moment. Then his expression sobered.

"What all this means, of course, is that it's time. I'm sure none of you are surprised to hear me say that I'm formally activating the Alignment's constitutional agreements today."

It was very, very quiet in the conference room, and he let the quiet linger. There was no need for any theatrical emphasis with these people. Every single one of them was the product of an alpha line—most of them of lines almost as old and highly developed as the Detweiler genotype itself—and they'd been aware for the better part of two decades that the end towards which they and their ancestors had worked was almost certain to come in their own lifetimes.

He considered them one at a time.

Stanley Hurskainen, the President of the Republic of Mannerheim, sat to Albrecht's right. He was a reassuringly solid presence, a hundred and ninety centimeters tall, with powerful shoulders, intense brown eyes, and dark, straight hair. No one could have been more cosmopolitan than he, yet he wore his hair in a wrist-thick braid that fell below his shoulders, like a throwback to some barbarian warrior ancestor. It should have struck the eye as anachronistic; instead, it suited him just as much—and just as inevitably, somehow—as his exquisite tailoring and perfect manicure. Which was probably appropriate, given that the Mannerheim System-Defense Force was far and away the most powerful of the Alignment's component navies.

Chancellor Walter Ford, who headed the most colorfully named of the alignment's political units—the Second Chance Republic of the Matagorda System—sat on the other side of Hurskanien. Ford was the oldest person in the room, a good twenty-five T-years older than Albrecht himself, and his seniority often made him a sort of unofficial spokesman for the others. He'd allowed his dark brown hair to go silver which, coupled with his warm brown eyes and pleasantly worn-looking face, made him someone any HD director would cheerfully have cast as anyone's favorite uncle, but there was a deadly quick brain behind that comfortable, low-key façade.

Clinton Thompson, King Clinton III of the Kingdom of New Madagascar, sat to Ford's right. The king was a dynamic-looking, striking man, with auburn hair, coal-black eyes, and an intense, focused face. He sat with a curiously catlike relaxation which was both total and yet seemed poised for instant motion, and he had the powerful wrists of the champion-grade fencer he'd been before he ascended to the throne.

Board Chairman Joan Kubrick, one of the only two women in the current generation of the Alignment's heads of state, sat between the king and Anton Polanski. Kubrick was the smallest person in the room. In fact, at just under a hundred and fifty-five centimeters, she was downright tiny, extraordinarily petite and delicate looking. Which was deceiving. With her chestnut hair, blue eyes, and dark complexion, she looked almost child-like, belying the enhancement of her musculature and skeleton.

Polanski was the system president of the Line System, and if Ford was the oldest person in the room, Polanski was the second-youngest. Only Daniel was younger than he, but Polanski had established himself as a concert-level guitarist before he followed his family tradition and entered politics. He had golden hair, green eyes, a very pale complexion, and fine hands, with long, slender fingers.

Roman Hitchcock, the president of the Visigoth System, was the most rugged looking of the people around the table, at least as far as his features were concerned. He had black hair, dark-gray eyes, and a strong nose, but in comparison to Hurskainen, who could easily have served as an artist's model for a barbarian king, Hitchcock was not only ten centimeters shorter, but built for speed and agility instead of raw power.

Nikomedes Kakadelis, Chief Counsel of the Democratic Republic of Thrace, was the only person there whose appearance really suited the traditional Old Earth ethnicity of his name. He had dark, curly hair, blue eyes, a strong nose and chin, and a slightly olive complexion. He was barely eight centimeters taller than Kubrick, but that was the only physical similarity between them. He had a weight lifter's physique and a wrestler's arms.

Beyond Kakadelis, Director Vincent Stone, who headed the Directorate of New Orkney, was almost too pretty. He had extraordinarily regular features, and a nose just on the masculine side of delicate, liquid brown eyes, a cleft chin, and hair as dark as a raven's wing. In fact, he was so "pretty" people often overlooked his powerful physique. Despite his youthful appearance, he was one of the older people in the room, and he'd also been a highly decorated naval officer before *he* entered politics... which, of course, had been part of the plan for his career from the beginning.

Coming around the end of the table, back toward the Detweilers, was Rebecca Monticelli, president of the Comstock Republic and the only other woman present. She could have been deliberately designed by the Alignment's geneticists to contrast with Kubrick, although it had actually just worked out that way. She had black hair, dark eyes, and a skier's tan—not surprisingly, since her favorite recreational pastime was cross-country skiing. She was also a good two centimeters taller than the famous Honor Alexander-Harrington—in fact, she and Hurskanien were the two tallest people in the room—and *her* genotype included even more musculature enhancement than the Meyerdahl first wave's.

Next was Chancellor Robert Tarantino of the Republic of New Bombay. Personally, Detweiler found Tarantino just a bit on the irritating side. It wasn't really the chancellor's fault, but one of the quirks in the Tarantino genotype had expressed unusually vigorously in his case, with the result that he was one of the most physically restless people Detweiler had ever met. He had platinum hair, brown eyes, and a slightly swarthy complexion, and he was constantly fiddling with something. In fact, Detweiler had once experimented by taking Tarantino's old-fashioned "worry rock" away from him to see what would happen, only to find the chancellor tapping his toes under the table in time with his fingers' drumming on his knees. Despite that, he was an extremely capable political leader, with multiple advanced degrees—in economics and physics—and he enjoyed a League-wide reputation as an economic policymaker.

And, finally, to Albrecht's left, was Reynaldo Lucas—Marquis Reynaldo IV, of the Marquisate of Denver. He was sandy-haired, with hazel eyes and a neatly trimmed beard. Like Hurskainen, he favored long hair, and the Lucas genome shared some of the Polanski genome's musical talent. In Lucas's case, it expressed as a magnificent baritone singing voice rather than an instrumental ability, however.

An extraordinarily capable group of people by any standard, he thought, trying hard not to feel complacent. And they, and their families (and a substantial portion of the *rest* of their home-worlds' political and economic elites, for that matter), were every one of them part of the Alignment. Part of its strategy, proof of its genetic superiority, recruited—or, in some cases, inserted—generations before. The Hurskainen genome, for example, had been placed in Visigoth over three T-centuries ago. Stanley Hurskainen represented the fifteenth generation of that alpha line, and the Thompson genome on New Madagascar was even older. None were as old and prestigious as the Detweiler genome, yet unlike the Detweilers, they and their parents and grandparents and great-grandparents and great-great-grandparents had been open parts of their homeworlds' societies. Indeed, they'd been put in place for exactly this moment.

"I hope you'll forgive me for saying this, Albrecht," Ford said after a moment, "but I wish you could come into the open at the same time. We all understand why you can't, but it just seems... wrong, somehow."

"Thank you, Walt. I appreciate that," Detweiler said, and he did. It wasn't flattery or sycophancy on Ford's part, and he saw agreement in most of the others' faces.

"I appreciate it, but we all know why I can't."

Ford nodded, as did a couple of the others, and Detweiler reminded himself—again—of all the manifold reasons what he'd just said was true.

The last thing they could afford at this critical juncture was for the rest of the galaxy to decide that the corrupt, outlaw corporations of Mesa were secretly pulling the strings behind these men and women. The very thing that made them so critical to the Alignment's ultimate success was the fact that there had never been a single trace of a connection between one of them and Mesa. All of them came from families which had been part of their native societies for so long their bona fides were beyond question. All had well-earned reputations as capable, farsighted, deeply involved heads of state. Each had expressed his or her own condemnation of genetic slavery, and most had been actively involved in stamping it out in their own societies. And unlike the vast majority of Solarian League politicians, there had never been even a hint of corruption or venality attached to any of them.

Which meant they were absolutely essential. When the Manties hammered the SLN into wreckage yet again—when the carefully primed "spontaneous rebellions" broke out in a dozen places simultaneously in the Verge as the League Navy's reputation crumbled, and when the score of Frontier Security governors who'd been carefully prepared by their own versions of Aldona Anisimovna followed the example of the Maya Sector and unilaterally assumed emergency powers in order to "protect" the citizens of their sectors—the men and women around this table with Albert Detweiler would emerge as the leaders of a new interstellar power.

The Alignment's strategists had picked the name for that power—the Renaissance Factor—decades ago, and the exquisitely orchestrated crescendo of disasters would "force" them into taking steps to protect their own star systems from the tide of anarchy. They wouldn't *call* themselves a star nation—not immediately—but that was what they would be. And, in the fullness of time, when it was obvious to the entire galaxy that they were simply responding to the catastrophic, totally unanticipated disintegration of the League, they would finally, regretfully, exercise their constitutional right to secede from the League and formally assume their position as a sovereign star nation.

A star nation which had grown solely out of their emergency association to stave off collapse. On which had nothing at all to do with Mesa...and which would painstakingly avoid anything that could be even remotely construed as a eugenics policy.

Until, that was, the rest of the galaxy discovered that the Renaissance Factor had become exactly what it called itself—the reinvigorated successor of the Solarian League, at least as big and powerful as the League itself had ever been, and dedicated, indeed, to the rebirth of humanity in a new and glorious future of potential fully realized at last.

Albrecht Detweiler wasn't at all certain he himself, even with prolong and the "natural" longevity engineered into his genes, would live long enough to see that day arrive. But that was all right, for he was seeing something even more important. He was seeing *this* day, when centuries of sacrifice, planning, and unceasing labor had finally come to fruition and forced the path of human history into the rightful direction from which the sanctimonious Beowulf Code and the human race's hysterical reaction to Old Earth's Final War had diverted it so long ago. None of them would live long enough to see the completion of the journey upon which their entire species had just unknowingly set out, but every one of them knew it would come, and that *they*—they and their ancestors—were the ones who had made that so.

"We all know why I can't," Albrecht Detweiler repeated softly. "But when the eleven of you stand up and announce the Factor's existence, believe me, I'll be standing right there with you. And I can't think of anyone I could possibly be prouder to have representing all of us."

Chapter Forty

"YES, DENIS?"

Eloise Pritchart tried—tried *hard*—not to sound irritated as Denis LePic's face appeared on her com display, but LePic had known her too long and too well for her to fool him. Besides, even a saint (which Eloise Pritchart had never pretended to be) would have been irritated by a call which came in exactly one hour and seventeen minutes after she'd *finally* gotten to bed.

"I'm very sorry to disturb you, Madam President," he said, rather more formally than he normally addressed her when no one else was present, "but I thought about it very carefully, first. Technically, there's no reason I *had* to screen you right this moment, but the more I thought about it, the more I realized you'd never forgive me if I waited till morning."

"I beg your pardon?" Pritchart's topaz eyes had narrowed intently.

"You may remember that we've all been concerned about a certain intelligence operative who'd dropped out of sight?"

He paused, and the eyes which had just narrowed flared wide.

"Yes," she said rather more slowly, "as a matter of fact, I *do* remember. Why?"

"Because he's just reappeared," LePic said. "And he has a friend with him. And the two of them have a new friend—one I think you're going to want to talk to yourself."

"And is Sheila going to be willing to let me into the same room with this 'new friend' of his?"

"As a matter of fact, I think she's likely to pitch five kinds of fit at the mere prospect," LePic said a bit wryly. "But since I'm quite positive Kevin is going to want to be there, as well—not to mention Tom, Wilhelm, and Linda Trenis—I feel fairly confident about your security."

"I see." Pritchart gazed at him for several seconds, her mind accelerating to full speed as it brushed off the remnants of sleep. "Tell me," she said, "did our friend find his new friend where we thought he might?"

"Oh, I think you could say that, Madam President. Not only that, but he's a very *impressive* new friend. I've only managed to skim the report our wandering lad finally got around to delivering, but based just on what I've seen so far, I think I can safely say you're about to discover that just about everything we thought we knew, we don't. Know, I mean."

Pritchart inhaled deeply as LePic's expression finally penetrated fully. What she'd mistaken for humor, possibly even amusement at having awakened her, was something else entirely. A mask. Or perhaps not so much a *mask* as a thin surface veneer of calm, a fragile shield for the shocked echoes of a universe turned upside down still rumbling around somewhere deep inside him.

"Well, in that case," she heard her own voice saying calmly, "I think you'd better go ahead and start waking up a few other people."

✧   ✧   ✧

"So, our wandering boy returns, I see," Eloise Pritchart murmured, an hour later, as Victor Cachat, a troll-like man who looked suspiciously like the officially deceased Anton Zilwicki, and a sandy-haired, hazel-eyed man were escorted into the Octagon briefing room. "Welcome home, Officer Cachat. We'd been wondering why you hadn't written."

Somewhat to her surprise, Cachat actually colored with what looked a lot like embarrassment. It probably wasn't, she told herself—that would be too much to hope for, although she couldn't think of anything else it might have been—and turned her attention to the young man's companions. "And this, I take it, is the redoubtable Captain Zilwicki?"

If Cachat might have looked a little embarrassed—or harried, at least—Zilwicki, despite the fact that (as a Manticoran) he was in the very presence of his enemies, didn't. In fact, he didn't really look like a troll, either, she admitted. He actually looked more like a granite boulder, or perhaps an artist's model for a mountain dwarf. The grim, *dangerous* sort of mountain dwarf. If he felt any emotion at this moment, it was probably amusement, she decided. Well, that and something else. An odd fusion of emotions that were almost like grim triumph coupled with singing anxiety, all under the control of iron self-discipline. It was the first time she'd ever actually laid eyes on the Manticoran, and he was even more impressive in person than she'd expected. No wonder he and Cachat made such a formidable combination.

"I'm afraid the galaxy at large thinks you're, well, *dead*, Captain Ziliwicki," she said. "I'm pleased to see the reports were in error. Although I'm sure quite a few people in Manticore are going to be just as curious to know where you've been for the last several months as we are about Officer Cachat's whereabouts."

"I'm sure there are, too, Madam President." Zilwicki's voice was exactly the deep, rolling one she would have expected out of his physique. "Unfortunately, we had a little, um, engine trouble on the way home. It took us several months to make repairs." He grimaced. "We played a lot of cards," he added.

"I imagine so." The President cocked her head. "And I imagine you've also discovered there have been a few developments since whatever happened—and I do trust you're going to tell us what it was that *did* happen—in Green Pines?"

"I'm sure that will be covered, Ma'am," Zilwicki said, and there was more than a trace of grimness in his tone. "It wasn't much like the 'official version' I've heard, but it was bad enough."

Pritchart gazed at him for a moment, then nodded slowly. So, he and Cachat had been involved, at least peripherally. Of course, when it turned out he was still alive, it was going to be a nasty blow to *Mesa's* version of events. She found that notion appealing.

"But I don't believe I know who *this* gentleman is," she continued, looking at the third member of the ill-assorted trio her security detail was watching like a bevy of particularly ill-tempered hawks.

The stranger's expression was the most interesting of the three, actually, she thought. He was obviously nervous as a cat at a dog show, and not just because of the way Shiela Thiessen and her cohorts were watching him. Yet there was something else, as well...something that seemed to mingle determination as grim and purposeful as Anton Zilwicki's with something very like...guilt?

"No, Madam President, you don't—yet." If Cachat had, in fact, felt anything approaching embarrassment, there was no sign of it in his reply. "This is Dr. Herlander Simões. Of the planet Mesa."

Pritchart felt her eyes narrowing again. She, Theisman, LePic, Linda Trenis, and Victor Lewis sat side by side across a conference table from the three chairs waiting for Cachat, Zilwicki, and Simões. Of them all, only LePic had had the opportunity to even skim Cachat's preliminary report, however, and the fact that the Attorney General hadn't even wasted any time personally debriefing Cachat and his companions before bringing them straight to her said a great deal about how *he'd* reacted to whatever it was they'd discovered.

Or *thought* they'd discovered, at least, she reminded herself.

"I see." She gazed speculatively at the Mesan, then cocked her head. "May I assume Dr. Simões is the reason you've been . . . out of touch, let's say, for the last, oh, six or seven T-months?" she asked after a moment.

"He's *one* of the reasons, Ma'am," Cachat replied.

"Then, by all means, be seated," she invited, waving a hand at the empty chairs, "and let's hear what you—and Dr. Simões, of course—have to tell us."

"My God," a visibly shaken Eloise Pritchart said several hours later. "My dear sweet God, Tom. Do you think this could possibly be *true*?"

Thomas Theisman hadn't seen the President's face that pale since Genevieve Chin and her battered survivors crawled home from the Battle of Manticore. In fact, he hadn't seen her this close to being literally stunned since he'd personally brought her the news of Javier Giscard's death. Not that he blamed her, since he was fairly certain his own expression was pretty much an exact mirror of hers.

"I . . . don't know," he admitted slowly, leaning back in his chair and shaking his head. "I don't know. But—"

He paused and closed his eyes for a moment, his mind running back over Dr. Simões' incredible rolling barrage of revelations. And the even more incredible—and maddeningly incomplete— hints of still more of them which a Mesan named Jack McBryde had doled out to prove the value of allowing him to defect to the Republic. At the time, he'd been able to do little more than sit there and listen, just trying to absorb the devastating series of blows to his understanding of how the galaxy was organized. Of course it couldn't possibly be true! And yet...

"As a matter of fact," he said, opening his eyes and bringing his chair back fully upright again, "I think it could be. True, I mean."

"It's got to be some kind of organized disinformation operation, Madam President," Linda Trenis argued. Yet even as she spoke, her tone said that, like Theisman, she thought it might just possibly be true. That it was her job to be skeptical, and so she would, even though, deep down inside, where instinct took over from trained intellect...

"I think Admiral Theisman may be right, Linda," Victor Lewis disagreed. "In fact, I think I actually believe it."

The CO of Operational Research sounded as if he were surprised to hear himself saying it, but his expression was probably closer to normal than that of anyone else in the President's office. Where the others' faces still looked rather like Pritchart had always assumed a poleaxed steer must look, his was intensely thoughtful.

"But—" Pritchart began.

"Think about it, Eloise," Theisman interrupted. She looked at him, and he shrugged. "Think about what Simões said—and what Cachat and Zilwicki both agree this McBryde had to say, as well. Crazy as it all sounds, it all hangs together, too."

Pritchart started to protest again, then made herself stop. Insane as it all seemed, Theisman was right. It *did* hang together. Of course, if Trenis was right about its being some sort of disinformation effort, it *would* hang together. On the other hand, she thought, there probably wouldn't be quite so many gaps in their information, either. If someone had wanted to sell the Republic a bill of goods, they would have come up with plausible excuses and lies to plug more of those holes.

And they would have known Zilwicki was alive, since they needed him to get the disinformation home. So they'd hardly have announced he was dead! Except, of course, that according to McBryde's story, the system government in Mesa doesn't even realize how riddled it is with agents of this "Alignment," so the government might've put the Green Pines story together without any orders from its... puppet masters.

Oh, lord! Did I really just think all that? She shook her head. *My brain hurts already, and it's not even dawn yet.*

"I agree with Admiral Theisman," Lewis said quietly but firmly. "And, no offense, Linda, but if it's a case of disinformation, I don't

see what the hell—pardon me, Madam President—it's supposed
to be disinforming us *about*! Try as I might, I can't think of any
conceivable reason for anyone on Mesa to try to convince the
Republic of Haven we're on some centuries-long interstellar hit
list right along with the Manties. Can anyone else in this office
come up with a reason any Mesan would be doing anything that
could so radically shake up our relations with the Star Empire?
Something which might convince us we actually have an enemy
in *common* and point both of us directly at *them*?"

"Admiral Lewis has a point there, Madam President," Denis LePic
agreed, his own eyes narrowing in thought. "And there's another
point, too. Cachat and Zilwicki independently confirmed the explosion that took out this 'Gamma Center' of Simões'. While I'm willing
to concede that a good disinformation operation requires enough
capital investment to make it convincing, somehow I find it a bit
difficult to believe that even someone like Manpower would set
off a high-kiloton-range nuke right on top of one of their own top
management's bedroom communities just to sell us on it."

"And assuming McBryde knew what he was talking about, it
makes at least a little sense out of the fact that Manpower—or
this 'Mesan Alignment,' at least—has been acting so much like a
belligerent star nation," Theisman pointed out. "It *is* a belligerent
star nation; it's just that no one else realized it."

"Oh, how I *wish* they'd been able to get McBryde out, too,"
Pritchart said with soft, terrible passion, then waved both hands
contritely when Theisman gave her a speaking glance.

"I know—I know!" she said. "*If* this is true, we're incredibly
lucky to have even a clue of it, much less Simões. I'm sure he's
going to turn out to be incredibly valuable—if this is true—in
the long run, but he's a tech geek." Theisman's lips twitched at
the President's choice of noun, and she shook a finger at him.
"Don't you dare smile at that, Tom Theisman! Instead, think of
him as Shannon Foraker." Theisman's nascent smile disappeared,
and she nodded. "Right. That's *exactly* the kinds of holes we're
going to have in any political or strategic military information
he can give us, no matter how good the debrief is."

"And assuming there's any way to verify that what he's telling
us is the truth," Trenis observed. They all looked at her, and she
shrugged. "All our critical naval personnel are supplied with anti-
interrogation protection. It's effective against every drug therapy

we know about, but we've always recognized there are likely to be therapies we *don't* know about. I think we have to assume the Mesans are at least as aware of that as we are—I mean, let's remember where all their traditional expertise is focused. And given anyone as ruthless as McBryde and Simões have described, and anyone whose security's been good enough to keep all of this black literally for centuries, I have to think they've probably included some kind of suicide protocol to keep anyone from pumping someone as critical as Simões sounds like being."

"Or, for that matter, if McBryde was telling the truth about this new nanotech of theirs, God only knows what he might be programmed to do under, um, rigorous interrogation," LePic said.

"Well, so far, at least, they don't appear to have installed anything to keep him from *voluntarily* spilling the beans when he's not under duress," Lewis pointed out. "If we sit him down with our own hyper physicists and let them start going over what he can tell them about this 'streak drive' of theirs, we should at least be able to tell whether or not the math holds together. Which would tend to verify—or disprove—one large chunk of what he's already told us."

"Maybe—eventually," Pritchart replied. "On the other hand, I'm no hyper physicist, obviously, but I'd be surprised if they could confirm or disprove what he's got to say very quickly." She grimaced. "To be honest, the Manties could probably do that faster than we could, given how far ahead of us they are in compensators and grav-pulse bandwidth."

"For that matter," Theisman said with a crooked smile, "it's a pity Duchess Harrington's not around anymore. I'll bet Nimitz could tell us whether or not he's lying. Or whether he's lying to us knowingly, at least."

Pritchart nodded, but she also leaned back in her own chair, her lips pursed, her expression intent. Trenis started to say something more, only to stop as Theisman raised his hand and shook his head. He, LePic, and the two admirals sat silently, watching the President think, while endless seconds ticked past. Then, finally, she looked back at Theisman, and there was something at the backs of her topaz eyes. Something that made the Secretary of War distinctly uneasy.

"I think we have to assume at least the possibility that McBryde and Simões were both genuine defectors and both of them were telling the truth," she said. "As Denis has pointed out, nuking one of your own towns—even a small one, if it happens to be a luxury satellite suburb for your own elite and their families—is an awful steep price to pay just to sell a lie to someone light-centuries away from you. Especially what could only be a *pointless* lie, since, like Admiral Lewis, I can't see any way having us believe all this would *help* Manpower."

No one else said anything, and she smiled wryly. The expression went oddly with that bleak, hard fire behind her eyes.

"It's going to take a while for me to get my mind wrapped around the concept that for the last five or six centuries a bunch of would-be genetic supermen have been plotting to impose their own view of the future on the human race. In one way, it's actually easier for me because it includes those Manpower bastards. I'm so used to thinking of them as the scum of the galaxy, capable of anything as long as it suits their purposes, that I can actually see them as the villains of any piece. But this master plan of theirs, this 'Alignment,' is something else."

"If McBryde was right about the Alignment having been involved with the Legislaturalists—and especially with DuQuesne—then it may be possible for us to turn up evidence of it," LePic said thoughtfully. "I know we'd be going back a long way," he continued when the others looked at him, "but we never had any reason to suspect outside influence before. That puts a whole new perspective on how we got stuck with the 'People's Republic' in the first place, and if we look at the records from that angle, we may spot something no one even had a reason to look for at the time."

"You really think they could've played any significant role in that, Sir?" Trenis asked. He raised an eyebrow at her, and she grimaced. "To be honest, that was one of the bells and whistles that most strongly suggested disinformation to me. I mean," she turned to Pritchart, "I'm always up for a good conspiracy theory, Madam President—God knows the history of the People's Republic's left all of us ready for that! But managing to overthrow someone else's Constitution without leaving a single fingerprint—?"

The admiral waved her own hands in a baffled gesture, but Pritchart shook her head.

"Actually, I'm inclined to see that as a point in McBryde's favor," she replied, and snorted harshly at Trenis' surprised expression. "If there's anything to this at all, these people obviously think in terms of century-long operational frameworks, Admiral. For that matter, think of the chutzpah involved in anyone's thinking they could actually overthrow something as big and powerful as the Solarian League! Anybody willing to take *that* on would look at destabilizing something as small as the Old Republic as an exercise in light lifting. For that matter, they may even've seen it as a setting up exercise—a chance to practice their technique before the main event!"

"Assuming someone's actually managed to put something like this together, the fact that they've taken such a long view would make them extraordinarily dangerous," Theisman said thoughtfully. LePic, Trenis, and Lewis looked at him interrogatively, but Pritchart only nodded with an odd blend of curtness and grim approval, as if he was following her own chain of logic.

"Think about it," he told the others. "If they're willing to approach something like this on a *generational* basis—if their strategists at any given moment have been willing to work towards something that's not going to happen until their grandchildren's or their great-grandchildren's time—think about the kinds of covers they could build for their agents. We could be looking at twenty or thirty *generations* of sleepers, for God's sake! There could be people right here in Nouveau Paris, people whose families have been solid citizens of the Republic for three or four hundred years, who are actually part of this Alignment. Think about the kind of intelligence penetration that implies. Or about how long and subtly they could work on influencing political trends and policies. Or the media."

The others weren't looking confused anymore. In fact, all three of them were rather pale as Theisman's implications sank home.

"You're right," Pritchart agreed. "On the other hand, let's not get too carried away. *They* may think they're superwomen, but I don't see why we should start thinking of them that way. I don't doubt they could do exactly what you're describing, Tom. In fact, that may well be what they did to the Old Republic. But however long they've been planning, they've still got to hold themselves to a manageable level of complexity. They've got to be able to *coordinate* everything, and we've had enough experience trying to coordinate the Republic to know how tall an order that can be even when we don't have to worry about keeping communications lines covert. Which has particular point in a case like this, I suspect, since I tend to doubt they could bury their sleepers quite as deeply as you've just suggested. There's got to be at least some contact somewhere if they aren't going to lose their assets simply because someone dies before she gets around to telling her son or daughter 'Oh, by the way. We're actually secret agents for the Mesan Alignment. Here's your secret decoder kit. Be ready to be contacted by the Galactic Evil Overlord on Frequency X with orders to betray the society you've been raised all your life to think of as your own.'"

"Granted." Theisman nodded. "But that contact could be damned well hidden, especially when no one's had any reason to look for it in the first place."

"I agree, Sir," Victor Lewis said. "Still, the President just made another excellent point. For them to make this work, they have to have an almost fanatical respect for the KISS principle." LePic laughed harshly, and the admiral smiled—briefly—at him. "I'm not talking about their overall strategy, Sir. Obviously, they haven't been afraid to think big where *that's* concerned! But if they've genuinely managed to keep all this under wraps for so long, and if they've actually gotten far enough along they're really ready to pull the trigger, then they have got to be some of the best covert operators in the history of humanity. And from our own experience, I can tell you that for them to have managed that, they have to have been pretty damned ruthless about prioritizing and assessing risks. They're probably willing to be as complicated as they have to be to accomplish anything they feel is genuinely critical, and they're probably operating on a huge scale, but they're not going to operate on any *huger* scale than they think they absolutely have to."

"That actually fits in with what we've seen so far, assuming what's been happening to the Manties is actually part of this strategy McBryde described to Cachat and Zilwicki," LePic acknowledged with a thoughtful expression. "They've got pieces in motion all over the board, but when you come right down to it, aside from the actual attack on the Manties' home system, none of it's required a lot of manpower"—he winced at his own unintentional double entendre but continued gamely—"or military muscle of their *own*. In fact, almost all the movement we've seen could have been produced very economically. Get to Byng and Crandall, and maybe one or two of the Kolokoltsov group, then add somebody around *your* level in the military, Tom, and you get the fleet movements that brought the Manties into conflict with the Sollies. And then momentum—Solly arrogance, the inherent corruption of the League's system, the lack of meaning-ful political control, the competition between Frontier Security satrapies, the desire for revenge because of the way the Manties had humiliated them militarily—pushes things along with very little additional effort on your part. Meanwhile, you concentrate your intensive efforts somewhere else—organizing whatever was in some of those 'bargaining points' McBryde was hanging on to to encourage Cachat to get him out—where *informed* cooperation is critical to your final strategy."

"Which brings us back to Nouveau Paris," Pritchart said grimly.

The others looked at her, and she barked a metallic, snarling laugh.

"Of course it does! For that matter, Tom, you and I have already discussed this, in a way. If McBryde was telling the truth about the existence of this 'assassination nanotech' of theirs, I think we finally know what happened to Yves Grosclaude, don't we?" She showed her teeth, and this time the glare at the backs of her eyes burned like a topaz balefire. "Frankly, it ties in rather neatly with the only bits and pieces of forensic evidence Kevin and Inspector Abrioux managed to come up with at the time. And just why, do you think, was this 'Mesan Alignment' kind enough to provide Arnold with one of its most closely held, top secret toys? Remember what you were just saying about sleepers, Tom? And that little comment of yours, Denis, about producing movement economically?"

The others were staring at her in shock, and she wondered why. From the instant she'd heard about McBryde's description of the new Mesan nanotechnology, she'd realized what had happened to Grosclaude. And if one of this "Alignment's" critical objectives was the destruction of both the Star Empire of Manticore and the Republic of Haven, what better, more elegant way to go about it than to send them back to war with one another?

"It makes sense, doesn't it?" she pressed. "They played us *mo* by having Arnold doctor the diplomatic correspondence. Hell, they may've had someone at the other end doing the same thing for High Ridge! No one's seen hide nor hair of Descroix ever since the wheels came off, now have they? And then, when we figured out what Arnold had done, they played *Elizabeth* by convincing her we'd killed Webster and tried to kill her niece exactly the same way the Legislaturalists killed her father and Saint-Just tried to kill *her*! God only knows how many millions of civilians and spacers—ours and the Manties'—these . . . *people* have gotten killed over the past eighty T-years or so, and Elizabeth—and I—both walked straight into it when it was *our* turn!"

The President's rage was a bare-fanged, bristling presence in the office now. Then Theisman raised one hand in a cautionary gesture.

"Assuming a single word of what McBryde told Cachat and Zilwicki is true, you may well be right, Eloise," he said quietly. "In fact, assuming there's any truth to it, I think you almost certainly *are* right. But at the same time, it may *not* be true. I don't know about you, but there's a part of *me* that would really, really like to be able to blame all the people we've killed—and the people we've had killed on our own side—on someone else's evil machinations instead of our own inherent ability to screw up. It may be that that's what happened. But before we start operating on that assumption, we've got to find some way to test whether or not it is."

"Oh, I agree with you entirely, Tom," Pritchart said. "At the same time, though, I think we've already got enough, what with the records Cachat and Zilwicki brought home of the Green Pines explosions and how they *don't* match the Mesa version, what Simões can tell us, what our own scientists can tell us about his new drive claims, to justify very quietly reaching out to Congress."

Theisman looked distinctly alarmed, as did LePic. Trenis and Lewis, on the other hand, were obviously trying very hard *not* to look alarmed. In fact, they were trying so hard—and failing so completely—that the President chuckled much more naturally.

"I'm not planning on talking to anyone unless Leslie, Kevin Usher, and probably you, Tom, all agree that, whoever it is, she's at least her own woman. And, trust me, I'm thinking in terms of a preliminary security vetting *God* might not pass! And I'm certainly not going to bring anyone like McGwire or Younger in on this until and unless we feel absolutely certain McBryde's and Simões's information is credible. But if we *do* come to that conclusion, this is going to change every single one of our foreign policy assumptions. That being the case, I think we need to start doing a little very careful, very circumspect spadework as soon as possible."

MAY 1922 POST DIASPORA

"If the Solarian League wants a war, the Solarian League will *have* one."

—Queen Elizabeth III of Manticore

Chapter Forty-One

"GOOD MORNING," Albrecht Detweiler said, looking into the camera. "I know it's only been a couple of weeks since we last met, but since then, we've received confirmation the Sollies are going to employ Filareta as we'd hoped."

He paused, reflecting on just how disastrous it could be if the message he was recording fell into someone else's hands. The odds of that happening were literally too minute even to be calculated, or he would never have recorded it in the first place, of course. Only eleven copies of it would be made—one for each of the "Renaissance Factor's" heads of state, on high-security, DNA-coded chips—and each of them would be transported by streak boat in locked, dead-man's switch-controlled, self-destruct-equipped cases for hand-delivery by the Alignment's most trusted couriers. Every precaution for transporting secure information which had been developed during six centuries of successful conspiracy and covert operations had been integrated into the conduits connecting his office to the message's recipients. If anyone had managed to compromise one of those conduits, the entire strategy was doomed anyway, so there really wasn't much point resorting to circumlocution to keep any unauthorized souls who might hypothetically see it from figuring out what he was saying.

"Assuming he manages to meet the specified movement schedule," he went on after a moment, "he should reach Manticore almost exactly three T-weeks from today. Although he's probably clever enough to have at least a few suspicions about how Crandall came to be placed where she was, which means he's probably cherishing a few second thoughts about his own relationship with Manpower, there's not much wiggle room in the orders Rajampet and the Security Board have cut for him. And it's clear from those orders that they've bought into the theory that Manticore's 'mysterious attackers' must have pretty thoroughly gutted the home system's defenses."

Profound satisfaction glittered in his eyes with the last sentence. Getting that particular "conclusion" into the SLN's thought processes had been simpler than he'd expected, although the latest reports from both Collin and Franklin indicated that was going to get harder in the next few months. Well, it wasn't as if that hadn't been anticipated all along. As the catastrophic scope of ONI's threat appreciation failures was driven home in gutted starships and dead spacers, even *Solly* admirals were bound to realize a thorough housecleaning of their intelligence services was in order. It would be interesting to see if the present senior officers at ONI and OpAn were publicly scapegoated or simply shuffled out to pasture, but it was inevitable that more competent successors (after all, there couldn't be any *less* competent successors) would replace them.

"So, unless something totally unanticipated happens—which, of course, is always possible, unfortunately," he continued, "Filareta will follow his orders and demand Manticore's surrender. At which point, the Manties will refuse and he and most of his superdreadnoughts will get exactly the same treatment Crandall got at Spindle. And if it should happen that restraint seems likely to rear its ugly head at the critical moment, we've taken a few precautions to . . . help the situation along, let's say."

He paused again, smiling thinly.

"Frankly, it seems most likely to us from our sources in Old Chicago that if, in fact, Filareta gets himself as thoroughly smashed as Crandall did, the follow-up wave Rajampet is currently planning will get put on indefinite hold. There has to be a limit to how many superdreadnoughts even the SLN is willing to pour down a rat hole, after all.

"Even if that happens, however, we have . . . arrangements in place to see to it that at least a dozen members of of the Assembly will demand explanations. There's even a possibility—which, to be honest, I find particularly delicious—that Beowulf will be leading the pack. At the same time, we'll be sending the execute order to our first wave of 'spontaneous uprisings' against Frontier Security and its tyrannical ways. When that happens, it will be time for the Factor to come out into the open."

His expression turned much more intent, and he leaned slightly forward, towards the camera.

"The groundwork is all in place, and, so far, things have gone very much as planned. There's always room for that to change, though, and it's critical the next stage be properly handled. With only one or two exceptions, all of your first wave 'annexations' should be programmed to welcome the Faction's protection, but those exceptions—if they arise—are going to have to be very carefully approached. I know we've talked about this, but let me reemphasize that even though we've picked all of these systems because of their potential industrial and economic contributions, it's absolutely essential that the Faction be seen as a beneficial, *voluntary* association. So, if it turns out any of your targets are unwilling to voluntarily join, accept that. There'll be time to add them later, and for the immediate future, it's much more important that all of you are self-evidently acting solely in self-defense in the face of the chaos and anarchy spreading steadily through the Shell and Verge."

He paused again for emphasis, then settled back in his chair more comfortably.

"I'm perfectly well aware that all of you already knew all of that." He smiled slightly. "Put it down to the executive producer's last-minute, pre-curtain anxiety. Or, more likely, envy." His smile grew broader. "All of you are going to be operating openly from here on out. I've just discovered exactly how much I wish *I* were doing the same thing, and it turns out I'm not quite as philosopical about it as I thought I was. So, what I suppose I'm really doing here, is nagging all of you over the details out of sheer frustration."

He allowed his smile to grow broader still, then shrugged.

"But, while I'm nagging, let's go over a couple of my concerns about our potential problem children. Clinton, I know you and Prince Felix have been friends for years, but our latest analysis is that the Siegfried Parliament is likely to balk, at least initially, when you invite Felix to join the Factor. It looks to us like an alliance—for now, at least—is likely to emerge between the most conservative of his nobles, because they're afraid of losing the power they already have, and of the growing Siegfried industrial class, which is afraid of seeing the rules change just when it's on the brink of *acquiring* significant political clout. The thing that worries me about it is that you and Felix *are* so close. I think he's likely to try to force the issue, and our analysts' opinion is that there's about a forty percent chance he'd fail. On the other hand, the very nature of the alliance we're afraid of means it's ultimately going to come apart as the nobility's and the industrialists' interests diverge or even come into direct conflict. The steady worsening of the situation around them is going to have an effect, as well, so according to those same analysts' projections, the chance that Siegfried will ultimately request annexation by the Factor rises to well above *ninety* percent if we indicate we're prepared to accept their decision *against* joining—for now—gracefully. So, I think you're going to have to handle your impulsive old fencing partner rather delicately. The invitation has to be extended, but you need to stress to him that—"

"Well, I suppose word had to get out eventually," William Alexander said glumly.

He and his brother sat at the poolside, watching Honor Alexander-Harrington swim laps. The Earl of White Haven nursed a stein of beer, and his blue eyes were more than a little anxious as he watched his wife swim with such single-minded determination and dolphin-like grace. She'd always loved to swim, but her sheer focus, the way she lost herself in the physical exertion as if it were a way for her to simply shut down her mind, was new for her. It was something he'd never seen out of her before, and it worried him more than he was prepared to admit. Worried him almost as much as the nightmares he wasn't supposed to know she was having. For that matter, Nimitz was sprawled across the seat of the lawn chair next to his, and from the way the 'cat's eyes followed Honor, Hamish knew Nimitz was concerned about her, as well.

Although, the earl admitted, probably not for the same reasons. Nimitz didn't like Honor's sorrow, or her dreams, or—especially—her gnawing anxiety over her father's lingering grief, but the treecat had no qualms at all about what she intended to do about the attack on Sphinx. In fact, he agreed with her, with every fiber of his being. Nor did he doubt for a moment that she would succeed. Hamish, despite a much more realistic grasp of the military realities, had discovered he shared Nimitz's confidence, but he was much more deeply concerned about the ultimate price she might pay to achieve that success.

And it's eating you up inside to realize how much she's still hurting, he admitted to himself. *You have to wonder if all the vengeance in the universe is ever going to fix* that.

He shook that thought aside and looked at William.

"Do we have any idea how it leaked?" he asked.

"Not really." Baron Grantville shrugged, then sipped from his own glass of iced tea. "It came from somewhere on Beowulf, though. I suppose it's possible Patricia Givens' source leaked it deliberately, although I can't imagine why. Or it may just be that some Beowulfan newsy picked up on something coming out of Sol. Anyway, the cat's out of the bag, unless we want to be stupid enough to try to deny it."

"That *would* be outstandingly stupid," White Haven agreed.

"I know. In fact, if it hadn't leaked on its own, we'd have had to break the news ourselves before much longer. So, in a way, it's only forced our hand a bit earlier than we'd planned. But that still leaves the question of exactly what we do about it."

"Do about it?" White Haven repeated, arching one eyebrow in obvious puzzlement. "Do about what?"

"About how we respond publicly," Grantville explained with more than a hint of exasperation. "Specifically, about why it came in the form of a leak instead of from us. You *know* how critical it is that we—"

He paused suddenly, eyes narrowing in abrupt suspicion, then snorted at his brother's quick grin.

"I suppose you think you're clever, Ham?" he said witheringly.

"Maybe not, but at least I've got a sense of humor," White Haven replied.

"That's *one* man's opinion."

White Haven chuckled. It really hadn't been all that funny, but anything that could amuse William even briefly was worth it at the moment.

"How *are* we going to respond?" he asked rather more seriously.

"You'll find out at nineteen-hundred, local," William told him. "That's when Elizabeth is going live system-wide."

✧   ✧   ✧

Elizabeth Winton's expression was solemn as she looked out of HD displays throughout the entire Manticore Binary System while the totally unnecessary official introduction came to an end.

It wasn't as if anyone was going to fail to recognize her, even though as a general rule the Queen of Manticore seldom addressed all her subjects at the same time. In fact, these days she couldn't. She couldn't even simultaneously address all of the subjects of the "Old Star Kingdom," far less the entire Star Empire, since no one could drive a signal through a wormhole junction to Trevor's Star or the Lynx Terminus. Normally, when she spoke publicly at all, it was to relatively small gatherings—at "town hall meetings," civic organizations, charitable associations, and similar events. Clips of her remarks from those occasions, and sometimes even entire speeches, were frequently rebroadcast, but the tradition was that the reigning monarch did not engage in partisan politics. Everyone knew she (or he) really did, given that the monarch was acting head of government as well as head of state, but not in the rough-and-tumble of political strife. Which meant the Prime Minister was the usual face of Her Majesty's Government, except on particularly critical occasions.

Like tonight's.

"Good evening," she said quietly. "I'm speaking to you tonight because the Star Empire—*our* Star Empire—faces what is undoubtedly the greatest challenge and threat in our history."

She paused and reached up to gently touch the ears of the treecat stretched across the back of her chair, letting that sentence settle into her subjects' minds. Then she lowered her arm, folded her hands together on the antique desk blotter in front of her, and continued unflinchingly.

"The events of the past fifteen T-months have been the most traumatic period in the lives of every man, woman and child of the Old Star Kingdom of Manticore. No one could have imagined in her worst nightmares the sequence of events which began with the Battle of Monica, then continued through the proposed summit meeting between myself and President Pritchart, then the assassination of Admiral Webster thirteen months ago, and the simultaneous attack on Queen Berry of Torch and my own niece. Then came the Battle of Lovat, one T-year ago—a decisive victory...followed less than three T-months later by the Battle of Manticore, with all the millions of dead and shattered ships which were left in its wake. And no sooner had we begun to recover from that desperate struggle, than we found ourselves plunged into a fresh confrontation—this time with the Solarian League itself—at New Tuscany. All of you know what happened when Admiral Josef Byng treacherously, and cravenly, massacred three ships of our Navy—three *destroyers*, fired upon by seventeen Solarian *battlecruisers* when they hadn't even raised their wedges or sidewalls. And all of you know what happened when Count ess Gold Peak arrived at New Tuscany to demand an explanation and an accounting."

She paused once more, then allowed herself to inhale deeply.

"The confrontation with the Solarian League was not of our seeking. We endeavored to make that point clear to the Solarian government, but our diplomatic efforts were rebuffed, and our warnings about the seriousness of our impending collision—and of the outside forces we had come to believe were deliberately bringing that collision about—were ignored. Which led, just under four T-months ago, to the Battle of Spindle, where a handful of our heavy cruisers completely defeated over seventy Solarian superdreadnoughts."

An edge of iron pride showed in her voice, but her expression remained solemn, serious and focused.

"I'm sure all of you recall that moment of combined fear for the future and pride in our uniformed men and women when we realized not a single Manticoran, not one of our Grayson allies, had even been injured at Spindle. It seemed impossible that the vaunted Solarian Navy could have been so summarily and completely defeated.

"Which"—her voice dropped and hardened—"made the shock and horror of the attack on our home system immeasurably worse than it would have been anyway. It hit us at the very moment when our confidence and relief were highest, and it took us completely by surprise. The truth is that no one—not the Admiralty, not our intelligence services, not our diplomats, not our political leaders, not I, but *no one*—even saw that attack coming."

She made the admission unflinchingly.

"We believe the attack was made possible through the development of a radically new starship drive technology. We believe we have, after a painstaking analysis of Perimeter Security's records, identified the hyper footprint of the attackers' arrival, although it wasn't recognized as such at the time. We also believe it would be extraordinarily difficult, if not outright impossible, for a similar operation to be repeated without the attackers being detected and engaged far short of their targets.

"Yet despite all that, the truth remains—we *were* attacked. The attack *was* totally successful. Millions of our citizens, thousands of visitors to our star system, and an unconscionable percentage of the intelligent species native to this, our home system, died in a deliberate, callous attack whose very nature precluded the notice to evacuate nonmilitary personnel required under the universally recognized rules of warfare. It was, by any standard anyone might choose to apply, the most successful, most devastating, and bloodiest surprise attack in the history of human warfare, and it left our industrial infrastructure crippled and in ruins."

She paused once more, and throughout the Manticore Binary System literally billions of other human beings sat silent with her, staring at her face, wondering what she would say—what she *could* say—next.

"Even if we'd attempted to, there would have been no way we could have kept what happened here a secret," she resumed finally. "Although no one could definitively say even who was responsible for it, the fact that the attack had occurred, and its consequences, spread rapidly throughout the League. We do believe we know who was behind the attack upon us." Her eyes hardened, and surprise rippled through her enormous audience. "At this point, we can't prove our suspicions, but looking at everything which has happened over the past T-year, there is a very clear and discernible pattern. We know, without doubt, that we're still merely scratching the surface, that there are far more things we *don't* know than things we do know. But I am totally confident that we'll find the proof we require. We *will* discover who was behind that attack, where that attack originated, and who carried it out, and when we've proven those things to our complete satisfaction, we *will* act."

Her voice was a sword, chilled steel with a razor edge, and her treecat companion's ears flattened as he showed bared, needle-pointed canines.

"In the meantime, however," she continued, "those in the League whose stupidity and arrogance made them so amenable to our enemies' manipulation have not suddenly become wise. As some in the media have been reporting, the Solarian League Navy, having failed to learn its lesson at Spindle, has decided to move directly against the Manticore System. We anticipate the arrival of several hundred Solarian superdreadnoughts in our space within the next two to three T-weeks."

If the silence of her audience had been profound before, it became absolute as she made that admission.

"When those ships arrive, they will not be here on a peaceful diplomatic mission. All of us have known for our entire lives how corrupt the Solarian League has truly become. We know who truly runs the Solarian bureaucracy. We know about the 'sweetheart deals' between Solarian transstellars and the venal, utterly dishonest Frontier Security commissioners who pimp for them. We know about the vast gulf between the League's soaring professions of belief in human dignity and human worth and OFS' support of debt peonage throughout the Verge. Between the League's solemn condemnation of the interstellar genetic slave trade and the reality of high League officials and bureaucrats on the payrolls of criminal enterprises like Manpower Incorporated."

Her lip curled, and her brown eyes glittered like ice.

"Knowing what we know, none of us can be surprised by the fact that the Solarian League Navy intends to demand the Star Empire of Manticore's unconditional surrender. The intention is to turn us into yet another OFS-administered satellite of the League. We've all seen, only too often, what happens to local government, local administration of justice, local economies, and the right of self-determination when the 'enlightened' supervision of the Office of Frontier Security engulfs an independent star nation. Make no mistake about it—that is precisely what the League intends to do to us.

"It intends to do so out of a desire for vengeance for the defeats it's suffered at our Navy's hands. It intends to do so because it cannot tolerate the example of a 'neobarb' out-system star nation which refuses to slavishly comply with the League's whims. It intends to do so because it resents the size and power of our merchant marine. And it intends to do so out of the basest motives of greed as it contemplates the potential revenue source of the Manticoran Wormhole Junction."

She paused yet again, briefly, and her shoulders squared and her head rose proudly.

"There is no hope of dissuading the Solarians from their chosen course," she said slowly and distinctly. "The Solarian League, for all its past glories and high achievements, has become an *appetite*, a voracious hunger, and trillions of its citizens, living safe, satisfied, self-centered, and secure lives on its core worlds, have no concept of what routinely happens to the weak and the helpless along its frontiers.

"It's time they found out."

The eyes which had been cold as ice glittered with a sudden fire, and Ariel half-rose on the back of her chair, lips curling back from his fangs in challenge.

"The Star Empire of Manticore has been wounded as we've never been wounded before," she said flatly. "But a hexapuma or a peak bear or a Kodiak max is most dangerous when it's wounded. Perhaps the men and women secure at the heart of the Solarian League's bureaucracy have forgotten that fact. If so, we're about to remind them.

"I do not say this lightly. I know, even better than any of you, how badly we've been weakened, how seriously our industrial and economic power has been reduced, what that means ultimately for our military capacity. I *know* the stakes."

The woman the treecats had named "Soul of Steel" looked out of all those countless HD displays, and there wasn't a single millimeter of retreat in those eyes of blazing ice.

"Despite the damage we've suffered, Home Fleet remains intact. Despite the damage to our production lines, Home Fleet's magazines are fully loaded. Our system-defense missiles are untouched. If the Solarian League wants a war, the Solarian League will *have* one. If that is the choice the League makes, then the war which began at New Tuscany and continued at Spindle will resume right here. Whatever they may think, the fleet they've dispatched against us is no match for our remaining combat power. If they choose to send a second, equally large, fleet after this one, the Admiralty is confident we have sufficient strength to defeat it, as well. No doubt the League believes we'll refuse to fight because of the vast difference between our ultimate capabilities. The League is wrong.

"Within six T-months, we will have reestablished our missile production capability. It won't be as great as it was prior to the recent attack, but it will be sufficient to guarantee the security of our own star systems against any ships or weapons currently in the Solarian League Navy's inventory. That is the bottom-line analysis of the Admiralty, and you have my word—and the word of the House of Winton—that I am telling you the absolute truth when I say that."

She paused once more, letting that soak into her audience's minds. Then she smiled thinly.

"There is, of course, a vast difference between being able to guarantee our own security in the near term and being able to defeat a behemoth like the Solarian League in the long term. I don't pretend to have a magic bullet to guarantee our ultimate victory. But I do have this. I have the courage of the Manticoran people. I have my own refusal to fail the trust those people have placed in the House of Winton. I have the determination of all Manticorans—those of the Old Star Kingdom and those of the Star Empire who have newly and freely joined us—to live in freedom. I have the skill and the high professionalism and the dauntless determination of the men and women of the Manticoran armed forces. And I have the absolute certainty that those things will never fail me . . . or you.

"I don't bring you any 'magic bullet,' because there is none. I make no promises of easy triumphs, because there will be no easy triumphs. I promise you only the truth, and the truth is that the price we will ultimately pay will be even higher than the one we've already paid. That the cost of the battle which waits for us will be sacrifice, loss, backbreaking toil, blood, and grief. But I also promise you this one more thing. I promise you *victory*. For seventy-plus T-years, the Star Empire has lived under sentence of death, yet we're still here. And we will *still* be here when the smoke finally clears. However long it takes, whatever sacrifice it entails, wherever the battle takes us, and no matter what foe we may face, we *will* triumph, and those who have wrought such destruction and suffering upon us, who have butchered our civilians, who have attacked us from the shadows like assassins, will discover to their infinite regret that in the defense of our homes, our families, and our children, *we* can be just as merciless as *them*."

Chapter Forty-Two

THE ALARM BUZZED in the darkness, and Honor Alexander-Harrington sat up in bed, reached out a long arm, and pressed the acceptance key.

Nimitz had rolled off of her chest when she moved, and his green eyes glowed like molten emeralds in the com terminal's reflected light as he blinked sleepily. She felt his mind-glow nestled close to her own, and she gave him a quick caress with her free hand as the display came fully alive with the crown and crossed swords of HMS *Imperator*'s wallpaper.

"Yes?"

She hadn't slept well over the three months since the attack on the home system. She'd hoped that might change once she got back aboard her flagship here at Trevor's Star, but it hadn't. Yet there was no sign of that in her crisp acknowledgment as she accepted the com request audio only.

"Your Grace," Captain Rafael Cardones' voice replied, "I think we need you on Flag Bridge. Now."

Honor's eyebrows rose as Cardones' strained tone registered. She'd seen him in the midst of combat, seen him cradling broken ribs while he continued to man his station, seen him in the most stressful situations she could imagine, and yet she'd never heard that note in his voice before.

"What is it, Rafe?" she asked sharply.

"Your Grace, we've just picked up a hyper footprint. It's a

single ship, about four light-minutes outside the system limit. It's quite near one of the FTL platforms, and it's squawking its transponder code."

"And?" she prompted a bit sharply when he paused.

"And it's a Havenite ship, Ma'am. In fact, according to its transponder, it's *Haven One*."

"All right, Hamish, what's this all about?" Elizabeth Winton demanded irritably as she sat down in front of the com. She'd just gotten to bed after yet another incredibly long day, the two T-weeks since her defiant speech hadn't been particularly restful, the anticipated arrival of Admiral Filareta's fleet within the next week to ten days wasn't likely to improve things one bit, and she was not amused at being reawakened after less than two hours of sleep.

No one replied, and Elizabeth's eyebrows rose in surprise. It wasn't exactly like Hamish Alexander-Harrington to wake her up in the middle of the night just to play silly buggers, yet the Admiralty House wallpaper on her display bore the personal sigil of the First Lord of Admiralty. No one else was going to be using that wallpaper, even assuming they'd been able to somehow get access to Admiralty House or Mount Royal Palace's secure communications net. So where the hell was Hamish?

Seconds ticked past. Then a minute. Then a full minute. Then *two* minutes, and Elizabeth Winton, who had never been known as the most patient person in the world, began to frown in something so much stronger than mere irritation.

"I'm sorry, Elizabeth. It isn't Hamish," a voice finally said, after better than six full minutes, and Elizabeth's eyebrows widened in astonishment as the Admiralty House wallpaper disappeared and a white-bereted woman looked back at her from what was obviously a warship's briefing room and not Hamish Alexander-Harrington's office.

"Honor?" The Queen shook her head. "What are you doing on this channel? Or even here, instead of at Trevor's Star, for that matter? I thought you weren't due back until the middle of next week!"

There was another of those interminable pauses, and then—

"There's been a slight . . . change in plans," Honor said. "I ended up having to accelerate my schedule, and I got Hamish to tap me in through Admiralty House's secure channels as soon as we came through from Trevor's Star. That's why his identifier showed on your com. And why this conversation seems to be taking so long between pieces." She smiled crookedly. "But *Imperator* should be making Manticore orbit in about nineteen hours, and I thought I should probably give you a heads-up. You see, something's come up rather unexpectedly that I thought I should come home to discuss with you personally."

Elizabeth frowned. Something about Honor's expression perplexed her, and she wondered why the other woman had gone to such obvious lengths to wake her up in the middle of the night only to sit down in front of a secure com and be told that *Imperator* was still nineteen hours out from the capital planet. Just exactly what sort of "heads up" did Honor have in mind?

"What 'came up rather unexpectedly'?" she asked.

"It seems we have an unanticipated visitor," Honor said simply, six minutes later, and expanded her own com's field of view.

For a moment, it failed to register. But then Elizabeth Winton's jaw dropped as she recognized the platinum-haired, topaz-eyed woman standing at Honor's side.

"I apologize for waking you up in the middle of the night, Your Majesty," President Elizabeth Pritchart said calmly, "but I think we need to talk."

Chapter Forty-Three

THE PINNACE WHICH DOCKED with HMS *Imperator*'s forward boat bay was Duchess Harrington's personal small craft. As such, it had priority over any other auxiliary assigned to her flagship, although it was just a bit unusual for even her pinnace to be accompanied—one might have said "escorted"—by a pair of Royal Manticoran Army trans-atmospheric sting ships.

The flight operations officer in charge of *Imperator*'s small craft movements didn't seem surprised to see them, however. He simply acknowledged their presence and assigned them berthing slots on either side of Duchess Harrington's craft.

But if *he'd* been warned what to expect, it quickly became evident that the boat bay officer of the deck (who, at this extremely late hour of *Imperator*'s shipboard day, was an extremely *junior* ensign with red hair, fair skin, and blue eyes, rejoicing in the name of Hieronymus Thistlewaite) hadn't been. That young man had spotted the duchess' arrival and mustered the proper side party for an admiral of her towering seniority. He looked just a bit nervous, since there were no older and wiser heads looking over his shoulder this time, but Ensign Thistlewaite seemed reasonably confident he had the situation under control.

Until, that was, Elizabeth Adrienne Samantha Annette Winton, Grand Commander of the Order of King Roger, Grand Commander of the Order of Queen Elizabeth I, Grand Commander of the Order of the Golden Lion, Baroness of Crystal Pine, Baroness of

White Sand, Countess of Tannerman, Countess of High Garnet, Grand Duchess of Basilisk, Princess Protector of the Realm, and, by God's grace and the will of Parliament, Queen Elizabeth III of the Star Kingdom of Manticore, and Empress Elizabeth I of the Star Empire of Manticore, swung lithely out of the boarding tube at Duchess Harrington's heels.

None of the side party had expected their monarch's sudden arrival, and not even naval discipline was enough to hide their astonishment.

"Eighth Fleet, arri—" a voice began over the boat bay speakers, then chopped off abruptly as the petty officer behind it realized who else had just appeared aboard his ship.

The smooth efficiency of the side party's formalities slithered to a halt, and Ensign Thistlewaite's jaw dropped. Then it closed with an almost audible snap, his face turned a considerably darker red than his hair, and he stared appealingly at the duchess.

"*Manticore*, arriving!" the speakers said suddenly as the petty officer recovered abruptly, and the bosun's pipes began to twitter again while three additional side boys came dashing up from somewhere.

"Permission to come aboard, Sir?" Elizabeth said gravely, managing not to smile, as the twitter of pipes came to an end. The first two bodyguards who'd emerged from the tube behind her, wearing the uniform of the Queen's Own, appeared rather less amused than she obviously was, but Thistlewaite's blue eyes looked back at her with desperate gratitude.

"Permission granted, Ma'am—I mean, Your Majesty!"

Honor hadn't believed the young man could turn even redder, but she'd been wrong.

"Permission to come aboard, Sir?" she repeated as Elizabeth stepped past her.

"Permission granted, Your Grace." Thistlewaite's relief at getting back to *something* familiar was obvious as she returned his salute, and she smiled slightly.

"My apologies, Ensign," she said. "We organized this on the fly, as it were, and we didn't want the newsies getting word of Her Majesty's visit. Apparently you didn't get the word in time, either."

"Uh, no, Ma'am," he admitted, blushing a bit less blindingly.

"Well, it happens," she said philosophically while another passel of armsmen and bodyguards appeared behind her and the

Queen, then nodded to him and turned to Elizabeth. "This way, Your Majesty," she said.

"Thank you, Admiral," Elizabeth replied. She nodded and smiled to Thistlewaite in turn, then headed towards the lift banks at Honor's side, accompanied by three Grayson armsmen, six members of the Queen's Own, one plainclothes officer from Palace Security, and two treecats, who appeared inordinately amused by the two-legs' antics as they rode their persons' shoulders.

Elizabeth's amusement at poor Thistlewaite's reaction to her arrival had completely dissipated by the time they reached the door to Honor's day cabin.

It was once again the middle of the night by Elizabeth's personal chrono, and she was glad she was accustomed to working late. Although, all things considered, she couldn't remember the last time she'd had to deal with any diplomatic question quite this pressing so late at night. She snorted in harsh amusement at the thought.

Oh, be honest, Beth! she told herself. *You don't remember the last time you've ever had to deal with "any diplomatic question quite this pressing" at all, whatever the time of day—or night! And certainly not the last time you had so little warning you were going to have to deal with it!*

Honor's "heads up" had given her almost a full day to think and confer, yet she still didn't know—because Pritchart hadn't said—exactly what it was the Havenite head of state thought they might have to discuss. Fortunately, no one else on Manticore, outside the circle of her very closest advisers, knew anything particularly interesting was going on at all. Honor had taken her personal pinnace down to Landing in order to get Elizabeth aboard *Imperator* without the newsies finding out anything was toward, so at least no one was busy raising any hysterical hopes—or mongering any panic—about Eloise Pritchart's sudden, unanticipated visit. That was probably a good thing, yet the Queen could wish that she herself had at least some idea of what Pritchart had in mind. Unfortunately, the only thing she knew for certain was that neither Nimitz nor Honor had detected any indications of chicanery or treachery in any of the Havenites' mind-glows. Whatever Pritchart was up to, at least she seemed to be sincere about it.

Which was all very well, but still seemed remarkably cold comfort at the moment.

Now the Queen paused with extremely atypical hesitation as the door opened. Her spine was absolutely straight, her lips were tight, and she visibly braced herself before she continued into the cabin.

A dozen people had risen and turned to face the door, and despite decades of experience at the highest levels of politics, Elizabeth's nostrils flared as she found herself face to face with Eloise Pritchart.

The President was accompanied by her Secretary of State, and Elizabeth recognized Secretary of War Thomas Theisman, as well. She also recognized Anton Zilwicki (who, fortunately, Honor had already warned her wasn't quite as dead as people had been assuming), and it didn't require much imagination to figure out that the young, coarse-haired man standing beside him must be Victor Cachat. Commodore Mercedes Brigham, Honor's chief of staff, Commander George Reynolds, her intelligence officer, and Waldemar Tümmel, her flag lieutenant, were also known faces, as was James MacGuiness. But she didn't have a clue who the others were, and she felt her bodyguards bristling as they faced the formidable crowd.

"Your Majesty," Honor said quietly into what could have become an awkward silence, "allow me to present President Eloise Pritchart, Secretary of State Leslie Montrose, Secretary of War Thomas Theisman, Attorney General Denis LePic, Director Kevin Usher of the Federal Investigation Agency, Special Officer Victor Cachat, and Dr. Herlander Simões." She smiled crookedly. "I believe you already know everyone else."

"Yes," Elizabeth said after a moment. "I believe I do."

Pritchart bowed to her very slightly, and the Queen returned the courtesy with a nod, but even a space the size of Honor's day cabin was crowded by so many people, and the tension level could have been carved with a knife. Elizabeth glanced around for a moment, then looked at Honor.

"Please, everyone, be seated," Honor invited, acknowledging the silent command to continue in her role as official hostess.

Her "guests" obeyed, settling down around their two principals with a sort of instinctive social ranking, and she glanced at MacGuiness.

"May I assume your pantry is its normally efficient self despite the lateness of the hour, Mac?"

"Of course, Your Grace." MacGuiness bowed with perfect aplomb. "Would anyone care for refreshment?" he continued, turning to the others.

Although Elizabeth had just discovered a rather sudden craving for a strong whiskey, she suppressed it. No one seemed inclined to venture where she hadn't led the way, and after a moment, Honor shrugged slightly.

"It would appear not," she told the steward. "If anyone changes her mind, I'll buzz."

"Of course, Your Grace," MacGuiness murmured again, and withdrew.

Honor waited until the pantry door had closed behind him, then turned back to the others.

"In case any of you had managed to remain unaware of it," she said with another of those off-center smiles, "the tension level in this room is rather high, according to Nimitz." All eyes flitted to the treecat sitting on the back of her chair. "I can't imagine why that might be," she added.

Elizabeth surprised herself with a snort of laughter. It was harsh, but it was also genuine, and she shook her head reprovingly.

"I think I might be able to think of a reason or two," she said, then turned her own attention to Pritchart. "I must say, Madam President, that of all the possible scenarios under which you and I might have come face to face at last, this one would never have occurred to me." She let her eyes sweep over the cabinet secretaries flanking Pritchart. "If anything were to happen to this delegation, it would make a serious hole in your government, I believe."

"I thought that since you'd trusted us enough to send Admiral Alexander-Harrington to us, I should return the compliment, Your Majesty," Pritchart replied.

"Perhaps so," Elizabeth said. "But there was that one minor difference, I believe. I sent Duchess Harrington accompanied by an entire battle fleet."

"Indeed you did." Pritchart nodded, those striking topaz eyes meeting Elizabeth's levelly. "And I assure you, we missed neither element of the message behind that...arrangement. Neither the pointed suggestion, shall we say, that it would be wise of us to pay attention to her message and see to it that nothing untoward happened to her, nor the fact that you could have sent *just* the fleet...and its laser heads. Believe me, after all that's happened between our star nations, after the collapse of our own summit, after the Battle of Manticore, against the backdrop of the tensions mounting between the Star Empire and the League, I was as pleased as I was astonished that you were willing to talk instead of simply attacking when your advantage was so overwhelming."

"I suppose I could say the same thing, given your unexpected arrival after what happened to our system infrastructure," Elizabeth replied.

"Your Majesty, what happened to your star system has a lot to do with my presence here, but not, perhaps, in the way you believe."

"No?" Elizabeth regarded her intently, wishing with all her heart that she possessed even a hint of the empathic ability Honor had developed.

Honor had already briefed her fully on what she herself had sensed from Pritchart and the others—both during her time in Nouveau Paris, and since the President's totally unexpected arrival at Trevor's Star—but that wasn't the same thing as sensing it for herself. In fact, it wasn't even remotely the same thing.

Elizabeth Winton tried to be ruthlessly honest with herself. History was unfortunately replete with examples of kings and queens—and presidents—whose advisers had told them what they thought their rulers wanted to hear. And there'd been just as many—at least—of those kings and queens (and presidents) who'd told *themselves* what they wanted to hear. That was one of the lessons her father had always emphasized to her, and since taking the throne herself, she'd discovered just how wise he'd been to do that. And how difficult it was, at times, to remember it.

Yet because of that self honesty, she was well aware of her own temper, of how hard it was for her to forgive anyone who injured those she was responsible for protecting or those she loved. At this moment, in this day cabin, as she sat on Honor's couch, she looked into the eyes of the President of the Republic of Haven—the very personification of the star nation which had murdered her own father, her uncle, her cousin, and her prime minister. Of the conquering empire which had engulfed dozens of star systems, cost the lives of untold thousands of her military personnel, and forced the expenditure of literally incalculable floods of her people's treasure, as well as their blood. Every bulldog fiber of her being quivered with the tension of all that remembered bloodshed and violence, of the need to keep her guard up, to recall all those decades of treachery. It was her *job* to remember that, her duty to protect her people, and she would have given her own right arm to be able to know—not to be told, by someone else, however much she trusted that someone, but to *know*, beyond question or doubt—what the person behind those topaz eyes was truly thinking.

A soft, silken warmth pressed against the side of her neck, and Ariel's bone-deep, buzzing purr vibrated into her. She reached up to him, and he stroked his head against the palm of her hand, but his own fingers were still. They never moved, never signed a single word, and that, she realized suddenly, was the most eloquent thing he could possibly have told her.

"All right, Madam President," she said, and wondered if the others in that cabin were as surprised as she was by the gentleness of her own voice, "why don't you *tell* me why you're here?"

"Thank you," Pritchart said very quietly, as if she understood exactly what had been going through Elizabeth's mind. Then the President drew a deep breath and sat back in her chair.

"Before I say anything else, Your Majesty, there's one point I want to clear up. One which has bedeviled the relations between the Republic of Haven and the Star Empire for far too long."

She paused a moment, as if even now it was difficult to steel herself, then continued levelly.

"Your Majesty, we know who tampered with our prewar diplomatic correspondence. We did *not* know at the time the Republic resumed hostilities." She looked squarely at Elizabeth, facing the sudden resurgence of the Queen's tension. "You have my word—my personal word, as well as that of the Republic of Haven—that it was only well after Operation Thunderbolt that we discovered, essentially by a fluke, that in fact the Star Empire was telling the truth about the High Ridge Government's correspondence. That the version which *I* saw in Nouveau Paris, and which my cabinet colleagues saw with me, had been altered before it ever reached us . . . and, despite the fact that it carried your own Foreign Office's valid authentication codes, *not* by any Manticoran. The two men responsible for it were Yves Grosclaude, our special envoy to you, and Secretary of State Arnold Giancola."

With the exception of Honor Alexander-Harrington and Anton Zilwicki, every Manticoran in the cabin stiffened in shock, and

Elizabeth Winton's eyes blazed. She opened her mouth quickly, angrily... then forced herself to close it and sat back.

"We weren't aware of what Giancola had done until Mr. Grosclaude was killed in a highly suspicious 'air car accident.' One which looked remarkably like a suicide... or"—Pritchart's eyes bored into Elizabeth's, then flicked sideways to Honor—"like someone who'd been *compelled* to kill himself by flying into a cliff wall. Almost, you might say, like someone who'd been *adjusted*."

Elizabeth's eyes narrowed. She didn't have any idea where Pritchart was headed, but Ariel was still purring against her neck, and Honor's expression was still composed and calm, and so she made herself wait.

"Kevin, here," Pritchart nodded sideways at Usher, "has a nasty, suspicious mind which was already chewing the correspondence question over. When Grosclaude died so spectacularly, those suspicions of his started working overtime. It didn't take long for him to discover proof that the correspondence had been altered at our end. Unfortunately, the 'proof' had clearly been manufactured, apparently to implicate Giancola."

She smiled very thinly at Elizabeth's evident confusion.

"We came to the conclusion that Giancola had arranged it himself on the theory that if obviously forged evidence indicated he was the guilty party, it would be blindingly apparent to everyone that he'd been framed, and who would bother to frame a *guilty* man? In other words, he *wanted* us to bring that evidence forward publicly—or that was our theory, at least. And then," her expression hardened with remembered fury and frustration, "*Giancola* was killed in *another* air car accident, this time—as far as we've been able to determine—a *real* accident.

"So there we were. We had no real evidence, only documentation which had obviously been forged. The only two men we could be relatively certain knew what had happened were both dead. And, just to make matters worse, they'd both died in *air car accidents*... which just happened to have been State Security's favorite means for removing 'inconvenient' individuals. Given the strength of the war party in Congress, the fact that we couldn't *prove* any of it, and the enormous suspicion which was going to be produced throughout the entire Republic by the way in which Grosclaude and Giancola had died, we couldn't simply present our theory and expect Congress to go along with an admission that it was someone in the Republic—*not* the Republic itself, but a rogue element in the very highest levels of our administration—who'd manipulated our correspondence. Who'd manipulated us—manipulated *me*—into calling for a resumption of hostilities because we honestly believed the government of our adversaries was not simply using diplomacy for its own cynical ends but then lying about *our* diplomatic notes."

There was an edge of raw appeal in her quiet voice, and Elizabeth paused long enough to be sure she had control of her own voice.

"How long have you known—or suspected, at least?" she asked then.

"Giancola was killed in September 1920," Pritchart replied unflinchingly. "We already suspected what had happened, but as long as he was alive, it was an ongoing investigation. There was always the chance we might find the real evidence we needed."

"But you've known—known for almost *two T-years*—that we were telling the truth. That it was *your* man who'd falsified the correspondence! And you said *nothing*!"

Elizabeth glared at Pritchart, and some of the other Havenites stirred angrily as her accusatory anger flooded over them, but their President only nodded.

"In as much as we 'knew' anything, yes," she said. "And that, Your Majesty, was the reason I proposed the summit meeting between us. Because it was time, once it became evident we'd never be able to find *proof* of what had happened, to end the fighting however we had to do it, even if that meant admitting the truth to you—to you, personally, where you and your treecat could evaluate my truthfulness. We still couldn't have gone public with the information back home, any more than you could remove High Ridge before the war." Her eyes hardened ever so slightly as she reminded Elizabeth of her own experience with the limitations political considerations could impose. "But I was willing to tell *you*—and to surrender considerable military advantages on our part—to achieve peace. And so, when your Captain Terekhov sailed off to Monica, I sent your cousin home to you to do just that. And we both remember what happened then."

She held Elizabeth's angry eyes steadily, and a cold shock went through the Manticoran Queen as she remembered. Remembered her fury, her rejection of the summit—*her* decision to resume military operations instead of talking.

Silence fell, fragile and singing with its own tension, and Pritchart let it linger for several seconds before she spoke again.

"When you attacked Lovat," she said quietly, and Elizabeth's eyes flickered as she remembered who'd been killed there, "we knew your new targeting system gave you a decisive military advantage. Or that it would, assuming you could get it into general deployment. So we—Thomas and I—" she nodded in Theisman's direction, "mounted Operation Beatrice. Thomas planned it, but I asked for it. Neither of us expected it to be as bloody—on both sides—as it finally was, but I won't pretend we thought the cost in lives would be cheap. Yet since the summit had been killed, since you were pushing the offensive against us, and since your new combat advantage was going to be so overwhelming, we felt our only hope was to strike for outright military victory before you could get your new systems deployed throughout your navy. And from our own analysis of the Battle of Manticore, we almost succeeded."

She paused for just a moment, then shrugged.

"When we lost the Battle of Manticore, we lost the war, Your Majesty. We knew that. But then, to our surprise, you sent us Admiral Alexander-Harrington. You'll never know how tempted I was to tell her the truth then. Not at first, but after I'd come to know her. Yet I couldn't. Partly, that was because of more of those domestic political constraints. When an administration's been as badly damaged as mine was by the Battle of Manticore, managing the internal dynamics gets just as hard as fighting an external enemy, but that was only part of it. Maybe the rest of it was simply because we'd kept it secret for so long. Maybe I *would* have told her, if she hadn't been recalled so precipitously. I don't know. But when your home system was attacked, there were those on our side who saw it almost as an act of divine intervention. An opportunity to win after all—or, at least, to avoid losing."

She made the admission without flinching, and Elizabeth nodded slowly. Of course there had. If what had happened to the Star Empire had happened to the Republic, exactly the same thought would have occurred to any number of Manticorans.

Including me, she admitted to herself.

"Obviously," she heard her own voice say, "that wasn't the option you chose to pursue."

"No, it wasn't. In fact, it was the last thing I wanted to do, for a lot of reasons. Including the fact that, as Admiral Alexander-Harrington had pointed out to us, if there's ever going to be an end to the cycle of violence between Haven and Manticore, it has to be achieved on some sort of equitable basis, not because one of us simply pounds the other into such bloody ruin that she has to yield.

"But, what I never anticipated for a moment was what happened when Officer Cachat and Mr. Zilwicki turned up in Nouveau Paris last month."

"Excuse me?" Elizabeth blinked at the apparent *non sequitur*, and Pritchart smiled. It was not a pleasant expression. In fact, it reminded Elizabeth forcefully of one she'd seen in her own mirror upon occasion.

"We have reason to believe we now know why events in Talbott were orchestrated the way they were," the President said. "Moreover, we know—or we think we do—at least approximately how the attack on your home system was carried out, and by whom. And we believe we know who's been supplying the advanced bio-nanotech which has been turning people into programmed assassins...or suicides. And"—she looked deep into Elizabeth's eyes once more—"we think we know who Arnold Giancola was working for, who manipulated *me* into going back to war against you, and who manipulated *you* into going back to war against me."

Elizabeth stared at her, brain whirling, unable to believe what she was hearing.

"Your Majesty, the Republic of Haven—not just the current Republic, but the *Old* Republic—and the Star Empire of Manticore have been on the same list for centuries. We have a common enemy—one which has manipulated us into killing millions of our own for its own purposes. One which has reached a critical point in its own plans, set events in motion which require the destruction—not the defeat, the *destruction*—of both the Star Empire *and* the Republic. And for the better part of a T-century, the two of us have been doing exactly what that enemy wanted."

Pritchart paused once more, then shook her head slowly.

"I think it's time we stopped," she said very quietly.

✧   ✧   ✧

"More coffee, Your Majesty?"

Elizabeth looked up at the murmured question, then smiled and extended her cup. James MacGuiness poured, then moved on around the table, refilling other cups, and she watched him go before she sipped. It was, as always, delicious, and she thought yet again what a pity it was that MacGuiness made such splendid coffee when Honor couldn't stand the beverage.

The familiar reflection trickled through her brain, and she set the cup back down and gave herself a mental shake. No doubt her staff back at Mount Royal Palace had its hands full covering for her absence, but they were just going to have to go on coping for a while longer. Despite the grinding fatigue of far too many hours, too much adrenaline, and far too many shocks to the universe she'd thought she understood, she knew she and Eloise Pritchart were still far from finished.

She looked across the table at the Havenite President, who'd just finished a serving of MacGuiness' trademark eggs Benedict, and picked up her own coffee cup. Despite a sleepless night, following a day even longer than Elizabeth's had been, the other woman still looked improbably beautiful. And still radiated that formidable presence, as well. Elizabeth doubted anyone could have intentionally planned a greater physical contrast than the one between her own mahogany skin and dark eyes and Pritchart's platinum and topaz, and they'd been producd by political and social systems which were at least as different as their appearances. Yet she'd come—unwillingly, almost kicking and screaming—to the conclusion that the two of them were very much alike under the surface.

"So," she said, sitting back from the table she shared with only Honor, Pritchart, and Theisman, "is Simões telling the truth or not, Honor?"

The two Havenites looked at Honor with slightly surprised expressions, and Honor smiled. Nimitz was sound asleep on his perch, and after the night which had just passed, she saw no point in waking him up.

"There's a reason Her Majesty's asking me, instead of Nimitz or Ariel," she told her guests. "As it happens, I've been hanging around with treecats long enough to have caught to at least some of their abilities. I can't read minds, but I can read emotions, and I know when someone's lying."

It was astonishingly easy for her to make that admission to the leaders of the star nation she'd fought her entire adult life.

Pritchart blinked at her, then those topaz eyes narrowed in thought, and the President began nodding—slowly, at first, then more rapidly.

"So *that's* why you make such a fiendishly effective diplomat!" she said with something very like an air of triumph. "I couldn't believe how well a total novice was reading us. Now I know—you were *cheating*!"

The last word came out in something very like a laugh, and Honor nodded back.

"Where diplomacy's concerned, according to my mentors in the Foreign Office, there *is* no such thing as 'cheating,' Madam President. In fact, one of those mentors quoted an old axiom to me. Where diplomacy is involved, he said, if you aren't cheating, you aren't trying hard enough."

Elizabeth snorted in amusement, and Theisman shook his head.

"In this instance, however," Honor continued more seriously, "what Her Majesty is asking me is whether or not I can tell if Dr. Simões is telling the truth. I already informed her"—she looked directly at Pritchart "—that I knew *you* were, Madam President. On the other hand, I also assumed you would have expected from the beginning that Nimitz would have been able to tell me and that I would have passed his observations on to Her Majesty, so I didn't feel any particular scruples about that."

Pritchart nodded again, and Honor shrugged.

"What I can tell you about Simões is that his anger—his outrage—at this 'Alignment' is absolutely genuine. The *pain* inside that man is incredible."

She closed her eyes for a moment, and her nostrils flared.

"Everything I can 'taste' about his 'mind-glow' tells me he's telling us the truth, in so far as he knows the truth. Whether or not McBryde might have been passing along disinformation is more than I could say, of course. But, on balance, I think he was telling the truth, as well. It all fits together too well with what we've already seen, and with what Simões can tell us about their hardware."

"And there are still so *damned* many holes in it," Elizabeth half-snarled.

"Yes, there are," Honor agreed. "On the other hand, I'd say the Star Empire knows infinitely more than we knew yesterday, Elizabeth . . . given that we didn't know *anything* at that point."

Elizabeth nodded slowly, then looked at Pritchart.

"So I guess what it comes down to," she said slowly, "is where we go from here. Whatever happens, I want you to know I'm enormously grateful for the information you've provided us. And I think we can both agree that the war between Haven and Manticore is over."

She shook her head, as if, even now, she couldn't quite believe what she'd just said. Not because she didn't want to, but because it seemed impossible, like something which couldn't possibly be true because of how badly everyone *wanted* it to be true.

"Mind you," she continued, "I don't expect everyone to be delighted about that. For that matter, a few days ago, I probably would have been one of the people who wasn't delighted myself," she admitted.

"Trust me, there's the odd couple of billion Havenites who probably feel exactly the same way," Pritchart said dryly.

"And that's the sticking point, isn't it?" Elizabeth asked softly. "Stopping shooting at each other—that much I'm sure we can manage. But it's not enough. Not if Simões' and McBryde's story is true after all."

"No, it's not," Pritchart agreed quietly.

"Well," Elizabeth smiled with very little humor at all, "at least I can feel confident now that you'll keep the Republican Navy off our backs long enough for us to deal with this Admiral Filareta."

"Actually," Pritchart said, "I had something else in mind."

"Something else?" Elizabeth's eyebrows rose.

"Your Majesty—Elizabeth—the Mesan Alignment wants both of us destroyed, starting with the Star Empire. I don't know if it honestly believes the SLN can do the job where you're concerned, or if it was anticipating *we'd* do it when we recognized the opportunity it had given us. But it doesn't really matter. What *matters* is that this Solarian attack on you is simply one more step in a strategy directed against *both* of us. So I think something a bit more pointed than simply stopping shooting at each other might be in order."

"Such as?" Elizabeth asked slowly, eyes slitted in concentration.

"I understand your missile production facilities have been taken off-line," Pritchart said. "Tom here tells me you've undoubtedly got enough of those ungodly super missiles in your magazines to thoroughly kick the ass of this Filareta if he really insists on following his orders. But that's going to cut into your reserves, and given that the Alignment managed to rip the hell out of your home system, I think it would be a good idea for you to conserve as much ammunition as you can in hopes we'll find someone a bit better suited to playing the role of target."

"And?" Elizabeth's eyes were opening wider in speculation.

"Well, it just happens that Thomas here has a modest little fleet— two or three hundred of the wall, I believe—waiting approximately eight hours from Trevor's Star in hyper. If you're willing to trust us in Manticoran space, perhaps we could help you encourage Filareta to see reason. And while I'm well aware our hardware isn't as good as *yours*, every indication I've seen is that it's one hell of a lot better than anything the *Sollies* have."

"Are you offering me a *military alliance* against the *Solarian League*?" Elizabeth asked very carefully.

"If McBryde was right, there isn't going to be much of a Solarian League very much longer," Pritchart replied grimly. "And given the fact that the same bunch of murderous bastards who shot up your home system are also directly responsible for you and I having killed a couple of million of our own people, I think we could say we have a certain commonality of interest where they're concerned. And it's not a case of selfless altruism on my part, you know. We're *both* on the Alignment's list. Don't you think it would be sort of stupid of either of us to let the other one go down and leave us all alone?"

Brown eyes and topaz met across a table littered with the remnants of breakfast, and it was very, very quiet.

"We're still going to have those problems, you know," Elizabeth said almost conversationally after a moment. "All those people on both sides who don't like each other. All that legacy of suspicion."

"Of course." Pritchart nodded.

"And then there's the little matter of figuring out where this Alignment's real headquarters is, and who else is fronting for it, and what other weapons it has, and where else it has programmed assassins tucked away, and exactly what it's got in mind for the Republic once the Star Empire's been polished off."

"True."

"And, now that I think about it, there's the question of how we're going to rebuild our capabilities here, and how much technology sharing—and how quickly—we can convince our separate navies and our allies to put up with. You know there's going to be heel-dragging and tantrum-throwing the minute I start suggesting anything like that!"

"I'm sure there will."

The two women looked at one another, and then, slowly, both of them began to smile.

"What the hell," Elizabeth Winton said. "I've always liked a challenge."

She extended her hand across the table.

Pritchart took it.

✦ Characters

Abercrombie, Sir Tyler—Home Secretary, Star Kingdom of Manticore.

Abrioux, Special Senior Inspector Danielle—one of Kevin Usher's top investigators, Federal Investigation Agency, Republic of Haven.

Abruzzi, Malachai—Permanent Senior Undersecretary of Information, Solarian League.

Adenauer, Commander Dominica Adenauer, Royal Manticoran Navy—operations officer, Tenth Fleet.

Adriopoulos, Commander Alexandros, Royal Manticoran Navy—Commodore James Tanner's chief of staff.

Agnelli, Chief Steward Joanna, Royal Manticoran Navy—Sir Aivars Terekhov's personal steward.

Alexander, The Honorable William—Baron Grantville, Prime Minister of the Star Empire of Manticore; Hamish Alexander-Harrington's younger brother.

Alexander-Harrington, Admiral Hamish—Earl of White Haven; First Lord of Admiralty; husband of Emily and Honor Alexander-Harrington.

Alexander-Harrington, Admiral Lady Dame Honor, Royal Manticoran Navy, Grayson Space Navy—Duchess and Steadholder Harrington; CO, Eighth Fleet. Wife of Hamish and Emily Alexander-Harrington. Special envoy to the Republic of Haven.

Alexander-Harrington, Lady Emily—Countess of White Haven; wife of Hamish and Honor Alexander-Harrington.

al-Fanudahi, Captain Daud ibn Mamoun, Solarian League Navy—a Battle Fleet officer assigned as an analyst to the Office of Operational Analysis.

Alonso y Yáñez, Fleet Admiral Engracia, Solarian League Navy—CO, Frontier Fleet.

Alquezar, Joachim—Prime Minister, Talbott Quadrant.

Anisimovna, Aldona—senior operative for Mesan Strategy Council and Mesan Alignment.

Archer, Lieutenant Gervais Winston Erwin Neville ("Gwen"), Royal Manticoran Navy—Admiral Michelle Henke's flag lieutenant.

Armstrong, Captain Victoria ("Vicki"), Royal Manticoran Navy—CO, HMS *Artemis*; Admiral Michelle Henke's flag captain.

Atkins, Corporal Joshua, Harrington Steadholder's Guard—one of Honor Alexander-Harrington's personal armsmen.

Attunga, Marguerite—a reporter for Manticoran News Service, Incorporated.

Bardasano, Isabel—Jessyk Combine cadet board member and senior director Mesan Alignment security services.

Barloi, Henrietta—Secretary of Technology, Republic of Haven.

Bautista, Vice Admiral Pépé, Solarian League Navy—Fleet Admiral Sandra Crandall's chief of staff.

Beaupré, Lieutenant (JG) Andre, Republic of Haven Navy—Admiral Thomas Theisman's personal shuttle pilot.

Belardinelli, Antoine—President Eloise Pritchart's senior secretary.

Berkeley, Lieutenant (SG) Anthony, Royal Manticoran Navy—assigned Manufacturing and Prototyping Command, HMSS *Weyland*.

Bernard, Fleet Admiral Evangeline, Solarian League Navy—CO, Office of Strategy and Planning.

Billingsley, Master Steward Chris, Royal Manticoran Navy—Michelle Henke's personal steward.

Blackett, Sergeant Luke, Harrington Steadholder's Guard—James Harrington's personal armsman.

Blaine, Vice Admiral Jessup, Royal Manticoran Navy—CO, Lynx Terminus Home Fleet detachment.

Boisvin, Lieutenant Édouard, Royal Manticoran Navy—XO, HMS *Stevedore*.

Boltitz, Helga—Henri Krietzmann's personal aide.

Borderwijk, Captain Alenka, Republic of Haven Navy—Admiral Thomas Theisman's senior aide.

Bouchard, Lieutenant Commander Jerod, Royal Manticoran Navy—astrogator, HMS *Artemis*.

Bourchier, Senator Ninon—Senator, Republic of Haven; Constitutional Progressive Party.

Brantley, Lieutenant Commander Harper, Royal Manticoran Navy—communications officer, Eighth Fleet.

Brigham, Commodore Mercedes, Grayson Space Navy—Admiral Honor Alexander-Harrington's chief of staff, Eighth Fleet.

Browne, Commander Ishmael, Solarian League Navy—XO, SLNS *Joseph Buckley*.

Burrows, Admiral John, Solarian League Navy—Fleet Admiral Massimo Filareta's chief of staff.

Cabeçadas, Jennifer—John and Laura Cabeçadas' older daughter.

Cabeçadas, John—a tourist passing through HMSS *Hephaestus* with his family.

Cabeçadas, Laura—John Cabeçadas' wife.

Cabeçadas, Miguel—John and Laura Cabeçadas' son.

Cabeçadas, Serafina—John and Laura Cabeçadas' infant daughter.

Cachat, Special Officer Victor—station chief, Erewhon Sector, Foreign Intelligence Service, Republic of Haven.

Caparelli, Admiral Sir Thomas, Royal Manticoran Navy—First Space Lord, Royal Manticoran Navy.

Carlson, Captain Frederick, Royal Manticoran Navy—CO, HMS *Quentin Saint-James*; Sir Aivars Terekhov's flag captain.

Carmichael, Sir Lyman—Admiral James Webster's replacement as Manticoran ambassador to the Solarian League.

Carus, Commander Michael, Royal Manticoran Navy—CO, *HMS Javelin* and senior officer, Destroyer Division 265.2 ("The Silver Cepheids").

Casterlin, Commander Sterling, Royal Manticoran Navy—staff astrogator, Tenth Fleet.

Chamberlain, Vice Admiral Hansen, Solarian League Navy—Admiral Keeley O'Cleary's chief of staff.

Chandler, Commander Ambrose, Royal Manticoran Navy—Vice Admiral Khumalo's staff intelligence officer.

Chase, Lieutenant Commander Julie, Royal Manticoran Navy—CO, HMS *Lodestone*, Division 265.2.

Chatfield, Captain Darryl, Solarian League Navy—Fleet Admiral Sandra Crandall's communications officer.

Cheng, Admiral Hai-shwun, Solarian League Navy—CO, Office of Operational Analysis division of the Office of Naval Intelligence.

Chernevsky, Anastasia—head of naval research and development for Mesan Alignment.

Chin, Captain Marjorie, Solarian League Navy—XO, SLNS *Anton von Leeuwenhoek.*

Chol, Yeou Kun—President of the Solarian League.

Coleman, Commander Theresa, Mesan Alignment Navy—Admiral Frederick Topolev's chief of staff.

Colenso, Admiral Jennifer, Mesan Alignment Navy—CO, Task Force Two, Oyster Bay operation.

Colombo, Rear Admiral Thomas, Royal Manticoran Navy—Vice Admiral Claudio Faraday's predecessor as CO, HMSS *Weyland.*

Conner, Captain Jerome, Royal Manticoran Navy—CO, Battlecruiser Division 106.1.

Cortez, Admiral Sir Lucien, Royal Manticoran Navy—Fifth Space Lord, Royal Manticoran Navy; CO, Bureau of personnel.

Cottolengo, Lieutenant Commander Chikosi, Royal Manticoran Navy—electronic warfare officer, Battlecruiser Squadron 108.

Crandall, Fleet Admiral Sandra, Solarian League Navy—CO, Task Force 496.

Culpepper, Commander Martin, Royal Manticoran Navy—Admiral Michael Oversteegen's chief of staff.

da Orta e Diadoro, Jacinta—Interior Minister of the Solarian League.

Da Silva, Lieutenant Chantelle, Royal Manticoran Navy—logistics officer, Battlecruiser Squadron 108.

Danko, Sergeant Major Evelyn, Royal Manticoran Marine Corps—"Gunny" Danko; HMS *Rigel*'s senior Marine noncom.

Danvers, Vice Admiral Lilian, Royal Manticoran Navy—Third Space Lord, Royal Manticoran Navy; CO Bureau of Ships.

d'Arezzo, Ensign Paulo, Royal Manticoran Navy—junior officer, assigned Manufacturing and Prototyping Command, HMSS *Weyland.*

Deangelo, Captain Severino, Royal Manticoran Navy—Sir Lyman Carmichael's naval attaché on Old Terra.

Denton, Lieutenant Commander Lewis, Royal Manticoran Navy—CO, HMS *Reprise.*

Detweiler, Albrecht—chief executive, Mesan Alignment; director, Mesan Strategy Council.

Detweiler, Benjamin—Albrecht Detweiler's son; Mesan Alignment chief for military affairs.

Detweiler, Collin—Albrecht Detweiler's son, Mesan Alignment chief for intelligence operations.

Detweiler, Daniel—Albrecht Detweiler's son, Mesan Alignment chief for nongenetic R&D.

Detweiler, Evelina—Albrecht Detweiler's wife and a senior scientist for the Mesan Alignment in her own right.

Detweiler, Everett—Albrecht Detweiler's son, Mesan Alignment chief for genetic R&D.

Detweiler, Franklin—Albrecht Detweiler's son, Mesan Alignment chief for political strategy.

Detweiler, Gervais—Albrecht Detweiler's son, Mesan Alignment chief for foreign affairs.

Dicey, Royal Manticoran Navy—Master Steward Chris Billingsley's Maine Coon cat.

Diego, Commander Wilton, Royal Manticoran Navy—tactical officer, HMS *Artemis*.

Dombroski, Lieutenant (JG) Tabatha, Royal Manticoran Navy—junior tactical officer, HMS *Star Witch*.

Doyle, Surgeon Commander Lamprecht, Royal Manticoran Navy—ship's surgeon, HMS *Artemis*.

Dzung-ming, Rear Admiral Tang, Solarian League Navy—Admiral Keeley O'Cleary's operations officer.

Edwards, Lieutenant Commander William ("Bill"), Royal Manticoran Navy—communications officer, Tenth Fleet.

Epstein, Lieutenant Commander Jessica, Royal Manticoran Navy—supervisory officer assigned to Perimeter Security Command, Manticore binary system.

Fairfax, Rear Admiral Lavinia, Solarian League Navy—Admiral Keeley O'Cleary's intelligence officer.

Faraday, Vice Admiral Claudio, Royal Manticoran Navy—CO, HMSS *Weyland*.

Fariñas, Lieutenant Sebastián, Royal Manticoran Navy—Admiral Michael Oversteegen's flag lieutenant.

Fernandez, Lieutenant Commander Kyle, Royal Manticoran Navy— communications officer, HMS *Artemis*.

Filareta, Fleet Admiral Massimo, Solarian League Navy—commanding officer of SLN fleet stationed in the Tasmania System.

FitzCummings, Dame Charlotte—Countess Maiden Hill; Minister of industry, Star Empire of Manticore.

FitzGerald, Captain (JG) Ansten, Royal Manticoran Navy—CO, HMS *Hexapuma*.

Flynn, Commander Sheila, Mesan Alignment Navy—Commodore Karol Østby's chief of staff.

Fonzarelli, Captain Karaamat, Royal Manticoran Navy—senior officer, Repair & Refit Command, HMSS *Hephaestus*.

Ford, Walter ("Walt")—Chancellor, Second Chance Republic, Matagorda System.

Foreman, Commander Clement, Mesan Alignment Navy—Commodore Karol Østby's ops officer.

Frankel, Steward First-Class Benjamin, Royal Manticoran Navy— Ansten FitzGerald's steward.

Givens, Admiral Patricia, Royal Manticoran Navy—Second Space Lord, Royal Manticoran Navy, and CO, Office of Naval Intelligence.

Gregory, Stan—Secretary of Urban Affairs, Republic of Haven.

Gruner, Lieutenant Aloysius, Solarian League Navy—CO, Dispatch Boat 17709, attached to Admiral Josef Byng's squadron at New Tuscany.

Gyulay, Shona—Prime Minister of the Solarian League.

Haarhuis, Captain Berend, Solarian League Navy—Fleet Admiral Sandra Crandall's staff astrogator.

Haftner, Abednego—Henri Krietzmann's chief of staff.

Halstead, Captain Raymond, Royal Manticoran Navy—one of Admiral Hemphill's project officers at BuWeaps.

Hampton, Alicia—Secretary of State Leslie Montreau's personal secretary, Republic of Haven.

Hanriot, Rachel—Secretary of the Treasury, Republic of Haven.

Hardy, Captain George—CO, RMS *Paul Tankersley*.

Harkness, Chief Warrant Officer Sir Horace, Royal Manticoran Navy—staff electronic warfare officer, Heavy Cruiser Division 96.1.

Harper, Platoon Sergeant Frances ("Frankie"), Royal Manticoran Marine Corps—platoon sergeant, First Platoon, Alpha Company, Marine detachment, HMS *Rigel*.

Hawke, Captain Spencer, Harrington Steadholder's Guard—Honor Alexander-Harrington's senior personal armsman.

Hemphill, Admiral Sonja, Royal Manticoran Navy—Baroness of Low Delhi, Fourth Space Lord, Royal Manticoran Navy; CO Bureau of Weapons.

Henke, Admiral Gloria Michelle Samantha Evelyn, Royal Manticoran Navy—Countess Gold Peak; CO, Tenth Fleet.

Hennessy, Lieutenant Commander Coleman, Royal Manticoran Navy—Admiral Sonja Hemphill's chief of staff.

Henning, Lieutenant Commander Vivienne, Mesan Alignment Navy—Admiral Frederick Topolev's staff astrogator.

Higgins, Admiral Allen, Royal Manticoran Navy—CO, Home Fleet.

Hitchcock, Roman—System President, Visigoth System.

Hongbo, Junyan—Vice-Commissioner, Office of Frontier Security, for the Madras Sector.

Howard, Albert—Innokentiy Kolokoltsov's butler.

Hübner, Captain Lieselotte "Liesel," Royal Manticoran Navy—Sir Thomas Caparelli's chief of staff.

Hurskainen, Stanley—President, Republic of Mannerheim, Mannerheim System.

Imbar, Efron—a reporter for Star Kingdom News.

Inbari, Lieutenant Commander Mazal, Royal Manticoran Navy—astrogator, Cruiser Squadron 94.

Ingebrigtsen, Captain Luciana, Royal Manticoran Marine Corps—CO, Alpha Company, Marine detachment, HMS *Rigel*.

Iwasaki, Corporal Dunstan, Royal Manticoran Marine Corps—section leader, First Platoon, Alpha Company, Marine detachment, HMS *Rigel*.

Jackson, Chief Petty Officer Manitoba, Royal Manticoran Navy—primary helmsman, HMS *Quay*.

Jackson, Lieutenant Sylvester ("Sly"), Royal Manticoran Marine Corps—CO, Second Platoon, Alpha Company, Marine detachment, HMS *Rigel*.

Jaruwalski, Captain (JG) Andrea, Royal Manticoran Navy—operations officer, Eighth Fleet.

Jefferson, Captain (SG) George, Royal Manticoran Navy—senior officer, Delta Division, Research and Development Command, HMSS *Weyland*.

Jennings, Admiral Willis, Solarian League Navy—Fleet Admiral Winston Kingsford's chief of staff.

Johansen, Lieutenant Commander Barnabé, Royal Manticoran Navy—astrogator, HMS *Quentin Saint-James*.

Juppé, Baltasar—an influential Old Terran reporter specializing in financial news.

Justice, Special Officer Sharon—special officer Victor Cachat's second-in-command, Erewhon Sector, Foreign Intelligence Service, Republic of Haven.

Kagiyama, Ensign Aikawa, Royal Manticoran Navy—junior officer serving in HMS *Hexapuma*.

Kakadelis, Nikomedes ("Nicky")—Chief Councilor, Democratic Republic of Thrace, Thrace System.

Karlberg, Commodore Emil, Nuncio Space Force—senior officer, Nuncio Space Force.

Karpova, Senior Chief Petty Officer Oxana, Royal Manticoran Navy—helmswoman, HMS *Stevedore*.

Kew, Sir Barnabas—permanent undersecretary; Manticoran foreign office, special envoy to the Republic of Haven.

Kgari, Lieutenant Commander Theophile, Royal Manticoran Navy—staff astrogator, Eighth Fleet.

Khumalo, Vice Admiral Augustus, Royal Manticoran Navy—CO, Talbott Station.

King Clinton III—see Clinton Thompson.

Kingsford, Fleet Admiral Winston Seth, Solarian League Navy—CO, Battle Fleet.

Kittow, Commander Joshua, Royal Manticoran Navy—XO, HMS *Quentin Saint-James*.

Kolokoltsov, Innokentiy Arsenovich—Permanent Senior Undersecretary for Foreign Affairs, Solarian League.

Kolosov, Lieutenant Peter, Royal Manticoran Navy—XO, HMS *Reprise*.

Kolstad, Commander Felicidad, Mesan Alignment Navy—Admiral Frederick Topolev's operations officer.

Krietzmann, Henri—Minister of War, Alquezar Government, Talbott Quadrant.

Kubrick, Joan—Board Chairman, Maxwell Association, Maxwell System.

Kunimichi, Taketomo—retired Solarian League Navy admiral and Defense Minister of the Solarian League.

Maddox, Captain Baruti—CO, Aldona Anisimovna's "yacht" *Bolide*.

Mang, Sywan—Minister of Commerce of the Solarian League.

Manning, Rear Admiral Nathalie, Royal Manticoran Navy—CO, Battlecruiser Division 108.2

Manston, Lieutenant (JG) Heather, Royal Manticoran Navy—astrogator, dispatch boat HMS *Hare*.

Marcos, Captain Madison, Royal Manticoran Navy—CO, HMS *Star Dance*; Commodore James Tanner's flag captain.

Markiewicz, Major Evgeny, Royal Manticoran Marine Corps—CO, Marine detachment, HMS *Rigel*.

Markussen, Leontina—Minister of Education and Information, Solarian League.

Marquette, Admiral Arnaud, Republic of Haven Navy—chief of the naval staff, Republic of Haven.

Marquis Reynaldo IV—see Reynaldo Lucas.

Maslov, Lieutenant Isaiah, Royal Manticoran Navy—electronic warfare officer, HMS *Artemis*.

Matsuko, Dame Estelle—Baroness Medusa; Imperial Governor, Talbott Quadrant.

Maurier, Francine—Baroness Morncreek; Chancellor of the Exchequer of the Star Empire of Manticore.

McBryde, Jack—Chief of Security, Gamma Center, Mesan Alignment.

McClelland, Commander Martin, Mesan Alignment Navy—Admiral Frederick Topolev's staff electronics warfare officer.

McClure, Sergeant Jefferson, Harrington Steadholder's Guard—Emily Alexander-Harrington's personal armsman.

McCormick, Lieutenant Clinton, Royal Manticoran Navy—tracking officer assigned to Perimeter Security Command, Manticore binary system.

McGill, Lieutenant Heather, Royal Manticoran Navy—tactical officer, HMS *Reprise*.

McGillicuddy, Commander Anastasia, Royal Manticoran Navy—officer assigned Manufacturing and Prototyping Command, HMSS *Weyland*.

McGraw, Sergeant Clifford, Harrington Steadholder's Guard—one of Honor Alexander-Harrington's personal armsmen.

McGwire, Senator Samson—Senator, Republic of Haven; New Conservative Party.

McMahon, Captain Vince, Royal Manticoran Navy—CO, HMS *Star Witch*.

Milne, Captain Hayden, Mesan Alignment Navy—CO, MANS *Genesis*, Albrecht Detweiler's "yacht."

Monahan, Ensign Rachel, Royal Manticoran Navy—junior officer assigned to HMS *Reprise*.

Montella, Lieutenant (SG) Atalante, Royal Manticoran Navy—communications officer, Cruiser Squadron 94.

Monticelli, Rebecca ("Becky")—President, Comstock Republic, Comstock System.

Montoya, Commodore Alvin, Royal Manticoran Navy—CO, Battle-cruiser Division 108.1.

Montreau, Leslie—Secretary of State, Republic of Haven.

Moorehead, Sybil—Prime Minister Alquezar's chief of staff.

Morozov, Lieutenant (SG) Ramón, Royal Manticoran Navy—logistics officer, Cruiser Squadron 94.

Mulcahey, Carissa—Baroness Selleck; special envoy to the Republic of Haven.

Myau, Surgeon Lieutenant Zhin, Royal Manticoran Navy—ship's surgeon, HMS *Quentin Saint-James*.

Myerson, Chief Petty Officer Wesley, Royal Manticoran Navy—second helmswoman, HMS *Quay*.

Nagchaudhuri, Commander Amal, Royal Manticoran Navy—XO, HMS *Hexapuma*.

Navarro, Lieutenant Aldonza, Royal Manticoran Marine Corps—CO, Third Platoon, Alpha Company, Marine detachment, HMS *Rigel*.

Nesbitt, Colonel Jean-Claude—chief security officer, Department of State, Republic of Haven.

Nesbitt, Tony—Secretary of Commerce, Republic of Haven.

Neukirch, Lieutenant Commander Gilderoy, Royal Manticoran Navy—tactical officer, HMS *Star Witch*.

Noorlander, Harbrecht—Treasury Minister of the Solarian League.

O'Cleary, Admiral Keeley, Solarian League Navy—CO, Battle Squadron 326; Fleet Admiral Sandra Crandall's third-in-command.

Ødcgaard, Lieutenant Commander Mateuz, Royal Manticoran Navy—intelligence officer, Cruiser Squadron 94.

O'Hanrahan, Audrey—an influential Old Terran reporter specializing in "muckraking journalism."

Pritchart, Eloise—President of the Republic of Haven.

Quartermain, Omosupe—Permanent Senior Undersecretary of Commerce, Solarian League.

Rajampet, Fleet Admiral Kaushal Rajani, Solarian League Navy—Chief of Naval Operations for the Solarian League.

Redondo, Consuelo—a reporter for the Sphinx News Association.

Retallack, Commander Steren, Royal Manticoran Navy—operations officer, Battlecruiser Squadron 108.

Reynolds, Commander George, Royal Manticoran Navy—intelligence officer, Eighth Fleet.

Richardson, Lieutenant Osama, Royal Manticoran Navy—engineer, HMS *Reprise*.

Rivera, Jacqueline—a reporter for Solarian News Services.

Rodriguez, Lieutenant Sinead, Royal Manticoran Navy—communications officer, HMS *Rigel*.

Roelas y Valiente, Marcelito Lorenzo—Foreign Minister of the Solarian League.

Ronayne, Brangwen—Attorney General of the Solarian League.

Roquefort, Rear Admiral Benesek, Royal Manticoran Navy—CO, HMSS *Vulcan*.

Rousseau, Angela—President Eloise Pritchart's personal assistant.

Sackett, Commodore Lemuel, Montana System Navy—senior officer, Montana System Navy.

Sambroth, Commander Nicolette, Solarian League Navy—tactical officer, SLNS *Joseph Buckley*.

Sanderson, Walter—Secretary of the Interior, Republic of Haven.

Saunders, Captain Victoria, Royal Manticoran Navy—CO, HMS *Hercules*; Vice Admiral Khumalo's flag captain.

Schreiber, Lieutenant Commander Utako, Mesan Alignment Navy—Commodore Roderick Sung's operations officer.

Scidel, Lieutenant Landbert, Royal Manticoran Navy—Engineer, HMS *Stevedore*.

Shavarshyan, Commander Hago, Solarian League Navy—Frontier Fleet intelligence officer attached to Fleet Admiral Sandra Crandall's staff.

Shaw, Captain Terence, Royal Manticoran Navy—Admiral Sir Lucien Cortez's chief of staff.

Shoupe, Captain Loretta, Royal Manticoran Navy—Vice Admiral Khumalo's chief of staff.

Simões, Dr. Herlander—Mesan Alignment hyper-physicist assigned to Gamma Center, Green Pines, Mesa.

Sloan, Chief Petty Officer Tamara, Royal Manticoran Navy—a noncom aboard HMS *Reprise*.

Stabolis, Ericka—Evelina Detweiler's genetically enhanced bodyguard.

Stabolis, Heinrich—Albrecht Detweiler's genetically enhanced bodyguard.

Staunton, Sandra—Secretary of Biosciences, Republic of Haven.

Stimson, Sergeant Tobias, Harrington Steadholder's Guard—Hamish Alexander-Harrington's personal armsman.

Stone, Vincent—Director, Directorate of New Orkney, New Orkney System.

Strickland, Lieutenant Commander Sharon, Royal Manticoran Navy—CO, HMS *Stevedore*.

Sugihara, Captain (SG) Brian, Royal Manticoran Navy—Rear Admiral Warren Trammell's chief of staff.

Sugimatsu, Lieutenant Commander Andrew, Royal Manticoran Navy—CO, HMS *Quay*.

Sullivan, Captain Ambrose, Royal Manticoran Navy—CO, HMS *Rigel*; Admiral Michael Oversteegen's flag captain.

Sung, Commodore Roderick, Mesan Alignment Navy—CO, Task Group 2.2, Oyster Bay operation.

Taliadoros, Kyrillos—Aldona Anisimovna's genetically enhanced bodyguard.

Tanner, Commodore James, Royal Manticoran Navy—CO, Cruiser Squadron 114.1.

Tarantino, Robert ("Bob")—Chancellor, Republic of New Bombay, New Bombay System.

Teague, Captain Irene, Solarian League Navy—a Frontier Fleet officer assigned as an analyst to the Office of Operational Analysis.

Telmachi, Robert—Archbishop of Manticore.

Tennard, Sergeant Jeremiah, Harrington Steadholder's Guard—Faith Harrington's personal armsman.

Terekhov, Commodore Sir Aivars, Royal Manticoran Navy—CO, Cruiser Squadron 94.

Tersteeg, Lieutenant Commander Maxwell, Royal Manticoran Navy—electronic warfare officer, Tenth Fleet.

Theisman, Admiral Thomas, Republic of Haven Navy—Secretary of War, Republic of Haven, and Chief of Naval Operations, Republic of Haven Navy.

Thiessen, Sheila—senior member of President Eloise Pritchart's personal security detachment, Republic of Haven.

Thimár, Admiral Karl-Heinz, Solarian League Navy—CO, Office of Naval Intelligence.

Thomas, Lieutenant Irena, Royal Manticoran Navy—communications officer, Battlecruiser Squadron 108.

Thompson, Clinton—King Clinton III, ruler of the Kingdom of New Madagascar, Oceana System.

Thurgood, Commodore Francis, Solarian League Navy—Lorcan Verrochio's senior Frontier Fleet officer, Madras Sector.

Timmons, Chief Petty Officer Randall, Royal Manticoran Navy—Rear Admiral Tina Yeager's senior yeoman.

Tobolowski, Lieutenant Basil, Royal Manticoran Navy—staff astrogator, Battlecruiser Squadron 108.

Topolev, Admiral Frederick, Mesan Alignment Navy—CO, Task Force One, Oyster Bay operation.

Török, Lieutenant Commander Iona, Royal Manticoran Navy—communications officer, HMS *Quentin Saint-James*.

Trajan, Wilhelm—Director, Foreign Intelligence Service, Republic of Haven.

Trammell, Rear Admiral Warren, Royal Manticoran Navy—CO, Manufacturing and Prototyping Command, HMSS *Weyland*.

Treacher, Lieutenant Commander Jackson, Royal Manticoran Navy—logistics officer, Tenth Fleet.

Tremaine, Captain Prescott ("Scotty") David, Royal Manticoran Navy—CO, HMS *Alistair McKeon*; senior officer, Heavy Cruiser Division 96.1.

Trenis, Vice Admiral Linda, Republic of Haven Navy—CO, Bureau of Planning, Republic of Haven Navy.

Truman, Rear Admiral Margaret, Royal Manticoran Navy—CO, HMSS *Hephaestus*.

Tsau, Commodore Travis, Mesan Alignment Navy—Commodore Roderick Sung's chief of staff.

Tullingham, Chief Justice Jeffrey—Chief Justice, Supreme Court, Republic of Haven.

Tümmel, Lieutenant Waldemar, Royal Manticoran Navy—Admiral Honor Alexander-Harrington's flag lieutenant.

Tuominen, The Honorable Voitto—permanent secretary, Manticoran foreign office; special envoy to the Republic of Haven.

Usher, Kevin—Director, Federal Investigation Agency, Republic of Haven.

Van Dort, Bernardus—founder and ex-chairman of the Rembrandt Trade Union; special minister without portfolio, Alquezar Government, Talbott Quadrant.

Van Heutz, Captain Jacomina, Solarian League Navy—CO, SLNS *Joseph Buckley*; Fleet Admiral Sandra Crandall's flag captain.

Van Scheldt, Paul—Prime Minister Alquezar's appointments secretary.

Verrochio, Lorcan—Commissioner, Office of Frontier Security, for the Madras Sector.

Verstappen, Lieutenant Truida, Royal Manticoran Navy—XO, HMS *Quay*.

Walsh, Captain Joshua, Mesan Alignment Navy—CO, MANS *Mako*; Admiral Frederick Topolev's flag captain.

Wanderman, Senior Chief Petty Officer Aubrey, Royal Manticoran Navy—noncommissioned officer, assigned Manufacturing and Prototyping Command, HMSS *Weyland*.

Wang, Astrid—Innokentiy Kolokoltsov's personal assistant and chief of staff.

Weaver, Lieutenant Samuel, Royal Manticoran Navy—Rear Admiral Tina Yeager's flag lieutenant.

Wijenberg, Bruce—Minister of Trade, Star Empire of Manticore.

Wodoslawski, Agatá—Permanent Senior Undersecretary of the Treasury, Solarian League.

Yeager, Rear Admiral Tina, Royal Manticoran Navy—CO, Research and Development Command, HMSS *Weyland*.

Younger, Representative Gerald—Representative, Republic of Haven; New Conservative Party.

Zhing-wei, Vice Admiral Ou-yang, Solarian League Navy—Fleet Admiral Sandra Crandall's operations officer.

Zilwicki, Captain Anton—retired Royal Manticoran Navy officer; senior intelligence operative for Kingdom of Torch.

Zilwicki, Ensign Helen, Royal Manticoran Navy—Sir Aivars Terekhov's flag lieutenant.